The Fourth Ghost Story MEGAPACK®

IN THE SAME SERIES

The Fourth Ghost Story MEGAPACK®

Edited by John Gregory Betancourt

WILDSIDE PRESS

COPYRIGHT INFO

CONTENTS

A NOTE FROM THE PUBLISHER

We love ghost stories here at Wildside Press. If you've read the first 3 volumes in this series, plus *The Macabre MEGAPACK®* series, you're pretty well caught up with the classic supernatural fiction we've been reading lately.

Enjoy...and don't worry, there will be more Ghost Story volumes!

—John Betancourt
Publisher, Wildside Press LLC
www.wildsidepress.com

ABOUT THE SERIES

Over the last few years, our MEGAPACK® ebook series has grown to be our most popular endeavor. (Maybe it helps that we sometimes offer them as premiums to our mailing list!) One question we keep getting asked is, "Who's the editor?"

The MEGAPACK® ebook series (except where specifically credited) are a group effort. Everyone at Wildside works on them. This includes John Betancourt (me), Carla Coupe, Steve Coupe, Shawn Garrett, Helen McGee, Bonner Menking, Colin Azariah-Kribbs, A.E. Warren, and many of Wildside's authors... who often suggest stories to include (and not just their own!)

THE FOUR-FIFTEEN EXPRESS,
by Amelia B. Edwards

Originally published in 1867.

The events which I am about to relate took place between nine and ten years ago. Sebastopol had fallen in the early spring, the peace of Paris had been concluded since March, our commercial relations with the Russian empire were but recently renewed; and I, returning home after my first northward journey since the war, was well pleased with the prospect of spending the month of December under the hospitable and thoroughly English roof of my excellent friend, Jonathan Jelf, Esq., of Dumbleton Manor, Clayborough, East Anglia. Travelling in the interests of the well-known firm in which it is my lot to be a junior partner, I had been called upon to visit not only the capitals of Russia and Poland, but had found it also necessary to pass some weeks among the trading ports of the Baltic; whence it came that the year was already far spent before I again set foot on English soil, and that, instead of shooting pheasants with him, as I had hoped, in October, I came to be my friend's guest during the more genial Christmas-tide.

My voyage over, and a few days given up to business in Liverpool and London, I hastened down to Clayborough with all the delight of a schoolboy whose holidays are at hand. My way lay by the Great East Anglian line as far as Clayborough station, where I was to be met by one of the Dumbleton carriages and conveyed across the remaining nine miles of country. It was a foggy afternoon, singularly warm for the 4th of December, and I had arranged to leave London by the 4.15 express. The early darkness of winter had already closed in; the lamps were lighted in the carriages; a clinging damp dimmed the windows, adhered to the door-handles, and pervaded all the atmosphere; while the gas-jets at the neighbouring book-stand diffused a luminous haze that only served to make the gloom of the terminus more visible. Having arrived some seven minutes before the starting of the train, and, by the connivance of the guard, taken sole possession of an empty compartment, I lighted my travelling-lamp, made myself particularly snug, and settled down to the undisturbed enjoyment of a book and a cigar. Great, therefore, was my disappointment when, at the last moment, a gentleman came hurrying along the platform, glanced into my carriage, opened the locked door with a private key, and stepped in.

It struck me at the first glance that I had seen him before—a tall, spare man, thin-lipped, light-eyed, with an ungraceful stoop in the shoulders, and scant grey hair worn somewhat long upon the collar. He carried a light waterproof coat, an umbrella, and a large brown japanned deed-box, which last he placed under the seat. This done, he felt carefully in his breast-pocket, as if to make certain of the safety of his purse or pocket-book, laid his umbrella in the netting overhead, spread the waterproof across his knees, and exchanged his hat for a travelling-cap of some Scotch material. By this time the train was moving out of the station and into the faint grey of the wintry twilight beyond.

I now recognized my companion. I recognized him from the moment when he removed his hat and uncovered the lofty, furrowed, and somewhat narrow brow beneath. I had met him, as I distinctly remembered, some three years before, at the very house for which, in all probability, he was now bound, like myself. His name was Dwerrihouse, he was a lawyer by profession, and, if I was not greatly mistaken, was first cousin to the wife of my host. I knew also that he was a man eminently "well-to-do", both as regarded his professional and private means. The Jelfs entertained him with that sort of observant courtesy which falls to the lot of the rich relation, the children made much of him, and the old butler, albeit somewhat surly "to the general", treated him with deference. I thought, observing him by the vague mixture of lamplight and twilight, that Mrs. Jelf's cousin looked all the worse for the three years' wear and tear which had gone over his head since our last meeting. He was very pale, and had a restless light in his eye that I did not remember to have observed before. The anxious lines, too, about his mouth were deepened, and there was a cavernous, hollow look about his cheeks and temples which seemed to speak of sickness or sorrow. He had glanced at me as he came in, but without any gleam of recognition in his face. Now he glanced again, as I fancied, somewhat doubtfully. When he did so for the third or fourth time I ventured to address him.

"Mr. John Dwerrihouse, I think?"

"That is my name," he replied.

"I had the pleasure of meeting you at Dumbleton about three years ago."

"I thought I knew your face," he said; "but your name, I regret to say—"

"Langford—William Langford. I have known Jonathan Jelf since we were boys together at Merchant Taylors', and I generally spend a few weeks at Dumbleton in the shooting season. I suppose we are bound for the same destination."

"Not if you are on your way to the manor," he replied. "I am travelling upon business—rather troublesome business, too—while you, doubtless, have only pleasure in view."

"Just so. I am in the habit of looking forward to this visit as to the brightest three weeks in all the year."

"It is a pleasant house," said Mr. Dwerrihouse.

"The pleasantest I know."

"And Jelf is thoroughly hospitable."

"The best and kindest fellow in the world."

"They have invited me to spend Christmas week with them," pursued Mr. Dwerrihouse, after a moment's pause.

"And you are coming?"

"I cannot tell. It must depend on the issue of this business which I have in hand. You have heard perhaps that we are about to construct a branch line from Blackwater to Stockbridge."

I explained that I had been for some months away from England, and had therefore heard nothing of the contemplated improvement. Mr. Dwerrihouse smiled complacently.

"It *will* be an improvement," he said, "a great improvement. Stockbridge is a flourishing town, and needs but a more direct railway communication with the metropolis to become an important centre of commerce. This branch was my own idea. I brought the project before the board, and have myself superintended the execution of it up to the present time."

"You are an East Anglian director, I presume?"

"My interest in the company," replied Mr. Dwerrihouse, "is threefold. I am a director, I am a considerable shareholder, and, as head of the firm of Dwerrihouse, Dwerrihouse and Craik, I am the company's principal solicitor."

Loquacious, self-important, full of his pet project, and apparently unable to talk on any other subject, Mr. Dwerrihouse then went on to tell of the opposition he had encountered and the obstacles he had overcome in the cause of the Stockbridge branch. I was entertained with a multitude of local details and local grievances. The rapacity of one squire, the impracticability of another, the indignation of the rector whose glebe was threatened, the culpable indifference of the Stockbridge townspeople, who could *not* be brought to see that their most vital interests hinged upon a junction with the Great East Anglian line; the spite of the local newspaper, and the unheard-of difficulties attending the Common question, were each and all laid before me with a circumstantiality that possessed the deepest interest for my excellent fellow-traveller, but none whatever for myself. From these, to my despair, he went on to more intricate matters: to the approximate expenses of construction per mile; to the estimates sent in by different contractors; to the probable traffic returns of the new line; to the provisional clauses of the new act as enumerated in Schedule D of the company's last half-yearly report; and so on and on and on, till my head ached and my attention flagged and my eyes kept closing in spite of every effort that I made to keep them open. At length I was roused by these words:

"Seventy-five thousand pounds, cash down."

"Seventy-five thousand pounds, cash down," I repeated, in the liveliest tone I could assume. "That is a heavy sum."

"A heavy sum to carry here," replied Mr. Dwerrihouse, pointing significantly to his breast-pocket, "but a mere fraction of what we shall ultimately have to pay."

"You do not mean to say that you have seventy-five thousand pounds at this moment upon your person?" I exclaimed.

"My good sir, have I not been telling you so for the last half-hour?" said Mr. Dwerrihouse, testily. "That money has to be paid over at half-past eight o'clock this evening, at the office of Sir Thomas's solicitors, on completion of the deed of sale."

"But how will you get across by night from Blackwater to Stockbridge with seventy-five thousand pounds in your pocket?"

"To Stockbridge!" echoed the lawyer. "I find I have made myself very imperfectly understood. I thought I had explained how this sum only carries us as far as Mallingford—the first stage, as it were, of our journey—and how our route from Blackwater to Mallingford lies entirely through Sir Thomas Liddell's property."

"I beg your pardon," I stammered. I fear my thoughts were wandering. So you only go as far as Mallingford tonight?"

"Precisely. I shall get a conveyance from the Blackwater Arms. And you?"

"Oh, Jelf sends a trap to meet me at Clayborough! Can I be the bearer of any message from you?"

"You may say, if you please, Mr. Langford, that I wished I could have been your companion all the way, and that I will come over, if possible, before Christmas."

"Nothing more?"

Mr. Dwerrihouse smiled grimly. "Well," he said, "you may tell my cousin that she need not burn the hall down in my honour this time, and that I shall be obliged if she will order the blue-room chimney to be swept before I arrive."

"That sounds tragic. Had you a conflagration on the occasion of your last visit to Dumbleton?"

"Something like it. There had been no fire lighted in my bedroom since the spring, the flue was foul, and the rooks had built in it; so when I went up to dress for dinner I found the room full of smoke and the chimney on fire. Are we already at Blackwater?"

The train had gradually come to a pause while Mr. Dwerrihouse was speaking, and, on putting my head out of the window, I could see the station some few hundred yards ahead. There was another train before us blocking the way, and the guard was making use of the delay to collect the Blackwater tickets. I had scarcely ascertained our position when the ruddy-faced official appeared at our carriage door.

"Tickets, sir!" said he.

"I am for Clayborough," I replied, holding out the tiny pink card.

He took it, glanced at it by the light of his little lantern, gave it back, looked, as I fancied, somewhat sharply at my fellow-traveller, and disappeared.

"He did not ask for yours," I said, with some surprise.

"They never do," replied Mr. Dwerrihouse; "they all know me, and of course I travel free."

"Blackwater! Blackwater!" cried the porter, running along the platform beside us as we glided into the station.

Mr. Dwerrihouse pulled out his deed-box, put his travelling-cap in his pocket, resumed his hat, took down his umbrella, and prepared to be gone.

"Many thanks, Mr. Langford, for your society," he said, with old-fashioned courtesy. "I wish you a good-evening."

"Good-evening," I replied, putting out my hand.

But he either did not see it or did not choose to see it, and, slightly lifting his hat, stepped out upon the platform. Having done this, he moved slowly away and mingled with the departing crowd.

Leaning forward to watch him out of sight, I trod upon something which proved to be a cigar-case. It had fallen, no doubt, from the pocket of his water-proof coat, and was made of dark morocco leather, with a silver monogram upon the side. I sprang out of the carriage just as the guard came up to lock me in.

"Is there one minute to spare?" I asked, eagerly. "The gentleman who travelled down with me from town has dropped his cigar-case; he is not yet out of the station."

"Just a minute and a half, sir," replied the guard. "You must be quick."

I dashed along the platform as fast as my feet could carry me. It was a large station, and Mr. Dwerrihouse had by this time got more than half-way to the farther end.

I, however, saw him distinctly, moving slowly with the stream. Then, as I drew nearer, I saw that he had met some friend, that they were talking as they walked, that they presently fell back somewhat from the crowd and stood aside in earnest conversation. I made straight for the spot where they were waiting. There was a vivid gas-jet just above their heads, and the light fell upon their faces. I saw both distinctly—the face of Mr. Dwerrihouse and the face of his companion. Running, breathless, eager as I was, getting in the way of porters and passengers, and fearful every instant lest I should see the train going on without me, I yet observed that the newcomer was considerably younger and shorter than the director, that he was sandy-haired, moustachioed, small-featured, and dressed in a close-cut suit of Scotch tweed. I was now within a few yards of them. I ran against a stout gentleman, I was nearly knocked down by a luggage-truck, I stumbled over a carpet-bag; I gained the spot just as the driver's whistle warned me to return.

To my utter stupefaction, they were no longer there. I had seen them but two seconds before—and they were gone! I stood still; I looked to right and left; I saw no sign of them in any direction. It was as if the platform had gaped and swallowed them.

"There were two gentlemen standing here a moment ago," I said to a porter at my elbow; "which way can they have gone?"

"I saw no gentlemen, sir," replied the man.

The whistle shrilled out again. The guard, far up the platform, held up his arm, and shouted to me to "come on!"

"If you're going on by this train, sir," said the porter, "you must run for it."

I did run for it, just gained the carriage as the train began to move, was shoved in by the guard, and left, breathless and bewildered, with Mr. Dwerrihouse's cigar-case still in my hand.

It was the strangest disappearance in the world; it was like a transformation trick in a pantomime. They were there one moment—palpably there, talking, with the gaslight full upon their faces—and the next moment they were gone. There was no door near, no window, no staircase; it was a mere slip of barren platform, tapestried with big advertisements. Could anything be more mysterious?

It was not worth thinking about, and yet, for my life, I could not help pondering upon it—pondering, wondering, conjecturing, turning it over and over in my mind, and beating my brains for a solution of the enigma. I thought of it all the way from Blackwater to Clayborough. I thought of it all the way from Clayborough to Dumbleton, as I rattled along the smooth highway in a trim dog-cart, drawn by a splendid black mare and driven by the silentest and dapperest of East Anglian grooms.

We did the nine miles in something less than an hour, and pulled up before the lodge-gates just as the church clock was striking half-past seven. A couple of minutes more, and the warm glow of the lighted hall was flooding out upon the gravel, a hearty grasp was on my hand, and a clear jovial voice was bidding me "welcome to Dumbleton."

"And now, my dear fellow," said my host, when the first greeting was over, "you have no time to spare. We dine at eight, and there are people coming to meet you, so you must just get the dressing business over as quickly as may be. By the way, you will meet some acquaintances; the Biddulphs are coming, and Prendergast (Prendergast of the Skirmishers) is staying in the house. Adieu! Mrs. Jelf will be expecting you in the drawing-room."

I was ushered to my room—not the blue room, of which Mr. Dwerrihouse had made disagreeable experience, but a pretty little bachelor's chamber, hung with a delicate chintz and made cheerful by a blazing fire. I unlocked my portmanteau.

I tried to be expeditious, but the memory of my railway adventure haunted me. I could not get free of it; I could not shake it off. It impeded me, it worried me, it tripped me up, it caused me to mislay my studs, to mistie my cravat, to wrench the buttons off my gloves. Worst of all, it made me so late that the party had all assembled before I reached the drawing-room. I had scarcely paid my respects to Mrs. Jelf when dinner was announced, and we paired off, some eight or ten couples strong, into the dining-room.

I am not going to describe either the guests or the dinner. All provincial parties bear the strictest family resemblance, and I am not aware that an East Anglian banquet offers any exception to the rule. There was the usual country baronet and his wife; there were the usual country parsons and their wives; there was the sempiternal turkey and haunch of venison. *Vanitas vanitatum.* There is nothing new under the sun.

I was placed about midway down the table. I had taken one rector's wife down to dinner, and I had another at my left hand. They talked across me, and their talk was about babies; it was dreadfully dull. At length there came a pause. The entrées had just been removed, and the turkey had come upon the scene. The conversation had all along been of the languidest, but at this moment it happened to have stagnated altogether. Jelf was carving the turkey; Mrs. Jelf looked as if she was trying to think of something to say; everybody else was silent. Moved by an unlucky impulse, I thought I would relate my adventure.

"By the way, Jelf," I began, "I came down part of the way today with a friend of yours."

"Indeed!" said the master of the feast, slicing scientifically into the breast of the turkey. "With whom, pray?"

"With one who bade me tell you that he should, if possible, pay you a visit before Christmas."

"I cannot think who that could be," said my friend, smiling.

"It must be Major Thorp," suggested Mrs. Jelf.

I shook my head.

"It was not Major Thorp," I replied; "it was a near relation of your own, Mrs. Jelf."

"Then I am more puzzled than ever," replied my hostess. "Pray tell me who it was."

"It was no less a person than your cousin, Mr. John Dwerrihouse."

Jonathan Jelf laid down his knife and fork. Mrs. Jelf looked at me in a strange, startled way, and said never a word.

"And he desired me to tell you, my dear madam, that you need not take the trouble to burn the hall down in his honour this time, but only to have the chimney of the blue room swept before his arrival."

Before I had reached the end of my sentence I became aware of something ominous in the faces of the guests. I felt I had said something which I had better have left unsaid, and that for some unexplained reason my words had evoked a general consternation. I sat confounded, not daring to utter another syllable, and for at least two whole minutes there was dead silence round the table. Then Captain Prendergast came to the rescue.

"You have been abroad for some months, have you not, Mr. Langford?" he said, with the desperation of one who flings himself into the breach. "I heard you had been to Russia. Surely you have something to tell us of the state and temper of the country after the war?"

I was heartily grateful to the gallant Skirmisher for this diversion in my favour. I answered him, I fear, somewhat lamely; but he kept the conversation up, and presently one or two others joined in, and so the difficulty, whatever it might have been, was bridged over—bridged over, but not repaired. A something, an awkwardness, a visible constraint remained. The guests hitherto had been simply dull, but now they were evidently uncomfortable and embarrassed.

The dessert had scarcely been placed upon the table when the ladies left the room. I seized the opportunity to select a vacant chair next Captain Prendergast.

"In Heaven's name," I whispered, "what was the matter just now? What had I said?"

"You mentioned the name of John Dwerrihouse."

"What of that? I had seen him not two hours before."

"It is a most astounding circumstance that you should have seen him," said Captain Prendergast. "Are you sure it was he?"

"As sure as of my own identity. We were talking all the way between London and Blackwater. But why does that surprise you?"

"*Because*," replied Captain Prendergast, dropping his voice to the lowest whisper—"*because John Dwerrihouse absconded three months ago with s seventy-five thousand pounds of the company's money, and has never been heard of since.*"

John Dwerrihouse had absconded three months ago—and I had seen him only a few hours back! John Dwerrihouse had embezzled seventy-five thousand pounds of the company's money, yet told me that he carried that sum upon his person! Were ever facts so strangely incongruous, so difficult to reconcile? How should he have ventured again into the light of day? How dared he show himself along the line? Above all, what had he been doing throughout those mysterious three months of disappearance?

Perplexing questions these—questions which at once suggested themselves to the minds of all concerned, but which admitted of no easy solution. I could find no reply to them. Captain Prendergast had not even a suggestion to offer. Jonathan Jelf, who seized the first opportunity of drawing me aside and learning all that I had to tell, was more amazed and bewildered than either of us. He came to my room that night, when all the guests were gone, and we talked the thing over from every point of view; without, it must be confessed, arriving at any kind of conclusion.

"I do not ask you," he said, "whether you can have mistaken your man. That is impossible."

"As impossible as that I should mistake some stranger for yourself."

"It is not a question of looks or voice, but of facts. That he should have alluded to the fire in the blue room is proof enough of John Dwerrihouse's identity. How did he look?"

"Older, I thought; considerably older, paler, and more anxious."

"He has had enough to make him look anxious, anyhow," said my friend, gloomily, "be he innocent or guilty."

"I am inclined to believe that he is innocent," I replied. "He showed no embarrassment when I addressed him, and no uneasiness when the guard came round. His conversation was open to a fault. I might almost say that he talked too freely of the business which he had in hand."

"That again is strange, for I know no one more reticent on such subjects. He actually told you that he had the seventy-five thousand pounds in his pocket?"

"He did."

"Humph! My wife has an idea about it, and she may be right—"

"What idea?"

"Well, she fancies—women are so clever, you know, at putting themselves inside people's motives—she fancies that he was tempted, that he did actually take the money, and that he has been concealing himself these three months in some wild part of the country, struggling possibly with his conscience all the time, and daring neither to abscond with his booty nor to come back and restore it."

"But now that he has come back?"

"That is the point. She conceives that he has probably thrown himself upon the company's mercy, made restitution of the money, and, being forgiven, is permitted to carry the business through as if nothing whatever I had happened."

"The last," I replied, "is an impossible case. Mrs. Jelf thinks like a generous and delicate-minded woman, but not in the least like a board of railway directors. They would never carry forgiveness so far."

"I fear not; and yet it is the only conjecture that bears a semblance of likelihood. However, we can run over to Clayborough tomorrow and see if anything is to be learned. By the way, Prendergast tells me you picked up his cigar-case."

"I did so, and here it is."

Jelf took the cigar-case, examined it by the light of the lamp, and said at once that it was beyond doubt Mr. Dwerrihouse's property, and that he remembered to have seen him use it.

"Here, too, is his monogram on the side," he added—"a big J transfixing a capital D. He used to carry the same on his note-paper."

"It offers, at all events, a proof that I was not dreaming."

"Ay, but it is time you were asleep and dreaming now. I am ashamed to have kept you up so long. Good night."

"Good night, and remember that I am more than ready to go with you to Clayborough or Blackwater or London or anywhere, if I can be of the least service."

"Thanks! I know you mean it, old friend, and it may be that I shall put you to the test. Once more, good night."

So we parted for that night, and met again in the breakfast-room at half-past eight next morning. It was a hurried, silent, uncomfortable meal; none of us had slept well, and all were thinking of the same subject. Mrs. Jelf had evidently been crying, Jelf was impatient to be off, and both Captain Prendergast and myself felt ourselves to be in the painful position of outsiders who are involuntarily brought into a domestic trouble. Within twenty minutes after we had left the breakfast-table the dog-cart was brought round, and my friend and I were on the road to Clayborough.

"Tell you what it is, Langford," he said, as we sped along between the wintry hedges, "I do not much fancy to bring up Dwerrihouse's name at Clayborough. All the officials know that he is my wife's relation, and the subject just now is hardly a pleasant one. If you don't much mind, we will take the 11.10 to Blackwater. It's an important station, and we shall stand a far better chance of picking up information there than at Clayborough."

So we took the 11.10, which happened to be an express, and, arriving at Blackwater about a quarter before twelve, proceeded at once to prosecute our inquiry.

We began by asking for the station-master, a big, blunt, businesslike person, who at once averred that he knew Mr. John Dwerrihouse perfectly well, and that there was no director on the line whom he had seen and spoken to so frequently. "He used to be down here two or three times a week about three months ago," said he, "when the new line was first set afoot; but since then, you know, gentlemen—"

He paused significantly.

Jelf flushed scarlet.

"Yes, yes," he said, hurriedly; "we know all about that. The point now to be ascertained is whether anything has been seen or heard of him lately."

"Not to my knowledge," replied the station-master.

"He is not known to have been down the line any time yesterday, for instance?"

The station-master shook his head.

"The East Anglian, sir,"said he,"is about the last place where he would dare to show himself. Why, there isn't a station-master, there isn't a guard, there isn't a porter, who doesn't know Mr. Dwerrihouse by sight as well as he knows his own face in the looking-glass, or who wouldn't telegraph for the police as soon as he had set eyes on him at any point along the line. Bless you, sir! there's been a standing order out against him ever since the 25th of September last."

"And yet," pursued my friend, "a gentleman who travelled down yesterday from London to Clayborough by the afternoon express testifies that he saw Mr. Dwerrihouse in the train, and that Mr. Dwerrihouse alighted at Blackwater station."

"Quite impossible, sir," replied the station-master, promptly.

"Why impossible?"

"Because there is no station along the line where he is so well known or where he would run so great a risk. It would be just running his head into the lion's mouth; he would have been mad to come nigh Blackwater station; and if he had come he would have been arrested before he left the platform."

"Can you tell me who took the Blackwater tickets of that train?"

"I can, sir. It was the guard, Benjamin Somers."

"And where can I find him?"

"You can find him, sir, by staying here, if you please, till one o'clock. He will be coming through with the up express from Crampton, which stays at Blackwater for ten minutes."

We waited for the up express, beguiling the time as best we could by strolling along the Blackwater road till we came almost to the outskirts of the town, from which the station was distant nearly a couple of miles. By one o'clock we were back again upon the platform and waiting for the train. It came punctually, and I at once recognized the ruddy-faced guard who had gone down with my train the evening before.

"The gentlemen want to ask you something about Mr. Dwerrihouse Somers," said the station-master, by way of introduction.

The guard flashed a keen glance from my face to Jelf's and back again to mine.

"Mr. John Dwerrihouse, the late director?" said he, interrogatively.

"The same," replied my friend. "Should you know him if you saw him?"

"Anywhere, sir."

"Do you know if he was in the 4.15 express yesterday afternoon?"

"He was not, sir."

"How can you answer so positively?"

"Because I looked into every carriage and saw every face in that train, and I could take my oath that Mr. Dwerrihouse was not in it. This gentleman was," he added, turning sharply upon me. "I don't know that I ever saw him before in my life, but I remember his face perfectly. You nearly missed taking your seat in time at this station, sir, and you got out at Clayborough."

"Quite true, guard," I replied; "but do you not also remember the face of the gentleman who travelled down in the same carriage with me as far as here?"

"It was my impression, sir, that you travelled down alone," said Somers, with a look of some surprise.

"By no means. I had a fellow-traveller as far as Blackwater, and it was in try-ing to restore him the cigar-case which he had dropped in the carriage that I so nearly let you go on without me."

"I remember your saying something about a cigar-case, certainly," replied the guard; "but—"

"You asked for my ticket just before we entered the station."

"I did, sir."

"Then you must have seen him. He sat in the corner next the very door to which you came."

"No, indeed; I saw no one."

I looked at Jelf I began to think the guard was in the ex-director's confidence, and paid for his silence.

"If I had seen another traveller I should have asked for his ticket," added Somers. "Did you see me ask for his ticket, sir?"

"I observed that you did not ask for it, but he explained that by saying—" I hesitated. I feared I might be telling too much, and so broke off abruptly.

The guard and the station-master exchanged glances. The former looked im-patiently at his watch.

"I am obliged to go on in four minutes more, sir," he said.

"One last question, then," interposed Jelf, with a sort of desperation. "If this gentleman's fellow-traveller had been Mr. John Dwerrihouse, and he had been sitting in the corner next door by which you took the tickets, could you have failed to see and recognize him?"

"No, sir; it would have been quite impossible."

"And you are certain you did *not* see him?"

"As I said before, sir, I could take my oath I did not see him. And if it wasn't that I don't like to contradict a gentleman, I would say I could also take my oath that this gentleman was quite alone in the carriage the whole way from London to Clayborough. Why, sir," he added, dropping his voice so as to be inaudible to the station-master, who had been called away to speak to some person close by, "you expressly asked me to give you a compartment to yourself, and I did so. I locked you in, and you were so good as to give me something for myself."

"Yes; but Mr. Dwerrihouse had a key of his own."

"I never saw him, sir; I saw no one in that compartment but yourself. Beg pardon, sir; my time's up."

And with this the ruddy guard touched his cap and was gone. In another minute the heavy panting of the engine began afresh, and the train glided slowly out of the station.

We looked at each other for some moments in silence. I was the first to speak.

"Mr. Benjamin Somers knows more than he chooses to tell," I said.

"Humph! do you think so?"

"It must be. He could not have come to the door without seeing him; it's impossible."

"There is one thing not impossible, my dear fellow."

"What is that?"

"That you may have fallen asleep and dreamed the whole thing."

"Could I dream of a branch line that I had never heard of? Could I dream of a hundred and one business details that had no kind of interest for me? Could I dream of the seventy-five thousand pounds?"

"Perhaps you might have seen or heard some vague account of the affair while you were abroad. It might have made no impression upon you at the time, and might have come back to you in your dreams, recalled perhaps by the mere names of the stations on the line."

"What about the fire in the chimney of the blue room—should I have heard of that during my journey?"

"Well, no; I admit there is a difficulty about that point."

"And what about the cigar-case?"

"Ay, by jove! there is the cigar-case. That is a stubborn fact. Well, it's a mysterious affair, and it will need a better detective than myself, I fancy, to clear it up. I suppose we may as well go home."

A week had not gone by when I received a letter from the secretary of the East Anglian Railway Company, requesting the favour of my attendance at a special board meeting not then many days distant. No reasons were alleged and no apologies offered for this demand upon my time, but they had heard, it was clear, of my inquiries anent the missing director, and had a mind to put me through some sort Of official examination upon the subject. Being still a guest at Dumbleton Hall, I had to go up to London for the purpose, and Jonathan Jelf accompanied me. I found the direction of the Great East Anglian line represented by a party of some twelve or fourteen gentlemen seated in solemn conclave round a huge green baize table, in a gloomy boardroom adjoining the London terminus.

Being courteously received by the chairman (who at once began by saying that certain statements of mine respecting Mr. John Dwerrihouse had come to the knowledge ofthe direction, and that they in consequence desired to confer with me on those points), we were placed at the table, and the inquiry proceeded in due form.

I was first asked if I knew Mr. John Dwerrihouse, how long I had been acquainted with him, and whether I could identify him at sight. I was then asked when I had seen him last. To which I replied, "On the 4th of this present month, December, 1856." Then came the inquiry of where I had seen him on that fourth day of December; to which I replied that I met him in a first-class compartment of the 4.15 down express, that he got in just as the train was leaving the London terminus, and that he alighted at Blackwater station. The chairman then inquired whether I had held any communication with my fellow-traveller; whereupon I related, as nearly as I could remember it, the whole bulk and substance of Mr. John Dwerrihouse's diffuse information respecting the new branch line.

To all this the board listened with profound attention, while the chairman presided and the secretary took notes. I then produced the cigar-case. It was passed from hand to hand, and recognized by all. There was not a man present who did not remember that plain cigar-case with its silver monogram, or to whom it seemed anything less than entirely corroborative of my evidence. When at length I had told all that I had to tell, the chairman whispered something to the secretary; the secretary touched a silver hand-bell, and the guard, Benjamin Somers, was ushered into the room. He was then examined as carefully as myself. He declared that he knew Mr. John Dwerrihouse perfectly well, that he could not be mistaken in him, that he remembered going down with the 4.15 express on the afternoon in question, that he remembered me, and that, there being one or two empty first-class compartments on that especial afternoon, he had, in compliance with my request, placed me in a carriage by myself. He was positive that I remained alone in that compartment all the way from London to Clayborough. He was ready to take his oath that Mr. Dwerrihouse was neither in that carriage with me, nor in any compartment of that train. He remembered distinctly to have examined my ticket at Blackwater; was certain that there was no one else at that time in the carriage; could not have failed to observe a second person, if there had been one; had that second person been Mr. John Dwerrihouse, should have quietly double-locked the door of the carriage and have at once given information to the Blackwater station-master. So clear, so decisive, so ready, was Somers with this testimony, that the board looked fairly puzzled.

"You hear this person's statement, Mr. Langford," said the chairman. "It contradicts yours in every particular. What have you to say in reply?"

"I can only repeat what I said before. I am quite as positive of the truth of my own assertions as Mr. Somers can be of the truth of his."

"You say that Mr. Dwerrihouse alighted at Blackwater, and that he was in possession of a private key. Are you sure that he had not alighted by means of that key before the guard came round for the tickets?"

"I am quite positive that he did not leave the carriage till the train had fairly entered the station, and the other Blackwater passengers alighted. I even saw that he was met there by a friend."

"Indeed! Did you see that person distinctly?"

"Quite distinctly."

"Can you describe his appearance?"

"I think so. He was short and very slight, sandy-haired, with a bushy moustache and beard, and he wore a closely fitting suit of grey tweed. His age I should take to be about thirty-eight or forty."

"Did Mr. Dwerrihouse leave the station in this person's company?"

"I cannot tell. I saw them walking together down the platform, and then I saw them standing aside under a gas-jet, talking earnestly. After that I lost sight of them quite suddenly, and just then my train went on, and I with it."

The chairman and secretary conferred together in an undertone. The directors whispered to one another. One or two looked suspiciously at the guard. I could see that my evidence remained unshaken, and that, like myself, they suspected some complicity between the guard and the defaulter.

"How far did you conduct that 4.15 express on the day in question, Somers?" asked the chairman.

"All through, sir," replied the guard, "from London to Crampton."

"How was it that you were not relieved at Clayborough? I thought there was always a change of guards at Clayborough."

"There used to be, sir, till the new regulations came in force last midsummer, since when the guards in charge of express trains go the whole way through."

The chairman turned to the secretary.

"I think it would be as well," he said, "if we had the day-book to refer to upon this point."

Again the secretary touched the silver hand-bell, and desired the porter in attendance to summon Mr. Raikes. From a word or two dropped by another of the directors I gathered that Mr. Raikes was one of the under-secretaries.

He came, a small, slight, sandy-haired, keen-eyed man, with an eager, nervous manner, and a forest of light beard and moustache. He just showed himself at the door of the board-room, and, being requested to bring a certain day-book from a certain shelf in a certain room, bowed and vanished.

He was there such a moment, and the surprise of seeing him was so great and sudden, that it was not till the door had closed upon him that I found voice to speak. He was no sooner gone, however, than I sprang to my feet.

"That person," I said, "is the same who met Mr. Dwerrihouse upon the platform at Blackwater!"

There was a general movement of surprise. The chairman looked grave and somewhat agitated.

"Take care, Mr. Langford," he said; "take care what you say."

"I am as positive of his identity as of my own."

"Do you consider the consequences of your words? Do you consider that you are bringing a charge of the gravest character against one of the company's servants?"

"I am willing to be put upon my oath, if necessary. The man who came to that door a minute since is the same whom I saw talking with Mr. Dwerrihouse on the Blackwater platform. Were he twenty times the company's servant, I could say neither more nor less."

The chairman turned again to the guard.

"Did you see Mr. Raikes in the train or on the platform?" he asked. Somers shook his head.

"I am confident Mr. Raikes was not in the train," he said, "and I certainly did not see him on the platform."

The chairman turned next to the secretary.

"Mr. Raikes is in your office, Mr. Hunter," he said. "Can you remember if he was absent on the 4th instant?"

"I do not think he was," replied the secretary, "but I am not prepared to speak positively. I have been away most afternoons myself lately, and Mr. Raikes might easily have absented himself if he had been disposed."

At this moment the under-secretary returned with the day-book under his arm.

"Be pleased to refer, Mr. Raikes," said the chairman, "to the entries of the 4th instant, and see what Benjamin Somers's duties were on that day."

Mr. Raikes threw open the cumbrous volume, and ran a practised eye and finger down some three or four successive columns of entries. Stopping suddenly at the foot of a page, he then read aloud that Benjamin Somers had on that day conducted the 4.15 express from London to Crampton.

The chairman leaned forward in his seat, looked the under-secretary full in the face, and said, quite sharply and suddenly:

"Where were *you*, Mr. Raikes, on the same afternoon?"

"*I*, sir?"

"You, Mr. Raikes. Where were you on the afternoon and evening of the 4th of the present month?"

"Here, sir, in Mr. Hunter's office. Where else should I be?"

There was a dash of trepidation in the under-secretary's voice as he said this, but his look of surprise was natural enough.

"We have some reason for believing, Mr. Raikes, that you were absent that afternoon without leave. Was this the case?"

"Certainly not, sir. I have not had a day's holiday since September. Mr. Hunter will bear me out in this."

Mr. Hunter repeated what he had previously said on the subject, but added that the clerks in the adjoining office would be certain to know. Whereupon the senior clerk, a grave, middle-aged person in green glasses, was summoned and interrogated.

His testimony cleared the under-secretary at once. He declared that Mr. Raikes had in no instance, to his knowledge, been absent during office hours since his return from his annual holiday in September.

I was confounded. The chairman turned to me with a smile, in which a shade of covert annoyance was scarcely apparent.

"You hear, Mr. Langford?" he said.

"I hear, sir; but my conviction remains unshaken."

"I fear, Mr. Langford, that your convictions are very insufficiently based," replied the chairman, with a doubtful cough. "I fear that you 'dream dreams', and mistake them for actual occurrences. It is a dangerous habit of mind, and might lead to dangerous results. Mr. Raikes here would have found himself in an unpleasant position had he not proved so satisfactory an alibi."

I was about to reply, but he gave me no time.

"I think, gentlemen," he went on to say, addressing the board, "that we should be wasting time to push this inquiry further. Mr. Langford's evidence would seem to be of an equal value throughout. The testimony of Benjamin Somers disproves his first statement, and the testimony of the last witness disproves his second. I think we may conclude that Mr. Langford fell asleep in the train on the occasion of his journey to Clayborough, and dreamed an unusually vivid and circumstantial dream, of which, however, we have now heard quite enough."

There are few things more annoying than to find one's positive convictions met with incredulity. I could not help feeling impatience at the turn that affairs had taken. I was not proof against the civil sarcasm of the chairman's manner. Most intolerable of all, however, was the quiet smile lurking about the corners of Benjamin Somers's mouth, and the half-triumphant, half-malicious gleam in the eyes of the under-secretary. The man was evidently puzzled and somewhat alarmed. His looks seemed furtively to interrogate me. Who was I? What did I want? Why had I come here to do him an ill turn with his employers? What was it to me whether or not he was absent without leave?

Seeing all this, and perhaps more irritated by it than the thing deserved, I begged leave to detain the attention of the board for a moment longer. Jelf plucked me impatiently by the sleeve.

"Better let the thing drop," he whispered. "The chairman's right enough; you dreamed it, and the less said now the better."

I was not to be silenced, however, in this fashion. I had yet something to say, and I would say it. It was to this effect: that dreams were not usually productive of tangible results, and that I requested to know in what way the chairman conceived I had evolved from my dream so substantial and well-made a delusion as the cigar-case which I had had the honour to place before him at the commencement of our interview.

"The cigar-case, I admit, Mr. Langford," the chairman replied, "is a very strong point in your evidence. It is your only strong point, however, and there is just a possibility that we may all be misled by a mere accidental resemblance. Will you permit me to see the case again?"

"It is unlikely," I said, as I handed it to him, "that any other should bear precisely this monogram, and yet be in all other particulars exactly similar."

The chairman examined it for a moment in silence, and then passed it to Mr. Hunter. Mr. Hunter turned it over and over, and shook his head.

"This is no mere resemblance,"he said. "It isjohn Dwerrihouse's cigar-case to a certainty. I remember it perfectly; I have seen it a hundred times."

"I believe I may say the same," added the chairman; "yet how account for the way in which Mr. Langford asserts that it came into his possession?"

"I can only repeat," I replied, "that I found it on the floor of the carriage after Mr. Dwerrihouse had alighted. It was in leaning out to look after him that I trod upon it, and it was in running after him for the purpose of restoring it that I saw, or believed I saw, Mr. Raikes standing aside with him in earnest conversation."

Again I felt Jonathan Jelf plucking at my sleeve.

"Look at Raikes," he whispered; "look at Raikes!"

I turned to where the under-secretary had been standing a moment before, and saw him, white as death, with lips trembling and livid, stealing towards the door.

To conceive a sudden, strange, and indefinite suspicion, to fling myself in his way, to take him by the shoulders as if he were a child, and turn his craven face, perforce, towards the board, were with me the work of an instant.

"Look at him!" I exclaimed. "Look at his face! I ask no better witness to the truth of my words."

The chairman's brow darkened.

"Mr. Raikes," he said, sternly, "if you know anything you had better speak."

Vainly trying to wrench himself from my grasp, the under-secretary stammered out an incoherent denial.

"Let me go," he said. "I know nothing—you have no right to detain me—let me go!"

"Did you, or did you not, meet Mr. John Dwerrihouse at Blackwater station? The charge brought against you is either true or false. If true, you will do well to throw yourself upon the mercy of the board and make full confession of all that you know."

The under-secretary wrung his hands in an agony of helpless terror.

"I was away!" he cried. "I was two hundred miles away at the time! I know nothing about it—I have nothing to confess—I am innocent—I call God to witness I am innocent!"

"Two hundred miles away!" echoed the chairman. "What do you mean?"

"I was in Devonshire. I had three weeks' leave of absence—I appeal to Mr. Hunter—Mr. Hunter knows I had three weeks' leave of absence! I was in Devonshire all the time; I can prove I was in Devonshire!"

Seeing him so abject, so incoherent, so wild with apprehension, the directors began to whisper gravely among themselves, while one got quietly up and called the porter to guard the door.

"What has your being in Devonshire to do with the matter?" said the chairman. "When were you in Devonshire?"

"Mr. Raikes took his leave in September," said the secretary, "about the time when Mr. Dwerrihouse disappeared."

"I never even heard that he had disappeared till I came back!"

"That must remain to be proved," said the chairman. "I shall at once put this matter in the hands of the police. In the meanwhile, Mr. Raikes being myself a magistrate and used to deal with these cases, I advise you to offer no resistance, but to confess while confession may yet do you service. As for your accomplice —"

The frightened wretch fell upon his knees.

"I had no accomplice!" he cried. "Only have mercy upon me—only spare my life, and I will confess all! I didn't mean to harm him! I didn't mean to hurt a hair of his head! Only have mercy upon me, and let me go!"

The chairman rose in his place, pale and agitated. "Good heavens!" he exclaimed, "what horrible mystery is this? What does it mean?"

"As sure as there is a God in heaven,"said Jonathan Jelf, "it means that murder has been done."

"No! No! No!" shrieked Raikes, still upon his knees, and cowering like a beaten hound. "Not murder! No jury that ever sat could bring it in murder. I thought I had only stunned him—I never meant to do more than stun him! Manslaughter—manslaughter—not murder!"

Overcome by the horror of this unexpected revelation, the chairman covered his face with his hand and for a moment or two remained silent.

"Miserable man," he said at length, "you have betrayed yourself!"

"You made me confess! You urged me to throw myself upon the mercy of the board!"

"You have confessed to a crime which no one suspected you of having committed," replied the chairman, "and which this board has no power either to punish or forgive. All that I can do for you is to advise you to submit to the law, to plead guilty, and to conceal nothing. When did you do this deed?"

The guilty man rose to his feet, and leaned heavily against the table. His answer came reluctantly, like the speech of one dreaming.

"On the 22nd of September!"

On the 22nd of September! I looked in Jonathan Jelf's face, and he in mine. I felt my own paling with a strange sense of wonder and dread. I saw his blanch suddenly, even to the lips.

"Merciful heaven!" he whispered. "*What was it, then, that you saw in the train?*"

What was it that I saw in the train? That question remains unanswered to this day. I have never been able to reply to it. I only know that it bore the living likeness of the murdered man, whose body had then been lying some ten weeks under a rough pile of branches and brambles and rotting leaves, at the bottom of a deserted chalk-pit about half-way between Blackwater and Mallingford. I know that it spoke and moved and looked as that man spoke and moved and looked in life; that I heard, or seemed to hear, things related which I could never otherwise have learned; that I was guided, as it were, by that vision on the platform to the identification of the murderer; and that, a passive instrument myself, I was destined, by means of these mysterious teachings, to bring about the ends of Justice. For these things I have never been able to account.

As for that matter of the cigar-case, it proved, on inquiry, that the carriage in which I travelled down that afternoon to Clayborough had not been in use for several weeks, and was, in point of fact, the same in which poor John Dwerrihouse had performed his last journey. The case had doubtless been dropped by him, and had lain unnoticed till I found it.

Upon the details of the murder I have no need to dwell. Those who desire more ample particulars may find them, and the written confession of Augustus Raikes, in the files of *The Times* for 1856. Enough that the under-secretary, knowing the history of the new line, and following the negotiation step by step through all its stages, determined to waylay Mr. Dwerrihouse, rob him of the seventy-five thousand pounds, and escape to America with his booty.

In order to effect these ends he obtained leave of absence a few days before the time appointed for the payment of the money, secured his passage across the Atlantic in a steamer advertised to start on the 23rd, provided himself with a heavily loaded "life-preserver", and went down to Blackwater to await the arrival of his victim. How he met him on the platform with a pretended message from the board, how he offered to conduct him by a short cut across the fields to Mallingford, how, having brought him to a lonely place, he struck him down with the life-preserver, and so killed him, and how, finding what he had done, he dragged the body to the verge of an out-of-the-way chalk-pit, and there flung it in and piled it over with branches and brambles, are facts still fresh in the memories of those who, like the connoisseurs in De Quincey's famous essay, regard murder as a fine art. Strangely enough, the murderer, having done his work, was afraid to leave the country. He declared that he had not intended to take the director's life, but only to stun and rob him; and that, finding the blow had killed, he dared not fly for fear of drawing down suspicion upon his own head. As a mere robber he would have been safe in the States, but as a murderer he would inevitably have been pursued and given up to justice. So he forfeited his passage, returned to the office as usual at the end of his leave, and locked up his ill-gotten thousands till a more convenient opportunity. In the meanwhile he had the satisfaction of finding that Mr. Dwerrihouse was universally believed to have absconded with the money, no one knew how or whither.

Whether he meant murder or not, however, Mr. Augustus Raikes paid the full penalty of his crime, and was hanged at the Old Bailey, in the second week in January, 1857. Those who desire to make his further acquaintance may see him any day (admirably done in wax) in the Chamber of Horrors at Madame Tussaud's exhibition, in Baker Street. He is there to be found in the midst of a select society of ladies and gentlemen of atrocious memory, dressed in the close-cut tweed suit which he wore on the evening of the murder, and holding in his hand the identical life-preserver with which he committed it.

THREE SPANISH LADIES,
by Walter E. Marconette

Originally published in *Spaceways* #1, November 1938.

A Tale Told by a Wraith....

"Si, Si, Senor Saint Petair! It was at Irun that I lost my life. You wish to hear the story? Very well, but first you must understand that I have loved, or thought I loved, three women at the same time."

"Do not smile, senor Saint; it is not a frivolous matter. To love one woman, that is bad enough; but to love two, that is terrible. Just imagine my woes with three!"

At this point the wraith with the very Spanish accent shifted his position on the cloud he occupied with St. Peter. Finally he settled back with a loud sigh, if ghosts may be said to sigh, and continued his narration.

"The first was Juanita. She was tall and slim and lithe. The second was Carlotta. She eked out a bare existence by selling flowers on the street for a few coppers an ounce. Her figure was short and rather plump with skin as brown as a nut.

"The third was quite different, senor Saint, a blonde. Delores, the daughter of old Don Hernandez, was half French. You see, her father met his wife on one of his annual visits to Paris."

"Well, senor Saint, I loved the three and became more miserable as the days slid by. I might still be in the dilemma, but then the revolution came."

"When France's legions marched to attack Irun (that is my home city up on the French frontier), I joined the loyalist forces. They pounded us with heavy artillery for days, shelling, shelling ceaselessly until men began to go mad from it. Then, our vigilance relaxed, the rebels poured in. All that day we fought like demons, but ever we were pushed back."

"And then, by one of those weird coincidences which do occur at times to mystify us, I rounded a corner and found, crouched low in a doorway, my three loves. Not knowing each other, yet hiding together!"

"I had hardly perceived the girls when suddenly I was struck. I felt the slug's deadening impact, felt it tear its fiery way through my flesh, and heard a sickening crunch and splintering as my bones gave way."

"As I crumpled, I was glad. Yes, glad, for I knew my love problems were solved. Regardless of the seething hell about me, the one girl who really loved me would reach my side. And, senor Saint, would you believe it, I calmly wondered which of the three it would be as I lay there!"

"A hand touched my shoulder; I heard someone call my name softly. With a mighty effort I opened my eyes...and peered into those of...Dios!....Jose, my sergeant!"

"There and then I wished I might die. Si, those fascists were very, very obliging fellows, for they dropped a heavy shell almost on top of us.

"By the way, Senor Saint Petair, is my friend Jose here? He isn't? My, can it be that he is in...in...in...in the other place?"

BRICKETT BOTTOM,
by Amyas Northcote

Originally appeared in *In Ghostly Company* **(1921).**

The Reverend Arthur Maydew was the hard-working incumbent of a large parish in one of our manufacturing towns. He was also a student and a man of no strong physique, so that when an opportunity was presented to him to take an annual holiday by exchanging parsonages with an elderly clergyman, Mr. Roberts, the Squarson of the Parish of Overbury, and an acquaintance of his own, he was glad to avail himself of it.

Overbury is a small and very remote village in one of our most lovely and rural counties, and Mr. Roberts had long held the living of it.

Without further delay we can transport Mr. Maydew and his family, which consisted only of two daughters, to their temporary home. The two young ladies, Alice and Maggie, the heroines of this narrative, were at that time aged twenty-six and twenty-four years respectively. Both of them were attractive girls, fond of such society as they could find in their own parish and, the former especially, always pleased to extend the circle of their acquaintance. Although the elder in years, Alice in many ways yielded place to her sister, who was the more energetic and practical and upon whose shoulders the bulk of the family cares and responsibilities rested. Alice was inclined to be absent-minded and emotional and to devote more of her thoughts and time to speculations of an abstract nature than her sister.

Both of the girls, however, rejoiced at the prospect of a period of quiet and rest in a pleasant country neighbourhood, and both were gratified at knowing that their father would find in Mr. Roberts' library much that would entertain his mind, and in Mr. Roberts' garden an opportunity to indulge freely in his favourite game of croquet. They would have, no doubt, preferred some cheerful neighbours, but Mr. Roberts was positive in his assurances that there was no one in the neighbourhood whose acquaintance would be of interest to them.

The first few weeks of their new life passed pleasantly for the Maydew family. Mr. Maydew quickly gained renewed vigour in his quiet and congenial surroundings, and in the delightful air, while his daughters spent much of their time in long walks about the country and in exploring its beauties.

One evening late in August the two girls were returning from a long walk along one of their favourite paths, which led along the side of the Downs. On their right, as they walked, the ground fell away sharply to a narrow glen, named Brickett Bottom, about three-quarters of a mile in length, along the bottom of which ran a little-used country road leading to a farm, known as Blaise's Farm, and then onward and upward to lose itself as a sheep track on the higher Downs. On their side of the slope some scattered trees and bushes grew, but beyond the lane and running up over the farther slope of the glen was a thick wood, which extended away to Carew Court, the seat of a neighbouring magnate, Lord Carew. On their left the open Down rose above them and beyond its crest lay Overbury.

The girls were walking hastily, as they were later than they had intended to be and were anxious to reach home. At a certain point at which they had now arrived the path forked, the right hand branch leading down into Brickett Bottom and the left hand turning up over the Down to Overbury.

Just as they were about to turn into the left hand path Alice suddenly stopped and pointing downwards exclaimed:

"How very curious, Maggie! Look, there is a house down there in the Bottom, which we have, or at least I have, never noticed before, often as we have walked up the Bottom."

Maggie followed with her eyes her sister's pointing finger. "I don't see any house," she said.

"Why, Maggie," said her sister, "can't you see it! A quaint-looking, old-fashioned red brick house, there just where the road bends to the right. It seems to be standing in a nice, well- kept garden too."

Maggie looked again, but the light was beginning to fade in the glen and she was short-sighted to boot.

"I certainly don't see anything," she said. "But then I am so blind and the light is getting bad; yes, perhaps I do see a house," she added, straining her eyes.

"Well, it is there," replied her sister, "and to-morrow we will come and explore it." Maggie agreed readily enough, and the sisters went home, still speculating on how they had happened not to notice the house before and resolving firmly on an expedition thither the next day. However, the expedition did not come off as planned, for that evening Maggie slipped on the stairs and fell, spraining her ankle in such a fashion as to preclude walking for some time.

Notwithstanding the accident to her sister, Alice remained possessed by the idea of making further investigations into the house she had looked down upon from the hill the evening before; and the next day, having seen Maggie carefully settled for the afternoon, she started off for Brickett Bottom. She returned in triumph and much intrigued over her discoveries, which she eagerly narrated to her sister.

Yes. There was a nice, old-fashioned red brick house, not very large and set in a charming, old- world garden in the Bottom. It stood on a tongue of land jutting out from the woods, just at the point where the lane, after a fairly straight course from its junction with the main road half a mile away, turned sharply to the right in the direction of Blaise's Farm. More than that, Alice had seen the people of the house, whom she described as an old gentleman and a lady, presumably his wife. She had not clearly made out the gentleman, who was sitting in the porch, but the old lady, who had been in the garden busy with her flowers, had looked up and smiled pleasantly at her as she passed. She was sure, she said, that they were nice people and that it would be pleasant to make their acquaintance.

Maggie was not quite satisfied with Alice's story. She was of a more prudent and retiring nature than her sister; she had an uneasy feeling that, if the old couple had been desirable or attractive neighbours, Mr. Roberts would have mentioned them, and knowing Alice's nature she said what she could to discourage her vague idea of endeavouring to make acquaintance with the owners of the red brick house.

On the following morning, when Alice came to her sister's room to inquire how she did, Maggie noticed that she looked pale and rather absent-minded, and, after a few commonplace remarks had passed, she asked:

"What is the matter, Alice? You don't look yourself this morning." Her sister gave a slightly embarrassed laugh.

"Oh, I am all right," she replied, "only I did not sleep very well. I kept on dreaming about the house. It was such an odd dream too; the house seemed to be home, and yet to be different."

"What, that house in Brickett Bottom?" said Maggie. "Why, what is the matter with you, you seem to be quite crazy about the place?"

"Well, it is curious, isn't it, Maggie, that we should have only just discovered it, and that it looks to be lived in by nice people? I wish we could get to know them."

Maggie did not care to resume the argument of the night before and the subject dropped, nor did Alice again refer to the house or its inhabitants for some little time. In fact, for some days the weather was wet and Alice was forced to abandon her walks, but when the weather once more became fine she resumed them, and Maggie suspected that Brickett Bottom formed one of her sister's favourite expeditions. Maggie became anxious over her sister, who seemed to grow daily more absent-minded and silent, but she refused to be drawn into any confidential talk, and Maggie was nonplussed.

One day, however, Alice returned from her afternoon walk in an unusually excited state of mind, of which Maggie sought an explanation. It came with a rush. Alice said that, that afternoon, as she approached the house in Brickett Bottom, the old lady, who as usual was busy in her garden, had walked down to the gate as she passed and had wished her good day.

Alice had replied and, pausing, a short conversation had followed. Alice could not remember the exact tenor of it, but, after she had paid a compliment to the old lady's flowers, the latter had rather diffidently asked her to enter the garden for a closer view. Alice had hesitated, and the old lady had said "Don't be afraid of me, my dear, I like to see young ladies about me and my husband finds their society quite necessary to him." After a pause she went on: "Of course nobody has told you about us. My husband is Colonel Paxton, late of the Indian Army, and we have been here for many, many years. It's rather lonely, for so few people ever see us. Do come in and meet the Colonel."

"I hope you didn't go in," said Maggie rather sharply.

"Why not?" replied Alice.

"Well, I don't like Mrs. Paxton asking you in that way," answered Maggie. "I don't see what harm there was in the invitation," said Alice.

"I didn't go in because it was getting late and I was anxious to get home; but —"

"But what?" asked Maggie.

Alice shrugged her shoulders. "Well," she said, "I have accepted Mrs. Paxton's invitation to pay her a little visit to-morrow." And she gazed defiantly at Maggie.

Maggie became distinctly uneasy on hearing of this resolution. She did not like the idea of her impulsive sister visiting people on such slight acquaintance, especially as they had never heard them mentioned before. She endeavoured by all means, short of appealing to Mr. Maydew, to dissuade her sister from going, at any rate until there had been time to make some inquiries as to the Paxtons. Alice, however, was obdurate.

What harm could happen to her? she asked. Mrs. Paxton was a charming old lady. She was going early in the afternoon for a short visit. She would be back for tea and croquet with her father and, anyway, now that Maggie was laid up, long solitary walks were unendurable and she was not going to let slip the chance of following up what promised to be a pleasant acquaintance.

Maggie could do nothing more. Her ankle was better and she was able to get down to the garden and sit in a long chair near her father, but walking was still quite out of the question, and it was with some misgivings that on the following day she watched Alice depart gaily for her visit, promising to be back by half-past four at the very latest.

The afternoon passed quietly till nearly five, when Mr. Maydew, looking up from his book, noticed Maggie's uneasy expression and asked:

"Where is Alice?"

"Out for a walk," replied Maggie; and then after a short pause she went on: "And she has also gone to pay a call on some neighbours whom she has recently discovered."

"Neighbours," ejaculated Mr. Maydew, "what neighbours? Mr. Roberts never spoke of any neighbours to me."

"Well, I don't know much about them," answered Maggie. "Only Alice and I were out walking the day of my accident and saw or at least she saw, for I am so blind I could not quite make it out, a house in Brickett Bottom. The next day she went to look at it closer, and yesterday she told me that she had made the acquaintance of the people living in it. She says that they are a retired Indian officer and his wife, a Colonel and Mrs. Paxton, and Alice describes Mrs. Paxton as a charming old lady, who pressed her to come and see them. So she has gone this afternoon, but she promised me she would be back long before this."

Mr. Maydew was silent for a moment and then said:

"I am not well pleased about this. Alice should not be so impulsive and scrape acquaintance with absolutely unknown people. Had there been nice neighbours in Brickett Bottom, I am certain Mr. Roberts would have told us."

The conversation dropped; but both father and daughter were disturbed and uneasy and, tea having been finished and the clock striking half-past five, Mr. Maydew asked Maggie:

"When did you say Alice would be back?"

"Before half-past four at the latest, father."

"Well, what can she be doing? What can have delayed her? You say you did not see the house," he went on.

"No," said Maggie, "I cannot say I did. It was getting dark and you know how short-sighted I am."

"But surely you must have seen it at some other time," said her father.

"That is the strangest part of the whole affair," answered Maggie. "We have often walked up the Bottom, but I never noticed the house, nor had Alice till that evening. I wonder," she went on after a short pause, "if it would not be well to ask Smith to harness the pony and drive over to bring her back. I am not happy about her—I am afraid—"

"Afraid of what?" said her father in the irritated voice of a man who is growing frightened. "What can have gone wrong in this quiet place? Still, I'll send

Smith over for her."

So saying he rose from his chair and sought out Smith, the rather dull-witted gardener- groom attached to Mr. Roberts' service.

"Smith," he said, "I want you to harness the pony at once and go over to Colonel Paxton's in Brickett Bottom and bring Miss Maydew home."

The man stared at him.

"Go where, sir?" he said.

Mr. Maydew repeated the order and the man, still staring stupidly, answered: "I never heard of Colonel Paxton, sir. I don't know what house you mean." Mr. Maydew was now growing really anxious.

"Well, harness the pony at once," he said; and going back to Maggie he told her of what he called Smith's stupidity, and asked her if she felt that her ankle would be strong enough to permit her to go with him and Smith to the Bottom to point out the house.

Maggie agreed readily and in a few minutes the party started off. Brickett Bottom, although not more than three-quarters of a mile away over the Downs, was at least three miles by road; and as it was nearly six o'clock before Mr. Maydew left the Vicarage, and the pony was old and slow, it was getting late before the entrance to Brickett Bottom was reached. Turning into the lane the cart proceeded slowly up the Bottom, Mr. Maydew and Maggie looking anxiously from side to side, whilst Smith drove stolidly on looking neither to the right nor left.

"Where is the house?" said Mr. Maydew presently.

"At the bend of the road," answered Maggie, her heart sickening as she looked out through the failing light to see the trees stretching their ranks in unbroken formation along it. The cart reached the bend. "It should be here," whispered Maggie.

They pulled up. Just in front of them the road bent to the right round a tongue of land, which, unlike the rest of the right hand side of the road, was free from trees and was covered only by rough grass and stray bushes. A closer inspection disclosed evident signs of terraces having once been formed on it, but of a house there was no trace.

"Is this the place?" said Mr. Maydew in a low voice.

Maggie nodded.

"But there is no house here," said her father. "What does it all mean? Are you sure of yourself, Maggie? Where is Alice?"

Before Maggie could answer a voice was heard calling "Father! Maggie!" The sound of the voice was thin and high and, paradoxically, it sounded both very near and yet as if it came from some infinite distance. The cry was thrice repeated and then silence fell. Mr. Maydew and Maggie stared at each other.

"That was Alice's voice," said Mr. Maydew huskily, "she is near and in trouble, and is calling us. Which way did you think it came from, Smith?" he added, turning to the gardener.

"I didn't hear anybody calling," said the man. "Nonsense!" answered Mr. Maydew.

And then he and Maggie both began to call "Alice. Alice. Where are you?" There was no reply and Mr. Maydew sprang from the cart, at the same time bidding Smith to hand the reins to Maggie and come and search for the missing girl. Smith obeyed him and both men, scrambling up the turfy bit of ground, began to search and call through the neighbouring wood. They heard and saw nothing, however, and after an agonised search Mr. Maydew ran down to the cart and begged Maggie to drive on to Blaise's Farm for help leaving himself and Smith to continue the search. Maggie followed her father's instructions and was fortunate enough to find Mr. Rumbold, the farmer, his two sons and a couple of labourers just returning from the harvest field. She explained what had happened, and the farmer and his men promptly volunteered to form a search party, though Maggie, in spite of her anxiety, noticed a queer expression on Mr. Rumbold's face as she told him her tale.

The party, provided with lanterns, now went down the Bottom, joined Mr. Maydew and Smith and made an exhaustive but absolutely fruitless search of the woods near the bend of the road. No trace of the missing girl was to be found, and after a long and anxious time the search was abandoned, one of the young Rumbolds volunteering to ride into the nearest town and notify the police.

Maggie, though with little hope in her own heart, endeavoured to cheer her father on their homeward way with the idea that Alice might have returned to Overbury over the Downs whilst they were going by road to the Bottom, and that she had seen them and called to them in jest when they were opposite the tongue of land.

However, when they reached home there was no Alice and, though the next day the search was resumed and full inquiries were instituted by the police, all was to no purpose. No trace of Alice was ever found, the last human being that saw her having been an old woman, who had met her going down the path into the Bottom on the afternoon of her disappearance, and who described her as smiling but looking "queerlike."

This is the end of the story, but the following may throw some light upon it.

The history of Alice's mysterious disappearance became widely known through the medium of the Press and Mr. Roberts, distressed beyond measure at what had taken place, returned in all haste to Overbury to offer what comfort and help he could give to his afflicted friend and tenant. He called upon the Maydews and, having heard their tale, sat for a short time in silence. Then he said:

"Have you ever heard any local gossip concerning this Colonel and Mrs. Paxton?"

"No," replied Mr. Maydew, "I never heard their names until the day of my poor daughter's fatal visit."

"Well," said Mr. Roberts, "I will tell you all I can about them, which is not very much, I fear." He paused and then went on: "I am now nearly seventy-five years old, and for nearly seventy years no house has stood in Brickett Bottom. But when I was a child of about five there was an old-fashioned, red brick house standing in a garden at the bend of the road, such as you have described. It was owned and lived in by a retired Indian soldier and his wife, a Colonel and Mrs. Paxton. At the time I speak of, certain events having taken place at the house and the old couple having died, it was sold by their heirs to Lord Carew, who shortly after pulled it down on the ground that it interfered with his shooting. Colonel and Mrs. Paxton were well known to my father, who was the clergyman here before me, and to the neighbourhood in general. They lived quietly and were not unpopular, but the Colonel was supposed to possess a violent and vindictive temper. Their family consisted only of themselves, their daughter and a couple of servants, the Colonel's old Army servant and his Eurasian wife. Well, I cannot tell you details of what happened, I was only a child; my father never liked gossip and in later years, when he talked to me on the subject, he always avoided any appearance of exaggeration or sensationalism. However, it is known that Miss Paxton fell in love with and became engaged to a young man to whom her parents took a strong dislike. They used every possible means to break off the match, and many rumours were set on foot as to their conduct—undue influence, even cruelty were charged against them. I do not know the truth, all I can say is that Miss Paxton died and a very bitter feeling against her parents sprang up. My father, however, continued to call, but was rarely admitted. In fact, he never saw Colonel Paxton after his daughter's death and only saw Mrs. Paxton once or twice. He described her as an utterly broken woman, and was not surprised at her following her daughter to the grave in about three months' time. Colonel Paxton became, if possible, more of a recluse than ever after his wife's death and himself died not more than a month after her under circumstances which pointed to suicide. Again a crop of rumours sprang up, but there was no one in particular to take action, the doctor certified Death from Natural Causes, and Colonel Paxton, like his wife and daughter, was buried in this churchyard. The property passed to a distant relative, who came down to it for one night shortly afterwards; he never came again, having apparently conceived a violent dislike to the place, but arranged to pension off the servants and then sold the house to Lord Carew, who was glad to purchase this little island in the middle of his property. He pulled it down soon after he had bought it, and the garden was left to relapse into a wilderness."

Mr. Roberts paused. "Those are all the facts," he added.

"But there is something more," said Maggie.

Mr. Roberts hesitated for a while. "You have a right to know all," he said almost to himself; then louder he continued: "What I am now going to tell you is really rumour, vague and uncertain; I cannot fathom its truth or its meaning. About five years after the house had been pulled down a young maidservant at Carew Court was out walking one afternoon. She was a stranger to the village and a new-comer to the Court. On returning home to tea she told her fellow-servants that as she walked down Brickett Bottom, which place she described clearly, she passed a red brick house at the bend of the road and that a kind-faced old lady had asked her to step in for a while. She did not go in, not because she had any suspicions of there being anything uncanny, but simply because she feared to be late for tea.

"I do not think she ever visited the Bottom again and she had no other similar experience, so far as I am aware.

"Two or three years later, shortly after my father's death, a travelling tinker with his wife and daughter camped for the night at the foot of the Bottom. The girl strolled away up the glen to gather blackberries and was never seen or heard of again. She was searched for in vain—of course, one does not know the truth—and she may have run away voluntarily from her parents, although there was no known cause for her doing so.

"That," concluded Mr. Roberts, "is all I can tell you of either facts or rumours; all that I can now do is to pray for you and for her."

ACROSS THE GULF,
by Henry S. Whitehead

Originally published in *Weird Tales*, May 1926.

For the first year, or thereabouts, after his Scotch mother's death the successful lawyer Alan Carrington was conscious, among his other feelings, of a kind of vague dread that she might appear as a character in one of his dreams, as, she had often assured him, her mother had come to her. Being the man he was, he resented this feeling as an incongruity. Yet, there was a certain background for the feeling of dread. It had been one of his practical mother's convictions that such an appearance of her long-dead mother always preceded a disaster in the family.

Such aversions as he might possess against the maternal side of his ancestry were all included in his dislike for belief in this kind of thing. When he agreed that "the Scotch are a dour race," he always had reference, at least mentally, to this superstitious strain, associated with that race from time immemorial, concrete to his experience because of this belief of his mother's, against which he had always fought.

He carried out dutifully, and with a high degree of professional skill, all her various expressed desires, and continued, after her death, to live in their large, comfortable house. Perhaps because his mother never did appear in such dreams as he happened to remember, his dread became less and less poignant. At the end of two years or so, occupied with the thronging interests of a public man in the full power of his early maturity, it had almost ceased to be so much as a memory.

In the spring of his forty-fourth year, Carrington, who had long worked at high pressure and virtually without vacations, was apprized by certain mental and physical indications which his physician interpreted vigorously, that he must take at least the whole summer off and devote himself to recuperation. Rest, said the doctor, for his overworked mind and under-exercised body, was imperatively indicated.

Carrington was able to set his nearly innumerable interests and affairs in order in something like three weeks by means of highly concentrated efforts to that end. Then, exceedingly nervous, and not a little debilitated physically from this extra strain upon his depleted resources, he had to meet the problem of where he was to go and what he was to do. He was, of course, too deeply set in the rut of his routines to find such a decision easy. Fortunately, this problem was solved for him by a letter which he received unexpectedly from one of his cousins on his mother's side, the Reverend Fergus MacDonald, a gentleman with whom he had had only slight contacts.

Dr. MacDonald was a middle-aged, retired clergyman, whom an imminent decline had removed eight or ten years before from a brilliant, if underpaid, career in his own profession. After a few years sojourn in the Adirondacks he had emerged cured, and with an already growing reputation as a writer of that somewhat inelastic literary product emphasized by certain American magazines which seem to embalm a spinsterish austerity of the literary form under the label of distinction.

Dr. MacDonald had retained a developed pastoral instinct which he could no longer satisfy in the management of a parish. He was, besides, too little robust to risk assuming, at least for some time to come, the wearing burden of teaching. He compromised the matter by establishing a summer camp for boys in his still-desirable Adirondacks. Being devoid of experience in business matters he associated with himself a certain Thomas Starkey, a young man whom the ravages of the White Plague had snatched away from a sales-managership and driven into the quasi-exile of Saranac, where Dr. MacDonald had met him.

This association proved highly successful for the half-dozen years that it had lasted. Then Starkey, after a brave battle for his health, had succumbed, just at a period when his trained business intelligence would have been most helpful to the affairs of the camp.

Dazed at this blow, Dr. MacDonald had desisted from his labors after literary distinction long enough to write to his cousin Carrington, beseeching his legal and financial counsel. When Carrington had read the last of his cousin's finished periods, he decided at once, and dispatched a telegram announcing his immediate setting out for the camp, his intention to remain through the summer, and the promise to assume full charge of the business management. He started for the Adirondacks the next afternoon.

His presence brought immediate order out of confusion. Dr. MacDonald, on the evening of the second day of his cousin's administration of affairs, got down on his knees and returned thanks to his Maker for the undeserved beneficence which had sent this financial angel of light into the midst of his affairs, in this, his hour of dire need! Thereafter the reverend doctor immersed himself more and more deeply in his wonted task of producing the solid literature dear to the hearts of his editors.

But if Carrington's coming had improved matters at the camp, the balance of indebtedness was far from being one-sided. For the first week or so the reaction from his accustomed way of life had caused him to feel, if anything, even staler and more nerve-racked than before. But that first unpleasantness past, the invigorating air of the balsam-laden pine woods began to show its restorative effects rapidly. He found that he was sleeping like the dead. He could not get enough sleep, it appeared. His appetite increased, and he found that he was putting on needed weight. The business management of a boys' camp, absurdly simple after the complex matters of Big Business with which he had long been occupied, was only a spice to this new existence among the deep shadows and sunny spaces of the Adirondack country. At the end of a month of this, he confidently declared himself a new man. By the first of August, instead of the nervous wreck who had arrived, sharp-visaged and cadaverous, two months before, Carrington presented the appearance of a robust, hard-muscled athlete of thirty, twenty-two pounds heavier and "without a nerve in his body."

* * * *

On the evening of the fourth day of August, healthily weary after a long day's hike, Carrington retired soon after 9 o'clock, and fell immediately into a deep and restful sleep. Toward morning he dreamed of his mother for the first time since her death more than six years before. His dream took the form that he was lying here, in his own bed, awake,—a not altogether uncommon form of dream,

—and that he was very chilly in the region of the left shoulder. As is well-known to those skilled in the scientific phenomena of the dream-state, now a very prominent portion of the material used in psychological study, this kind of sensation in a dream virtually always is the result of an actual physical condition, and is reproduced in the dream because of that actual background as a stimulus. Carrington's cold shoulder was toward the left-hand, or outside of the bed, which stood against the wall of his large, airy room.

In his dream he thought that he reached out his hand to replace the bed clothes, and as he did so his hand was softly, though firmly, taken, and his mother's well-remembered voice said: "Lie still, laddie; I'll tuck you in." Then he thought his mother replaced the loosened covers and tucked them in about his shoulder with her competent touch. He wanted to thank her, and as he could not see her because of the position in which he was lying, he endeavored to open his eyes and turn over, being in that state commonly thought of as between sleep and waking. With some considerable effort he succeeded in forcing open his reluctant eyes; but turning over was a much more difficult matter, it appeared. He had to fight against an overpowering inclination to sink back comfortably into the deep sleep, from which, in his dream, he had awakened to find his shoulder disagreeably uncomfortable. The warmth of the replaced covers was an additional inducement to sleep.

At last, with a determined wrench he overcame his desire to go to sleep again and rolled over to his left side by dint of a strong effort of his will, smiling gratefully and about to express his thanks. But at the instant of accomplishing this victory of the will, he actually awakened, in precisely the position recorded in his mind in the dream-state.

Where he had expected to meet his mother's eyes, he saw nothing, but there remained with him a persistent impression that he had felt the withdrawal of her hand from where, on his shoulder, it had rested caressingly. The grateful warmth of the bedclothes in that cool morning remained, however, and he observed that they were well tucked in about that shoulder.

His dream had clearly been of the type which George Du Maurier speaks of in *Peter Ibbetson*. He had "dreamed true," and it required several minutes before he could rid himself of the impression that his mother, moved by some strange whimsicality, had stepped out of his sight, perhaps hidden herself behind the bed! He was actually about to look back of the bed before the utter absurdity of the idea became fully apparent to him. The back of the bed stood close against the wall of the room. His mother had been dead more than six years.

He jumped out of bed at the sound of reveille, blown by the camp bugler, and this abrupt action dissipated his impressions. Their memory remained, however, very clear-cut in his mind for the next two days. The impression of his mother's nearness in the course of that vivid dream had recalled her to his mind with the greatest clarity. With this revived impression of her, too, there marched, almost of necessity he supposed, in his mind the old idea which he had dreaded,—the idea that she would come to him to warn him of some impending danger.

Curiously enough, as he analyzed his sensations, he found that there remained none of the old resentment connected with this speculation, such as had characterized it during the period immediately after his mothers death. His maturity, the preoccupations of an exceptionally full and active life, and the tenderness which marked all his memories of his mother had served to remove from his mind all traces of that idea. The possibility of a "warning" in his dream of his dear mother only caused him to smile during those days after the dream during which the revived impression of his mother slowly faded thin, but it was the indulgent, slightly melancholy smile of a revived nostalgia, a gentle, faint sense of "homesickness" for her, such as might affect any middle-aged man recently reminded of a beloved mother in some rather intense fashion.

On the evening of the second day after his dream he was walking toward the camp garage with some visitors, a man and woman, parents of one of the boys at the camp, intending to drive with them to the village to guide them in some minor purchases. Just beside the well-worn trail through the great pine trees, halfway up the hill to the garage, the woman noticed a clump of large, brownish mushrooms, and enquired if they were of an edible variety. Carrington picked one and examined it. To his limited knowledge it seemed to have several of the marks of an edible mushroom. While they were standing beside the place where the mushrooms grew, one of the younger boys passed them.

"Crocker," called Mr. Carrington.

"Yes, Mr. Carrington," replied young Crocker, pausing.

"Crocker, your cabin is the one farthest south, isn't it?"

"Yes, sir."

"Were you going there just now?"

"Yes, Mr. Carrington; can I do anything for you?"

"Well, if it isn't too much trouble, you might take this mushroom over to Professor Benjamin's—you know where his camp is, just the other side of the wire fence beyond your cabin,—and ask him to let us know whether or not this is an edible mushroom. I'm not quite sure myself."

"Certainly," replied the boy, pleased to be allowed "out of bounds" even to the extent of the few rods separating the camp property from that of the gentleman named by Carrington, a university teacher regarded locally as a great expert on mushrooms, fungi, and suchlike things.

Carrington called after the disappearing boy.

"Oh, Crocker!"

"Yes, Mr. Carrington?"

"Throw it away if Dr. Benjamin says it's no good; but if he says it's all right, bring it back, please, and leave it on the mantel-shelf in the big living room. Do you mind?"

"All right, sir," shouted Crocker over his shoulder, and trotted on.

Returning from the village an hour later, Carrington found the mushroom on the mantel-shelf in the living room.

He placed it in a large paper bag, left it in the kitchen in a safe place, and, the next morning before breakfast, walked up the trail toward the garage and filled his paper bag with mushrooms.

He liked mushrooms, and so, doubtless, did the people who had noticed these. He decided he would prepare the mushrooms himself. There would be just about enough for three generous portions. Mushrooms were not commonly eaten as a breakfast dish, but—this was camp!

Exchanging a pleasant "good morning" with the young colored man who served as assistant cook, and who was engaged in getting breakfast ready, and smilingly declining his offer to prepare the mushrooms, he peeled them, warmed a generous lump of fresh, country butter in a large frying pan, and began cooking them.

A delightfully appetizing odor arising from the pan provoked respectful banter from the young cook, amused at the camp-director's efforts along the lines of his own profession, and the two chatted while Carrington turned his mushrooms over and over in the butter with a long fork. When they were done exactly to a turn, and duly peppered and salted, Carrington left them in the pan, which he took off the stove, and set about the preparation of three canapés of fried toast. He was going to serve his mushrooms in style, as the grinning young cook slyly remarked. He grinned back, and divided the mushrooms into three equal portions, each on its canapé, which he asked the under-cook to keep hot in the oven during the brief interval until mess call should bring everybody at camp in to breakfast.

Then with his long fork he speared several small pieces of mushroom which had got broken in the pan. After blowing these cool on the fork, Carrington, grinning like a boy, put them into his mouth and began to eat them.

"Good, suh?" enquired the assistant cook.

"Delicious," mumbled Carrington, enthusiastically, his mouth full of the succulent bits. After he had swallowed his mouthful, he remarked:

"But I must have left a bit of the hide on one of 'em. There's a little trace of bitter."

"Look out for 'em, suh," enjoined the under-cook, suddenly grave. "They're plumb wicked when they ain't jus' right, suh."

"These are all right," returned Carrington, reassuringly. "I had Professor Benjamin look them over."

He sauntered out on the veranda, waiting for the bugle call. From many directions the boys and a few visitors were straggling in toward the mess hall after a morning dip in the lake and cabin inspection. From their room in the guest house the people with whom he had been the evening before came across the broad veranda toward him. He was just turning toward them with a smile of pleasant greeting when the very hand of death fell on him.

Without warning, a sudden terrible griping, accompanied by a deadly coldness, and this immediately followed by a pungent, burning heat, ran through his body. Great beads of sweat sprang out on his forehead. His knees began to give under him. Everything, all this pleasant world about him, of brilliant morning sunshine and deep, sharply-defined shadow, turned greenish and dim. His senses started to slip away from him in the numbness which closed down like a relentless hand, crushing out his consciousness.

With an effort which seemed to wrench his soul and tear him with unimagined pain, he gathered all his waning forces, and, sustained only by a mighty effort of his powerful will, he staggered through the open doorway of the mess hall into the kitchen. He nearly collapsed as he leaned against the nearest table, articulating between fast-paralyzing lips:

"Water,—and mustard! Quick. The mushrooms!"

The head-cook, that moment arrived in the kitchen, happened to be quick-minded. The under-cook, too, had had, of course, some preparation for this possibility.

One of the men seized a bowl just used for beating eggs and with shaking hands poured it half-full of warm water from a heating kettle on the stove. Into this the other emptied nearly half a tin of dry mustard which he stirred about frantically with his floury hand. This, his eyes rolling with terror, he held to Carrington's lips, and Carrington, concentrating afresh all his remaining faculties, forced the nauseous fluid through his blue lips, and swallowed, painfully, great saving gulps of the powerful emetic.

Again and yet again the two negroes renewed the dose.

One of the counselors, on dining room duty, coming into the kitchen sensed something terribly amiss, and ran to support Carrington.

* * * *

Ten minutes later, vastly nauseated, trembling with weakness, but safe, Carrington, leaning heavily on the young counselor, walked up and down behind the mess hall. His first words, after he could speak coherently, were to order the assistant cook to burn the contents of the three hot plates in the oven....

He had eaten a large mouthful of one of the most deadly varieties of poisonous mushroom, one containing the swiftly-acting vegetable alkaloids which spell certain death. His few moments' respite, as he reasoned the matter out afterward, had been undoubtedly due to his having cooked the mushrooms in butter, of which he had been lavish. This, thoroughly soaked up by the mushrooms, had, for a brief period, resisted digestion.

Very gradually, as he walked up and down, taking in deep breaths of the sweet, pine-scented air, his strength returned to him. After he had thoroughly walked off the faintness which had followed the violent treatment to which he had subjected himself, he went up to his room, and, still terribly shaken by his experience and narrow escape from death, went to bed to rest.

Crocker, it appeared, had duly carried out his instructions. Dr. Benjamin had looked at the specimen and told the boy that there were several varieties of this mushroom, not easily to be distinguished from one another, of which some were wholesome, and one contained a deadly alkaloid. Being otherwise occupied at the time, he would have to defer his opinion until he had had an opportunity for a more thorough examination. He had handed back the mushroom submitted to him and the lad had given it to a counselor, who had put it on the mantel-shelf intending to report to Mr. Carrington the following morning.

Weak still, and very drowsy, Carrington lay on his bed and silently thanked the Powers above for having preserved his life.

Abruptly he thought of his mother. The warning!

At once it was as though she stood in the room beside his bed; as though their long, close companionship had not been interrupted by death.

A wave of affectionate gratitude suffused him. Under its influence he rose, wearily, and sank to his knees beside the bed, his head on his arms, in the very spot where his mother had seemed to stand in his dream.

Tears welled into his eyes, and fell, unnoticed, as he communed silently with her who had brought him into the world, whose watchful love and care not even death could interrupt or vitiate.

Silently, fervently, he spoke across the gulf to his mother....

He choked with silent sobs as understanding of her invincible love came to him and overwhelmed him. Then, to the accompaniment of a tremulous calmness which seemed to fall upon him abruptly, he had the sense of her, standing close beside him, as she had stood in his dream. He dared not raise his eyes, because now he knew that he was awake. It seemed to him as though she spoke, though there came to him no sensation of anything that could be compared to sound.

"Ye must be getting back into your bed, laddie."

And keeping his eyes tightly shut, lest he disturb this visitation, he awkwardly fumbled his way back into bed. He settled himself on his back, and an overpowering drowsiness, perhaps begotten of his recent shock and its attendant bodily weakness, ran through him like a benediction and a refreshing wind.

As he drifted down over the threshold of consciousness into the deep and prolonged sleep of physical exhaustion which completely restored him, his last remembrance was of the lingering caress of his mother's firm hand resting on his shoulder.

THE NIGHT CALL,
by Henry van Dyke

This story is taken from *The Unknown Quantity* (1913).

I

The first caprice of November snow had sketched the world in white for an hour in the morning. After mid-day, the sun came out, the wind turned warm, and the whiteness vanished from the landscape. By evening, the low ridges and the long plain of New Jersey were rich and sad again, in russet and dull crimson and old gold; for the foliage still clung to the oaks and elms and birches, and the dying monarchy of autumn retreated slowly before winter's cold republic.

In the old town of Calvinton, stretched along the highroad, the lamps were lit early as the saffron sunset faded into humid night. A mist rose from the long, wet street and the sodden lawns, muffling the houses and the trees and the college towers with a double veil, under which a pallid aureole encircled every light, while the moon above, languid and tearful, waded slowly through the mounting fog. It was a night of delay and expectation, a night of remembrance and mystery, lonely and dim and full of strange, dull sounds.

In one of the smaller houses on the main street the light in the window burned late. Leroy Carmichael was alone in his office reading Balzac's story of "The Country Doctor." He was not a gloomy or despondent person, but the spirit of the night had entered into him. He had yielded himself, as young men of ardent temperament often do, to the subduing magic of the fall. In his mind, as in the air, there was a soft, clinging mist, and blurred lights of thought, and a still foreboding of change. A sense of the vast tranquil movement of Nature, of her sympathy and of her indifference, sank deeply into his heart. For a time he realised that all things, and he, too, some day, must grow old; and he felt the universal pathos of it more sensitively, perhaps, than he would ever feel it again.

If you had told Carmichael that this was what he was thinking about as he sat in his bachelor quarters on that November night, he would have stared at you and then laughed.

"Nonsense," he would have answered, cheerfully. "I'm no sentimentalist: only a bit tired by a hard afternoon's work and a rough ride home. Then, Balzac always depresses me a little. The next time I'll take some quinine and Dumas: he is a tonic."

But, in fact, no one came in to interrupt his musings and rouse him to that air of cheerfulness with which he always faced the world, and to which, indeed (though he did not know it), he owed some measure of his delay in winning the confidence of Calvinton.

He had come there some five years ago with a particularly good outfit to practice medicine in that quaint and alluring old burgh, full of antique hand-made furniture and traditions. He had not only been well trained for his profession in the best medical school and hospital of New York, but he was also a graduate of Calvinton College (in which his father had been a professor for a time), and his granduncle was a Grubb, a name high in the Golden Book of Calvintonian aristocracy and inscribed upon tombstones in every village within a radius of fifteen miles. Consequently the young doctor arrived well accredited, and was received in his first year with many tokens of hospitality in the shape of tea-parties and suppers.

But the final and esoteric approval of Calvinton was a thing apart from these mere fashionable courtesies and worldly amenities—a thing not to be bestowed without due consideration and satisfactory reasons. Leroy Carmichael failed, somehow or other, to come up to the requirements for a leading physician in such a conservative community. In the judgment of Calvinton he was a clever young man; but he lacked poise and gravity. He walked too lightly along the streets, swinging his stick, and greeting his acquaintances blithely, as if he were rather glad to be alive. Now this is a sentiment, if you analyse it, near akin to vanity, and, therefore, to be discountenanced in your neighbour and concealed in yourself. How can a man be glad that he is alive, and frankly show it, without a touch of conceit and a reprehensible forgetfulness of the presence of original sin even in the best families? The manners of a professional man, above all, should at once express and impose humility.

Young Dr. Carmichael, Calvinton said, had been spoiled by his life in New York. It had made him too gay, light-hearted, almost frivolous. It was possible that he might know a good deal about medicine, though doubtless that had been exaggerated; but it was certain that his temperament needed chastening before he could win the kind of confidence that Calvinton had given to the venerable Dr. Coffin, whose face was like a monument, and whose practice rested upon the two pillars of podophyllin and predestination.

So Carmichael still felt, after his five years' work, that he was an outsider; felt it rather more indeed than when he had first come. He had enough practice to keep him in good health and spirits. But his patients were along the side streets and in the smaller houses and out in the country. He was not called, except in a chance emergency, to the big houses with the white pillars. The inner circle had not yet taken him in.

He wondered how long he would have to work and wait for that. He knew that things in Calvinton moved slowly; but he knew also that its silent and subconscious judgments sometimes crystallised with incredible rapidity and hardness. Was it possible that he was already classified in the group that came near but did not enter, an inhabitant but not a real burgher, a half-way citizen and a lifelong new-comer? That would be rough; he would not like growing old in that way.

But perhaps there was no such invisible barrier hemming in his path. Perhaps it was only the naturally slow movement of things that hindered him. Some day the gate would open. He would be called in behind those white pillars into the world of which his father had often told him stories and traditions. There he would prove his skill and his worth. He would make himself useful and trusted by his work. Then he could marry the girl he loved, and win a firm place and a real home in the old town whose strange charm held him so strongly even in the vague sadness of this autumnal night.

He turned again from these musings to his Balzac, and read the wonderful pages in which Benassis tells the story of his consecration to his profession and Captain Genestas confides the little Adrien to his care, and then the beautiful letter in which the boy describes the country doctor's death and burial. The simple pathos of it went home to Carmichael's heart.

"It is a fine life, after all," said he to himself, as he shut the book at midnight and laid down his pipe. "No man has a better chance than a doctor to come close to the real thing. Human nature is his patient, and each case is a symptom. It's worth while to work for the sake of getting nearer to the reality and doing some definite good by the way. I'm glad that this isn't one of those mystical towns where Christian Science and Buddhism and all sorts of vagaries flourish. Calvinton may be difficult, but it's not obscure. And some day I'll feel its pulse and get at the heart of it."

The silence of the little office was snapped by the nervous clamour of the electric bell, shrilling with a night call.

II

Dr. Carmichael turned on the light in the hall, and opened the front door. A tall, dark man of military aspect loomed out of the mist, and, behind him, at the curbstone, the outline of a big motorcar was dimly visible. He held out a visiting-card inscribed "Baron de Mortemer," and spoke slowly and courteously, but with a strong nasal accent and a tone of insistent domination.

"You are the Dr. Carmichael, yes? You speak French—no? It is a pity. There is need of you at once—a patient—it is very pressing. You will come with me, yes?"

"But I do not know you, sir," said the doctor; "you are—"

"The Baron de Mortemer," broke in the stranger, pointing to the card as if it answered all questions. "It is the Baroness who is very suffering—I pray you to come without delay."

"But what is it?" asked the doctor. "What shall I bring with me? My instrument-case?"

The Baron smiled with his lips and frowned with his eyes. "Not at all," he said, "Madame expects not an arrival—it is not so bad as that—but she has had a sudden access of anguish—she has demanded you. I pray you to come at the instant. Bring what pleases you, what you think best, but come!"

The man's manner was not agitated, but it was strangely urgent, overpowering, constraining; his voice was like a pushing hand. Carmichael threw on his coat and hat, hastily picked up his medicine-satchel and a portable electric battery, and followed the Baron to the motor.

The great car started easily and rolled softly purring down the deserted street. The houses were all asleep, and the college buildings dark as empty fortresses. The moon-threaded mist clung closely to the town like a shroud of gauze, not concealing the form beneath, but making its immobility more mysterious. The trees drooped and dripped with moisture, and the leaves seemed ready, almost longing, to fall at a touch. It was one of those nights when the solid things of the world, the houses and the hills and the woods and the very earth itself, grow unreal to the point of vanishing; while the impalpable things, the presences of life and death which travel on the unseen air, the influences of the far-off starry lights, the silent messages and presentiments of darkness, the ebb and flow of vast currents of secret existence all around us, seem so close and vivid that they absorb and overwhelm us with their intense reality.

Through this realm of indistinguishable verity and illusion, strangely imposed upon the familiar, homely street of Calvinton, the machine ran smoothly, faintly humming, as the Frenchman drove it with master-skill—itself a dream of embodied power and speed. Gliding by the last cottages of Town's End where the street became the highroad, the car ran swiftly through the open country for a mile until it came to a broad entrance. The gate was broken from the leaning posts and thrown to one side. Here the machine turned in and laboured up a rough, grass-grown carriage-drive.

Carmichael knew that they were at Castle Gordon, one of the "old places" of Calvinton, which he often passed on his country drives. The house stood well back from the road, on a slight elevation, looking down over the oval field that was once a lawn, and the scattered elms and pines and Norway firs that did their best to preserve the memory of a noble plantation. The building was colonial; heavy stone walls covered with yellow stucco; tall white wooden pillars ranged along a narrow portico; a style which seemed to assert that a Greek temple was good enough for the residence of an American gentleman. But the clean buff and white of the house had long since faded. The stucco had cracked, and, here and there, had fallen from the stones. The paint on the pillars was dingy, peeling in round blisters and narrow strips from the grey wood underneath. The trees were ragged and untended, the grass uncut, the driveway overgrown with weeds and gullied by rains—the whole place looked forsaken. Carmichael had always supposed that it was vacant. But he had not passed that way for nearly a month, and, meantime, it might have been reopened and tenanted.

The Baron drove the car around to the back of the house and stopped there.

"Pardon," said he, "that I bring you not to the door of entrance; but this is the more convenient."

He knocked hurriedly and spoke a few words in French. The key grated in the lock and the door creaked open. A withered, wiry little man, dressed in dark grey, stood holding a lighted candle, which flickered in the draught. His head was nearly bald; his sallow, hairless face might have been of any age from twenty to a hundred years; his eyes between their narrow red lids were glittering and inscrutable as those of a snake. As he bowed and grinned, showing his yellow, broken teeth, Carmichael thought that he had never seen a more evil face or one more clearly marked with the sign of the drug-fiend.

"My chauffeur, Gaspard," said the Baron, "also my valet, my cook, my chambermaid, my man to do all, what you call factotum, is it not? But he speaks not English, so pardon me once more."

He spoke a few words to the man, who shrugged his shoulders and smiled with the same deferential grimace while his unchanging eyes gleamed through their slits. Carmichael caught only the word "Madame" while he was slipping off his overcoat, and understood that they were talking of his patient.

"Come," said the Baron, "he says that it goes better, at least not worse—that is always something. Let us mount at the instant."

The hall was bare, except for a table on which a kitchen lamp was burning, and two chairs with heavy automobile coats and rugs and veils thrown upon them. The stairway was uncarpeted, and the dust lay thick under the banisters. At

46

the door of the back room on the second floor the Baron paused and knocked softly. A low voice answered, and he went in, beckoning the doctor to follow.

III

If Carmichael lived to be a hundred he could never forget that first impression. The room was but partly furnished, yet it gave at once the idea that it was inhabited; it was even, in some strange way, rich and splendid. Candles on the mantelpiece and a silver travelling-lamp on the dressing-table threw a soft light on little articles of luxury, and photographs in jewelled frames, and a couple of well-bound books, and a gilt clock marking the half-hour after midnight. A wood fire burned in the wide chimney-place, and before it a rug was spread. At one side there was a huge mahogany four-post bedstead, and there, propped up by the pillows, lay the noblest-looking woman that Carmichael had ever seen.

She was dressed in some clinging stuff of soft black, with a diamond at her breast, and a deep-red cloak thrown over her feet. She must have been past middle age, for her thick, brown hair was already touched with silver, and one lock of snow-white lay above her forehead. But her face was one of those which time enriches; fearless and tender and high-spirited, a speaking face in which the dark-lashed grey eyes were like words of wonder and the sensitive mouth like a clear song. She looked at the young doctor and held out her hand to him.

"I am glad to see you," she said, in her low, pure voice, "very glad! You are Roger Carmichael's son. Oh, I am glad to see you indeed."

"You are very kind," he answered, "and I am glad also to be of any service to you, though I do not yet know who you are."

The Baron was bending over the fire rearranging the logs on the andirons. He looked up sharply and spoke in his strong nasal tone.

"*Pardon! Madame la Baronne de Mortemer, j'ai l'honneur de vous presenter Monsieur le Docteur Carmichael.*"

The accent on the "doctor" was marked. A slight shadow came upon the lady's face. She answered, quietly:

"Yes, I know. The doctor has come to see me because I was ill. We will talk of that in a moment. But first I want to tell him who I am—and by another name. Dr. Carmichael, did your father ever speak to you of Jean Gordon?"

"Why, yes," he said, after an instant of thought, "it comes back to me now quite clearly. She was the young girl to whom he taught Latin when he first came here as a college instructor. He was very fond of her. There was one of her books in his library—I have it now—a little volume of Horace, with a few translations in verse written on the fly-leaves, and her name on the title-page—Jean Gordon. My father wrote under that, 'My best pupil, who left her lessons unfinished.' He was very fond of the book, and so I kept it when he died."

The lady's eyes grew moist, but the tears did not fall. They trembled in her voice.

"I was that Jean Gordon—a girl of fifteen—your father was the best man I ever knew. You look like him, but he was handsomer than you. Ah, no, I was not his best pupil, but his most wilful and ungrateful one. Did he never tell you of my running away—of the unjust suspicions that fell on him—of his voyage to Europe?"

"Never," answered Carmichael. "He only spoke, as I remember, of your beauty and your brightness, and of the good times that you all had when this old

47

house was in its prime."

"Yes, yes," she said, quickly and with strong feeling, "they were good times, and he was a man of honour. He never took an unfair advantage, never boasted of a woman's favour, never tried to spare himself. He was an American man. I hope you are like him."

The Baron, who had been leaning on the mantel, crossed the room impatiently and stood beside the bed. He spoke in French again, dragging the words in his insistent, masterful voice, as if they were something heavy which he laid upon his wife.

Her grey eyes grew darker, almost black, with enlarging pupils. She raised herself on the pillows as if about to get up. Then she sank back again and said, with an evident effort:

"Rene, I must beg you not to speak in French again. The doctor does not understand it. We must be more courteous. And now I will tell him about my sudden illness to-night. It was the first time—like a flash of lightning—an ice-cold hand of pain—"

Even as she spoke a swift and dreadful change passed over her face. Her colour vanished in a morbid pallor; a cold sweat lay like death-dew on her forehead; her eyes were fixed on some impending horror; her lips, blue and rigid, were strained with an unspeakable, intolerable anguish. Her left arm stiffened as if it were gripped in a vise of pain. Her right hand fluttered over her heart, plucking at an unseen weight. It seemed as if an invisible, silent death-wind were quenching the flame of her life. It flickered in an agony of strangulation.

"Be quick," cried the doctor; "lay her head lower on the pillows, loosen her dress, warm her hands."

He had caught up his satchel, and was looking for a little vial. He found it almost empty. But there were four or five drops of the yellowish, oily liquid. He poured them on his handkerchief and held it close to the lady's mouth. She was still breathing regularly though slowly, and as she inhaled the pungent, fruity smell, like the odour of a jargonelle pear, a look of relief flowed over her face, her breathing deepened, her arm and her lips relaxed, the terror faded from her eyes.

He went to his satchel again and took out a bottle of white tablets marked "Nitroglycerin." He gave her one of them, and when he saw her look of peace grow steadier, after a minute, he prepared the electric battery. Softly he passed the sponges charged with their mysterious current over her temples and her neck and down her slender arms and blue-veined wrists, holding them for a while in the palms of her hands, which grew rosy.

In all this the Baron had helped as he could, and watched closely, but without a word. He was certainly not indifferent; neither was he distressed; the expression of his black eyes and heavy, passionless face was that of presence of mind, self-control covering an intense curiosity. Carmichael conceived a vague sentiment of dislike for the man.

When the patient rested easily they stepped outside the room together for a moment.

"It is the *angina*, I suppose," droned the Baron, "hein? That is of great inconvenience. But I think it is the false one, that is much less grave—not truly dangerous, hein?"

"My dear sir," answered Carmichael, "who can tell the difference between a false and a true *angina pectoris*, except by a post-mortem? The symptoms are much alike, the result is sometimes identical, if the paroxysm is severe enough. But in this case I hope that you may be right. Your wife's illness is severe, dangerous, but not necessarily fatal. This attack has passed and may not recur for months or even years."

The lip-smile came back under the Baron's sullen eyes.

"Those are the good news, my dear doctor," said he, slowly. "Then we shall be able to travel soon, perhaps to-morrow or the next day. It is of an extreme importance. This place is insufferable to me. We have engagements in Washington —a gay season."

Carmichael looked at him steadily and spoke with deliberation.

"Baron, you must understand me clearly. This is a serious case. If I had not come in time your wife might be dead now. She cannot possibly be moved for a week, perhaps it may take a month fully to restore her strength. After that she must have a winter of absolute quiet and repose."

The Frenchman's face hardened; his brows drew together in a black line, and he lifted his hand quickly with a gesture of irritation. Then he bowed.

"As you will, doctor! And for the present moment, what is it that I may have the honour to do for your patient?"

"Just now," said the doctor, "she needs a stimulant—a glass of sherry or of brandy, if you have it—and a hot-water bag—you have none? Well, then, a couple of bottles filled with hot water and wrapped in a cloth to put at her feet. Can you get them?"

The Baron bowed again, and went down the stairs. As Carmichael returned to the bedroom he heard the droning, insistent voice below calling "Gaspard, Gaspard!"

The great grey eyes were open as he entered the room, and there was a sense of release from pain and fear in them that was like the deepest kind of pleasure.

"Yes, I am much better," said she; "the attack has passed. Will it come again? No? Not soon, you mean. Well, that is good. You need not tell me what it is— time enough for that to-morrow. But come and sit by me. I want to talk to you. Your first name is—"

"Leroy," he answered. "But you are weak; you must not talk much."

"Only a little," she replied, smiling; "it does me good. Leroy was your mother's name—yes? It is not a Calvinton name. I wonder where your father met her. Perhaps in France when he came to look for me. But he did not find me— no, indeed—I was well hidden then—but he found your mother. You are young enough to be my son. Will you be a friend to me for your father's sake?"

She spoke gently, in a tone of infinite kindness and tender grace, with pauses in which a hundred unspoken recollections and appeals were suggested. The young man was deeply moved. He took her hand in his firm clasp.

"Gladly," he said, "and for your sake too. But now I want you to rest."

"Oh," she answered, "I am resting now. But let me talk a little more. It will not harm me. I have been through so much! Twice married—a great fortune to spend—all that the big world can give. But now I am very tired of the whirl. There is only one thing I want—to stay here in Calvinton. I rebelled against it once; but it draws me back. There is a strange magic in the place. Haven't you felt it? How do you explain it?"

"Yes," he said, "I have felt it surely, but I can't explain it, unless it is a kind of ancient peace that makes you wish to be at home here even while you rebel."

She nodded her head and smiled softly.

"That is it," she said, hesitating for a moment. "But my husband—you see he is a very strong man, and he loves the world, the whirling life—he took a dislike to this place at once. No wonder, with the house in such a state! But I have plenty of money—it will be easy to restore the house. Only, sometimes I think he cares more for the money than—but no matter what I think. He wishes to go on at once—to-morrow, if we can. I hate the thought of it. Is it possible for me to stay? Can you help me?"

"Dear lady," he answered, lifting her hand to his lips, "set your mind at rest. I have already told him that it is impossible for you to go for many days. You can arrange to move to the inn to-morrow, and stay there while you direct the putting of your house in order."

A sound in the hallway announced the return of the Baron and Gaspard with the hot-water bottles and the cognac. The doctor made his patient as comfortable as possible for the night, prepared a sleeping-draught, and gave directions for the use of the tablets in an emergency.

"Good night," he said, bending over her. "I will see you in the morning. You may count upon me."

"I do," she said, with her eyes resting on his; "thank you for all. I shall expect you—*au revoir.*"

As they went down the stairs he said to the Baron, "Remember, absolute repose is necessary. With that you are safe enough for to-night. But you may possibly need more of the nitrite of amyl. My vial is empty. I will write the prescription, if you will allow me."

"In the dining-room," said the Baron, taking up the lamp and throwing open the door of the back room on the right. The floor had been hastily swept and the rubbish shoved into the fireplace. The heavy chairs stood along the wall. But two of them were drawn up at the head of the long mahogany table, and dishes and table utensils from a travelling-basket were lying there, as if a late supper had been served.

"You see," said the Baron, drawling, "our banquet-hall! Madame and I have dined in this splendour to-night. Is it possible that you write here?"

His secret irritation, his insolence, his contempt spoke clearly enough in his tone. The remark was almost like an intentional insult. For a second Carmichael hesitated. "No," he thought, "why should I quarrel with him? He is only sullen. He can do no harm."

He pulled a chair to the foot of the table, took out his tablet and his fountain-pen, and wrote the prescription. Tearing off the leaf, he folded it crosswise and left it on the table.

In the hall, as he put on his coat he remembered the paper.

"My prescription," he said, "I must take it to the druggist to-night."

"Permit me," said the Baron, "the room is dark. I will take the paper, and procure the drug as I return from escorting the doctor to his residence."

He went into the dark room, groped about for a moment, and returned, closing the door behind him.

"Come, Monsieur," he said, "your work at the Chateau Gordon is finished for this night. I shall leave you with yourself—at home, as you say—in a few moments. Gaspard—Gaspard, *fermez la porte a cle*!"

The strong nasal voice echoed through the house, and the servant ran lightly down the stairs. His master muttered a few sentences to him, holding up his right hand as he did so, with the five fingers extended, as if to impress something on the man's mind.

"Pardon," he said, turning to Carmichael, "that I speak always French, after the rebuke. But this time it is of necessity. I repeat the instruction for the pilules. One at each hour until eight o'clock—five, not more—it is correct? Come, then, our equipage is always harnessed, always ready, how convenient!"

The two men did not speak as the car rolled through the brumous night. A rising wind was sifting the fog. The moon had set. The loosened leaves came whirling, fluttering, sinking through the darkness like a flight of huge dying moths. Now and then they brushed the faces of the travellers with limp, moist wings.

The red night-lamp in the drug-store was still burning. Carmichael called the other's attention to it.

"You have the prescription?"

"Without doubt!" he answered. "After I have escorted you, I shall procure the drug."

The doctor's front door was lit up as he had left it. The light streamed out rather brightly and illumined the Baron's sullen black eyes and smiling lips as he leaned from the car, lifting his cap.

"A thousand thanks, my dear doctor, you have been excessively kind; yes, truly of an excessive goodness for us. It is a great pleasure—how do you tell it in English?—it is a great pleasure to have met you. *Adieu*."

"Till to-morrow morning!" said Carmichael, cheerfully, waving his hand.

The Baron stared at him curiously, and lifted his cap again.

"*Adieu*!" droned the insistent voice, and the great car slid into the dark.

IV

The next morning was of crystal. It was after nine when Carmichael drove his electric-phaeton down the leaf-littered street, where the country wagons and the decrepit hacks were already meandering placidly, and out along the highroad, between the still green fields. It seemed to him as if the experience of the past night were "such stuff as dreams are made of." Yet the impression of what he had seen and heard in that firelit chamber—of the eyes, the voice, the hand of that strangely lovely lady—of her vision of sudden death, her essentially lonely struggle with it, her touching words to him when she came back to life—all this was so vivid and unforgettable that he drove straight to Castle Gordon.

The great house was shut up like a tomb: every door and window was closed, except where half of one of the shutters had broken loose and hung by a single hinge. He drove around to the back. It was the same there. A cobweb was spun across the lower corner of the door and tiny drops of moisture jewelled it. Perhaps it had been made in the early morning. If so, no one had come out of the door since night.

Carmichael knocked, and knocked again. No answer. He called. No reply. Then he drove around to the portico with the tall white pillars and tried the front door. It was locked. He peered through the half-open window into the drawing-room. The glass was crusted with dirt and the room was dark. He was trying to make out the outlines of the huddled furniture when he heard a step behind him. It was the old farmer from the nearest cottage on the road.

"Mornin', doctor! I seen ye comin' in, and tho't ye might want to see the house."

"Good morning, Scudder! I do, if you'll let me in. But first tell me about these automobile tracks in the drive."

The old man gazed at him with a kind of dull surprise as if the question were foolish.

"Why, ye made 'em yerself, comin' up, didn't ye?"

"I mean those larger tracks—they were made by a much heavier car than mine."

"Oh," said the old man, nodding, "them was made by a big machine that come in here las' week. You see this house's bin shet up 'bout ten years, ever sence ol' Jedge Gordon died. B'longs to Miss Jean—her that run off with the Eye-talyin. She kinder wants to sell it, and kinder not—ye see—"

"Yes," interrupted Carmichael, "but about that big machine—when did you say it was here?"

"P'raps four or five days ago; I think it was a We'nsday. Two fellers from Philadelfy—said they wanted to look at the house, tho't of buyin' it. So I bro't 'em in, but when they seen the outside of it they said they didn't want to look at it no more—too big and too crumbly!"

"And since then no one has been here?"

"Not a soul—leastways nobody that I seen. I don't s'pose you think o' buyin' the house, doc'! It's too lonely for an office, ain't it?"

"You're right, Scudder, much too lonely. But I'd like to look through the old place, if you will take me in."

The hall, with the two chairs and the table, on which a kitchen lamp with a half-inch of oil in it was standing, gave no sign of recent habitation. Carmichael glanced around him and hurried up the stairway to the bedroom. A tall four-poster stood in one corner, with a coverlet apparently hiding a mattress and some pillows. A dressing-table stood against the wall, and in the middle of the floor there were a few chairs. A half-open closet door showed a pile of yellow linen. The daylight sifted dimly into the room through the cracks of the shutters.

"Scudder," said Carmichael, "I want you to look around carefully and tell me whether you see any signs of any one having been here lately."

The old man stared, and turned his eyes slowly about the room. Then he shook his head.

"Can't say as I do. Looks pretty much as it did when me and my wife breshed it up in October. Ye see it's kinder clean fer an old house—not much dust from the road here. That linen and that bed's bin here since I c'n remember. Them burnt logs mus' be left over from old Jedge Gordon's time. He died in here. But what's the matter, doc'? Ye think tramps or burglers—"

"No," said Carmichael, "but what would you say if I told you that I was called here last night to see a patient, and that the patient was the Miss Jean Gordon of whom you have just told me?"

"What d'ye mean?" said the old man, gaping. Then he gazed at the doctor pityingly, and shook his head. "I know ye ain't a drinkin' man, doc', so I wouldn't say nothin'. But I guess ye bin dreamin'. Why, las' time Miss Jean writ to me—her name's Mortimer now, and her husband's a kinder Barrin or some sorter furrin noble,—she was in Paris, not mor'n two weeks ago! Said she was dyin' to come back to the ol' place agin, but she wa'n't none too well, and didn't guess she c'd manage it. Ef ye said ye seen her here las' night—why—well, I'd jest think ye'd bin dreamin'. P'raps ye're a little under the weather—bin workin' too hard?"

"I never was better, Scudder, but sometimes curious notions come to me. I wanted to see how you would take this one. Now we'll go downstairs again."

The old man laughed, but doubtfully, as if he was still puzzled by the talk, and they descended the creaking, dusty stairs. Carmichael turned at once into the dining-room.

The rubbish was still in the fireplace, the chairs ranged along the wall. There were no dishes on the long table; but at the head of it two chairs; and at the foot, one; and in front of that, lying on the table, a folded bit of paper. Carmichael picked it up and opened it.

It was his prescription for the nitrite of amyl.

He hesitated a moment; then refolded the paper and put it in his vest-pocket.

Seated in his car, with his hand on the lever, he turned to Scudder, who was watching him with curious eyes.

"I'm very much obliged to you, Scudder, for taking me through the house. And I'll be more obliged to you if you'll just keep it to yourself—what I said to you about last night."

"Sure," said the old man, nodding gravely. "I like ye, doc', and that kinder talk might do ye harm here in Calvinton. We don't hold much to dreams and visions down this way. But, say, 'twas a mighty interestin' dream, wa'n't it? I guess Miss Jean hones for them white pillars, many a day—they sorter stand for old times. They draw ye, don't they?"

"Yes, my friend," said Carmichael as he moved the lever, "they speak of the past. There is a magic in those white pillars. They draw you."

HIS UNQUIET GHOST,
by Mary Noailles Murfree

Originally published in 1911.

The moon was high in the sky. The wind was laid. So silent was the vast stretch of mountain wilderness, aglint with the dew, that the tinkle of a rill far below in the black abyss seemed less a sound than an evidence of the pervasive quietude, since so slight a thing, so distant, could compass so keen a vibration. For an hour or more the three men who lurked in the shadow of a crag in the narrow mountain-pass, heard nothing else. When at last they caught the dull reverberation of a slow wheel and the occasional metallic clank of a tire against a stone, the vehicle was fully three miles distant by the winding road in the valley. Time lagged. Only by imperceptible degrees the sound of deliberate approach grew louder on the air as the interval of space lessened. At length, above their ambush at the summit of the mountain's brow the heads of horses came into view, distinct in the moonlight between the fibrous pines and the vast expanse of the sky above the valley. Even then there was renewed delay. The driver of the wagon paused to rest the team.

The three lurking men did not move; they scarcely ventured to breathe. Only when there was no retrograde possible, no chance of escape, when the vehicle was fairly on the steep declivity of the road, the precipice sheer on one side, the wall of the ridge rising perpendicularly on the other, did two of them, both revenue-raiders disguised as mountaineers, step forth from the shadow. The other, the informer, a genuine mountaineer, still skulked motionless in the darkness. The "revenuers," ascending the road, maintained a slow, lunging gait, as if they had toiled from far.

Their abrupt appearance had the effect of a galvanic shock to the man handling the reins, a stalwart, rubicund fellow, who visibly paled. He drew up so suddenly as almost to throw the horses from their feet.

"G' evenin'," ventured Browdie, the elder of the raiders, in a husky voice affecting an untutored accent. He had some special ability as a mimic, and, being familiar with the dialect and manners of the people, this gift greatly facilitated the rustic impersonation he had essayed. "Ye're haulin' late," he added, for the hour was close to midnight.

"Yes, stranger; haulin' late, from Eskaqua—a needcessity."

"What's yer cargo?" asked Browdie, seeming only ordinarily inquisitive.

A sepulchral cadence was in the driver's voice, and the disguised raiders noted that the three other men on the wagon had preserved, throughout, a solemn silence. "What we-uns mus' all be one day, stranger—a corpus."

Browdie was stultified for a moment Then, sustaining his assumed character, he said: "I hope it be nobody I know. I be fairly well acquainted in Eskaqua, though I hail from down in Lonesome Cove. Who be dead!"

There was palpably a moment's hesitation before the spokesman replied: "Watt Wyatt; died day 'fore yestiddy."

At the words, one of the silent men in the wagon turned his face suddenly, with such obvious amazement depicted upon it that it arrested the attention of the "rev-enuers." This face was so individual that it was not likely to be easily mistaken or forgotten. A wild, breezy look it had, and a tricksy, incorporeal expression that might well befit some fantastic, fabled thing of the woods. It was full of fine script of elusive meanings, not registered in the lineaments of the prosaic man of the day, though perchance of scant utility, not worth interpretation. His full gray eyes were touched to glancing brilliancy by a moonbeam; his long, fibrously floating brown hair was thrown backward; his receding chin was peculiarly delicate; and though his well-knit frame bespoke a hardy vigor, his pale cheek was soft and thin. All the rustic grotesquery of garb and posture was cancelled by the deep shadow of a bough, and his delicate face showed isolated in the moonlight.

Browdie silently pondered his vague suspicions for a moment "Whar did he die at?" he then demanded at a venture.

"At his daddy's house, fur sure. Whar else?" responded the driver. "I hev got what's lef' of him hyar in the coffin-box. We expected ter make it ter Shiloh buryin'-ground 'fore dark; but the road is middlin' heavy, an' 'bout five mile' back Ben cast a shoe. The funeral warn't over much 'fore noon."

"Whyn't they bury him in Eskaqua, whar he died!" persisted Browdie.

"Waal, they planned ter bury him alongside his mother an' gran'dad, what used ter live in Tanglefoot Cove. But we air wastin' time hyar, an' we hev got none ter spare. Gee, Ben! Git up, John!"

The wagon gave a lurch; the horses, holding back in bracing attitudes far from the pole, went teetering down the steep slant, the locked wheel dragging heavily; the four men sat silent, two in slouching postures at the head of the coffin; the third, with the driver, was at its foot. It seemed drearily suggestive, the last journey of this humble mortality, in all the splendid environment of the mountains, under the vast expansions of the aloof skies, in the mystic light of the unnoting moon.

"Is this bona-fide?" asked Browdie, with a questioning glance at the informer, who had at length crept forth.

"I dunno," sullenly responded the mountaineer. He had acquainted the two officers, who were of a posse of revenue-raiders hovering in the vicinity, with the mysterious circumstance that a freighted wagon now and then made a midnight transit across these lonely ranges. He himself had heard only occasionally in a wakeful hour the roll of heavy wheels, but he interpreted this as the secret transportation of brush whisky from the still to its market. He had thought to fix the transgression on an old enemy of his own, long suspected of moonshining; but he was acquainted with none of the youngsters on the wagon, at whom he had peered cautiously from behind the rocks. His actuating motive in giving information to the emissaries of the government had been the rancor of an old feud, and his detection meant certain death. He had not expected the revenue-raiders to be outnumbered by the supposed moonshiners, and he would not fight in the open. He had no sentiment of fealty to the law, and the officers glanced at each other in uncertainty.

"This evidently is not the wagon in question," said Browdie, disappointed.

"I'll follow them a bit," volunteered Bonan, the younger and the more active of the two officers. "Seems to me they'll bear watching."

Indeed, as the melancholy cortège fared down and down the steep road, dwindling in the sheeny distance, the covert and half-suppressed laughter of the sepulchral escort was of so keen a relish that it was well that the scraping of the locked wheel aided the distance to mask the incongruous sound.

"What ailed you-uns ter name *me* as the corpus, 'Gene Barker?" demanded Walter Wyatt, when he had regained the capacity of coherent speech.

"Oh, I hed ter do suddint murder on somebody," declared the driver, all bluff and reassured and red-faced again, "an' I couldn't think quick of nobody else. Besides, I helt a grudge agin' you fer not stuffin' mo' straw 'twixt them jimmyjohns in the coffin-box."

"That's a fac'. Ye air too triflin' ter be let ter live, Watt," cried one of their comrades. "I hearn them jugs clash tergether in the coffin-box when 'Gene checked the team up suddint, I tell you. An' them men sure 'peared ter me powerful suspectin'."

"*I* hearn the clash of them jimmyjohns," chimed in the driver. "I really thunk my hour war come. Some informer must hev set them men ter spyin' round fer moonshine."

"Oh, surely nobody wouldn't dare," urged one of the group, uneasily; for the identity of an informer was masked in secrecy, and his fate, when discovered, was often gruesome.

"They couldn't hev noticed the clash of them jimmyjohns, nohow," declared the negligent Watt, nonchalantly. "But namin' *me* fur the dead one! Supposin' they air revenuers fur true, an' hed somebody along, hid out in the bresh, ez war acquainted with me by sight—"

"Then they'd hev been skeered out'n thar boots, that's all," interrupted the self-sufficient 'Gene. "They would hev 'lowed they hed viewed yer brazen ghost, bold ez brass, standin' at the head of yer own coffin-box."

"Or mebbe they mought hev recognized the Wyatt favor, ef they warn't acquainted with *me*," persisted Watt, with his unique sense of injury.

Eugene Barker defended the temerity of his inspiration. "They would hev jes thought ye war kin ter the deceased, an' at-tendin' him ter his long home."

"'Gene don't keer much fur ye ter be alive nohow, Watt Wyatt," one of the others suggested tactlessly, "'count o' Minta Elladine Biggs."

Eugene Barker's off-hand phrase was incongruous with his sudden gravity and his evident rancor as he declared: "*I* ain't carin' fur sech ez Watt Wyatt. An' they *do* say in the cove that Minta Elladine Biggs hev gin him the mitten, anyhow, on account of his gamesome ways, playin' kyerds, a-bet-tin' his money, drinkin' apple-jack, an' sech."

The newly constituted ghost roused himself with great vitality as if to retort floutingly; but as he turned, his jaw suddenly fell; his eyes widened with a ghastly distension. With an unsteady arm extended he pointed silently. Distinctly outlined on the lid of the coffin was the simulacrum of the figure of a man.

One of his comrades, seated on the tailboard of the wagon, had discerned a significance in the abrupt silence. As he turned, he, too, caught a fleeting glimpse of that weird image on the coffin-lid. But he was of a more mundane pulse. The apparition roused in him only a wonder whence could come this shadow in the midst of the moon-flooded road. He lifted his eyes to the verge of the bluff above, and there he descried an indistinct human form, which suddenly disappeared as he looked, and at that moment the simulacrum vanished from the lid of the box.

The mystery was of instant elucidation. They were suspected, followed. The number of their pursuers of course they could not divine, but at least one of the revenue-officers had trailed the wagon between the precipice and the great wall of the ascent on the right, which had gradually dwindled to a diminished height. Deep gullies were here and there washed out by recent rains, and one of these indentations might have afforded an active man access to the summit. Thus the pursuer had evidently kept abreast of them, speeding along in great leaps through the lush growth of huckleberry bushes, wild grasses, pawpaw thickets, silvered by the moon, all fringing the great forests that had given way on the shelving verge of the steeps where the road ran. Had he overheard their unguarded, significant words? Who could divine, so silent were the windless mountains, so deep a-dream the darksome woods, so spellbound the mute and mystic moonlight?

The group maintained a cautious reticence now, each revolving the problematic disclosure of their secret, each canvassing the question whether the pursuer himself was aware of his betrayal of his stealthy proximity. Not till they had reached the ford of the river did they venture on a low-toned colloquy. The driver paused in midstream and stepped out on the pole between the horses to let down the check-reins, as the team manifested an inclination to drink in transit; and thence, as he stood thus perched, he gazed to and fro, the stretch of dark and lustrous ripples baffling all approach within ear-shot, the watering of the horses justifying the pause and cloaking its significance to any distant observer.

But the interval was indeed limited; the mental processes of such men are devoid of complexity, and their decisions prompt. They advanced few alternatives; their prime object was to be swiftly rid of the coffin and its inculpating contents, and with the "revenuer" so hard on their heels this might seem a troublous problem enough.

"Put it whar a coffin b'longs—in the churchyard," said Wyatt; for at a considerable distance beyond the rise of the opposite bank could be seen a barren clearing in which stood a gaunt, bare, little white frame building that served all the country-side for its infrequent religious services.

"We couldn't dig a grave before that spy—ef he be a revenuer sure enough—could overhaul us," Eugene Barker objected.

"We could turn the yearth right smart, though," persisted Wyatt, for pickax and shovel had been brought in the wagon for the sake of an aspect of verisimilitude and to mask their true intent.

Eugene Barker acceded to this view. "That's the dinctum—dig a few jes fer a blind. We kin slip the coffin-box under the church-house 'fore he gits in sight,—he'll be feared ter follow too close,—an' leave it thar till the other boys kin wagon it ter the cross-roads' store ter-morrer night."

The horses, hitherto held to the sober gait of funeral travel, were now put to a speedy trot, unmindful of whatever impression of flight the pace might give to the revenue-raider in pursuit. The men were soon engrossed in their deceptive enterprise in the churchyard, plying pickax and shovel for dear life; now and again they paused to listen vainly for the sound of stealthy approach. They knew that there was the most precarious and primitive of foot-bridges across the deep stream, to traverse which would cost an unaccustomed wayfarer both time and pains; thus the interval was considerable before the resonance of rapid footfalls gave token that their pursuer had found himself obliged to sprint smartly along the country road to keep any hope of ever again' viewing the wagon which the intervening water-course had withdrawn from his sight. That this hope had grown tenuous was evident in his relinquishment of his former caution, for when they again caught a glimpse of him he was forging along in the middle of the road without any effort at concealment. But as the wagon appeared in the perspective, stationary, hitched to the hedge of the graveyard, he recurred to his previous methods. The four men still within the in-closure, now busied in shovelling the earth back again into the excavation they had so swiftly made, covertly watched him as he skulked into the shadow of the wayside. The little "church-house," with all its windows whitely aglare in the moonlight, reflected the pervasive sheen, and silent, spectral, remote, it seemed as if it might well harbor at times its ghastly neighbors from the quiet cemetery without, dimly ranging themselves once more in the shadowy ranks of its pews or grimly stalking down the drear and deserted aisles. The fact that the rising ground toward the rear of the building necessitated a series of steps at the entrance, enabled the officer to mask behind this tall flight his crouching approach, and thus he ensconced himself in the angle between the wall and the steps, and looked forth in fancied security.

The shadows multiplied the tale of the dead that the head-boards kept, each similitude askew in the moonlight on the turf below the slanting monument To judge by the motions of the men engaged in the burial and the mocking antics of their silhouettes on the ground, it must have been obvious to the spectator that they were already filling in the earth. The interment may have seemed to him suspiciously swift, but the possibility was obvious that the grave might have been previously dug in anticipation of their arrival. It was plain that he was altogether unprepared for the event when they came slouching forth to the wagon, and the stalwart and red-faced driver, with no manifestation of surprise, hailed him as he still crouched in his lurking-place. "Hello, stranger! Warn't that you-uns runnin' arter the wagon a piece back yonder jes a while ago?"

The officer rose to his feet, with an intent look both dismayed and embarrassed. He did not venture on speech; he merely acceded with a nod.

"Ye want a lift, I reckon."

The stranger was hampered by the incongruity between his rustic garb, common to the coves, and his cultivated intonation; for, unlike his comrade Browdie, he had no mimetic faculties whatever. Nevertheless, he was now constrained to "face the music."

"I didn't want to interrupt you," he said, seeking such excuse as due consideration for the circumstances might afford; "but I'd like to ask where I could get lodging for the night."

"What's yer name?" demanded Barker, unceremoniously.

"Francis Bonan," the raider replied, with more assurance. Then he added, by way of explaining his necessity, "I'm a stranger hereabouts."

"Ye air so," assented the sarcastic 'Gene. "Ye ain't even acquainted with yer own clothes. Ye be a town man."

"Well, I'm not the first man who has had to hide out," Ronan parried, seeking to justify his obvious disguise.

"Shot somebody?" asked 'Gene, with an apparent accession of interest.

"It's best for me not to tell."

"So be." 'Gene acquiesced easily. "Waal, ef ye kin put up with sech accommodations ez our'n, I'll take ye home with me."

Ronan stood aghast. But there was no door of retreat open. He was alone and helpless. He could not conceal the fact that the turn affairs had taken was equally unexpected and terrifying to him, and the moonshiners, keenly watchful, were correspondingly elated to discern that he had surely no reinforcements within reach to nerve him to resistance or to menace their liberty. He had evidently followed them too far, too recklessly; perhaps without the consent and against the counsel of his comrades, perhaps even without their knowledge of his movements and intention.

Now and again as the wagon jogged on and on toward their distant haven, the moonlight gradually dulling to dawn, Wyatt gave the stranger a wondering, covert glance, vaguely, shrinkingly curious as to the sentiments of a man vacillating between the suspicion of capture and the recognition of a simple hospitality without significance or danger. The man's face appealed to him, young, alert, intelligent, earnest, and the anguish of doubt and anxiety it expressed went to his heart. In the experience of his sylvan life as a hunter Wyatt's peculiar and subtle temperament evolved certain fine-spun distinctions which were unique; a trapped thing had a special appeal to his commiseration that a creature ruthlessly slaughtered in the open was not privileged to claim. He did not accurately and in words discriminate the differences, but he felt that the captive had sounded all the gamut of hope and despair, shared the gradations of an appreciated sorrow that makes all souls akin and that even lifts the beast to the plane of brotherhood, the bond of emotional woe. He had often with no other or better reason liberated the trophy of his snare, calling after the amazed and franticly fleeing creature, "Bye-bye, Buddy!" with peals of his whimsical, joyous laughter.

He was experiencing now a similar sequence of sentiments in noting the wild-eyed eagerness with which the captured raider took obvious heed of every minor point of worthiness that might mask the true character of his entertainers. But, indeed, these deceptive hopes might have been easily maintained by one not so desirous of reassurance when, in the darkest hour before the dawn, they reached a large log-cabin sequestered in dense woods, and he found himself an inmate of a simple, typical mountain household. It held an exceedingly venerable grandfather, wielding his infirmities as a rod of iron; a father and mother, hearty, hospitable, subservient to the aged tyrant, but keeping in filial check a family of sons and daughters-in-law, with an underfoot delegation of grandchildren, who seemed to spend their time in a bewildering manouver of dashing out at one door to dash in at another. A tumultuous rain had set in shortly after dawn, with lightning and wind,—"the tail of a harricane," as the host called it,—and a terrible bird the actual storm must have been to have a tail of such dimensions. There was no getting forth, no living creature of free will "took water" in this elemental crisis. The numerous dogs crowded the children away from the hearth, and the hens strolled about the large living-room, clucking to scurrying broods. Even one of the horses tramped up on the porch and looked in ever and anon, solicitous of human company.

"I brung Ben up by hand, like a bottle-fed baby," the hostess apologized, "an' he ain't never fund out fur sure that he ain't folks."

There seemed no possible intimation of moonshine in this entourage, and the coffin filled with jugs, a-wagoning from some distillers' den in the range to the cross-roads' store, might well have been accounted only the vain phantasm of an overtired brain surcharged with the vexed problems of the revenue service. The disguised revenue-raider was literally overcome with drowsiness, the result of his exertions and his vigils, and observing this, his host gave him one of the big feather beds under the low slant of the eaves in the roof-room, where the other men, who had been out all night, also slept the greater portion of the day. In fact, it was dark when Wyatt wakened, and, leaving the rest still torpid with slumber and fatigue, descended to the large main room of the cabin.

The callow members of the household had retired to rest, but the elders of the band of moonshiners were up and still actively astir, and Wyatt experienced a prescient vicarious qualm to note their lack of heed or secrecy—the noisy shifting of heavy weights (barrels, kegs, bags of apples, and peaches for pomace), the loud voices and unguarded words. When a door in the floor was lifted, the whiff of chill, subterranean air that pervaded the whole house was heavily freighted with spirituous odors, and gave token to the meanest intelligence, to the most unobservant inmate, that the still was operated in a cellar, peculiarly immune to suspicion, for a cellar is never an adjunct to the ordinary mountain cabin. Thus the infraction of the revenue law went on securely and continuously beneath the placid, simple, domestic life, with its reverent care for the very aged and its tender nurture of the very young.

It was significant, indeed, that the industry should not be pretermitted, however, when a stranger was within the gates. The reason to Wyatt, familiar with the moonshiners' methods and habits of thought, was only too plain. They intended that the "revenuer" should never go forth to tell the tale. His comrades had evidently failed to follow his trail, either losing it in the wilderness or from ignorance of his intention. He had put himself hopelessly into the power of these desperate men, whom his escape or liberation would menace with incarceration for a long term as Federal prisoners in distant penitentiaries, if, indeed, they were not already answerable to the law for some worse crime than illicit distilling. His murder would be the extreme of brutal craft, so devised as to seem an accident, against the possibility of future investigation.

The reflection turned Wyatt deathly cold, he who could not bear unmoved the plea of a wild thing's eye. He sturdily sought to pull himself together. It was none of his decree; it was none of his deed, he argued. The older moonshiners, who managed all the details of the enterprise, would direct the event with absolute authority and the immutability of fate. But whatever should be done, he revolted from any knowledge of it, as from any share in the act. He had risen to leave the place, all strange of aspect now, metamorphosed,—various disorderly details of the prohibited industry ever and anon surging up from the still-room below,—when a hoarse voice took cognizance of his intention with a remonstrance.

"Why, Watt Wyatt, ye can't go out in the cove. Ye air dead! Ye will let that t'other revenue-raider ye seen into the secret o' the bresh whisky in our wagon ef ye air viewed about whenst 'Gene hev spread the report that ye air dead. Wait till them raiders hev cleared out of the kentry."

The effort at detention, to interfere with his liberty, added redoubled impetus to Wyatt's desire to be gone. He suddenly devised a cogent necessity. "I be feared my dad mought hear that fool tale. I ain't much loss, but dad would feel it."

"Oh, I sent Jack thar ter tell him better whenst he drove ter mill ter-day ter git the meal fer the mash. Jack made yer dad understand 'bout yer sudden demise."

"Oh, yeh," interposed the glib Jack; "an' he said ez *he* couldn't abide sech jokes."

"Shucks!" cried the filial Wyatt. "Dad war full fresky himself in his young days; I hev hearn his old frien's say so."

"I tried ter slick things over," said the diplomatic Jack. "I 'lowed young folks war giddy by nature. I 'lowed 't war jes a flash o' fun. An' he say: 'Flash o' fun be con-sarned! My son is more like a flash o' lightning; ez suddint an' mischee-vious an' totally ondesirable.'"

The reproach obviously struck home, for Wyatt maintained a disconsolate si-lence for a time. At length, apparently goaded by his thoughts to attempt a de-fense, he remonstrated:

"Nobody ever war dead less of his own free will. I never elected ter be a harnt. 'Gene Barker hed no right ter nominate *me* fer the dear departed, nohow."

One of the uncouth younger fellows, his shoulders laden with a sack of meal, paused on his way from the porch to the trap-door to look up from beneath his burden with a sly grin as he said, "'Gene war wishin' it war true, that's why."

"'Count o' Minta Elladine Riggs," gaily chimed in another.

"But 'Gene needn't gredge Watt foothold on this yearth fer sech; *she* ain't keerin' whether Watt lives or dies," another contributed to the rough, rallying fun.

But Wyatt was of sensitive fibre. He had flushed angrily; his eyes were alight; a bitter retort was trembling on his lips when one of the elder Barkers, discrimi-nating the elements of an uncontrollable fracas, seized on the alternative.

"Could you-uns *sure* be back hyar by daybreak, Watt!" he asked, fixing the young fellow with a stern eye.

"No 'spectable ghost roams around arter sun-up," cried Wyatt, fairly jovial at the prospect of liberation.

"Ye mus' be heedful not ter be viewed," the senior admonished him.

"I be goin' ter slip about keerful like a reg'lar, stiddy-goin' harnt, an' eaves-drop a bit. It's worth livin' a hard life ter view how a feller's friends will take his demise."

"I reckon ye kin make out ter meet the wagin kemin' back from the cross-roads' store. It went out this evenin' with that coffin full of jugs that ye lef' las' night under the church-house, whenst 'Gene seen you-uns war suspicioned. They will hev time ter git ter the cross-roads with the whisky on' back little arter mid-night, special' ez we-uns hev got the raider that spied out the job hyar fast by the leg."

The mere mention of the young prisoner rendered Wyatt the more eager to be gone, to be out of sight and sound. But he had no agency in the disaster, he urged against some inward clamor of protest; the catastrophe was the logical result of the fool-hardiness of the officer in following these desperate men with no back-ing, with no power to apprehend or hold, relying on his flimsy disguise, and risk-ing delivering himself into their hands, fettered as he was with the knowledge of his discovery of their secret.

"It's nothin' ter *me*, nohow," Wyatt was continually repeating to himself, though when he sprang through the door he could scarcely draw his breath be-cause of some mysterious, invisible clutch at his throat.

He sought to ascribe this symptom to the density of the pervasive fog without, that impenetrably cloaked all the world; one might wonder how a man could find his way through the opaque white vapor. It was, however, an accustomed medium to the young mountaineer, and his feet, too, had something of that unclassified muscular instinct, apart from reason, which guides in an oft-trodden path. Once he came to a halt, from no uncertainty of locality, but to gaze apprehensively through the blank, white mists over a shuddering shoulder. "I wonder ef thar be any other harnts aloose ter-night, a-boguing through the fog an' the moon," he speculated. Presently he went on again, shaking his head sagely. "I ain't wantin' ter collogue with sech," he averred cautiously.

Occasionally the moonlight fell in expansive splendor through a rift in the white vapor; amidst the silver glintings a vague, illusory panorama of promontory and island, bay and inlet, far ripplings of gleaming deeps, was presented like some magic reminiscence, some ethereal replica of the past, the simulacrum of the seas of these ancient coves, long since ebbed away and vanished.

The sailing moon visibly rocked, as the pulsing tides of the cloud-ocean rose and fell, and ever and anon this supernal craft was whelmed in its surgings, and once more came majestically into view, freighted with fancies and heading for the haven of the purple western shores.

In one of these clearances of the mists a light of an alien type caught the eye of the wandering spectre—a light, red, mundane, of prosaic suggestion. It filtered through the crevice of a small batten shutter.

The ghost paused, his head speculatively askew. "Who sits so late at the forge!" he marvelled, for he was now near the base of the mountain, and he recognized the low, dark building looming through the mists, its roof aslant, its chimney cold, the big doors closed, the shutter fast. As he neared the place a sudden shrill guffaw smote the air, followed by a deep, gruff tone of disconcerted remonstrance. Certain cabalistic words made the matter plain.

"High, Low, Jack, *and* game! Fork! Fork!" Once more there arose a high falsetto shriek of jubilant laughter.

Walter Wyatt crept noiselessly down the steep slant toward the shutter. He had no sense of intrusion, for he was often one of the merry blades wont to congregate at the forge at night and take a hand at cards, despite the adverse sentiment of the cove and the vigilance of the constable of the district, bent on enforcing the laws prohibiting gaming. As Wyatt stood at the crevice of the shutter the whole interior was distinct before him—the disabled wagon-wheels against the walls, the horse-shoes on a rod across the window, the great hood of the forge, the silent bellows, with its long, motionless handle. A kerosene lamp, perched on the elevated hearth of the forge, illumined the group of wild young mountaineers clustered about a barrel on the head of which the cards were dealt. There were no chairs; one of the gamesters sat on a keg of nails; another on an inverted splint basket; two on a rude bench that was wont to be placed outside the door for the accommodation of customers waiting for a horse to be shod or a plow to be laid. An onlooker, not yet so proficient as to attain his ambition of admission to the play, had mounted the anvil, and from this coign of vantage beheld all the outspread landscape of the "hands." More than once his indiscreet, inadvertent betrayal of some incident of his survey of the cards menaced him with a broken head. More innocuous to the interests of the play was a wight humbly ensconced on the shoeing-stool, which barely brought his head to the level of the board; but as he was densely ignorant of the game, he took no disadvantage from his lowly posture. His head was red, and as it moved erratically about in the gloom, Watt Wyatt thought for a moment that it was the smith's red setter. He grinned as he resolved that some day he would tell the fellow this as a pleasing gibe; but the thought was arrested by the sound of his own name.

"Waal, sir," said the dealer, pausing in shuffling the cards, "I s'pose ye hev all hearn 'bout Walter Wyatt's takin' off."

"An' none too soon, sartain." A sour visage was glimpsed beneath the wide brim of the speaker's hat.

"Waal," drawled the semblance of the setter from deep in the clare-obscure, "Watt war jes a fool from lack o' sense."

"That kind o' fool can't be cured," said another of the players. Then he sharply adjuxed the dealer. "Look out what ye be doin'! Ye hev gimme *two* ky-erds."

"'Gene Barker will git ter marry Minta Elladine Biggs now, I reckon," suggested the man on the anvil.

"An' I'll dance at the weddin' with right good will an' a nimble toe," declared the dealer, vivaciously. "I'll be glad ter see that couple settled. That gal couldn't make up her mind ter let Walter Wyatt go, an' yit no woman in her senses would hev been willin, ter marry him. He war ez onresponsible ez—ez—fox-fire."

"An' ez onstiddy ez a harricane," commented another.

"An' no more account than a mole in the yearth," said a third.

The ghost at the window listened in aghast dismay and became pale in sober truth, for these boon companions he had accounted the best friends he had in the world. They had no word of regret, no simple human pity; even that facile meed of casual praise that he was "powerful pleasant company" was withheld. And for these and such as these he had bartered the esteem of the community at large and his filial duty and obedience; had spurned the claims of good citizenship and placed himself in jeopardy of the law; had forfeited the hand of the woman he loved.

"Minta Elladine Biggs ain't keerin' nohow fer sech ez Watt," said the semblance of the setter, with a knowing nod of his red head. "I war up thar at the mill whenst the news kem ter-day, an' she war thar ter git some seconds. I hev hearn women go off in high-strikes fer a lovyer's death—even Mis' Simton, though hem was jes her husband, an' a mighty pore one at that. But Minta Elladine jes listened quiet an' composed, an' never said one word."

The batten shutter was trembling in the ghost's hand. In fact, so convulsive was his grasp that it shook the hook from the staple, and the shutter slowly opened as he stood at gaze.

Perhaps it was the motion that attracted the attention of the dealer, perhaps the influx of a current of fresh air. He lifted his casual glance and beheld, distinct in the light from the kerosene lamp and imposed on the white background of the mist, that familiar and individual face, pallid, fixed, strange, with an expression that he had never seen it wear hitherto. One moment of suspended faculties, and he sprang up with a wild cry that filled the little shanty with its shrill terror. The others gazed astounded upon him, then followed the direction of his starting eyes, and echoed his frantic fright. There was a wild scurry toward the door. The overturning of the lamp was imminent, but it still burned calmly on the elevated hearth, while the shoeing-stool capsized in the rush, and the red head of its lowly occupant was lowlier still, rolling on the dirt floor. Even with this disadvantage, however, he was not the hindmost, and reached the exit unhurt. The only specific damage wrought by the panic was to the big barnlike doors of the place. They had been stanchly barred against the possible intrusion of the constable of the district, and the fastenings in so critical an emergency could not be readily loosed. The united weight and impetus of the onset burst the flimsy doors into fragments, and as the party fled in devious directions in the misty moonlight, the calm radiance entered at the wide-spread portal and illuminated the vacant place where late had been so merry a crew.

Walter Wyatt had known the time when the incident would have held an incomparable relish for him. But now he gazed all forlorn into the empty building with a single thought in his mind. "Not one of 'em keered a mite! Nare good word, nare sigh, not even, 'Fare ye well, old mate!'"

His breast heaved, his eyes flashed.

"An' I hev loant money ter Jim, whenst I hed need myself; an' holped George in the mill, when his wrist war sprained, without a cent o' pay; an' took the blame when 'Dolphus war faulted by his dad fur lamin' the horse-critter; an' stood back an' let Pete git the meat whenst we-uns shot fur beef, bein' he hev got a wife an' chil'ren ter feed. All *leetle* favors, but nare *leetle* word."

He had turned from the window and was tramping absently down the road, all unmindful of the skulking methods of the spectral gentry. If he had chanced to be observed, his little farce, that had yet an element of tragedy in its presentation, must soon have reached its close. But the fog hung about him like a cloak, and when the moon cast aside the vapors, it was in a distant silver sheen illumining the far reaches of the valley. Only when its light summoned forth a brilliant and glancing reflection on a lower level, as if a thousand sabers were unsheathed at a word, he recognized the proximity of the river and came to a sudden halt.

"Whar is this fool goin'?" he demanded angrily of space. "To the graveyard, I declar', ez ef I war a harnt fur true, an' buried sure enough. An' I wish I war. I wish I war."

He realized, after a moment's consideration, that he had been unconsciously actuated by the chance of meeting the wagon, returning by this route from the cross-roads' store. He was tired, disheartened; his spirit was spent; he would be glad of the lift. He reflected, however, that he must needs wait some time, for this was the date of a revival-meeting at the little church, and the distillers' wagon would lag, that its belated night journey might not be subjected to the scrutiny and comment of the church-goers. Indeed, even now Walter Wyatt saw in the distance the glimmer of a lantern, intimating homeward-bound worshipers not yet out of sight.

"The saints kep' it up late ter-night," he commented.

He resolved to wait till the roll of wheels should tell of the return of the moonshiners' empty wagon.

He crossed the river on the little footbridge and took his way languidly along the road toward the deserted church. He was close to the hedge that grew thick and rank about the little inclosure when he suddenly heard the sound of lamentation from within. He drew back precipitately, with a sense of sacrilege, but the branches of the unpruned growth had caught in his sleeve, and he sought to disengage the cloth without such rustling stir as might disturb or alarm the mourner, who had evidently lingered here, after the dispersal of the congregation, for a moment's indulgence of grief and despair. He had a glimpse through the shaking boughs and the flickering mist of a woman's figure kneeling on the crude red clods of a new-made grave. A vague, anxious wonder as to the deceased visited him, for in the sparsely settled districts a strong community sense prevails. Suddenly in a choking gust of sobs and burst of tears he recognized his own name in a voice of which every inflection was familiar. For a moment his heart seemed to stand still. His brain whirled with a realization of this unforeseen result of the fantastic story of his death in Eskaqua Cove, which the moonshiners, on the verge of detection and arrest, had circulated in Tanglefoot as a measure of safety. They had fancied that when the truth was developed it would be easy enough to declare the men drunk or mistaken. The "revenuers" by that time would be far away, and the pervasive security, always the sequence of a raid, successful or otherwise, would once more promote the manufacture of the brush whisky. The managers of the moon-shining interest had taken measures to guard Wyatt's aged father from this fantasy of woe, but they had not dreamed that the mountain coquette might care. He himself stood appalled that this ghastly fable should delude his heart's beloved, amazed that it should cost her one sigh, one sob. Her racking paroxysms of grief over this gruesome figment of a grave he was humiliated to hear, he was woeful to see. He felt that he was not worth one tear of the floods with which she bewept his name, uttered in every cadence of tender regret that her melancholy voice could compass. It must cease, she must know the truth at whatever cost. He broke through the hedge and stood in the flicker of the moonlight before her, pale, agitated, all unlike his wonted self.

She did not hear, amid the tumult of her weeping, the rustling of the boughs, but some subtle sense took cognizance of his presence. She half rose, and with one hand holding back her dense yellow hair, which had fallen forward on her forehead, she looked up at him fearfully, tremulously, with all the revolt of the corporeal creature for the essence of the mysterious incorporeal. For a moment he could not speak. So much he must needs explain. The next instant he was whelmed in the avalanche of her words.

"Te hev kem!" she exclaimed in a sort of shrill ecstasy. "Te hev kem so far ter hear the word that I would give my life ter hev said before. Te knowed it in heaven! an' how like ye ter kem ter gin me the chanst ter say it at last! How like the good heart of ye, worth all the hearts on yearth—an' *buried hyar!*"

With her open palm she smote the insensate clods with a gesture of despair. Then she went on in a rising tide of tumultuous emotion. "I love ye! Oh, I *always* loved ye! I never keered fur nobody else! an' I war tongue-tied, an' full of fool pride, an' faultin' ye fur yer ways; an' I wouldn't gin ye the word I knowed ye war wantin' ter hear. But now I kin tell the pore ghost of ye—I kin tell the pore, pore ghost!"

She buried her swollen, tear-stained face in her hands, and shook her head to and fro with the realization of the futility of late repentance. As she once more lifted her eyes, she was obviously surprised to see him still standing there, and the crisis seemed to restore to him the faculty of speech.

"Minta Elladine," he said huskily and prosaically, "I ain't dead!"

She sprang to her feet and stood gazing at him, intent and quivering.

"I be truly alive an' kicking an' ez worthless ez ever," he went on.

She said not a word, but bent and pallid, and, quaking in every muscle, stood peering beneath her hand, which still held back her hair.

"It's all a mistake," he urged. "This ain't no grave. The top war dug a leetle ter turn off a revenuer's suspicions o' the moonshiners. They put that tale out."

Still, evidently on the verge of collapse, she did not speak.

"Ye needn't be afeared ez I be goin' ter take fur true all I hearn ye say; folks air gin ter vauntin' the dead," he paused for a moment, remembering the caustic comments over the deal of the cards, then added, "though I reckon *I* hev hed some cur'ous 'speriences ez a harnt."

She suddenly threw up both arms with a shrill scream, half nervous exhaustion, half inexpressible delight. She swayed to and fro, almost fainting, her balance failing. He caught her in his arms, and she leaned sobbing against his breast.

"I stand ter every word of it," she cried, her voice broken and lapsed from control. "I love ye, an' I despise all the rest!"

"I be powerful wild," he suggested contritely.

"I ain't keerin' ef ye be ez wild ez a deer."

"But I'm goin' to quit gamesome company an' playin' kyerds an' sech. I expec' ter mend my ways now," he promised eagerly.

"Ye kin mend 'em or let 'em stay tore, jes ez ye please," she declared recklessly. "I ain't snatched my lovyer from the jaws o' death ter want him otherwise; ye be plumb true-hearted, *I know*."

"I mought ez well hev been buried in this grave fer the last ten year' fer all the use I hev been," he protested solemnly; "but I hev learnt a lesson through bein' a harnt fer a while—I hev jes kem ter life. I'm goin' ter *live* now. I'll make myself some use in the world, an' fust off I be goin' ter hinder the murder of a man what they hev got trapped up yander at the still."

This initial devoir of his reformation, however, Wyatt found no easy matter. The event had been craftily planned to seem an accident, a fall from a cliff in pursuing the wagon, and only the most ardent and cogent urgency on Wyatt's part prevailed at length. He argued that this interpretation of the disaster would not satisfy the authorities. To take the raider's life insured discovery, retribution. But as he had been brought to the still in the night, it was obvious that if he were conveyed under cover of darkness and by roundabout trails within striking distance of the settlements, he could never again find his way to the locality in the dense wilderness. In his detention he had necessarily learned nothing fresh, for the only names he could have overheard had long been obnoxious to suspicion of moonshining, and afforded no proof. Thus humanity, masquerading as caution, finally triumphed, and the officer, blindfolded, was conducted through devious and winding ways many miles distant, and released within a day's travel of the county town.

Walter Wyatt was scarcely welcomed back to life by the denizens of the cove generally with the enthusiasm attendant on the first moments of his resuscitation, so to speak. He never forgot the solemn ecstasy of that experience, and in later years he was wont to annul any menace of discord with his wife by the warning, half jocose, half tender: "Ye hed better mind; ye'll be sorry some day fur treatin' me so mean. Remember, I hev viewed ye a-weepin' over my grave before now."

A reformation, however complete and salutary, works no change of identity, and although he developed into an orderly, industrious, law-abiding citizen, his prankish temperament remained recognizable in the fantastic fables which he delighted to recount at some genial fireside of what he had seen and heard as a ghost.

"Pears like, Watt, ye hed more experiences whenst dead than living," said an auditor, as these stories multiplied.

"I did, fur a fack," Watt protested. "I war a powerful onchancy, onquiet ghost. I even did my courtin' whilst in my reg'lar line o' business a-hanatin' a grave-yard."

THE DREAM-GOWN OF THE JAPANESE AMBASSADOR, by Brander Matthews

(1896.)

I

After arranging the Egyptian and Mexican pottery so as to contrast agreeably with the Dutch and the German beer-mugs on the top of the bookcase that ran along one wall of the sitting-room, Cosmo Waynflete went back into the bed-room and took from a half-empty trunk the little cardboard boxes in which he kept the collection of playing-cards, and of all manner of outlandish equivalents for these simple instruments of fortune, picked up here and there during his two or three years of dilettante travelling in strange countries. At the same time he brought out a Japanese crystal ball, which he stood upon its silver tripod, placing it on a little table in one of the windows on each side of the fireplace; and there the rays of the westering sun lighted it up at once into translucent loveliness.

The returned wanderer looked out of the window and saw on one side the graceful and vigorous tower of the Madison Square Garden, with its Diana turn-ing in the December wind, while in the other direction he could look down on the frozen paths of Union Square, only a block distant, but as far below him al-most as though he were gazing down from a balloon. Then he stepped back into the sitting-room itself, and noted the comfortable furniture and wood-fire crack-ling in friendly fashion on the hearth, and his own personal belongings, scattered here and there as though they were settling themselves for a stay. Having arrived from Europe only that morning, he could not but hold himself lucky to have found these rooms taken for him by the old friend to whom he had announced his return, and with whom he was to eat his Christmas dinner that evening. He had not been on shore more than six or seven hours, and yet the most of his odds and ends were unpacked and already in place as though they belonged in this new abode. It was true that he had toiled unceasingly to accomplish this, and as he stood there in his shirt-sleeves, admiring the results of his labors, he was con-scious also that his muscles were fatigued, and that the easy-chair before the fire opened its arms temptingly.

He went again into the bedroom, and took from one of his many trunks a long, loose garment of pale-gray silk. Apparently this beautiful robe was in-tended to serve as a dressing-gown, and as such Cosmo Waynflete utilized it im-mediately. The ample folds fell softly about him, and the rich silk itself seemed to be soothing to his limbs, so delicate was its fibre and so carefully had it been woven. Around the full skirt there was embroidery of threads of gold, and again on the open and flowing sleeves. With the skilful freedom of Japanese art the pattern of this decoration seemed to suggest the shrubbery about a spring, for there were strange plants with huge leaves broadly outlined by the golden threads, and in the midst of them water was seen bubbling from the earth and lapping gently over the edge of the fountain. As the returned wanderer thrust his arms into the dressing-gown with its symbolic embroidery on the skirt and sleeves, he remembered distinctly the dismal day when he had bought it in a little curiosity-shop in Nuremberg; and as he fastened across his chest one by one the loops of silken cord to the three coins which served as buttons down the front of the robe, he recalled also the time and the place where he had picked up each of these pieces of gold and silver, one after another. The first of them was a Persian daric, which he had purchased from a dealer on the Grand Canal in Venice; and the second was a Spanish peso struck under Philip II. at Potosi, which he had found in a stall on the embankment of the Quay Voltaire, in Paris; and the third was a York shilling, which he had bought from the man who had turned it up in ploughing a field that sloped to the Hudson near Sleepy Hollow.

Having thus wrapped himself in this unusual dressing-gown with its unexpected buttons of gold and silver, Cosmo Waynflete went back into the front room. He dropped into the arm-chair before the fire. It was with a smile of physical satisfaction that he stretched out his feet to the hickory blaze.

The afternoon was drawing on, and in New York the sun sets early on Christmas day. The red rays shot into the window almost horizontally, and they filled the crystal globe with a curious light. Cosmo Waynflete lay back in his easy-chair, with his Japanese robe about him, and gazed intently at the beautiful ball which seemed like a bubble of air and water. His mind went back to the afternoon in April, two years before, when he had found that crystal sphere in a Japanese shop within sight of the incomparable Fugiyama.

II

As he peered into its transparent depths, with his vision focused upon the spot of light where the rays of the setting sun touched it into flame, he was but little surprised to discover that he could make out tiny figures in the crystal. For the moment this strange thing seemed to him perfectly natural. And the movements of these little men and women interested him so much that he watched them as they went to and fro, sweeping a roadway with large brooms. Thus it happened that the fixity of his gaze was intensified. And so it was that in a few minutes he saw with no astonishment that he was one of the group himself, he himself in the rich and stately attire of a samurai. From the instant that Cosmo Waynflete discovered himself among the people whom he saw moving before him, as his eyes were fastened on the illuminated dot in the transparent ball, he ceased to see them as little figures, and he accepted them as of the full stature of man. This increase in their size was no more a source of wonderment to him than it had been to discern himself in the midst of them. He accepted both of these marvellous things without question—indeed, with no thought at all that they were in any way peculiar or abnormal. Not only this, but thereafter he seemed to have transferred his personality to the Cosmo Waynflete who was a Japanese samurai and to have abandoned entirely the Cosmo Waynflete who was an American traveller, and who had just returned to New York that Christmas morning. So completely did the Japanese identity dominate that the existence of the American identity was wholly unknown to him. It was as though the American had gone to sleep in New York at the end of the nineteenth century, and had waked a Japanese in Nippon in the beginning of the eighteenth century.

With his sword by his side—a Murimasa blade, likely to bring bad luck to the wearer sooner or later—he had walked from his own house in the quarter of Kioto which is called Yamashina to the quarter which is called Yoshiwara, a place of ill repute, where dwell women of evil life, and where roysterers and drunkards come by night. He knew that the sacred duty of avenging his master's death had led him to cast off his faithful wife so that he might pretend to riot in debauchery at the Three Sea-Shores. The fame of his shameful doings had spread abroad, and it must soon come to the ears of the man whom he wished to take unawares. Now he was lying prone in the street, seemingly sunk in a drunken slumber, so that men might see him and carry the news to the treacherous assassin of his beloved master. As he lay there that afternoon, he revolved in his mind the devices he should use to make away with his enemy when the hour might be ripe at last for the accomplishment of his holy revenge. To himself he called the roll of his fellow-ronins, now biding their time, as he was, and ready always to obey his orders and to follow his lead to the death, when at last the sun should rise on the day of vengeance.

So he gave no heed to the scoffs and the jeers of those who passed along the street, laughing him to scorn as they beheld him lying there in a stupor from excessive drink at that inordinate hour of the day. And among those who came by at last was a man from Satsuma, who was moved to voice the reproaches of all that saw this sorry sight.

"Is not this Oishi Kuranosuke," said the man from Satsuma, "who was a councillor of Asano Takumi no Kami, and who, not having the heart to avenge his lord, gives himself up to women and wine? See how he lies drunk in the public street! Faithless beast! Fool and craven! Unworthy of the name of a samurai!"

And with that the man from Satsuma trod on him as he lay there, and spat upon him, and went away indignantly. The spies of Kotsuke no Suke heard what the man from Satsuma had said, and they saw how he had spurned the prostrate samurai with his foot; and they went their way to report to their master that he need no longer have any fear of the councillors of Asano Takumi no Kami. All this the man, lying prone in the dust of the street, noted; and it made his heart glad, for then he made sure that the day was soon coming when he could do his duty at last and take vengeance for the death of his master.

III

He lay there longer than he knew, and the twilight settled down at last, and the evening stars came out. And then, after a while, and by imperceptible degrees, Cosmo Waynflete became conscious that the scene had changed and that he had changed with it. He was no longer in Japan, but in Persia. He was no longer lying like a drunkard in the street of a city, but slumbering like a weary soldier in a little oasis by the side of a spring in the midst of a sandy desert. He was asleep, and his faithful horse was unbridled that it might crop the grass at will.

The air was hot and thick, and the leaves of the slim tree above him were never stirred by a wandering wind. Yet now and again there came from the darkness a faintly fetid odor. The evening wore on and still he slept, until at length in the silence of the night a strange huge creature wormed its way steadily out of its lair amid the trees, and drew near the sleeping man to devour him fiercely. But the horse neighed vehemently and beat the ground with his hoofs and waked his master. Then the hideous monster vanished; and the man, aroused from his sleep, saw nothing, although the evil smell still lingered in the sultry atmosphere. He lay down again once more, thinking that for once his steed had given a false alarm. Again the grisly dragon drew nigh, and again the courser notified its rider, and again the man could make out nothing in the darkness of the night; and again he was wellnigh stifled by the foul emanation that trailed in the wake of the misbegotten creature. He rebuked his horse and laid him down once more.

A third time the dreadful beast approached, and a third time the faithful charger awoke its angry master. But there came the breath of a gentle breeze, so that the man did not fear to fill his lungs; and there was a vague light in the heavens now, so that he could dimly discern his mighty enemy; and at once he girded himself for the fight. The scaly monster came full at him with dripping fangs, its mighty body thrusting forward its huge and hideous head. The man met the attack without fear and smote the beast full on the crest, but the blow rebounded from its coat of mail.

Then the faithful horse sprang forward and bit the dreadful creature full upon the neck and tore away the scales, so that its master's sword could pierce the armored hide. So the man was able to dissever the ghastly head and thus to slay the monstrous dragon. The blackness of night wrapped him about once more as he fell on his knees and gave thanks for his victory; and the wind died away again.

IV

Only a few minutes later, so it seemed to him, Cosmo Waynflete became doubtfully aware of another change of time and place—of another transformation of his own being. He knew himself to be alone once more, and even without his trusty charger. Again he found himself groping in the dark. But in a little while there was a faint radiance of light, and at last the moon came out behind a tower. Then he saw that he was not by the roadside in Japan or in the desert of Persia, but now in some unknown city of Southern Europe, where the architecture was hispano-moresque. By the silver rays of the moon he was able to make out the beautiful design damascened upon the blade of the sword which he held now in his hand ready drawn for self-defence.

Then he heard hurried footfalls down the empty street, and a man rushed around the corner pursued by two others, who had also weapons in their hands. For a moment Cosmo Waynflete was a Spaniard, and to him it was a point of honor to aid the weaker party. He cried to the fugitive to pluck up heart and to withstand the enemy stoutly. But the hunted man fled on, and after him went one of the pursuers, a tall, thin fellow, with a long black cloak streaming behind him as he ran.

The other of the two, a handsome lad with fair hair, came to a halt and crossed swords with Cosmo, and soon showed himself to be skilled in the art of fence. So violent was the young fellow's attack that in the ardor of self-defence Cosmo ran the boy through the body before he had time to hold his hand or even to reflect.

The lad toppled over sideways. "Oh, my mother!" he cried, and in a second he was dead. While Cosmo bent over the body, hasty footsteps again echoed along the silent thoroughfare. Cosmo peered around the corner, and by the struggling moonbeams he could see that it was the tall, thin fellow in the black cloak, who was returning with half a score of retainers, all armed, and some of them bearing torches.

Cosmo turned and fled swiftly, but being a stranger in the city he soon lost himself in its tortuous streets. Seeing a light in a window and observing a vine that trailed from the balcony before it, he climbed up boldly, and found himself face to face with a gray-haired lady, whose visage was beautiful and kindly and noble. In a few words he told her his plight and besought sanctuary. She listened to him in silence, with exceeding courtesy of manner, as though she were weighing his words before making up her mind. She raised the lamp on her table and let its beams fall on his lineaments. And still she made no answer to his appeal.

Then came a glare of torches in the street below and a knocking at the door. Then at last the old lady came to a resolution; she lifted the tapestry at the head of her bed and told him to bestow himself there. No sooner was he hidden than the tall, thin man in the long black cloak entered hastily. He greeted the elderly lady as his aunt, and he told her that her son had been set upon by a stranger in the street and had been slain. She gave a great cry and never took her eyes from his face. Then he said that a servant had seen an unknown man climb to the balcony of her house. What if it were the assassin of her son? The blood left her face and she clutched at the table behind her, as she gave orders to have the house searched.

When the room was empty at last she went to the head of the bed and bade the man concealed there to come forth and begone, but to cover his face, that she might not be forced to know him again. So saying, she dropped on her knees before a crucifix, while he slipped out of the window again and down to the deserted street.

He sped to the corner and turned it undiscovered, and breathed a sigh of relief and of regret. He kept on steadily, gliding stealthily along in the shadows, until he found himself at the city gate as the bell of the cathedral tolled the hour of midnight.

V

How it was that he passed through the gate he could not declare with precision, for seemingly a mist had settled about him. Yet a few minutes later he saw that in some fashion he must have got beyond the walls of the town, for he recognized the open country all around. And, oddly enough, he now discovered himself to be astride a bony steed. He could not say what manner of horse it was he was riding, but he felt sure that it was not the faithful charger that had saved his life in Persia, once upon a time, in days long gone by, as it seemed to him then. He was not in Persia now—of that he was certain, nor in Japan, nor in the Iberian peninsula. Where he was he did not know.

In the dead hush of midnight he could hear the barking of a dog on the opposite shore of a dusky and indistinct waste of waters that spread itself far below him. The night grew darker and darker, the stars seemed to sink deeper in the sky, and driving clouds occasionally hid them from his sight. He had never felt so lonely and dismal. In the centre of the road stood an enormous tulip-tree; its limbs were gnarled and fantastic, large enough to form trunks for ordinary trees, twisting down almost to the earth, and rising again into the air. As he approached this fearful tree he thought he saw something white hanging in the midst of it, but on looking more narrowly he perceived it was a place where it had been scathed by lightning and the white wood laid bare. About two hundred yards from the tree a small brook crossed the road; and as he drew near he beheld—on the margin of this brook, and in the dark shadow of the grove—he beheld something huge, misshapen, black, and towering. It stirred not, but seemed gathered up in the gloom like some gigantic monster ready to spring upon the traveller.

He demanded, in stammering accents, "Who are you?" He received no reply. He repeated his demand in a still more agitated voice. Still there was no answer. And then the shadowy object of alarm put itself in motion, and with a scramble and a bound stood in the middle of the road. He appeared to be a horseman of large dimensions and mounted on a black horse of powerful frame. Having no relish for this strange midnight companion, Cosmo Waynflete urged on his steed in hopes of leaving the apparition behind; but the stranger quickened his horse also to an equal pace. And when the first horseman pulled up, thinking to lag behind, the second did likewise. There was something in the moody and dogged silence of this pertinacious companion that was mysterious and appalling. It was soon fearfully accounted for. On mounting a rising ground which brought the figure of his fellow-traveller against the sky, gigantic in height and muffled in a cloak, he was horror-struck to discover the stranger was headless!—but his horror was still more increased in observing that the head which should have rested on the shoulders was carried before the body on the pommel of the saddle.

The terror of Cosmo Waynflete rose to desperation, and he spurred his steed suddenly in the hope of giving his weird companion the slip. But the headless horseman started full jump with him. His own horse, as though possessed by a demon, plunged headlong down the hill. He could hear, however, the black steed panting and blowing close behind him; he even fancied that he felt the hot breath of the pursuer. When he ventured at last to cast a look behind, he saw the goblin rising in the stirrups, and in the very act of hurling at him the grisly head. He fell out of the saddle to the ground; and the black steed and the goblin rider passed by him like a whirlwind.

VI

How long he lay there by the roadside, stunned and motionless, he could not guess; but when he came to himself at last the sun was already high in the heavens. He discovered himself to be reclining on the tall grass of a pleasant graveyard which surrounded a tiny country church in the outskirts of a pretty little village. It was in the early summer, and the foliage was green above him as the boughs swayed gently to and fro in the morning breeze. The birds were singing gayly as they flitted about over his head. The bees hummed along from flower to flower. At last, so it seemed to him, he had come into a land of peace and quiet, where there was rest and comfort and where no man need go in fear of his life. It was a country where vengeance was not a duty and where midnight combats were not a custom he found himself smiling as he thought that a grisly dragon and a goblin rider would be equally out of place in this laughing landscape.

Then the bell in the steeple of the little church began to ring merrily, and he rose to his feet in expectation. All of a sudden the knowledge came to him why it was that they were ringing. He wondered then why the coming of the bride was thus delayed. He knew himself to be a lover, with life opening brightly before him; and the world seemed to him sweeter than ever before and more beautiful.

Then at last the girl whom he loved with his whole heart and who had promised to marry him appeared in the distance, and he thought he had never seen her look more lovely. As he beheld his bridal party approaching, he slipped into the church to await her at the altar. The sunshine fell full upon the portal and made a halo about the girl's head as she crossed the threshold.

But even when the bride stood by his side and the clergyman had begun the solemn service of the church the bells kept on, and soon their chiming became a clangor, louder and sharper and more insistent.

VII

So clamorous and so persistent was the ringing that Cosmo Waynflete was roused at last. He found himself suddenly standing on his feet, with his hand clutching the back of the chair in which he had been sitting before the fire when the rays of the setting sun had set long ago. The room was dark, for it was lighted now only by the embers of the burnt-out fire; and the electric bell was ringing steadily, as though the man outside the door had resolved to waken the seven sleepers.

Then Cosmo Waynflete was wide-awake again; and he knew where he was once more—not in Japan, not in Persia, not in Lisbon, not in Sleepy Hollow, but here in New York, in his own room, before his own fire. He opened the door at once and admitted his friend, Paul Stuyvesant.

"It isn't dinner-time, is it?" he asked. "I'm not late, am I? The fact is, I've been asleep."

"It is so good of you to confess that," his friend answered, laughing; "although the length of time you kept me waiting and ringing might have led me to suspect it. No, you are not late and it is not dinner-time. I've come around to have another little chat with you before dinner, that's all."

"Take this chair, old man," said Cosmo, as he threw another hickory-stick on the fire. Then he lighted the gas and sat down by the side of his friend.

"This chair is comfortable, for a fact," Stuyvesant declared, stretching himself out luxuriously. "No wonder you went to sleep. What did you dream of?—strange places you had seen in your travels or the homely scenes of your native land."

Waynflete looked at his friend for a moment without answering the question. He was startled as he recalled the extraordinary series of adventures which had fallen to his lot since he had fixed his gaze on the crystal ball. It seemed to him as though he had been whirled through space and through time.

"I suppose every man is always the hero of his own dreams," he began, doubtfully.

"Of course," his friend returned; "in sleep our natural and healthy egotism is absolutely unrestrained. It doesn't make any matter where the scene is laid or whether the play is a comedy or a tragedy, the dreamer has always the centre of the stage, with the calcium light turned full on him."

"That's just it," Waynflete went on; "this dream of mine makes me feel as if I were an actor, and as if I had been playing many parts, one after the other, in the swiftest succession. They are not familiar to me, and yet I confess to a vague feeling of unoriginality. It is as though I were a plagiarist of adventure—if that be a possible supposition. I have just gone through these startling situations myself, and yet I'm sure that they have all of them happened before—although, perhaps, not to any one man. Indeed, no one man could have had all these adventures of mine, because I see now that I have been whisked through the centuries and across the hemispheres with a suddenness possible only in dreams. Yet all my experiences seem somehow second-hand, and not really my own."

"Picked up here and there—like your bric-à-brac?" suggested Stuyvesant. "But what are these alluring adventures of yours that stretched through the ages and across the continents?"

Then, knowing how fond his friend was of solving mysteries and how proud he was of his skill in this art, Cosmo Waynflete narrated his dream as it has been set down in these pages.

When he had made an end, Paul Stuyvesant's first remark was: "I'm sorry I happened along just then and waked you up before you had time to get married."

His second remark followed half a minute later.

"I see how it was," he said; "you were sitting in this chair and looking at that crystal ball, which focussed the level rays of the setting sun, I suppose? Then it is plain enough—you hypnotized yourself!"

"I have heard that such a thing is possible," responded Cosmo."

"Possible?" Stuyvesant returned, "it is certain! But what is more curious is the new way in which you combined your self-hypnotism with crystal-gazing. You have heard of scrying, I suppose?"

"You mean the practice of looking into a drop of water or a crystal ball or anything of that sort," said Cosmo, "and of seeing things in it—of seeing people moving about?"

"That's just what I do mean," his friend returned. "And that's just what you have been doing. You fixed your gaze on the ball, and so hypnotized yourself; and then, in the intensity of your vision, you were able to see figures in the crystal—with one of which visualized emanations you immediately identified yourself. That's easy enough, I think. But I don't see what suggested to you your separate experiences. I recognize them, of course—"

"You recognize them?" cried Waynflete, in wonder.

"I can tell you where you borrowed every one of your adventures," Stuyvesant replied, "But what I'd like to know now is what suggested to you just those particular characters and situations, and not any of the many others also stored away in your subconsciousness."

So saying, he began to look about the room.

"My subconsciousness?" repeated Waynflete. "Have I ever been a samurai in my subconsciousness?"

Paul Stuyvesant looked at Cosmo Waynflete for nearly a minute without reply. Then all the answer he made was to say: "That's a queer dressing-gown you have on."

"It is time I took it off," said the other, as he twisted himself out of its clinging folds. "It is a beautiful specimen of weaving, isn't it? I call it the dream-gown of the Japanese ambassador, for although I bought it in a curiosity-shop in Nuremberg, it was once, I really believe, the slumber-robe of an Oriental envoy."

Stuyvesant took the silken garment from his friend's hand.

"Why did the Japanese ambassador sell you his dream-gown in a Nuremberg curiosity-shop?" he asked.

"He didn't," Waynflete explained. "I never saw the ambassador, and neither did the old German lady who kept the shop. She told me she bought it from a Japanese acrobat who was out of an engagement and desperately hard up. But she told me also that the acrobat had told her that the garment had belonged to an ambassador who had given it to him as a reward of his skill, and that he never would have parted with it if he had not been dead-broke."

Stuyvesant held the robe up to the light and inspected the embroidery on the skirt of it.

"Yes," he said, at last, "this would account for it, I suppose. This bit here was probably meant to suggest 'the well where the head was washed,'—see?"

"I see that those lines may be meant to represent the outline of a spring of water, but I don't see what that has to do with my dream," Waynflete answered.

"Don't you?" Stuyvesant returned. "Then I'll show you. You had on this silk garment embroidered here with an outline of the well in which was washed the head of Kotsuke no Suke, the man whom the Forty-Seven Ronins killed. You know the story?"

"I read it in Japan, but—" began Cosmo.

"You had that story stored away in your subconsciousness," interrupted his friend. "And when you hypnotized yourself by peering into the crystal ball, this embroidery it was which suggested to you to see yourself as the hero of the tale —Oishi Kuranosuke, the chief of the Forty-Seven Ronins, the faithful follower who avenged his master by pretending to be vicious and dissipated—just like Brutus and Lorenzaccio—until the enemy was off his guard and open to attack."

"I think I do recall the tale of the Forty-Seven Ronins, but only very vaguely," said the hero of the dream. "For all I know I may have had the adventure of Oishi Kuranosuke laid on the shelf somewhere in my subconsciousness, as you want me to believe. But how about my Persian dragon and my Iberian noble-woman?"

Paul Stuyvesant was examining the dream-gown of the Japanese ambassador with minute care. Suddenly he said, "Oh!" and then he looked up at Cosmo Waynflete and asked: "What are those buttons? They seem to be old coins."

"They are old coins," the other answered; "it was a fancy of mine to utilize them on that Japanese dressing-gown. They are all different, you see. The first is —"

"Persian, isn't it?" interrupted Stuyvesant.

"Yes," Waynflete explained, "it is a Persian daric. And the second is a Spanish peso made at Potosi under Philip II. for use in America. And the third is a York shilling, one of the coins in circulation here in New York at the time of the Revolution—I got that one, in fact, from the farmer who ploughed it up in a field at Tarrytown, near Sunnyside."

"Then there are three of your adventures accounted for, Cosmo, and easily enough," Paul commented, with obvious satisfaction at his own explanation. "Just as the embroidery on the silk here suggested to you—after you had hypnotized yourself—that you were the chief of the Forty-Seven Ronins, so this first coin here in turn suggested to you that you were Rustem, the hero of the 'Epic of Kings.' You have read the 'Shah-Nameh?'"

"I remember Firdausi's poem after a fashion only," Cosmo answered. "Was not Rustem a Persian Hercules, so to speak?"

"That's it precisely," the other responded, "and he had seven labors to perform; and you dreamed the third of them, the slaying of the grisly dragon. For my own part, I think I should have preferred the fourth of them, the meeting with the lovely enchantress; but that's neither here nor there."

"It seems to me I do recollect something about that fight of Rustem and the strange beast. The faithful horse's name was Rakush, wasn't it?" asked Waynflete.

"If you can recollect the 'Shah-Nameh,'" Stuyvesant pursued, "no doubt you can recall also Beaumont and Fletcher's 'Custom of the Country?' That's where you got the midnight duel in Lisbon and the magnanimous mother, you know."

"No, I didn't know," the other declared.

"Well, you did, for all that," Paul went on. "The situation is taken from one in a drama of Calderon's, and it was much strengthened in the taking. You may not now remember having read the play, but the incident must have been familiar to you, or else your subconsciousness couldn't have yielded it up to you so readily at the suggestion of the Spanish coin, could it?"

"I did read a lot of Elizabethan drama in my senior year at college," admitted Cosmo, "and this piece of Beaumont and Fletcher's may have been one of those I read; but I totally fail to recall now what it was all about."

"You won't have the cheek to declare that you don't remember the 'Legend of Sleepy Hollow,' will you?" asked Stuyvesant. "Very obviously it was the adventure of Ichabod Crane and the Headless Horseman that the York shilling suggested to you."

"I'll admit that I do recollect Irving's story now," the other confessed.

"So the embroidery on the dream-gown gives the first of your strange situations; and the three others were suggested by the coins you have been using as buttons," said Paul Stuyvesant. "There is only one thing now that puzzles me: that is the country church and the noon wedding and the beautiful bride."

And with that he turned over the folds of the silken garment that hung over his arm.

Cosmo Waynflete hesitated a moment and a blush mantled his cheek. Then he looked his friend in the face and said: "I think I can account for my dreaming about her—I can account for that easily enough."

"So can I," said Paul Stuyvesant, as he held up the photograph of a lovely American girl that he had just found in the pocket of the dream-gown of the Japanese ambassador.

THE MAN IN THE MIRROR,
by Lillian B. Hunt

In the twinkling of an eye, he shot past me. The reception-hall was shaded, but the massive gilt mirror at the far end, scintillating under twin clusters of light, caught his image and held it for an instant.

A clean-cut fellow he was, an artist in appearance, slender and agile—a young man with a face at once fascinating and repellent. The features showed the ravages of dissipation, of poverty, and unfulfilled ambition. The cheeks were hollow and of a bluish pallor; the eyes wildly startled, like those of the hunted deer.

Under the rembrandt, banded with black, hung straight, wet wisps of hair whose tawny glint harmonized well with the stains of modeling clay on hands and sculptor's apron. But what startled me most in that brief glimpse of him was a great wound in the center of his forehead, seared and livid, like the brand of a murderer.

For a quarter hour at least I had been pacing the open conservatory in the right wing of the reception-hall which, in the form of a broad balcony, overlooks the boxwood shrubbery and terrace-gardens. The heavy fragrance of blossoms with the drowsy damp of the river air had gone to my head like a drug.

I felt unsteady, uncertain. The studio garments I wore actually burdened my brain and clogged my steps, for I seemed to be searching, searching everywhere — for what? Well, I hardly knew. For some time my memory had played the knave with me. It was simply that nature had turned Shylock and was exacting from the prodigal even more than her rightful pound.

There were times of late when, without warning, my head would spin and seethe, and my body quiver in a frenzy. Such attacks invariably left my nerves in shreds, and made the dread of the future unspeakably terrifying. To-night I seemed both unnerved and fearful. The perfumed air of the balcony oppressed me, the shrubbery below haunted me.

Thus, in striding up and down, I felt that something extraordinary had happened. The very atmosphere in its heaviness breathed mystery. I peered over the trim lawns set with flower-beds and cone-cut bays, and back again at the dense wall of shrubbery barely distinguishable in the wan starlight.

I stared inside the reception-hall, shadowed save for the clusters of light over the mirror at the far end, and, staring, I stumbled; something crackled and shivered under my feet.

Perhaps you know the shock of stumbling when the nerves are keyed to a certain tension. Perhaps you have heard that sharp, crunching sound that tingles through your tense body like a sword-thrust, and leaves you weak and trembling!

Well, I found myself tottering in a mass of broken porcelain, and, looking down, noticed hundreds of fragments scattered about the tiled pavement. At first I was puzzled, and yet I should have known.

With no feeling other than sadness, I bent and gathered a few of the fragments in my shaking hands. They startled me with a fiendish suggestion. Even as I handled them, they flashed in my eyes wicked as witch-fires, they darted serpents' fangs at me and glowed a vivid scarlet. I flung them over the balustrade in a quick revulsion of feeling, and they fell, sparkling and clinking, on the concrete path below.

At that very instant there came to me the muffled sound of voices and the slow tramp of feet. I counted five silhouettes in the group, and the foremost carried a large-sized pocket flash-light which revolved persistently at every step.

Naturally I was curious to learn their errand, and in my eagerness groped my way over heaps of broken plants, earth, and pottery to a long gap in the floral ranks where I could lean over the balustrade with ease.

The men paused directly beneath me and, as I had surmised, pounced headlong on the brilliant bits of porcelain, jabbering and gesticulating like true natives of the jungle. Of course, I laughed aloud—it was so absurd, so contemptible, their clawing over those atoms in their puny efforts at deduction. And as I laughed the glare of the electric lantern shot upward—full in my face.

The smile froze on my lips. I was blinded, alarmed, too; but what of that? I merely dropped to my knees and huddled there in the darkness.

This incident happened directly before I saw the strange man in the mirror—I rushed quickly back into the house just in time to see him pass. He startled me, too, because he was so close to me, not more than an arm's length away.

I sprang back from him in momentary fright—and suddenly he was gone. There wasn't the faintest trace of him anywhere; yet his image was still clear and distinct in my mind—the wild, protruding eyes, the haggard face, the scarlet mark on the forehead.

For ten minutes, perhaps, I moved about that portion of the hall where he had been, watching and listening for another sign of his presence. Then, impelled by the wariness of his footfall and the weird terror in his face, I began to explore the adjoining parlors and library.

But he had vanished.

Certainly, then, he was the criminal! Why did I think so? I didn't know. All that concerned me was that a suspicious young man lurked beneath my brother's roof.

I leaned against the newel-post and considered. It still lacked two hours of midnight, and Harmon had hosts of friends whom I had never met and who would be likely to drop in after dinner for a round of cards or billiards. Yet, I felt this visitor was no ordinary one, and decided to lose no time in rallying the servants and running him down.

I whirled around toward the nearest push-bell, but before I could place a finger upon it there came to my ears the noise of loud thumping and the prolonged buzzing of an electric bell. By intent listening I concluded that the well-spring of sound was the main front door which opened upon the verandas. Evidently, then, my visitors of the terrace had decided to go further into the heart of things.

I stood quiet for a moment. I hardly knew where to go or what to do. If the refugee was to be caught in my brother's house, should not the glory of the capture be mine? I had found him first; to me belonged the praise and the reward.

However, as I shifted from one foot to the other in nervous uncertainty, I was again amazed. In the midst of the ringing and rapping the parlor portieres swayed violently, and the man of the mirror stood before me. He was ghastly, and when he saw me he shivered and raised his hand to hide the scar on his forehead.

"What is it?" I shrilled at him. "What have you done?"

He said nothing; his dry lips moved, but made no sound. I was quick to see the mockery of his attitude, and I reached for him in a fury. But hardly had my fist swung out than he vanished as before, even as a specter might have dissolved in air.

All I remember is that I crashed into a great gilt frame, and that the mirror went swaying and straining like a thing bewitched. When I regained my footing there was nothing for me to see save the portieres still swinging in his wake.

This time I did not even try to follow him. My one impulse was to compose myself and tidy my person before opening the door. I rushed into the coat-room, tore off my outer garments, and threw them on the floor. Then, quietly and with a dignity befitting my Vaughan ancestors, I opened the door, which by this time was well-nigh parted from its hinges.

"Diana' is not here!" I explained hastily to the five men without. "She is gone! A strange man with a strange scar stole her. I tried to catch him, but failed. He is still here. Search every room! Guard every door!"

After that my memory is a blank. But it seems I must have remained in the reception-room to await developments. On a leather couch I huddled, sick and very weak. My brain was throbbing, and my fingers plucked the cushions in a semidelirium.

Finally I heard the tramp of returning feet, and felt a strong hand on my shoulder. Raising my head, I instantly encountered the searching eyes of Detective Robesart, a man of high standing in the profession. I bowed socially, and while doing so, recognized in his four associates, the servants of the house, including Dombey, the chauffeur.

"Have you found him?" I questioned feverishly.

"Not yet," answered Robesart. "At least, no one answering his description. Were you alone when you saw him?"

I nodded. Robesart fastened his magnetic gaze upon me, examining me from head to heel. He was a short man and stout, with eyes like ebony pin-points and a jaw of grim power. He was a man to be feared, and I feared him.

Quietly he swung about and stepped outside on the veranda, the four attendants and myself in close file behind him. Once there, he paused abruptly and turned to me.

"Go first, Mr. Vaughan," he said.

I asked no questions, but in a dim way understood his request. I took the flashlight from his hand and walked a straight course to the shrubbery. Then, as the servants crowded breathlessly about me, my courage failed, and I slipped behind, hoping they might be the first to make the discovery.

But they carried me with them, every step, and forced me to level my light full at the piteous object. I shrieked at the bare glimpse of it, and tried to beat my way back through the shrubbery. Failing in this, I stood quietly aside and looked at it, timidly at first, then boldly, then sorrowfully.

It was the white marble torso of Harmon's masterpiece— "Diana in Flight," valued at a hundred thousand—the "Diana" I had always worshiped and coveted, had tried for years to imitate in my humble attic workshop. It was crushed to atoms.

Robesart knelt for examination. And as I dropped beside him and placed my hand on a portion of the fair young head, so piteously mutilated, a sudden, sharp grief convulsed me, and I moaned and wept uncontrollably.

Who—oh, who could have done this damnable act?

But Robesart cut short my ravings. With kindly patience and stern practicability, he drew my attention to the exquisite hands twined with the roots and foliage of rare plants, the crumbled hair, and the enfolding studio-curtain of sea-green velvet glittering with flecks of rainbow porcelain.

Beyond all question, she had been thrown from a height—from the balcony—after first being stolen from the drawing-room!

Again I screamed, and lurched forward. Two of the servants lifted me to a standing position and stood on either side for support.

"How did this happen?" Robesart asked abruptly. "Tell us, Mr. Vaughan."

Thus suddenly addressed, I must have swooned. The shock had completely wrecked my nerves. My tongue was stiff; my head seemed to pound with a sledgehammer's precision.

"I do not know," I heard myself saying in an unfamiliar voice. "This is the first I have seen her since my brother Harmon left for New York at four o'clock."

"How, then, did you know of her destruction and the place?" Robesart continued.

His eyes were gleaming at me with an intensity that roused my fury. I felt in his glance and in the tone of his blunt questioning all the shafts and spear-points of accusation.

I glanced at him with stubborn defiance, but said nothing.

"When you opened the door to us, a halfhour ago, you stated that 'Diana was gone,' and you brought us here where she lies," the detective explained patiently. "Therefore, the natural question to ask you is, how did you learn of all this?"

"I surmised it!" I replied, cautioned by the brutal menace in his tone. "I didn't know positively!"

Robesart turned to Lunston, the butler. "When did you last see this statue in its accustomed place, Lunston?"

"Directly after tea, sir!" was the answer. "I was carrying the silver tray, sir, and I saw she had been moved to the conservatory."

"Was there any one else in the house beside the servants?"

"No one, sir!"

"Certainly no enemy, no suspicious stranger?"

Lunston denied such a possibility.

"But there was a strange man!" I shouted, enraged. "I know there was, for I saw him. I met him face to face— I talked with him. If these hirelings here had tended their duties and taken charge of the house instead of crying 'Thief!' and racing away four strong, they might have caught him easily."

"I assure you, Mr. Vaughan," Robesart declared earnestly, "if any human being besides yourself was inside the house when these men left it, he has not yet escaped. Every door, every window from roof to cellar was locked, and locked on the inside—excepting the front door which has been constantly guarded; every door, every window is still locked on the inside according to last investigation. The chef, Pierre, had the presence of mind to order all this done before giving the alarm—

"Perhaps you'd care to hear their version of the affair, Mr. Vaughan," he continued. "According to their joint testimony, the four servants were gathered in the kitchen at dusk previous to the serving of dinner. While there they were terrified by a series of crashes that came from the open conservatory where they had last seen you at work on a small clay model of the 'Diana.'

"Pierre and Lunston ventured immediately into the reception-hall. The front door stood wide open, and as they passed they heard a heavy thud outside as of a mass of stone falling from a height. Together they examined the conservatory. There was no sign of human presence, though they had every reason to believe you were hiding there."

"They lie!" I screamed, but the detective raised his hand imperatively and I held my breath.

"They found the conservatory much disturbed. Plants had been knocked down and trampled upon; jardinieres and flower-pots lay crushed among heaps of black earth. There had been a struggle, a fight to a finish, but the principals were missing. 'Diana' was gone from her pedestal; even the velvet draperies of her niche were gone. They searched every room and as they went along closed every door and window.

"Lunston hastened to the telephone and Dombey to the garage that he might run out the car and pick up the first policeman he met. The car, however, had gone wrong. It could not be started till a quarter-hour later when, with the greatest possible despatch, they brought me here. And," he added, rising, "here I stay till I find my man."

"He was in the house!" I exclaimed in shrill treble. "I saw him, studio-togs and all!" Robesart stared at my blanched face. "You're not well, Mr. Vaughan!" he said with sudden concern.

Immediately the terrific pains in my forehead returned. They were carrying her in from the terrace—reverently as though she were human dead, and I shrieked like a maniac and tore the air with clawlike fingers.

However, they grappled with me and poured a stimulant down my throat, and in time the agony passed. I recognized Robesart beside me.

"The man in the mirror!" I cried.

"Have you found him?"

He shook his head thoughtfully.

"No person, strange or otherwise, has been in the house, save ourselves," he replied. "The place has been thoroughly searched. However, I wish you to describe the fellow7 in detail. You say he wore studio-clothes?"

"Yes, yes." I replied in eager haste, and then I frankly met his gaze and told him all I remembered. During the recital Robesart stood motionless, staring at me till I was fully conscious of the great, silent question in his piercing gaze.

"But there was no mysterious vandal!" he blurted out. "There was no strange man in the whole affair from start to finish! He is merely a creature of your imagination."

"What?" I roared, leaping to my feet, snarling with anger. "Do you mean—"

"Candidly now, Mr. Vaughan, why did you steal and destroy the famous 'Diana'?" Robesart asked forcefully.

"Destroy the 'Diana'!" I howled. "How dare you—"

"Your forehead—the brand on your forehead!" he cried dramatically, "Your victim was marble, but she put the murderer's mark upon you that all men may see and beware!"

I clapped my hand to my head, bewildered, fearful. A wound! A great wound where the flesh had been broken! I could actually feel it. The pain of it was almost intolerable—how odd that I had not noticed it before. Small wonder that Robesart suspected me—

Again I lost consciousness and for a long time lay like one dead. At last Robesart roused me.

"Mr. Vaughan," he said with great solemnity, "while you were sleeping I phoned your brother and physician in New York. Dr. Rossmore has known your family for generations and your own personal history from the day of your birth, and I may add that neither are surprised at to-night's affair!"

"You mean," I raved, "that hey have been expecting this thing of me?"

"They have imagined such an outcome!"

"What would be my motive?"

"Jealousy." His lips were rigid. "You have failed in your chosen art—failed miserably. What more natural than you should be jealous of your brother Harmon's success, and resenting his most valuable work—"

"Just so!" I exclaimed, shifting easily into the thread of the argument. "Why shouldn't Harmon divide with me? He has fame and money and I'm a—a nobody!"

"That's exactly the motive!" was the quiet answer. "Are you ready to make your confession?"

"I have no confession!" I told him fiercely. "I deny the charge. I know you believe me insane—you believe my story of the real criminal in the mirror a fabrication. Of course the strange mark on my head is damning evidence, but—"

Robesart smiled whimsically. My teeth began chattering and my shoulders shook.

"Lunston," he called to one of the men, "Go to the coat-closet and bring Mr. Vaughan's wraps!"

I grasped his sleeve and he turned toward me expectantly.

"You must find that man in the mirror!" I chattered. "There is a man and you must be convinced of it! You must insist upon his being found!"

The detective nodded earnestly. As the servant stepped forward with my belongings, Robesart took the long, full, sculptor's apron in his hand. "This is yours, Mr. Vaughan?"

"It is mine!" I answered, ramming my arms in the sleeves.

"And this?" He held a brown rembrandt in his hand which I recognized at once by the shabby black velvet stretched around its band.

"Yes, mine!" I exclaimed.

I put on the cap and apron, not that I felt the need of them, but because I firmly believed I could convince him of my innocence and make him my friend for life—if only we might find the man—

Suddenly a subtle change swept over his stern face and manner.

"I have news for you, Vaughan," his great voice boomed. "Our investigation is now ended! We have found the criminal—the man of the mirror! Come inside! We need you for identification!" I tried to cry out my relief, my joy. But I couldn't.

"Come inside with us," Robesart whispered. "Show us the man in the mirror!"

I could only babble incoherent words of delight. But even before I reached the threshold the wound on my forehead seethed and agonies unspeakable crashed through my brain.

The columns of the veranda spun about me and I clung to both men for support. But through it all I was conscious only that my innocence and veracity were proved at last beyond all question, and that I was about to see my brother's enemy again face to face.

"Your story is a plausible one, after all!" Robesart was saying in a cool, monotonous tone as we stumbled into the vestibule.

The electrolier had been turned out, the reception-hall was shaded save for the twin clusters of light twinkling over the great gilt mirror at the far end. As Robesart walked beside me, his face showed a perceptible triumph, his eyes glittered suspiciously.

We traversed the hallway in silence, and then I paused directly in front of the mirror, and my heart ceased its beat.

I simply stared straight ahead, and there he stood—the vandal—the same haunted face, the same bulging eyes, heavy cap, black band, tawny hair, and apron with its stains of modeling clay, the brand in the center of the forehead.

"Yes, yes, it's he!" I screamed. "It's he! It's he!"

The torments of the inferno fairly riddled me. I threw out my arms and sprang forward to throttle him. Before the men could interfere, I had crashed into the mirror, reeled, and fallen with the unwieldy mass of it upon me.

And then—at last—I knew—it was I—I—

But I can say no more.

HIS DAY BACK, by Jack Brant

There was a knock at the door. At my request, it opened and in walked, or rather glided, my man, Mullbury. A strange thing about Mullbury is that he whenever he knocks, I realize instantly that I have something to say to him.

"Mullbury, pack my suitcase for a week of travel. I'm going West."

Mullbury immediately withdrew. He is a most remarkable man, and save for the one time when he asked for an increase in wages because of the court's decision that he should pay alimony, his sole object in knocking has been to take my expected command.

Why I should start for the West I could not understand. I knew no one in New Mexico. I had seen it on the map when a small boy—a square of pink, I think, though I am not sure now of the color—and learned that it was one of those lawless places called territories.

Beyond that, being what is known as a narrow man, which means that more vital interests absorb my attentions, I have never taken the slightest interest in New Mexico until startled by Mullbury's knock. Then, moved by some unexplainable impulse, I threw away my cigar, telephoned for accommodations to Las Cruces, and started on the midnight express.

During the three days' journey, I had ample time to reflect on the folly of this move. I realized perfectly that I should not have left my business at this time. That I had always intended, when able to take a vacation, to visit my brother in Cuba.

Cuba would do me good, and I would have the opportunity to gratify an abnormal craving to see a cockfight. Yet I found it absolutely impossible to turn back.

On the afternoon of the third day, I arrived in Las Cruces on a train I would not have caught but for the fortunate fact that it was twelve hours late. I took passage in what might have been the original overland stage, slightly modified, and was conveyed safely through the dust, to the taste of which I had become accustomed on the sleeper, to a one-story mud fort bearing the name "hotel" in red and black over its door.

I engaged a narrow but surprisingly cool room. Then I ventured forth on the one long business street, still compelled by the unaccountable impulse, and purchased a complete costume more in accord with my surroundings than the one suit which I had brought with me, and which was already attracting more attention than was pleasing to a man of my retiring nature.

I also purchased an elaborate prospecting outfit, provisions to last several days, and a sleeping-bag. This last was forced upon me by an attractive Mexican maiden with perfect teeth who thrust it laughingly into my arms, repeating what appeared to be the only English she knew, "You buy! You buy!" as if it all was a huge joke.

And it was a joke. That bag would have been all right for a trip to the north pole, but was slightly unnecessary for the burning sands of New Mexico.

As a final act of folly I engaged transportation with a mule-team which would start in the morning for Organ. Organ is a small mining settlement at the base of the Organ Mountains, which rise very much like the pipe-stems of an organ above the level desert in the east.

Rugged and steep the mountains look, like the edge of the world. I felt somewhere that they were my destination, and watched them—gorgeously lighted with purple and gold by the brilliant sunset— with interest.

There was a great deal of mystery and awe about them. They seemed a fitting haunt for wild, inhuman spirits, whose unholy groans could echo through the deep canyons; for lone, ghostly shapes, floating sadly from their heights at dusk to bring terror and disaster to the surrounding world. Standing there so tall, and plainly outlined in the clear, dry air. I could scarcely believe when told that they were ten miles away, so near they seemed.

I never believed in fairies. At least, not very much. You can't if you happen to live in a city with proof on all sides that no such things exist. But I couldn't help thinking, as I looked at those mountains, that if there were any anywhere you would find them among those red and pink and purple rocks.

* * * *

At daybreak the next morning, the hotel furnished me with a fine breakfast, and I was relieved to find that my madness had not affected my appetite. I had not slept very well—a reddish stain on the wall over my head, framed by about a hundred and fifty disconnected red legs, had reminded me of what a man on the train had told me regarding tarantulas and centipedes. But I don't think I saw any real ones.

I found my mule team and put my pack in and climbed up on the front seat with the driver. The first part of the drive was very pleasant until the sun discovered us and came a little nearer to see what a man of my make was doing with a prospector's outfit.

The desert, which had looked so flat in the distance, was a series of sandy hills partly covered with cactus and what I think was sage (I am not sure that I know what sage is, so it might have been sage), populated by lizards and horned toads and fat little prairie dogs and thousands upon thousands of long-eared rabbits. I understood what the man meant who said that when he got out on the desert, the ground got up and started to run away from him.

Every now and then we would come upon a bird about as big as a spring chicken, which looked like an over-grown and very unkempt sandpeep, employed in killing a snake or making a tasty breakfast off of centipedes and tarantulas. If I had to live in that country, I would tame one of those birds and keep it with me constantly.

I tried to learn something of the country from the driver, but without success. He was cheerful enough, but his vocabulary was not much more extensive than that of the girl who had sold me the sleeping-bag. He was evidently used to prospectors of my type, for he made no comment when I asked to be put off just before reaching Organ.

He waved to me as I entered a deep ravine, and I waved back. Then I passed out of sight among the rocks, and found myself absolutely alone in the wildest country I had ever seen.

Up and up I climbed, winding in and out through massive boulders and tangles of knotted and twisted trees. I had no idea where I was going, but the something that had brought me this far kept leading me on, and I followed passively.

Once in a patch of sand I saw tracks as big as my head, with claws; but I was not afraid. The reason that I did not feel worried I attribute to my belief in fate—since my marriage I have been content to take calmly whatever may be in store for me.

After scrambling over an impossible trail that branched from the main gorge —a thing no man would have done of his own free will—I found myself in a narrow defile between towering cliffs. I followed this until it ended in a circular platform shut in on all sides except the front by steep, unscalable walls of rocks.

I walked to the edge and peered over—and drew back hastily. There was a sheer drop of about five hundred feet, with ugly looking rocks at the bottom. The only means of access was the narrow defile through which I had entered. I could go no farther.

"Well, here I am!" I said aloud, perfectly unconsciously.

"It's about time," answered a gruff voice above me.

I sat down and mopped my brow. To be expected at this place and at this time was a good deal of a shock, even to such a believer in fate as myself.

"Don't be alarmed," said the voice, less gruff this time and with a tone of amusement in it. "It's a little uncanny at first, but you will get used to it. I did."

This gave me courage to look up in the direction from which the voice came. There, some fifty feet directly over my head, sitting calmly on the only projecting piece of rock on that whole smooth surface, his legs swinging idly over the edge, was a man!

For a few minutes we looked at each other in silence. He was about my size, dressed in a prospector's outfit similar to my own, and as new. His face was kindly, showing nothing but amused curiosity, and I began to feel more at ease. There was something even familiar about him, and I wondered where I had seen him before.

"How did you get up there?" I asked, my wonder prompting the question.

"It's easy when you are in my condition," he replied casually. "Are you Mr. Bent?"

"Benjamin Bent is my name," I answered "Who are you?"

"My name is Adams—Jonathan Adams. You have probably heard a great deal about me."

I gasped. Jonathan Adams was the name of my wife's second husband, the one before she married me.

"Not the Jonathan Adams who married Mrs. Hayes?" I stammered.

"The same," he answered. "You, I believe, had the pleasure of marrying her next."

"But," I remonstrated, beginning to feel dizzy, "you were supposed to have died five years ago!"

"That's right," said Mr. Adams. "I did die. I committed suicide by jumping off this very cliff, as Mr. Hayes did before me."

"See here," I said, trying to appear calm. "This is no time to joke. You don't expect me to believe that you are my wife's second husband's ghost!"

"That's just what I am," he answered with a grin. "Aren't you beginning to see through me."

I looked at him closely. To my astonishment, I could follow a crack in the rock behind him through his shoulders. I sat down and pressed my head between my hands, trying to think.

"There, there!" said the ghost. "Don't take it so hard. I know just how you feel. I felt the same way when I first saw Mr. Hayes. But, good Heavens, there is nothing to be afraid of. I wouldn't hurt you if I could. I know what you have been through already. I came down here to help you, the same as Mr. Hayes did for me."

He was so reassuring and polite and apologetic that most of my fear left me, and my curiosity got the better of what remained. I looked up again with interest.

"I never saw a ghost before," I said, trying to explain my fright. "I suppose you just floated up to that rock?"

"Sure," answered Mr. Adams. "I'll come down to show you."

With that he slipped off the ledge and slowly floated to my side. He put out his hand, but drew it away hastily when I reached out to shake it. I recognized him now from his likeness to the big picture in the gilt frame which my wife kept hung in the sitting-room beside the one of Mr. Hayes.

"I'm sorry," he said, referring with evident confusion to his action in withdrawing his hand. "but I can't get over some of those habits. Of course, you couldn't shake hands with me, for there is nothing there to shake."

I saw he was sensitive about it, so I merely laughed, though I was curious to try the effect.

"It's mighty good of you to take it so well," he continued. "I was in a blue funk for quite a time before Mr. Hayes could comfort me. A very nice man, that Mr. Hayes. Have you ever met him?"

I shook my head.

"Well, never mind; you will. He didn't come now because he thought two of us might be too much for you. But we are always together, and I am sure we three will be great friends. Bond of sympathy, you know."

He sat down beside me and asked me to fill my pipe. It all seemed so natural that I did this with as much unconcern as if he had been Jonathan Adams in the flesh. He apologized for not joining me in my smoke, saying that he had lost his taste for it.

"It's not a very long story," he began, after I was nicely puffing, "and my being here is all through Mr. Hayes. He was Amelia's first husband, you know. He stood it as long as he could, which was just five years. Then he came out here, discovered this place where we are now, and jumped over. It was taking awful chances, when you think that he didn't know anything of what was coming after. But he was a nervous, high-strung man, and had reached the point where he was willing to take chances. He says now that he would have done it two or three years earlier if he had known the relief and rest he was going to get. It was perfect bliss, all right, after his five years of married life. For a number of years he just sat back and enjoyed it.

"Then he got to thinking, in his generous way, that perhaps some poor fellow was suffering just as he had suffered. This thought kept bothering him so much, being of a tender nature, that he made inquiries and found out about me. After that, the knowledge of my troubles bothered him still more, till at last he couldn't stand it any longer and began to plan how he could help me out.

"Now, there is a rule where we are that every five years we can come back to Earth on the same day that we snuffed out. There aren't many of us that do it, because we are satisfied where we are and are content to let the worth go its way undisturbed. But Mr. Hayes was so worried over my troubles that five years ago this very day, which was his 'day back,' as we call it, he made arrangements to meet me here.

"We met. It was a meeting that I will never forget, and it took me a long time to get over it. But finally I became accustomed to him, and in an hour he had convinced me, and I jumped off. And I may say that I have never regretted it since.

"Then through some mutual friend we found out about you, and we agreed that it was only fair that you should have the benefit of our experiences. So I have come back to clear up any of the points you may be in doubt about.

"Of course, there are some drawbacks, and we don't get all the privileges of those who pass out naturally. But it's so much better than the life you have been leading that there is no comparison."

Here I stopped him with a gesture of my hand.

"Mr. Adams," I said brokenly, "I think I understand what you are driving at, and I am very grateful. But did you know that I buried my dear wife last Tuesday?"

"No!" he cried, "You don't mean to tell me that Amelia is dead?"

For a few moments he remained silent, his head bowed.

"Dear, dear!" he finally said. "I should read the papers more thoroughly. Allow me to condole with you."

Mechanically he extended his hand. I reached out to grasp it, but my fingers closed on the empty air. He was too much worked up to notice.

"I will take the news back to Mr. Hayes," he said quietly.

"I am very grateful to you both," I said after a few moments of respectful silence, "for your kind intentions and your interest in me. Please express to Mr. Hayes my deepest gratitude."

"Yes, yes," said Mr. Adams a little absently "I have enjoyed meeting you, and it is somewhat of a disappointment that you are not to join us. But, of course. I will not urge that now."

"Poor Amelia!" was all I could say.

"And now," said Mr. Adams, straightening up, "if you expect to get back before dark, I will not detain you longer."

He was right—time had gone faster than I had noticed. I turned toward the pass through which I had come. Then we both jumped with fright.

A deep growl came rolling up among the rocks!

Mr. Adams was the first to recover himself. "Grizzly!" he said, smiling. "Funny how strong habit is. Of course, he can't do a thing to me, yet for a moment I was as frightened as if I was alive."

"How about me?" I asked, still trembling.

Mr. Adams became serious at once.

"I think I can manage it," he said. "The bear smells you, but he can see me, and if you will step behind that rock, I may be able to decoy him off. He will think it is me he smells. So I will say good-bye, for I may have to leave hastily."

I dropped obediently behind the rock, but peered over the top to watch developments. If Mr. Adams failed I preferred jumping off the cliff to being eaten gradually by a hungry bear.

The shaggy head and shoulders of a huge grizzly appeared round the corner. I knew he was a grizzly from a rug which we once owned. Mr. Adams approached him fearlessly, and the bear opened his mouth to receive him. I shuddered with horror.

But when within only a few feet of the bear, Mr. Adams jumped lightly over his head and landed somewhere behind him. The effect on the grizzly was astonished disappointment. He turned quickly round and dashed after Mr. Adams, who was disappearing round the corner.

After a few minutes had elapsed, I rose from my hiding-place and followed them.

There was no sign of them in the narrow defile, and I did not see them again until I reached the main ravine. There I caught sight of them far up the mountain: Mr. Adams sailing serenely over the rough ground, the bear panting in hot pursuit a few feet behind.

Mr. Adams turned and waved me a polite farewell, which I returned. Then I walked quietly to Organ, chartered a mule-team, and three days later arrived back in Boston.

* * * *

The first thing I then did was to visit a famous brain and nerve specialist. If science had any explanation for my experience, I wanted to hear it before I began boasting about my acquaintance with real ghosts.

"My dear sir," said the specialist after I had told him everything, "your case, though interesting, is not at all unusual. It has nothing to do with mental telepathy or telegy which are the only so-called supernatural effects recognized by science. You are no doubt familiar with the phenomenon of walking in the sleep, the walker being awake to all appearances and with eyes wide open. You, sir, have the opposite malady of dreaming while you are actually awake. I prescribe complete rest and a change of climate."

"But, doctor," I expostulated, "if it was all a dream, why did the bear follow Mr. Adams out of the canyon?"

"Do not think," answered the wise doctor, "that because the bear ran out of the canyon that he was necessarily following anyone. Unless cornered or wounded, they are timid animals, and your sudden appearance in a prospector's outfit would ordinarily be enough to protect you. And then it is possible that this was also part of your dream and there wasn't any bear."

This was all I could get out of him.

Of course he is right, and there are no ghosts. But he'll never get me to believe it, just the same!

MY OWN TRUE GHOST STORY,
by Rudyard Kipling

As I came through the Desert thus it was—
As I came through the Desert.
The City of Dreadful Night.

Somewhere in the Other World, where there are books and pictures and plays and shop windows to look at, and thousands of men who spend their lives in building up all four, lives a gentleman who writes real stories about the real insides of people; and his name is Mr. Walter Besant. But he will insist upon treating his ghosts—he has published half a workshopful of them—with levity. He makes his ghost-seers talk familiarly, and, in some cases, flirt outrageously, with the phantoms. You may treat anything, from a Viceroy to a Vernacular Paper, with levity; but you must behave reverently toward a ghost, and particularly an Indian one.

There are, in this land, ghosts who take the form of fat, cold, pobby corpses, and hide in trees near the roadside till a traveler passes. Then they drop upon his neck and remain. There are also terrible ghosts of women who have died in child-bed. These wander along the pathways at dusk, or hide in the crops near a village, and call seductively. But to answer their call is death in this world and the next. Their feet are turned backward that all sober men may recognize them. There are ghosts of little children who have been thrown into wells. These haunt well curbs and the fringes of jungles, and wail under the stars, or catch women by the wrist and beg to be taken up and carried. These and the corpse ghosts, however, are only vernacular articles and do not attack Sahibs. No native ghost has yet been authentically reported to have frightened an Englishman; but many English ghosts have scared the life out of both white and black.

Nearly every other Station owns a ghost. There are said to be two at Simla, not counting the woman who blows the bellows at Syree dâk-bungalow on the Old Road; Mussoorie has a house haunted of a very lively Thing; a White Lady is supposed to do night-watchman round a house in Lahore; Dalhousie says that one of her houses "repeats" on autumn evenings all the incidents of a horrible horse-and-precipice accident; Murree has a merry ghost, and, now that she has been swept by cholera, will have room for a sorrowful one; there are Officers' Quarters in Mian Mir whose doors open without reason, and whose furniture is guaranteed to creak, not with the heat of June but with the weight of Invisibles who come to lounge in the chairs; Peshawur possesses houses that none will willingly rent; and there is something—not fever—wrong with a big bungalow in Allahabad. The older Provinces simply bristle with haunted houses, and march phantom armies along their main thoroughfares.

Some of the dâk-bungalows on the Grand Trunk Road have handy little cemeteries in their compound—witnesses to the "changes and chances of this mortal life" in the days when men drove from Calcutta to the Northwest. These bungalows are objectionable places to put up in. They are generally very old, always dirty, while the *khansamah* is as ancient as the bungalow. He either chatters senilely, or falls into the long trances of age. In both moods he is useless. If you get angry with him, he refers to some Sahib dead and buried these thirty years, and says that when he was in that Sahib's service not a *khansamah* in the Province could touch him. Then he jabbers and mows and trembles and fidgets among the dishes, and you repent of your irritation.

In these dâk-bungalows, ghosts are most likely to be found, and when found, they should be made a note of. Not long ago it was my business to live in dâk-bungalows. I never inhabited the same house for three nights running, and grew to be learned in the breed. I lived in Government-built ones with red brick walls and rail ceilings, an inventory of the furniture posted in every room, and an excited snake at the threshold to give welcome. I lived in "converted" ones—old houses officiating as dâk-bungalows—where nothing was in its proper place and there wasn't even a fowl for dinner. I lived in second-hand palaces where the wind blew through open-work marble tracery just as uncomfortably as through a broken pane. I lived in dâk-bungalows where the last entry in the visitors' book was fifteen months old, and where they slashed off the curry-kid's head with a sword. It was my good luck to meet all sorts of men, from sober traveling missionaries and deserters flying from British Regiments, to drunken loafers who threw whisky bottles at all who passed; and my still greater good fortune just to escape a maternity case. Seeing that a fair proportion of the tragedy of our lives out here acted itself in dâk-bungalows, I wondered that I had met no ghosts. A ghost that would voluntarily hang about a dâk-bungalow would be mad of course; but so many men have died mad in dâk-bungalows that there must be a fair percentage of lunatic ghosts.

In due time I found my ghost, or ghosts rather, for there were two of them. Up till that hour I had sympathized with Mr. Besant's method of handling them, as shown in "The Strange Case of Mr. Lucraft and Other Stories." I am now in the Opposition.

We will call the bungalow Katmal dâk-bungalow. But *that* was the smallest part of the horror. A man with a sensitive hide has no right to sleep in dâk-bungalows. He should marry. Katmal dâk-bungalow was old and rotten and unrepaired. The floor was of worn brick, the walls were filthy, and the windows were nearly black with grime. It stood on a bypath largely used by native Sub-Deputy Assistants of all kinds, from Finance to Forests; but real Sahibs were rare. The *khansamah*, who was nearly bent double with old age, said so.

When I arrived, there was a fitful, undecided rain on the face of the land, accompanied by a restless wind, and every gust made a noise like the rattling of dry bones in the stiff toddy palms outside. The *khansamah* completely lost his head on my arrival. He had served a Sahib once. Did I know that Sahib? He gave me the name of a well-known man who has been buried for more than a quarter of a century, and showed me an ancient daguerreotype of that man in his prehistoric youth. I had seen a steel engraving of him at the head of a double volume of Memoirs a month before, and I felt ancient beyond telling.

The day shut in and the *khansamah* went to get me food. He did not go through the, pretense of calling it "*khana*"—man's victuals. He said "*ratub*," and that means, among other things, "grub"—dog's rations. There was no insult in his choice of the term. He had forgotten the other word, I suppose.

While he was cutting up the dead bodies of animals, I settled myself down, after exploring the dâk-bungalow. There were three rooms, beside my own, which was a corner kennel, each giving into the other through dingy white doors fastened with long iron bars. The bungalow was a very solid one, but the partition walls of the rooms were almost jerry-built in their flimsiness. Every step or bang of a trunk echoed from my room down the other three, and every footfall came back tremulously from the far walls. For this reason I shut the door. There were no lamps—only candles in long glass shades. An oil wick was set in the bathroom.

For bleak, unadulterated misery that dâk-bungalow was the worst of the many that I had ever set foot in. There was no fireplace, and the windows would not open; so a brazier of charcoal would have been useless. The rain and the wind splashed and gurgled and moaned round the house, and the toddy palms rattled and roared. Half a dozen jackals went through the compound singing, and a hyena stood afar off and mocked them. A hyena would convince a Sadducee of the Resurrection of the Dead—the worst sort of Dead. Then came the *ratub*—a curious meal, half native and half English in composition—with the old *khansamah* babbling behind my chair about dead and gone English people, and the wind-blown candles playing shadow-bo-peep with the bed and the mosquito-curtains. It was just the sort of dinner and evening to make a man think of every single one of his past sins, and of all the others that he intended to commit if he lived.

Sleep, for several hundred reasons, was not easy. The lamp in the bathroom threw the most absurd shadows into the room, and the wind was beginning to talk nonsense.

Just when the reasons were drowsy with blood-sucking I heard the regular —"Let-us-take-and-heave-him-over" grunt of doolie-bearers in the compound. First one doolie came in, then a second, and then a third. I heard the doolies dumped on the ground, and the shutter in front of my door shook. "That's some one trying to come in," I said. But no one spoke, and I persuaded myself that it was the gusty wind. The shutter of the room next to mine was attacked, flung back, and the inner door opened. "That's some Sub-Deputy Assistant," I said, "and he has brought his friends with him. Now they'll talk and spit and smoke for an hour."

But there were no voices and no footsteps. No one was putting his luggage into the next room. The door shut, and I thanked Providence that I was to be left in peace. But I was curious to know where the doolies had gone. I got out of bed and looked into the darkness. There was never a sign of a doolie. Just as I was getting into bed again, I heard, in the next room, the sound that no man in his senses can possibly mistake—the whir of a billiard ball down the length of the slates when the striker is stringing for break. No other sound is like it. A minute afterwards there was another whir, and I got into bed. I was not frightened—indeed I was not. I was very curious to know what had become of the doolies. I jumped into bed for that reason.

Next minute I heard the double click of a cannon and my hair sat up. It is a mistake to say that hair stands up. The skin of the head tightens and you can feel a faint, prickly, bristling all over the scalp. That is the hair sitting up.

There was a whir and a click, and both sounds could only have been made by one thing—a billiard ball. I argued the matter out at great length with myself;

and the more I argued the less probable it seemed that one bed, one table, and two chairs—all the furniture of the room next to mine—could so exactly duplicate the sounds of a game of billiards. After another cannon, a three-cushion one to judge by the whir, I argued no more. I had found my ghost and would have given worlds to have escaped from that dâk-bungalow. I listened, and with each listen the game grew clearer. There was whir on whir and click on click. Sometimes there was a double click and a whir and another click. Beyond any sort of doubt, people were playing billiards in the next room. And the next room was not big enough to hold a billiard table!

Between the pauses of the wind I heard the game go forward—stroke after stroke. I tried to believe that I could not hear voices; but that attempt was a failure.

Do you know what fear is? Not ordinary fear of insult, injury or death, but abject, quivering dread of something that you cannot see—fear that dries the inside of the mouth and half of the throat—fear that makes you sweat on the palms of the hands, and gulp in order to keep the uvula at work? This is a fine Fear—a great cowardice, and must be felt to be appreciated. The very improbability of billiards in a dâk-bungalow proved the reality of the thing. No man—drunk or sober—could imagine a game at billiards, or invent the spitting crack of a "screw-cannon."

A severe course of dâk-bungalows has this disadvantage—it breeds infinite credulity. If a man said to a confirmed dâk-bungalow-haunter:—"There is a corpse in the next room, and there's a mad girl in the next but one, and the woman and man on that camel have just eloped from a place sixty miles away," the hearer would not disbelieve because he would know that nothing is too wild, grotesque, or horrible to happen in a dâk-bungalow.

This credulity, unfortunately, extends to ghosts. A rational person fresh from his own house would have turned on his side and slept. I did not. So surely as I was given up as a bad carcass by the scores of things in the bed because the bulk of my blood was in my heart, so surely did I hear every stroke of a long game at billiards played in the echoing room behind the iron-barred door. My dominant fear was that the players might want a marker. It was an absurd fear; because creatures who could play in the dark would be above such superfluities. I only know that that was my terror; and it was real.

After a long, long while the game stopped, and the door banged. I slept because I was dead tired. Otherwise I should have preferred to have kept awake. Not for everything in Asia would I have dropped the door-bar and peered into the dark of the next room.

When the morning came, I considered that I had done well and wisely, and inquired for the means of departure.

"By the way, *khansamah*," I said, "what were those three doolies doing in my compound in the night?"

"There were no doolies," said the *khansamah*.

I went into the next room and the daylight streamed through the open door. I was immensely brave. I would, at that hour, have played Black Pool with the owner of the big Black Pool down below.

"Has this place always been a dâk-bungalow?" I asked.

"No," said the *khansamah*. "Ten or twenty years ago, I have forgotten how long, it was a billiard room."

"A how much?"

"A billiard room for the Sahibs who built the Railway. I was *khansamah* then in the big house where all the Railway-Sahibs lived, and I used to come across with brandy-*shrab*. These three rooms were all one, and they held a big table on which the Sahibs played every evening. But the Sahibs are all dead now, and the Railway runs, you say, nearly to Kabul."

"Do you remember anything about the Sahibs?"

"It is long ago, but I remember that one Sahib, a fat man and always angry, was playing here one night, and he said to me:—'Mangal Khan, brandy-*pani do*,' and I filled the glass, and he bent over the table to strike, and his head fell lower and lower till it hit the table, and his spectacles came off, and when we—the Sahibs and I myself—ran to lift him he was dead. I helped to carry him out. Aha, he was a strong Sahib! But he is dead and I, old Mangal Khan, am still living, by your favor."

That was more than enough! I had my ghost—a first-hand, authenticated article. I would write to the Society for Psychical Research—I would paralyze the Empire with the news! But I would, first of all, put eighty miles of assessed crop land between myself and that dâk-bungalow before nightfall. The Society might send their regular agent to investigate later on.

I went into my own room and prepared to pack after noting down the facts of the case. As I smoked I heard the game begin again,—with a miss in balk this time, for the whir was a short one.

The door was open and I could see into the room. *Click—click!* That was a cannon. I entered the room without fear, for there was sunlight within and a fresh breeze without. The unseen game was going on at a tremendous rate. And well it might, when a restless little rat was running to and fro inside the dingy ceiling-cloth, and a piece of loose window-sash was making fifty breaks off the window-bolt as it shook in the breeze!

Impossible to mistake the sound of billiard balls! Impossible to mistake the whir of a ball over the slate! But I was to be excused. Even when I shut my enlightened eyes the sound was marvelously like that of a fast game.

Entered angrily the faithful partner of my sorrows, Kadir Baksh.

"This bungalow is very bad and low-caste! No wonder the Presence was disturbed and is speckled. Three sets of doolie-bearers came to the bungalow late last night when I was sleeping outside, and said that it was their custom to rest in the rooms set apart for the English people! What honor has the *khansamah*? They tried to enter, but I told them to go. No wonder, if these *Oorias* have been here, that the Presence is sorely spotted. It is shame, and the work of a dirty man!"

Kadir Baksh did not say that he had taken from each gang two annas for rent in advance, and then, beyond my earshot, had beaten them with the big green umbrella whose use I could never before divine. But Kadir Baksh has no notions of morality.

There was an interview with the *khansamah*, but as he promptly lost his head, wrath gave place to pity, and pity led to a long conversation, in the course of which he put the fat Engineer-Sahib's tragic death in three separate stations—two of them fifty miles away. The third shift was to Calcutta, and there the Sahib died while driving a dog-cart.

If I had encouraged him the *khansamah* would have wandered all through Bengal with his corpse.

I did not go away as soon as I intended. I stayed for the night, while the wind and the rat and the sash and the window-bolt played a ding-dong "hundred and fifty up." Then the wind ran out and the billiards stopped, and I felt that I had ruined my one genuine, hall-marked ghost story.

Had I only stopped at the proper time, I could have made *anything* out of it.

That was the bitterest thought of all!

THE LONG CHAMBER,
by Olivia Howard Dunbar

There was perhaps no warrant for the vaguely swelling disquiet that possessed me from the moment that, late in the sultry August after noon, there arrived the delayed telegram that announced the immediate coming of Beatrice Vesper.

...Beatrice Vesper abruptly on her way to me, and alone—it was the most strangely unlikely news. Yet I had no cause for real concern. She would find ready conveyance over the three steep miles from the railroad—our pleasantly decaying village being unlinked with the contemporary world. And, as the others reminded me, it wasn't as though the redundant spaciousness of Burleigh House didn't seem to invite, almost to select and compel, unaccustomed guests; or as though the Long Chamber, our supreme source of pride, hadn't that morning received the final touches that consecrated it to the utmost hospitality we could offer. As for Beatrice, she would delight in the survival of Burleigh House as unfailingly as she herself would prove its most harmonious ornament. And that matter of ornament wasn't one that David and I could be said to have taken at all lightly. How prodigally, how passionately, we had spent our love and labor on the precious house, in the months since it had so unexpectedly fallen into our hands—only to admit to each other, at the end of it all, in almost hysterical dismay, that the stately interiors seemed always empty, however vociferously we strove to be at home in them. There were void, waiting spaces that not the sum of all our alien, cheerful presences could fill. We had achieved a background, but a background for brilliant life; and it was as though we, living in terms of the palest prose, defiled past it almost invisibly. The truth was that we had established no spiritual tenancy, and that we didn't, ourselves, belong there. But though I was far from guessing with what mysterious tentacles the past would seize her, I knew that Beatrice Vesper would belong.

It was plain enough, however, from the first sight of my old friend, that she had come to me in no unhappy stress. Her secure and unvexed air was for an instant disconcerting; I had, in my panic, so prepared myself for haggard pathos. And indeed it was almost incredible that the hurrying, untender years should not have bruised so delicate a creature. With swiftly relaxing nerves I surrendered to the flattery of her explanation that when, only the day before, her husband had been summoned to Europe by cable—she herself being kept behind by the important final proof-reading of a technical work of Dr. Vesper's, to be published in the early autumn—she had from all her social resources chosen Burleigh House as her temporary refuge.... So that, after all, it seemed stupid to have taken fright. Beatrice and I had been the closest companions in earlier days. And doubtless I had exaggerated those conditions of her life which, for years past, had led her friends into the way of speaking of her ruefully, reminiscently, almost as if she were dead.

It was in this latter spirit that I had been speaking of her to David, only the day before, picturing her as the only woman I knew whose marriage had been complete self-immolation. Those of us who wore our fetters with a more modern jauntiness had resented, from our ill-informed distance, what seemed to be her slavish submission. She might as well have been chained in a cave—the rest of the world had not a glimpse of her. Dr. Vesper—a mild enough tyrant in appearance—did not care for society, so they had literally no visitors. There prevailed a legend that he was the most miserable of dyspeptics; and that Beatrice devoted most of her time to preparing the unheard-of substances that fed him. His financial concerns—for important mining interests had sprung from the geological work in which he had become famous—kept him in the city throughout the year, and Beatrice had never left him for a day, even in torrid midsummer.

But David, who is sturdily unmodern, refused to be astonished. "Why not, if she's in love with him?" he asked.

"But she's not," I insisted "or—she wasn't. It's her husband who's in love, and with the most unheard-of concentration. He has cared for her ever since she was a child, so the thing hung over her—though I suppose that's not a romantic way of putting it—for years before they were married. So isn't it rather extreme for her to relinquish everything else in the world for the sake of the man she merely—likes?"

David may have submitted a discreet version of this to our old friend Anthony Lloyd, who had been with us all that summer, and I imagine that in consequence both men looked to find in Beatrice Vesper the dull, heavy-domestic type. So when, an hour after her arrival, they saw her vivid smile and smooth black hair and her young, slim figure in its mulberry-colored taffeta against the dark panels of our candle-lighted dining-room, they both bore very definite evidence of response to her loveliness. Anthony even betrayed his admiration a shade too markedly, for he had rather an assured way of paying court to women who attracted him. But his advance was deftly and unmistakably cut off. Beatrice Vesper's wifely attitude remained true, I saw, to its severely classic pattern.

However, pitfalls of this order were easily avoided, teased as we all were by the irresistible topic of our dazzling inheritance. And David was shortly embarked upon his familiar contention that we cared much more for the place than if he had been the direct heir and we had been able to anticipate the glory of ownership.

"Oh, we're very humble," David conceded, "but we do claim credit as resuscitators. That's what we've really felt ourselves to be doing for months—breathing life into a beautiful thing that had been left for dead. And it has begun to live again, don't you think, in a feeble way? But it's as showmen that we're so shockingly deficient. You see a house that Judge Timothy Burleigh built in 1723 and that was continuously lived in until they deserted it a generation ago, must—well, must have its secrets. But we have to admit we don't know them!"

"Oh, do you think you can live here without knowing?" Beatrice broke out with an intensity that surprised us all. "You'll divine them, if you learn them in no other way. Family traditions can never be smothered, you know—they cling too imperishably!"

"But the legend famine has already been relieved," Anthony announced, "or we assume that it has. At least, we've found a group of old trunks, filled with papers, and they've all been assigned to me, to dig secrets from. I'm going to begin in the morning."

"It's not that Molly and I haven't longed to dig for ourselves," David hastily defended us, "but we haven't had time. And as for divination—our imaginations lack the necessary point of departure because our cousins have kept all the portraits. That's the really serious gap, you'll notice, in our conscientious furnishing —that apparently we've sprung from the soil, that we haven't an ancestor. Though of course we have seen the old pictures, long ago, or I have."

"Oh, what were they—" Beatrice began.

"Mrs. Vesper, need you ask?" Anthony interrupted. "Wigged men with heavy, hawk-nosed faces—"

"And meek-eyed women," David assented, laughing. "Yes, they do look like that, mostly. The Burleighs were a formidable race and their wives must have been unnaturally submissive.

"But that's according to the Colonial portrait-painter's conventions," Anthony argued. "The very earliest of your portraits must have been painted less than two hundred years ago. Well, that's time enough for fashions in portraits to change; but do human beings alter essentially? The old Burleighs cannot have been so different, inside their Colonial purple and fine linen, from you and Molly. Your hawk-nosed grandfathers must have enjoyed a joke, now and then, and those meek-eyed Patiences and Charities—mustn't they have had their emotions?"

"There must be conditions so harsh that emotions remain latent," I suggested, carelessly.

But Anthony never missed an occasion to dogmatize, after his own fashion: "I admit there are temperaments that cannot love, for instance. But to those that can the opportunity doesn't fail."

"But surely," he roused me to protest, "there is a type of woman who never learns her own capacity, who remains ingenuous, undeveloped—"

"Only until her appointed time," Anthony extravagantly persisted.

"What you are trying to express," David flouted, "is the old-fashioned schoolgirlish belief in predestined lovers. And perhaps it has remained for you to explain what happens in case the predestined lover dies?"

"In that case he'll come back from the dead to teach her!" But this point was made amid a shout of laughter, and we all conceded that the subject had been carried as far as it could be.

Almost immediately after dinner, Beatrice confessing that she was very tired, I rather self-consciously took a pewter candlestick from its stand in the lower hall and guided her upstairs. And I found myself weakly unable to bid her good night without a fond proprietary emphasis on the treasures of the Long Chamber, its ancient oaken chests and still more ancient powdering-table, its carved bed and woven counterpane, even the long mirror, faintly time-blurred, in which we had been told that Anne Burleigh, the first mistress of the house, used once to contemplate her charming face and towering head-dress.

"Then, of course, it contains her image still." Beatrice's smiling, confident glance seemed to penetrate with singular ease the delicate clouds with which two centuries had lightly flecked the glass. "I shall see it, of course, after she gets used to me. I wonder if this was her room?"

"That is one of the thousand things we don't know," I lamented. "But it may well have been. It is the finest, we think, of all the rooms. Judge Timothy's lovely young wife should have had it!"

"Don't you think it's almost heartless to have preserved her mere possessions," Beatrice admonished me, "and yet allow the memories of her life to be so scattered? We must gather them up and piece them together!"

"Reconstruction ought not to be too difficult in her case," I laughed. "I imagine she was a simple creature."

* * * *

It was our household custom to breakfast in our rooms, and after that to pursue our independent occupations throughout the greater part of the day. But Beatrice's proof-sheets and documents, which were of the most inordinate bulk, and which further depressingly renewed themselves by express every few days, often consumed her evenings likewise. It had struck me that we might achieve an arid semblance of friendly intercourse if she would assign to me some clerkly and mechanical part of her labors. But I saw from her look that it was as though I had asked a priestess to delegate to me her hieratic function. Her fealty to her dingy religion of ink and paper and chemical symbols was inflexible. And unreasoning, I thought, since it had cost her the look of freshness and vigor she had worn on coming to us. The thing was consuming her—her altered face told the story. Two weeks, indeed, after she had come, I realized that we had not yet had a comfortable talk together. What, after all, did I know of this new Beatrice, except that her highly decorative presence justified our otherwise empty splendor, and that for her own part she was working herself into an illness. She had come to us, she said, for rest and country peace and a season of friendship, but it was patent to the point of irony that she was profiting by none of these. And I did confess to myself, I remember, a secret hurt that there were so many days when she was unable, or ostensibly so, to join us at the hour of frank idleness when we took our tea under the oak-tree on the lawn, and when we always, sooner or later, fell to talking of our somewhat shadowy guest.

"Is it I whom Mrs. Vesper is avoiding?" Anthony asked, rather wistfully, one afternoon. "I'll admit I didn't seize her tone directly she arrived, but I have it now—completely! She would find me irreproachable if she would only mingle with us a little. How comforting it would be if she had a human liking for tennis and riding!"

"My dear Anthony, I don't think she knows you are under the same roof, except when she sees you at dinner," I assured him. "But she's under the thrall of an inhuman husband who is overworking her from the other end of the world and practically denying us any share in her."

"Are you so sure it's overwork," David demanded, "and not the beginning of typhoid? She does look downright ill, you know. My own impulse would be to send for a doctor. Could there be anything unwholesome about the house—any eighteenth-century germ that has escaped our scourings?"

We all brooded for a moment on the possibility this opened.

"Do you think distraction would help her?" Anthony asked. "Because I have it here!"—he tapped his breast-pocket, triumphantly. "I've patched together in the last few days a good part of the history of Burleigh House. I had meant not to tell you yet, but secrecy is consuming me."

"Dole the stories out to us one at a time," David lazily suggested, his interest half-paralyzed by the sheer weight of the August atmosphere. "We'll inaugurate a series of Nights—if not a Thousand and One, then as many as you please. And you'll begin to-night, of course. Can you go as far back as Judge Timothy?"

"Yes—if you would rather begin there. Though I hadn't planned—"

"Then it's settled," I interrupted. And this was indeed so precisely I what we had all been thirstily waiting for that I thought it a sufficient pretext for disturbing Beatrice on the spot. Moreover, David's hints had freshly stimulated my own smoldering anxiety in regard to my friend. I had been too passive—I should have forced her to spare herself. The unnamable fears that I had felt on the day of her arrival recurred and pierced me.

In the Long Chamber I found her rather wearily putting away her work for the day. She stood by her table, a slender, drooping figure with a sheaf of fluttering papers in her hand, and faced me—still without the look of affectionate welcome I had so missed of late; merely with a sweet patience and courtesy. I should perhaps have approached my end by gentle, gradual arts, but my concern for her abruptly overflowed in unconsidered words. I begged her to admit to me that she wasn't well, that I might insist on proper care for her. I blamed bitterly my own laxity in allowing her to wear herself out as she had done. The publication of her husband's book on a certain day could not, I urged, be a matter so imperative that she must sacrifice her youth, her life, to it. By every obligation of our old friendship I implored her to intrust herself to me—and I laid especial stress on my responsibility to her absent husband.

"You were all vigor and loveliness when you came to us," I reminded her. "And now—now—you are so changed!"

She looked at me in a half-startled fashion as I said this, and a dim, ambiguous smile trembled on her lips.

"Yes—he will find me changed." She spoke thoughtfully, but quite without emphasis. "But that is something I must face alone."

If she had said no more than this she would have left me with the impression that the distant Dr. Vesper was a subtler Bluebeard. And indeed a look of secrecy and dread that I now for the first time caught flowing darkly over her candid face was wretchedly that of the wife who has opened the forbidden door and is haunted by the intolerable knowledge that must shortly betray her. Could it, after all, be a worse than physical suffering that was draining her eyes of their look of life? She had begun to move uneasily about, and I felt that she would have been glad to have me leave her. But unable longer to endure the intervening shield, I made a desperate effort to demolish it, to force her reluctant confidence; and with hot cheeks and trembling voice I stammered crude, disconnected sentences on the frequent failure of men to understand women and situations…on the indulgence with which we were forced to regard many masculine traits…

"Oh, you have thought that?" she interrupted me, almost shrilly—"that my husband caused me suffering? Why, Molly, I supposed you knew, that everybody knew, how utterly, stainlessly good he is. It is I, oh, always I, who fall short." She took my hand gently. "You must not go until I have told you how it is." And we sat down together.

Much of what she then told me I did indeed already know, but under a different complexion from that with which she now invested it—how at nineteen she had married Edward Vesper almost frivolously, with no sense of sacredness, lightly assuming—though this was, of course, true enough—that she was bestowing a blessing by becoming the wife of the man for whom she felt a merely childlike affection. How, afterward, she had discovered that the marriage had been urged, hurried, by her poor, desperate mother, who, with four younger children, was at the end of everything; and how Dr. Vesper's money had supported them all ever since....

"Then I saw," Beatrice slowly went on, after a little, though I saw what the words were costing her, "how narrowly my own foolish ignorance had saved me from baseness. I had married for my own advantage a man who gave me perfect love. Facing this, I saw that from that moment I was bound to give more than I had ever dreamed of giving. And that, if I couldn't love my husband as he so wonderfully loved me, I must at least offer him the most sedulous counterfeit I could muster. That the least abatement of unremitting devotion would be treachery.... Well, that has been my life, and always, until now, I have known that no woman could do more—"

She would have gone on, the momentum of an impulsive confidence is so great, but at that point the maid came in search of me, announcing dinner. So, after a violent flurry of dressing, Beatrice and I contrived, ten minutes later, to be with the others in the dining-room. The disclosure she had made to me, with its intensely characteristic light on the apparent enigmas of her marriage, seemed for the time to have loosed a painful restraint. She talked with gentle gaiety, exchanging swift jests with the imperturbable Anthony, for whom I knew she had come to have a genuine liking, and seeming humanly at home with all of us, rather than driven, as one could fancy her latterly to have been, by some invisible harriers.

It even seemed natural and expected when, after dinner, Beatrice, who had so often spent her evenings alone, chose to seat herself at the old spinet and coax from it a few dim spectral chords.

"There's the prelude for your story, Anthony," David remarked when she had finished.

"It's a perfect one," Anthony declared. "Those are, of course, the very sounds with which Anne Burleigh beguiled her solemn days."

I had caught a note in his voice that awed me a little. "Anne Burleigh—you're to tell us of her! Then it won't, of course, be a cheerful story. Why is it that it has always been she, rather than any of the others, for whom our hearts have vaguely ached?"

"Cheerful? But of course not," Anthony rejoined with energy. "It can't be that you wanted me to discover simple tales of domestic lethargy. That isn't the sort of thing that leaves its impress on a family—and a house. That wouldn't be a story."

Then, as we urged him to begin, he altered his tone and turned to David a serious face. "You'll have to understand," he said, "that I'm taking a great liberty —with you and with your ancestors. This story that I've made out and that I'll repeat to you is, as a matter of fact, very largely—inferred. It's by no means an explicit tradition. But the inference seems to me so plain—and after living here in the house it is, oddly, so credible—and, well, you must forgive me, if, after all, you prefer to leave the inference unformulated."

None of us spoke; and I let my sewing drop in my lap.

"As you know," Anthony began, "Judge Timothy Burleigh married Anne Steele when she was seventeen. A year or two afterward, when they were living in this new and splendid Burleigh House, Sophia Steele, the young wife's sister,

came to pay a visit. In this young girl's diary, which tells so much else, and which I've had the astonishing fortune to discover, she records her impression of her sister, who looked 'very maidenly, though the wife of so great a man and the mistress of so fine a house.' But I won't read you her crabbed little sentences—you can see them for yourselves later; I'll simply try to make a connected story.
...

"Judge Timothy does not appear to have markedly played the lover to his charming little bride, but Sophia heard him praise her for her obedience, saying that it was the prime virtue in a wife. I had supposed that the housewives of that day had exacting responsibilities, but possibly because it was so fine a thing to be the Judge's wife, or else because her youth exempted her, little Mistress Burleigh seems to have had abundant leisure. She would play the spinet for hours at a time or she would sit with her baby boy—"

"The boy must have been Colonel Jonathan," David, who has always been rather too fond of facts, interposed. "Anne Burleigh had but one child."

"You see her, don't you, as I do," Anthony went on, "forlorn little Maeterlinckian heroine, treated as a child by her husband and practising rigidly the submission he exacted of her? It must have been a dull household, in spite of the splendid entertaining that took place at intervals, or sister Sophia wouldn't have had so much leisure to write in her diary. And it must have been an unnatural one, or—the climax wouldn't have flamed so suddenly. Something had to happen in such a house—and it did happen, as I make out, when a young relative of the Burleighs from Virginia came North to seek advancement in the law through his distinguished relative, the Judge. This young man, Brian Calvert, was asked to Burleigh House as a guest. It is very plain that he was keenly admired from the first by little sister Sophia, who meticulously describes his height and beauty and 'merry manners.' The Judge, I imagine, did not diffuse much merriment through the house. But the Virginian probably didn't see little Sophia; his attention was too completely and frankly absorbed. So she stayed apart, a sad, involuntary little spy, not critical or even fully comprehending, but vaguely and innocently envious, I gather, of an unknown mysterious thing with which the air about her had suddenly become surcharged. Anne Burleigh herself, poor child, was doubtless almost as far from understanding what had befallen her. At all events, there seems to have been no concealment. Anne and Calvert spent long days together, sitting under the trees in the garden. No one knows whether he said a word of love to her—I could almost believe that he did not. But the young, innocent creatures were none the less firmly in the grasp of the elemental force that was about to shatter them. It may have been love of the kind that absolutely cannot yield to reason, and that could never adapt itself to a slow cooling and decline—"

"Of course, they had to die," Beatrice Vesper broke in. "One cannot love like that—and live."

Her voice held somber secrets. It was as though she were speaking of something intimately real. I tried to see her face, but the shadow veiled it.

Anthony paused for a moment as though he, too, were amazed at her interruption. "Yes," he said, "there had to be a tragic issue.... The happenings of a certain day were told long after, but vaguely, in Sophia's journal. Perhaps the child herself only suspected.... One day Brian Calvert was ill and remained in his room. When evening came Anne suggested taking some supper to him. The

Judge reminded her, and rather ungently, that such an errand was for a servant to perform.... An hour later she burst into her sister's bedroom in a passion of fear. She had for the first time eluded and disobeyed her husband, taking to Calvert's room a porringer of gruel that she had made herself. The Judge, whom she doubtless supposed busy with his books, heard her step, followed her, and, entering the room a moment later, discovered her in Calvert's arms. I am sure they had never kissed before, but to her husband this was no extenuation. The Judge forced Anne from the room. Listening outside, she heard the sound of swords—and more—and worse.... Brian Calvert was never seen again. Anne Burleigh herself fell ill, and a few months later she died."

I felt that we had heard as much as we could bear, but David did not understand my signal, and advanced his literal and perfectly reasonable inquiry:

"Are you sure that Calvert was killed?"

"Entirely sure," Anthony said, a little dryly, "though there isn't a shadow of proof. Can you imagine such a husband hesitating or failing of his purpose?"

"You believe that they fought each other in this house?" David went on, in his solemn effort to realize the thing. "And there is no record of it? But where can it have been? You don't know that, of course?"

"Yes, I know," Anthony admitted, slowly. "It was in the guest-room. They called it the Long Chamber."

"The Long Chamber!" David repeated. And he turned toward Beatrice his honest, unperceiving eyes.

Beatrice had been sitting motionless. Now she rose hastily. "Why should you feel it tragic that he died?" she demanded, almost with brusqueness, but without looking at any one of us. "He would have chosen it. It was no unwilling death—that much I know." Her voice, usually so calm, was roughened with agitation. "I have stayed too long," she added. "I am very tired and should have gone earlier. But the story held us so.

She was gone before I had found words to detain her, and we all sat silent. Then Anthony said:

"I felt it before I had half finished the story. I know it now. She has seen Calvert's ghost!"

"That's preposterous!" David exclaimed.

"Because you haven't seen it yourself'?" our friend inquired, quietly. "But, my dear David, have you ever slept in that room? And in any case what would the ghost of that young lover have to say to you?"

"Or to Beatrice Vesper, for that matter?" I added.

Anthony shrugged his shoulders. "Who knows?" he said. "I admit that if it were the usual family specter, I can't conceive her risking a second encounter. But Calvert's apparition—that might perhaps be less formidable.... Still, it's all much queerer than I like—and I'm not even sure I want her to tell."

David began to be troubled. "Molly, you know her. We don't. Is she so infernally secretive? Could she see a ghost in our house without telling us? And why shouldn't she tell?"

I sat brooding, conscious that I was trembling a response to every lightest breath of air. There were secrets about; the troubled atmosphere was heavy with them. Something had happened to Beatrice, as any one but my dear dull David could have seen. But since we three were so blindly in the dark, how and whence could it have come? Anthony was, of course, uncommonly astute, yet I had no curiosity as to the guesses I saw him shrewdly elaborating. He did not know Beatrice's sound, unassailable simplicity as I knew it.

We were all, indeed, unnaturally alert, tensely awaiting we knew not what, so that when the door-bell rang we all started as though the sound had some portentous significance—holding our breath, fairly, until the maid came in with an envelope which she said was for Mrs. Vesper.

"It's a cable," I said. "I'll take it up to her."

A half-hour must have passed since she had gone upstairs, yet when I knocked she came to her door fully dressed. When she saw the envelope she asked me to stay until she had read the message—which was, she told me, a moment later, from her husband. He was sailing and would arrive in a week.

With a sense of relief that was almost disloyal I welcomed this definite, prosaic event. At least it would dissipate the vapors that had gathered. "Can't we send for him to come directly here?" I suggested. "Must you meet him in New York when it is so hot and you're not really well?"

She laid her hand gently on my arm, instinctively trying to soften the harsh abruptness of what she was about to say.

"Why shouldn't I tell you? I shall never see him again."

The words sounded so unreasoning that I felt myself growing literally cold. "But, dear Beatrice—it was such a little time ago—in this very room—that you told me—"

"Of his goodness and his love. And of the obligations they imposed on me. But now—if I can't fully meet them—if I'm not the same—"

Her phrases were still without meaning to me. I tried vaguely to protest. "But your courage—"

"Oh, I had courage—for a lifetime. But I was mercifully blindfolded. Now, when I know—"

Anthony's confident statement recurred to me, precipitating dim suspicions, intimations, of my own.

"Beatrice, what is it that you have learned to know?" I demanded, firmly. "What is it that you have—seen?"

She cast a quick glance toward the old mirror, dull-rimmed, garlanded, in which she had gaily told me that she expected to see Anne Burleigh's child—like face. "Seen?" she repeated. "Oh, dear Molly, it's not alone what I have seen.... But there is something that lives on here, in this room, of which I merely knew the name.... I have felt it almost from the first moment. And there have been hours when I have so shared in it—when I have lived with an intensity I had never dreamed of—"

"Beatrice,"—I pressed her for something more definite—"you have seen Anne Burleigh?"

"Oh, it's not she who has left the deathless element," Beatrice said. "It's the man who loved her, who loved so well that he did not need to live. You see his love was so complete that it gained an earthly immortality of its own. It is here—now. I did not know such things could be. And, oh, Molly, I have tried not to know! You have seen how I have struggled to fill up my time and thought with work. I have not welcomed this other new thing, I have shrunk from it. But it has seized me and stripped my eyes and dazzled them—and I know what love can be."

"Brian Calvert has taught you!" I could not help the words. And, in spite of me, they sounded like an accusation.

"If it were only a lesson I could unlearn," she answered, quietly. "If I could only forget the sweet terror of it all."

"The terror of dreams and visions? But, dear Beatrice, that fades and vanishes."

"It is already vanished. But not before it has changed me past all helping. You can see how, after this, I can never—pretend to love."

I did not try to press her further, for I hoped that the next day, when Anthony's story would be less vivid to us all, I could prevail on the desperation of her attitude. I did insist, however, that she should not spend the night alone, and she consented, after a little, that I should sleep with her. Or so, at least, we termed it. But my patient vigil told me plainly enough that poor Beatrice slept no more than I. It is true that I assumed—though how could I be sure?—that I had dispelled her disturbing phantasms. I did not, though I lay there expectant at her side, feel the clutch at my own heart of Brian Calvert's strangely inextinguishable love; and though in the first few pale moments of dawn I saw Beatrice's strained eyes bent steadily on Anne Burleigh's garlanded mirror, to me its unrevealing surface presented merely a reticent blur.

It did not surprise me when, an hour later, Beatrice told me that she must leave Burleigh House that morning. And indeed it seemed that to let her go—out of the reach of the ghostliness that had so preyed upon her sensitive spirit—was, at that critical moment, the best that I could do for her. Yet, strangely, even after all that she had told me, I did not guess into what utter darkness she was going. Immune as I then believed myself to spectral invasions of my own serenity, I did not know at that time, nor until long after, how the reverberations of spent lives may sometimes sound so loud as to muffle the merely human cry. All that Beatrice Vesper saw and felt as she sat in the Long Chamber and battled ineffectually with the insistent presence, or presences, that may have abided within the distances of the dim, garlanded mirror, is still, I know, beyond my vain conjecture. And there are certain bare and almost intolerable facts that seem indeed to close the door on such imaginings.... For Edward Vesper never saw his wife again, and a month after Beatrice's going word came to me that she was dead. We have closed the Long Chamber for all time.

THE PAST, by Ellen Glasgow

I had no sooner entered the house than I knew something was wrong. Though I had never been in so splendid a place before—it was one of those big houses just off Fifth Avenue—I had a suspicion from the first that the magnificence covered a secret disturbance. I was always quick to receive impressions, and when the black iron doors swung together behind me, I felt as if I were shut inside a prison.

When I gave my name and explained that I was the new secretary, I was delivered into the charge of an elderly lady's-maid, who looked as if she had been crying. Without speaking a word, though she nodded kindly enough, she led me down the hall, and then up a flight of stairs at the back of the house to a pleasant bedroom in the third storey. There was a great deal of sunshine, and the walls, which were painted a soft yellow, made the room very cheerful. It would be a comfortable place to sit in when I was not working, I thought, while the sad-faced maid stood watching me remove my wraps and hat.

"If you are not tired, Mrs. Vanderbridge would like to dictate a few letters," she said presently, and they were the first words she had spoken.

"I am not a bit tired. Will you take me to her?" One of the reasons, I knew, which had decided Mrs. Vanderbridge to engage me was the remarkable similarity of our handwriting. We were both Southerners, and though she was now famous on two continents for her beauty, I couldn't forget that she had got her early education at the little academy for young ladies in Fredericksburg. This was a bond of sympathy in my thoughts at least, and, heaven knows, I needed to remember it while I followed the maid down the narrow stairs and along the wide hall to the front of the house.

In looking back after a year, I can recall every detail of that first meeting. Though it was barely four o'clock, the electric lamps were turned on in the hall, and I can still see the mellow light that shone over the staircase and lay in pools on the old pink rugs, which were so soft and fine that I felt as if I were walking on flowers. I remember the sound of music from a room somewhere on the first floor, and the scent of lilies and hyacinths that drifted from the conservatory. I remember it all, every note of music, every whiff of fragrance; but most vividly I remember Mrs. Vanderbridge as she looked round, when the door opened, from the wood fire into which she had been gazing. Her eyes caught me first. They were so wonderful that for a moment I couldn't see anything else; then I took in slowly the dark red of her hair, the clear pallor of her skin, and the long, flowing lines of her figure in a tea-gown of blue silk. There was a white bearskin rug under her feet, and while she stood there before the wood fire, she looked as if she had absorbed the beauty and colour of the house as a crystal vase absorbs the light. Only when she spoke to me, and I went nearer, did I detect the heaviness beneath her eyes and the nervous quiver of her mouth, which drooped a little at the corners. Tired and worn as she was, I never saw her afterwards—not even when she was dressed for the opera—look quite so lovely, so much like an exquisite flower, as she did on that first afternoon. When I knew her better, I discovered that she was a changeable beauty; there were days when all the colour seemed to go out of her, and she looked dull and haggard; but at her best no one I've ever seen could compare with her.

She asked me a few questions, and though she was pleasant and kind, I knew that she scarcely listened to my responses. While I sat down at the desk and dipped my pen into the ink, she flung herself on the couch before the fire with a movement which struck me as hopeless. I saw her feet tap the white fur rug, while she plucked nervously at the lace on the end of one of the gold-coloured sofa pillows. For an instant the thought flashed through my mind that she had been taking something—drug of some sort—and that she was suffering now from the effects of it. Then she looked at me steadily, almost as if she were reading my thoughts, and I knew that I was wrong. Her large radiant eyes were as innocent as a child's.

She dictated a few notes—all declining invitations—and then, while I still waited pen in hand, she sat up on the couch with one of her quick movements, and said in a low voice, "I am not dining out tonight, Miss Wrenn. I am not well enough."

"I am sorry for that." It was all I could think of to say, for I did not understand why she should have told me.

"If you don't mind, I should like you to come down to dinner. There will be only Mr. Vanderbridge and myself."

"Of course I will come if you wish it." I couldn't very well refuse to do what she asked me, yet I told myself, while I answered, that if I had known she expected me to make one of the family, I should never, not even at twice the salary, have taken the place. It didn't take me a minute to go over my slender wardrobe in my mind and realize that I had nothing to wear that would look well enough.

"I can see you don't like it," she added after a moment, almost wistfully, "but it won't be often. It is only when we are dining alone."

This, I thought, was even queerer than the request—or command—for I knew from her tone, just as plainly as if she had told me in words, that she did not wish to dine alone with her husband.

"I am ready to help you in any way—in any way that I can," I replied, and I was so deeply moved by her appeal that my voice broke in spite of my effort to control it. After my lonely life I dare say I should have loved any one who really needed me, and from the first moment that I read the appeal in Mrs. Vanderbridge's face I felt that I was willing to work my fingers to the bone for her. Nothing that she asked of me was too much when she asked it in that voice, with that look.

"I am glad you are nice," she said, and for the first time she smiled—a charming, girlish smile with a hint of archness. "We shall get on beautifully, I know, because I can talk to you. My last secretary was English, and I frightened her almost to death whenever I tried to talk to her." Then her tone grew serious. "You won't mind dining with us. Roger—Mr. Vanderbridge—is the most charming man in the world."

"Is that his picture?"

"Yes, the one in the Florentine frame. The other is my brother. Do you think we are alike?"

"Since you've told me, I notice a likeness." Already I had picked up the Florentine frame from the desk, and was eagerly searching the features of Mr. Vanderbridge. It was an arresting face, dark, thoughtful, strangely appealing, and picturesque—though this may have been due, of course, to the photographer. The more I looked at it, the more there grew upon me an uncanny feeling of familiarity; but not until the next day, while I was still trying to account for the impression that I had seen the picture before, did there flash into my mind the memory of an old portrait of a Florentine nobleman in a loan collection last winter. I can't remember the name of the painter—I am not sure that it was known—but this photograph might have been taken from the painting. There was the same imaginative sadness in both faces, the same haunting beauty of feature, and one surmised that there must be the same rich darkness of colouring. The only striking difference was that the man in the photograph looked much older than the original of the portrait, and I remembered that the lady who had engaged me was the second wife of Mr. Vanderbridge and some ten or fifteen years younger, I had heard, than her husband.

"Have you ever seen a more wonderful face?" asked Mrs. Vanderbridge. "Doesn't he look as if he might have been painted by Titian?"

"Is he really so handsome as that?"

"He is a little older and sadder, that is all. When we were married it was exactly like him." For an instant she hesitated and then broke out almost bitterly, "Isn't that a face any woman might fall in love with, a face any woman—living or dead—would not be willing to give up?"

Poor child, I could see that she was overwrought and needed someone to talk to, but it seemed queer to me that she should speak so frankly to a stranger. I wondered why any one so rich and so beautiful should ever be unhappy—for I had been schooled by poverty to believe that money is the first essential of happiness—and yet her unhappiness was as evident as her beauty, or the luxury that enveloped her. At that instant I felt that I hated Mr. Vanderbridge, for whatever the secret tragedy of their marriage might be, I instinctively knew that the fault was not on the side of the wife. She was as sweet and winning as if she were still the reigning beauty in the academy for young ladies. I knew with a knowledge deeper than any conviction that she was not to blame, and if she wasn't to blame, then who under heaven could be at fault except her husband?

In a few minutes a friend came in to tea, and I went upstairs to my room, and unpacked the blue taffeta dress I had bought for my sister's wedding. I was still doubtfully regarding it when there was a knock at my door, and the maid with the sad face came in to bring me a pot of tea. After she had placed the tray on the table, she stood nervously twisting a napkin in her hands while she waited for me to leave my unpacking and sit down in the easy chair she had drawn up under the lamp.

"How do you think Mrs. Vanderbridge is looking?" she asked abruptly in a voice that held a breathless note of suspense. Her nervousness and the queer look in her face made me stare at her sharply. This was a house, I was beginning to feel, where everybody, from the mistress down, wanted to question me. Even the silent maid had found voice for interrogation.

"I think her the loveliest person I've ever seen," I answered after a moment's hesitation. There couldn't be any harm in telling her how much I admired her mistress.

"Yes, she is lovely—everyone thinks so—and her nature is as sweet as her face." She was becoming loquacious. "I have never had a lady who was so sweet and kind. She hasn't always been rich, and that may be the reason she never seems to grow hard and selfish, the reason she spends so much of her life thinking of other people. It's been six years now, ever since her marriage, that I've lived with her, and in all that time I've never had a cross word from her."

"One can see that. With everything she has she ought to be as happy as the day is long."

"She ought to be." Her voice dropped, and I saw her glance suspiciously at the door, which she had closed when she entered. "She ought to be, but she isn't. I have never seen any one so unhappy as she has been of late—ever since last summer. I suppose I oughtn't to talk about it, but I've kept it to myself so long that I feel as if it was killing me. If she was my own sister, I couldn't be any fonder of her, and yet I have to see her suffer day after day, and not say a word—not even to her. She isn't the sort of lady you could speak to about a thing like that."

She broke down, and dropping on the rug at my feet, hid her face in her hands. It was plain that she was suffering acutely, and while I patted her shoulder, I thought what a wonderful mistress Mrs. Vanderbridge must be to have attached a servant to her so strongly.

"You must remember that I am a stranger in the house, that I scarcely know her, that I've never so much as laid eyes on her husband," I said warningly, for I've always avoided, as far as possible, the confidences of servants.

"But you look as if you could be trusted." The maid's nerves, as well as the mistress's, were on edge, I could see. "And she needs somebody who can help her. She needs a real friend—somebody who will stand by her no matter what happens." Again, as in the room downstairs, there flashed through my mind the suspicion that I had got into a place where people took drugs or drink—or were all out of their minds. I had heard of such houses.

"How can I help her? She won't confide in me, and even if she did, what could I do for her?"

"You can stand by and watch. You can come between her and harm—if you see it." She had risen from the floor and stood wiping her reddened eyes on the napkin. "I don't know what it is, but I know it is there. I feel it even when I can't see it."

Yes, they were all out of their minds; there couldn't be any other explanation. The whole episode was incredible. It was the kind of thing, I kept telling myself, that did not happen. Even in a book nobody could believe it.

"But her husband? He is the one who must protect her."

She gave me a blighting look. "He would if he could. He isn't to blame—you mustn't think that. He is one of the best men in the world, but he can't help her. He can't help her because he doesn't know. He doesn't see it."

A bell rang somewhere, and catching up the tea-tray, she paused just long enough to throw me a pleading word, "Stand between her and harm, if you see it."

When she had gone I locked the door after her, and turned on all the lights in the room. Was there really a tragic mystery in the house, or were they all mad, as I had first imagined? The feeling of apprehension, of vague uneasiness, which had come to me when I entered the iron doors, swept over me in a wave while I sat there in the soft glow of the shaded electric light. Something was wrong. Somebody was making that lovely woman unhappy, and who, in the name of reason, could this somebody be except her husband? Yet the maid had spoken of him as "one of the best men in the world," and it was impossible to doubt the tearful sincerity of her voice. Well, the riddle was too much for me. I gave it up at last with a sigh—dreading the hour that would call me downstairs to meet Mr. Vanderbridge. I felt in every nerve and fibre of my body that I should hate him the moment I looked at him.

But at eight o'clock, when I went reluctantly downstairs, I had a surprise. Nothing could have been kinder than the way Mr. Vanderbridge greeted me, and I could tell as soon as I met his eyes that there wasn't anything vicious or violent in his nature. He reminded me more than ever of the portrait in the loan collection, and though he was so much older than the Florentine nobleman, he had the same thoughtful look. Of course I am not an artist, but I have always tried, in my way, to be a reader of personality; and it didn't take a particularly keen observer to discern the character and intellect in Mr. Vanderbridge's face. Even now I remember it as the noblest face I have ever seen; and unless I had possessed at least a shade of penetration, I doubt if I should have detected the melancholy. For it was only when he was thinking deeply that this sadness seemed to spread like a veil over his features. At other times he was cheerful and even gay in his manner; and his rich dark eyes would light up now and then with irrepressible humour. From the way he looked at his wife I could tell that there was no lack of love or tenderness on his side any more than there was on hers. It was obvious that he was still as much in love with her as he had been before his marriage, and my immediate perception of this only deepened the mystery that enveloped them. If the fault wasn't his and wasn't hers, then who was responsible for the shadow that hung over the house?

For the shadow was there. I could feel it, vague and dark, while we talked about the war and the remote possibilities of peace in the spring. Mrs. Vanderbridge looked young and lovely in her gown of white satin with pearls on her bosom, but her violet eyes were almost black in the candlelight, and I had a curious feeling that this blackness was the colour of thought. Something troubled her to despair, yet I was as positive as I could be of anything I had ever been told that she had breathed no word of this anxiety or distress to her husband. Devoted as they were, a nameless dread, fear, or apprehension divided them. It was the thing I had felt from the moment I entered the house; the thing I had heard in the tearful voice of the maid. One could scarcely call it horror, because it was too vague, too impalpable, for so vivid a name; yet, after all these quiet months, horror is the only word I can think of that in any way expresses the emotion which pervaded the house.

I had never seen so beautiful a dinner table, and I was gazing with pleasure at the damask and glass and silver—there was a silver basket of chrysanthemums, I remember, in the centre of the table—when I noticed a nervous movement of Mrs. Vanderbridge's head, and saw her glance hastily towards the door and the staircase beyond. We had been talking animatedly, and as Mrs. Vanderbridge turned away, I had just made a remark to her husband, who appeared to have fallen into a sudden fit of abstraction, and was gazing thoughtfully over his soup-plate at the white and yellow chrysanthemums. It occurred to me, while I watched him, that he was probably absorbed in some financial problem, and I regretted that I had been so careless as to speak to him. To my surprise, however, he replied immediately in a natural tone, and I saw, or imagined that I saw, Mrs. Vanderbridge throw me a glance of gratitude and relief. I can't remember what we were talking about, but I recall perfectly that the conversation kept up pleasantly, without a break, until dinner was almost half over. The roast had been served, and I was in the act of helping myself to potatoes, when I became aware that Mr. Vanderbridge had again fallen into his reverie. This time he scarcely seemed to hear his wife's voice when she spoke to him, and I watched the sadness cloud his face while he continued to stare straight ahead of him with a look that was almost yearning in its intensity.

Again I saw Mrs. Vanderbridge, with her nervous gesture, glance in the direction of the hall, and to my amazement, as she did so, a woman's figure glided noiselessly over the old Persian rug at the door, and entered the dining-room. I was wondering why no one spoke to her, why she spoke to no one, when I saw her sink into a chair on the other side of Mr. Vanderbridge and unfold her napkin. She was quite young, younger even than Mrs. Vanderbridge, and though she was not really beautiful, she was the most graceful creature I had ever imagined. Her dress was of grey stuff, softer and more clinging than silk, and of a peculiar misty texture and colour, and her parted hair lay like twilight on either side of her forehead. She was not like any one I had ever seen before—she appeared so much frailer, so much more elusive, as if she would vanish if you touched her. I can't describe, even months afterwards, the singular way in which she attracted and repelled me.

At first I glanced inquiringly at Mrs. Vanderbridge, hoping that she would introduce me, but she went on talking rapidly in an intense, quivering voice, without noticing the presence of her guest by so much as the lifting of her eyelashes. Mr. Vanderbridge still sat there, silent and detached, and all the time the eyes of the stranger—starry eyes with a mist over them—looked straight through me at the tapestried wall at my back. I knew she didn't see me and that it wouldn't have made the slightest difference to her if she had seen me. In spite of her grace and her girlishness I did not like her, and I felt that this aversion was not on my side alone. I do not know how I received the impression that she hated Mrs. Vanderbridge—never once had she glanced in her direction—yet I was aware, from the moment of her entrance, that she was bristling with animosity, though animosity is too strong a word for the resentful spite, like the jealous rage of a spoiled child, which gleamed now and then in her eyes. I couldn't think of her as wicked any more than I could think of a bad child as wicked. She was merely wilful and undisciplined and—I hardly know how to convey what I mean—selfish.

After her entrance the dinner dragged on heavily. Mrs. Vanderbridge still kept up her nervous chatter, but nobody listened, for I was too embarrassed to pay any attention to what she said, and Mr. Vanderbridge had never recovered from his abstraction. He was like a man in a dream, not observing a thing that happened before him, while the strange woman sat there in the candlelight with her curious look of vagueness and unreality. To my astonishment not even the servants appeared to notice her, and though she had unfolded her napkin when she sat down, she wasn't served with either the roast or the salad. Once or twice, particularly when a new course was served, I glanced at Mrs. Vanderbridge to see if she would rectify the mistake, but she kept her gaze fixed on her plate. It was just as if there were a conspiracy to ignore the presence of the stranger, though she had been, from the moment of her entrance, the dominant figure at the table. You tried to pretend she wasn't there, and yet you knew—you knew vividly that she was gazing insolently straight through you.

The dinner lasted, it seemed, for hours, and you may imagine my relief when at last Mrs. Vanderbridge rose and led the way back into the drawing-room. At first I thought the stranger would follow us, but when I glanced round from the hall she was still sitting there beside Mr. Vanderbridge, who was smoking a cigar with his coffee.

"Usually he takes his coffee with me," said Mrs. Vanderbridge, "but tonight he has things to think over."

"I thought he seemed absent-minded."

"You noticed it, then?" She turned to me with her straightforward glance, "I always wonder how much strangers notice. He hadn't been well of late, and he has these spells of depression. Nerves are dreadful things, aren't they?"

I laughed. "So I've heard, but I've never been able to afford them."

"Well, they do cost a great deal, don't they?" She had a trick of ending her sentences with a question, "I hope your room is comfortable, and that you don't feel timid about being alone on that floor. If you haven't nerves, you can't get nervous, can you?"

"No, I can't get nervous." Yet while I spoke, I was conscious of a shiver deep down in me, as if my senses reacted again to the dread that permeated the atmosphere.

As soon as I could, I escaped to my room, and I was sitting there over a book, when the maid—her name was Hopkins, I had discovered—came in on the pretext of inquiring if I had everything I needed. One of the innumerable servants had already turned down my bed, so when Hopkins appeared at the door, I suspected at once that there was a hidden motive underlying her ostensible purpose.

"Mrs. Vanderbridge told me to look after you," she began. "She is afraid you will be lonely until you learn the way of things."

"No, I'm not lonely," I answered. "I've never had time to be lonely."

"I used to be like that; but time hangs heavy on my hands now. That's why I've taken to knitting." She held out a grey yarn muffler. "I had an operation a year ago, and since then Mrs. Vanderbridge has had another maid—a French one —to sit up for her at night and undress her. She is always so fearful of overtaxing us, though there isn't really enough work for two lady's maids, because she is so thoughtful that she never gives any trouble if she can help it."

"It must be nice to be rich," I said idly, as I turned a page of my book. Then I added almost before I realized what I was saying, "The other lady doesn't look as if she had so much money."

Her face turned paler if that were possible, and for a minute I thought she was going to faint. "The other lady?"

"I mean the one who came down late to dinner—the one in the grey dress. She wore no jewels, and her dress wasn't low in the neck."

"Then you saw her?" There was a curious flicker in her face as if her pallor came and went.

"We were at the table when she came in. Has Mr. Vanderbridge a secretary who lives in the house?"

"No, he hasn't a secretary except at his office. When he wants one at the house, he telephones to his office."

"I wondered why she came, for she didn't eat any dinner, and nobody spoke to her—not even Mr. Vanderbridge."

"Oh, he never speaks to her. Thank God, it hasn't come to that yet."

"Then why does she come? It must be dreadful to be treated like that, and before the servants, too. Does she come often?"

"There are months and months when she doesn't. I can always tell by the way Mrs. Vanderbridge picks up. You wouldn't know her, she is so full of life—the very picture of happiness. Then one evening she—the Other One, I mean—comes back again, just as she did tonight, just as she did last summer, and it all begins over from the beginning."

"But can't they keep her out—the Other One? Why do they let her in?"

"Mrs. Vanderbridge tries hard. She tries all she can every minute. You saw her tonight?"

"And Mr. Vanderbridge? Can't he help her?"

She shook her head with an ominous gesture. "He doesn't know."

"He doesn't know she is there? Why, she was close by him. She never took her eyes off him except when she was staring through me at the wall."

"Oh, he knows she is there, but not in that way. He doesn't know that any one else knows."

I gave it up, and after a minute she said in an oppressed voice, "It seems strange that you should have seen her. I never have."

"But you know all about her."

"I know and I don't know. Mrs. Vanderbridge lets things drop sometimes—she gets ill and feverish very easily—but she never tells me anything outright. She isn't that sort."

"Haven't the servants told you about her—the Other One?"

At this, I thought, she seemed startled. "Oh, they don't know anything to tell. They feel that something is wrong; that is why they never stay longer than a week or two—we've had eight butlers since autumn—but they never see what it is."

She stooped to pick up the ball of yarn which had rolled under my chair. "If the time ever comes when you can stand between them, you will do it?" she asked.

"Between Mrs. Vanderbridge and the Other One?"

Her look answered me.

"You think, then, that she means harm to her?"

"I don't know. Nobody knows—but she is killing her."

The clock struck ten, and I returned to my book with a yawn, while Hopkins gathered up her work and went out, after wishing me a formal goodnight. The odd part about our secret conferences was that as soon as they were over, we began to pretend so elaborately to each other that they had never been.

"I'll tell Mrs. Vanderbridge that you are very comfortable," was the last remark Hopkins made before she sidled out of the door and left me alone with the mystery. It was one of those situations—I am obliged to repeat this over and over —that was too preposterous for me to believe in even while I was surrounded and overwhelmed by its reality. I didn't dare face what I thought, I didn't dare face even what I felt; but I went to bed shivering in a warm room, while I resolved passionately that if the chance ever came to me I would stand between Mrs. Vanderbridge and this unknown evil that threatened her.

* * * *

In the morning Mrs. Vanderbridge went out shopping, and I did not see her until the evening, when she passed me on the staircase as she was going out to dinner and the opera. She was radiant in blue velvet, with diamonds in her hair and at her throat, and I wondered again how any one so lovely could ever be troubled.

"I hope you had a pleasant day, Miss Wrenn," she said kindly. "I have been too busy to get off any letters, but tomorrow we shall begin early." Then, as if from an afterthought, she looked back and added, "There are some new novels in my sitting-room. You might care to look over them."

When she had gone, I went upstairs to the sitting-room and turned over the books, but I couldn't, to save my life, force an interest in printed romances, after meeting Mrs. Vanderbridge and remembering the mystery that surrounded her. I wondered if "the Other One," as Hopkins called her, lived in the house, and I was still wondering this when the maid came in and began putting the table to rights.

"Do they dine out often?" I asked.

"They used to, but since Mr. Vanderbridge hasn't been so well, Mrs. Vanderbridge doesn't like to go without him. She only went tonight because he begged her to."

She had barely finished speaking when the door opened, and Mr. Vanderbridge came in and sat down in one of the big velvet chairs before the wood fire. He had not noticed us, for one of his moods was upon him, and I was about to slip out as noiselessly as I could when I saw that the Other One was standing in the patch of firelight on the hearthrug. I had not seen her come in, and Hopkins evidently was still unaware of her presence, for while I was watching, I saw the maid turn towards her with a fresh log for the fire. At the moment it occurred to me that Hopkins must be either blind or drunk, for without hesitating in her advance, she moved on the stranger, holding the huge hickory log out in front of her. Then, before I could utter a sound or stretch out a hand to stop her, I saw her walk straight through the grey figure and carefully place the log on the andirons.

So she isn't real, after all, she is merely a phantom, I found myself thinking, as I fled from the room, and hurried along the hall to the staircase. She is only a ghost, and nobody believes in ghosts any longer. She is something that I know doesn't exist, yet even, though she can't possibly be, I can swear that I have seen her. My nerves were so shaken by the discovery that as soon as I reached my room I sank in a heap on the rug, and it was here that Hopkins found me a little later when she came to bring me an extra blanket.

"You looked so upset I thought you might have seen something," she said. "Did anything happen while you were in the room?"

"She was there all the time—every blessed minute. You walked right through her when you put the log on the fire. Is it possible that you didn't see her?"

"No, I didn't see anything out of the way." She was plainly frightened. "Where was she standing?"

"On the hearthrug in front of Mr. Vanderbridge. To reach the fire you had to walk straight through her, for she didn't move. She didn't give way an inch."

115

"Oh, she never gives way. She never gives way living or dead."

This was more than human nature could stand.

"In heavens name," I cried irritably, "who is she?"

"Don't you know?" She appeared genuinely surprised. "Why, she is the other Mrs. Vanderbridge. She died fifteen years ago, just a year after they were married, and people say a scandal was hushed up about her, which he never knew. She isn't a good sort, that's what I think of her, though they say he almost worshipped her."

"And she still has this hold on him?"

"He can't shake it off, that's what's the matter with him, and if it goes on, he will end his days in an asylum. You see, she was very young, scarcely more than a girl, and he got the idea in his head that it was marrying him that killed her. If you want to know what I think, I believe she put it there for a purpose."

"You mean—?" I was so completely at sea that I couldn't frame a rational question. "I mean she haunts him purposely in order to drive him out of his mind. She was always that sort, jealous and exacting, the kind that clutches and strangles a man, and I've often thought, though I've no head for speculation, that we carry into the next world the traits and feelings that have got the better of us in this one. It seems to me only common sense to believe that we're obliged to work them off somewhere until we are free of them. That is the way my first lady used to talk, anyhow, and I've never found anybody that could give me a more sensible idea."

"And isn't there any way to stop it? What has Mrs. Vanderbridge done?"

"Oh, she can't do anything now. It has got beyond her, though she has had doctor after doctor, and tried everything she could think of. But, you see, she is handicapped because she can't mention it to her husband. He doesn't know that she knows."

"And she won't tell him?"

"She is the sort that would die first—just the opposite from the Other One—for she leaves him free, she never clutches and strangles. It isn't her way." For a moment she hesitated, and then added grimly—"I've wondered if you could do anything?"

"If I could? Why, I am a perfect stranger to them all."

"That's why I've been thinking it. Now, if you could corner her some day—the Other One—and tell her up and down to her face what you think of her."

The idea was so ludicrous that it made me laugh in spite of my shaken nerves. "They would fancy me out of my wits! Imagine stopping an apparition and telling it what you think of it!"

"Then you might try talking it over with Mrs. Vanderbridge. It would help her to know that you see her also."

But the next morning, when I went down to Mrs. Vanderbridge's room, I found that she was too ill to see me. At noon a trained nurse came on the case, and for a week we took our meals together in the morning-room upstairs. She appeared competent enough, but I am sure that she didn't so much as suspect that there was anything wrong in the house except the influenza which had attacked Mrs. Vanderbridge the night of the opera. Never once during that week did I catch a glimpse of the Other One, though I felt her presence whenever I left my room and passed through the hall below. I knew all the time as well as if I had seen her that she was hidden there, watching, watching—

At the end of the week Mrs. Vanderbridge sent for me to write some letters, and when I went into her room, I found her lying on the couch with a tea-table in front of her. She asked me to make the tea because she was still so weak, and I saw that she looked flushed and feverish, and that her eyes were unnaturally large and bright. I hoped she wouldn't talk to me, because people in that state are apt to talk too much and then to blame the listener; but I had hardly taken my seat at the tea-table before she said in a hoarse voice—the cold had settled on her chest:

"Miss Wrenn, I have wanted to ask you ever since the other evening—did you—did you see anything unusual at dinner? From your face when you came out I thought—I thought—"

I met this squarely. "That I might have? Yes, I did see something."

"You saw her?"

"I saw a woman come in and sit down at the table, and I wondered why no one served her. I saw her quite distinctly."

"A small woman, thin and pale, in a grey dress?"

"She was so vague and—and misty, you know what I mean, that it is hard to describe her; but I should know her again anywhere. She wore her hair parted and drawn down over her ears. It was very dark and fine—as fine as spun silk."

We were speaking in low voices, and unconsciously we had moved closer together while my idle hands left the tea things.

"Then you know," she said earnestly, "that she really comes—that I am not out of my mind—that it is not an hallucination?"

"I know that I saw her. I would swear to it. But doesn't Mr. Vanderbridge see her also?"

"Not as we see her. He thinks that she is in his mind only." Then, after an uncomfortable silence, she added suddenly, "She is really a thought, you know. She is his thought of her—but he doesn't know that she is visible to the rest of us."

"And he brings her back by thinking of her?"

She leaned nearer while a quiver passed over her features and the flush deepened in her cheeks. "That is the only way she comes back—the only way she has the power to come back—as a thought. There are months and months when she leaves us in peace because he is thinking of other things, but of late, since his illness, she has been with him almost constantly." A sob broke from her, and she buried her face in her hands. "I suppose she is always trying to come—only she is too vague—and hasn't any form that we can see except when he thinks of her as she used to look when she was alive. His thought of her is like that, hurt and tragic and revengeful. You see, he feels that he ruined her life because she died when the child was coming—a month before it would have been born."

"And if he were to see her differently, would she change? Would she cease to be revengeful if he stopped thinking her so?"

"God only knows. I've wondered and wondered how I might move her to pity."

"Then you feel that she is really there? That she exists outside of his mind?"

"How can I tell? What do any of us know of the world beyond? She exists as much as I exist to you or you to me. Isn't thought all that there is—all that we know?"

This was deeper than I could follow; but in order not to appear stupid, I murmured sympathetically,

"And does she make him unhappy when she comes?"

"She is killing him—and me. I believe that is why she does it."

"Are you sure that she could stay away? When he thinks of her isn't she obliged to come back?"

"Oh, I've asked that question over and over! In spite of his calling her so unconsciously, I believe she comes of her own will, I have always the feeling—it has never left me for an instant—that she could appear differently if she would. I have studied her for years until I know her like a book, and though she is only an apparition, I am perfectly positive that she wills evil to us both. Don't you think he would change that if he could? Don't you think he would make her kind instead of vindictive if he had the power?"

"But if he could remember her as loving and tender?"

"I don't know. I give it up—but it is killing me."

It was killing her. As the days passed I began to realize that she had spoken the truth. I watched her bloom fade slowly and her lovely features grow pinched and thin like the features of a starved person. The harder she fought the apparition, the more I saw that the battle was a losing one, and that she was only wasting her strength. So impalpable yet so pervasive was the enemy that it was like fighting a poisonous odour. There was nothing to wrestle with, and yet there was everything. The struggle was wearing her out—was, as she had said, actually "killing her"; but the physician who dosed her daily with drugs—there was need now of a physician—had not the faintest idea of the malady he was treating. In those dreadful days I think that even Mr. Vanderbridge hadn't a suspicion of the truth. The past was with him so constantly—he was so steeped in the memories of it—that the present was scarcely more than a dream to him. It was, you see, a reverse of the natural order of things; the thought had become more vivid to his perceptions than any object. The phantom had been victorious so far, and he was like a man recovering from the effects of a narcotic. He was only half awake, only half alive to the events through which he lived and the people who surrounded him. Oh, I realize that 1 am telling my story badly!—that I am slurring over the significant interludes! My mind has dealt so long with external details that I have almost forgotten the words that express invisible things. Though the phantom in the house was more real to me than the bread I ate or the floor on which I trod, I can give you no impression of the atmosphere in which we lived day after day—of the suspense, of the dread of something we could not define, of the brooding horror that seemed to lurk in the shadows of the firelight, of the feeling always, day and night, that some unseen person was watching us. How Mrs. Vanderbridge stood it without losing her reason I have never known; and even now I am not sure that she could have kept her reason if the end had not come when it did. That I accidentally brought it about is one of the things in my life I am most thankful to remember.

It was an afternoon in late winter, and I had just come up from luncheon, when Mrs. Vanderbridge asked me to empty an old desk in one of the upstairs rooms "I am sending all the furniture in that room away," she said; "it was bought in a bad period, and I want to clear it out and make room for the lovely things we picked up in Italy. There is nothing in the desk worth saving except some old letters from Mr. Vanderbridge's mother before her marriage."

I was glad that she could think of anything so practical as furniture, and it was with relief that I followed her into the dim, rather musty room over the library, where the windows were all tightly closed. Years ago, Hopkins had once told me, the first Mrs. Vanderbridge had used this room for a while, and after her death her husband had been in the habit of shutting himself up alone here in the evenings. This, I inferred, was the secret reason why my employer was sending the furniture away. She had resolved to clear the house of every association with the past.

For a few minutes we sorted the letters in the drawers of the desk, and then, as I expected, Mrs. Vanderbridge became suddenly bored by the task she had undertaken. She was subject to these nervous reactions, and I was prepared for them even when they seized her so spasmodically. I remember that she was in the very act of glancing over an old letter when she rose impatiently, tossed it into the fire unread, and picked up a magazine she had thrown down on a chair.

"Go over them by yourself, Miss Wrenn," she said, and it was characteristic of her nature that she should assume my trustworthiness. "If anything seems worth saving you can file it—but I'd rather die than have to wade through all this."

They were mostly personal letters, and while I went on, carefully filing them, I thought how absurd it was of people to preserve so many papers that were entirely without value. Mr. Vanderbridge I had imagined to be a methodical man, and yet the disorder of the desk produced a painful effect on my systematic temperament. The drawers were filled with letters evidently unsorted, for now and then I came upon a mass of business receipts and acknowledgements crammed in among wedding invitations or letters from some elderly lady, who wrote interminable pale epistles in the finest and most feminine of Italian hands. That a man of Mr. Vanderbridge's wealth and position should have been so careless about his correspondence amazed me until I recalled the dark hints Hopkins had dropped in some of her midnight conversations. Was it possible that he had actually lost his reason for months after the death of his first wife, during that year when he had shut himself alone with her memory? The question was still in my mind when my eyes fell an the envelope in my hand, and I saw that it was addressed to Mrs. Roger Vanderbridge. So this explained, in a measure at least, the carelessness and the disorder! The desk was not his, but hers, and after her death he had used it only during those desperate months when he barely opened a letter. What he had done in those long evenings when he sat alone here it was beyond me to imagine. Was it any wonder that the brooding should have permanently unbalanced his mind?

At the end of an hour I had sorted and filed the papers, with the intention of asking Mrs. Vanderbridge if she wished me to destroy the ones that seemed to be unimportant. The letters she had instructed me to keep had not come to my hand, and I was about to give up the search for them, when, in shaking the lock of one of the drawers, the door of a secret compartment fell open, and I discovered a dark object, which crumbled and dropped apart when I touched it. Bending nearer, I saw that the crumbled mass had once been a bunch of flowers, and that a streamer of purple ribbon still held together the frail structure of wire and stems. In this drawer someone had hidden a sacred treasure, and moved by a sense of romance and adventure, I gathered the dust tenderly in tissue paper, and prepare to take it downstairs to Mrs. Vanderbridge. It was not until then that some letters tied loosely together with a silver cord caught my eye, and while I picked them up, I remember thinking that they must be the ones for which I had been looking so long. Then, as the cord broke in my grasp and I gathered the letters from the lid of the desk, a word or two flashed back at me through the torn edges of the envelopes, and I realized that they were love letters written, I surmised, some fifteen years ago, by Mr. Vanderbridge to his first wife.

"It may hurt her to see them," I thought, "but I don't dare destroy them. There is nothing I can do except give them to her."

As I left the room, carrying the letters and the ashes of the flowers, the idea of taking them to the husband instead of to the wife flashed through my mind. Then —I think it was some jealous feeling about the phantom that decided me—I quickened my steps to a run down the staircase.

"They would bring her back. He would think of her more than ever," I told myself, "so he shall never see them. He shall never see them if I can prevent it." I believe it occurred to me that Mrs. Vanderbridge would be generous enough to give them to him—she was capable of rising above her jealousy, I knew—but I determined that she shouldn't do it until I had reasoned it out with her. "If anything on earth would bring back the Other One for good; it would be his seeing these old letters," I repeated as I hastened down the hall.

Mrs. Vanderbridge was lying on the couch before the fire, and I noticed at once that she had been crying. The drawn look in her sweet face went to my heart, and I felt that I would do anything in the world to comfort her. Though she had a book in her hand, I could see that she had not been reading. The electric lamp on the table by her side was already lighted, leaving the rest of the room in shadow, for it was a grey day with a biting edge of snow in the air. It was all very charming in the soft light; but as soon as I entered I had a feeling of oppression that made me want to run out into the wind. If you have ever lived in a haunted house—a house pervaded by an unforgettable past—you will understand the sensation of melancholy that crept over me the minute the shadows began to fall. It was not in myself—of this I am sure, for I have naturally a cheerful temperament —it was in the space that surrounded us and the air we breathed.

I explained to her about the letters, and then, kneeling on the rug in front of her, I emptied the dust of the flowers into the fire. There was though I hate to confess it, a vindictive pleasure in watching it melt into the flames; and at the moment I believe I could have burned the apparition as thankfully. The more I saw of the Other One, the more I found myself accepting Hopkins's judgment of her. Yes, her behavior, living and dead, proved that she was not "a good sort."

My eyes were still on the flames when a sound from Mrs. Vanderbridge—half a sigh, half a sob—made me turn quickly and look up at her.

"But this isn't his handwriting," she said in a puzzled tone. "They are love letters, and they are to her—but they are not from him." For a moment or two she was silent, and I heard the pages rustle in her hands as she turned them impatiently. "They are not from him," she repeated presently, with an exultant ring in her voice. "They are written after her marriage, but they are from another man." She was as sternly tragic as an avenging fate. "She wasn't faithful to him while she lived. She wasn't faithful to him even while he was hers—"

With a spring I had risen from my knees and was bending over her.

"Then you can save him from her. You can win him back! You have only to show him the letters, and he will believe."

"Yes, I have only to show him the letters." She was looking beyond me into the dusky shadows of the firelight, as if she saw the Other One standing there before her, "I have only to show him the letters," I knew now that she was not speaking to me, "and he will believe."

"Her power over him will be broken," I cried out. "He will think of her differently. Oh, don't you see? Can't you see? It is the only way to make him think of her differently. It is the only way to break for ever the thought that draws her back to him."

"Yes, I see, it is the only way," she said slowly; and the words were still on her lips when the door opened and Mr. Vanderbridge entered.

"I came for a cup of tea," he began, and added with playful tenderness, "What is the only way?"

It was the crucial moment, I realized—it was the hour of destiny for these two —and while he sank wearily into a chair, I looked imploringly at his wife and then at the letters lying scattered loosely about her. If I had had my will I should have flung them at him with a violence which would have startled him out of his lethargy. Violence, I felt, was what he needed—violence, a storm, tears, reproaches—all the things he would never get from his wife.

For a minute or two she sat there, with the letters before her, and watched him with her thoughtful and tender gaze. I knew from her face, so lovely and yet so sad, that she was looking again at invisible things—at the soul of the man she loved, not at the body. She saw him, detached and spiritualized, and she saw also the Other One—for while we waited I became slowly aware of the apparition in the firelight—of the white face and the cloudy hair and the look of animosity and bitterness in the eyes. Never before had I been so profoundly convinced of the malignant will veiled by that thin figure. It was as if the visible form were only a spiral of grey smoke covering a sinister purpose.

"The only way," said Mrs. Vanderbridge, "is to fight fairly even when one fights evil." Her voice was like a bell, and as she spoke, she rose from the couch and stood there in her glowing beauty confronting the pale ghost of the past. There was a light about her that was almost unearthly—the light of triumph. The radiance of it blinded me for an instant. It was like a flame, clearing the atmosphere of all that was evil, of all that was poisonous and deadly. She was looking directly at the phantom, and there was no hate in her voice—there was only a great pity, a great sorrow and sweetness.

"I can't fight you that way," she said, and I knew that for the first time she had swept aside subterfuge and evasion, and was speaking straight to the presence before her. "After all, you are dead and I am living, and I cannot fight you that way. I give up everything. I give him back to you. Nothing is mine that I cannot win and keep fairly. Nothing is mine that belongs really to you."

Then, while Mr. Vanderbridge rose, with a start of fear, and came towards her, she bent quickly, and flung the letters into the fire. When he would have stooped to gather the unburned pages, her lovely flowing body curved between his hands and the flames; and so transparent, so ethereal she looked, that I saw—or imagined that I saw—the firelight shine through her. "The only way, my dear, is the right way," she said softly.

The next instant—I don't know to this day how or when it began—I was aware that the apparition had drawn nearer, and that the dread and fear, the evil purpose, were no longer a part of her. I saw her clearly for a moment—saw her as I had never seen her before—young and gentle and—yes, this is the only word for it—loving. It was just as if a curse had turned into a blessing, for, while she stood there, I had a curious sensation of being enfolded in a kind of spiritual glow and comfort—only words are useless to describe the feeling because it wasn't in the least like anything else I had ever known in my life. It was light without heat, glow without light—and yet it was none of these things. The nearest I can come to it is to call it a sense of blessedness—of blessedness that made you at peace with everything you had once hated.

Not until afterwards did I realize that it was the victory of good over evil. Not until afterwards did I discover that Mrs. Vanderbridge had triumphed over the past in the only way that she could triumph. She had won, not by resisting, but by accepting; not by violence, but by gentleness; not by grasping, but by renouncing. Oh, long, long afterwards, I knew that she had robbed the phantom of power over her by robbing it of hatred. She had changed the thought of the past, in that lay her victory.

At the moment I did not understand this. I did not understand it even when I looked again for the apparition in the firelight, and saw that it had vanished. There was nothing there—nothing except the pleasant flicker of light and shadow on the old Persian rug.

MISS TEMPY'S WATCHERS,
by Sarah Orne Jewett

The time of year was April; the place was a small farming town in New Hampshire, remote from any railroad. One by one the lights had been blown out in the scattered houses near Miss Tempy Dent's; but as her neighbors took a last look out-of-doors, their eyes turned with instinctive curiosity toward the old house, where a lamp burned steadily. They gave a little sigh. "Poor Miss Tempy!" said more than one bereft acquaintance; for the good woman lay dead in her north chamber, and the light was a watcher's light. The funeral was set for the next day, at one o'clock.

The watchers were two of the oldest friends, Mrs. Crowe and Sarah Ann Binson. They were sitting in the kitchen, because it seemed less awesome than the unused best room, and they beguiled the long hours by steady conversation. One would think that neither topics nor opinions would hold out, at that rate, all through the long spring night; but there was a certain degree of excitement just then, and the two women had risen to an unusual level of expressiveness and confidence. Each had already told the other more than one fact that she had determined to keep secret; they were again and again tempted into statements that either would have found impossible by daylight. Mrs. Crowe was knitting a blue yarn stocking for her husband; the foot was already so long that it seemed as if she must have forgotten to narrow it at the proper time. Mrs. Crowe knew exactly what she was about, however; she was of a much cooler disposition than Sister Binson, who made futile attempts at some sewing, only to drop her work into her lap whenever the talk was most engaging.

Their faces were interesting—of the dry, shrewd, quick-witted New England type, with thin hair twisted neatly back out of the way. Mrs. Crowe could look vague and benignant, and Miss Binson was, to quote her neighbors, a little too sharp-set: but the world knew that she had need to be, with the load she must carry of supporting an inefficient widowed sister and six unpromising and unwilling nieces and nephews.

The eldest boy was at last placed with a good man to learn the mason's trade. Sarah Ann Binson, for all her sharp, anxious aspect, never defended herself, when her sister whined and fretted. She was told every week of her life that the poor children never would have had to lift a finger if their father had lived, and yet she had kept her steadfast way with the little farm, and patiently taught the young people many useful things, for which, as everybody said, they would live to thank her. However pleasureless her life appeared to outward view, it was brimful of pleasure to herself.

Mrs. Crowe, on the contrary, was well to do, her husband being a rich farmer and an easy-going man. She was a stingy woman, but for all that she looked kindly; and when she gave away anything, or lifted a finger to help anybody, it was thought a great piece of beneficence, and a compliment, indeed, which the recipient accepted with twice as much gratitude as double the gift that came from a poorer and more generous acquaintance. Everybody liked to be on good terms with Mrs. Crowe. Socially she stood much higher than Sarah Ann Binson. They were both old schoolmates and friends of Temperance Dent, who had asked them, one day, not long before she died, if they would not come together and look after the house, and manage everything, when she was gone. She may have had some hope that they might become closer friends in this period of intimate partnership, and that the richer woman might better understand the burdens of the poorer. They had not kept the house the night before; they were too weary with the care of their old friend, whom they had not left until all was over.

There was a brook which ran down the hillside very near the house, and the sound of it was much louder than usual. When there was silence in the kitchen, the busy stream had a strange insistence in its wild voice, as if it tried to make the watchers understand something that related to the past.

"I declare, I can't begin to sorrow for Tempy yet. I am so glad to have her at rest," whispered Mrs. Crowe. "It is strange to set here without her, but I can't make it clear that she has gone. I feel as if she had got easy and dropped off to sleep, and I'm more scared about waking her up than knowing any other feeling."

"Yes," said Sarah Ann, "it's just like that, ain't it? But I tell you we are goin' to miss her worse than we expect. She's helped me through with many a trial, has Temperance. I ain't the only one who says the same, neither."

These words were spoken as if there were a third person listening; somebody beside Mrs. Crowe. The watchers could not rid their minds of the feeling that they were being watched themselves. The spring wind whistled in the window crack, now and then, and buffeted the little house in a gusty way that had a sort of companionable effect. Yet, on the whole, it was a very still night, and the watchers spoke in a half-whisper.

"She was the freest-handed woman that ever I knew," said Mrs. Crowe, decidedly. "According to her means, she gave away more than anybody. I used to tell her 'twa'n't right. I used really to be afraid that she went without too much, for we have a duty to ourselves."

Sister Binson looked up in a half-amused, unconscious way, and then recollected herself.

Mrs. Crowe met her look with a serious face. "It ain't so easy for me to give as it is for some," she said simply, but with an effort which was made possible only by the occasion. "I should like to say, while Tempy is laying here yet in her own house, that she has been a constant lesson to me. Folks are too kind, and shame me with thanks for what I do. I ain't such a generous woman as poor Tempy was, for all she had nothin' to do with, as one may say."

Sarah Binson was much moved at this confession, and was even pained and touched by the unexpected humility. "You have a good many calls on you," she began, and then left her kind little compliment half finished.

"Yes, yes, but I've got means enough. My disposition's more of a cross to me as I grow older, and I made up my mind this morning that Tempy's example should be my pattern henceforth." She began to knit faster than ever.

"'Tain't no use to get morbid: that's what Tempy used to say herself," said Sarah Ann, after a minute's silence. "Ain't it strange to say 'used to say'?" and her own voice choked a little. "She never did like to hear folks git goin' about themselves."

"'Twas only because they're apt to do it so as other folks will say 'twasn't so, an' praise 'em up," humbly replied Mrs. Crowe, "and that ain't my object. There wa'n't a child but what Tempy set herself to work to see what she could do to please it. One time my brother's folks had been stopping here in the summer, from Massachusetts. The children was all little, and they broke up a sight of toys, and left 'em when they were going away. Tempy come right up after they rode by, to see if she couldn't help me set the house to rights, and she caught me just as I was going to fling some of the clutter into the stove. I was kind of tired out, starting 'em off in season. 'Oh, give me them!' says she, real pleading; and she wropped 'em up and took 'em home with her when she went, and she mended 'em up and stuck 'em together, and made some young one or other happy with every blessed one. You'd thought I'd done her the biggest favor. 'No thanks to me. I should ha' burnt 'em, Tempy,' says I."

"Some of 'em came to our house, I know," said Miss Binson. "She'd take a lot o' trouble to please a child, 'stead o' shoving of it out o' the way, like the rest of us when we're drove."

"I can tell you the biggest thing she ever done, and I don't know 's there's anybody left but me to tell it. I don't want it forgot," Sarah Binson went on, looking up at the clock to see how the night was going. "It was that pretty-look-ing Trevor girl, who taught the Corners school, and married so well afterwards, out in New York State. You remember her, I dare say?"

"Certain," said Mrs. Crowe, with an air of interest.

"She was a splendid scholar, folks said, and give the school a great start; but she'd overdone herself getting her education, and working to pay for it, and she all broke down one spring, and Tempy made her come and stop with her a while —you remember that? Well, she had an uncle, her mother's brother, out in Chicago, who was well off and friendly, and used to write to Lizzie Trevor, and I dare say make her some presents; but he was a lively, driving man, and didn't take time to stop and think about his folks. He hadn't seen her since she was a little girl. Poor Lizzie was so pale and weakly that she just got through the term o' school. She looked as if she was just going straight off in a decline. Tempy, she cosseted her up a while, and then, next thing folks knew, she was tellin' round how Miss Trevor had gone to see her uncle, and meant to visit Niagary Falls on the way, and stop over night. Now I happened to know, in ways I won't dwell on to explain, that the poor girl was in debt for her schoolin' when she come here, and her last quarter's pay had just squared it off at last, and left her without a cent ahead, hardly; but it had fretted her thinking of it, so she paid it all; they might have dunned her that she owed it to. An' I taxed Tempy about the girl's goin' off on such a journey till she owned up, rather 'n have Lizzie blamed, that she'd given her sixty dollars, same 's if she was rolling in riches, and sent her off to have a good rest and vacation."

"Sixty dollars!" exclaimed Mrs. Crowe. "Tempy only had ninety dollars a year that came in to her; rest of her livin' she got by helpin' about, with what she raised off this little piece o' ground, sand one side an' clay the other. An' how often I've heard her tell, years ago, that she'd rather see Niagary than any other sight in the world!"

The women looked at each other in silence; the magnitude of the generous sacrifice was almost too great for their comprehension.

"She was just poor enough to do that!" declared Mrs. Crowe at last, in an abandonment of feeling. "Say what you may, I feel humbled to the dust," and her companion ventured to say nothing. She never had given away sixty dollars at once, but it was simply because she never had it to give. It came to her very lips to say in explanation, "Tempy was so situated;" but she checked herself in time, for she would not betray her own loyal guarding of a dependent household.

"Folks say a great deal of generosity, and this one's being public-sperited, and that one free-handed about giving," said Mrs. Crowe, who was a little nervous in the silence. "I suppose we can't tell the sorrow it would be to some folks not to give, same 's 'twould be to me not to save. I seem kind of made for that, as if 'twas what I'd got to do. I should feel sights better about it if I could make it evident what I was savin' for. If I had a child, now, Sarah Ann," and her voice was a little husky, "if I had a child, I should think I washeapin' of it up because he was the one trained by the Lord to scatter it again for good. But here's Mr. Crowe and me, we can't do anything with money, and both of us like to keep things same 's they've always been. Now Priscilla Dance was talking away like a mill-clapper, week before last. She'd think I would go right off and get one o' them new-fashioned gilt-and-white papers for the best room, and some new furniture, an' a marble-top table. And I looked at her, all struck up. 'Why,' says I, 'Priscilla, that nice old velvet paper ain't hurt a mite. I shouldn't feel 'twas my best room without it. Dan'el says 'tis the first thing he can remember rubbin' his little baby fingers on to it, and how splendid he thought them red roses was.' I maintain," continued Mrs. Crowe stoutly, "that folks wastes sights o' good money doin' just such foolish things. Tearin' out the insides o' meetin'-houses, and fixin' the pews different; 'twas good enough as 'twas with mendin'; then times come, an' they want to put it all back same 's 'twas before."

This touched upon an exciting subject to active members of that parish. Miss Binson and Mrs. Crowe belonged to opposite parties, and had at one time come as near hard feelings as they could, and yet escape them. Each hastened to speak of other things and to show her untouched friendliness.

"I do agree with you," said Sister Binson, "that few of us know what use to make of money, beyond everyday necessities. You've seen more o' the world than I have, and know what's expected. When it comes to taste and judgment about such things, I ought to defer to others;" and with this modest avowal the critical moment passed when there might have been an improper discussion.

In the silence that followed, the fact of their presence in a house of death grew more clear than before. There was something disturbing in the noise of a mouse gnawing at the dry boards of a closet wall near by. Both the watchers looked up anxiously at the clock; it was almost the middle of the night, and the whole world seemed to have left them alone with their solemn duty. Only the brook was awake.

"Perhaps we might give a look upstairs now," whispered Mrs. Crowe, as if she hoped to hear some reason against their going just then to the chamber of death; but Sister Binson rose, with a serious and yet satisfied countenance, and lifted the small lamp from the table. She was much more used to watching than Mrs. Crowe, and much less affected by it. They opened the door into a small entry with a steep stairway; they climbed the creaking stairs, and entered the cold upper room on tiptoe. Mrs. Crowe's heart began to beat very fast as the lamp was put on a high bureau, and made long, fixed shadows about the walls. She went hesitatingly toward the solemn shape under its white drapery, and felt a sense of remonstrance as Sarah Ann gently, but in a businesslike way, turned back the thin sheet.

"Seems to me she looks pleasanter and pleasanter," whispered Sarah Ann Binson impulsively, as they gazed at the white face with its wonderful smile. "Tomorrow 'twill all have faded out. I do believe they kind of wake up a day or two after they die, and it's then they go." She replaced the light covering, and they both turned quickly away; there was a chill in this upper room.

"'Tis a great thing for anybody to have got through, ain't it?" said Mrs. Crowe softly, as she began to go down the stairs on tiptoe. The warm air from the kitchen beneath met them with a sense of welcome and shelter.

"I don' know why it is, but I feel as near again to Tempy down here as I do up there," replied Sister Binson. "I feel as if the air was full of her, kind of. I can sense things, now and then, that she seems to say. Now I never was one to take up with no nonsense of sperits and such, but I declare I felt as if she told me just now to put some more wood into the stove."

Mrs. Crowe preserved a gloomy silence. She had suspected before this that her companion was of a weaker and more credulous disposition than herself. "'Tis a great thing to have got through," she repeated, ignoring definitely all that had last been said. "I suppose you know as well as I that Tempy was one that always feared death. Well, it's all put behind her now; she knows what 'tis." Mrs. Crowe gave a little sigh, and Sister Binson's quick sympathies were stirred toward this other old friend, who also dreaded the great change.

"I'd never like to forgit almost those last words Tempy spoke plain to me," she said gently, like the comforter she truly was. "She looked up at me once or twice, that last afternoon after I come to set by her, and let Mis' Owen go home; and I says, 'Can I do anything to ease you, Tempy?' and the tears come into my eyes so I couldn't see what kind of a nod she give me. 'No, Sarah Ann, you can't, dear,' says she; and then she got her breath again, and says she, looking at me real meanin', 'I'm only a-gettin' sleepier and sleepier; that's all there is,' says she, and smiled up at me kind of wishful, and shut her eyes. I knew well enough all she meant. She'd been lookin' out for a chance to tell me, and I don' know 's she ever said much afterwards."

Mrs. Crowe was not knitting; she had been listening too eagerly. "Yes, 'twill be a comfort to think of that sometimes," she said, in acknowledgment.

"I know that old Dr. Prince said once, in evenin' meetin', that he'd watched by many a dyin' bed, as we well knew, and enough o' his sick folks had been scared o' dyin' their whole lives through; but when they come to the last, he'd never seen one but was willin', and most were glad, to go. ''Tis as natural as bein' born or livin' on,' he said. I don't know what had moved him to speak that night. You know he wa'n't in the habit of it, and 'twas the monthly concert of prayer for foreign missions anyways," said Sarah Ann; "but 'twas a great stay to the mind to listen to his words of experience."

"There never was a better man," responded Mrs. Crowe, in a really cheerful tone. She had recovered from her feeling of nervous dread, the kitchen was so comfortable with lamplight and firelight; and just then the old clock began to tell the hour of twelve with leisurely whirring strokes.

Sister Binson laid aside her work, and rose quickly and went to the cupboard. "We'd better take a little to eat," she explained. "The night will go fast after this. I want to know if you went and made some o' your nice cupcake, while you was home today?" she asked, in a pleased tone; and Mrs. Crowe acknowledged such a gratifying piece of thoughtfulness for this humble friend who denied herself all luxuries. Sarah Ann brewed a generous cup of tea, and the watchers drew their chairs up to the table presently, and quelled their hunger with good country appetites. Sister Binson put a spoon into a small, old-fashioned glass of preserved quince, and passed it to her friend. She was most familiar with the house, and played the part of hostess. "Spread some o' this on your bread and butter," she said to Mrs. Crowe. "Tempy wanted me to use some three or four times, but I never felt to. I know she'd like to have us comfortable now, and would urge us to make a good supper, poor dear."

"What excellent preserves she did make!" mourned Mrs. Crowe. "None of us has got her light hand at doin' things tasty. She made the most o' everything, too. Now, she only had that one old quince-tree down in the far corner of the piece, but she'd go out in the spring and tend to it, and look at it so pleasant and kind of expect the old thorny thing into bloomin'."

"She was just the same with folks," said Sarah Ann. "And she'd never git more'n a little apernful o' quinces, but she'd have every mite o' goodness out o' those, and set the glasses up onto her best-room closet shelf, *so* pleased. 'Twa'n't but a week ago tomorrow mornin' I fetched her a little taste o' jelly in a tea-spoon; and she says 'Thank ye,' and took it, an' the minute she tasted it she looked up at me as worried as could be. 'Oh, I don't want to eat that,' says she. 'I always keep that in case o' sickness.' 'You're goin' to have the good o' one tumbler yourself,' says I. 'I'd just like to know who's sick now, if you ain't!' An' she couldn't help laughin', I spoke up so smart. Oh, dear me, how I shall miss talkin' over things with her! She always sensed things, and got just the p'int you meant."

"She didn't begin to age until two or three years ago, did she?" asked Mrs. Crowe. "I never saw anybody keep her looks as Tempy did. She looked young long after I begun to feel like an old woman. The doctor used to say 'twas her young heart, and I don't know but what he was right. How she did do for other folks! There was one spell she wasn't at home a day to a fortnight. She got most of her livin' so, and that made her own potatoes and things last her through. None o' the young folks could get married without her, and all the old ones was disappointed if she wa'n't round when they was down with sickness and had to go. An' cleanin', or tailorin' for boys, or rug-hookin'—there was nothin' but what she could do as handy as most. 'I do love to work,'—ain't you heard her say that twenty times a week?"

Sarah Ann Binson nodded, and began to clear away the empty plates. "We may want a taste o' somethin' more towards mornin'," she said. "There's plenty in the closet here; and in case some comes from a distance to the funeral, we'll have a little table spread after we get back to the house."

"Yes, I was busy all the mornin'. I've cooked up a sight o' things to bring over," said Mrs. Crowe. "I felt 'twas the last I could do for her."

They drew their chairs near the stove again, and took up their work. Sister Binson's rocking-chair creaked as she rocked; the brook sounded louder than ever. It was more lonely when nobody spoke, and presently Mrs. Crowe returned to her thoughts of growing old.

"Yes, Tempy aged all of a sudden. I remember I asked her if she felt as well as common, one day, and she laughed at me good. There, when Mr. Crowe begun to look old, I couldn't help feeling as if somethin' ailed him, and like as not 'twas somethin' he was goin' to git right over, and I dosed him for it stiddy, half of one summer."

"How many things we shall be wanting to ask Tempy!" exclaimed Sarah Ann Binson, after a long pause. "I can't make up my mind to doin' without her. I wish folks could come back just once, and tell us how 'tis where they've gone. Seems then we could do without 'em better."

The brook hurried on, the wind blew about the house now and then; the house itself was a silent place, and the supper, the warm fire, and an absence of any new topics for conversation made the watchers drowsy. Sister Binson closed her eyes first, to rest them for a minute; and Mrs. Crowe glanced at her compassionately, with a new sympathy for the hard-worked little woman. She made up her mind to let Sarah Ann have a good rest, while she kept watch alone; but in a few minutes her own knitting was dropped, and she, too, fell asleep. Overhead, the pale shape of Tempy Dent, the outworn body of that generous, loving-hearted, simple soul, slept on also in its white raiment. Perhaps Tempy herself stood near, and saw her own life and its surroundings with new understanding. Perhaps she herself was the only watcher.

Later, by some hours, Sarah Ann Binson woke with a start. There was a pale light of dawn outside the small windows. Inside the kitchen, the lamp burned dim. Mrs. Crowe awoke, too.

"I think Tempy'd be the first to say 'twas just as well we both had some rest," she said, not without a guilty feeling.

Her companion went to the outer door, and opened it wide. The fresh air was none too cold, and the brook's voice was not nearly so loud as it had been in the midnight darkness. She could see the shapes of the hills, and the great shadows that lay across the lower country. The east was fast growing bright.

"'Twill be a beautiful day for the funeral," she said, and turned again, with a sigh, to follow Mrs. Crowe up the stairs.

THE HAUNTED MAN AND THE GHOST'S BARGAIN, by Charles Dickens

CHAPTER I

The Gift Bestowed

Everybody said so.

Far be it from me to assert that what everybody says must be true. Everybody is, often, as likely to be wrong as right. In the general experience, everybody has been wrong so often, and it has taken, in most instances, such a weary while to find out how wrong, that the authority is proved to be fallible. Everybody may sometimes be right; "but *that's* no rule," as the ghost of Giles Scroggins says in the ballad.

The dread word, Ghost, recalls me.

Everybody said he looked like a haunted man. The extent of my present claim for everybody is, that they were so far right. He did.

Who could have seen his hollow cheek; his sunken brilliant eye; his black-attired figure, indefinably grim, although well-knit and well-proportioned; his grizzled hair hanging, like tangled sea-weed, about his face,—as if he had been, through his whole life, a lonely mark for the chafing and beating of the great deep of humanity,—but might have said he looked like a haunted man?

Who could have observed his manner, taciturn, thoughtful, gloomy, shadowed by habitual reserve, retiring always and jocund never, with a distraught air of reverting to a bygone place and time, or of listening to some old echoes in his mind, but might have said it was the manner of a haunted man?

Who could have heard his voice, slow-speaking, deep, and grave, with a natural fulness and melody in it which he seemed to set himself against and stop, but might have said it was the voice of a haunted man?

Who that had seen him in his inner chamber, part library and part laboratory, —for he was, as the world knew, far and wide, a learned man in chemistry, and a teacher on whose lips and hands a crowd of aspiring ears and eyes hung daily,— who that had seen him there, upon a winter night, alone, surrounded by his drugs and instruments and books; the shadow of his shaded lamp a monstrous beetle on the wall, motionless among a crowd of spectral shapes raised there by the flickering of the fire upon the quaint objects around him; some of these phantoms (the reflection of glass vessels that held liquids), trembling at heart like things that knew his power to uncombine them, and to give back their component parts to fire and vapour;—who that had seen him then, his work done, and he pondering in his chair before the rusted grate and red flame, moving his thin mouth as if in speech, but silent as the dead, would not have said that the man seemed haunted and the chamber too?

Who might not, by a very easy flight of fancy, have believed that everything about him took this haunted tone, and that he lived on haunted ground?

His dwelling was so solitary and vault-like,—an old, retired part of an ancient endowment for students, once a brave edifice, planted in an open place, but now the obsolete whim of forgotten architects; smoke-age-and-weather-darkened, squeezed on every side by the overgrowing of the great city, and choked, like an old well, with stones and bricks; its small quadrangles, lying down in very pits formed by the streets and buildings, which, in course of time, had been constructed above its heavy chimney stalks; its old trees, insulted by the neighbouring smoke, which deigned to droop so low when it was very feeble and the weather very moody; its grass-plots, struggling with the mildewed earth to be grass, or to win any show of compromise; its silent pavements, unaccustomed to the tread of feet, and even to the observation of eyes, except when a stray face looked down from the upper world, wondering what nook it was; its sun-dial in a little bricked-up corner, where no sun had straggled for a hundred years, but where, in compensation for the sun's neglect, the snow would lie for weeks when it lay nowhere else, and the black east wind would spin like a huge humming-top, when in all other places it was silent and still.

His dwelling, at its heart and core—within doors—at his fireside—was so lowering and old, so crazy, yet so strong, with its worn-eaten beams of wood in the ceiling, and its sturdy floor shelving downward to the great oak chimney-piece; so environed and hemmed in by the pressure of the town yet so remote in fashion, age, and custom; so quiet, yet so thundering with echoes when a distant voice was raised or a door was shut,—echoes, not confined to the many low passages and empty rooms, but rumbling and grumbling till they were stifled in the heavy air of the forgotten Crypt where the Norman arches were half-buried in the earth.

You should have seen him in his dwelling about twilight, in the dead winter time.

When the wind was blowing, shrill and shrewd, with the going down of the blurred sun. When it was just so dark, as that the forms of things were indistinct and big—but not wholly lost. When sitters by the fire began to see wild faces and figures, mountains and abysses, ambuscades and armies, in the coals. When people in the streets bent down their heads and ran before the weather. When those who were obliged to meet it, were stopped at angry corners, stung by wandering snow-flakes alighting on the lashes of their eyes,—which fell too sparingly, and were blown away too quickly, to leave a trace upon the frozen ground. When windows of private houses closed up tight and warm. When lighted gas began to burst forth in the busy and the quiet streets, fast blackening otherwise. When stray pedestrians, shivering along the latter, looked down at the glowing fires in kitchens, and sharpened their sharp appetites by sniffing up the fragrance of whole miles of dinners.

When travellers by land were bitter cold, and looked wearily on gloomy landscapes, rustling and shuddering in the blast. When mariners at sea, outlying upon icy yards, were tossed and swung above the howling ocean dreadfully. When lighthouses, on rocks and headlands, showed solitary and watchful; and benighted sea-birds breasted on against their ponderous lanterns, and fell dead. When little readers of story-books, by the firelight, trembled to think of Cassim Baba cut into quarters, hanging in the Robbers' Cave, or had some small misgivings that the fierce little old woman, with the crutch, who used to start out of the box in the merchant Abudah's bedroom, might, one of these nights, be found upon the stairs, in the long, cold, dusky journey up to bed.

When, in rustic places, the last glimmering of daylight died away from the ends of avenues; and the trees, arching overhead, were sullen and black. When, in parks and woods, the high wet fern and sodden moss, and beds of fallen leaves, and trunks of trees, were lost to view, in masses of impenetrable shade. When mists arose from dyke, and fen, and river. When lights in old halls and in cottage windows, were a cheerful sight. When the mill stopped, the wheelwright and the blacksmith shut their workshops, the turnpike-gate closed, the plough and harrow were left lonely in the fields, the labourer and team went home, and the striking of the church clock had a deeper sound than at noon, and the church-yard wicket would be swung no more that night.

When twilight everywhere released the shadows, prisoned up all day, that now closed in and gathered like mustering swarms of ghosts. When they stood lowering, in corners of rooms, and frowned out from behind half-opened doors. When they had full possession of unoccupied apartments. When they danced upon the floors, and walls, and ceilings of inhabited chambers, while the fire was low, and withdrew like ebbing waters when it sprang into a blaze. When they fantastically mocked the shapes of household objects, making the nurse an ogress, the rocking-horse a monster, the wondering child, half-scared and half-amused, a stranger to itself,—the very tongs upon the hearth, a straddling giant with his arms a-kimbo, evidently smelling the blood of Englishmen, and wanting to grind people's bones to make his bread.

When these shadows brought into the minds of older people, other thoughts, and showed them different images. When they stole from their retreats, in the likenesses of forms and faces from the past, from the grave, from the deep, deep gulf, where the things that might have been, and never were, are always wandering.

When he sat, as already mentioned, gazing at the fire. When, as it rose and fell, the shadows went and came. When he took no heed of them, with his bodily eyes; but, let them come or let them go, looked fixedly at the fire. You should have seen him, then.

When the sounds that had arisen with the shadows, and come out of their lurking-places at the twilight summons, seemed to make a deeper stillness all about him. When the wind was rumbling in the chimney, and sometimes croon-ing, sometimes howling, in the house. When the old trees outside were so shaken and beaten, that one querulous old rook, unable to sleep, protested now and then, in a feeble, dozy, high-up "Caw!" When, at intervals, the window trembled, the rusty vane upon the turret-top complained, the clock beneath it recorded that an-other quarter of an hour was gone, or the fire collapsed and fell in with a rattle.

—When a knock came at his door, in short, as he was sitting so, and roused him.

"Who's that?" said he. "Come in!"

Surely there had been no figure leaning on the back of his chair; no face look-ing over it. It is certain that no gliding footstep touched the floor, as he lifted up his head, with a start, and spoke. And yet there was no mirror in the room on whose surface his own form could have cast its shadow for a moment; and, Something had passed darkly and gone!

"I'm humbly fearful, sir," said a fresh-coloured busy man, holding the door open with his foot for the admission of himself and a wooden tray he carried, and letting it go again by very gentle and careful degrees, when he and the tray had got in, lest it should close noisily,"that it's a good bit past the time to-night. But Mrs. William has been taken off her legs so often"—

"By the wind? Ay! I have heard it rising."

"—By the wind, sir—that it's a mercy she got home at all. Oh dear, yes. Yes. It was by the wind, Mr. Redlaw. By the wind."

He had, by this time, put down the tray for dinner, and was employed in lighting the lamp, and spreading a cloth on the table. From this employment he desisted in a hurry, to stir and feed the fire, and then resumed it; the lamp he had lighted, and the blaze that rose under his hand, so quickly changing the appearance of the room, that it seemed as if the mere coming in of his fresh red face and active manner had made the pleasant alteration.

"Mrs. William is of course subject at any time, sir, to be taken off her balance by the elements. She is not formed superior to *that*."

"No," returned Mr. Redlaw good-naturedly, though abruptly.

"No, sir. Mrs. William may be taken off her balance by Earth; as for example, last Sunday week, when sloppy and greasy, and she going out to tea with her newest sister-in-law, and having a pride in herself, and wishing to appear perfectly spotless though pedestrian. Mrs. William may be taken off her balance by Air; as being once over-persuaded by a friend to try a swing at Peckham Fair, which acted on her constitution instantly like a steam-boat. Mrs. William may be taken off her balance by Fire; as on a false alarm of engines at her mother's, when she went two miles in her nightcap. Mrs. William may be taken off her balance by Water; as at Battersea, when rowed into the piers by her young nephew, Charley Swidger junior, aged twelve, which had no idea of boats whatever. But these are elements. Mrs. William must be taken out of elements for the strength of *her* character to come into play."

As he stopped for a reply, the reply was "Yes," in the same tone as before.

"Yes, sir. Oh dear, yes!" said Mr. Swidger, still proceeding with his preparations, and checking them off as he made them. "That's where it is, sir. That's what I always say myself, sir. Such a many of us Swidgers!—Pepper. Why there's my father, sir, superannuated keeper and custodian of this Institution, eighty-seven year old. He's a Swidger!—Spoon."

"True, William," was the patient and abstracted answer, when he stopped again.

"Yes, sir," said Mr. Swidger. "That's what I always say, sir. You may call him the trunk of the tree!—Bread. Then you come to his successor, my unworthy self —Salt—and Mrs. William, Swidgers both.—Knife and fork. Then you come to all my brothers and their families, Swidgers, man and woman, boy and girl. Why, what with cousins, uncles, aunts, and relationships of this, that, and t'other degree, and whatnot degree, and marriages, and lyings-in, the Swidgers—Tumbler—might take hold of hands, and make a ring round England!"

Receiving no reply at all here, from the thoughtful man whom he addressed, Mr. William approached, him nearer, and made a feint of accidentally knocking the table with a decanter, to rouse him. The moment he succeeded, he went on, as if in great alacrity of acquiescence.

"Yes, sir! That's just what I say myself, sir. Mrs. William and me have often said so. 'There's Swidgers enough,' we say, 'without *our* voluntary contributions,'—Butter. In fact, sir, my father is a family in himself—Castors—to take care of; and it happens all for the best that we have no child of our own, though it's made Mrs. William rather quiet-like, too. Quite ready for the fowl and mashed potatoes, sir? Mrs. William said she'd dish in ten minutes when I left the Lodge."

"I am quite ready," said the other, waking as from a dream, and walking slowly to and fro.

"Mrs. William has been at it again, sir!" said the keeper, as he stood warming a plate at the fire, and pleasantly shading his face with it. Mr. Redlaw stopped in his walking, and an expression of interest appeared in him.

"What I always say myself, sir. She *will* do it! There's a motherly feeling in Mrs. William's breast that must and will have went."

"What has she done?"

"Why, sir, not satisfied with being a sort of mother to all the young gentlemen that come up from a variety of parts, to attend your courses of lectures at this ancient foundation—its surprising how stone-chaney catches the heat this frosty weather, to be sure!" Here he turned the plate, and cooled his fingers.

"Well?" said Mr. Redlaw.

"That's just what I say myself, sir," returned Mr. William, speaking over his shoulder, as if in ready and delighted assent. "That's exactly where it is, sir! There ain't one of our students but appears to regard Mrs. William in that light. Every day, right through the course, they puts their heads into the Lodge, one after another, and have all got something to tell her, or something to ask her. 'Swidge' is the appellation by which they speak of Mrs. William in general, among themselves, I'm told; but that's what I say, sir. Better be called ever so far out of your name, if it's done in real liking, than have it made ever so much of, and not cared about! What's a name for? To know a person by. If Mrs. William is known by something better than her name—I allude to Mrs. William's qualities and disposition—never mind her name, though it *is* Swidger, by rights. Let 'em call her Swidge, Widge, Bridge—Lord! London Bridge, Blackfriars, Chelsea, Putney, Waterloo, or Hammersmith Suspension—if they like."

The close of this triumphant oration brought him and the plate to the table, upon which he half laid and half dropped it, with a lively sense of its being thoroughly heated, just as the subject of his praises entered the room, bearing another tray and a lantern, and followed by a venerable old man with long grey hair.

Mrs. William, like Mr. William, was a simple, innocent-looking person, in whose smooth cheeks the cheerful red of her husband's official waistcoat was very pleasantly repeated. But whereas Mr. William's light hair stood on end all over his head, and seemed to draw his eyes up with it in an excess of bustling readiness for anything, the dark brown hair of Mrs. William was carefully smoothed down, and waved away under a trim tidy cap, in the most exact and quiet manner imaginable. Whereas Mr. William's very trousers hitched themselves up at the ankles, as if it were not in their iron-grey nature to rest without looking about them, Mrs. William's neatly-flowered skirts—red and white, like her own pretty face—were as composed and orderly, as if the very wind that blew so hard out of doors could not disturb one of their folds. Whereas his coat had something of a fly-away and half-off appearance about the collar and breast, her little bodice was so placid and neat, that there should have been protection for her, in it, had she needed any, with the roughest people. Who could have had the heart to make so calm a bosom swell with grief, or throb with fear, or flutter with a thought of shame! To whom would its repose and peace have not appealed against disturbance, like the innocent slumber of a child!

"Punctual, of course, Milly," said her husband, relieving her of the tray, "or it wouldn't be you. Here's Mrs. William, sir!—He looks lonelier than ever to-night," whispering to his wife, as he was taking the tray, "and ghostlier altogether."

Without any show of hurry or noise, or any show of herself even, she was so calm and quiet, Milly set the dishes she had brought upon the table,—Mr. William, after much clattering and running about, having only gained possession of a butter-boat of gravy, which he stood ready to serve.

"What is that the old man has in his arms?" asked Mr. Redlaw, as he sat down to his solitary meal.

"Holly, sir," replied the quiet voice of Milly.

"That's what I say myself, sir," interposed Mr. William, striking in with the butter-boat. "Berries is so seasonable to the time of year!—Brown gravy!"

"Another Christmas come, another year gone!"murmured the Chemist, with a gloomy sigh. "More figures in the lengthening sum of recollection that we work and work at to our torment, till Death idly jumbles all together, and rubs all out. So, Philip!" breaking off, and raising his voice as he addressed the old man, standing apart, with his glistening burden in his arms, from which the quiet Mrs. William took small branches, which she noiselessly trimmed with her scissors, and decorated the room with, while her aged father-in-law looked on much interested in the ceremony.

"My duty to you, sir," returned the old man. "Should have spoke before, sir, but know your ways, Mr. Redlaw—proud to say—and wait till spoke to! Merry Christmas, sir, and Happy New Year, and many of'em. Have had a pretty many of 'em myself—ha, ha!—and may take the liberty of wishing'em. I'm eighty-seven!"

"Have you had so many that were merry and happy?"asked the other.

"Ay, sir, ever so many," returned the old man.

"Is his memory impaired with age? It is to be expected now," said Mr. Redlaw, turning to the son, and speaking lower.

"Not a morsel of it, sir," replied Mr. William. "That's exactly what I say myself, sir. There never was such a memory as my father's. He's the most wonderful man in the world. He don't know what forgetting means. It's the very observation I'm always making to Mrs. William, sir, if you'll believe me!"

Mr. Swidger, in his polite desire to seem to acquiesce at all events, delivered this as if there were no iota of contradiction in it, and it were all said in unbounded and unqualified assent.

The Chemist pushed his plate away, and, rising from the table, walked across the room to where the old man stood looking at a little sprig of holly in his hand.

"It recalls the time when many of those years were old and new, then?" he said, observing him attentively, and touching him on the shoulder. "Does it?"

"Oh many, many!" said Philip, half awaking from his reverie. "I'm eighty-seven!"

"Merry and happy, was it?" asked the Chemist in a low voice. "Merry and happy, old man?"

"Maybe as high as that, no higher," said the old man, holding out his hand a little way above the level of his knee, and looking retrospectively at his questioner, "when I first remember 'em! Cold, sunshiny day it was, out a-walking, when some one—it was my mother as sure as you stand there, though I don't know what her blessed face was like, for she took ill and died that Christmastime—told me they were food for birds. The pretty little fellow thought—that's me, you understand—that birds' eyes were so bright, perhaps, because the berries that they lived on in the winter were so bright. I recollect that. And I'm eighty-seven!"

"Merry and happy!" mused the other, bending his dark eyes upon the stooping figure, with a smile of compassion. "Merry and happy—and remember well?"

"Ay, ay, ay!" resumed the old man, catching the last words. "I remember 'em well in my school time, year after year, and all the merry-making that used to come along with them. I was a strong chap then, Mr. Redlaw; and, if you'll believe me, hadn't my match at football within ten mile. Where's my son William? Hadn't my match at football, William, within ten mile!"

"That's what I always say, father!" returned the son promptly, and with great respect. "You ARE a Swidger, if ever there was one of the family!"

"Dear!" said the old man, shaking his head as he again looked at the holly. "His mother—my son William's my youngest son—and I, have sat among 'em all, boys and girls, little children and babies, many a year, when the berries like these were not shining half so bright all round us, as their bright faces. Many of 'em are gone; she's gone; and my son George (our eldest, who was her pride more than all the rest!) is fallen very low: but I can see them, when I look here, alive and healthy, as they used to be in those days; and I can see him, thank God, in his innocence. It's a blessed thing to me, at eighty-seven."

The keen look that had been fixed upon him with so much earnestness, had gradually sought the ground.

"When my circumstances got to be not so good as formerly, through not being honestly dealt by, and I first come here to be custodian," said the old man, "—which was upwards of fifty years ago—where's my son William? More than half a century ago, William!"

"That's what I say, father," replied the son, as promptly and dutifully as before, "that's exactly where it is. Two times ought's an ought, and twice five ten, and there's a hundred of 'em."

"It was quite a pleasure to know that one of our founders—or more correctly speaking," said the old man, with a great glory in his subject and his knowledge of it, "one of the learned gentlemen that helped endow us in Queen Elizabeth's time, for we were founded afore her day—left in his will, among the other bequests he made us, so much to buy holly, for garnishing the walls and windows, come Christmas. There was something homely and friendly in it. Being but strange here, then, and coming at Christmas time, we took a liking for his very picter that hangs in what used to be, anciently, afore our ten poor gentlemen commuted for an annual stipend in money, our great Dinner Hall.—A sedate gentleman in a peaked beard, with a ruff round his neck, and a scroll below him, in old English letters, 'Lord! keep my memory green!' You know all about him, Mr. Redlaw?"

"I know the portrait hangs there, Philip."

"Yes, sure, it's the second on the right, above the panelling. I was going to say —he has helped to keep *my* memory green, I thank him; for going round the building every year, as I'm a doing now, and freshening up the bare rooms with these branches and berries, freshens up my bare old brain. One year brings back another, and that year another, and those others numbers! At last, it seems to me as if the birth-time of our Lord was the birth-time of all I have ever had affection for, or mourned for, or delighted in,—and they're a pretty many, for I'm eighty-seven!"

"Merry and happy," murmured Redlaw to himself.

The room began to darken strangely.

"So you see, sir," pursued old Philip, whose hale wintry cheek had warmed into a ruddier glow, and whose blue eyes had brightened while he spoke, "I have plenty to keep, when I keep this present season. Now, where's my quiet Mouse? Chattering's the sin of my time of life, and there's half the building to do yet, if the cold don't freeze us first, or the wind don't blow us away, or the darkness don't swallow us up."

The quiet Mouse had brought her calm face to his side, and silently taken his arm, before he finished speaking.

"Come away, my dear," said the old man. "Mr. Redlaw won't settle to his dinner, otherwise, till it's cold as the winter. I hope you'll excuse me rambling on, sir, and I wish you good night, and, once again, a merry—"

"Stay!" said Mr. Redlaw, resuming his place at the table, more, it would have seemed from his manner, to reassure the old keeper, than in any remembrance of his own appetite. "Spare me another moment, Philip. William, you were going to tell me something to your excellent wife's honour. It will not be disagreeable to her to hear you praise her. What was it?"

"Why, that's where it is, you see, sir,"returned Mr. William Swidger, looking towards his wife in considerable embarrassment. "Mrs. William's got her eye upon me."

"But you're not afraid of Mrs. William's eye?"

"Why, no, sir," returned Mr. Swidger,"that's what I say myself. It wasn't made to be afraid of. It wouldn't have been made so mild, if that was the intention. But I wouldn't like to—Milly!—him, you know. Down in the Buildings."

Mr. William, standing behind the table, and rummaging disconcertedly among the objects upon it, directed persuasive glances at Mrs. William, and secret jerks of his head and thumb àt Mr. Redlaw, as alluring her towards him.

"Him, you know, my love," said Mr. William. "Down in the Buildings. Tell, my dear! You're the works of Shakespeare in comparison with myself. Down in the Buildings, you know, my love.—Student."

"Student?" repeated Mr. Redlaw, raising his head.

"That's what I say, sir!" cried Mr. William, in the utmost animation of assent. "If it wasn't the poor student down in the Buildings, why should you wish to hear it from Mrs. William's lips? Mrs. William, my dear—Buildings."

"I didn't know," said Milly, with a quiet frankness, free from any haste or confusion, "that William had said anything about it, or I wouldn't have come. I asked him not to. It's a sick young gentleman, sir—and very poor, I am afraid— who is too ill to go home this holiday-time, and lives, unknown to any one, in but a common kind of lodging for a gentleman, down in Jerusalem Buildings. That's all, sir."

"Why have I never heard of him?" said the Chemist, rising hurriedly. "Why has he not made his situation known to me? Sick!—give me my hat and cloak. Poor!—what house?—what number?"

"Oh, you mustn't go there, sir," said Milly, leaving her father-in-law, and calmly confronting him with her collected little face and folded hands.

"Not go there?"

"Oh dear, no!" said Milly, shaking her head as at a most manifest and self-evident impossibility. "It couldn't be thought of!"

"What do you mean? Why not?"

"Why, you see, sir," said Mr. William Swidger, persuasively and confidentially, "that's what I say. Depend upon it, the young gentleman would never have made his situation known to one of his own sex. Mrs. Williams has got into his confidence, but that's quite different. They all confide in Mrs. William; they all trust *her*. A man, sir, couldn't have got a whisper out of him; but woman, sir, and Mrs. William combined—!"

"There is good sense and delicacy in what you say, William," returned Mr. Redlaw, observant of the gentle and composed face at his shoulder. And laying his finger on his lip, he secretly put his purse into her hand.

"Oh dear no, sir!" cried Milly, giving it back again. "Worse and worse! Couldn't be dreamed of!"

Such a staid matter-of-fact housewife she was, and so unruffled by the momentary haste of this rejection, that, an instant afterwards, she was tidily picking up a few leaves which had strayed from between her scissors and her apron, when she had arranged the holly.

Finding, when she rose from her stooping posture, that Mr. Redlaw was still regarding her with doubt and astonishment, she quietly repeated—looking about, the while, for any other fragments that might have escaped her observation:

"Oh dear no, sir! He said that of all the world he would not be known to you, or receive help from you—though he is a student in your class. I have made no terms of secrecy with you, but I trust to your honour completely."

"Why did he say so?"

"Indeed I can't tell, sir," said Milly, after thinking a little, "because I am not at all clever, you know; and I wanted to be useful to him in making things neat and comfortable about him, and employed myself that way. But I know he is poor, and lonely, and I think he is somehow neglected too.—How dark it is!"

The room had darkened more and more. There was a very heavy gloom and shadow gathering behind the Chemist's chair.

"What more about him?" he asked.

"He is engaged to be married when he can afford it," said Milly, "and is studying, I think, to qualify himself to earn a living. I have seen, a long time, that he has studied hard and denied himself much.—How very dark it is!"

"It's turned colder, too," said the old man, rubbing his hands. "There's a chill and dismal feeling in the room. Where's my son William? William, my boy, turn the lamp, and rouse the fire!"

Milly's voice resumed, like quiet music very softly played:

"He muttered in his broken sleep yesterday afternoon, after talking to me" (this was to herself) "about some one dead, and some great wrong done that could never be forgotten; but whether to him or to another person, I don't know. Not *by* him, I am sure."

"And, in short, Mrs. William, you see—which she wouldn't say herself, Mr. Redlaw, if she was to stop here till the new year after this next one—" said Mr. William, coming up to him to speak in his ear, "has done him worlds of good! Bless you, worlds of good! All at home just the same as ever—my father made as snug and comfortable—not a crumb of litter to be found in the house, if you were to offer fifty pound ready money for it—Mrs. William apparently never out of the way—yet Mrs. William backwards and forwards, backwards and forwards, up and down, up and down, a mother to him!"

The room turned darker and colder, and the gloom and shadow gathering behind the chair was heavier.

"Not content with this, sir, Mrs. William goes and finds, this very night, when she was coming home (why it's not above a couple of hours ago), a creature more like a young wild beast than a young child, shivering upon a door-step. What does Mrs. William do, but brings it home to dry it, and feed it, and keep it till our old Bounty of food and flannel is given away, on Christmas morning! If it ever felt a fire before, it's as much as ever it did; for it's sitting in the old Lodge chimney, staring at ours as if its ravenous eyes would never shut again. It's sitting there, at least," said Mr. William, correcting himself, on reflection, "unless it's bolted!"

"Heaven keep her happy!" said the Chemist aloud,"and you too, Philip! and you, William! I must consider what to do in this. I may desire to see this student, I'll not detain you any longer now. Good-night!"

"I thank'ee, sir, I thank'ee!" said the old man, "for Mouse, and for my son William, and for myself. Where's my son William? William, you take the lantern and go on first, through them long dark passages, as you did last year and the year afore. Ha ha! *I* remember—though I'm eighty-seven! 'Lord, keep my memory green!' It's a very good prayer, Mr. Redlaw, that of the learned gentleman in the peaked beard, with a ruff round his neck—hangs up, second on the right above the panelling, in what used to be, afore our ten poor gentlemen commuted, our great Dinner Hall. 'Lord, keep my memory green!' It's very good and pious, sir. Amen! Amen!"

As they passed out and shut the heavy door, which, however carefully withheld, fired a long train of thundering reverberations when it shut at last, the room turned darker.

As he fell a musing in his chair alone, the healthy holly withered on the wall, and dropped—dead branches.

As the gloom and shadow thickened behind him, in that place where it had been gathering so darkly, it took, by slow degrees,—or out of it there came, by some unreal, unsubstantial process—not to be traced by any human sense,—an awful likeness of himself!

Ghastly and cold, colourless in its leaden face and hands, but with his features, and his bright eyes, and his grizzled hair, and dressed in the gloomy shadow of his dress, it came into his terrible appearance of existence, motionless, without a sound. As *he* leaned his arm upon the elbow of his chair, ruminating before the fire, *it* leaned upon the chair-back, close above him, with its appalling copy of his face looking where his face looked, and bearing the expression his face bore.

This, then, was the Something that had passed and gone already. This was the dread companion of the haunted man!

It took, for some moments, no more apparent heed of him, than he of it. The Christmas Waits were playing somewhere in the distance, and, through his thoughtfulness, he seemed to listen to the music. It seemed to listen too.

At length he spoke; without moving or lifting up his face.

"Here again!" he said.

"Here again," replied the Phantom.

"I see you in the fire," said the haunted man;"I hear you in music, in the wind, in the dead stillness of the night."

The Phantom moved its head, assenting.

"Why do you come, to haunt me thus?"

"I come as I am called," replied the Ghost.

"No. Unbidden," exclaimed the Chemist.

"Unbidden be it," said the Spectre. "It is enough. I am here."

Hitherto the light of the fire had shone on the two faces—if the dread lineaments behind the chair might be called a face—both addressed towards it, as at first, and neither looking at the other. But, now, the haunted man turned, suddenly, and stared upon the Ghost. The Ghost, as sudden in its motion, passed to before the chair, and stared on him.

The living man, and the animated image of himself dead, might so have looked, the one upon the other. An awful survey, in a lonely and remote part of an empty old pile of building, on a winter night, with the loud wind going by upon its journey of mystery—whence or whither, no man knowing since the world began—and the stars, in unimaginable millions, glittering through it, from eternal space, where the world's bulk is as a grain, and its hoary age is infancy.

"Look upon me!" said the Spectre. "I am he, neglected in my youth, and miserably poor, who strove and suffered, and still strove and suffered, until I hewed out knowledge from the mine where it was buried, and made rugged steps thereof, for my worn feet to rest and rise on."

"I *am* that man," returned the Chemist.

"No mother's self-denying love," pursued the Phantom, "no father's counsel, aided *me*. A stranger came into my father's place when I was but a child, and I was easily an alien from my mother's heart. My parents, at the best, were of that sort whose care soon ends, and whose duty is soon done; who cast their offspring loose, early, as birds do theirs; and, if they do well, claim the merit; and, if ill, the pity."

It paused, and seemed to tempt and goad him with its look, and with the manner of its speech, and with its smile.

"I am he," pursued the Phantom, "who, in this struggle upward, found a friend. I made him—won him—bound him to me! We worked together, side by side. All the love and confidence that in my earlier youth had had no outlet, and found no expression, I bestowed on him."

"Not all," said Redlaw, hoarsely.

"No, not all," returned the Phantom. "I had a sister."

The haunted man, with his head resting on his hands, replied"I had!" The Phantom, with an evil smile, drew closer to the chair, and resting its chin upon its folded hands, its folded hands upon the back, and looking down into his face with searching eyes, that seemed instinct with fire, went on:

"Such glimpses of the light of home as I had ever known, had streamed from her. How young she was, how fair, how loving! I took her to the first poor roof that I was master of, and made it rich. She came into the darkness of my life, and made it bright.—She is before me!"

"I saw her, in the fire, but now. I hear her in music, in the wind, in the dead stillness of the night,"returned the haunted man.

"*Did* he love her?" said the Phantom, echoing his contemplative tone. "I think he did, once. I am sure he did. Better had she loved him less—less secretly, less dearly, from the shallower depths of a more divided heart!"

"Let me forget it!" said the Chemist, with an angry motion of his hand. "Let me blot it from my memory!"

The Spectre, without stirring, and with its unwinking, cruel eyes still fixed upon his face, went on:

"A dream, like hers, stole upon my own life."

"It did," said Redlaw.

"A love, as like hers," pursued the Phantom,"as my inferior nature might cherish, arose in my own heart. I was too poor to bind its object to my fortune then, by any thread of promise or entreaty. I loved her far too well, to seek to do it. But, more than ever I had striven in my life, I strove to climb! Only an inch gained, brought me something nearer to the height. I toiled up! In the late pauses of my labour at that time,—my sister (sweet companion!) still sharing with me the expiring embers and the cooling hearth,—when day was breaking, what pictures of the future did I see!"

"I saw them, in the fire, but now," he murmured. "They come back to me in music, in the wind, in the dead stillness of the night, in the revolving years."

"—Pictures of my own domestic life, in aftertime, with her who was the inspiration of my toil. Pictures of my sister, made the wife of my dear friend, on equal terms—for he had some inheritance, we none—pictures of our sobered age and mellowed happiness, and of the golden links, extending back so far, that should bind us, and our children, in a radiant garland," said the Phantom.

"Pictures," said the haunted man, "that were delusions. Why is it my doom to remember them too well!"

"Delusions," echoed the Phantom in its changeless voice, and glaring on him with its changeless eyes. "For my friend (in whose breast my confidence was locked as in my own), passing between me and the centre of the system of my hopes and struggles, won her to himself, and shattered my frail universe. My sister, doubly dear, doubly devoted, doubly cheerful in my home, lived on to see me famous, and my old ambition so rewarded when its spring was broken, and then —"

"Then died," he interposed. "Died, gentle as ever; happy; and with no concern but for her brother. Peace!"

The Phantom watched him silently.

"Remembered!" said the haunted man, after a pause. "Yes. So well remembered, that even now, when years have passed, and nothing is more idle or more visionary to me than the boyish love so long outlived, I think of it with sympathy, as if it were a younger brother's or a son's. Sometimes I even wonder when her heart first inclined to him, and how it had been affected towards me.—Not lightly, once, I think.—But that is nothing. Early unhappiness, a wound from a hand I loved and trusted, and a loss that nothing can replace, outlive such fancies."

"Thus," said the Phantom, "I bear within me a Sorrow and a Wrong. Thus I prey upon myself. Thus, memory is my curse; and, if I could forget my sorrow and my wrong, I would!"

"Mocker!" said the Chemist, leaping up, and making, with a wrathful hand, at the throat of his other self. "Why have I always that taunt in my ears?"

"Forbear!" exclaimed the Spectre in an awful voice. "Lay a hand on Me, and die!"

He stopped midway, as if its words had paralysed him, and stood looking on it. It had glided from him; it had its arm raised high in warning; and a smile passed over its unearthly features, as it reared its dark figure in triumph.

"If I could forget my sorrow and wrong, I would,"the Ghost repeated. "If I could forget my sorrow and my wrong, I would!"

"Evil spirit of myself," returned the haunted man, in a low, trembling tone, "my life is darkened by that incessant whisper."

"It is an echo," said the Phantom.

"If it be an echo of my thoughts—as now, indeed, I know it is," rejoined the haunted man, "why should I, therefore, be tormented? It is not a selfish thought. I suffer it to range beyond myself. All men and women have their sorrows,—most of them their wrongs; ingratitude, and sordid jealousy, and interest, besetting all degrees of life. Who would not forget their sorrows and their wrongs?"

"Who would not, truly, and be happier and better for it?" said the Phantom.

"These revolutions of years, which we commemorate," proceeded Redlaw, "what do *they* recall! Are there any minds in which they do not re-awaken some sorrow, or some trouble? What is the remembrance of the old man who was here to-night? A tissue of sorrow and trouble."

"But common natures," said the Phantom, with its evil smile upon its glassy face, "unenlightened minds and ordinary spirits, do not feel or reason on these things like men of higher cultivation and profounder thought."

"Tempter," answered Redlaw, "whose hollow look and voice I dread more than words can express, and from whom some dim foreshadowing of greater fear is stealing over me while I speak, I hear again an echo of my own mind."

"Receive it as a proof that I am powerful,"returned the Ghost. "Hear what I offer! Forget the sorrow, wrong, and trouble you have known!"

"Forget them!" he repeated.

"I have the power to cancel their remembrance—to leave but very faint, confused traces of them, that will die out soon," returned the Spectre. "Say! Is it done?"

"Stay!" cried the haunted man, arresting by a terrified gesture the uplifted hand. "I tremble with distrust and doubt of you; and the dim fear you cast upon me deepens into a nameless horror I can hardly bear.—I would not deprive myself of any kindly recollection, or any sympathy that is good for me, or others. What shall I lose, if I assent to this? What else will pass from my remembrance?"

"No knowledge; no result of study; nothing but the intertwisted chain of feelings and associations, each in its turn dependent on, and nourished by, the banished recollections. Those will go."

"Are they so many?" said the haunted man, reflecting in alarm.

"They have been wont to show themselves in the fire, in music, in the wind, in the dead stillness of the night, in the revolving years," returned the Phantom scornfully.

"In nothing else?"

The Phantom held its peace.

But having stood before him, silent, for a little while, it moved towards the fire; then stopped.

"Decide!" it said, "before the opportunity is lost!"

"A moment! I call Heaven to witness," said the agitated man, "that I have never been a hater of any kind,—never morose, indifferent, or hard, to anything around me. If, living here alone, I have made too much of all that was and might have been, and too little of what is, the evil, I believe, has fallen on me, and not on others. But, if there were poison in my body, should I not, possessed of anti-dotes and knowledge how to use them, use them? If there be poison in my mind, and through this fearful shadow I can cast it out, shall I not cast it out?"

"Say," said the Spectre, "is it done?"

"A moment longer!" he answered hurriedly. "*I would forget it if I could*! Have *I* thought that, alone, or has it been the thought of thousands upon thousands, generation after generation? All human memory is fraught with sorrow and trouble. My memory is as the memory of other men, but other men have not this choice. Yes, I close the bargain. Yes! I WILL forget my sorrow, wrong, and trouble!"

"Say," said the Spectre, "is it done?"

"It is!"

"It is. And take this with you, man whom I here renounce! The gift that I have given, you shall give again, go where you will. Without recovering yourself the power that you have yielded up, you shall henceforth destroy its like in all whom you approach. Your wisdom has discovered that the memory of sorrow, wrong, and trouble is the lot of all mankind, and that mankind would be the happier, in its other memories, without it. Go! Be its benefactor! Freed from such remembrance, from this hour, carry involuntarily the blessing of such freedom with you. Its diffusion is inseparable and inalienable from you. Go! Be happy in the good you have won, and in the good you do!"

The Phantom, which had held its bloodless hand above him while it spoke, as if in some unholy invocation, or some ban; and which had gradually advanced its eyes so close to his, that he could see how they did not participate in the terrible smile upon its face, but were a fixed, unalterable, steady horror melted before him and was gone.

As he stood rooted to the spot, possessed by fear and wonder, and imagining he heard repeated in melancholy echoes, dying away fainter and fainter, the words, "Destroy its like in all whom you approach!" a shrill cry reached his ears. It came, not from the passages beyond the door, but from another part of the old building, and sounded like the cry of some one in the dark who had lost the way.

He looked confusedly upon his hands and limbs, as if to be assured of his identity, and then shouted in reply, loudly and wildly; for there was a strangeness and terror upon him, as if he too were lost.

The cry responding, and being nearer, he caught up the lamp, and raised a heavy curtain in the wall, by which he was accustomed to pass into and out of the theatre where he lectured,—which adjoined his room. Associated with youth and animation, and a high amphitheatre of faces which his entrance charmed to interest in a moment, it was a ghostly place when all this life was faded out of it, and stared upon him like an emblem of Death.

"Halloa!" he cried. "Halloa! This way! Come to the light!" When, as he held the curtain with one hand, and with the other raised the lamp and tried to pierce the gloom that filled the place, something rushed past him into the room like a wild-cat, and crouched down in a corner.

"What is it?" he said, hastily.

He might have asked "What is it?" even had he seen it well, as presently he did when he stood looking at it gathered up in its corner.

A bundle of tatters, held together by a hand, in size and form almost an infant's, but in its greedy, desperate little clutch, a bad old man's. A face rounded and smoothed by some half-dozen years, but pinched and twisted by the experiences of a life. Bright eyes, but not youthful. Naked feet, beautiful in their childish delicacy,—ugly in the blood and dirt that cracked upon them. A baby savage, a young monster, a child who had never been a child, a creature who might live to take the outward form of man, but who, within, would live and perish a mere beast.

Used, already, to be worried and hunted like a beast, the boy crouched down as he was looked at, and looked back again, and interposed his arm to ward off the expected blow.

"I'll bite," he said, "if you hit me!"

The time had been, and not many minutes since, when such a sight as this would have wrung the Chemist's heart. He looked upon it now, coldly; but with a heavy effort to remember something—he did not know what—he asked the boy what he did there, and whence he came.

"Where's the woman?" he replied. "I want to find the woman."

"Who?"

"The woman. Her that brought me here, and set me by the large fire. She was so long gone, that I went to look for her, and lost myself. I don't want you. I want the woman."

He made a spring, so suddenly, to get away, that the dull sound of his naked feet upon the floor was near the curtain, when Redlaw caught him by his rags.

"Come! you let me go!" muttered the boy, struggling, and clenching his teeth. "I've done nothing to you. Let me go, will you, to the woman!"

"That is not the way. There is a nearer one," said Redlaw, detaining him, in the same blank effort to remember some association that ought, of right, to bear upon this monstrous object. "What is your name?"

"Got none."

"Where do you live?"

"Live! What's that?"

The boy shook his hair from his eyes to look at him for a moment, and then, twisting round his legs and wrestling with him, broke again into his repetition of "You let me go, will you? I want to find the woman."

The Chemist led him to the door. "This way," he said, looking at him still confusedly, but with repugnance and avoidance, growing out of his coldness. "I'll take you to her."

The sharp eyes in the child's head, wandering round the room, lighted on the table where the remnants of the dinner were.

"Give me some of that!" he said, covetously.

"Has she not fed you?"

"I shall be hungry again to-morrow, sha'n't I? Ain't I hungry every day?"

Finding himself released, he bounded at the table like some small animal of prey, and hugging to his breast bread and meat, and his own rags, all together, said:

"There! Now take me to the woman!"

As the Chemist, with a new-born dislike to touch him, sternly motioned him to follow, and was going out of the door, he trembled and stopped.

"The gift that I have given, you shall give again, go where you will!"

The Phantom's words were blowing in the wind, and the wind blew chill upon him.

"I'll not go there, to-night," he murmured faintly. "I'll go nowhere to-night. Boy! straight down this long-arched passage, and past the great dark door into the yard,—you see the fire shining on the window there."

"The woman's fire?" inquired the boy.

He nodded, and the naked feet had sprung away. He came back with his lamp, locked his door hastily, and sat down in his chair, covering his face like one who was frightened at himself.

For now he was, indeed, alone. Alone, alone.

CHAPTER II

The Gift Diffused

A small man sat in a small parlour, partitioned off from a small shop by a small screen, pasted all over with small scraps of newspapers. In company with the small man, was almost any amount of small children you may please to name —at least it seemed so; they made, in that very limited sphere of action, such an imposing effect, in point of numbers.

Of these small fry, two had, by some strong machinery, been got into bed in a corner, where they might have reposed snugly enough in the sleep of innocence, but for a constitutional propensity to keep awake, and also to scuffle in and out of bed. The immediate occasion of these predatory dashes at the waking world, was the construction of an oyster-shell wall in a corner, by two other youths of tender age; on which fortification the two in bed made harassing descents (like those accursed Picts and Scots who beleaguer the early historical studies of most young Britons), and then withdrew to their own territory.

In addition to the stir attendant on these inroads, and the retorts of the invaded, who pursued hotly, and made lunges at the bed-clothes under which the marauders took refuge, another little boy, in another little bed, contributed his mite of confusion to the family stock, by casting his boots upon the waters; in other words, by launching these and several small objects, inoffensive in themselves, though of a hard substance considered as missiles, at the disturbers of his repose,—who were not slow to return these compliments.

Besides which, another little boy—the biggest there, but still little—was tottering to and fro, bent on one side, and considerably affected in his knees by the weight of a large baby, which he was supposed by a fiction that obtains sometimes in sanguine families, to be hushing to sleep. But oh! the inexhaustible regions of contemplation and watchfulness into which this baby's eyes were then only beginning to compose themselves to stare, over his unconscious shoulder!

It was a very Moloch of a baby, on whose insatiate altar the whole existence of this particular young brother was offered up a daily sacrifice. Its personality may be said to have consisted in its never being quiet, in any one place, for five consecutive minutes, and never going to sleep when required. "Tetterby's baby" was as well known in the neighbourhood as the postman or the pot-boy. It roved from door-step to door-step, in the arms of little Johnny Tetterby, and lagged heavily at the rear of troops of juveniles who followed the Tumblers or the Monkey, and came up, all on one side, a little too late for everything that was attractive, from Monday morning until Saturday night. Wherever childhood congregated to play, there was little Moloch making Johnny fag and toil. Wherever Johnny desired to stay, little Moloch became fractious, and would not remain. Whenever Johnny wanted to go out, Moloch was asleep, and must be watched. Whenever Johnny wanted to stay at home, Moloch was awake, and must be taken out. Yet Johnny was verily persuaded that it was a faultless baby, without its peer in the realm of England, and was quite content to catch meek glimpses of things in general from behind its skirts, or over its limp flapping bonnet, and to go staggering about with it like a very little porter with a very large parcel, which was not directed to anybody, and could never be delivered anywhere.

The small man who sat in the small parlour, making fruitless attempts to read his newspaper peaceably in the midst of this disturbance, was the father of the family, and the chief of the firm described in the inscription over the little shop front, by the name and title of A. Tetterby and Co., Newsmen. Indeed, strictly speaking, he was the only personage answering to that designation, as Co. was a mere poetical abstraction, altogether baseless and impersonal.

Tetterby's was the corner shop in Jerusalem Buildings. There was a good show of literature in the window, chiefly consisting of picture-newspapers out of date, and serial pirates, and footpads. Walking-sticks, likewise, and marbles, were included in the stock in trade. It had once extended into the light confectionery line; but it would seem that those elegancies of life were not in demand about Jerusalem Buildings, for nothing connected with that branch of commerce remained in the window, except a sort of small glass lantern containing a languishing mass of bull's-eyes, which had melted in the summer and congealed in the winter until all hope of ever getting them out, or of eating them without eating the lantern too, was gone for ever. Tetterby's had tried its hand at several things. It had once made a feeble little dart at the toy business; for, in another lantern, there was a heap of minute wax dolls, all sticking together upside down, in the direst confusion, with their feet on one another's heads, and a precipitate of broken arms and legs at the bottom. It had made a move in the millinery direction, which a few dry, wiry bonnet-shapes remained in a corner of the window to attest. It had fancied that a living might lie hidden in the tobacco trade, and had stuck up a representation of a native of each of the three integral portions of the British Empire, in the act of consuming that fragrant weed; with a poetic legend attached, importing that united in one cause they sat and joked, one chewed tobacco, one took snuff, one smoked: but nothing seemed to have come of it—except flies. Time had been when it had put a forlorn trust in imitative jewellery, for in one pane of glass there was a card of cheap seals, and another of pencil-cases, and a mysterious black amulet of inscrutable intention, labelled ninepence.

But, to that hour, Jerusalem Buildings had bought none of them. In short, Tetterby's had tried so hard to get a livelihood out of Jerusalem Buildings in one way or other, and appeared to have done so indifferently in all, that the best position in the firm was too evidently Co.'s; Co., as a bodiless creation, being untroubled with the vulgar inconveniences of hunger and thirst, being chargeable neither to the poor's-rates nor the assessed taxes, and having no young family to provide for.

Tetterby himself, however, in his little parlour, as already mentioned, having the presence of a young family impressed upon his mind in a manner too clamorous to be disregarded, or to comport with the quiet perusal of a newspaper, laid down his paper, wheeled, in his distraction, a few times round the parlour, like an undecided carrier-pigeon, made an ineffectual rush at one or two flying little figures in bed-gowns that skimmed past him, and then, bearing suddenly down upon the only unoffending member of the family, boxed the ears of little Moloch's nurse.

"You bad boy!" said Mr. Tetterby,"haven't you any feeling for your poor father after the fatigues and anxieties of a hard winter's day, since five o'clock in the morning, but must you wither his rest, and corrode his latest intelligence, with *your* wicious tricks? Isn't it enough, sir, that your brother 'Dolphus is toiling and moiling in the fog and cold, and you rolling in the lap of luxury with a— with a baby, and everything you can wish for," said Mr. Tetterby, heaping this up as a great climax of blessings, "but must you make a wilderness of home, and maniacs of your parents? Must you, Johnny? Hey?" At each interrogation, Mr. Tetterby made a feint of boxing his ears again, but thought better of it, and held his hand.

"Oh, father!" whimpered Johnny, "when I wasn't doing anything, I'm sure, but taking such care of Sally, and getting her to sleep. Oh, father!"

"I wish my little woman would come home!" said Mr. Tetterby, relenting and repenting, "I only wish my little woman would come home! I ain't fit to deal with'em. They make my head go round, and get the better of me. Oh, Johnny! Isn't it enough that your dear mother has provided you with that sweet sister?" indicating Moloch; "isn't it enough that you were seven boys before without a ray of gal, and that your dear mother went through what she *did* go through, on purpose that you might all of you have a little sister, but must you so behave yourself as to make my head swim?"

Softening more and more, as his own tender feelings and those of his injured son were worked on, Mr. Tetterby concluded by embracing him, and immediately breaking away to catch one of the real delinquents. A reasonably good start occurring, he succeeded, after a short but smart run, and some rather severe cross-country work under and over the bedsteads, and in and out among the intricacies of the chairs, in capturing this infant, whom he condignly punished, and bore to bed. This example had a powerful, and apparently, mesmeric influence on him of the boots, who instantly fell into a deep sleep, though he had been, but a moment before, broad awake, and in the highest possible feather. Nor was it lost upon the two young architects, who retired to bed, in an adjoining closet, with great privacy and speed. The comrade of the Intercepted One also shrinking into his nest with similar discretion, Mr. Tetterby, when he paused for breath, found himself unexpectedly in a scene of peace.

"My little woman herself," said Mr. Tetterby, wiping his flushed face, "could hardly have done it better! I only wish my little woman had had it to do, I do indeed!"

Mr. Tetterby sought upon his screen for a passage appropriate to be impressed upon his children's minds on the occasion, and read the following.

"'It is an undoubted fact that all remarkable men have had remarkable mothers, and have respected them in after life as their best friends.' Think of your own remarkable mother, my boys," said Mr. Tetterby, "and know her value while she is still among you!"

He sat down again in his chair by the fire, and composed himself, cross-legged, over his newspaper.

"Let anybody, I don't care who it is, get out of bed again," said Tetterby, as a general proclamation, delivered in a very soft-hearted manner, "and astonishment will be the portion of that respected contemporary!"—which expression Mr. Tetterby selected from his screen. "Johnny, my child, take care of your only sister, Sally; for she's the brightest gem that ever sparkled on your early brow."

Johnny sat down on a little stool, and devotedly crushed himself beneath the weight of Moloch.

"Ah, what a gift that baby is to you, Johnny!"said his father, "and how thankful you ought to be! 'It is not generally known, Johnny,'" he was now referring to the screen again, "'but it is a fact ascertained, by accurate calculations, that the following immense percentage of babies never attain to two years old; that is to say—'"

"Oh, don't, father, please!" cried Johnny. "I can't bear it, when I think of Sally."

Mr. Tetterby desisting, Johnny, with a profound sense of his trust, wiped his eyes, and hushed his sister.

"Your brother 'Dolphus," said his father, poking the fire, "is late to-night, Johnny, and will come home like a lump of ice. What's got your precious mother?"

"Here's mother, and 'Dolphus too, father!" exclaimed Johnny, "I think."

"You're right!" returned his father, listening. "Yes, that's the footstep of my little woman."

The process of induction, by which Mr. Tetterby had come to the conclusion that his wife was a little woman, was his own secret. She would have made two editions of himself, very easily. Considered as an individual, she was rather remarkable for being robust and portly; but considered with reference to her husband, her dimensions became magnificent. Nor did they assume a less imposing proportion, when studied with reference to the size of her seven sons, who were but diminutive. In the case of Sally, however, Mrs. Tetterby had asserted herself, at last; as nobody knew better than the victim Johnny, who weighed and measured that exacting idol every hour in the day.

Mrs. Tetterby, who had been marketing, and carried a basket, threw back her bonnet and shawl, and sitting down, fatigued, commanded Johnny to bring his sweet charge to her straightway, for a kiss. Johnny having complied, and gone back to his stool, and again crushed himself, Master Adolphus Tetterby, who had by this time unwound his torso out of a prismatic comforter, apparently interminable, requested the same favour. Johnny having again complied, and again gone back to his stool, and again crushed himself, Mr. Tetterby, struck by a sudden thought, preferred the same claim on his own parental part. The satisfaction of this third desire completely exhausted the sacrifice, who had hardly breath enough left to get back to his stool, crush himself again, and pant at his relations.

"Whatever you do, Johnny," said Mrs. Tetterby, shaking her head, "take care of her, or never look your mother in the face again."

"Nor your brother," said Adolphus.

"Nor your father, Johnny," added Mr. Tetterby.

Johnny, much affected by this conditional renunciation of him, looked down at Moloch's eyes to see that they were all right, so far, and skilfully patted her back (which was uppermost), and rocked her with his foot.

"Are you wet, 'Dolphus, my boy?" said his father. "Come and take my chair, and dry yourself."

"No, father, thank'ee," said Adolphus, smoothing himself down with his hands. "I an't very wet, I don't think. Does my face shine much, father?"

"Well, it *does* look waxy, my boy," returned Mr. Tetterby.

"It's the weather, father," said Adolphus, polishing his cheeks on the worn sleeve of his jacket. "What with rain, and sleet, and wind, and snow, and fog, my face gets quite brought out into a rash sometimes. And shines, it does—oh, don't it, though!"

Master Adolphus was also in the newspaper line of life, being employed, by a more thriving firm than his father and Co., to vend newspapers at a railway station, where his chubby little person, like a shabbily-disguised Cupid, and his shrill little voice (he was not much more than ten years old), were as well known as the hoarse panting of the locomotives, running in and out. His juvenility might have been at some loss for a harmless outlet, in this early application to traffic, but for a fortunate discovery he made of a means of entertaining himself, and of dividing the long day into stages of interest, without neglecting business. This ingenious invention, remarkable, like many great discoveries, for its simplicity, consisted in varying the first vowel in the word "paper," and substituting, in its stead, at different periods of the day, all the other vowels in grammatical succession. Thus, before daylight in the winter-time, he went to and fro, in his little oil-skin cap and cape, and his big comforter, piercing the heavy air with his cry of "Morn-ing Pa-per!" which, about an hour before noon, changed to "Morn-ing Pepper!" which, at about two, changed to "Morn-ing Pip-per!" which in a couple of hours changed to "Morn-ing Pop-per!" and so declined with the sun into "Eve-ning Pup-per!" to the great relief and comfort of this young gentleman's spirits.

Mrs. Tetterby, his lady-mother, who had been sitting with her bonnet and shawl thrown back, as aforesaid, thoughtfully turning her wedding-ring round and round upon her finger, now rose, and divesting herself of her out-of-door attire, began to lay the cloth for supper.

"Ah, dear me, dear me, dear me!" said Mrs. Tetterby. "That's the way the world goes!"

"Which is the way the world goes, my dear?" asked Mr. Tetterby, looking round.

"Oh, nothing," said Mrs. Tetterby.

Mr. Tetterby elevated his eyebrows, folded his newspaper afresh, and carried his eyes up it, and down it, and across it, but was wandering in his attention, and not reading it.

Mrs. Tetterby, at the same time, laid the cloth, but rather as if she were punishing the table than preparing the family supper; hitting it unnecessarily hard with the knives and forks, slapping it with the plates, dinting it with the salt-cellar, and coming heavily down upon it with the loaf.

"Ah, dear me, dear me, dear me!" said Mrs. Tetterby. "That's the way the world goes!"

"My duck," returned her husband, looking round again, "you said that before. Which is the way the world goes?"

"Oh, nothing!" said Mrs. Tetterby.

"Sophia!" remonstrated her husband, "you said *that* before, too."

"Well, I'll say it again if you like,"returned Mrs. Tetterby. "Oh nothing—there! And again if you like, oh nothing—there! And again if you like, oh nothing—now then!"

Mr. Tetterby brought his eye to bear upon the partner of his bosom, and said, in mild astonishment:

"My little woman, what has put you out?"

"I'm sure *I* don't know," she retorted. "Don't ask me. Who said I was put out at all? *I* never did."

Mr. Tetterby gave up the perusal of his newspaper as a bad job, and, taking a slow walk across the room, with his hands behind him, and his shoulders raised —his gait according perfectly with the resignation of his manner—addressed himself to his two eldest offspring.

"Your supper will be ready in a minute,'Dolphus," said Mr. Tetterby. "Your mother has been out in the wet, to the cook's shop, to buy it. It was very good of your mother so to do. *You* shall get some supper too, very soon, Johnny. Your mother's pleased with you, my man, for being so attentive to your precious sister."

Mrs. Tetterby, without any remark, but with a decided subsidence of her animosity towards the table, finished her preparations, and took, from her ample basket, a substantial slab of hot pease pudding wrapped in paper, and a basin covered with a saucer, which, on being uncovered, sent forth an odour so agreeable, that the three pair of eyes in the two beds opened wide and fixed themselves upon the banquet. Mr. Tetterby, without regarding this tacit invitation to be seated, stood repeating slowly, "Yes, yes, your supper will be ready in a minute, 'Dolphus—your mother went out in the wet, to the cook's shop, to buy it. It was very good of your mother so to do"—until Mrs. Tetterby, who had been exhibiting sundry tokens of contrition behind him, caught him round the neck, and wept.

"Oh, Dolphus!" said Mrs. Tetterby, "how could I go and behave so?"

This reconciliation affected Adolphus the younger and Johnny to that degree, that they both, as with one accord, raised a dismal cry, which had the effect of immediately shutting up the round eyes in the beds, and utterly routing the two remaining little Tetterbys, just then stealing in from the adjoining closet to see what was going on in the eating way.

"I am sure, 'Dolphus," sobbed Mrs. Tetterby,"coming home, I had no more idea than a child unborn—"

Mr. Tetterby seemed to dislike this figure of speech, and observed, "Say than the baby, my dear."

"—Had no more idea than the baby," said Mrs. Tetterby.—"Johnny, don't look at me, but look at her, or she'll fall out of your lap and be killed, and then you'll die in agonies of a broken heart, and serve you right.—No more idea I hadn't than that darling, of being cross when I came home; but somehow, 'Dolphus—" Mrs. Tetterby paused, and again turned her wedding-ring round and round upon her finger.

"I see!" said Mr. Tetterby. "I understand! My little woman was put out. Hard times, and hard weather, and hard work, make it trying now and then. I see, bless your soul! No wonder! Dolf, my man," continued Mr. Tetterby, exploring the basin with a fork, "here's your mother been and bought, at the cook's shop, besides pease pudding, a whole knuckle of a lovely roast leg of pork, with lots of crackling left upon it, and with seasoning gravy and mustard quite unlimited. Hand in your plate, my boy, and begin while it's simmering."

Master Adolphus, needing no second summons, received his portion with eyes rendered moist by appetite, and withdrawing to his particular stool, fell upon his supper tooth and nail. Johnny was not forgotten, but received his rations on bread, lest he should, in a flush of gravy, trickle any on the baby. He was required, for similar reasons, to keep his pudding, when not on active service, in his pocket.

There might have been more pork on the knucklebone,—which knucklebone the carver at the cook's shop had assuredly not forgotten in carving for previous customers—but there was no stint of seasoning, and that is an accessory dreamily suggesting pork, and pleasantly cheating the sense of taste. The pease pudding, too, the gravy and mustard, like the Eastern rose in respect of the nightingale, if they were not absolutely pork, had lived near it; so, upon the whole, there was the flavour of a middle-sized pig. It was irresistible to the Tetterbys in bed, who, though professing to slumber peacefully, crawled out when unseen by their parents, and silently appealed to their brothers for any gastronomic token of fraternal affection. They, not hard of heart, presenting scraps in return, it resulted that a party of light skirmishers in nightgowns were careering about the parlour all through supper, which harassed Mr. Tetterby exceedingly, and once or twice imposed upon him the necessity of a charge, before which these guerilla troops retired in all directions and in great confusion.

Mrs. Tetterby did not enjoy her supper. There seemed to be something on Mrs. Tetterby's mind. At one time she laughed without reason, and at another time she cried without reason, and at last she laughed and cried together in a manner so very unreasonable that her husband was confounded.

"My little woman," said Mr. Tetterby, "if the world goes that way, it appears to go the wrong way, and to choke you."

"Give me a drop of water," said Mrs. Tetterby, struggling with herself, "and don't speak to me for the present, or take any notice of me. Don't do it!"

Mr. Tetterby having administered the water, turned suddenly on the unlucky Johnny (who was full of sympathy), and demanded why he was wallowing there, in gluttony and idleness, instead of coming forward with the baby, that the sight of her might revive his mother. Johnny immediately approached, borne down by its weight; but Mrs. Tetterby holding out her hand to signify that she was not in a condition to bear that trying appeal to her feelings, he was interdicted from advancing another inch, on pain of perpetual hatred from all his dearest connections; and accordingly retired to his stool again, and crushed himself as before.

After a pause, Mrs. Tetterby said she was better now, and began to laugh.

"My little woman," said her husband, dubiously, "are you quite sure you're better? Or are you, Sophia, about to break out in a fresh direction?"

"No, 'Dolphus, no," replied his wife. "I'm quite myself." With that, settling her hair, and pressing the palms of her hands upon her eyes, she laughed again.

"What a wicked fool I was, to think so for a moment!" said Mrs. Tetterby. "Come nearer, 'Dolphus, and let me ease my mind, and tell you what I mean. Let me tell you all about it."

Mr. Tetterby bringing his chair closer, Mrs. Tetterby laughed again, gave him a hug, and wiped her eyes.

"You know, Dolphus, my dear," said Mrs. Tetterby, "that when I was single, I might have given myself away in several directions. At one time, four after me at once; two of them were sons of Mars."

"We're all sons of Ma's, my dear," said Mr. Tetterby, "jointly with Pa's."

"I don't mean that," replied his wife, "I mean soldiers—serjeants."

"Oh!" said Mr. Tetterby.

"Well, 'Dolphus, I'm sure I never think of such things now, to regret them; and I'm sure I've got as good a husband, and would do as much to prove that I was fond of him, as—"

"As any little woman in the world," said Mr. Tetterby. "Very good. *Very* good."

If Mr. Tetterby had been ten feet high, he could not have expressed a gentler consideration for Mrs. Tetterby's fairy-like stature; and if Mrs. Tetterby had been two feet high, she could not have felt it more appropriately her due.

"But you see, 'Dolphus," said Mrs. Tetterby, "this being Christmas-time, when all people who can, make holiday, and when all people who have got money, like to spend some, I did, somehow, get a little out of sorts when I was in the streets just now. There were so many things to be sold—such delicious things to eat, such fine things to look at, such delightful things to have—and there was so much calculating and calculating necessary, before I durst lay out a sixpence for the commonest thing; and the basket was so large, and wanted so much in it; and my stock of money was so small, and would go such a little way;—you hate me, don't you, 'Dolphus?"

"Not quite," said Mr. Tetterby, "as yet."

"Well! I'll tell you the whole truth," pursued his wife, penitently, "and then perhaps you will. I felt all this, so much, when I was trudging about in the cold, and when I saw a lot of other calculating faces and large baskets trudging about, too, that I began to think whether I mightn't have done better, and been happier, if—I—hadn't—" the wedding-ring went round again, and Mrs. Tetterby shook her downcast head as she turned it.

"I see," said her husband quietly; "if you hadn't married at all, or if you had married somebody else?"

"Yes," sobbed Mrs. Tetterby. "That's really what I thought. Do you hate me now, 'Dolphus?"

"Why no," said Mr. Tetterby. "I don't find that I do, as yet."

Mrs. Tetterby gave him a thankful kiss, and went on.

"I begin to hope you won't, now, 'Dolphus, though I'm afraid I haven't told you the worst. I can't think what came over me. I don't know whether I was ill, or mad, or what I was, but I couldn't call up anything that seemed to bind us to each other, or to reconcile me to my fortune. All the pleasures and enjoyments we had ever had—*they* seemed so poor and insignificant, I hated them. I could have trodden on them. And I could think of nothing else, except our being poor, and the number of mouths there were at home."

"Well, well, my dear," said Mr. Tetterby, shaking her hand encouragingly, "that's truth, after all. We *are* poor, and there *are* a number of mouths at home here."

"Ah! but, Dolf, Dolf!" cried his wife, laying her hands upon his neck, "my good, kind, patient fellow, when I had been at home a very little while—how different! Oh, Dolf, dear, how different it was! I felt as if there was a rush of recollection on me, all at once, that softened my hard heart, and filled it up till it was bursting. All our struggles for a livelihood, all our cares and wants since we have been married, all the times of sickness, all the hours of watching, we have ever had, by one another, or by the children, seemed to speak to me, and say that they had made us one, and that I never might have been, or could have been, or would have been, any other than the wife and mother I am. Then, the cheap enjoyments that I could have trodden on so cruelly, got to be so precious to me—Oh so priceless, and dear!—that I couldn't bear to think how much I had wronged them; and I said, and say again a hundred times, how could I ever behave so,'Dolphus, how could I ever have the heart to do it!"

The good woman, quite carried away by her honest tenderness and remorse, was weeping with all her heart, when she started up with a scream, and ran behind her husband. Her cry was so terrified, that the children started from their sleep and from their beds, and clung about her. Nor did her gaze belie her voice, as she pointed to a pale man in a black cloak who had come into the room.

"Look at that man! Look there! What does he want?"

"My dear," returned her husband, "I'll ask him if you'll let me go. What's the matter! How you shake!"

"I saw him in the street, when I was out just now. He looked at me, and stood near me. I am afraid of him."

"Afraid of him! Why?"

"I don't know why—I—stop! husband!" for he was going towards the stranger.

She had one hand pressed upon her forehead, and one upon her breast; and there was a peculiar fluttering all over her, and a hurried unsteady motion of her eyes, as if she had lost something.

"Are you ill, my dear?"

"What is it that is going from me again?" she muttered, in a low voice. "What *is* this that is going away?"

Then she abruptly answered: "Ill? No, I am quite well," and stood looking vacantly at the floor.

Her husband, who had not been altogether free from the infection of her fear at first, and whom the present strangeness of her manner did not tend to reassure, addressed himself to the pale visitor in the black cloak, who stood still, and whose eyes were bent upon the ground.

"What may be your pleasure, sir," he asked,"with us?"

"I fear that my coming in unperceived," returned the visitor, "has alarmed you; but you were talking and did not hear me."

"My little woman says—perhaps you heard her say it," returned Mr. Tetterby, "that it's not the first time you have alarmed her to-night."

"I am sorry for it. I remember to have observed her, for a few moments only, in the street. I had no intention of frightening her."

As he raised his eyes in speaking, she raised hers. It was extraordinary to see what dread she had of him, and with what dread he observed it—and yet how narrowly and closely.

"My name," he said, "is Redlaw. I come from the old college hard by. A young gentleman who is a student there, lodges in your house, does he not?"

"Mr. Denham?" said Tetterby.

"Yes."

It was a natural action, and so slight as to be hardly noticeable; but the little man, before speaking again, passed his hand across his forehead, and looked quickly round the room, as though he were sensible of some change in its atmosphere. The Chemist, instantly transferring to him the look of dread he had directed towards the wife, stepped back, and his face turned paler.

"The gentleman's room," said Tetterby, "is upstairs, sir. There's a more convenient private entrance; but as you have come in here, it will save your going out into the cold, if you'll take this little staircase," showing one communicating directly with the parlour, "and go up to him that way, if you wish to see him."

"Yes, I wish to see him," said the Chemist. "Can you spare a light?"

The watchfulness of his haggard look, and the inexplicable distrust that darkened it, seemed to trouble Mr. Tetterby. He paused; and looking fixedly at him in return, stood for a minute or so, like a man stupefied, or fascinated.

At length he said, "I'll light you, sir, if you'll follow me."

"No," replied the Chemist, "I don't wish to be attended, or announced to him. He does not expect me. I would rather go alone. Please to give me the light, if you can spare it, and I'll find the way."

In the quickness of his expression of this desire, and in taking the candle from the newsman, he touched him on the breast. Withdrawing his hand hastily, almost as though he had wounded him by accident (for he did not know in what part of himself his new power resided, or how it was communicated, or how the manner of its reception varied in different persons), he turned and ascended the stair.

But when he reached the top, he stopped and looked down. The wife was standing in the same place, twisting her ring round and round upon her finger. The husband, with his head bent forward on his breast, was musing heavily and sullenly. The children, still clustering about the mother, gazed timidly after the visitor, and nestled together when they saw him looking down.

"Come!" said the father, roughly. "There's enough of this. Get to bed here!"

"The place is inconvenient and small enough," the mother added, "without you. Get to bed!"

The whole brood, scared and sad, crept away; little Johnny and the baby lagging last. The mother, glancing contemptuously round the sordid room, and tossing from her the fragments of their meal, stopped on the threshold of her task of clearing the table, and sat down, pondering idly and dejectedly. The father betook himself to the chimney-corner, and impatiently raking the small fire together, bent over it as if he would monopolise it all. They did not interchange a word.

The Chemist, paler than before, stole upward like a thief; looking back upon the change below, and dreading equally to go on or return.

"What have I done!" he said, confusedly. "What am I going to do!"

"To be the benefactor of mankind," he thought he heard a voice reply.

He looked round, but there was nothing there; and a passage now shutting out the little parlour from his view, he went on, directing his eyes before him at the way he went.

"It is only since last night," he muttered gloomily, "that I have remained shut up, and yet all things are strange to me. I am strange to myself. I am here, as in a dream. What interest have I in this place, or in any place that I can bring to my remembrance? My mind is going blind!"

There was a door before him, and he knocked at it. Being invited, by a voice within, to enter, he complied.

"Is that my kind nurse?" said the voice. "But I need not ask her. There is no one else to come here."

It spoke cheerfully, though in a languid tone, and attracted his attention to a young man lying on a couch, drawn before the chimney-piece, with the back towards the door. A meagre scanty stove, pinched and hollowed like a sick man's cheeks, and bricked into the centre of a hearth that it could scarcely warm, contained the fire, to which his face was turned. Being so near the windy house-top, it wasted quickly, and with a busy sound, and the burning ashes dropped down fast.

"They chink when they shoot out here," said the student, smiling, "so, according to the gossips, they are not coffins, but purses. I shall be well and rich yet, some day, if it please God, and shall live perhaps to love a daughter Milly, in remembrance of the kindest nature and the gentlest heart in the world."

He put up his hand as if expecting her to take it, but, being weakened, he lay still, with his face resting on his other hand, and did not turn round.

The Chemist glanced about the room;—at the student's books and papers, piled upon a table in a corner, where they, and his extinguished reading-lamp, now prohibited and put away, told of the attentive hours that had gone before this illness, and perhaps caused it;—at such signs of his old health and freedom, as the out-of-door attire that hung idle on the wall;—at those remembrances of other and less solitary scenes, the little miniatures upon the chimney-piece, and the drawing of home;—at that token of his emulation, perhaps, in some sort, of his personal attachment too, the framed engraving of himself, the looker-on. The time had been, only yesterday, when not one of these objects, in its remotest association of interest with the living figure before him, would have been lost on Redlaw. Now, they were but objects; or, if any gleam of such connexion shot upon him, it perplexed, and not enlightened him, as he stood looking round with a dull wonder.

The student, recalling the thin hand which had remained so long untouched, raised himself on the couch, and turned his head.

"Mr. Redlaw!" he exclaimed, and started up.

Redlaw put out his arm.

"Don't come nearer to me. I will sit here. Remain you, where you are!"

He sat down on a chair near the door, and having glanced at the young man standing leaning with his hand upon the couch, spoke with his eyes averted towards the ground.

"I heard, by an accident, by what accident is no matter, that one of my class was ill and solitary. I received no other description of him, than that he lived in this street. Beginning my inquiries at the first house in it, I have found him."

"I have been ill, sir," returned the student, not merely with a modest hesitation, but with a kind of awe of him,"but am greatly better. An attack of fever—of the brain, I believe—has weakened me, but I am much better. I cannot say I have been solitary, in my illness, or I should forget the ministering hand that has been near me."

"You are speaking of the keeper's wife,"said Redlaw.

"Yes." The student bent his head, as if he rendered her some silent homage.

The Chemist, in whom there was a cold, monotonous apathy, which rendered him more like a marble image on the tomb of the man who had started from his dinner yesterday at the first mention of this student's case, than the breathing man himself, glanced again at the student leaning with his hand upon the couch, and looked upon the ground, and in the air, as if for light for his blinded mind.

"I remembered your name," he said, "when it was mentioned to me down stairs, just now; and I recollect your face. We have held but very little personal communication together?"

"Very little."

"You have retired and withdrawn from me, more than any of the rest, I think?"

The student signified assent.

"And why?" said the Chemist; not with the least expression of interest, but with a moody, wayward kind of curiosity. "Why? How comes it that you have sought to keep especially from me, the knowledge of your remaining here, at this season, when all the rest have dispersed, and of your being ill? I want to know why this is?"

The young man, who had heard him with increasing agitation, raised his downcast eyes to his face, and clasping his hands together, cried with sudden earnestness and with trembling lips:

"Mr. Redlaw! You have discovered me. You know my secret!"

"Secret?" said the Chemist, harshly. "I know?"

"Yes! Your manner, so different from the interest and sympathy which endear you to so many hearts, your altered voice, the constraint there is in everything you say, and in your looks," replied the student, "warn me that you know me. That you would conceal it, even now, is but a proof to me (God knows I need none!) of your natural kindness and of the bar there is between us."

A vacant and contemptuous laugh, was all his answer.

"But, Mr. Redlaw," said the student, "as a just man, and a good man, think how innocent I am, except in name and descent, of participation in any wrong inflicted on you or in any sorrow you have borne."

"Sorrow!" said Redlaw, laughing. "Wrong! What are those to me?"

"For Heaven's sake," entreated the shrinking student, "do not let the mere interchange of a few words with me change you like this, sir! Let me pass again from your knowledge and notice. Let me occupy my old reserved and distant place among those whom you instruct. Know me only by the name I have assumed, and not by that of Longford—"

"Longford!" exclaimed the other.

He clasped his head with both his hands, and for a moment turned upon the young man his own intelligent and thoughtful face. But the light passed from it, like the sun-beam of an instant, and it clouded as before.

"The name my mother bears, sir," faltered the young man, "the name she took, when she might, perhaps, have taken one more honoured. Mr. Redlaw,"hesitating, "I believe I know that history. Where my information halts, my guesses at what is wanting may supply something not remote from the truth. I am the child of a marriage that has not proved itself a well-assorted or a happy one. From infancy, I have heard you spoken of with honour and respect—with something that was almost reverence. I have heard of such devotion, of such fortitude and tenderness, of such rising up against the obstacles which press men down, that my fancy, since I learnt my little lesson from my mother, has shed a lustre on your name. At last, a poor student myself, from whom could I learn but you?"

Redlaw, unmoved, unchanged, and looking at him with a staring frown, answered by no word or sign.

"I cannot say," pursued the other, "I should try in vain to say, how much it has impressed me, and affected me, to find the gracious traces of the past, in that certain power of winning gratitude and confidence which is associated among us students (among the humblest of us, most) with Mr. Redlaw's generous name. Our ages and positions are so different, sir, and I am so accustomed to regard you from a distance, that I wonder at my own presumption when I touch, however lightly, on that theme. But to one who—I may say, who felt no common interest in my mother once—it may be something to hear, now that all is past, with what indescribable feelings of affection I have, in my obscurity, regarded him; with what pain and reluctance I have kept aloof from his encouragement, when a word of it would have made me rich; yet how I have felt it fit that I should hold my course, content to know him, and to be unknown. Mr. Redlaw,"said the student, faintly, "what I would have said, I have said ill, for my strength is strange to me as yet; but for anything unworthy in this fraud of mine, forgive me, and for all the rest forget me!"

The staring frown remained on Redlaw's face, and yielded to no other expression until the student, with these words, advanced towards him, as if to touch his hand, when he drew back and cried to him:

"Don't come nearer to me!"

The young man stopped, shocked by the eagerness of his recoil, and by the sternness of his repulsion; and he passed his hand, thoughtfully, across his forehead.

"The past is past," said the Chemist. "It dies like the brutes. Who talks to me of its traces in my life? He raves or lies! What have I to do with your distempered dreams? If you want money, here it is. I came to offer it; and that is all I came for. There can be nothing else that brings me here," he muttered, holding his head again, with both his hands. "There *can* be nothing else, and yet—"

He had tossed his purse upon the table. As he fell into this dim cogitation with himself, the student took it up, and held it out to him.

"Take it back, sir," he said proudly, though not angrily. "I wish you could take from me, with it, the remembrance of your words and offer."

"You do?" he retorted, with a wild light in his eyes. "You do?"

"I do!"

The Chemist went close to him, for the first time, and took the purse, and turned him by the arm, and looked him in the face.

"There is sorrow and trouble in sickness, is there not?" he demanded, with a laugh.

The wondering student answered, "Yes."

"In its unrest, in its anxiety, in its suspense, in all its train of physical and mental miseries?" said the Chemist, with a wild unearthly exultation. "All best forgotten, are they not?"

The student did not answer, but again passed his hand, confusedly, across his forehead. Redlaw still held him by the sleeve, when Milly's voice was heard outside.

"I can see very well now," she said, "thank you, Dolf. Don't cry, dear. Father and mother will be comfortable again, to-morrow, and home will be comfortable too. A gentleman with him, is there!"

Redlaw released his hold, as he listened.

"I have feared, from the first moment," he murmured to himself, "to meet her. There is a steady quality of goodness in her, that I dread to influence. I may be the murderer of what is tenderest and best within her bosom."

She was knocking at the door.

"Shall I dismiss it as an idle foreboding, or still avoid her?" he muttered, looking uneasily around.

She was knocking at the door again.

"Of all the visitors who could come here," he said, in a hoarse alarmed voice, turning to his companion, "this is the one I should desire most to avoid. Hide me!"

The student opened a frail door in the wall, communicating where the garret-roof began to slope towards the floor, with a small inner room. Redlaw passed in hastily, and shut it after him.

The student then resumed his place upon the couch, and called to her to enter.

"Dear Mr. Edmund," said Milly, looking round, "they told me there was a gentleman here."

"There is no one here but I."

"There has been some one?"

"Yes, yes, there has been some one."

She put her little basket on the table, and went up to the back of the couch, as if to take the extended hand—but it was not there. A little surprised, in her quiet way, she leaned over to look at his face, and gently touched him on the brow.

"Are you quite as well to-night? Your head is not so cool as in the afternoon."

"Tut!" said the student, petulantly, "very little ails me."

A little more surprise, but no reproach, was expressed in her face, as she withdrew to the other side of the table, and took a small packet of needlework from her basket. But she laid it down again, on second thoughts, and going noiselessly about the room, set everything exactly in its place, and in the neatest order; even to the cushions on the couch, which she touched with so light a hand, that he hardly seemed to know it, as he lay looking at the fire. When all this was done, and she had swept the hearth, she sat down, in her modest little bonnet, to her work, and was quietly busy on it directly.

"It's the new muslin curtain for the window, Mr. Edmund," said Milly, stitching away as she talked. "It will look very clean and nice, though it costs very little, and will save your eyes, too, from the light. My William says the room should not be too light just now, when you are recovering so well, or the glare might make you giddy."

He said nothing; but there was something so fretful and impatient in his change of position, that her quick fingers stopped, and she looked at him anxiously.

"The pillows are not comfortable," she said, laying down her work and rising. "I will soon put them right."

"They are very well," he answered. "Leave them alone, pray. You make so much of everything."

He raised his head to say this, and looked at her so thanklessly, that, after he had thrown himself down again, she stood timidly pausing. However, she resumed her seat, and her needle, without having directed even a murmuring look towards him, and was soon as busy as before.

"I have been thinking, Mr. Edmund, that *you* have been often thinking of late, when I have been sitting by, how true the saying is, that adversity is a good teacher. Health will be more precious to you, after this illness, than it has ever been. And years hence, when this time of year comes round, and you remember the days when you lay here sick, alone, that the knowledge of your illness might not afflict those who are dearest to you, your home will be doubly dear and doubly blest. Now, isn't that a good, true thing?"

She was too intent upon her work, and too earnest in what she said, and too composed and quiet altogether, to be on the watch for any look he might direct towards her in reply; so the shaft of his ungrateful glance fell harmless, and did not wound her.

"Ah!" said Milly, with her pretty head inclining thoughtfully on one side, as she looked down, following her busy fingers with her eyes. "Even on me—and I am very different from you, Mr. Edmund, for I have no learning, and don't know how to think properly—this view of such things has made a great impression, since you have been lying ill. When I have seen you so touched by the kindness and attention of the poor people down stairs, I have felt that you thought even that experience some repayment for the loss of health, and I have read in your face, as plain as if it was a book, that but for some trouble and sorrow we should never know half the good there is about us."

His getting up from the couch, interrupted her, or she was going on to say more.

"We needn't magnify the merit, Mrs. William," he rejoined slightingly. "The people down stairs will be paid in good time I dare say, for any little extra service they may have rendered me; and perhaps they anticipate no less. I am much obliged to you, too."

Her fingers stopped, and she looked at him.

"I can't be made to feel the more obliged by your exaggerating the case," he said. "I am sensible that you have been interested in me, and I say I am much obliged to you. What more would you have?"

Her work fell on her lap, as she still looked at him walking to and fro with an intolerant air, and stopping now and then.

"I say again, I am much obliged to you. Why weaken my sense of what is your due in obligation, by preferring enormous claims upon me? Trouble, sorrow, affliction, adversity! One might suppose I had been dying a score of deaths here!"

"Do you believe, Mr. Edmund," she asked, rising and going nearer to him, "that I spoke of the poor people of the house, with any reference to myself? To me?"laying her hand upon her bosom with a simple and innocent smile of astonishment.

"Oh! I think nothing about it, my good creature," he returned. "I have had an indisposition, which your solicitude—observe! I say solicitude—makes a great deal more of, than it merits; and it's over, and we can't perpetuate it."

He coldly took a book, and sat down at the table.

She watched him for a little while, until her smile was quite gone, and then, returning to where her basket was, said gently:

"Mr. Edmund, would you rather be alone?"

"There is no reason why I should detain you here,"he replied.

"Except—" said Milly, hesitating, and showing her work.

"Oh! the curtain," he answered, with a supercilious laugh. "That's not worth staying for."

She made up the little packet again, and put it in her basket. Then, standing before him with such an air of patient entreaty that he could not choose but look at her, she said:

"If you should want me, I will come back willingly. When you did want me, I was quite happy to come; there was no merit in it. I think you must be afraid, that, now you are getting well, I may be troublesome to you; but I should not have been, indeed. I should have come no longer than your weakness and confinement lasted. You owe me nothing; but it is right that you should deal as justly by me as if I was a lady—even the very lady that you love; and if you suspect me of meanly making much of the little I have tried to do to comfort your sick room, you do yourself more wrong than ever you can do me. That is why I am sorry. That is why I am very sorry."

If she had been as passionate as she was quiet, as indignant as she was calm, as angry in her look as she was gentle, as loud of tone as she was low and clear, she might have left no sense of her departure in the room, compared with that which fell upon the lonely student when she went away.

He was gazing drearily upon the place where she had been, when Redlaw came out of his concealment, and came to the door.

"When sickness lays its hand on you again," he said, looking fiercely back at him, "—may it be soon!—Die here! Rot here!"

"What have you done?" returned the other, catching at his cloak. "What change have you wrought in me? What curse have you brought upon me? Give me back *my*self!"

"Give me back myself!" exclaimed Redlaw like a madman. "I am infected! I am infectious! I am charged with poison for my own mind, and the minds of all mankind. Where I felt interest, compassion, sympathy, I am turning into stone. Selfishness and ingratitude spring up in my blighting footsteps. I am only so much less base than the wretches whom I make so, that in the moment of their transformation I can hate them."

As he spoke—the young man still holding to his cloak—he cast him off, and struck him: then, wildly hurried out into the night air where the wind was blowing, the snow falling, the cloud-drift sweeping on, the moon dimly shining; and where, blowing in the wind, falling with the snow, drifting with the clouds, shining in the moonlight, and heavily looming in the darkness, were the Phantom's words, "The gift that I have given, you shall give again, go where you will!"

Whither he went, he neither knew nor cared, so that he avoided company. The change he felt within him made the busy streets a desert, and himself a desert, and the multitude around him, in their manifold endurances and ways of life, a mighty waste of sand, which the winds tossed into unintelligible heaps and made a ruinous confusion of. Those traces in his breast which the Phantom had told him would "die out soon,"were not, as yet, so far upon their way to death, but that he understood enough of what he was, and what he made of others, to desire to be alone.

This put it in his mind—he suddenly bethought himself, as he was going along, of the boy who had rushed into his room. And then he recollected, that of those with whom he had communicated since the Phantom's disappearance, that boy alone had shown no sign of being changed.

Monstrous and odious as the wild thing was to him, he determined to seek it out, and prove if this were really so; and also to seek it with another intention, which came into his thoughts at the same time.

So, resolving with some difficulty where he was, he directed his steps back to the old college, and to that part of it where the general porch was, and where, alone, the pavement was worn by the tread of the students' feet.

The keeper's house stood just within the iron gates, forming a part of the chief quadrangle. There was a little cloister outside, and from that sheltered place he knew he could look in at the window of their ordinary room, and see who was within. The iron gates were shut, but his hand was familiar with the fastening, and drawing it back by thrusting in his wrist between the bars, he passed through softly, shut it again, and crept up to the window, crumbling the thin crust of snow with his feet.

The fire, to which he had directed the boy last night, shining brightly through the glass, made an illuminated place upon the ground. Instinctively avoiding this, and going round it, he looked in at the window. At first, he thought that there was no one there, and that the blaze was reddening only the old beams in the ceiling and the dark walls; but peering in more narrowly, he saw the object of his search coiled asleep before it on the floor. He passed quickly to the door, opened it, and went in.

The creature lay in such a fiery heat, that, as the Chemist stooped to rouse him, it scorched his head. So soon as he was touched, the boy, not half awake, clutching his rags together with the instinct of flight upon him, half rolled and half ran into a distant corner of the room, where, heaped upon the ground, he struck his foot out to defend himself.

"Get up!" said the Chemist. "You have not forgotten me?"

"You let me alone!" returned the boy. "This is the woman's house—not yours."

The Chemist's steady eye controlled him somewhat, or inspired him with enough submission to be raised upon his feet, and looked at.

"Who washed them, and put those bandages where they were bruised and cracked?" asked the Chemist, pointing to their altered state.

"The woman did."

"And is it she who has made you cleaner in the face, too?"

"Yes, the woman."

Redlaw asked these questions to attract his eyes towards himself, and with the same intent now held him by the chin, and threw his wild hair back, though he loathed to touch him. The boy watched his eyes keenly, as if he thought it needful to his own defence, not knowing what he might do next; and Redlaw could see well that no change came over him.

"Where are they?" he inquired.

"The woman's out."

"I know she is. Where is the old man with the white hair, and his son?"

"The woman's husband, d'ye mean?"inquired the boy.

"Ay. Where are those two?"

"Out. Something's the matter, somewhere. They were fetched out in a hurry, and told me to stop here."

"Come with me," said the Chemist, "and I'll give you money."

"Come where? and how much will you give?"

"I'll give you more shillings than you ever saw, and bring you back soon. Do you know your way to where you came from?"

"You let me go," returned the boy, suddenly twisting out of his grasp. "I'm not a going to take you there. Let me be, or I'll heave some fire at you!"

He was down before it, and ready, with his savage little hand, to pluck the burning coals out.

What the Chemist had felt, in observing the effect of his charmed influence stealing over those with whom he came in contact, was not nearly equal to the cold vague terror with which he saw this baby-monster put it at defiance. It chilled his blood to look on the immovable impenetrable thing, in the likeness of a child, with its sharp malignant face turned up to his, and its almost infant hand, ready at the bars.

"Listen, boy!" he said. "You shall take me where you please, so that you take me where the people are very miserable or very wicked. I want to do them good, and not to harm them. You shall have money, as I have told you, and I will bring you back. Get up! Come quickly!" He made a hasty step towards the door, afraid of her returning.

"Will you let me walk by myself, and never hold me, nor yet touch me?" said the boy, slowly withdrawing the hand with which he threatened, and beginning to get up.

"I will!"

"And let me go, before, behind, or anyways I like?"

"I will!"

"Give me some money first, then, and go."

The Chemist laid a few shillings, one by one, in his extended hand. To count them was beyond the boy's knowledge, but he said "one," every time, and avariciously looked at each as it was given, and at the donor. He had nowhere to put them, out of his hand, but in his mouth; and he put them there.

Redlaw then wrote with his pencil on a leaf of his pocket-book, that the boy was with him; and laying it on the table, signed to him to follow. Keeping his rags together, as usual, the boy complied, and went out with his bare head and naked feet into the winter night.

Preferring not to depart by the iron gate by which he had entered, where they were in danger of meeting her whom he so anxiously avoided, the Chemist led the way, through some of those passages among which the boy had lost himself, and by that portion of the building where he lived, to a small door of which he had the key. When they got into the street, he stopped to ask his guide—who instantly retreated from him—if he knew where they were.

The savage thing looked here and there, and at length, nodding his head, pointed in the direction he designed to take. Redlaw going on at once, he followed, something less suspiciously; shifting his money from his mouth into his hand, and back again into his mouth, and stealthily rubbing it bright upon his shreds of dress, as he went along.

Three times, in their progress, they were side by side. Three times they stopped, being side by side. Three times the Chemist glanced down at his face, and shuddered as it forced upon him one reflection.

The first occasion was when they were crossing an old churchyard, and Redlaw stopped among the graves, utterly at a loss how to connect them with any tender, softening, or consolatory thought.

The second was, when the breaking forth of the moon induced him to look up at the Heavens, where he saw her in her glory, surrounded by a host of stars he still knew by the names and histories which human science has appended to them; but where he saw nothing else he had been wont to see, felt nothing he had been wont to feel, in looking up there, on a bright night.

The third was when he stopped to listen to a plaintive strain of music, but could only hear a tune, made manifest to him by the dry mechanism of the instruments and his own ears, with no address to any mystery within him, without a whisper in it of the past, or of the future, powerless upon him as the sound of last year's running water, or the rushing of last year's wind.

At each of these three times, he saw with horror that, in spite of the vast intellectual distance between them, and their being unlike each other in all physical respects, the expression on the boy's face was the expression on his own.

They journeyed on for some time—now through such crowded places, that he often looked over his shoulder thinking he had lost his guide, but generally finding him within his shadow on his other side; now by ways so quiet, that he could have counted his short, quick, naked footsteps coming on behind—until they arrived at a ruinous collection of houses, and the boy touched him and stopped.

"In there!" he said, pointing out one house where there were shattered lights in the windows, and a dim lantern in the doorway, with "Lodgings for Travellers" painted on it.

Redlaw looked about him; from the houses to the waste piece of ground on which the houses stood, or rather did not altogether tumble down, unfenced, undrained, unlighted, and bordered by a sluggish ditch; from that, to the sloping line of arches, part of some neighbouring viaduct or bridge with which it was surrounded, and which lessened gradually towards them, until the last but one was a mere kennel for a dog, the last a plundered little heap of bricks; from that, to the child, close to him, cowering and trembling with the cold, and limping on one little foot, while he coiled the other round his leg to warm it, yet staring at all these things with that frightful likeness of expression so apparent in his face, that Redlaw started from him.

"In there!" said the boy, pointing out the house again. "I'll wait."

"Will they let me in?" asked Redlaw.

"Say you're a doctor," he answered with a nod. "There's plenty ill here."

Looking back on his way to the house-door, Redlaw saw him trail himself upon the dust and crawl within the shelter of the smallest arch, as if he were a rat. He had no pity for the thing, but he was afraid of it; and when it looked out of its den at him, he hurried to the house as a retreat.

"Sorrow, wrong, and trouble," said the Chemist, with a painful effort at some more distinct remembrance,"at least haunt this place darkly. He can do no harm, who brings forgetfulness of such things here!"

With these words, he pushed the yielding door, and went in.

There was a woman sitting on the stairs, either asleep or forlorn, whose head was bent down on her hands and knees. As it was not easy to pass without treading on her, and as she was perfectly regardless of his near approach, he stopped, and touched her on the shoulder. Looking up, she showed him quite a young face, but one whose bloom and promise were all swept away, as if the haggard winter should unnaturally kill the spring.

With little or no show of concern on his account, she moved nearer to the wall to leave him a wider passage.

"What are you?" said Redlaw, pausing, with his hand upon the broken stair-rail.

"What do you think I am?" she answered, showing him her face again.

He looked upon the ruined Temple of God, so lately made, so soon disfigured; and something, which was not compassion—for the springs in which a true compassion for such miseries has its rise, were dried up in his breast—but which was nearer to it, for the moment, than any feeling that had lately struggled into the darkening, but not yet wholly darkened, night of his mind—mingled a touch of softness with his next words.

"I am come here to give relief, if I can," he said. "Are you thinking of any wrong?"

She frowned at him, and then laughed; and then her laugh prolonged itself into a shivering sigh, as she dropped her head again, and hid her fingers in her hair.

"Are you thinking of a wrong?" he asked once more.

"I am thinking of my life," she said, with a mometary look at him.

He had a perception that she was one of many, and that he saw the type of thousands, when he saw her, drooping at his feet.

"What are your parents?" he demanded.

"I had a good home once. My father was a gardener, far away, in the country."

"Is he dead?"

"He's dead to me. All such things are dead to me. You a gentleman, and not know that!" She raised her eyes again, and laughed at him.

"Girl!" said Redlaw, sternly, "before this death, of all such things, was brought about, was there no wrong done to you? In spite of all that you can do, does no remembrance of wrong cleave to you? Are there not times upon times when it is misery to you?"

So little of what was womanly was left in her appearance, that now, when she burst into tears, he stood amazed. But he was more amazed, and much disquieted, to note that in her awakened recollection of this wrong, the first trace of her old humanity and frozen tenderness appeared to show itself.

He drew a little off, and in doing so, observed that her arms were black, her face cut, and her bosom bruised.

"What brutal hand has hurt you so?" he asked.

"My own. I did it myself!" she answered quickly.

"It is impossible."

"I'll swear I did! He didn't touch me. I did it to myself in a passion, and threw myself down here. He wasn't near me. He never laid a hand upon me!"

In the white determination of her face, confronting him with this untruth, he saw enough of the last perversion and distortion of good surviving in that miserable breast, to be stricken with remorse that he had ever come near her.

"Sorrow, wrong, and trouble!" he muttered, turning his fearful gaze away. "All that connects her with the state from which she has fallen, has those roots! In the name of God, let me go by!"

Afraid to look at her again, afraid to touch her, afraid to think of having sundered the last thread by which she held upon the mercy of Heaven, he gathered his cloak about him, and glided swiftly up the stairs.

Opposite to him, on the landing, was a door, which stood partly open, and which, as he ascended, a man with a candle in his hand, came forward from within to shut. But this man, on seeing him, drew back, with much emotion in his manner, and, as if by a sudden impulse, mentioned his name aloud.

In the surprise of such a recognition there, he stopped, endeavouring to recollect the wan and startled face. He had no time to consider it, for, to his yet greater amazement, old Philip came out of the room, and took him by the hand.

"Mr. Redlaw," said the old man, "this is like you, this is like you, sir! you have heard of it, and have come after us to render any help you can. Ah, too late, too late!"

Redlaw, with a bewildered look, submitted to be led into the room. A man lay there, on a truckle-bed, and William Swidger stood at the bedside.

"Too late!" murmured the old man, looking wistfully into the Chemist's face; and the tears stole down his cheeks.

"That's what I say, father," interposed his son in a low voice. "That's where it is, exactly. To keep as quiet as ever we can while he's a dozing, is the only thing to do. You're right, father!"

Redlaw paused at the bedside, and looked down on the figure that was stretched upon the mattress. It was that of a man, who should have been in the vigour of his life, but on whom it was not likely the sun would ever shine again. The vices of his forty or fifty years' career had so branded him, that, in comparison with their effects upon his face, the heavy hand of Time upon the old man's face who watched him had been merciful and beautifying.

"Who is this?" asked the Chemist, looking round.

"My son George, Mr. Redlaw," said the old man, wringing his hands. "My eldest son, George, who was more his mother's pride than all the rest!"

Redlaw's eyes wandered from the old man's grey head, as he laid it down upon the bed, to the person who had recognised him, and who had kept aloof, in the remotest corner of the room. He seemed to be about his own age; and although he knew no such hopeless decay and broken man as he appeared to be, there was something in the turn of his figure, as he stood with his back towards him, and now went out at the door, that made him pass his hand uneasily across his brow.

"William," he said in a gloomy whisper, "who is that man?"

"Why you see, sir," returned Mr. William,"that's what I say, myself. Why should a man ever go and gamble, and the like of that, and let himself down inch by inch till he can't let himself down any lower!"

"Has *he* done so?" asked Redlaw, glancing after him with the same uneasy action as before.

"Just exactly that, sir," returned William Swidger, "as I'm told. He knows a little about medicine, sir, it seems; and having been wayfaring towards London with my unhappy brother that you see here," Mr. William passed his coat-sleeve across his eyes, "and being lodging up stairs for the night—what I say, you see, is that strange companions come together here sometimes—he looked in to attend upon him, and came for us at his request. What a mournful spectacle, sir! But that's where it is. It's enough to kill my father!"

Redlaw looked up, at these words, and, recalling where he was and with whom, and the spell he carried with him—which his surprise had obscured—retired a little, hurriedly, debating with himself whether to shun the house that moment, or remain.

Yielding to a certain sullen doggedness, which it seemed to be a part of his condition to struggle with, he argued for remaining.

"Was it only yesterday," he said, "when I observed the memory of this old man to be a tissue of sorrow and trouble, and shall I be afraid, to-night, to shake it? Are such remembrances as I can drive away, so precious to this dying man that I need fear for *him*? No! I'll stay here."

But he stayed in fear and trembling none the less for these words; and, shrouded in his black cloak with his face turned from them, stood away from the bedside, listening to what they said, as if he felt himself a demon in the place.

"Father!" murmured the sick man, rallying a little from stupor.

"My boy! My son George!" said old Philip.

"You spoke, just now, of my being mother's favourite, long ago. It's a dreadful thing to think now, of long ago!"

"No, no, no;" returned the old man. "Think of it. Don't say it's dreadful. It's not dreadful to me, my son."

"It cuts you to the heart, father." For the old man's tears were falling on him.

"Yes, yes," said Philip, "so it does; but it does me good. It's a heavy sorrow to think of that time, but it does me good, George. Oh, think of it too, think of it too, and your heart will be softened more and more! Where's my son William? William, my boy, your mother loved him dearly to the last, and with her latest breath said, 'Tell him I forgave him, blessed him, and prayed for him.' Those were her words to me. I have never forgotten them, and I'm eighty-seven!"

"Father!" said the man upon the bed, "I am dying, I know. I am so far gone, that I can hardly speak, even of what my mind most runs on. Is there any hope for me beyond this bed?"

"There is hope," returned the old man, "for all who are softened and penitent. There is hope for all such. Oh!" he exclaimed, clasping his hands and looking up, "I was thankful, only yesterday, that I could remember this unhappy son when he was an innocent child. But what a comfort it is, now, to think that even God himself has that remembrance of him!"

Redlaw spread his hands upon his face, and shrank, like a murderer.

"Ah!" feebly moaned the man upon the bed. "The waste since then, the waste of life since then!"

"But he was a child once," said the old man. "He played with children. Before he lay down on his bed at night, and fell into his guiltless rest, he said his prayers at his poor mother's knee. I have seen him do it, many a time; and seen her lay his head upon her breast, and kiss him. Sorrowful as it was to her and me, to think of this, when he went so wrong, and when our hopes and plans for him were all broken, this gave him still a hold upon us, that nothing else could have given. Oh, Father, so much better than the fathers upon earth! Oh, Father, so much more afflicted by the errors of Thy children! take this wanderer back! Not as he is, but as he was then, let him cry to Thee, as he has so often seemed to cry to us!"

As the old man lifted up his trembling hands, the son, for whom he made the supplication, laid his sinking head against him for support and comfort, as if he were indeed the child of whom he spoke.

When did man ever tremble, as Redlaw trembled, in the silence that ensued! He knew it must come upon them, knew that it was coming fast.

"My time is very short, my breath is shorter,"said the sick man, supporting himself on one arm, and with the other groping in the air, "and I remember there is something on my mind concerning the man who was here just now, Father and William—wait!—is there really anything in black, out there?"

"Yes, yes, it is real," said his aged father.

"Is it a man?"

"What I say myself, George," interposed his brother, bending kindly over him. "It's Mr. Redlaw."

"I thought I had dreamed of him. Ask him to come here."

The Chemist, whiter than the dying man, appeared before him. Obedient to the motion of his hand, he sat upon the bed.

"It has been so ripped up, to-night, sir," said the sick man, laying his hand upon his heart, with a look in which the mute, imploring agony of his condition was concentrated, "by the sight of my poor old father, and the thought of all the trouble I have been the cause of, and all the wrong and sorrow lying at my door, that—"

Was it the extremity to which he had come, or was it the dawning of another change, that made him stop?

"—that what I *can* do right, with my mind running on so much, so fast, I'll try to do. There was another man here. Did you see him?"

Redlaw could not reply by any word; for when he saw that fatal sign he knew so well now, of the wandering hand upon the forehead, his voice died at his lips. But he made some indication of assent.

"He is penniless, hungry, and destitute. He is completely beaten down, and has no resource at all. Look after him! Lose no time! I know he has it in his mind to kill himself."

It was working. It was on his face. His face was changing, hardening, deepening in all its shades, and losing all its sorrow.

"Don't you remember? Don't you know him?" he pursued.

He shut his face out for a moment, with the hand that again wandered over his forehead, and then it lowered on Redlaw, reckless, ruffianly, and callous.

"Why, d-n you!" he said, scowling round,"what have you been doing to me here! I have lived bold, and I mean to die bold. To the Devil with you!"

And so lay down upon his bed, and put his arms up, over his head and ears, as resolute from that time to keep out all access, and to die in his indifference.

If Redlaw had been struck by lightning, it could not have struck him from the bedside with a more tremendous shock. But the old man, who had left the bed while his son was speaking to him, now returning, avoided it quickly likewise, and with abhorrence.

"Where's my boy William?" said the old man hurriedly. "William, come away from here. We'll go home."

"Home, father!" returned William. "Are you going to leave your own son?"

"Where's my own son?" replied the old man.

"Where? why, there!"

"That's no son of mine," said Philip, trembling with resentment. "No such wretch as that, has any claim on me. My children are pleasant to look at, and they wait upon me, and get my meat and drink ready, and are useful to me. I've a right to it! I'm eighty-seven!"

"You're old enough to be no older," muttered William, looking at him grudgingly, with his hands in his pockets. "I don't know what good you are, myself. We could have a deal more pleasure without you."

"*My* son, Mr. Redlaw!" said the old man. "*My* son, too! The boy talking to me of *my* son! Why, what has he ever done to give me any pleasure, I should like to know?"

"I don't know what you have ever done to give *me* any pleasure," said William, sulkily.

"Let me think," said the old man. "For how many Christmas times running, have I sat in my warm place, and never had to come out in the cold night air; and have made good cheer, without being disturbed by any such uncomfortable, wretched sight as him there? Is it twenty, William?"

"Nigher forty, it seems," he muttered. "Why, when I look at my father, sir, and come to think of it," addressing Redlaw, with an impatience and irritation that were quite new, "I'm whipped if I can see anything in him but a calendar of ever so many years of eating and drinking, and making himself comfortable, over and over again."

"I—I'm eighty-seven," said the old man, rambling on, childishly and weakly, "and I don't know as I ever was much put out by anything. I'm not going to begin now, because of what he calls my son. He's not my son. I've had a power of pleasant times. I recollect once—no I don't—no, it's broken off. It was something about a game of cricket and a friend of mine, but it's somehow broken off. I wonder who he was—I suppose I liked him? And I wonder what became of him—I suppose he died? But I don't know. And I don't care, neither; I don't care a bit."

In his drowsy chuckling, and the shaking of his head, he put his hands into his waistcoat pockets. In one of them he found a bit of holly (left there, probably last night), which he now took out, and looked at.

"Berries, eh?" said the old man. "Ah! It's a pity they're not good to eat. I recollect, when I was a little chap about as high as that, and out a walking with—let me see—who was I out a walking with?—no, I don't remember how that was. I don't remember as I ever walked with any one particular, or cared for any one, or any one for me. Berries, eh? There's good cheer when there's berries. Well; I ought to have my share of it, and to be waited on, and kept warm and comfortable; for I'm eighty-seven, and a poor old man. I'm eigh-ty-seven. Eigh-ty-seven!"

The drivelling, pitiable manner in which, as he repeated this, he nibbled at the leaves, and spat the morsels out; the cold, uninterested eye with which his youngest son (so changed) regarded him; the determined apathy with which his eldest son lay hardened in his sin; impressed themselves no more on Redlaw's observation,—for he broke his way from the spot to which his feet seemed to have been fixed, and ran out of the house.

His guide came crawling forth from his place of refuge, and was ready for him before he reached the arches.

"Back to the woman's?" he inquired.

"Back, quickly!" answered Redlaw. "Stop nowhere on the way!"

For a short distance the boy went on before; but their return was more like a flight than a walk, and it was as much as his bare feet could do, to keep pace with the Chemist's rapid strides. Shrinking from all who passed, shrouded in his cloak, and keeping it drawn closely about him, as though there were mortal contagion in any fluttering touch of his garments, he made no pause until they reached the door by which they had come out. He unlocked it with his key, went in, accompanied by the boy, and hastened through the dark passages to his own chamber.

The boy watched him as he made the door fast, and withdrew behind the table, when he looked round.

"Come!" he said. "Don't you touch me! You've not brought me here to take my money away."

Redlaw threw some more upon the ground. He flung his body on it immediately, as if to hide it from him, lest the sight of it should tempt him to reclaim it; and not until he saw him seated by his lamp, with his face hidden in his hands, began furtively to pick it up. When he had done so, he crept near the fire, and, sitting down in a great chair before it, took from his breast some broken scraps of food, and fell to munching, and to staring at the blaze, and now and then to glancing at his shillings, which he kept clenched up in a bunch, in one hand.

"And this," said Redlaw, gazing on him with increased repugnance and fear, "is the only one companion I have left on earth!"

How long it was before he was aroused from his contemplation of this creature, whom he dreaded so—whether half-an-hour, or half the night—he knew not. But the stillness of the room was broken by the boy (whom he had seen listening) starting up, and running towards the door.

"Here's the woman coming!" he exclaimed.

The Chemist stopped him on his way, at the moment when she knocked.

"Let me go to her, will you?" said the boy.

"Not now," returned the Chemist. "Stay here. Nobody must pass in or out of the room now. Who's that?"

"It's I, sir," cried Milly. "Pray, sir, let me in!"

"No! not for the world!" he said.

"Mr. Redlaw, Mr. Redlaw, pray, sir, let me in."

"What is the matter?" he said, holding the boy.

"The miserable man you saw, is worse, and nothing I can say will wake him from his terrible infatuation. William's father has turned childish in a moment,

William himself is changed. The shock has been too sudden for him; I cannot understand him; he is not like himself. Oh, Mr. Redlaw, pray advise me, help me!"

"No! No! No!" he answered.

"Mr. Redlaw! Dear sir! George has been muttering, in his doze, about the man you saw there, who, he fears, will kill himself."

"Better he should do it, than come near me!"

"He says, in his wandering, that you know him; that he was your friend once, long ago; that he is the ruined father of a student here—my mind misgives me, of the young gentleman who has been ill. What is to be done? How is he to be followed? How is he to be saved? Mr. Redlaw, pray, oh, pray, advise me! Help me!"

All this time he held the boy, who was half-mad to pass him, and let her in.

"Phantoms! Punishers of impious thoughts!"cried Redlaw, gazing round in anguish, "look upon me! From the darkness of my mind, let the glimmering of contrition that I know is there, shine up and show my misery! In the material world as I have long taught, nothing can be spared; no step or atom in the wondrous structure could be lost, without a blank being made in the great universe. I know, now, that it is the same with good and evil, happiness and sorrow, in the memories of men. Pity me! Relieve me!"

There was no response, but her "Help me, help me, let me in!" and the boy's struggling to get to her.

"Shadow of myself! Spirit of my darker hours!" cried Redlaw, in distraction, "come back, and haunt me day and night, but take this gift away! Or, if it must still rest with me, deprive me of the dreadful power of giving it to others. Undo what I have done. Leave me benighted, but restore the day to those whom I have cursed. As I have spared this woman from the first, and as I never will go forth again, but will die here, with no hand to tend me, save this creature's who is proof against me,—hear me!"

The only reply still was, the boy struggling to get to her, while he held him back; and the cry, increasing in its energy,"Help! let me in. He was your friend once, how shall he be followed, how shall he be saved? They are all changed, there is no one else to help me, pray, pray, let me in!"

CHAPTER III

The Gift Reversed

Night was still heavy in the sky. On open plains, from hill-tops, and from the decks of solitary ships at sea, a distant low-lying line, that promised by-and-by to change to light, was visible in the dim horizon; but its promise was remote and doubtful, and the moon was striving with the night-clouds busily.

The shadows upon Redlaw's mind succeeded thick and fast to one another, and obscured its light as the night-clouds hovered between the moon and earth, and kept the latter veiled in darkness. Fitful and uncertain as the shadows which the night-clouds cast, were their concealments from him, and imperfect revelations to him; and, like the night-clouds still, if the clear light broke forth for a moment, it was only that they might sweep over it, and make the darkness deeper than before.

Without, there was a profound and solemn hush upon the ancient pile of building, and its buttresses and angles made dark shapes of mystery upon the ground, which now seemed to retire into the smooth white snow and now seemed to come out of it, as the moon's path was more or less beset. Within, the Chemist's room was indistinct and murky, by the light of the expiring lamp; a ghostly silence had succeeded to the knocking and the voice outside; nothing was audible but, now and then, a low sound among the whitened ashes of the fire, as of its yielding up its last breath. Before it on the ground the boy lay fast asleep. In his chair, the Chemist sat, as he had sat there since the calling at his door had ceased—like a man turned to stone.

At such a time, the Christmas music he had heard before, began to play. He listened to it at first, as he had listened in the church-yard; but presently—it playing still, and being borne towards him on the night air, in a low, sweet, melancholy strain—he rose, and stood stretching his hands about him, as if there were some friend approaching within his reach, on whom his desolate touch might rest, yet do no harm. As he did this, his face became less fixed and wondering; a gentle trembling came upon him; and at last his eyes filled with tears, and he put his hands before them, and bowed down his head.

His memory of sorrow, wrong, and trouble, had not come back to him; he knew that it was not restored; he had no passing belief or hope that it was. But some dumb stir within him made him capable, again, of being moved by what was hidden, afar off, in the music. If it were only that it told him sorrowfully the value of what he had lost, he thanked Heaven for it with a fervent gratitude.

As the last chord died upon his ear, he raised his head to listen to its lingering vibration. Beyond the boy, so that his sleeping figure lay at its feet, the Phantom stood, immovable and silent, with its eyes upon him.

Ghastly it was, as it had ever been, but not so cruel and relentless in its aspect —or he thought or hoped so, as he looked upon it trembling. It was not alone, but in its shadowy hand it held another hand.

And whose was that? Was the form that stood beside it indeed Milly's, or but her shade and picture? The quiet head was bent a little, as her manner was, and her eyes were looking down, as if in pity, on the sleeping child. A radiant light fell on her face, but did not touch the Phantom; for, though close beside her, it was dark and colourless as ever.

"Spectre!" said the Chemist, newly troubled as he looked, "I have not been stubborn or presumptuous in respect of her. Oh, do not bring her here. Spare me that!"

"This is but a shadow," said the Phantom;"when the morning shines seek out the reality whose image I present before you."

"Is it my inexorable doom to do so?" cried the Chemist.

"It is," replied the Phantom.

"To destroy her peace, her goodness; to make her what I am myself, and what I have made of others!"

"I have said seek her out," returned the Phantom. "I have said no more."

"Oh, tell me," exclaimed Redlaw, catching at the hope which he fancied might lie hidden in the words. "Can I undo what I have done?"

"No," returned the Phantom.

"I do not ask for restoration to myself," said Redlaw. "What I abandoned, I abandoned of my own free will, and have justly lost. But for those to whom I have transferred the fatal gift; who never sought it; who unknowingly received a curse of which they had no warning, and which they had no power to shun; can I do nothing?"

"Nothing," said the Phantom.

"If I cannot, can any one?"

The Phantom, standing like a statue, kept its gaze upon him for a while; then turned its head suddenly, and looked upon the shadow at its side.

"Ah! Can she?" cried Redlaw, still looking upon the shade.

The Phantom released the hand it had retained till now, and softly raised its own with a gesture of dismissal. Upon that, her shadow, still preserving the same attitude, began to move or melt away.

"Stay," cried Redlaw with an earnestness to which he could not give enough expression. "For a moment! As an act of mercy! I know that some change fell upon me, when those sounds were in the air just now. Tell me, have I lost the power of harming her? May I go near her without dread? Oh, let her give me any sign of hope!"

The Phantom looked upon the shade as he did—not at him—and gave no answer.

"At least, say this—has she, henceforth, the consciousness of any power to set right what I have done?"

"She has not," the Phantom answered.

"Has she the power bestowed on her without the consciousness?"

The phantom answered: "Seek her out."

And her shadow slowly vanished.

They were face to face again, and looking on each other, as intently and awfully as at the time of the bestowal of the gift, across the boy who still lay on the ground between them, at the Phantom's feet.

"Terrible instructor," said the Chemist, sinking on his knee before it, in an attitude of supplication, "by whom I was renounced, but by whom I am revisited (in which, and in whose milder aspect, I would fain believe I have a gleam of hope), I will obey without inquiry, praying that the cry I have sent up in the anguish of my soul has been, or will be, heard, in behalf of those whom I have injured beyond human reparation. But there is one thing—"

"You speak to me of what is lying here," the phantom interposed, and pointed with its finger to the boy.

"I do," returned the Chemist. "You know what I would ask. Why has this child alone been proof against my influence, and why, why, have I detected in its thoughts a terrible companionship with mine?"

"This," said the Phantom, pointing to the boy, "is the last, completest illustration of a human creature, utterly bereft of such remembrances as you have yielded up. No softening memory of sorrow, wrong, or trouble enters here, because this wretched mortal from his birth has been abandoned to a worse condition than the beasts, and has, within his knowledge, no one contrast, no humanising touch, to make a grain of such a memory spring up in his hardened breast. All within this desolate creature is barren wilderness. All within the man bereft of what you have resigned, is the same barren wilderness. Woe to such a man! Woe, tenfold, to the nation that shall count its monsters such as this, lying here, by hundreds and by thousands!"

Redlaw shrank, appalled, from what he heard.

"There is not," said the Phantom, "one of these—not one—but sows a harvest that mankind MUST reap. From every seed of evil in this boy, a field of ruin is grown that shall be gathered in, and garnered up, and sown again in many places in the world, until regions are overspread with wickedness enough to raise the waters of another Deluge. Open and unpunished murder in a city's streets would be less guilty in its daily toleration, than one such spectacle as this."

It seemed to look down upon the boy in his sleep. Redlaw, too, looked down upon him with a new emotion.

"There is not a father," said the Phantom,"by whose side in his daily or his nightly walk, these creatures pass; there is not a mother among all the ranks of loving mothers in this land; there is no one risen from the state of childhood, but shall be responsible in his or her degree for this enormity. There is not a country throughout the earth on which it would not bring a curse. There is no religion upon earth that it would not deny; there is no people upon earth it would not put to shame."

The Chemist clasped his hands, and looked, with trembling fear and pity, from the sleeping boy to the Phantom, standing above him with his finger pointing down.

"Behold, I say," pursued the Spectre, "the perfect type of what it was your choice to be. Your influence is powerless here, because from this child's bosom you can banish nothing. His thoughts have been in'terrible companionship' with yours, because you have gone down to his unnatural level. He is the growth of man's indifference; you are the growth of man's presumption. The beneficent design of Heaven is, in each case, overthrown, and from the two poles of the immaterial world you come together."

The Chemist stooped upon the ground beside the boy, and, with the same kind of compassion for him that he now felt for himself, covered him as he slept, and no longer shrank from him with abhorrence or indifference.

Soon, now, the distant line on the horizon brightened, the darkness faded, the sun rose red and glorious, and the chimney stacks and gables of the ancient building gleamed in the clear air, which turned the smoke and vapour of the city into a cloud of gold. The very sun-dial in his shady corner, where the wind was used to spin with such unwindy constancy, shook off the finer particles of snow that had accumulated on his dull old face in the night, and looked out at the little white wreaths eddying round and round him. Doubtless some blind groping of the morning made its way down into the forgotten crypt so cold and earthy, where the Norman arches were half buried in the ground, and stirred the dull sap in the lazy vegetation hanging to the walls, and quickened the slow principle of life within the little world of wonderful and delicate creation which existed there, with some faint knowledge that the sun was up.

The Tetterbys were up, and doing. Mr. Tetterby took down the shutters of the shop, and, strip by strip, revealed the treasures of the window to the eyes, so proof against their seductions, of Jerusalem Buildings. Adolphus had been out so long already, that he was halfway on to "Morning Pepper." Five small Tetterbys, whose ten round eyes were much inflamed by soap and friction, were in the tortures of a cool wash in the back kitchen; Mrs. Tetterby presiding. Johnny, who was pushed and hustled through his toilet with great rapidity when Moloch chanced to be in an exacting frame of mind (which was always the case), staggered up and down with his charge before the shop door, under greater difficulties than usual; the weight of Moloch being much increased by a complication of defences against the cold, composed of knitted worsted-work, and forming a complete suit of chain-armour, with a head-piece and blue gaiters.

It was a peculiarity of this baby to be always cutting teeth. Whether they never came, or whether they came and went away again, is not in evidence; but it had certainly cut enough, on the showing of Mrs. Tetterby, to make a handsome dental provision for the sign of the Bull and Mouth. All sorts of objects were impressed for the rubbing of its gums, notwithstanding that it always carried, dangling at its waist (which was immediately under its chin), a bone ring, large enough to have represented the rosary of a young nun. Knife-handles, umbrella-tops, the heads of walking-sticks selected from the stock, the fingers of the family in general, but especially of Johnny, nutmeg-graters, crusts, the handles of doors, and the cool knobs on the tops of pokers, were among the commonest instruments indiscriminately applied for this baby's relief. The amount of electricity that must have been rubbed out of it in a week, is not to be calculated. Still Mrs. Tetterby always said "it was coming through, and then the child would be herself;" and still it never did come through, and the child continued to be somebody else.

The tempers of the little Tetterbys had sadly changed with a few hours. Mr. and Mrs. Tetterby themselves were not more altered than their offspring. Usually they were an unselfish, good-natured, yielding little race, sharing short commons when it happened (which was pretty often) contentedly and even generously, and taking a great deal of enjoyment out of a very little meat. But they were fighting now, not only for the soap and water, but even for the breakfast which was yet in perspective. The hand of every little Tetterby was against the other little Tetterbys; and even Johnny's hand—the patient, much-enduring, and devoted Johnny —rose against the baby! Yes, Mrs. Tetterby, going to the door by mere accident, saw him viciously pick out a weak place in the suit of armour where a slap would tell, and slap that blessed child.

Mrs. Tetterby had him into the parlour by the collar, in that same flash of time, and repaid him the assault with usury thereto.

"You brute, you murdering little boy," said Mrs. Tetterby. "Had you the heart to do it?"

"Why don't her teeth come through, then,"retorted Johnny, in a loud rebellious voice, "instead of bothering me? How would you like it yourself?"

"Like it, sir!" said Mrs. Tetterby, relieving him of his dishonoured load.

"Yes, like it," said Johnny. "How would you? Not at all. If you was me, you'd go for a soldier. I will, too. There an't no babies in the Army."

Mr. Tetterby, who had arrived upon the scene of action, rubbed his chin thoughtfully, instead of correcting the rebel, and seemed rather struck by this view of a military life.

"I wish I was in the Army myself, if the child's in the right," said Mrs. Tetterby, looking at her husband,"for I have no peace of my life here. I'm a slave—a Virginia slave:" some indistinct association with their weak descent on the tobacco trade perhaps suggested this aggravated expression to Mrs. Tetterby. "I never have a holiday, or any pleasure at all, from year's end to year's end! Why, Lord bless and save the child," said Mrs. Tetterby, shaking the baby with an irritability hardly suited to so pious an aspiration,"what's the matter with her now?"

Not being able to discover, and not rendering the subject much clearer by shaking it, Mrs. Tetterby put the baby away in a cradle, and, folding her arms, sat rocking it angrily with her foot.

"How you stand there, 'Dolphus," said Mrs. Tetterby to her husband. "Why don't you do something?"

"Because I don't care about doing anything,"Mr. Tetterby replied.

"I am sure *I* don't," said Mrs. Tetterby.

"I'll take my oath *I* don't,"said Mr. Tetterby.

A diversion arose here among Johnny and his five younger brothers, who, in preparing the family breakfast table, had fallen to skirmishing for the temporary possession of the loaf, and were buffeting one another with great heartiness; the smallest boy of all, with precocious discretion, hovering outside the knot of combatants, and harassing their legs. Into the midst of this fray, Mr. and Mrs. Tetterby both precipitated themselves with great ardour, as if such ground were the only ground on which they could now agree; and having, with no visible remains of their late soft-heartedness, laid about them without any lenity, and done much execution, resumed their former relative positions.

"You had better read your paper than do nothing at all," said Mrs. Tetterby.

"What's there to read in a paper?" returned Mr. Tetterby, with excessive discontent.

"What?" said Mrs. Tetterby. "Police."

"It's nothing to me," said Tetterby. "What do I care what people do, or are done to?"

"Suicides," suggested Mrs. Tetterby.

"No business of mine," replied her husband.

"Births, deaths, and marriages, are those nothing to you?" said Mrs. Tetterby.

"If the births were all over for good, and all to-day; and the deaths were all to begin to come off to-morrow; I don't see why it should interest me, till I thought it was a coming to my turn," grumbled Tetterby. "As to marriages, I've done it myself. I know quite enough about *them*."

To judge from the dissatisfied expression of her face and manner, Mrs. Tetterby appeared to entertain the same opinions as her husband; but she opposed him, nevertheless, for the gratification of quarrelling with him.

"Oh, you're a consistent man," said Mrs. Tetterby, "an't you? You, with the screen of your own making there, made of nothing else but bits of newspapers, which you sit and read to the children by the half-hour together!"

"Say used to, if you please," returned her husband. "You won't find me doing so any more. I'm wiser now."

"Bah! wiser, indeed!" said Mrs. Tetterby. "Are you better?"

The question sounded some discordant note in Mr. Tetterby's breast. He ruminated dejectedly, and passed his hand across and across his forehead.

"Better!" murmured Mr. Tetterby. "I don't know as any of us are better, or happier either. Better, is it?"

He turned to the screen, and traced about it with his finger, until he found a certain paragraph of which he was in quest.

"This used to be one of the family favourites, I recollect," said Tetterby, in a forlorn and stupid way,"and used to draw tears from the children, and make 'em good, if there was any little bickering or discontent among 'em, next to the story of the robin redbreasts in the wood. 'Melancholy case of destitution. Yesterday a small man, with a baby in his arms, and surrounded by half-a-dozen ragged little ones, of various ages between ten and two, the whole of whom were evidently in a famishing condition, appeared before the worthy magistrate, and made the following recital:'—Ha! I don't understand it, I'm sure," said Tetterby; "I don't see what it has got to do with us."

"How old and shabby he looks," said Mrs. Tetterby, watching him. "I never saw such a change in a man. Ah! dear me, dear me, dear me, it was a sacrifice!"

"What was a sacrifice?" her husband sourly inquired.

Mrs. Tetterby shook her head; and without replying in words, raised a complete sea-storm about the baby, by her violent agitation of the cradle.

"If you mean your marriage was a sacrifice, my good woman—" said her husband.

"I *do* mean it," said his wife.

"Why, then I mean to say," pursued Mr. Tetterby, as sulkily and surlily as she, "that there are two sides to that affair; and that I was the sacrifice; and that I wish the sacrifice hadn't been accepted."

"I wish it hadn't, Tetterby, with all my heart and soul I do assure you," said his wife. "You can't wish it more than I do, Tetterby."

"I don't know what I saw in her," muttered the newsman, "I'm sure;—certainly, if I saw anything, it's not there now. I was thinking so, last night, after supper, by the fire. She's fat, she's ageing, she won't bear comparison with most other women."

"He's common-looking, he has no air with him, he's small, he's beginning to stoop and he's getting bald," muttered Mrs. Tetterby.

"I must have been half out of my mind when I did it," muttered Mr. Tetterby.

"My senses must have forsook me. That's the only way in which I can explain it to myself," said Mrs. Tetterby with elaboration.

In this mood they sat down to breakfast. The little Tetterbys were not habituated to regard that meal in the light of a sedentary occupation, but discussed it as a dance or trot; rather resembling a savage ceremony, in the occasionally shrill whoops, and brandishings of bread and butter, with which it was accompanied, as well as in the intricate filings off into the street and back again, and the hoppings up and down the door-steps, which were incidental to the performance. In the present instance, the contentions between these Tetterby children for the milk-and-water jug, common to all, which stood upon the table, presented so lamentable an instance of angry passions risen very high indeed, that it was an outrage on the memory of Dr. Watts. It was not until Mr. Tetterby had driven the whole herd out at the front door, that a moment's peace was secured; and even that was broken by the discovery that Johnny had surreptitiously come back, and was at that instant choking in the jug like a ventriloquist, in his indecent and rapacious haste.

"These children will be the death of me at last!"said Mrs. Tetterby, after banishing the culprit. "And the sooner the better, I think."

"Poor people," said Mr. Tetterby, "ought not to have children at all. They give *us* no pleasure."

He was at that moment taking up the cup which Mrs. Tetterby had rudely pushed towards him, and Mrs. Tetterby was lifting her own cup to her lips, when they both stopped, as if they were transfixed.

"Here! Mother! Father!" cried Johnny, running into the room. "Here's Mrs. William coming down the street!"

And if ever, since the world began, a young boy took a baby from a cradle with the care of an old nurse, and hushed and soothed it tenderly, and tottered away with it cheerfully, Johnny was that boy, and Moloch was that baby, as they went out together!

Mr. Tetterby put down his cup; Mrs. Tetterby put down her cup. Mr. Tetterby rubbed his forehead; Mrs. Tetterby rubbed hers. Mr. Tetterby's face began to smooth and brighten; Mrs. Tetterby's began to smooth and brighten.

"Why, Lord forgive me," said Mr. Tetterby to himself, "what evil tempers have I been giving way to? What has been the matter here!"

"How could I ever treat him ill again, after all I said and felt last night!" sobbed Mrs. Tetterby, with her apron to her eyes.

"Am I a brute," said Mr. Tetterby, "or is there any good in me at all? Sophia! My little woman!"

"'Dolphus dear," returned his wife.

"I—I've been in a state of mind," said Mr. Tetterby, "that I can't abear to think of, Sophy."

"Oh! It's nothing to what I've been in, Dolf," cried his wife in a great burst of grief.

"My Sophia," said Mr. Tetterby, "don't take on. I never shall forgive myself. I must have nearly broke your heart, I know."

"No, Dolf, no. It was me! Me!" cried Mrs. Tetterby.

"My little woman," said her husband, "don't. You make me reproach myself dreadful, when you show such a noble spirit. Sophia, my dear, you don't know what I thought. I showed it bad enough, no doubt; but what I thought, my little woman!—"

"Oh, dear Dolf, don't! Don't!" cried his wife.

"Sophia," said Mr. Tetterby, "I must reveal it. I couldn't rest in my conscience unless I mentioned it. My little woman—"

"Mrs. William's very nearly here!" screamed Johnny at the door.

"My little woman, I wondered how," gasped Mr. Tetterby, supporting himself by his chair, "I wondered how I had ever admired you—I forgot the precious children you have brought about me, and thought you didn't look as slim as I could wish. I—I never gave a recollection," said Mr. Tetterby, with severe self-accusation, "to the cares you've had as my wife, and along of me and mine, when you might have had hardly any with another man, who got on better and was luckier than me (anybody might have found such a man easily I am sure); and I quarrelled with you for having aged a little in the rough years you have lightened for me. Can you believe it, my little woman? I hardly can myself."

Mrs. Tetterby, in a whirlwind of laughing and crying, caught his face within her hands, and held it there.

"Oh, Dolf!" she cried. "I am so happy that you thought so; I am so grateful that you thought so! For I thought that you were common-looking, Dolf; and so you are, my dear, and may you be the commonest of all sights in my eyes, till you close them with your own good hands. I thought that you were small; and so you are, and I'll make much of you because you are, and more of you because I love my husband. I thought that you began to stoop; and so you do, and you shall lean on me, and I'll do all I can to keep you up. I thought there was no air about you; but there is, and it's the air of home, and that's the purest and the best there is, and God bless home once more, and all belonging to it, Dolf!"

"Hurrah! Here's Mrs. William!" cried Johnny.

So she was, and all the children with her; and so she came in, they kissed her, and kissed one another, and kissed the baby, and kissed their father and mother, and then ran back and flocked and danced about her, trooping on with her in triumph.

Mr. and Mrs. Tetterby were not a bit behind-hand in the warmth of their reception. They were as much attracted to her as the children were; they ran towards her, kissed her hands, pressed round her, could not receive her ardently or enthusiastically enough. She came among them like the spirit of all goodness, affection, gentle consideration, love, and domesticity.

"What! are *you* all so glad to see me, too, this bright Christmas morning?" said Milly, clapping her hands in a pleasant wonder. "Oh dear, how delightful this is!"

More shouting from the children, more kissing, more trooping round her, more happiness, more love, more joy, more honour, on all sides, than she could bear.

"Oh dear!" said Milly, "what delicious tears you make me shed. How can I ever have deserved this! What have I done to be so loved?"

"Who can help it!" cried Mr. Tetterby.

"Who can help it!" cried Mrs. Tetterby.

"Who can help it!" echoed the children, in a joyful chorus. And they danced and trooped about her again, and clung to her, and laid their rosy faces against her dress, and kissed and fondled it, and could not fondle it, or her, enough.

"I never was so moved," said Milly, drying her eyes, "as I have been this morning. I must tell you, as soon as I can speak.—Mr. Redlaw came to me at sunrise, and with a tenderness in his manner, more as if I had been his darling daughter than myself, implored me to go with him to where William's brother George is lying ill. We went together, and all the way along he was so kind, and so subdued, and seemed to put such trust and hope in me, that I could not help crying with pleasure. When we got to the house, we met a woman at the door (somebody had bruised and hurt her, I am afraid), who caught me by the hand, and blessed me as I passed."

"She was right!" said Mr. Tetterby. Mrs. Tetterby said she was right. All the children cried out that she was right.

"Ah, but there's more than that," said Milly. "When we got up stairs, into the room, the sick man who had lain for hours in a state from which no effort could rouse him, rose up in his bed, and, bursting into tears, stretched out his arms to me, and said that he had led a mis-spent life, but that he was truly repentant now, in his sorrow for the past, which was all as plain to him as a great prospect, from which a dense black cloud had cleared away, and that he entreated me to ask his poor old father for his pardon and his blessing, and to say a prayer beside his bed. And when I did so, Mr. Redlaw joined in it so fervently, and then so thanked and thanked me, and thanked Heaven, that my heart quite overflowed, and I could have done nothing but sob and cry, if the sick man had not begged me to sit down by him,—which made me quiet of course. As I sat there, he held my hand in his until he sank in a doze; and even then, when I withdrew my hand to leave him to come here (which Mr. Redlaw was very earnest indeed in wishing me to do), his hand felt for mine, so that some one else was obliged to take my place and make believe to give him my hand back. Oh dear, oh dear," said Milly, sobbing. "How thankful and how happy I should feel, and do feel, for all this!"

While she was speaking, Redlaw had come in, and, after pausing for a moment to observe the group of which she was the centre, had silently ascended the stairs. Upon those stairs he now appeared again; remaining there, while the young student passed him, and came running down.

"Kind nurse, gentlest, best of creatures," he said, falling on his knee to her, and catching at her hand,"forgive my cruel ingratitude!"

"Oh dear, oh dear!" cried Milly innocently,"here's another of them! Oh dear, here's somebody else who likes me. What shall I ever do!"

The guileless, simple way in which she said it, and in which she put her hands before her eyes and wept for very happiness, was as touching as it was delightful.

"I was not myself," he said. "I don't know what it was—it was some consequence of my disorder perhaps—I was mad. But I am so no longer. Almost as I speak, I am restored. I heard the children crying out your name, and the shade passed from me at the very sound of it. Oh, don't weep! Dear Milly, if you could read my heart, and only knew with what affection and what grateful homage it is glowing, you would not let me see you weep. It is such deep reproach."

"No, no," said Milly, "it's not that. It's not indeed. It's joy. It's wonder that you should think it necessary to ask me to forgive so little, and yet it's pleasure that you do."

"And will you come again? and will you finish the little curtain?"

"No," said Milly, drying her eyes, and shaking her head. "You won't care for my needlework now."

"Is it forgiving me, to say that?"

She beckoned him aside, and whispered in his ear.

"There is news from your home, Mr. Edmund."

"News? How?"

"Either your not writing when you were very ill, or the change in your handwriting when you began to be better, created some suspicion of the truth; however that is—but you're sure you'll not be the worse for any news, if it's not bad news?"

"Sure."

"Then there's some one come!" said Milly.

"My mother?" asked the student, glancing round involuntarily towards Redlaw, who had come down from the stairs.

"Hush! No," said Milly.

"It can be no one else."

"Indeed?" said Milly, "are you sure?"

"It is not—" Before he could say more, she put her hand upon his mouth.

"Yes it is!" said Milly. "The young lady (she is very like the miniature, Mr. Edmund, but she is prettier) was too unhappy to rest without satisfying her doubts, and came up, last night, with a little servant-maid. As you always dated your letters from the college, she came there; and before I saw Mr. Redlaw this morning, I saw her. *She* likes me too!" said Milly. "Oh dear, that's another!"

"This morning! Where is she now?"

"Why, she is now," said Milly, advancing her lips to his ear, "in my little parlour in the Lodge, and waiting to see you."

He pressed her hand, and was darting off, but she detained him.

"Mr. Redlaw is much altered, and has told me this morning that his memory is impaired. Be very considerate to him, Mr. Edmund; he needs that from us all."

The young man assured her, by a look, that her caution was not ill-bestowed; and as he passed the Chemist on his way out, bent respectfully and with an obvious interest before him.

Redlaw returned the salutation courteously and even humbly, and looked after him as he passed on. He dropped his head upon his hand too, as trying to reawaken something he had lost. But it was gone.

The abiding change that had come upon him since the influence of the music, and the Phantom's reappearance, was, that now he truly felt how much he had lost, and could compassionate his own condition, and contrast it, clearly, with the natural state of those who were around him. In this, an interest in those who were around him was revived, and a meek, submissive sense of his calamity was bred, resembling that which sometimes obtains in age, when its mental powers are weakened, without insensibility or sullenness being added to the list of its infirmities.

He was conscious that, as he redeemed, through Milly, more and more of the evil he had done, and as he was more and more with her, this change ripened itself within him. Therefore, and because of the attachment she inspired him with (but without other hope), he felt that he was quite dependent on her, and that she was his staff in his affliction.

So, when she asked him whether they should go home now, to where the old man and her husband were, and he readily replied "yes"—being anxious in that regard—he put his arm through hers, and walked beside her; not as if he were the wise and learned man to whom the wonders of Nature were an open book, and hers were the uninstructed mind, but as if their two positions were reversed, and he knew nothing, and she all.

He saw the children throng about her, and caress her, as he and she went away together thus, out of the house; he heard the ringing of their laughter, and their merry voices; he saw their bright faces, clustering around him like flowers; he witnessed the renewed contentment and affection of their parents; he breathed the simple air of their poor home, restored to its tranquillity; he thought of the unwholesome blight he had shed upon it, and might, but for her, have been diffusing then; and perhaps it is no wonder that he walked submissively beside her, and drew her gentle bosom nearer to his own.

When they arrived at the Lodge, the old man was sitting in his chair in the chimney-corner, with his eyes fixed on the ground, and his son was leaning against the opposite side of the fire-place, looking at him. As she came in at the door, both started, and turned round towards her, and a radiant change came upon their faces.

"Oh dear, dear, dear, they are all pleased to see me like the rest!" cried Milly, clapping her hands in an ecstasy, and stopping short. "Here are two more!"

Pleased to see her! Pleasure was no word for it. She ran into her husband's arms, thrown wide open to receive her, and he would have been glad to have her there, with her head lying on his shoulder, through the short winter's day. But the old man couldn't spare her. He had arms for her too, and he locked her in them.

"Why, where has my quiet Mouse been all this time?" said the old man. "She has been a long while away. I find that it's impossible for me to get on without Mouse. I—where's my son William?—I fancy I have been dreaming, William."

"That's what I say myself, father," returned his son. "I have been in an ugly sort of dream, I think.—How are you, father? Are you pretty well?"

"Strong and brave, my boy," returned the old man.

It was quite a sight to see Mr. William shaking hands with his father, and patting him on the back, and rubbing him gently down with his hand, as if he could not possibly do enough to show an interest in him.

"What a wonderful man you are, father!—How are you, father? Are you really pretty hearty, though?"said William, shaking hands with him again, and patting him again, and rubbing him gently down again.

"I never was fresher or stouter in my life, my boy."

"What a wonderful man you are, father! But that's exactly where it is," said Mr. William, with enthusiasm. "When I think of all that my father's gone through, and all the chances and changes, and sorrows and troubles, that have happened to him in the course of his long life, and under which his head has grown grey, and years upon years have gathered on it, I feel as if we couldn't do enough to honour the old gentleman, and make his old age easy.—How are you, father? Are you really pretty well, though?"

Mr. William might never have left off repeating this inquiry, and shaking hands with him again, and patting him again, and rubbing him down again, if the old man had not espied the Chemist, whom until now he had not seen.

"I ask your pardon, Mr. Redlaw," said Philip,"but didn't know you were here, sir, or should have made less free. It reminds me, Mr. Redlaw, seeing you here on a Christmas morning, of the time when you was a student yourself, and worked so hard that you were backwards and forwards in our Library even at Christmas time. Ha! ha! I'm old enough to remember that; and I remember it right well, I do, though I am eighty-seven. It was after you left here that my poor wife died. You remember my poor wife, Mr. Redlaw?"

The Chemist answered yes.

"Yes," said the old man. "She was a dear creetur.—I recollect you come here one Christmas morning with a young lady—I ask your pardon, Mr. Redlaw, but I think it was a sister you was very much attached to?"

The Chemist looked at him, and shook his head. "I had a sister," he said vacantly. He knew no more.

"One Christmas morning," pursued the old man,"that you come here with her —and it began to snow, and my wife invited the lady to walk in, and sit by the fire that is always a burning on Christmas Day in what used to be, before our ten poor gentlemen commuted, our great Dinner Hall. I was there; and I recollect, as I was stirring up the blaze for the young lady to warm her pretty feet by, she read the scroll out loud, that is underneath that pictur, 'Lord, keep my memory green!' She and my poor wife fell a talking about it; and it's a strange thing to think of, now, that they both said (both being so unlike to die) that it was a good prayer, and that it was one they would put up very earnestly, if they were called away young, with reference to those who were dearest to them. 'My brother,' says the young lady—'My husband,' says my poor wife.—'Lord, keep his memory of me, green, and do not let me be forgotten!'"

Tears more painful, and more bitter than he had ever shed in all his life, coursed down Redlaw's face. Philip, fully occupied in recalling his story, had not observed him until now, nor Milly's anxiety that he should not proceed.

"Philip!" said Redlaw, laying his hand upon his arm, "I am a stricken man, on whom the hand of Providence has fallen heavily, although deservedly. You speak to me, my friend, of what I cannot follow; my memory is gone."

"Merciful power!" cried the old man.

"I have lost my memory of sorrow, wrong, and trouble," said the Chemist, "and with that I have lost all man would remember!"

To see old Philip's pity for him, to see him wheel his own great chair for him to rest in, and look down upon him with a solemn sense of his bereavement, was to know, in some degree, how precious to old age such recollections are.

The boy came running in, and ran to Milly.

"Here's the man," he said, "in the other room. I don't want *him*."

"What man does he mean?" asked Mr. William.

"Hush!" said Milly.

Obedient to a sign from her, he and his old father softly withdrew. As they went out, unnoticed, Redlaw beckoned to the boy to come to him.

"I like the woman best," he answered, holding to her skirts.

"You are right," said Redlaw, with a faint smile. "But you needn't fear to come to me. I am gentler than I was. Of all the world, to you, poor child!"

The boy still held back at first, but yielding little by little to her urging, he consented to approach, and even to sit down at his feet. As Redlaw laid his hand upon the shoulder of the child, looking on him with compassion and a fellow-feeling, he put out his other hand to Milly. She stooped down on that side of him, so that she could look into his face, and after silence, said:

"Mr. Redlaw, may I speak to you?"

"Yes," he answered, fixing his eyes upon her. "Your voice and music are the same to me."

"May I ask you something?"

"What you will."

"Do you remember what I said, when I knocked at your door last night? About one who was your friend once, and who stood on the verge of destruction?"

"Yes. I remember," he said, with some hesitation.

"Do you understand it?"

He smoothed the boy's hair—looking at her fixedly the while, and shook his head.

"This person," said Milly, in her clear, soft voice, which her mild eyes, looking at him, made clearer and softer, "I found soon afterwards. I went back to the house, and, with Heaven's help, traced him. I was not too soon. A very little and I should have been too late."

He took his hand from the boy, and laying it on the back of that hand of hers, whose timid and yet earnest touch addressed him no less appealingly than her voice and eyes, looked more intently on her.

"He *is* the father of Mr. Edmund, the young gentleman we saw just now. His real name is Longford.—You recollect the name?"

"I recollect the name."

"And the man?"

"No, not the man. Did he ever wrong me?"

"Yes!"

"Ah! Then it's hopeless—hopeless."

He shook his head, and softly beat upon the hand he held, as though mutely asking her commiseration.

"I did not go to Mr. Edmund last night," said Milly,—"You will listen to me just the same as if you did remember all?"

"To every syllable you say."

"Both, because I did not know, then, that this really was his father, and because I was fearful of the effect of such intelligence upon him, after his illness, if it should be. Since I have known who this person is, I have not gone either; but that is for another reason. He has long been separated from his wife and son— has been a stranger to his home almost from this son's infancy, I learn from him —and has abandoned and deserted what he should have held most dear. In all that time he has been falling from the state of a gentleman, more and more, until —" she rose up, hastily, and going out for a moment, returned, accompanied by the wreck that Redlaw had beheld last night.

"Do you know me?" asked the Chemist.

"I should be glad," returned the other, "and that is an unwonted word for me to use, if I could answer no."

The Chemist looked at the man, standing in self-abasement and degradation before him, and would have looked longer, in an ineffectual struggle for enlightenment, but that Milly resumed her late position by his side, and attracted his attentive gaze to her own face.

"See how low he is sunk, how lost he is!" she whispered, stretching out her arm towards him, without looking from the Chemist's face. "If you could remember all that is connected with him, do you not think it would move your pity to reflect that one you ever loved (do not let us mind how long ago, or in what belief that he has forfeited), should come to this?"

"I hope it would," he answered. "I believe it would."

His eyes wandered to the figure standing near the door, but came back speedily to her, on whom he gazed intently, as if he strove to learn some lesson from every tone of her voice, and every beam of her eyes.

"I have no learning, and you have much," said Milly; "I am not used to think, and you are always thinking. May I tell you why it seems to me a good thing for us, to remember wrong that has been done us?"

"Yes."

"That we may forgive it."

"Pardon me, great Heaven!" said Redlaw, lifting up his eyes, "for having thrown away thine own high attribute!"

"And if," said Milly, "if your memory should one day be restored, as we will hope and pray it may be, would it not be a blessing to you to recall at once a wrong and its forgiveness?"

He looked at the figure by the door, and fastened his attentive eyes on her again; a ray of clearer light appeared to him to shine into his mind, from her bright face.

"He cannot go to his abandoned home. He does not seek to go there. He knows that he could only carry shame and trouble to those he has so cruelly neglected; and that the best reparation he can make them now, is to avoid them. A very little money carefully bestowed, would remove him to some distant place, where he might live and do no wrong, and make such atonement as is left within his power for the wrong he has done. To the unfortunate lady who is his wife, and to his son, this would be the best and kindest boon that their best friend could give them—one too that they need never know of; and to him, shattered in reputation, mind, and body, it might be salvation."

He took her head between her hands, and kissed it, and said:"It shall be done. I trust to you to do it for me, now and secretly; and to tell him that I would forgive him, if I were so happy as to know for what."

As she rose, and turned her beaming face towards the fallen man, implying that her mediation had been successful, he advanced a step, and without raising his eyes, addressed himself to Redlaw.

"You are so generous," he said, "—you ever were—that you will try to banish your rising sense of retribution in the spectacle that is before you. I do not try to banish it from myself, Redlaw. If you can, believe me."

The Chemist entreated Milly, by a gesture, to come nearer to him; and, as he listened looked in her face, as if to find in it the clue to what he heard.

"I am too decayed a wretch to make professions; I recollect my own career too well, to array any such before you. But from the day on which I made my first step downward, in dealing falsely by you, I have gone down with a certain, steady, doomed progression. That, I say."

Redlaw, keeping her close at his side, turned his face towards the speaker, and there was sorrow in it. Something like mournful recognition too.

"I might have been another man, my life might have been another life, if I had avoided that first fatal step. I don't know that it would have been. I claim nothing for the possibility. Your sister is at rest, and better than she could have been with me, if I had continued even what you thought me: even what I once supposed myself to be."

Redlaw made a hasty motion with his hand, as if he would have put that subject on one side.

"I speak," the other went on, "like a man taken from the grave. I should have made my own grave, last night, had it not been for this blessed hand."

"Oh dear, he likes me too!" sobbed Milly, under her breath. "That's another!"

"I could not have put myself in your way, last night, even for bread. But, to-day, my recollection of what has been is so strongly stirred, and is presented to me, I don't know how, so vividly, that I have dared to come at her suggestion, and to take your bounty, and to thank you for it, and to beg you, Redlaw, in your dying hour, to be as merciful to me in your thoughts, as you are in your deeds."

He turned towards the door, and stopped a moment on his way forth.

"I hope my son may interest you, for his mother's sake. I hope he may deserve to do so. Unless my life should be preserved a long time, and I should know that I have not misused your aid, I shall never look upon him more."

Going out, he raised his eyes to Redlaw for the first time. Redlaw, whose steadfast gaze was fixed upon him, dreamily held out his hand. He returned and touched it—little more—with both his own; and bending down his head, went slowly out.

In the few moments that elapsed, while Milly silently took him to the gate, the Chemist dropped into his chair, and covered his face with his hands. Seeing him thus, when she came back, accompanied by her husband and his father (who were both greatly concerned for him), she avoided disturbing him, or permitting him to be disturbed; and kneeled down near the chair to put some warm clothing on the boy.

"That's exactly where it is. That's what I always say, father!" exclaimed her admiring husband. "There's a motherly feeling in Mrs. William's breast that must and will have went!"

"Ay, ay," said the old man; "you're right. My son William's right!"

"It happens all for the best, Milly dear, no doubt," said Mr. William, tenderly, "that we have no children of our own; and yet I sometimes wish you had one to love and cherish. Our little dead child that you built such hopes upon, and that never breathed the breath of life—it has made you quiet-like, Milly."

"I am very happy in the recollection of it, William dear," she answered. "I think of it every day."

"I was afraid you thought of it a good deal."

"Don't say, afraid; it is a comfort to me; it speaks to me in so many ways. The innocent thing that never lived on earth, is like an angel to me, William."

"You are like an angel to father and me," said Mr. William, softly. "I know that."

"When I think of all those hopes I built upon it, and the many times I sat and pictured to myself the little smiling face upon my bosom that never lay there, and the sweet eyes turned up to mine that never opened to the light," said Milly, "I can feel a greater tenderness, I think, for all the disappointed hopes in which there is no harm. When I see a beautiful child in its fond mother's arms, I love it all the better, thinking that my child might have been like that, and might have made my heart as proud and happy."

Redlaw raised his head, and looked towards her.

"All through life, it seems by me," she continued, "to tell me something. For poor neglected children, my little child pleads as if it were alive, and had a voice I knew, with which to speak to me. When I hear of youth in suffering or shame, I think that my child might have come to that, perhaps, and that God took it from me in His mercy. Even in age and grey hair, such as father's, it is present: saying that it too might have lived to be old, long and long after you and I were gone, and to have needed the respect and love of younger people."

Her quiet voice was quieter than ever, as she took her husband's arm, and laid her head against it.

"Children love me so, that sometimes I half fancy—it's a silly fancy, William —they have some way I don't know of, of feeling for my little child, and me, and understanding why their love is precious to me. If I have been quiet since, I have been more happy, William, in a hundred ways. Not least happy, dear, in this —that even when my little child was born and dead but a few days, and I was weak and sorrowful, and could not help grieving a little, the thought arose, that if I tried to lead a good life, I should meet in Heaven a bright creature, who would call me, Mother!"

Redlaw fell upon his knees, with a loud cry.

"O Thou," he said, "who through the teaching of pure love, hast graciously restored me to the memory which was the memory of Christ upon the Cross, and of all the good who perished in His cause, receive my thanks, and bless her!"

Then, he folded her to his heart; and Milly, sobbing more than ever, cried, as she laughed, "He is come back to himself! He likes me very much indeed, too! Oh, dear, dear, dear me, here's another!"

Then, the student entered, leading by the hand a lovely girl, who was afraid to come. And Redlaw so changed towards him, seeing in him and his youthful choice, the softened shadow of that chastening passage in his own life, to which, as to a shady tree, the dove so long imprisoned in his solitary ark might fly for rest and company, fell upon his neck, entreating them to be his children.

Then, as Christmas is a time in which, of all times in the year, the memory of every remediable sorrow, wrong, and trouble in the world around us, should be active with us, not less than our own experiences, for all good, he laid his hand upon the boy, and, silently calling Him to witness who laid His hand on children in old time, rebuking, in the majesty of His prophetic knowledge, those who kept them from Him, vowed to protect him, teach him, and reclaim him.

Then, he gave his right hand cheerily to Philip, and said that they would that day hold a Christmas dinner in what used to be, before the ten poor gentlemen commuted, their great Dinner Hall; and that they would bid to it as many of that Swidger family, who, his son had told him, were so numerous that they might join hands and make a ring round England, as could be brought together on so short a notice.

And it was that day done. There were so many Swidgers there, grown up and children, that an attempt to state them in round numbers might engender doubts, in the distrustful, of the veracity of this history. Therefore the attempt shall not be made. But there they were, by dozens and scores—and there was good news and good hope there, ready for them, of George, who had been visited again by his father and brother, and by Milly, and again left in a quiet sleep. There, present at the dinner, too, were the Tetterbys, including young Adolphus, who arrived in his prismatic comforter, in good time for the beef. Johnny and the baby were too late, of course, and came in all on one side, the one exhausted, the other in a supposed state of double-tooth; but that was customary, and not alarming.

It was sad to see the child who had no name or lineage, watching the other children as they played, not knowing how to talk with them, or sport with them, and more strange to the ways of childhood than a rough dog. It was sad, though in a different way, to see what an instinctive knowledge the youngest children there had of his being different from all the rest, and how they made timid approaches to him with soft words and touches, and with little presents, that he might not be unhappy. But he kept by Milly, and began to love her—that was another, as she said!—and, as they all liked her dearly, they were glad of that, and when they saw him peeping at them from behind her chair, they were pleased that he was so close to it.

All this, the Chemist, sitting with the student and his bride that was to be, Philip, and the rest, saw.

Some people have said since, that he only thought what has been herein set down; others, that he read it in the fire, one winter night about the twilight time; others, that the Ghost was but the representation of his gloomy thoughts, and Milly the embodiment of his better wisdom. *I* say nothing.

—Except this. That as they were assembled in the old Hall, by no other light than that of a great fire (having dined early), the shadows once more stole out of their hiding-places, and danced about the room, showing the children marvellous shapes and faces on the walls, and gradually changing what was real and familiar there, to what was wild and magical. But that there was one thing in the Hall, to which the eyes of Redlaw, and of Milly and her husband, and of the old man, and of the student, and his bride that was to be, were often turned, which the shadows did not obscure or change. Deepened in its gravity by the fire-light, and gazing from the darkness of the panelled wall like life, the sedate face in the portrait, with the beard and ruff, looked down at them from under its verdant wreath of holly, as they looked up at it; and, clear and plain below, as if a voice had uttered them, were the words.

Lord keep my Memory green.

THE BULLY OF BROCAS COURT,
by Arthur Conan Doyle

A Legend of the Ring

That year—it was in 1878—the South Midland Yeomanry were out near Luton, and the real question which appealed to every man in the great camp was not how to prepare for a possible European war, but the far more vital one how to get a man who could stand up for ten rounds to Farrier-Sergeant Burton. Slogger Burton was a fine upstanding fourteen stone of bone and brawn, with a smack in either hand which would leave any ordinary mortal senseless. A match must be found for him somewhere or his head would outgrow his dragoon helmet. Therefore Sir Fred Milburn, better known as Mumbles, was dispatched to London to find if among the fancy there was no one who would make a journey in order to take down the number of the bold dragoon.

They were bad days, those, in the prize-ring. The old knuckle-fighting had died out in scandal and disgrace, smothered by the pestilent crowd of betting men and ruffians of all sorts who hung upon the edge of the movement and brought disgrace and ruin upon the decent fighting men, who were often humble heroes whose gallantry has never been surpassed. An honest sportsman who desired to see a fight was usually set upon by villains, against whom he had no redress, since he was himself engaged on what was technically an illegal action. He was stripped in the open Street, his purse taken, and his head split open if he ventured to resist. The ring-side could only be reached by men who were prepared to fight their way there with cudgels and hunting crops. No wonder that the classic sport was attended now by those only who had nothing to lose.

On the other hand, the era of the reserved building and the legal glove-fight had not yet arisen, and the cult was in a strange intermediate condition. It was impossible to regulate it, and equally impossible to abolish it, since nothing appeals more directly and powerfully to the average Briton. Therefore there were scrambling contests in stableyards and barns, hurried visits to France, secret meetings at dawn in wild parts of the country, and all manner of evasions and experiments. The men themselves became as unsatisfactory as their surroundings. There could be no honest open contest, and the loudest bragger talked his way to the top of the list. Only across the Atlantic had the huge figure of John Lawrence Sullivan appeared, who was destined to be the last of the earlier system and the first of the later one.

Things being in this condition, the sporting Yeomanry Captain found it no easy matter among the boxing saloons and sporting pubs of London to find a man who could be relied upon to give a good account of the huge Famer-Sergeant. Heavy-weights were at a premium. Finally his choice fell upon Alf Stevens of Kentish Town, an excellent rising middle-weight who had never yet known defeat and had indeed some claims to the championship. His professional experience and craft would surely make up for the three stone of weight which separated him from the formidable dragoon. It was in this hope that Sir Fred Milburn engaged him, and proceeded to convey him in his dog-cart behind a pair of spanking greys to the camp of the Yeomen. They were to start one evening, drive up the Great North Road, sleep at St. Albans, and finish their journey next day.

The prize-fighter met the sporting Baronet at the Golden Cross, where Bates, the little groom, was standing at the head of the spirited horses. Stevens, a pale-faced, clean-cut young fellow, mounted beside his employer and waved his hand to a little knot of fighting men, rough, collarless, reefer-coated fellows who had gathered to bid their comrade good-bye. "Good luck, Alf!" came in a hoarse chorus as the boy released the horses' heads and sprang in behind, while the high dog-cart swung swiftly round the curve into Trafalgar Square.

Sir Frederick was so busy steering among the traffic in Oxford Street and the Edgware Road that he had little thought for anything else, but when he got into the edges of the country near Hendon, and the hedges had at last taken the place of that endless panorama of brick dwellings, he let his horses go easy with a loose rein while he turned his attention to the young man at his side. He had found him by correspondence and recommendation, so that he had some curiosity now in looking him over. Twilight was already falling and the light dim, but what the Baronet saw pleased him well. The man was a fighter every inch, clean-cut, deep-chested, with the long straight cheek and deep-set eye which goes with an obstinate courage. Above all, he was a man who had never yet met his master and was still upheld by the deep sustaining confidence which is never quite the same after a single defeat. The Baronet chuckled as he realized what a surprise packet was being carried north for the Farrier-Sergeant.

"I suppose you are in some sort of training, Stevens?" he remarked, turning to his companion. "Yes, sir; I am fit to fight for my life."

"So I should judge by the look of you."

"I live regular all the time, sir, but I was matched against Mike Connor for this last week-end and scaled down to eleven four. Then he paid forfeit, and here I am at the top of my form."

"That's lucky. You'll need it all against a man who has a pull of three stone and four inches." The young man smiled.

"I have given greater odds than that, sir."

"I dare say. But he's a game man as well."

"Well, sir, one can but do one's best."

The Baronet liked the modest but assured tone of the young pugilist. Suddenly an amusing thought struck him, and he burst out laughing.

"By Jove!" he cried. "What a lark if the Bully is out to-night!"

Alf Stevens pricked up his ears.

"Who might he be, sir?"

"Well, that's what the folk are asking. Some say they've seen him, and some say he's a fairy tale, but there's good evidence that he is a real man with a pair of rare good fists that leave their marks behind him."

"And where might he live?"

"On this very road. It's between Finchley and Elstree, as I've heard. There are two chaps, and they come out on nights when the moon is at full and challenge the passers-by to fight in the old style. One fights and the other picks up. By George! the fellow can fight, too, by all accounts. Chaps have been found in the morning with their faces all cut to ribbons to show that the Bully had been at work upon them."

Alf Stevens was full of interest.

"I've always wanted to try an old-style battle, sir, but it never chanced to come my way. I believe it would suit me better than the gloves."

"Then you won't refuse the Bully?"

"Refuse him! I'd go ten miles to meet him."

"By George! it would be great!" cried the Baronet. "Well, the moon is at the full, and the place should be about here."

"If he's as good as you say," Stevens remarked, "he should be known in the ring, unless he is just an amateur who amuses himself like that."

"Some think he's an ostler, or maybe a racing man from the training stables over yonder. Where there are horses there is boxing. If you can believe the accounts, there is something a bit queer and outlandish about the fellow. Hi! Look out, damn you, look out!"

The Baronet's voice had risen to a sudden screech of surprise and of anger. At this point the road dips down into a hollow, heavily shaded by trees, so that at night it arches across like the mouth of a tunnel. At the foot of the slope there stand two great stone pillars, which, as viewed by daylight, are lichen-stained and weathered, with heraldic devices on each which are so mutilated by time that they are mere protuberances of stone. An iron gate of elegant design, hanging loosely upon rusted hinges, proclaims both the past glories and the present decay of Brocas Old Hall, which lies at the end of the weed-encumbered avenue. It was from the shadow of this ancient gateway that an active figure had sprung suddenly into the centre of the road and had, with great dexterity, held up the horses, who ramped and pawed as they forced back upon their haunches.

"Here, Rowe, you 'old the tits, will ye?" cried a high strident voice. "I've a little word to say to this 'ere slap-up Corinthian before 'e goes any farther."

A second man had emerged from the shadows and without a word took hold of the horses' heads. He was a short, thick fellow, dressed in a curious brown many-caped overcoat, which came to his knees, with gaiters and boots beneath it. He wore no hat, and those in the dog-cart had a view, as he came in front of the side-lamps, of a surly red face with an ill-fitting lower lip clean shaven, and a high black cravat swathed tightly under the chin. As he gripped the leathers his more active comrade sprang forward and rested a bony hand upon the side of the splashboard while he looked keenly up with a pair of fierce blue eyes at the faces of the two travellers, the light beating full upon his own features. He wore a hat low upon his brow, but in spite of its shadow both the Baronet and the pugilist could see enough to shrink from him, for it was an evil face, evil but very formidable, stern, craggy, high-nosed, and fierce, with an inexorable mouth which bespoke a nature which would neither ask for mercy nor grant it. As to his age, one could only say for certain that a man with such a face was young enough to have all his virility and old enough to have experienced all the wickedness of life. The cold, savage eyes took a deliberate survey, first of the Baronet and then of the young man beside him.

"Aye, Rowe, it's a slap-up Corinthian, same as I said," he remarked over his shoulder to his companion. "But this other is a likely chap. If 'e isn't a millin' cove 'e ought to be. Any'ow, we'll try 'im out."

"Look here," said the Baronet, "I don't know who you are, except that you are a damned impertinent fellow. I'd put the lash of my whip across your face for two pins!"

"Stow that gammon, gov'nor! It ain't safe to speak to me like that."

"I've heard of you and your ways!" cried the angry soldier. "I'll teach you to stop my horses on the Queen's high road! You've got the wrong men this time, my fine fellow, as you will soon learn."

"That's as it may be," said the stranger. "May'ap, master, we may all learn something before we part. One or other of you 'as got to get down and put up your 'ands before you get any farther."

Stevens had instantly sprung down into the road.

"If you want a fight you've come to the right shop," said he; "it's my trade, so don't say I took you unawares."

The stranger gave a cry of satisfaction.

"Blow my dickey!" he shouted. "It is a millin' cove, Joe, same as I said. No more chaw-bacons for us, but the real thing. Well, young man, you've met your master to-night. Happen you never 'eard what Lord Longmore said o' me? 'A man must be made special to beat you,' says 'e. That's wot Lord Longmore said."

"That was before the Bull came along," growled the man in front, speaking for the first time. "Stow your chaffing, Joe! A little more about the Bull and you and me will quarrel. 'E bested me once, but it's all betters and no takers that I glut 'im if ever we meet again. Well, young man, what d'ye think of me?"

"I think you've got your share of cheek."

"Cheek. Wot's that?"

"Impudence, bluff—gas, if you like."

The last word had a surprising effect upon the stranger. He smote his leg with his hand and broke out into a high neighing laugh, in which he was joined by his gruff companion.

"You've said the right word, my beauty," cried the latter, "Gas is the word and no error. Well, there's a good moon, but the clouds are comin' up. We had best use the light while we can."

Whilst this conversation had been going on the Baronet had been looking with an ever-growing amazement at the attire of the stranger. A good deal of it confirmed his belief that he was connected with some stables, though making every allowance for this his appearance was very eccentric and old-fashioned. Upon his head he wore a yellowish-white top-hat of long-haired beaver, such as is still affected by some drivers of four-in-hands, with a bell crown and a curling brim. His dress consisted of a shortwaisted swallow-tail coat, snuff-coloured, with steel buttons. It opened in front to show a vest of striped silk, while his legs were encased in buff knee-breeches with blue stockings and low shoes. The figure was angular and hard, with a great suggestion of wiry activity. This Bully of Brocas was clearly a very great character, and the young dragoon officer chuckled as he thought what a glorious story he would carry back to the mess of this queer old-world figure and the thrashing which he was about to receive from the famous London boxer.

Billy, the little groom, had taken charge of the horses, who were shivering and sweating.

"This way!" said the stout man, turning towards the gate. It was a sinister place, black and weird, with the crumbling pillars and the heavy arching trees. Neither the Baronet nor the pugilist liked the look of it.

"Where are you going, then?"

"This is no place for a fight," said the stout man. "We've got as pretty a place as ever you saw inside the gate here. You couldn't beat it on Molesey Hurst."

"The road is good enough for me," said Stevens.

"The road is good enough for two Johnny Raws," said the man with the beaver hat. "It ain't good enough for two slap-up millin' coves like you an' me. You ain't afeard, are you?"

"Not of you or ten like you," said Stevens, stoutly.

"Well, then, come with me and do it as it ought to be done."

Sir Frederick and Stevens exchanged glances.

"I'm game," said the pugilist.

"Come on, then."

The little party of four passed through the gateway. Behind them in the darkness the horses stamped and reared, while the voice of the boy could be heard as he vainly tried to soothe them. After walking fifty yards up the grass-grown drive the guide turned to the right through a thick belt of trees, and they came out upon a circular plot of grass, white and clear in the moonlight. It had a raised bank, and on the farther side was one of those little pillared stone summer-houses beloved by the early Georgians.

"What did I tell you?" cried the stout man, triumphantly. "Could you do better than this within twenty mile of town? It was made for it. Now, Tom, get to work upon him, and show us what you can do."

It had all become like an extraordinary dream. The strange men, their odd dress, their queer speech, the moonlit circle of grass, and the pillared summer-house all wove themselves into one fantastic whole. It was only the sight of Alf Stevens's ill-fitting tweed suit, and his homely English face surmounting it, which brought the Baronet back to the workaday world. The thin stranger had taken off his beaver hat, his swallow-tailed coat, his silk waistcoat, and finally his shirt had been drawn over his head by his second. Stevens in a cool and leisurely fashion kept pace with the preparations of his antagonist. Then the two fighting men turned upon each other.

But as they did so Stevens gave an exclamation of surprise and horror. The removal of the beaver hat had disclosed a horrible mutilation of the head of his antagonist. The whole upper forehead had fallen in, and there seemed to be a broad red weal between his close-cropped hair and his heavy brows.

"Good Lord," cried the young pugilist. "What's amiss with the man?" The question seemed to rouse a cold fury in his antagonist.

"You look out for your own head, master," said he. "You'll find enough to do, I'm thinkin', without talkin' about mine."

This retort drew a shout of hoarse laughter from his second. "Well said, my Tommy!" he cried. "It's Lombard Street to a China orange on the one and only."

The man whom he called Tom was standing with his hands up in the centre of the natural ring. He looked a big man in his clothes, but he seemed bigger in the buff, and his barrel chest, sloping shoulders, and loosely-slung muscular arms were all ideal for the game. His grim eyes gleamed fiercely beneath his misshapen brows, and his lips were set in a fixed hard smile, more menacing than a scowl. The pugilist confessed, as he approached him, that he had never seen a more formidable figure. But his bold heart rose to the fact that he had never yet found the man who could master him, and that it was hardly credible that he would appear as an old-fashioned stranger on a country road. Therefore, with an answering smile, he took up his position and raised his hands.

But what followed was entirely beyond his experience. The stranger feinted quickly with his left, and sent in a swinging hit with his right, so quick and hard that Stevens had barely time to avoid it and to counter with a short jab as his opponent rushed in upon him. Next instant the man's bony arms were round him, and the pugilist was hurled into the air in a whirling cross-buttock, coming down with a heavy thud upon the grass. The stranger stood back and folded his arms while Stevens scrambled to his feet with a red flush of anger upon his cheeks.

"Look here," he cried. "What sort of game is this?"

"We claim foul!" the Baronet shouted.

"Foul be damned! As clean a throw as ever I saw!" said the stout man. "What rules do you fight under?"

"Queensberry, of course."

"I never heard of it. It's London prize-ring with us."

"Come on, then!" cried Stevens, furiously. "I can wrestle as well as another. You won't get me napping again."

* * * *

Nor did he. The next time that the stranger rushed in Stevens caught him in as strong a grip, and after swinging and swaying they came down together in a dog-fall. Three times this occurred, and each time the stranger walked across to his friend and seated himself upon the grassy bank before he recommenced.

"What d'ye make of him?" the Baronet asked, in one of these pauses.

Stevens was bleeding from the ear, but otherwise showed no sign of damage.

"He knows a lot," said the pugilist. "I don't know where he learned it, but he's had a deal of practice somewhere. He's as strong as a lion and as hard as a board, for all his queer face."

"Keep him at out-fighting. I think you are his master there."

"I'm not so sure that I'm his master anywhere, but I'll try my best."

It was a desperate fight, and as round followed round it became clear, even to the amazed Baronet, that the middle-weight champion had met his match. The stranger had a clever draw and a rush which, with his springing hits, made him a most dangerous foe. His head and body seemed insensible to blows, and the horribly malignant smile never for one instant flickered from his lips. He hit very hard with fists like flints, and his blows whizzed up from every angle. He had one particularly deadly lead, an uppercut at the jaw, which again and again nearly came home, until at last it did actually fly past the guard and brought Stevens to the ground. The stout man gave a whoop of triumph.

"The whisker hit, by George! It's a horse to a hen on my Tommy! Another like that, lad, and you have him beat."

"I say, Stevens, this is going too far," said the Baronet, as he supported his weary man. "What will the regiment say if I bring you up all knocked to pieces in a bye-battle! Shake hands with this fellow and give him best, or you'll not be fit for your job."

"Give him best? Not I!" cried Stevens, angrily. "I'll knock that damned smile off his ugly mug before I've done."

"What about the Sergeant?"

"I'd rather go back to London and never see the Sergeant than have my number taken down by this chap."

"Well, 'ad enough?" his opponent asked, in a sneering voice, as he moved from his seat on the bank.

For answer young Stevens sprang forward and rushed at his man with all the strength that was left to him. By the fury of his onset he drove him back, and for a long minute had all the better of the exchanges. But this iron fighter seemed never to tire. His step was as quick and his blow as hard as ever when this long rally had ended. Stevens had eased up from pure exhaustion. But his opponent did not ease up. He came back on him with a shower of furious blows which beat down the weary guard of the pugilist. Alf Stevens was at the end of his strength and would in another instant have sunk to the ground but for a singular intervention.

It has been said that in their approach to the ring the party had passed through a grove of trees. Out of these there came a peculiar shrill cry, a cry of agony, which might be from a child or from some small woodland creature in distress. It was inarticulate, high-pitched, and inexpressibly melancholy. At the sound the stranger, who had knocked Stevens on to his knees, staggered back and looked round him with an expression of helpless horror upon his face. The smile had left his lips and there only remained the loose-lipped weakness of a man in the last extremity of terror.

"It's after me again, mate!" he cried.

"Stick it out, Tom! You have him nearly beat! It can't hurt you."

"It can 'urt me! It will 'urt me!" screamed the fighting man. "My God! I can't face it! Ah, I see it! I see it!"

With a scream of fear he turned and bounded off into the brushwood. His companion, swearing loudly, picked up the pile of clothes and darted after him, the dark shadows swallowing up their flying figures.

Stevens, half-senselessly, had staggered back and lay upon the grassy bank, his head pillowed upon the chest of the young Baronet, who was holding his flask of brandy to his lips. As they sat there they were both aware that the cries had become louder and shriller. Then from among the bushes there ran a small white terrier, nosing about as if following a trail and yelping most piteously. It squattered across the grassy sward, taking no notice of the two young men. Then it also vanished into the shadows. As it did so the two spectators sprang to their feet and ran as hard as they could tear for the gateway and the trap. Terror had seized them—a panic terror far above reason or control. Shivering and shaking, they threw themselves into the dog-cart, and it was not until the willing horses had put two good miles between that ill-omened hollow and themselves that they at last ventured to speak.

"Did you ever see such a dog?" asked the Baronet.

"No," cried Stevens. "And, please God, I never may again."

Late that night the two travellers broke their journey at the Swan Inn, near Harpenden Common. The landlord was an old acquaintance of the Baronet's, and gladly joined him in a glass of port after supper. A famous old sport was Mr. Joe Homer, of the Swan, and he would talk by the hour of the legends of the ring, whether new or old. The name of Alf Stevens was well known to him, and he looked at him with the deepest interest.

"Why, sir, you have surely been fighting," said he. "I hadn't read of any engagement in the papers."

"Enough said of that," Stevens answered, in a surly voice.

"Well, no offence! I suppose"—his smiling face became suddenly very serious—"I suppose you didn't, by chance, see anything of him they call the Bully of Brocas as you came north?"

"Well, what if we did?"

The landlord was tense with excitement.

"It was him that nearly killed Bob Meadows. It was at the very gate of Brocas Old Hall that he stopped him. Another man was with him. Bob was game to the marrow, but he was found hit to pieces on the lawn inside the gate where the summer-house stands."

The Baronet nodded.

"Ah, you've been there!" cried the landlord.

"Well, we may as well make a clean breast of it," said the Baronet, looking at Stevens. "We have been there, and we met the man you speak of—an ugly customer he is, too!"

"Tell me!" said the landlord, in a voice that sank to a whisper. "Is it true what Bob Meadows says, that the men are dressed like our grandfathers, and that the fighting man has his head all caved in?"

"Well, he was old-fashioned, certainly, and his head was the queerest ever I saw."

"God in Heaven!" cried the landlord. "Do you know, sir, that Tom Hickman, the famous prize-fighter, together with his pal, Joe Rowe, a silversmith of the City, met his death at that very point in the year 1822, when he was drunk, and tried to drive on the wrong side of a wagon? Both were killed and the wheel of the wagon crushed in Hickman's forehead."

"Hickman! Hickman!" said the Baronet. "Not the gasman?"

"Yes, sir, they called him Gas. He won his fights with what they called the 'whisker hit,' and no one could stand against him until Neate—him that they called the Bristol Bull—brought him down."

Stevens had risen from the table as white as cheese.

"Let's get out of this, sir. I want fresh air. Let us get on our way." The landlord clapped him on the back.

"Cheer up, lad! You've held him off, anyhow, and that's more than anyone else has ever done. Sit down and have another glass of wine, for if a man in England has earned it this night it is you. There's many a debt you would pay if you gave the Gasman a welting, whether dead or alive. Do you know what he did in this very room?"

The two travellers looked round with startled eyes at the lofty room, stone-flagged and oak-panelled, with great open grate at the farther end.

"Yes, in this very room. I had it from old Squire Scotter, who was here that very night. It was the day when Shelton beat Josh Hudson out St. Albans way, and Gas had won a pocketful of money on the fight. He and his pal Rowe came in here upon their way, and he was mad-raging drunk. The folk fairly shrunk into the corners and under the tables, for he was stalkin' round with the great kitchen poker in his hand, and there was murder behind the smile upon his face. He was like that when the drink was in him—cruel, reckless, and a terror to the world. Well, what think you that he did at last with the poker? There was a little dog, a terrier as I've heard, coiled up before the fire, for it was a bitter December night. The Gasman broke its back with one blow of the poker. Then he burst out laughin', flung a curse or two at the folk that shrunk away from him, and so out to his high gig that was waiting outside. The next we heard was that he was carried down to Finchley with his head ground to a jelly by the wagon wheel. Yes, they do say the little dog with its bleeding skin and its broken back has been seen since then, crawlin' and yelpin' about Brocas Corner, as if it were bookin' for the swine that killed it. So you see, Mr. Stevens, you were fightin' for more than yourself when you put it across the Gasman."

"Maybe so," said the young prize-fighter, "but I want no more fights like that. The Farrier-Sergeant is good enough for me, sir, and if it is the same to you, we'll take a railway train back to town."

THE SPIRAL STONE,
by Arthur Willis Colton

The graveyard on the brow of the hill was white with snow. The marbles were white, the evergreens black. One tall spiral stone stood painfully near the centre. The little brown church outside the gates turned its face in the more comfortable direction of the village.

Only three were out among the graves: "Ambrose Chillingworth, *aetat* 30, 1675"; "Margaret Vane, *aetat* 19, 1839"; and "Thy Little One, O God, *aetat* 2," from the Mercer Lot. It is called the "Mercer Lot," but the Mercers are all dead or gone from the village.

The Little One trotted around busily, putting his tiny finger in the lettering and patting the faces of the cherubs. The other two sat on the base of the spiral, which twisted in the moonlight over them.

"I wonder why it is?" Margaret said. "Most of them never come out at all. We and the Little One come out so often. You were wise and learned. I knew so little. Will you tell me?"

"Learning is not wisdom," Ambrose answered. "But of this matter it was said that our containment in the grave depended on the spirit in which we departed. I made certain researches. It appeared by common report that only those came out whom desperate sin tormented, or labors incomplete and great desire at the point of death made restless. I had doubts the matter were more subtle, the reasons of it reaching out distantly." He sighed faintly, following with his eyes, tomb by tomb, the broad white path that dropped down the hillside to the church. "I desired greatly to live."

"I too. Is it because we desired it so much, then? But the Little One—"

"I do not know," he said.

The Little One trotted gravely here and there, seeming to know very well what he was about, and presently came to the spiral stone. The lettering on it was new, and there was no cherub. He dropped down suddenly on the snow with a faint whimper. His small feet came out from under his gown, as he sat upright gazing at the letters with round, troubled eyes, and up to the top of the monument, for the solution of some unstated problem.

"The stone is but newly placed," said Ambrose, "and the new-comer would seem to be of those who rest in peace."

They went and sat down on either side of him, on the snow. The peculiar cutting of the stone, with spirally ascending lines, together with the moon's illusion, gave it a semblance of motion. Something twisted and climbed continually, and vanished continually from the point. But the base was broad, square, and heavily lettered: "John Mareschelli Vane."

"Vane? That was thy name," said Ambrose.

1890. AETAT 72.

AN EMINENT CITIZEN, A PUBLIC BENEFACTOR,
AND WIDELY ESTEEMED.

FOR THE LOVE OF HIS NATIVE PLACE RETURNED
TO LAY HIS DUST THEREIN.

The Just Made Perfect.

"It would seem he did well and rounded his labors to a goodly end, lying down among his kindred as a sheaf that is garnered in the autumn. He was fortunate."

And Margaret spoke, in the thin, emotionless voice which those who are long in the graveyard use: "He was my brother."

"Thy brother?" said Ambrose.

The Little One looked up and down the spiral with wide eyes. The other two looked past it into the deep white valley, where the river, covered with ice and snow, was marked only by the lines of skeleton willows and poplars. A night wind, listless but continual, stirred the evergreens. The moon swung low over the opposite hills, and for a moment slipped behind a cloud.

"Says it is not so, 'For the Love of his Native Place'?" murmured Ambrose.

And as the moon came out, there leaned against the pedestal, pointing with a finger at the epitaph, one that seemed an old man, with bowed shoulders and keen, restless face, but in his manner cowed and weary.

"It is a lie," he said slowly. "I hated it, Margaret. I came because Ellen Mercer called me."

"Ellen isn't buried here."

"Not here?"

"Not here."

"Was it you, then, Margaret? Why?"

"I didn't call you."

"Who then?" he shrieked. "Who called me?"

The night wind moved on monotonously, and the moonlight was undisturbed, like glassy water.

"When I came away," she said, "I thought you would marry her. You didn't, then? But why should she call you?"

"I left the village suddenly!" he cried. "I grew to dread and then to hate it. I buried myself from the knowledge of it, and the memory of it was my enemy. I wished for a distant death, and these fifty years have heard the summons to come and lay my bones in this graveyard. I thought it was Ellen. You, sir, wear an antique dress; you have been long in this strange existence. Can you tell who called me? If not Ellen, where is Ellen?" He wrung his hands, and rocked to and fro.

"The mystery is with the dead as with the living," said Ambrose. "The shadows of the future and the past come among us. We look in their eyes, and understand them not. Now and again there is a call even here, and the grave is henceforth untenanted of its spirit. Here, too, we know a necessity which binds us, which speaks not with audible voice and will not be questioned."

"But tell me," moaned the other, "does the weight of sin depend upon its consequences? Then what weight do I bear? I do not know whether it was ruin or death, or a thing gone by and forgotten. Is there no answer here to this?"

"Death is but a step in the process of life," answered Ambrose. "I know not if any are ruined or anything forgotten. Look up, to the order of the j, stars, and handwriting on the wall of the firmament. But who hath read it? Mark this night wind, a still small voice. But what speaketh it? The earth is clothed in white garments as a bride. What mean the ceremonials of the seasons? The will from without is only known as it is manifested. Nor does it manifest where the consequences of the deed end or its causes began. Have they any end or a beginning? I can not answer you."

"Who called me, Margaret?"

And she said again monotonously:

"I didn't call you."

The Little One sat between Ambrose and Margaret, chuckling to himself and gazing up at the newcomer, who suddenly bent forward and looked into his eyes, with a gasp.

"What is this?" he whispered.

"Thy Little One, O God, *aetat* 2, from the Mercer Lot," returned Ambrose gently.

"He is very quiet. Art not neglecting thy business, Little One? The lower walks are unvisited tonight."

"They are Ellen's eyes!" cried the other; moaning and rocking. "Did you call me? Were you mine?"

"It is written, 'Thy Little One, O God,'" murmured Ambrose.

But the Little One only curled his feet up under his gown, and now chuckled contentedly.

THE GHOST OF THE BLUE CHAMBER,
by Jerome K. Jerome

"I don't want to make you fellows nervous," began my uncle in a peculiarly impressive, not to say blood-curdling, tone of voice, "and if you would rather that I did not mention it, I won't; but, as a matter of fact, this very house, in which we are now sitting, is haunted."

"You don't say that!" exclaimed Mr. Coombes.

"What's the use of your saying I don't say it when I have just said it?" retorted my uncle somewhat pettishly. "You do talk so foolishly. I tell you the house is haunted. Regularly on Christmas Eve the Blue Chamber [they called the room next to the nursery the 'blue chamber,' at my uncle's, most of the toilet service being of that shade] is haunted by the ghost of a sinful man—a man who once killed a Christmas wait with a lump of coal."

"How did he do it?" asked Mr. Coombes, with eager anxiousness. "Was it difficult?"

"I do not know how he did it," replied my uncle; "he did not explain the process. The wait had taken up a position just inside the front gate, and was singing a ballad. It is presumed that, when he opened his mouth for B flat, the lump of coal was thrown by the sinful man from one of the windows, and that it went down the wait's throat and choked him."

"You want to be a good shot, but it is certainly worth trying," murmured Mr. Coombes thoughtfully.

"But that was not his only crime, alas!" added my uncle. "Prior to that he had killed a solo cornet-player."

"No! Is that really a fact?" exclaimed Mr. Coombes.

"Of course it's a fact," answered my uncle testily; "at all events, as much a fact as you can expect to get in a case of this sort.

"How very captious you are this evening. The circumstantial evidence was overwhelming. The poor fellow, the cornet-player, had been in the neighbourhood barely a month. Old Mr. Bishop, who kept the 'Jolly Sand Boys' at the time, and from whom I had the story, said he had never known a more hardworking and energetic solo cornet-player. He, the cornet-player, only knew two tunes, but Mr. Bishop said that the man could not have played with more vigour, or for more hours in a day, if he had known forty. The two tunes he did play were 'Annie Laurie' and 'Home, Sweet Home;' and as regarded his performance of the former melody, Mr. Bishop said that a mere child could have told what it was meant for.

"This musician—this poor, friendless artist used to come regularly and play in this street just opposite for two hours every evening. One evening he was seen, evidently in response to an invitation, going into this very house, *but was never seen coming out of it!*"

"Did the townsfolk try offering any reward for his recovery?" asked Mr. Coombes.

"Not a ha'penny," replied my uncle.

"Another summer," continued my uncle, "a German band visited here, intending—so they announced on their arrival—to stay till the autumn.

"On the second day from their arrival, the whole company, as fine and healthy a body of men as one could wish to see, were invited to dinner by this sinful man, and, after spending the whole of the next twenty-four hours in bed, left the town a broken and dyspeptic crew; the parish doctor, who had attended them, giving it as his opinion that it was doubtful if they would, any of them, be fit to play an air again."

"You—you don't know the recipe, do you?" asked Mr. Coombes.

"Unfortunately I do not," replied my uncle; "but the chief ingredient was said to have been railway refreshment-room pork-pie.

"I forget the man's other crimes," my uncle went on; "I used to know them all at one time, but my memory is not what it was. I do not, however, believe I am doing his memory an injustice in believing that he was not entirely unconnected with the death, and subsequent burial, of a gentleman who used to play the harp with his toes; and that neither was he altogether unresponsible for the lonely grave of an unknown stranger who had once visited the neighbourhood, an Italian peasant lad, a performer upon the barrel-organ.

"Every Christmas Eve," said my uncle, cleaving with low impressive tones the strange awed silence that, like a shadow, seemed to have slowly stolen into and settled down upon the room, "the ghost of this sinful man haunts the Blue Chamber, in this very house. There, from midnight until cock-crow, amid wild muffled shrieks and groans and mocking laughter and the ghostly sound of horrid blows, it does fierce phantom fight with the spirits of the solo cornet-player and the murdered wait, assisted at intervals, by the shades of the German band; while the ghost of the strangled harpist plays mad ghostly melodies with ghostly toes on the ghost of a broken harp.

Uncle said the Blue Chamber was comparatively useless as a sleeping-apartment on Christmas Eve.

"Hark!" said uncle, raising a warning hand towards the ceiling, while we held our breath, and listened; "Hark! I believe they are at it now—in the *blue chamber*!"

I rose up, and said that I would sleep in the Blue Chamber.

Before I tell you my own story, however—the story of what happened in the Blue Chamber—I would wish to preface it with—

A PERSONAL EXPLANATION

I feel a good deal of hesitation about telling you this story of my own. You see it is not a story like the other stories that I have been telling you, or rather that Teddy Biffles, Mr. Coombes, and my uncle have been telling you: it is a true story. It is not a story told by a person sitting round a fire on Christmas Eve, drinking whisky punch: it is a record of events that actually happened.

Indeed, it is not a 'story' at all, in the commonly accepted meaning of the word: it is a report. It is, I feel, almost out of place in a book of this kind. It is more suitable to a biography, or an English history.

There is another thing that makes it difficult for me to tell you this story, and that is, that it is all about myself. In telling you this story, I shall have to keep on talking about myself; and talking about ourselves is what we modern-day authors have a strong objection to doing. If we literary men of the new school have one praiseworthy yearning more ever present to our minds than another it is the yearning never to appear in the slightest degree egotistical.

I myself, so I am told, carry this coyness—this shrinking reticence concerning anything connected with my own personality, almost too far; and people grumble at me because of it. People come to me and say—

"Well, now, why don't you talk about yourself a bit? That's what we want to read about. Tell us something about yourself."

But I have always replied, "No." It is not that I do not think the subject an interesting one. I cannot myself conceive of any topic more likely to prove fascinating to the world as a whole, or at all events to the cultured portion of it. But I will not do it, on principle. It is inartistic, and it sets a bad example to the younger men. Other writers (a few of them) do it, I know; but I will not—not as a rule.

Under ordinary circumstances, therefore, I should not tell you this story at all. I should say to myself, "No! It is a good story, it is a moral story, it is a strange, weird, enthralling sort of a story; and the public, I know, would like to hear it; and I should like to tell it to them; but it is all about myself—about what I said, and what I saw, and what I did, and I cannot do it. My retiring, anti-egotistical nature will not permit me to talk in this way about myself."

But the circumstances surrounding this story are not ordinary, and there are reasons prompting me, in spite of my modesty, to rather welcome the opportunity of relating it.

As I stated at the beginning, there has been unpleasantness in our family over this party of ours, and, as regards myself in particular, and my share in the events I am now about to set forth, gross injustice has been done me.

As a means of replacing my character in its proper light—of dispelling the clouds of calumny and misconception with which it has been darkened, I feel that my best course is to give a simple, dignified narration of the plain facts, and allow the unprejudiced to judge for themselves. My chief object, I candidly confess, is to clear myself from unjust aspersion. Spurred by this motive—and I think it is an honourable and a right motive—I find I am enabled to overcome my usual repugnance to talking about myself, and can thus tell—

MY OWN STORY

As soon as my uncle had finished his story, I, as I have already told you, rose up and said that *I* would sleep in the Blue Chamber that very night.

"Never!" cried my uncle, springing up. "You shall not put yourself in this deadly peril. Besides, the bed is not made."

"Never mind the bed," I replied. "I have lived in furnished apartments for gentlemen, and have been accustomed to sleep on beds that have never been made from one year's end to the other. Do not thwart me in my resolve. I am young, and have had a clear conscience now for over a month. The spirits will not harm me. I may even do them some little good, and induce them to be quiet and go away. Besides, I should like to see the show."

Saying which, I sat down again. (How Mr. Coombes came to be in my chair, instead of at the other side of the room, where he had been all the evening; and why he never offered to apologise when I sat right down on top of him; and why young Biffles should have tried to palm himself off upon me as my Uncle John, and induced me, under that erroneous impression, to shake him by the hand for nearly three minutes, and tell him that I had always regarded him as father,—are matters that, to this day, I have never been able to fully understand.)

They tried to dissuade me from what they termed my foolhardy enterprise, but I remained firm, and claimed my privilege. I was 'the guest.' 'The guest' always sleeps in the haunted chamber on Christmas Eve; it is his perquisite.

They said that if I put it on that footing, they had, of course, no answer; and they lighted a candle for me, and accompanied me upstairs in a body.

Whether elevated by the feeling that I was doing a noble action, or animated by a mere general consciousness of rectitude, is not for me to say, but I went up-stairs that night with remarkable buoyancy. It was as much as I could do to stop at the landing when I came to it; I felt I wanted to go on up to the roof. But, with the help of the banisters, I restrained my ambition, wished them all good-night, and went in and shut the door.

Things began to go wrong with me from the very first. The candle tumbled out of the candlestick before my hand was off the lock. It kept on tumbling out of the candlestick, and every time I picked put it up and put it in, it tumbled out again: I never saw such a slippery candle. I gave up attempting to use the candle-stick at last, and carried the candle about in my hand; and, even then, it would not keep upright. So I got wild and threw it out of window, and undressed and went to bed in the dark.

I did not go to sleep,—I did not feel sleepy at all,—I lay on my back, looking up at the ceiling, and thinking of things. I wish I could remember some of the ideas that came to me as I lay there, because they were so amusing. I laughed at them myself till the bed shook.

I had been lying like this for half an hour or so, and had forgotten all about the ghost, when, on casually casting my eyes round the room, I noticed for the first time a singularly contented-looking phantom, sitting in the easy-chair by the fire, smoking the ghost of a long clay pipe.

I fancied for the moment, as most people would under similar circumstances, that I must be dreaming. I sat up, and rubbed my eyes.

No! It was a ghost, clear enough. I could see the back of the chair through his body. He looked over towards me, took the shadowy pipe from his lips, and nod-ded.

The most surprising part of the whole thing to me was that I did not feel in the least alarmed. If anything, I was rather pleased to see him. It was company.

I said, "Good evening. It's been a cold day!"

He said he had not noticed it himself, but dared say I was right.

We remained silent for a few seconds, and then, wishing to put it pleasantly, I said, "I believe I have the honour of addressing the ghost of the gentleman who had the accident with the wait?"

He smiled, and said it was very good of me to remember it. One wait was not much to boast of, but still, every little helped.

I was somewhat staggered at his answer. I had expected a groan of remorse. The ghost appeared, on the contrary, to be rather conceited over the business. I thought that, as he had taken my reference to the wait so quietly, perhaps he would not be offended if I questioned him about the organ-grinder. I felt curious about that poor boy.

"Is it true," I asked, "that you had a hand in the death of that Italian peasant lad who came to the town once with a barrel-organ that played nothing but Scotch airs?"

He quite fired up. "Had a hand in it!" he exclaimed indignantly. "Who has dared to pretend that he assisted me? I murdered the youth myself. Nobody helped me. Alone I did it. Show me the man who says I didn't."

I calmed him. I assured him that I had never, in my own mind, doubted that he was the real and only assassin, and I went on and asked him what he had done with the body of the cornet-player he had killed.

He said, "To which one may you be alluding?"

"Oh, were there any more then?" I inquired.

He smiled, and gave a little cough. He said he did not like to appear to be boasting, but that, counting trombones, there were seven.

"Dear me!" I replied, "you must have had quite a busy time of it, one way and another."

He said that perhaps he ought not to be the one to say so, but that really, speaking of ordinary middle-society, he thought there were few ghosts who could look back upon a life of more sustained usefulness.

He puffed away in silence for a few seconds, while I sat watching him. I had never seen a ghost smoking a pipe before, that I could remember, and it interested me.

I asked him what tobacco he used, and he replied, "The ghost of cut cavendish, as a rule."

He explained that the ghost of all the tobacco that a man smoked in life belonged to him when he became dead. He said he himself had smoked a good deal of cut cavendish when he was alive, so that he was well supplied with the ghost of it now.

I observed that it was a useful thing to know that, and I made up my mind to smoke as much tobacco as ever I could before I died.

I thought I might as well start at once, so I said I would join him in a pipe, and he said, "Do, old man"; and I reached over and got out the necessary paraphernalia from my coat pocket and lit up.

We grew quite chummy after that, and he told me all his crimes. He said he had lived next door once to a young lady who was learning to play the guitar, while a gentleman who practised on the bass-viol lived opposite. And he, with fiendish cunning, had introduced these two unsuspecting young people to one another, and had persuaded them to elope with each other against their parents' wishes, and take their musical instruments with them; and they had done so, and, before the honeymoon was over, *she* had broken his head with the bass-viol, and *he* had tried to cram the guitar down her throat, and had injured her for life.

My friend said he used to lure muffin-men into the passage and then stuff them with their own wares till they burst and died. He said he had quieted eighteen that way.

Young men and women who recited long and dreary poems at evening parties, and callow youths who walked about the streets late at night, playing concertinas, he used to get together and poison in batches of ten, so as to save expense; and park orators and temperance lecturers he used to shut up six in a small room with a glass of water and a collection-box apiece, and let them talk each other to death.

It did one good to listen to him.

I asked him when he expected the other ghosts—the ghosts of the wait and the cornet-player, and the German band that Uncle John had mentioned. He smiled, and said they would never come again, any of them.

I said, "Why; isn't it true, then, that they meet you here every Christmas Eve for a row?"

He replied that it *was* true. Every Christmas Eve, for twenty-five years, had he and they fought in that room; but they would never trouble him nor anybody else again. One by one, had he laid them out, spoilt, and utterly useless for all haunting purposes. He had finished off the last German-band ghost that very evening, just before I came upstairs, and had thrown what was left of it out through the slit between the window-sashes. He said it would never be worth calling a ghost again.

"I suppose you will still come yourself, as usual?" I said. "They would be sorry to miss you, I know."

"Oh, I don't know," he replied; "there's nothing much to come for now. Unless," he added kindly, "*you* are going to be here. I'll come if you will sleep here next Christmas Eve."

"I have taken a liking to you," he continued; "you don't fly off, screeching, when you see a party, and your hair doesn't stand on end. You've no idea," he said, "how sick I am of seeing people's hair standing on end."

He said it irritated him.

Just then a slight noise reached us from the yard below, and he started and turned deathly black.

"You are ill," I cried, springing towards him; "tell me the best thing to do for you. Shall I drink some brandy, and give you the ghost of it?"

He remained silent, listening intently for a moment, and then he gave a sigh of relief, and the shade came back to his cheek.

"It's all right," he murmured; "I was afraid it was the cock."

"Oh, it's too early for that," I said. "Why, it's only the middle of the night."

"Oh, that doesn't make any difference to those cursed chickens," he replied bitterly. "They would just as soon crow in the middle of the night as at any other time—sooner, if they thought it would spoil a chap's evening out. I believe they do it on purpose."

He said a friend of his, the ghost of a man who had killed a water-rate collector, used to haunt a house in Long Acre, where they kept fowls in the cellar, and every time a policeman went by and flashed his bull's-eye down the grating, the old cock there would fancy it was the sun, and start crowing like mad; when, of course, the poor ghost had to dissolve, and it would, in consequence, get back home sometimes as early as one o'clock in the morning, swearing fearfully because it had only been out for an hour.

I agreed that it seemed very unfair.

"Oh, it's an absurd arrangement altogether," he continued, quite angrily. "I can't imagine what our old man could have been thinking of when he made it. As I have said to him, over and over again, 'Have a fixed time, and let everybody stick to it—say four o'clock in summer, and six in winter. Then one would know what one was about.'"

"How do you manage when there isn't any cock handy?" I inquired.

He was on the point of replying, when again he started and listened. This time I distinctly heard Mr. Bowles's cock, next door, crow twice.

"There you are," he said, rising and reaching for his hat; "that's the sort of thing we have to put up with. What *is* the time?"

I looked at my watch, and found it was half-past three.

"I thought as much," he muttered. "I'll wring that blessed bird's neck if I get hold of it." And he prepared to go.

"If you can wait half a minute," I said, getting out of bed, "I'll go a bit of the way with you."

"It's very good of you," he rejoined, pausing, "but it seems unkind to drag you out."

"Not at all," I replied; "I shall like a walk." And I partially dressed myself, and took my umbrella; and he put his arm through mine, and we went out together.

Just by the gate we met Jones, one of the local constables.

"Good-night, Jones," I said (I always feel affable at Christmas-time).

"Good-night, sir," answered the man a little gruffly, I thought. "May I ask what you're a-doing of?"

"Oh, it's all right," I responded, with a wave of my umbrella; "I'm just seeing my friend part of the way home."

He said, "What friend?"

"Oh, ah, of course," I laughed; "I forgot. He's invisible to you. He is the ghost of the gentleman that killed the wait. I'm just going to the corner with him."

"Ah, I don't think I would, if I was you, sir," said Jones severely. "If you take my advice, you'll say good-bye to your friend here, and go back indoors. Perhaps you are not aware that you are walking about with nothing on but a night-shirt and a pair of boots and an opera-hat. Where's your trousers?"

I did not like the man's manner at all. I said, "Jones! I don't wish to have to report you, but it seems to me you've been drinking. My trousers are where a man's trousers ought to be—on his legs. I distinctly remember putting them on."

"Well, you haven't got them on now," he retorted.

"I beg your pardon," I replied. "I tell you I have; I think I ought to know."

"I think so, too," he answered, "but you evidently don't. Now you come along indoors with me, and don't let's have any more of it."

Uncle John came to the door at this point, having been awaked, I suppose, by the altercation; and, at the same moment, Aunt Maria appeared at the window in her nightcap.

I explained the constable's mistake to them, treating the matter as lightly as I could, so as not to get the man into trouble, and I turned for confirmation to the ghost.

He was gone! He had left me without a word—without even saying good-bye!

It struck me as so unkind, his having gone off in that way, that I burst into tears; and Uncle John came out, and led me back into the house.

On reaching my room, I discovered that Jones was right. I had not put on my trousers, after all. They were still hanging over the bed-rail. I suppose, in my anxiety not to keep the ghost waiting, I must have forgotten them.

Such are the plain facts of the case, out of which it must, doubtless, to the healthy, charitable mind appear impossible that calumny could spring.

But it has.

Persons—I say 'persons'—have professed themselves unable to understand the simple circumstances herein narrated, except in the light of explanations at once misleading and insulting. Slurs have been cast and aspersions made on me by those of my own flesh and blood.

But I bear no ill-feeling. I merely, as I have said, set forth this statement for the purpose of clearing my character from injurious suspicion.

THE MINIATURE, by J. Y. Akerman

Calling one day on a friend, who had amassed a large collection of autographs, and other manuscript curiosities, he showed me a small quarto volume, which had been bequeathed to him by a relative, a physician, who for many years had been in extensive practice in London.

"He attended the patients at a private asylum for insane persons of the better classes," said my friend, "and I have often heard him speak of the writer of that beautiful MS, a gentleman of good family, who had been an inmate of —— House upwards of thirty years, at the time he was first called to attend him."

On looking over the volume, I found it filled with scraps of poetry, extracts from classic authors, and even from the Talmudic writers; but what interested me most was a narrative of several pages, which appeared so circumstantially related as to leave little doubt of its being partly, if not wholly, founded on fact. I begged permission to make a transcript, which was readily granted, and the result is before the reader.

* * * *

We laugh at what we call the folk of our ancestors, and their notions of destiny, and the malignant influences of the stars. For what will our children deride us? Perhaps for dreaming that friendship was a reality, and that constant love dwelt upon Earth. I once believed that friendship was not a vain name, and thought, with the antique sage, that one mind sometimes dwelt in two bodies. I dreamt, and woke to find that I had been dreaming!

George S—— was my chum at school, and my inseparable companion at college. We quitted it at the same time, he to proceed to London, where he was in expectation of obtaining a lucrative appointment in one of the English colonies, and I to return for a short period to the family mansion, When I reached —— Hall, I found several visitors, among whom was my cousin, Maria D——. She had grown into a woman since I had last met her, and I now thought I had never seen a more perfect figure, or a more bewitching countenance. Then she sang like a siren, and was an elegant horsewoman. Will those who read this wonder that I fell in love with her, that I spent nearly the whole of the day in her company, and that I could think of nothing in the world besides.

Something occurred to delay my friend George's departure from England, and, as he was idling about town, I invited him to —— Hall. Great as was my regard for him, I now, however, discovered that I could live less in his company. No marvel! I preferred the society of my lovely cousin, upon whose heart, I had the happiness to learn, my constant attentions had already made a sensible impression. I hesitated to make her an offer, though I had every reason to believe our attachment was mutual, partly, perhaps, from that excessive delicacy which constantly attends on true love, and partly because I wished to do so when my friend should have left us less exposed to intrusion. Would that the deep sea had swallowed him up, or that he had rotted under a tropical sun, ere he had come to —— Hall!

One morning I arose earlier than usual, and was looking from my chamber window on the beautiful prospect which the house commanded. Wrapped in a delightful reverie, of which my lovely cousin was the principal subject, I paid but little attention to the sound of voices below.

Suddenly, however, I awoke to consciousness: for the sweet tones of a woman in earnest conversation struck on my ear. Yes, it was hers—it was Maria's. What could have called her forth at so early an hour? As I looked earnestly towards the walk which ran through the plantation, I saw emerge from it my cousin and my friend! My heart rose to my lips and choked my utterance, or I should have cried out at the sight. I withdrew from the window and threw myself on the sofa, tormented with surmises a thousand times more painful even than realities.

At the breakfast table I was moody and thoughtful. My friend, perceiving this, attempted a joke; but I was in no humour to receive it. Then Maria, in a compassionating tone, remarked that I looked unwell, and that I should take a walk or ride before breakfast, adding that she and George S —— had walked for an hour and more in the plantation near the house. Though this announcement was certainly but ill calculated to afford perfect ease to my mind, it was yet made with such an artless air that my more gloomy surmises vanished, and I rallied; but I wished my friend would take his departure. Right truly says the Italian proverb, "Love's guerdon is jealousy."

After breakfast, George S—— proposed a stroll on foot to the ruins of the Cistercian Abbey, about a mile distant from the Hall, to which I at once assented. As we walked along the beautiful and shady lane which led to the ruin, George was as loquacious as ever, talking of everybody and everything, and of his confident expectation of realizing a fortune abroad. I was, however, in no humour for talking, and made few remarks in reply; but he appeared not to heed my taciturnity, and, when he arrived at the spot, broke forth into raptures at the sight of the noble ruin.

And truly it was a scene the contemplation of which might have lulled the minds of most men!

A thousand birds were caroling around us; the grass near the ruin was not long and rank, but short, close, studded with trefoil, and soft as a rich carpet. Luxuriant ivy climbed the shattered walls, bleached by the winds of centuries; and the lizards, basking in the sun, darted beneath the fallen fragments at the sound of our footsteps as we approached the spot.

We both sat down on a large stone and surveyed the noble oriel. I was passionately fond of Gothic architecture and had often admired this window, but I thought I had never seen it look so beautiful before. My moody thoughts fled, and I was wrapped in the contemplation of the exquisite tracery, when I was suddenly roused by my friend, who, patting me familiarly on the back, exclaimed,

"It is a beautiful ruin, Dick! How I wish thy sweet cousin, Maria, had accompanied us!"

I was struck dumb by this declaration; but my look was sufficiently eloquent to be understood by him, and he did not fail to interpret it aright. He appeared confused, and I, regaining my self-possession, arose from my seat with the laconic remark, "Indeed!"

George S—— attempted a laugh, but it failed; he was evidently as much disconcerted and disquieted as myself How lynx-eyed is love! We mutually read each other's hearts at the same moment.

"I am sorry for you, Dick," said he, after a short pause, affecting very awkwardly an air of indifference; "'pon my soul, I am; but I'm over head and ears in love with the girl, and should die at the bare thought of her encouraging another."

I wished for the strength of Milo, that I might have dashed out his brains against the huge stone on which we had been sitting. I felt my very blood seethe and simmer at the declaration, and with my clenched fist I struck him a violent and stunning blow, which, though it did not beat him to the ground, sent him staggering several paces backward.

"Liar!" screamed I frantically, "take that! You dare not proceed with your folly."

Recovering his feet, George S—— laid his hand on his sword, which he half unsheathed; but, as if conscious of there being no witness present, or wishing, perhaps, still further to convince me of the advantage he possessed, he did not draw.

"Nay," said I, "out with your weapon; nothing less will do. I would rather lose my birthright than yield to thee one, without whom life would be valueless."

He smiled bitterly, wiped his bruised and bloody face, and slowly drew from his bosom a small miniature, encircled with diamonds, which he held before my eyes. One glance was sufficient—it was a portrait of Maria! It was that face which, sleeping or waking, has haunted me these thirty years past.

"Villain!" I cried, clutching at the portrait with my left hand, while I snatched with my right hand my sword from its sheath, "you have stolen it."

With assumed coolness, which it was impossible he could feel, he smiled again, put back the miniature in his bosom, and drew his sword. The next moment our weapons crossed with an angry clash, and were flashing in the morning's sun.

My adversary was a perfect master of his weapon, and he pressed upon me with a vigour which any attempt to retaliate would have rendered dangerous in one so much inferior to him in skill. Maddened as I was, I yet restrained myself, and stood on my guard, my eyes fixed on his, and watching every glance: my wish to destroy him was intense. The fiend nerved my arm, and, while he warmed with the conflict, I became more cool and vigilant. At length he appeared to grow weary, and then I pressed upon him with the fixed determination of taking his life; but he rallied instantly, and, in returning a thrust, which I intended for his heart, and which he parried scarcely in time, his foot slipped, and he fell on one knee, the point of my sword entering the left breast by accident. It was not a deep wound, and perhaps he felt it not; for he attempted to master my sword with his left hand, while he shortened his own weapon and thrust fiercely at my throat, making at the same time a spring to regain his feet. But his fate was sealed:

as he rose, I dashed aside the thrust intended for me, and sheathed my weapon in his left breast. I believe I must have pierced his heart, for he sank on his knees with a gasp, and the next moment fell heavily on his face, with his sword still clutched tightly in his hand.'

Wearied and panting from the effects of the violent struggle, I threw myself on the large stone which had so recently served us for a seat, and looked on the body of my adversary. He was dead!—that fatal thrust had destroyed all rivalry, but at the price of murder, the murder of one who had been my friend from boyhood upwards!

A thousand conflicting emotions racked me as I beheld the piteous sight. Hatred was extinguished, and remorse succeeded; yet I still thought of the audacity of him who had provoked such deadly resentment. Fear, too, fear of the consequences of this fatal encounter in a solitary spot, without witnesses, added to the intensity of my misery, and I groaned in anguish. What was to be done? Should I go and deliver myself up to justice and declare the whole truth? Should I fly and leave the body of my friend to tell the dismal tale?—or should I bury him secretly, and leave it to be supposed that he had been robbed and murdered? As each suggestion was canvassed and rejected, in my despair, I even thought of dying by my own hand.

"Ah! miserable wretch!" I exclaimed, "what hast thou done?—to what dire necessity has a fair and false face driven thee? Yet I will look once more on those bewitching features which have brought me to this wretched pass!"

I stooped and turned the dead man on his back. His pallid face was writhen and distorted, his lips were bloody, and his eyes, which were wide open, seemed still to glare with hatred and defiance, as when he stood before me in the desperate struggle for life and death. I tore open his vest and discovered the wound which had killed him. It had collapsed, and looked no bigger than the puncture of a bodkin: but one little round crimson spot was visible; the haemorrhage was internal. There lay the miniature which, a few minutes before, had been held up exultingly to my frantic gaze. I seized it and pressed it to my lips, forgetting in my transports how dearly I had purchased it.

This delirium, however, soon subsided, and my next thoughts were of the dead body. I looked about me for some nook where I might deposit it. There was a chasm in the ground among the ruins a few yards off, where the vaulted roof of the crypt had fallen in. It was scarcely large enough to admit the corpse; but I raised it in my arms, bore it thither, and with some difficulty thrust it through the aperture. I heard it fall, as if to some distance, with a dull, heavy sound; and, casting in after it my adversary's hat and sword, I hurried from the spot like another Cain.

At dinner, one glance from Maria—as I replied, in answer to her enquiry after George S——, that he was gone to make a call a few miles oft —one glance, I say, thrilled through my very soul and almost caused me to betray myself. All noticed my perturbed look, and, complaining of violent headache, I withdrew from the table ere the meal was ended, and betook myself to my chamber.'

How shall I paint the horror of that evening, of the night that succeeded it, and the mental darkness which fell upon my wretched self ere the morning dawned! Night came; I rang for lights, and attempted to read, but in vain; and, after pacing my chamber for some hours, overpowered by fatigue, I threw myself on the bed and slept, how long I know not. Though a succession of hideous dreams haunted my slumbers, still I was not awakened by them; the scenes shifted when arrived at their climax, and a new ordeal of horrors succeeded. Yet, like him who suffers from nightmare, with a vague consciousness that all was not real, I wished to awake.

Last of all, I dreamt that I was arraigned for the murder of my friend. The judge summed up the evidence, which, though purely circumstantial, was sufficient to condemn me; and, amidst the silence of the crowded court, broken only by the sobs of anxious and sympathizing friends and relatives, I received sentence of death, and was hurried back to my cell. Here, abandoned by all hope, I lay grovelling on my straw bed, and cursed the hour of my birth. A figure entered, and in gentle accents, which I thought I recognized, bade me arise, quit my prison-house, and follow. The figure was that of a woman closely veiled, She led the way and passed the gaolers, who seemed buried in profound sleep. We left the town, crossed the common, and entered a wood, when I threw myself at the feet of my deliverer, and passionately besought her to unveil. She shook her head mournfully, bade me wait a while till she should return with a change of apparel, and departed.

I cast myself down at the foot of an aged oak, drew from my bosom the portrait of Maria, and, rapt in the contemplation of those lovely features, I did not perceive the approach of a man, the ranger of the forest, who, recognizing my prison-dress, darted upon me, exclaiming, "Villain! you have escaped from gaol and stolen that miniature from the Hall!"

I sprang to my feet, thrust the fatal portrait into my bosom, and would have fled; but he seized, and closed with me. In the struggle which followed, we both fell, I undermost.

At that moment I awoke; I was in reality struggling with someone, but whom I could not tell; for my candles had burnt out and the chamber was in total darkness! A powerful, bony hand grasped me tightly by the throat, while another was thrust into my bosom, as if in search of the miniature, which I had placed there previous to lying down.

With a desperate effort, I disengaged myself and leaped from the bed; but I was again seized, and again my assailant attempted to reach my fatal prize. We struggled violently; at one time I seemed to be overpowering him, and for several moments there was a pause, during which I heard my own breathing and felt my own heart throbbing violently; but he with whom I contended seemed not to breathe, nor to feel like a warm and living man.

An indescribable tremor shook my frame. I attempted to cry out, but my throat was rigid and incapable of articulation. I made another effort to disengage myself from the grasp of my assailant, and in doing so drew him, as I found by the curtains, near to the window. Again the hand was thrust into my bosom, and again I repelled it.

Panting with the violence of the struggle, while a cold sweat burst out at every pore, I disengaged my right hand. Determined to see with whom I contended, I dashed aside the curtain.

The dim light of the waning moon shone into the chamber; it fell upon the face of my antagonist, and one glance froze the blood in my veins. It was he!—it was George S——; —he whom I had murdered, glaring upon me with eyes which no mortal could look upon a second time! My brain whirled, a sound like the discharge of artillery shook the place, and I fell to the ground, blasted at the sight!

* * * *

Here follows a few incoherent sentences, which I have not deemed it necessary to transcribe. The reader will probably supply the sequel to this sad story.

TO LET, by B. M. Croker

Some years ago, when I was a slim young spin, I came out to India to live with my brother Tom; he and I were members of a large and somewhat impecunious family, and I do not think my mother was sorry to have one of her four grown-up daughters thus taken off her hands. Tom's wife, Aggie, had been at school with my eldest sister; we had known and liked her all our lives.

She was quite one of ourselves, and as she and the children were at home when Tom's letter was received, and his offer accepted, she helped me to choose my slender outfit with judgement, zeal, and taste; endowed me with several pretty additions to my wardrobe; superintended the fitting of my gowns and the trying on of my hats, with most sympathetic interest; and finally escorted me out to Lucknow, under her own wing, and installed me in the only spare room in her comfortable bungalow in Dilkongha.

My sister-in-law is a pretty little brunette, rather pale, with dark hair, brilliant black eyes, a resolute mouth, and a bright, intelligent expression. She is orderly, trim, and feverishly energetic, and seems to live every moment of her life. Her children, her wardrobe, her house, her servants, and last, not least, her husband, are all models in their way; and yet she has plenty of time for tennis and dancing, and talking and walking. She is, undoubtedly, a remarkably talented little creature, and especially prides herself on her nerve and her power of will, or will-power. I suppose they are the same thing?—and I am sure they are all the same to Tom, who worships the sole of her small slipper. Strictly between ourselves, she is the ruling member of the family, and turns her lord and master round her little finger. Tom is big and fair, of course, the opposite to his wife, quiet, rather easy-going and inclined to be indolent, but Aggie rouses him up, and pushes him to the front, and keeps him there. She knows all about his department, his prospects of promotion, his prospects of furlough, of getting acting-appointments, and so on, even better than he does himself. The chief of Tom's department—have I said that Tom is in the Irritation Office?—has placed it solemnly on record that he considers little Mrs Shandon a surprisingly clever woman. The two children, Bob and Tor, are merry, oppressively active monkeys, aged three and five years respectively. As for myself, I am tall and fair, and I wish I could add pretty; but this is a true story. My eyes are blue, my teeth are white, my hair is red—alas, a blazing red; and I was, at this period, nineteen years of age; and now I think I have given a sufficient outline of the whole family.

We arrived at Lucknow in November, when the cold weather is delightful, and everything was delightful to me. The bustle and life of a great Indian station, the novelty of my surroundings, the early morning rides, picnics down the river, and dances at the "Chutter Munzil" made me look upon Lucknow as a paradise on Earth; and in this light I still regarded it, until a great change came over the temperature, and the month of April introduced me to red-hot winds, sleepless nights, and the intolerable "brain fever" bird. Aggie had made up her mind definitely on one subject: we were not to go away to the hills until the rains. Tom could only get two months' leave (July and August), and she did not intend to leave him to grill on the plains alone. As for herself and the children—not to speak of me—we had all come out from home so recently we did not require a change. The trip to Europe had made a vast hole in the family stocking, and she wished to economize; and who can economize with two establishments in full swing? Tell me this, ye Anglo-Indian matrons. With a large, cool bungalow, plenty of *punkhas, khuskhus* tatties, ice, and a thermantidote, surely we could manage to brave May and June—at any rate the attempt was made. Gradually the hills drained Lucknow week by week; family after family packed up, warned us of our folly in remaining on the plains, offered to look for houses for us, and left by the night mail. By the middle of May, the place was figuratively empty. Nothing can be more dreary than a large station in the hot weather, unless it is an equally forsaken hill station in the depths of winter, when the mountains are covered with snow: the mall no longer resounds with gay voices and the tramp of companies, but is visited by bears and panthers, and the houses are closed, and, as it were, put to bed in straw! As for Lucknow in the summer, it was a melancholy spot; the public gardens were deserted, the chairs at the Chutter Munzil stood empty, the shops were shut, the baked white roads—no longer thronged with carriages and bamboo carts—gave ample room to the humble *ekka*, or a Dhobie's meagre donkey, shuffling along in the dust.

Of course we were not the *only* people remaining in the place, grumbling at the heat and dust and life in general; but there can be no sociability with the thermometer above 100 degrees in the shade.

Through the long, long Indian day we sat and gasped, in darkened rooms, and consumed quantities of "Nimbo pegs," *i.e.* limes and soda water, and listened to the fierce hot winds roaring along the road and driving the roasted leaves before it; and in the evening, when the sun had set, we went for a melancholy drive through the Wingfield Park, or round by Martiniere College, and met our friends at the library and compared sensations and thermometers. The season was exceptionally bad, but people say that every year, and presently Bobby and Tor began to fade: their little white faces and listless eyes appealed to Aggie as Tom's anxious expostulations had never done. "Yes, they must go to the hills with *me*." But this idea I repudiated at once; I refused to undertake the responsibility—I, who could scarcely speak a word to the servants—who had no experience! Then Bobbie had a bad go of fever—intermittent fever; the beginning of the end to his alarmed mother; the end being represented by a large gravestone! She now became as firmly determined to go as she had previously been resolved to stay; but it was so late in the season to take a house. Alas, alas, for the beautiful tempting advertisements in the *Pioneer*, which we had seen and scorned!

Aggie wrote to a friend in a certain hill station, called for this occasion only "Kantia," and Tom wired to a house agent, who triumphantly replied by letter that there was not *one* unlet bungalow on his books. This missive threw us into the depths of despair; there seemed no alternative but a hill hotel, and the usual quarters that await the last comers, and the proverbial welcome for children and dogs (we had only four); but the next day brought us good news from Aggie's friend Mrs Chalmers.

Dear Mrs Shandon,

I received your letter, and went at once to Cursitjee, the agent. Every hole and corner up here seems full, and he had not a single house to let. Today I had a note from him, saying that Briarwood is vacant; the people who took it are not coming up, they have gone to Naini Tal. You *are* in luck. I have just been out to see the house, and have secured it for you. It is a mile and a half from the club, but I know that you and your sister are capital walkers. I envy you. Such a charming place—two sitting-rooms, four bedrooms, four bathrooms, a hall, servants' go-downs, stabling, and a splendid view from a very pretty garden, and only Rs. 800 for the season!

Why, I am paying Rs. 1,000 for a *very* inferior house, with scarcely a stick of furniture and no view. I feel so proud of myself, and I am longing to show you my treasure trove. Telegraph when you start, and I shall have a milk man in waiting and fires in all the rooms.

Yours sincerely,

Edith Chalmers.

We now looked upon Mrs Chalmers as our best and dearest friend, and began to get under way at once. A long journey in India is a serious business when the party comprises two ladies, two children, two ayahs and five other servants, three fox terriers, a mongoose and a Persian cat—all these animals going to the hills for the benefit of their health—not to speak of a ton of luggage, including crockery and lamps, a cottage piano, a goat and a pony. Aggie and I, the children, one ayah, two terriers, the cat and mongoose, our bedding and pillows, the tiffin basket and ice basket, were all stowed into one compartment, and I must confess that the journey was truly miserable. The heat was stifling, despite the water tatties. One of the terriers had a violent dispute with the cat, and the cat had a difference with the mongoose, and Bob and Tor had a pitched battle more than once. I actually wished myself back in Lucknow. I was most truly thankful to wake one morning to find myself under the shadow of the Himalayas—not a mighty, snow-clad range of everlasting hills, but merely the spurs—the moderate slopes, covered with scrub and loose shale and jungle, and deceitful little trickling watercourses. We sent the servants on ahead, whilst we rested at the Dâk bungalow near the railway station, and then followed them at our leisure.

We accomplished the ascent in dandies—open kind of boxes, half box, half chair—carried on the shoulders of four men. This was an entirely novel sensation to me, and at first an agreeable one, so long as the slopes were moderate and the paths wide; but the higher we went, the narrower became the path, the steeper the naked precipice; and as my coolies would walk at the extreme edge, with the utmost indifference to my frantic appeals to "Beetor! Beetor!"—and would change poles at the most agonizing corners—my feelings were very mixed, especially when droves of loose pack ponies came thundering downhill, with no respect for the rights of the road.

Late at night we passed through Kantia and arrived at Briarwood far too weary to be critical. Fires were blazing, supper was prepared, and we dispatched it in haste, and most thankfully went to bed and slept soundly, as anyone would do who had spent thirty-six hours in a crowded compartment and ten in a cramped wooden case.

* * * *

The next morning, rested and invigorated, we set out on a tour of inspection; and it is almost worthwhile to undergo a certain amount of baking on the sweltering heat of the plains in order to enjoy those deep first draughts of cool hill air, instead of a stifling, dust-laden atmosphere, and to appreciate the green valleys and blue hills by force of contrast to the far-stretching, eye-smarting, white glaring roads that intersect the burnt-up plains—roads and plains that even the pariah abandons, salamander though he be!

To our delight and surprise, Mrs Chalmers had by no means overdrawn the advantages of our new abode. The bungalow is as solidly built of stone, two storied, and ample in size. It stood on a kind of shelf, cut out of the hillside, and was surrounded by a pretty flower garden, full of roses, fuchsias, carnations. The high road passed the gate, from which the avenue descended direct to the entrance door, which was at the end of the house, and from whence ran a long passage. Off this passage three rooms opened to the right, all looking south, and all looking into a deep, delightful, flagged verandah.

The stairs were very steep. At the head of them, the passage and rooms were repeated. There were small nooks, and dressing-rooms, and convenient outhouses, and plenty of good water; but the glory of Briarwood was undoubtedly its verandah: it was fully twelve feet wide, roofed with zinc, and overhung a precipice of a thousand feet—not a startlingly sheer *khud*, but a tolerably straight descent of grey-blue shale rocks and low jungle. From it there was a glorious view, across a valley, far away, to the snowy range. It opened at one end into the avenue, and was not inclosed; but at the side next the precipice there was a stout wooden railing, with netting at the bottom, for the safety of too enterprising dogs or children. A charming spot, despite its rather bold situation; and as Aggie and I sat in it, surveying the scenery and inhaling the pure hill air, and watching Bob and Tor tearing up and down playing horses, we said to one another that "the verandah alone was worth half the rent."

"It's absurdly cheap," exclaimed my sister-in-law complacently. "I wish you saw the hovel I had, at Simla, for the same rent. I wonder if it is feverish, or badly drained, or what?"

"Perhaps it has a ghost," I suggested facetiously; and at such an absurd idea we both went into peals of laughter.

At this moment Mrs Chalmers appeared, brisk, rosy, and breathlessly benevolent, having walked over from Kantia.

"So you have found it," she said as we shook hands. "I said nothing about this delicious verandah! I thought I would keep it as a surprise. I did not say a word too much for Briarwood, did I?"

"Not half enough," we returned rapturously; and presently we went in a body, armed with a list from the agent, and proceeded to go over the house and take stock of its contents.

"It's not a bit like a hill furnished house," boasted Mrs Chalmers, with a glow of pride, as she looked round the drawing-room; "carpets, curtains, solid—very solid—chairs, and Berlin wool-worked screens, a card-table, and any quantity of pictures."

"Yes, don't they look like family portraits?" I suggested, as we gazed at them. There was one of an officer in faded water colours, another of his wife, two of a previous generation in oils and amply gilded frames, two sketches of an English country house, and some framed photographs, groups of grinning cricketers or wedding guests. All the rooms were well, almost handsomely, furnished in an old-fashioned style. There was no scarcity of wardrobes, looking-glasses, or even armchairs in the bedrooms, and the pantry was fitted out—a most singular circumstance—with a large supply of handsome glass and china, lamps, old moderators, coffee-pots and tea-pots, plated side-dishes and candlesticks, cooking utensils and spoons and forks, wine coasters, and a cake-basket.

These articles were all let with the house, much to our amazement, provided we were responsible for the same. The china was Spode, the plate old family heirlooms, with a crest—a winged horse—on everything, down to the very mustard spoons.

"The people who own this house must be lunatics," remarked Aggie as she peered round the pantry; "fancy hiring out one's best family plate and good old china! And I saw some ancient music books in the drawing-room, and there is a side-saddle in the bottle khana."

"My dear, the people who owned this house are dead," explained Mrs Chalmers. "I heard all about them last evening from Mrs Starkey."

"Oh, is *she* up there?" exclaimed Aggie somewhat fretfully.

"Yes, her husband is cantonment magistrate. This house belonged to an old retired colonel and his wife. They and his niece lived here. These were all their belongings. They died within a short time of one another, and the old man left a queer will, to say that the house was to remain precisely as they left it for twenty years, and at the end of that time it was to be sold and all the property dispersed. Mrs Starkey says she is sure that he never intended it to be let, but the heir-at-law insists on that, and is furious at the terms of the will."

"Well, it is a very good thing for us," remarked Aggie; "we are as comfortable here as if we were in our own house: there is a stove in the kitchen; there are nice boxes for firewood in every room; clocks, real hair mattresses—in short, it is as you said, a treasure trove."

We set to work to modernize the drawing-room with phoolkaries, Madras muslin curtains, photograph screens and frames, and such-like portable articles. We placed the piano across a corner, arranged flowers in some handsome Dresden china vases, and entirely altered and improved the character of the room. When Aggie had dispatched a most glowing description of our new quarters to Tom, and we had had tiffin, we set off to walk into Kantia to put our names down at the library and to enquire for letters at the post office.

Aggie met a good many acquaintances—who does not who has lived five years in India in the same district?—among them Mrs Starkey, an elderly lady with a prominent nose and goggle eyes, who greeted her loudly across the reading-room table in this agreeable fashion.

"And so you have come up after *all*, Mrs Shandon. Someone told me that you meant to remain below, but I knew you never could be so wicked as to keep your poor little children in that heat."

Then coming round and dropping into a chair beside her she said, "And I suppose this young lady is your sister-in-law?"

Mrs Starkey eyed me critically, evidently appraising my chances in the great marriage market. She herself had settled her own two daughters most satisfactorily, and had now nothing to do but interest herself in these people's affairs.

"Yes," acquiesced Aggie. "Miss Shandon—Mrs Starkey."

"And so you have taken Briarwood?"

"Yes, we have been most lucky to get it."

"I hope you will think so at the end of three months," observed Mrs Starkey with a significant pursing of her lips. "Mrs Chalmers is a stranger up here, or she would not have been in such a hurry to jump at it."

"Why, what is the matter with it?" enquired Aggie. "It is well built, well furnished, well situated, and very cheap."

"That's just it—*suspiciously* cheap. Why, my dear Mrs Shandon, if there was not something against it, it would let for two hundred rupees a month."

"And what is against it?"

"It's haunted! There you have the reason in two words."

"Is that all? I was afraid it was the drains. I don't believe in ghosts and haunted houses. What are we supposed to see?"

"Nothing," retorted Mrs Starkey, who seemed a good deal nettled at our smiling incredulity.

"Nothing!" with an exasperating laugh.

"No, but you will make up for it in hearing. Not now—you are all right for the next six weeks—but after the monsoon breaks, I give you a week at Briarwood. No one would stand it longer, and indeed you might as well bespeak your rooms at Cooper's Hotel now. There is always a rush up here in July by the two month's leave people, and you will be poked into some wretched go-down."

Aggie laughed rather a careless ironical little laugh and said, "Thank you, Mrs Starkey; but I think we will stay on where we are; at any rate for the present."

"Of course it will be as *you* please. What do you think of the verandah?" she enquired with a curious smile.

"I think, as I was saying to Susan, that it is worth half the rent of the house."

"And in *my* opinion the house is worth double rent without it," and with this enigmatic remark she rose and sailed away.

"Horrid old frump," exclaimed Aggie as we walked home in the starlight. "She is jealous and angry that she did not get Briarwood *herself*—I know her so well. She is always hinting and repeating stories about the nicest people—always decrying your prettiest dress or your best servant."

We soon forgot all about Mrs Starkey and her dismal prophecy, being too gay and too busy to give her, or it, a thought. We had so many engagements—tennis parties and tournaments, picnics, concerts, dances and little dinners. We ourselves gave occasional afternoon teas in the verandah, using the best Spode cups and saucers and the old silver cake-basket, and were warmly complimented on our good fortune in securing such a charming house and garden. One day the children discovered to their great joy that the old chowkidar belonging to the bungalow possessed an African grey parrot—a rare bird indeed in India; he had a battered Europe cage, doubtless a remnant of better days, and swung on his ring, looking up at us enquiringly out of his impudent little black eyes.

The parrot had been the property of the former inmates of Briarwood, and as it was a long-lived creature, had survived its master and mistress, and was boarded out with the chowkidar, at one rupee per month.

The chowkidar willingly carried the cage into the verandah, where the bird seemed perfectly at home.

We got a little table for its cage, and the children were delighted with him, as he swung to and fro, with a bit of cake in his wrinkled claw.

Presently be startled us all by suddenly calling "Lucy," in a voice that was as distinct as if it had come from a human throat, "Pretty Lucy—Lu—cy."

"That must have been the niece," said Aggie. "I expect she was the original of that picture over the chimney-piece in your room; she looks like a Lucy."

It was a large framed half-length photograph of a very pretty girl, in a white dress, with gigantic open sleeves. The ancient parrot talked incessantly now that he had been restored to society; he whistled for the dogs and brought them flying to his summons, to his great satisfaction and their equally great indignation. He called "Qui hye" so naturally, in a lady's shrill soprano, or a gruff male bellow, that I have no doubt our servants would have liked to have wrung his neck. He coughed and expectorated like an old gentleman, and whined like a puppy, and mewed like a cat, and I am sorry to add, sometimes swore like a trooper; but his most constant cry was, "Lucy, where are you, pretty Lucy—Lucy—Lu—cy?"

* * * *

Aggie and I went to various picnics, but to that given by the Chalmers (in honour of Mr Chalmers's brother Charlie, a captain in a Gurkha regiment, just come up to Kantia on leave) Aggie was unavoidably absent. Tor had a little touch of fever, and she did not like to leave him; but I went under my hostess's care, and expected to enjoy myself immensely. Alas! on that self-same afternoon the long expected monsoon broke, and we were nearly drowned! We rode to the selected spot, five miles from Kantia, laughing and chattering, indifferent to the big blue-black clouds that came slowly, but surely, sailing up from below; it was a way they had had for days and nothing had come of it. We spread the table-cloth, boiled the kettle, unpacked the hampers, in spite of sharp gusts of wind and warning rumbling thunder.

Just as we had commenced to reap the reward of our exertions, there fell a few huge drops, followed by a vivid flash, and then a tremendous crash of thunder, like a whole park of artillery, that seemed to shake the mountains, and after this the deluge. In less than a minute we were soaked through; we hastily gathered up the tablecloth by its four ends, gave it to the coolies, and fled. It was all I could do to stand against the wind; only for Captain Chalmers I believe I would have been blown away; as it was, I lost my hat; it was whirled into space. Mrs Chalmers lost her boa, and Mrs Starkey, not merely her bonnet, but some portion of her hair.

We were truly in a wretched plight, the water streaming down our faces and squelching in our boots; the little trickling mountain rivulets were now like racing seas of turbid water; the lightning was almost blinding; the trees rocked dangerously and lashed one another with their quivering branches. I had never been out in such a storm before, and I hope I never may again.

We reached Kantia more dead than alive, and Mrs Chalmers sent an express to Aggie, and kept me till the next day. After raining as it only can rain in the Himalayas, the weather cleared, the sun shone, and I rode home in borrowed plumes, full of my adventures and in the highest spirits. I found Aggie sitting over the fire in the drawing-room, looking ghastly white—that was nothing uncommon—but terribly depressed, which was most unusual.

"I am afraid you have neuralgia?" I said as I kissed her; she nodded and made no reply.

"How is Tor?" I enquired as I drew a chair up to the fire.

"Better—quite well."

"Any news—any letter?"

"Not a word—not a line."

"Has anything happened to Pip"—Pip was a fox terrier, renowned for having the shortest tail and being the most impertinent dog in Lucknow—"or the mongoose?"

"No, you silly girl! Why do you ask such questions?"

"I was afraid something was amiss; you seem rather down on your luck."

Aggie shrugged her shoulders and then said:

"What put such an absurd idea into your head? Tell me all about the picnic," and she began to talk rapidly and to ask me various questions; but I observed that once she had set me going—no difficult task—her attention flagged, her eyes wandered from my face to the fire. She was not listening to half I said, and my most thrilling descriptions were utterly lost on this indifferent, abstracted little creature! I noticed from this time that she had become strangely nervous for her.

She invited herself to the share of half my bed; she was restless, distrait, and even irritable; and when I was asked out to spend the day, dispensed with my company with an alacrity that was by no means flattering. Formerly, of an evening she used to herd the children home at sundown and tear me away from the delights of the reading-room at seven o'clock; now she hung about the library until almost the last moment, until it was time to put out the lamps, and kept the children with her, making transparent pretexts for their company. Often we did not arrive at home till half-past eight o'clock.

I made no objections to these late hours. Neither did Charlie Chalmers, who often walked back with us and remained to dinner. I was amazed to notice that Aggie seemed delighted to have his company, for she had always expressed a rooted aversion to what she called "tame young men," and here was this new acquaintance dining with us at least thrice a week!

About a month after the picnic we had a spell of dreadful weather—thunderstorms accompanied by torrents. One pouring afternoon, Aggie and I were sitting over the drawing-room fire, whilst the rain came fizzing down among the logs and ran in rivers off the roof and out of the spouts. There had been no going out that day, and we were feeling rather flat and dull, as we sat in a kind of ghostly twilight, with all outdoor objects swallowed up in mist, listening to the violent battering of the rain on the zinc verandah, and the storm which was growling round the hills.

"Oh, for a visitor!" I exclaimed; "but no one but a fish or a lunatic would be out on such an evening."

"No one, indeed," echoed Aggie in a melancholy tone. "We may as well draw the curtains and have in the lamp and tea to cheer us up."

She had scarcely finished speaking when I heard the brisk trot of a horse along the road. It stopped at the gate and came rapidly down our avenue. I heard the wet gravel crunching under hoofs and—yes—a man's cheery whistle. My heart jumped, and I half rose from my chair. It must be Charlie Chalmers braving the elements to see me!—such, I must confess, was my incredible vanity! He did not stop at the front door as usual, but rode straight into the verandah, which afforded ample room and shelter for half-a-dozen mounted men.

"Aggie," I said eagerly, "do you hear? It must be—"

I paused—my tongue silenced by the awful pallor of her face and the expression of her eyes as she sat with her little hands clutching the arms of her chair, and her whole figure bent forward in an attitude of listening—an attitude of terror.

"What is it, Aggie?" I said, "Are you ill?"

As I spoke, the horse's hoofs made a loud clattering noise on the stone-paved verandah outside, and a man's voice—a young man's eager voice—called, *"Lucy!"*

Instantly a chair near the writing-table was pushed back and someone went quickly to the window—a French one—and bungled for a moment with the fastening—I always had a difficulty with that window myself. Aggie and I were within the bright circle of the firelight, but the rest of the room was dim, and outside the streaming grey sky was spasmodically illuminated by occasional vivid flashes that lit up the surrounding hills as if it were daylight. The trampling of impatient hoofs and the rattling of a door handle were the only sounds that were audible for a few breathless seconds; but during those seconds Pip, bristling like a porcupine and trembling violently in every joint, had sprung off my lap and crawled abjectly under Aggie's chair, seemingly in a transport of fear. The door was opened audibly, and a cold, icy blast swept in, that seemed to freeze my very heart and made me shiver from head to foot.

At this moment there came with a sinister blue glare—the most vivid flash of lightning I ever saw. It lit up the whole room, which was empty save for ourselves, and was instantly followed by a clap of thunder that caused my knees to knock together and that terrified me and filled me with horror. It evidently terrified the horse too; there was a violent plunge, a clattering of hoofs on the stones, a sudden loud crash of smashing timber, a woman's long, loud, piercing shriek, which stopped the very beating of my heart, and then a frenzied struggle in the cruel, crumbling, treacherous shale, the rattle of loose stones and the hollow roar of something sliding down the precipice.

I rushed to the door and tore it open, with that awful despairing cry still ringing in my ears. The verandah was empty; there was not a soul to be seen or a sound to be heard, save the rain on the roof.

"Aggie," I screamed, "come here! Someone has gone over the verandah and down the *khud*! You heard him."

"Yes," she said, following me out; "but come in—come in."

"I believe it was Charlie Chalmers"—shaking her as I spoke. "He has been killed—killed—*killed!* And you stand and do nothing. Send people! Let us go ourselves! *Bearer! Ayah! Khidmatgar!"* I cried, raising my voice.

"Hush! It was *not* Charlie Chalmers," she said, vainly endeavouring to draw me into the drawing-room. "Come in—come in."

"No, no!"—pushing her away and wringing my hands. "How cruel you are! How inhuman! There is a path. Let us go at once—at once!"

"You need not trouble yourself, Susan," she interrupted; "and you need not cry and tremble—*they* will bring him up. What you heard was supernatural; it was not real."

"No—no—no! It was all real. Oh! That scream is in my ears still."

"I will convince you," said Aggie, taking my hand as she spoke. "Feel all along the verandah. Are the railings broken?"

I did as she bade me. No, though was wet and clammy, the railing was intact.

"Where is the broken place?" she asked.

Where, indeed?

"Now," she continued, "since you will not come in, look over, and you will see something more presently."

Shivering with fear and cold, drifting rain, I gazed down as she bade me, and there far below I saw lights moving rapidly to and fro, evidently in search of something. After a little delay they congregated in one place. There was a low, booming murmur—they had found him—and presently they commenced to ascend the hill, with the "hum-hum" of coolies carrying a burden.

Nearer and nearer the lights and sounds came up to the very brink of the khud, past the end of the verandah. Many steps and many torches—faint blue torches held by invisible hands—invisible but heavy-footed bearers carried their burden slowly upstairs and along the passage, and deposited it with a dump in Aggie's bedroom! As we stood clasped in one another's arms and shaking all over, the steps descended, the ghostly lights passed up the avenue and disappeared in the gathering darkness. The repetition of the tragedy was over for that day.

"Have you heard it before?" I asked with chattering teeth, as I bolted the drawing-room window.

"Yes, the evening of the picnic and twice since. That is the reason I have always tried to stay out till late and to keep you out. I was hoping and praying you might never hear it. It always happens just before dark. I am afraid you have thought me very queer of late. I have told no end of stories to keep you and the children from harm—I have—"

"I think you have been very kind," I interrupted. "Oh, Aggie, shall you ever get that crash and that awful cry out of your head?"

"Never!" hastily lighting the candles as she spoke.

"Is there anything more?" I asked tremulously.

"Yes; sometimes at night the most terrible weeping and sobbing in my bedroom," and she shuddered at the mere recollection.

"Do the servants know?" I asked anxiously.

"The ayah Mumà has heard it, and the khánsámáh says his mother is sick and he must go, and the bearer wants to attend his brother's wedding. They will *all* leave."

"I suppose most people know too?" I suggested dejectedly.

"Yes, don't you remember Mrs Starkey's warnings and her saying that without the verandah the house was worth double rent? We understand that dark speech of hers now, and we have not come to Cooper's Hotel yet."

"No, not *yet*. I wish we *had*. I wonder what Tom will say? He will be here in another fortnight. Oh, I wish he was here now."

In spite of our heart-shaking experience, we managed to eat and drink and sleep, yea, to play tennis—somewhat solemnly, it is true—and go to the club, where we remained to the very *last* moment; needless to mention that I now entered into Aggie's manoeuvre *con amore*. Mrs Starkey evidently divined the reason of our loitering in Kantia, and said in her most truculent manner, as she squared up to us:

"You keep your children out very late, Mrs Shandon."

"Yes, but we like to have them with us," rejoined Aggie in a meek apologetic voice.

"Then why don't you go home earlier?"

"Because it is so stupid and lonely," was the mendacious answer.

"Lonely is not the word *I* should use. I wonder if you are as wise as your neighbours now? Come now, Mrs Shandon."

"About what?" said Aggie with ill-feigned innocence.

"About Briarwood. Haven't you heard it yet? The ghastly precipice and horse affair?"

"Yes, I suppose we may as well confess that we *have*."

"Humph! You are a brave couple to stay on. The Tombs tried it last year for three weeks. The Paxtons took it the year before, and then sub-let it, not that they believed in ghosts—oh, dear no," and she laughed ironically.

"And what is the story?" I enquired eagerly.

"Well the story is this. An old retired officer and his wife and their pretty niece lived at Briarwood a good many years ago. The girl was engaged to be married to a fine young fellow in the Guides. The day before the wedding what you know of happened, and has happened every monsoon ever since. The poor girl went out of her mind and destroyed herself, and the old colonel and his wife did not long survive her. The house is uninhabitable in the monsoon, and there seems nothing for it but to auction off the furniture and pull it down; it will always be the same as long as it stands. Take my advice and come into Cooper's Hotel. I believe you can have that small set of rooms at the back. The sitting-room smokes, but beggars can't be choosers."

"That will only be our very last resource," said Aggie hotly.

"It's not very grand, I grant you, but any port in a storm."

Tom arrived, was doubly welcome, and was charmed with Briarwood. Chaffed us unmercifully and derided our fears until he himself had a similar experience, and he heard the phantom horse plunging in the verandah and that wild, unearthly and utterly appalling shriek. No, he could not laugh that away, and seeing that we had now a mortal abhorrence of the place, that the children had to be kept abroad in the damp till long after dark, that Aggie was a mere hollow-eyed spectre, and that we had scarcely a servant left, that—in short, one day we packed up precipitately and fled in a body to Cooper's Hotel. But we did not basely endeavour to sub-let, nor advertise Briarwood as "a delightfully situated *pucka*-built house, containing all the requirements of a gentleman's family." No, no. Tom bore the loss of the rent and—a more difficult feat—Aggie bore Mrs Starkey's insufferable, "I told you so."

Aggie was at Kantia again last season. She walked out early one morning to see our former abode. The chowkidar and parrot are still in possession, and are likely to remain the sole tenants on the premises. The parrot suns and dusts his ancient feathers in the empty verandah, which re-echoes with his cry of "Lucy, where are you, pretty Lucy?" The chowkidar inhabits a secluded go-down at the back, where he passes most of the day in sleeping, or smoking the soothing "hooka." The place has a forlorn, uncared-for appearance now. The flowers are nearly all gone; the paint has peeled off the doors and windows; the avenue is grass-grown. Briarwood appears to have resigned itself to emptiness, neglect, and decay, although outside the gate there still hangs a battered board on which, if you look very closely you can decipher the words "To Let."

THE FOREIGNER,
by Sarah Orne Jewett

CHAPTER 1

One evening, at the end of August, in Dunnet Landing, I heard Mrs. Todd's firm footstep crossing the small front entry outside my door, and her conventional cough which served as a herald's trumpet, or a plain New England knock, in the harmony of our fellowship.

"Oh, please come in!" I cried, for it had been so still in the house that I supposed my friend and hostess had gone to see one of her neighbors. The first cold northeasterly storm of the season was blowing hard outside. Now and then there was a dash of great raindrops and a flick of wet lilac leaves against the window, but I could hear that the sea was already stirred to its dark depths, and the great rollers were coming in heavily against the shore. One might well believe that Summer was coming to a sad end that night, in the darkness and rain and sudden access of autumnal cold. It seemed as if there must be danger offshore among the outer islands.

"Oh, there!" exclaimed Mrs. Todd, as she entered. "I know nothing ain't ever happened out to Green Island since the world began, but I always do worry about mother in these great gales. You know those tidal waves occur sometimes down to the West Indies, and I get dwellin' on 'em so I can't set still in my chair, not knit a common row to a stocking. William might get mooning, out in his small bo't, and not observe how the sea was making, an' meet with some accident. Yes, I thought i'd come in and set with you if you wa'n't busy. No, I never feel any concern about 'em in winter 'cause then they're prepared, and all ashore and everything snug. William ought to keep help, as I tell him; yes, he ought to keep help."

I hastened to reassure my anxious guest by saying that Elijah Tilley had told me in the afternoon, when I came along the shore past the fish houses, that Johnny Bowden and the Captain were out at Green Island; he had seen them beating up the bay, and thought they must have put into Burnt Island cove, but one of the lobstermen brought word later that he saw them hauling out at Green Island as he came by, and Captain Bowden pointed ashore and shook his head to say that he did not mean to try to get in. "The old Miranda just managed it, but she will have to stay at home a day or two and put new patches in her sail," I ended, not without pride in so much circumstantial evidence.

Mrs. Todd was alert in a moment. "Then they'll all have a very pleasant evening," she assured me, apparently dismissing all fears of tidal waves and other sea-going disasters. "I was urging Alick Bowden to go ashore some day and see mother before cold weather. He's her own nephew; she sets a great deal by him. And Johnny's a great chum o' William's; don't you know the first day we had Johnny out 'long of us, he took an' give William his money to keep for him that he'd been a-savin', and William showed it to me an' was so affected, I thought he was goin' to shed tears? 'Twas a dollar an' eighty cents; yes, they'll have a beautiful evenin' all together, and like's not the sea'll be flat as a doorstep come morning."

I had drawn a large wooden rocking-chair before the fire, and Mrs. Todd was sitting there jogging herself a little, knitting fast, and wonderfully placid of countenance. There came a fresh gust of wind and rain, and we could feel the small wooden house rock and hear it creak as if it were a ship at sea.

"Lord, hear the great breakers!" exclaimed Mrs. Todd. "How they pound!— there, there! I always run of an idea that the sea knows anger these nights and gets full o' fight. I can hear the rote o' them old black ledges way down the thoroughfare. Calls up all those stormy verses in the Book o' Psalms; David he knew how old sea-goin' folks have to quake at the heart."

I thought as I had never thought before of such anxieties. The families of sailors and coastwise adventurers by sea must always be worrying about somebody, this side of the world or the other. There was hardly one of Mrs. Todd's elder acquaintances, men or women, who had not at some time or other made a sea voyage, and there was often no news until the voyagers themselves came back to bring it.

"There's a roaring high overhead, and a roaring in the deep sea," said Mrs. Todd solemnly, "and they battle together nights like this. No, I couldn't sleep; some women folks always goes right to bed an' to sleep, so's to forget, but 'taint my way. Well, it's a blessin' we don't all feel alike; there's hardly any of our folks at sea to worry about, nowadays, but I can't help my feelin's, an' I got thinking of mother all alone, if William had happened to be out lobsterin' and couldn't make the cove gettin' back."

"They will have a pleasant evening," I repeated. "Captain Bowden is the best of good company."

"Mother'll make him some pancakes for his supper, like's not," said Mrs. Todd, clicking her knitting needles and giving a pull at her yarn. Just then the old cat pushed open the unlatched door and came straight toward her mistress's lap. She was regarded severely as she stepped about and turned on the broad expanse, and then made herself into a round cushion of fur, but was not openly admonished. There was another great blast of wind overhead, and a puff of smoke came down the chimney.

"This makes me think o' the night Mis' Cap'n Tolland died," said Mrs. Todd, half to herself. "Folks used to say these gales only blew when somebody's a-dyin', or the devil was a-comin' for his own, but the worst man I ever knew died a real pretty mornin' in June."

"You have never told me any ghost stories," said I; and such was the gloomy weather and the influence of the night that I was instantly filled with reluctance to have this suggestion followed. I had not chosen the best of moments; just before I spoke we had begun to feel as cheerful as possible. Mrs. Todd glanced doubtfully at the cat and then at me, with a strange absent look, and I was really afraid that she was going to tell me something that would haunt my thoughts on every dark stormy night as long as I lived.

"Never mind now; tell me to-morrow by daylight, Mrs. Todd," I hastened to say, but she still looked at me full of doubt and deliberation.

"Ghost stories!" she answered. "Yes, I don't know but I've heard a plenty of 'em first an' last. I was just sayin' to myself that this is like the night Mis' Cap'n

Tolland died. 'Twas the great line storm in September all of thirty, or maybe forty, year ago. I ain't one that keeps much account o' time."

"Tolland? That's a name I have never heard in Dunnet," I said.

"Then you haven't looked well about the old part o' the buryin' ground, no'theast corner," replied Mrs. Todd. "All their women folks lies there; the sea's got most o' the men. They were a known family o' shipmasters in early times. Mother had a mate, Ellen Tolland, that she mourns to this day; died right in her bloom with quick consumption, but the rest o' that family was all boys but one, and older than she, an' they lived hard seafarin' lives an' all died hard. They were called very smart seamen. I've heard that when the youngest went into one o' the old shippin' houses in Boston, the head o' the firm called out to him: 'Did you say Tolland from Dunnet? That's recommendation enough for any vessel!' There was some o' them old shipmasters as tough as iron, an' they had the name o' usin' their crews very severe, but there wa'n't a man that wouldn't rather sign with 'em an' take his chances, than with the slack ones that didn't know how to meet accidents."

CHAPTER 2

There was so long a pause, and Mrs. Todd still looked so absent-minded, that I was afraid she and the cat were growing drowsy together before the fire, and I should have no reminiscences at all. The wind struck the house again, so that we both started in our chairs and Mrs. Todd gave a curious, startled look at me. The cat lifted her head and listened too, in the silence that followed, while after the wind sank we were more conscious than ever of the awful roar of the sea. The house jarred now and then, in a strange, disturbing way.

"Yes, they'll have a beautiful evening out to the island," said Mrs. Todd again; but she did not say it gayly. I had not seen her before in her weaker moments.

"Who was Mrs. Captain Tolland?" I asked eagerly, to change the current of our thoughts.

"I never knew her maiden name; if I ever heard it, I've gone an' forgot; 'twould mean nothing to me," answered Mrs. Todd.

"She was a foreigner, an' he met with her out in the Island o' Jamaica. They said she'd been left a widow with property. Land knows what become of it; she was French born, an' her first husband was a Portugee, or somethin'."

I kept silence now, a poor and insufficient question being worse than none.

"Cap'n John Tolland was the least smartest of any of 'em, but he was full smart enough, an' commanded a good brig at the time, in the sugar trade; he'd taken out a cargo o' pine lumber to the islands from somewheres up the river, an' had been headin' for home in the port o' Kingston, an' had gone ashore that afternoon for his papers, an' remained afterwards 'long of three friends o' his, all shipmasters. They was havin' their suppers together in a tavern; 'twas late in the evenin' an' they was more lively than usual, an' felt boyish; and over opposite was another house full o' company, real bright and pleasant lookin', with a lot o' lights, an' they heard somebody singin' very pretty to a guitar. They wa'n't in no go-to-meetin' condition, an' one of 'em, he slapped the table an' said, 'Le's go over 'n' hear that lady sing!' an' over they all went, good honest sailors, but three sheets in the wind, and stepped in as if they was invited, an' made their bows inside the door, an' asked if they could hear the music; they were all respectable well-dressed men. They saw the woman that had the guitar, an' there was a company a-listenin', regular highbinders all of 'em; an' there was a long table all spread out with big candlesticks like little trees o' light, and a sight o' glass an' silver ware; an' part o' the men was young officers in uniform, an' the colored folks was steppin' round servin' 'em, an' they had the lady singin'. 'Twas a wasteful scene, an' a loud talkin' company, an' though they was three sheets in the wind themselves there wa'n't one o' them cap'ns but had sense to perceive it. The others had pushed back their chairs, an' their decanters an' glasses was standin' thick about, an' they was teasin' the one that was singin' as if they'd just got her in to amuse 'em. But they quieted down; one o' the young officers had beautiful manners, an' invited the four cap'ns to join 'em, very polite; 'twas a kind of public house, and after they'd all heard another song, he come to consult with 'em whether they wouldn't git up and dance a hornpipe or somethin' to the lady's music.

They was all elderly men an' shipmasters, and owned property; two of 'em was church members in good standin'," continued Mrs. Todd loftily, "an' they wouldn't lend theirselves to no such kick-shows as that, an' spite o' bein' three sheets in the wind, as I have once observed, they waved aside the tumblers of wine the young officer was pourin' out for 'em so freehanded, and said they should rather be excused. An' when they all rose, still very dignified, as I've been well informed, and made their partin' bows and was goin' out, them young sports got round 'em an' tried to prevent 'em, and they had to push an' strive considerable, but out they come. There was this Cap'n Tolland and two Cap'n Bowdens, and the fourth was my own father." (Mrs. Todd spoke slowly, as if to impress the value of her authority.) "Two of them was very religious, upright men, but they would have their night off sometimes, all o' them old-fashioned cap'ns, when they was free of business and ready to leave port.

"An' they went back to their tavern an' got their bills paid, an' set down kind o' mad with everybody by the front window, mistrusting some o' their tavern charges, like's not, by that time, an' when they got tempered down, they watched the house over across, where the party was.

"There was a kind of a grove o' trees between the house an' the road, an' they heard the guitar a-goin' an' a-stoppin' short by turns, and pretty soon somebody began to screech, an' they saw a white dress come runnin' out through the bushes, an' tumbled over each other in their haste to offer help; an' out she come, with the guitar, cryin' into the street, and they just walked off four square with her amongst 'em, down toward the wharves where they felt more to home. They couldn't make out at first what 'twas she spoke,—Cap'n Lorenzo Bowden was well acquainted in Havre an' Bordeaux, an' spoke a poor quality o' French, an' she knew a little mite o' English, but not much; and they come somehow or other to discern that she was in real distress. Her husband and her children had died o' yellow fever; they'd all come up to Kingston from one o' the far Wind'ard Islands to get passage on a steamer to France, an' a negro had stole their money off her husband while he lay sick o' the fever, an' she had been befriended some, but the folks that knew about her had died too; it had been a dreadful run o' the fever that season, an' she fell at last to playin' an' singin' for hire, and for what money they'd throw to her round them harbor houses.

'Twas a real hard case, an' when them cap'ns made out about it, there wa'n't one that meant to take leave without helpin' of her. They was pretty mellow, an'

228

whatever they might lack o' prudence they more'n made up with charity: they didn't want to see nobody abused, an' she was sort of a pretty woman, an' they stopped in the street then an' there an' drew lots who should take her aboard, bein' all bound home. An' the lot fell to Cap'n Jonathan Bowden who did act discouraged; his vessel had but small accommodations, though he could stow a big freight, an' she was a dreadful slow sailer through bein' square as a box, an' his first wife, that was livin' then, was a dreadful jealous woman. He threw himself right onto the mercy o' Cap'n Tolland."

Mrs. Todd indulged herself for a short time in a season of calm reflection.

"I always thought they'd have done better, and more reasonable, to give her some money to pay her passage home to France, or wherever she may have wanted to go," she continued.

I nodded and looked for the rest of the story.

"Father told mother," said Mrs. Todd confidentially, "that Cap'n Jonathan Bowden an' Cap'n John Tolland had both taken a little more than usual; I wouldn't have you think, either, that they both wasn't the best o' men, an' they was solemn as owls, and argued the matter between 'em, an' waved aside the other two when they tried to put their oars in. An' spite o' Cap'n Tolland's bein' a settled old bachelor they fixed it that he was to take the prize on his brig; she was a fast sailer, and there was a good spare cabin or two where he'd sometimes carried passengers, but he'd filled 'em with bags o' sugar on his own account an' was loaded very heavy beside. He said he'd shift the sugar an' get along somehow, an' the last the other three cap'ns saw of the party was Cap'n John handing the lady into his bo't, guitar and all, an' off they all set tow'ds their ships with their men rowin' 'em in the bright moonlight down to Port Royal where the anchorage was, an' where they all lay' goin' out with the tide an' mornin' wind at break o' day. An' the others thought they heard music of the guitar, two o' the bo'ts kept well together, but it may have come from another source."

"Well; and then?" I asked eagerly after a pause. Mrs. Todd was almost laughing aloud over her knitting and nodding emphatically. We had forgotten all about the noise of the wind and sea.

"Lord bless you! he come sailing into Portland with his sugar, all in good time, an' they stepped right afore a justice o' the peace, and Cap'n John Tolland come paradin' home to Dunnet Landin' a married man. He owned one o' them thin, narrow-lookin' houses with one room each side o' the front door, and two slim black spruces spindlin' up against the front windows to make it gloomy inside. There was no horse nor cattle of course, though he owned pasture land, an' you could see rifts o' light right through the barn as you drove by. And there was a good excellent kitchen, but his sister reigned over that; she had a right to two rooms, and took the kitchen an' a bedroom that led out of it; an' bein' given no rights in the kitchen had angered the cap'n so they weren't on no kind o' speakin' terms. He preferred his old brig for comfort, but now and then, between voyages he'd come home for a few days, just to show he was master over his part o' the house, and show Eliza she couldn't commit no trespass.

"They stayed a little while; 'twas pretty spring weather, an' I used to see Cap'n John rollin' by with his arms full o' bundles from the store, lookin' as pleased and important as a boy; an' then they went right off to sea again, an' was gone a good many months. Next time he left her to live there alone, after they'd stopped at home together some weeks, an' they said she suffered from bein' at sea, but some said that the owners wouldn't have a woman aboard. 'Twas before father was lost on that last voyage of his, an' he said mother went up once or twice to see them. Father said there wa'n't a mite o' harm in her, but somehow or other a sight o' prejudice arose; it may have been caused by the remarks of Eliza an' her feelin's tow'ds her brother. Even my mother had no regard for Eliza Tolland. But mother asked the cap'n's wife to come with her one evenin' to a social circle that was down to the meetin'-house vestry, so she'd get acquainted a little, an' she appeared very pretty until they started to have some singin' to the melodeon. Mari' Harris an' one o' the younger Caplin girls undertook to sing a duet, an' they sort o' flatted, an' she put her hands right up to her ears, and give a little squeal, an' went quick as could be an' give 'em the right notes, for she could read the music like plain print, an' made 'em try it over again. She was real willin' an' pleasant, but that didn't suit, an' she made faces when they got it wrong. An' then there fell a dead calm, an' we was all settin' round prim as dishes, an' my mother, that never expects ill feelin', asked her if she wouldn't sing somethin', an up she got—poor creatur', it all seems so different to me now —an' sung a lovely little song standin' in the floor; it seemed to have something gay about it that kept a-repeatin', an' nobody could help keepin' time, an' all of a sudden she looked round at the tables and caught up a tin plate that some-body'd fetched a Washin'ton pie in, an' she begun to drum on it with her fingers like one o' them tambourines, an' went right on singin' faster an' faster, and next minute she begun to dance a little pretty dance between the verses, just as light and pleasant as a child. You couldn't help seein' how pretty 'twas; we all got to trottin' a foot, an' some o' the men clapped their hands quite loud, a-keepin' time, 'twas so catchin', an' seemed so natural to her. There wa'n't one of 'em but enjoyed it; she just tried to do her part, an' some urged her on, till she stopped with a little twirl of her skirts an' went to her place again by mother. And I can see mother now, reachin' over an' smilin' an' pattin' her hand.

"But next day there was an awful scandal goin' in the parish, an' Mari' Harris reproached my mother to her face, an' I never wanted to see her since, but I've had to a good many times. I said Mis' Tolland didn't intend no impropriety—I reminded her of David's dancin' before the Lord; but she said such a man as David never would have thought o' dancin' right there in the Orthodox vestry, and she felt I spoke with irreverence.

"And next sunday Mis' Tolland come walkin' into our meeting, but I must say she acted like a cat in a strange garret, and went right out down the aisle with her head in air, from the pew Deacon Caplin had showed her into. 'Twas just in the beginning of the long prayer. I wish she'd stayed through, whatever her rea-sons were. Whether she'd expected somethin' different, or misunderstood some o' the pastor's remarks, or what 'twas, I don't really feel able to explain, but she kind o' declared war, at least folks thought so, an' war 'twas from that time. I see she was cryin', or had been, as she passed by me; perhaps bein' in meetin' was what had power to make her feel homesick and strange.

"Cap'n John Tolland was away fittin' out; that next week he come home to see her and say farewell. He was lost with his ship in the Straits of Malacca, and she lived there alone in the old house a few months longer till she died. He left her well off; 'twas said he hid his money about the house and she knew where 'twas. Oh, I expect you've heard that story told over an' over twenty times, since you've been here at the Landin'?"

"Never one word," I insisted.

"It was a good while ago," explained Mrs. Todd, with reassurance. "Yes, it all happened a great while ago."

CHAPTER 3

At this moment, with a sudden flaw of the wind, some wet twigs outside blew against the window panes and made a noise like a distressed creature trying to get in. I started with sudden fear, and so did the cat, but Mrs. Todd knitted away and did not even look over her shoulder.

"She was a good-looking woman; yes, I always thought Mis' Tolland was good-looking, though she had, as was reasonable, a sort of foreign cast, and she spoke very broken English, no better than a child. She was always at work about her house, or settin' at a front window with her sewing; she was a beautiful hand to embroider. Sometimes, summer evenings, when the windows was open, she'd set an' drum on her guitar, but I don't know as I ever heard her sing but once after the cap'n went away. She appeared very happy about havin' him, and took on dreadful at partin' when he was down here on the wharf, going back to Portland by boat to take ship for that last v'y'ge. He acted kind of ashamed, Cap'n John did; folks about here ain't so much accustomed to show their feelings. The whistle had blown an' they was waitin' for him to get aboard, an' he was put to it to know what to do and treated her very affectionate in spite of all impatience; but mother happened to be there and she went an' spoke, and I remember what a comfort she seemed to be. Mis' Tolland clung to her then, and she wouldn't give a glance after the boat when it had started, though the captain was very eager a-wavin' to her. She wanted mother to come home with her an' wouldn't let go her hand, and mother had just come in to stop all night with me an' had plenty o' time ashore, which didn't always happen, so they walked off together, an' 'twas some considerable time before she got back.

"'I want you to neighbor with that poor lonesome creatur',' says mother to me, lookin' reproachful. 'She's a stranger in a strange land,' says mother. 'I want you to make her have a sense that somebody feels kind to her.'

"'Shy, since that time she flaunted out o' meetin', folks have felt she liked other ways better'n our'n,' says I. I was provoked, because I'd had a nice supper ready, an' mother'd let it wait so long 'twas spoiled. 'I hope you'll like your supper!' I told her. I was dreadful ashamed afterward of speakin' so to mother.

"'What consequence is my supper?' says she to me; mother can be very stern —'or your comfort or mine, beside letting a foreign person an' a stranger feel so desolate; she's done the best a woman could do in her lonesome place, and she asks nothing of anybody except a little common kindness. Think if 'twas you in a foreign land!'

"And mother set down to drink her tea, an' I set down humbled enough over by the wall to wait till she finished. An' I did think it all over, an' next day I never said nothin', but I put on my bonnet, and went to see Mis' Cap'n Tolland, if 'twas only for mother's sake. 'Twas about three quarters of a mile up the road here, beyond the schoolhouse. I forgot to tell you that the cap'n had bought out his sister's right at three or four times what 'twas worth, to save trouble, so they'd got clear o' her, an' I went round into the side yard sort o' friendly an' so-ciable, rather than stop an' deal with the knocker an' the front door. It looked so pleasant an' pretty I was glad I come; she had set a little table for supper, though 'twas still early, with a white cloth on it, right out under an old apple tree close by the house. I noticed 'twas same as with me at home, there was only one plate. She was just coming out with a dish; you couldn't see the door nor the table from the road.

"In the few weeks she'd been there she'd got some bloomin' pinks an' other flowers next the doorstep. Somehow it looked as if she'd known how to make it homelike for the cap'n. She asked me to set down; she was very polite, but she looked very mournful, and I spoke of mother, an' she put down her dish and caught holt o' me with both hands an' said my mother was an angel. When I see the tears in her eyes 'twas all right between us, and we were always friendly after that, and mother had us come out and make a little visit that summer; but she come a foreigner and she went a foreigner, and never was anything but a stranger among our folks. She taught me a sight o' things about herbs I never knew before nor since; she was well acquainted with the virtues o' plants. She'd act awful secret about some things too, an' used to work charms for herself sometimes, an' some o' the neighbors told to an' fro after she died that they knew enough not to provoke her, but 'twas all nonsense; 'tis the believin' in such things that causes 'em to be any harm, an' so I told 'em," confided Mrs. Todd contemptuously. "That first night I stopped to tea with her she'd cooked some eggs with some herb or other sprinkled all through, and 'twas she that first led me to discern mushrooms; an' she went right down on her knees in my garden here when she saw I had my different officious herbs. Yes, 'twas she that learned me the proper use o' parsley too; she was a beautiful cook."

Mrs. Todd stopped talking, and rose, putting the cat gently in the chair, while she went away to get another stick of apple-tree wood. It was not an evening when one wished to let the fire go down, and we had a splendid bank of bright coals. I had always wondered where Mrs. Todd had got such an unusual knowledge of cookery, of the varieties of mushrooms, and the use of sorrel as a vegetable, and other blessings of that sort. I had long ago learned that she could vary her omelettes like a child of France, which was indeed a surprise in Dunnet Landing.

CHAPTER

All these revelations were of the deepest interest, and I was ready with a question as soon as Mrs. Todd came in and had well settled the fire and herself and the cat again.

"I wonder why she never went back to France, after she was left alone?"

"She come here from the French islands," explained Mrs. Todd. "I asked her once about her folks, an' she said they were all dead; 'twas the fever took 'em. She made this her home, lonesome as 'twas; she told me she hadn't been in France since she was 'so small,' and measured me off a child o' six. She'd lived right out in the country before, so that part wa'n't unusual to her. Oh yes, there was something very strange about her, and she hadn't been brought up in high circles nor nothing o' that kind. I think she'd been really pleased to have the cap'n marry her an' give her a good home, after all she'd passed through, and leave her free with his money an' all that. An' she got over bein' so strange-looking to me after a while, but 'twas a very singular expression: she wore a fixed smile that wa'n't a smile; there wa'n't no light behind it, same's a lamp can't shine if it ain't lit. I don't know just how to express it, 'twas a sort of made countenance."

One could not help thinking of Sir Philip Sidney's phrase, "A made countenance, between simpering and smiling."

"She took it hard, havin' the captain go off on that last voyage," Mrs. Todd went on. "She said somethin' told her when they was partin' that he would never come back. He was lucky to speak a home-bound ship this side o' the Cape o' Good Hope, an' got a chance to send her a letter, an' that cheered her up. You often felt as if you was dealin' with a child's mind, for all she had so much information that other folks hadn't. I was a sight younger than I be now, and she made me imagine new things, and I got interested watchin' her an' findin' out what she had to say, but you couldn't get to no affectionateness with her. I used to blame me sometimes; we used to be real good comrades goin' off for an afternoon, but I never give her a kiss till the day she laid in her coffin and it come to my heart there wa'n't no one else to do it."

"And Captain Tolland died," I suggested after a while.

"Yes, the cap'n was lost," said Mrs. Todd, "and of course word didn't come for a good while after it happened. The letter come from the owners to my uncle, Cap'n Lorenzo Bowden, who was in charge of Cap'n Tolland's affairs at home, and he come right up for me an' said I must go with him to the house. I had known what it was to be a widow, myself, for near a year, an' there was plenty o' widow women along this coast that the sea had made desolate, but I never saw a heart break as I did then.

"'Twas this way: we walked together along the road, me an' uncle Lorenzo. You know how it leads straight from just above the schoolhouse to the brook bridge, and their house was just this side o' the brook bridge on the left hand; the cellar's there now, and a couple or three good-sized gray birches growin' in it. And when we come near enough I saw that the best room, this way, where she most never set, was all lighted up, and the curtains up so that the light shone bright down the road, and as we walked, those lights would dazzle and dazzle in my eyes, and I could hear the guitar a-goin', an' she was singin'. She heard our steps with her quick ears and come running to the door with her eyes a-shinin', an' all that set look gone out of her face, an' begun to talk French, gay as a bird, an' shook hands and behaved very pretty an' girlish, sayin' 'twas her fete day. I didn't know what she meant then. And she had gone an' put a wreath o' flowers on her hair an' wore a handsome gold chain that the cap'n had given her; an' there she was, poor creatur', makin' believe have a party all alone in her best room; 'twas prim enough to discourage a person, with too many chairs set close to the walls, just as the cap'n's mother had left it, but she had put sort o' long garlands on the walls, droopin' very graceful, and a sight of green boughs in the corners, till it looked lovely, and all lit up with a lot o' candles."

"Oh dear!" I sighed. "Oh, Mrs. Todd, what did you do?"

"She beheld our countenances," answered Mrs. Todd solemnly. "I expect they was telling everything plain enough, but Cap'n Lorenzo spoke the sad words to her as if he had been her father; and she wavered a minute and then over she went on the floor before we could catch hold of her, and then we tried to bring her to herself and failed, and at last we carried her upstairs, an' I told uncle to run down and put out the lights, and then go fast as he could for Mrs. Begg, being very experienced in sickness, an' he so did. I got off her clothes and her poor

233

wreath, and I cried as I done it. We both stayed there that night, and the doctor said 'twas a shock when he come in the morning; he'd been over to Black Island an' had to stay all night with a very sick child."

"You said that she lived alone some time after the news came," I reminded Mrs. Todd then.

"Oh yes, dear," answered my friend sadly, "but it wa'n't what you'd call livin'; no, it was only dyin', though at a snail's pace. She never went out again those few months, but for a while she could manage to get about the house a little, and do what was needed, an' I never let two days go by without seein' her or hearin' from her. She never took much notice as I came an' went except to answer if I asked her anything. Mother was the one who gave her the only comfort."

"What was that?" I asked softly.

"She said that anybody in such trouble ought to see their minister, mother did, and one day she spoke to Mis' Tolland, and found that the poor soul had been believin' all the time that there weren't any priests here. We'd come to know she was a Catholic by her beads and all, and that had set some narrow minds against her. And mother explained it just as she would to a child; and uncle Lorenzo sent word right off somewheres up river by a packet that was bound up the bay, and the first o' the week a priest come by the boat, an' uncle Lorenzo was on the wharf 'tendin' to some business; so they just come up for me, and I walked with him to show him the house. He was a kind-hearted old man; he looked so benevolent an' fatherly I could ha' stopped an' told him my own troubles; yes, I was satisfied when I first saw his face, an' when poor Mis' Tolland beheld him enter the room, she went right down on her knees and clasped her hands together to him as if he'd come to save her life, and he lifted her up and blessed her, an' I left 'em together, and slipped out into the open field and walked there in sight so if they needed to call me, and I had my own thoughts. At last I saw him at the door; he had to catch the return boat. I meant to walk back with him and offer him some supper, but he said no, and said he was comin' again if needed, and signed me to go into the house to her, and shook his head in a way that meant he understood everything. I can see him now; he walked with a cane, rather tired and feeble; I wished somebody would come along, so's to carry him down to the shore.

"Mis' Tolland looked up at me with a new look when I went in, an' she even took hold o' my hand and kept it. He had put some oil on her forehead, but nothing anybody could do would keep her alive very long; 'twas his medicine for the soul rather 'n the body. I helped her to bed, and next morning she couldn't get up to dress her, and that was Monday, and she began to fail, and 'twas Friday night she died." (Mrs. Todd spoke with unusual haste and lack of detail.) "Mrs. Begg and I watched with her, and made everything nice and proper, and after all the ill will there was a good number gathered to the funeral. 'Twas in Reverend Mr. Bascom's day, and he done very well in his prayer, considering he couldn't fill in with mentioning all the near connections by name as was his habit. He spoke very feeling about her being a stranger and twice widowed, and all he said about her being reared among the heathen was to observe that there might be roads leadin' up to the New Jerusalem from various points. I says to myself that I guessed quite a number must ha' reached there that wa'n't able to set out from Dunnet Landin'!"

234

Mrs. Todd gave an odd little laugh as she bent toward the firelight to pick up a dropped stitch in her knitting, and then I heard a heartfelt sigh.

'Twas most forty years ago," she said; "most everybody's gone a'ready that was there that day."

CHAPTER 5

Suddenly Mrs. Todd gave an energetic shrug of her shoulders, and a quick look at me, and I saw that the sails of her narrative were filled with a fresh breeze.

"Uncle Lorenzo, Cap'n Bowden that I have referred to"—

"Certainly!" I agreed with eager expectation.

"He was the one that had been left in charge of Cap'n John Tolland's affairs, and had now come to be of unforeseen importance.

"Mrs. Begg an' I had stayed in the house both before an' after Mis' Tolland's decease, and she was now in haste to be gone, having affairs to call her home; but uncle come to me as the exercises was beginning, and said he thought I'd better remain at the house while they went to the buryin' ground. I couldn't understand his reasons, an' I felt disappointed, bein' as near to her as most anybody; 'twas rough weather, so mother couldn't get in, and didn't even hear Mis' Tolland was gone till next day. I just nodded to satisfy him, 'twa'n't no time to discuss anything. Uncle seemed flustered; he'd gone out deep-sea fishin' the day she died, and the storm I told you of rose very sudden, so they got blown off way down the coast beyond Monhegan, and he'd just got back in time to dress himself and come.

"I set there in the house after I'd watched her away down the straight road far's I could see from the door; 'twas a little short walkin' funeral an' a cloudy sky, so everything looked dull an' gray, an' it crawled along all in one piece, same's walking funerals do, an' I wondered how it ever come to the Lord's mind to let her begin down among them gay islands all heat and sun, and end up here among the rocks with a north wind blowin'. 'Twas a gale that begun the afternoon before she died, and had kept blowin' off an' on ever since. I'd thought more than once how glad I should be to get home an' out o' sound o' them black spruces a-beatin' an' scratchin' at the front windows.

"I set to work pretty soon to put the chairs back, an' set outdoors some that was borrowed, an' I went out in the kitchen, an' I made up a good fire in case somebody come an' wanted a cup o' tea; but I didn't expect any one to travel way back to the house unless 'twas uncle Lorenzo. 'Twas growin' so chilly that I fetched some kindlin' wood and made fires in both the fore rooms. Then I set down an' begun to feel as usual, and I got my knittin' out of a drawer. You can't be sorry for a poor creatur' that's come to the end o' all her troubles; my only discomfort was I thought I'd ought to feel worse at losin' her than I did; I was younger then than I be now. And as I set there, I begun to hear some long notes o' dronin' music from upstairs that chilled me to the bone."

Mrs. Todd gave a hasty glance at me.

"Quick's I could gather me, I went right upstairs to see what 'twas," she added eagerly, "an 'twas just what I might ha' known. She'd always kept her guitar hangin' right against the wall in her room; 'twas tied by a blue ribbon, and there was a window left wide open; the wind was veerin' a good deal, an' it slanted in and searched the room. The strings was jarrin' yet.

"'Twas growin' pretty late in the afternoon, an' I begun to feel lonesome as I shouldn't now, and I was disappointed at having to stay there, the more I thought it over, but after a while I saw Cap'n Lorenzo polin' back up the road all alone, and when he come nearer I could see he had a bundle under his arm and had shifted his best black clothes for his every-day ones. I run out and put some tea into the teapot and set it back on the stove to draw, an' when he come in I reached down a little jug o' spirits—Cap'n Tolland had left his house well provisioned as if his wife was goin' to put to sea same's himself, an' there she'd gone an' left it. There was some cake that Mis' Begg an' I had made the day before. I thought that uncle an' me had a good right to the funeral supper, even if there wa'n't any one to join us. I was lookin' forward to my cup o' tea; 'twas beautiful tea out of a green lacquered chest that I've got now."

"You must have felt very tired," said I, eagerly listening.

"I was 'most beat out, with watchin' an' tendin' and all," answered Mrs. Todd, with as much sympathy in her voice as if she were speaking of another person. "But I called out to uncle as he came in, 'Well, I expect it's all over now, an' we've all done what we could. I thought we'd better have some tea or somethin' before we go home. Come right out in the kitchen, sir,' says I, never thinking but we only had to let the fires out and lock up everything safe an' eat our refreshment, an' go home.

"'I want both of us to stop here to-night,' says uncle, looking at me very important.

"'Oh, what for?' says I, kind o' fretful.

"'I've got my proper reasons,' says uncle. 'I'll see you well satisfied, Almira. Your tongue ain't so easy-goin' as some o' the women folks, an' there's property here to take charge of that you don't know nothin' at all about.'

"'What do you mean?' says I.

"'Cap'n Tolland acquainted me with his affairs; he hadn't no sort o' confidence in nobody but me an' his wife, after he was tricked into signin' that Portland note, an' lost money. An' she didn't know nothin' about business; but what he didn't take to sea to be sunk with him he's hid somewhere in this house. I expect Mis' Tolland may have told you where she kept things?' said uncle.

"I see he was dependin' a good deal on my answer," said Mrs. Todd, "but I had to disappoint him; no, she had never said nothin' to me.

"'Well, then, we've got to make a search,' says he, with considerable relish; but he was all tired and worked up, and we set down to the table, an' he had somethin', an' I took my desired cup o' tea, and then I begun to feel more interested.

"'Where you goin' to look first?' says I, but he give me a short look an' made no answer, and begun to mix me a very small portion out of the jug, in another glass. I took it to please him; he said I looked tired, speakin' real fatherly, and I did feel better for it, and we set talkin' a few minutes, an' then he started for the cellar, carrying an old ship's lantern he fetched out o' the stairway an' lit.

"'What are you lookin' for, some kind of a chist?' I inquired, and he said yes. All of a sudden it come to me to ask who was the heirs; Eliza Tolland, Cap'n John's own sister, had never demeaned herself to come near the funeral, and uncle Lorenzo faced right about and begun to laugh, sort o' pleased. I thought queer of it' 'twa'n't what he'd taken, which would be nothin' to an old weathered sailor like him.

"'Who's the heir?' says I the second time.

"'Why, it's *you*, Almiry,' says he; and I was so took aback I set right down on the turn o' the cellar stairs.

"'Yes, 'tis,' said uncle Lorenzo. 'I'm glad of it too. Some thought she didn't have no sense but foreign sense, an' a poor stock o' that, but she said you was friendly to her, an' one day after she got news of Tolland's death, an' I had fetched up his will that left everything to her, she said she was goin' to make a writin', so's you could have things after she was gone, an' she give five hundred to me for bein' executor. Square Pease fixed up the paper, an' she signed it; it's all accordin' to law.' There, I begun to cry," said Mrs. Todd; "I couldn't help it. I wished I had her back again to do somethin' for, an' to make her know I felt sisterly to her more'n I'd ever showed, an' it come over me 'twas all too late, an' I cried the more, till uncle showed impatience, an' I got up an' stumbled along down cellar with my apern to my eyes the greater part of the time.

"'I'm goin' to have a clean search,' says he; 'you hold the light.' An' I held it, and he rummaged in the arches an' under the stairs, an' over in some old closet where he reached out bottles an' stone jugs an' canted some kags an' one or two casks, an' chuckled well when he heard there was somethin' inside—but there wa'n't nothin' to find but things usual in a cellar, an' then the old lantern was givin' out an' we come away.

"'He spoke to me of a chist, Cap'n Tolland did,' says uncle in a whisper. 'He said a good sound chist was as safe a bank as there was, an' I beat him out of such nonsense, 'count o' fire an' other risks.' 'There's no chist in the rooms above,' says I'; 'no, uncle, there ain't no sea-chist, for I've been here long enough to see what there was to be seen.' Yet he wouldn't feel contented till he'd mounted up into the toploft; 'twas one o' them single, hip-roofed houses that don't give proper accommodation for a real garret, like Cap'n Littlepage's down here at the Landin'. There was broken furniture and rubbish, an' he let down a terrible sight o' dust into the front entry, but sure enough there wasn't no chist. I had it all to sweep up next day.

"'He must have took it away to sea,' says I to the cap'n, an' even then he didn't want to agree, but we was both beat out. I told him where i'd always seen Mis' Tolland get her money from, and we found much as a hundred dollars there in an old red morocco wallet. Cap'n John had been gone a good while a'ready, and she had spent what she needed. 'Twas in an old desk o' his in the settin' room that we found the wallet."

"At the last minute he may have taken his money to sea," I suggested.

"Oh yes," agreed Mrs. Todd. "He did take considerable to make his venture to bring home, as was customary, an' that was drowned with him as uncle agreed; but he had other property in shipping, and a thousand dollars invested in Portland in a cordage shop, but 'twas about the time shipping begun to decay, and the cordage shop failed, and in the end I wa'n't so rich as I thought I was goin' to be for those few minutes on the cellar stairs. There was an auction that accumulated something. Old Mis' Tolland, the cap'n's mother, had heired some good furniture from a sister: there was above thirty chairs in all, and they're apt to sell well. I got over a thousand dollars when we come to settle up, and I made uncle take his five hundred; he was getting along in years and had met with losses in navigation, and he left it back to me when he died, so I had a real good lift. It all lays in the bank over to Rockland, and I draw my interest fall an' spring, with the little

Mr. Todd was able to leave me; but that's kind o' sacred money; 'twas earnt and saved with the hope o' youth, an' I'm very particular what I spend it for. Oh yes, what with ownin' my house, I've been enabled to get along very well, with prudence!" said Mrs. Todd contentedly.

"But there was the house and land," I asked—"what became of that part of the property?"

Mrs. Todd looked into the fire, and a shadow of disapproval flitted over her face.

"Poor old uncle!" she said, "he got childish about the matter. I was hoping to sell at first, and I had an offer, but he always run of an idea that there was more money hid away, and kept wanting me to delay; an' he used to go up there all alone and search, and dig in the cellar, empty an' bleak as 'twas in winter weather or any time. An' he'd come and tell me he'd dreamed he found gold behind a stone in the cellar wall, or somethin'. And one night we all see the light o' fire up that way, an' the whole Landin' took the road, and run to look, and the Tolland property was all in a light blaze. I expect the old gentleman had dropped fire about; he said he'd been up there to see if everything was safe in the afternoon. As for the land, 'twas so poor that everybody used to have a joke that the Tolland boys preferred to farm the sea instead. It's 'most all grown up to bushes now, where it ain't poor water grass in the low places. There's some upland that has a pretty view, after you cross the brook bridge. Years an' years after she died, there was some o' her flowers used to come up an' bloom in the door garden. I brought two or three that was unusual down here; they always come up and remind me of her constant as the spring. But I never did want to fetch home that guitar, some way or 'nother; I wouldn't let it go at the auction, either. It was hangin' right there in the house when the fire took place. I've got some o' her other little things scattered about the house: that picture on the mantelpiece belonged to her."

I had often wondered where such a picture had come from, and why Mrs. Todd had chosen it; it was a French print of the statue of the Empress Josephine in the Savane at old Fort Royal, in Martinique.

CHAPTER 6

Mrs. Todd drew her chair closer to mine; she held the cat and her knitting with one hand as she moved, but the cat was so warm and so sound asleep that she only stretched a lazy paw in spite of what must have felt like a slight earthquake. Mrs. Todd began to speak almost in a whisper.

"I ain't told you all," she continued; "no, I haven't spoken of all to but very few. The way it came was this," she said solemnly, and then stopped to listen to the wind, and sat for a moment in deferential silence, as if she waited for the wind to speak first. The cat suddenly lifted her head with quick excitement and gleaming eyes, and her mistress was leaning forward toward the fire with an arm laid on either knee, as if they were consulting the glowing coals for some augury. Mrs. Todd looked like an old prophetess as she sat there with the firelight shining on her strong face; she was posed for some great painter. The woman with the cat was as unconscious and as mysterious as any sibyl of the Sistine Chapel.

"There, that's the last struggle o' the gale," said Mrs. Todd, nodding her head with impressive certainty and still looking into the bright embers of the fire.

"You'll see!" She gave me another quick glance, and spoke in a low tone as if we might be overheard.

"'Twas such a gale as this the night Mis' Tolland died. She appeared more comfortable the first o' the evenin'; and Mrs. Begg was more spent than I, bein' older, and a beautiful nurse that was the first to see and think of everything, but perfectly quiet an' never asked a useless question. You remember her funeral when you first come to the Landing? And she consented to goin' an' havin' a good sleep while she could, and left me one o' those good little pewter lamps that burnt whale oil an' made plenty o' light in the room, but not too bright to be disturbin'.

"Poor Mis' Tolland had been distressed the night before, an' all that day, but as night come on she grew more and more easy, an' was layin' there asleep; 'twas like settin' by any sleepin' person, and I had none but usual thoughts. When the wind lulled and the rain, I could hear the seas, though more distant than this, and I don' know's I observed any other sound than what the weather made; 'twas a very solemn feelin' night. I set close by the bed; there was times she looked to find somebody when she was awake. The light was on her face, so I could see her plain; there was always times when she wore a look that made her seem a stranger you'd never set eyes on before. I did think what a world it was that her an' me should have come together so, and she have nobody but Dunnet Landin' folks about her in her extremity. 'You're one o' the stray ones, poor creatur',' I said. I remember those very words passin' through my mind, but I saw reason to be glad she had some comforts, and didn't lack friends at the last, though she'd seen misery an' pain. I was glad she was quiet; all day she'd been restless, and we couldn't understand what she wanted from her French speech. We had the window open to give her air, an' now an' then a gust would strike that guitar that was on the wall and set it swinging by the blue ribbon, and soundin' as if somebody begun to play it. I come near takin' it down, but you never know what'll fret a sick person an' put 'em on the rack, an' that guitar was one o' the few things she'd brought with her."

I nodded assent, and Mrs. Todd spoke still lower.

"I set there close by the bed; I'd been through a good deal for some days back, and I thought I might's well be droppin' asleep too, bein' a quick person to wake. She looked to me as if she might last a day longer, certain, now she'd got more comfortable, but I was real tired, an' sort o' cramped as watchers will get, an' a fretful feeling begun to creep over me such as they often do have. If you give way, there ain't no support for the sick person; they can't count on no composure o' their own. Mis' Tolland moved then, a little restless, an' I forgot me quick enough, an' begun to hum out a little part of a hymn tune just to make her feel everything was as usual an' not wake up into a poor uncertainty. All of a sudden she set right up in bed with her eyes wide open, an' I stood an' put my arm behind her; she hadn't moved like that for days. And she reached out both her arms toward the door, an' I looked the way she was lookin', an' I see some one was standin' there against the dark. No, 'twa'n't Mis' Begg; 'twas somebody a good deal shorter than Mis' Begg. The lamplight struck across the room between us. I couldn't tell the shape, but 'twas a woman's dark face lookin' right at us; 'twa'n't but an instant I could see. I felt dreadful cold, and my head begun to swim; I thought the light went out; 'twa'n't but an instant, as I say, an' when my sight come back I couldn't see nothing there. I was one that didn't know what it was to faint away, no matter what happened; time was I felt above it in others, but 'twas somethin' that made poor human natur' quail. I saw very plain while I could see; 'twas a pleasant enough face, shaped somethin' like Mis' Tolland's, and a kind of expectin' look.

"No, I don't expect I was asleep," Mrs. Todd assured me quietly, after a moment's pause, though I had not spoken. She gave a heavy sigh before she went on. I could see that the recollection moved her in the deepest way.

"I suppose if I hadn't been so spent an' quavery with long watchin', I might have kept my head an' observed much better," she added humbly; "but I see all I could bear. I did try to act calm, an' I laid Mis' Tolland down on her pillow, an' I was a-shakin' as I done it. All she did was to look up to me so satisfied and sort o' questioning, an I looked back to her.

"'You saw her, didn't you?' she says to me, speakin' perfectly reasonable. ''Tis my mother,' she says again, very feeble, but lookin' straight up at me, kind of surprised with the pleasure, and smiling as if she saw I was overcome, an' would have said more if she could, but we had hold of hands. I see then her change was comin', but I didn't call Mis' Begg, nor make no uproar. I felt calm then, an' lifted to somethin' different as I never was since. She opened her eyes just as she was goin'—

"'You saw her, didn't you?' she said the second time, an' I says, '*Yes, dear, I did; you ain't never goin' to feel strange an' lonesome no more.*' An' then in a few quiet minutes 'twas all over. I felt they'd gone away together. No, I wa'n't alarmed afterward; 'twas just that one moment I couldn't live under, but I never called it beyond reason I should see the other watcher. I saw plain enough there was somebody there with me in the room.

CHAPTER 7

"''Twas just such a night as this Mis' Tolland died," repeated Mrs. Todd, returning to her usual tone and leaning back comfortably in her chair as she took up her knitting. "''Twas just such a night as this. I've told the circumstances to but very few; but I don't call it beyond reason. When folks is goin' 'tis all natural, and only common things can jar upon the mind. You know plain enough there's somethin' beyond this world; the doors stand wide open. 'There's somethin' of us that must still live on; we've got to join both worlds together an' live in one but for the other.' The doctor said that to me one day, an' I never could forget it; he said 'twas in one o' his old doctor's books."

We sat together in silence in the warm little room; the rain dropped heavily from the eaves, and the sea still roared, but the high wind had done blowing. We heard the far complaining fog horn of a steamer up the Bay.

"There goes the Boston boat out, pretty near on time," said Mrs. Todd with satisfaction. "Sometimes these late August storms'll sound a good deal worse than they really be. I do hate to hear the poor steamers callin' when they're bewildered in thick nights in winter, comin' on the coast. Yes, there goes the boat; they'll find it rough at sea, but the storm's all over."1

THE STONEGROUND GHOST TALES,
by E. G. Swain

Originally published in 1912.

**COMPILED FROM THE RECOLLECTIONS OF THE REVEREND
ROLAND BATCHEL, VICAR OF THE PARISH
THE MAN WITH THE ROLLER**

On the edge of that vast tract of East Anglia, which retains its ancient name of the Fens, there may be found, by those who know where to seek it, a certain village called Stoneground. It was once a picturesque village. Today it is not to be called either a village, or picturesque. Man dwells not in one "house of clay," but in two, and the material of the second is drawn from the earth upon which this and the neighbouring villages stood. The unlovely signs of the industry have changed the place alike in aspect and in population. Many who have seen the fossil skeletons of great saurians brought out of the clay in which they have lain from pre-historic times, have thought that the inhabitants of the place have not since changed for the better. The chief habitations, however, have their foundations not upon clay, but upon a bed of gravel which anciently gave to the place its name, and upon the highest part of this gravel stands, and has stood for many centuries, the Parish Church, dominating the landscape for miles around.

Stoneground, however, is no longer the inaccessible village, which in the middle ages stood out above a waste of waters. Occasional floods serve to indicate what was once its ordinary outlook, but in more recent times the construction of roads and railways, and the drainage of the Fens, have given it freedom of communication with the world from which it was formerly isolated.

The Vicarage of Stoneground stands hard by the Church, and is renowned for its spacious garden, part of which, and that (as might be expected) the part nearest the house, is of ancient date. To the original plot successive Vicars have added adjacent lands, so that the garden has gradually acquired the state in which it now appears.

The Vicars have been many in number. Since Henry de Greville was instituted in the year 1140 there have been 30, all of whom have lived, and most of whom have died, in successive vicarage houses upon the present site.

The present incumbent, Mr. Batchel, is a solitary man of somewhat studious habits, but is not too much enamoured of his solitude to receive visits, from time to time, from schoolboys and such. In the summer of the year 1906 he entertained two, who are the occasion of this narrative, though still unconscious of their part in it, for one of the two, celebrating his 15th birthday during his visit to Stoneground, was presented by Mr. Batchel with a new camera, with which he proceeded to photograph, with considerable skill, the surroundings of the house.

One of these photographs Mr. Batchel thought particularly pleasing. It was a view of the house with the lawn in the foreground. A few small copies, such as the boy's camera was capable of producing, were sent to him by his young friend, some weeks after the visit, and again Mr. Batchel was so much pleased with the picture, that he begged for the negative, with the intention of having the view enlarged.

The boy met the request with what seemed a needlessly modest plea. There were two negatives, he replied, but each of them had, in the same part of the picture, a small blur for which there was no accounting otherwise than by carelessness. His desire, therefore, was to discard these films, and to produce something more worthy of enlargement, upon a subsequent visit.

Mr. Batchel, however, persisted in his request, and upon receipt of the negative, examined it with a lens. He was just able to detect the blur alluded to; an examination under a powerful glass, in fact revealed something more than he had at first detected. The blur was like the nucleus of a comet as one sees it represented in pictures, and seemed to be connected with a faint streak which extended across the negative. It was, however, so inconsiderable a defect that Mr. Batchel resolved to disregard it. He had a neighbour whose favourite pastime was photography, one who was notably skilled in everything that pertained to the art, and to him he sent the negative, with the request for an enlargement, reminding him of a long-standing promise to do any such service, when as had now happened, his friend might see fit to ask it.

This neighbour who had acquired such skill in photography was one Mr. Groves, a young clergyman, residing in the Precincts of the Minster near at hand, which was visible from Mr. Batchel's garden. He lodged with a Mrs. Rumney, a superannuated servant of the Palace, and a strong-minded vigorous woman still, exactly such a one as Mr. Groves needed to have about him. For he was a constant trial to Mrs. Rumney, and but for the wholesome fear she begot in him, would have converted his rooms into a mere den. Her carpets and tablecloths were continually bespattered with chemicals; her chimney-piece ornaments had been unceremoniously stowed away and replaced by labelled bottles; even the bed of Mr. Groves was, by day, strewn with drying films and mounts, and her old and favourite cat had a bald patch on his flank, the result of a mishap with the pyrogallic acid.

Mrs. Rumney's lodger, however, was a great favourite with her, as such helpless men are apt to be with motherly women, and she took no small pride in his work. A life-size portrait of herself, originally a peace-offering, hung in her parlour, and had long excited the envy of every friend who took tea with her.

"Mr. Groves," she was wont to say, "is a nice gentleman, AND a gentleman; and chemical though he may be, I'd rather wait on him for nothing than what I would on anyone else for twice the money."

Every new piece of photographic work was of interest to Mrs. Rumney, and she expected to be allowed both to admire and to criticise. The view of Stoneground Vicarage, therefore, was shown to her upon its arrival. "Well may it want enlarging," she remarked, "and it no bigger than a postage stamp; it looks more like a doll's house than a vicarage," and with this she went about her work, whilst Mr. Groves retired to his dark room with the film, to see what he could make of the task assigned to him.

Two days later, after repeated visits to his dark room, he had made something considerable; and when Mrs. Rumney brought him his chop for luncheon, she was lost in admiration. A large but unfinished print stood upon his easel, and such a picture of Stoneground Vicarage was in the making as was calculated to delight both the young photographer and the Vicar.

Mr. Groves spent only his mornings, as a rule, in photography. His afternoons he gave to pastoral work, and the work upon this enlargement was over for the day. It required little more than "touching up," but it was this "touching up" which made the difference between the enlargements of Mr. Groves and those of other men. The print, therefore, was to be left upon the easel until the morrow, when it was to be finished. Mrs. Rumney and he, together, gave it an admiring inspection as she was carrying away the tray, and what they agreed in admiring most particularly was the smooth and open stretch of lawn, which made so excellent a foreground for the picture. "It looks," said Mrs. Rumney, who had once been young, "as if it was waiting for someone to come and dance on it."

Mr. Groves left his lodgings—we must now be particular about the hours—at half-past two, with the intention of returning, as usual, at five. "As reg'lar as a clock," Mrs. Rumney was wont to say, "and a sight more reg'lar than some clocks I knows of."

Upon this day he was, nevertheless, somewhat late, some visit had detained him unexpectedly, and it was a quarter-past five when he inserted his latch-key in Mrs. Rumney's door.

Hardly had he entered, when his landlady, obviously awaiting him, appeared in the passage: her face, usually florid, was of the colour of parchment, and, breathing hurriedly and shortly, she pointed at the door of Mr. Groves' room.

In some alarm at her condition, Mr. Groves hastily questioned her; all she could say was: "The photograph! the photograph!" Mr. Groves could only suppose that his enlargement had met with some mishap for which Mrs. Rumney was responsible. Perhaps she had allowed it to flutter into the fire. He turned towards his room in order to discover the worst, but at this Mrs. Rumney laid a trembling hand upon his arm, and held him back. "Don't go in," she said, "have your tea in the parlour."

"Nonsense," said Mr. Groves, "if that is gone we can easily do another."

"Gone," said his landlady, "I wish to Heaven it was."

The ensuing conversation shall not detain us. It will suffice to say that after a considerable time Mr. Groves succeeded in quieting his landlady, so much so that she consented, still trembling violently, to enter the room with him. To speak truth, she was as much concerned for him as for herself, and she was not by nature a timid woman.

The room, so far from disclosing to Mr. Groves any cause for excitement, appeared wholly unchanged. In its usual place stood every article of his stained and ill-used furniture, on the easel stood the photograph, precisely where he had left it; and except that his tea was not upon the table, everything was in its usual state and place.

But Mrs. Rumney again became excited and tremulous, "It's there," she cried. "Look at the lawn."

Mr. Groves stepped quickly forward and looked at the photograph. Then he turned as pale as Mrs. Rumney herself.

There was a man, a man with an indescribably horrible suffering face, rolling the lawn with a large roller.

Mr. Groves retreated in amazement to where Mrs. Rumney had remained standing. "Has anyone been in here?" he asked.

"Not a soul," was the reply, "I came in to make up the fire, and turned to have another look at the picture, when I saw that dead-alive face at the edge. It gave me the creeps," she said, "particularly from not having noticed it before. If that's anyone in Stoneground, I said to myself, I wonder the Vicar has him in the garden with that awful face. It took that hold of me I thought I must come and look at it again, and at five o'clock I brought your tea in. And then I saw him moved along right in front, with a roller dragging behind him, like you see."

Mr. Groves was greatly puzzled. Mrs. Rumney's story, of course, was incredible, but this strange evil-faced man had appeared in the photograph somehow. That he had not been there when the print was made was quite certain.

The problem soon ceased to alarm Mr. Groves; in his mind it was investing itself with a scientific interest. He began to think of suspended chemical action, and other possible avenues of investigation. At Mrs. Rumney's urgent entreaty, however, he turned the photograph upon the easel, and with only its white back presented to the room, he sat down and ordered tea to be brought in.

He did not look again at the picture. The face of the man had about it something unnaturally painful: he could remember, and still see, as it were, the drawn features, and the look of the man had unaccountably distressed him.

He finished his slight meal, and having lit a pipe, began to brood over the scientific possibilities of the problem. Had any other photograph upon the original film become involved in the one he had enlarged? Had the image of any other face, distorted by the enlarging lens, become a part of this picture? For the space of two hours he debated this possibility, and that, only to reject them all. His optical knowledge told him that no conceivable accident could have brought into his picture a man with a roller. No negative of his had ever contained such a man; if it had, no natural causes would suffice to leave him, as it were, hovering about the apparatus.

His repugnance to the actual thing had by this time lost its freshness, and he determined to end his scientific musings with another inspection of the object. So he approached the easel and turned the photograph round again. His horror returned, and with good cause. The man with the roller had now advanced to the middle of the lawn. The face was stricken still with the same indescribable look of suffering. The man seemed to be appealing to the spectator for some kind of help. Almost, he spoke.

Mr. Groves was naturally reduced to a condition of extreme nervous excitement. Although not by nature what is called a nervous man, he trembled from head to foot. With a sudden effort, he turned away his head, took hold of the picture with his outstretched hand, and opening a drawer in his sideboard thrust the thing underneath a folded tablecloth which was lying there. Then he closed the drawer and took up an entertaining book to distract his thoughts from the whole matter.

In this he succeeded very ill. Yet somehow the rest of the evening passed, and as it wore away, he lost something of his alarm. At ten o'clock, Mrs. Rumney, knocking and receiving answer twice, lest by any chance she should find herself alone in the room, brought in the cocoa usually taken by her lodger at that hour.

A hasty glance at the easel showed her that it stood empty, and her face betrayed her relief. She made no comment, and Mr. Groves invited none.

The latter, however, could not make up his mind to go to bed. The face he had seen was taking firm hold upon his imagination, and seemed to fascinate him and repel him at the same time. Before long, he found himself wholly unable to resist the impulse to look at it once more. He took it again, with some indecision, from the drawer and laid it under the lamp.

The man with the roller had now passed completely over the lawn, and was near the left of the picture.

The shock to Mr. Groves was again considerable. He stood facing the fire, trembling with excitement which refused to be suppressed. In this state his eye lighted upon the calendar hanging before him, and it furnished him with some distraction. The next day was his mother's birthday. Never did he omit to write a letter which should lie upon her breakfast-table, and the pre-occupation of this evening had made him wholly forgetful of the matter. There was a collection of letters, however, from the pillar-box near at hand, at a quarter before midnight, so he turned to his desk, wrote a letter which would at least serve to convey his affectionate greetings, and having written it, went out into the night and posted it.

The clocks were striking midnight as he returned to his room. We may be sure that he did not resist the desire to glance at the photograph he had left on his table. But the results of that glance, he, at any rate, had not anticipated. The man with the roller had disappeared. The lawn lay as smooth and clear as at first, "looking," as Mrs. Rumney had said, "as if it was waiting for someone to come and dance on it."

The photograph, after this, remained a photograph and nothing more. Mr. Groves would have liked to persuade himself that it had never undergone these changes which he had witnessed, and which we have endeavoured to describe, but his sense of their reality was too insistent. He kept the print lying for a week upon his easel. Mrs. Rumney, although she had ceased to dread it, was obviously relieved at its disappearance, when it was carried to Stoneground to be delivered to Mr. Batchel. Mr. Groves said nothing of the man with the roller, but gave the enlargement, without comment, into his friend's hands. The work of enlargement had been skilfully done, and was deservedly praised.

Mr. Groves, making some modest disclaimer, observed that the view, with its spacious foreground of lawn, was such as could not have failed to enlarge well. And this lawn, he added, as they sat looking out of the Vicar's study, looks as well from within your house as from without. It must give you a sense of responsibility, he added, reflectively, to be sitting where your predecessors have sat for so many centuries and to be continuing their peaceful work. The mere presence before your window, of the turf upon which good men have walked, is an inspiration.

The Vicar made no reply to these somewhat sententious remarks. For a moment he seemed as if he would speak some words of conventional assent. Then he abruptly left the room, to return in a few minutes with a parchment book.

"Your remark, Groves," he said as he seated himself again, "recalled to me a curious bit of history: I went up to the old library to get the book. This is the journal of William Longue who was Vicar here up to the year 1602. What you said about the lawn will give you an interest in a certain portion of the journal. I will read it."

* * * *

Aug. 1, 1600.—I am now returned in haste from a journey to Brightelmstone whither I had gone with full intention to remain about the space of two months. Master Josiah Wilburton, of my dear College of Emmanuel, having consented to assume the charge of my parish of Stoneground in the meantime. But I had intelligence, after 12 days' absence, by a messenger from the Churchwardens, that Master Wilburton had disappeared last Monday sennight, and had been no more seen. So here I am again in my study to the entire frustration of my plans, and can do nothing in my perplexity but sit and look out from my window, before which Andrew Birch rolleth the grass with much persistence. Andrew passeth so many times over the same place with his roller that I have just now stepped without to demand why he so wasteth his labour, and upon this he hath pointed out a place which is not levelled, and hath continued his rolling.

Aug. 2.—There is a change in Andrew Birch since my absence, who hath indeed the aspect of one in great depression, which is noteworthy of so chearful a man. He haply shares our common trouble in respect of Master Wilburton, of whom we remain without tidings. Having made part of a sermon upon the seventh Chapter of the former Epistle of St. Paul to the Corinthians and the 27th verse, I found Andrew again at his task, and bade him desist and saddle my horse, being minded to ride forth and take counsel with my good friend John Palmer at the Deanery, who bore Master Wilburton great affection.

Aug. 2 continued.—Dire news awaiteth me upon my return. The Sheriff's men have disinterred the body of poor Master W. from beneath the grass Andrew was rolling, and have arrested him on the charge of being his cause of death.

Aug. 10—Alas! Andrew Birch hath been hanged, the Justice having mercifully ordered that he should hang by the neck until he should be dead, and not sooner molested. May the Lord have mercy on his soul. He made full confession before me, that he had slain Master Wilburton in heat upon his threatening to make me privy to certain peculation of which I should not have suspected so old a servant. The poor man bemoaned his evil temper in great contrition, and beat his breast, saying that he knew himself doomed for ever to roll the grass in the place where he had tried to conceal his wicked fact.

"Thank you," said Mr. Groves. "Has that little negative got the date upon it?"

"Yes," replied Mr. Batchel, as he examined it with his glass. "The boy has marked it August 10."

The Vicar seemed not to remark the coincidence with the date of Birch's execution. Needless to say that it did not escape Mr. Groves. But he kept silence about the man with the roller, who has been no more seen to this day.

Doubtless there is more in our photography than we yet know of. The camera sees more than the eye, and chemicals in a freshly prepared and active state, have a power which they afterwards lose. Our units of time, adopted for the convenience of persons dealing with the ordinary movements of material objects, are of course conventional. Those who turn the instruments of science upon nature will always be in danger of seeing more than they looked for. There is such a disaster as that of knowing too much, and at some time or another it may overtake each of us. May we then be as wise as Mr. Groves in our reticence, if our turn should come.

BONE TO HIS BONE.

William Whitehead, Fellow of Emmanuel College, in the University of Cambridge, became Vicar of Stoneground in the year 1731. The annals of his incumbency were doubtless short and simple: they have not survived. In his day were no newspapers to collect gossip, no Parish Magazines to record the simple events of parochial life. One event, however, of greater moment then than now, is recorded in two places. Vicar Whitehead failed in health after 23 years of work, and journeyed to Bath in what his monument calls "the vain hope of being restored." The duration of his visit is unknown; it is reasonable to suppose that he made his journey in the summer, it is certain that by the month of November his physician told him to lay aside all hope of recovery.

Then it was that the thoughts of the patient turned to the comfortable straggling vicarage he had left at Stoneground, in which he had hoped to end his days. He prayed that his successor might be as happy there as he had been himself. Setting his affairs in order, as became one who had but a short time to live, he executed a will, bequeathing to the Vicars of Stoneground, for ever, the close of ground he had recently purchased because it lay next the vicarage garden. And by a codicil, he added to the bequest his library of books. Within a few days, William Whitehead was gathered to his fathers.

A mural tablet in the north aisle of the church, records, in Latin, his services and his bequests, his two marriages, and his fruitless journey to Bath. The house he loved, but never again saw, was taken down 40 years later, and re-built by Vicar James Devie. The garden, with Vicar Whitehead's "close of ground" and other adjacent lands, was opened out and planted, somewhat before 1850, by Vicar Robert Towerson. The aspect of everything has changed. But in a convenient chamber on the first floor of the present vicarage the library of Vicar Whitehead stands very much as he used it and loved it, and as he bequeathed it to his successors "for ever."

The books there are arranged as he arranged and ticketed them. Little slips of paper, sometimes bearing interesting fragments of writing, still mark his places. His marginal comments still give life to pages from which all other interest has faded, and he would have but a dull imagination who could sit in the chamber amidst these books without ever being carried back 180 years into the past, to the time when the newest of them left the printer's hands.

Of those into whose possession the books have come, some have doubtless loved them more, and some less; some, perhaps, have left them severely alone. But neither those who loved them, nor those who loved them not, have lost them, and they passed, some century and a half after William Whitehead's death, into the hands of Mr. Batchel, who loved them as a father loves his children. He lived alone, and had few domestic cares to distract his mind. He was able, therefore, to enjoy to the full what Vicar Whitehead had enjoyed so long before him. During many a long summer evening would he sit poring over long-forgotten books; and since the chamber, otherwise called the library, faced the south, he could also spend sunny winter mornings there without discomfort. Writing at a small table, or reading as he stood at a tall desk, he would browse amongst the books like an ox in a pleasant pasture.

There were other times also, at which Mr. Batchel would use the books. Not being a sound sleeper (for book-loving men seldom are), he elected to use as a bedroom one of the two chambers which opened at either side into the library. The arrangement enabled him to beguile many a sleepless hour amongst the books, and in view of these nocturnal visits he kept a candle standing in a sconce above the desk, and matches always ready to his hand.

There was one disadvantage in this close proximity of his bed to the library. Owing, apparently, to some defect in the fittings of the room, which, having no mechanical tastes, Mr. Batchel had never investigated, there could be heard, in the stillness of the night, exactly such sounds as might arise from a person moving about amongst the books. Visitors using the other adjacent room would often remark at breakfast, that they had heard their host in the library at one or two o'clock in the morning, when, in fact, he had not left his bed. Invariably Mr. Batchel allowed them to suppose that he had been where they thought him. He disliked idle controversy, and was unwilling to afford an opening for supernatural talk. Knowing well enough the sounds by which his guests had been deceived, he wanted no other explanation of them than his own, though it was of too vague a character to count as an explanation. He conjectured that the window-sashes, or the doors, or "something," were defective, and was too phlegmatic and too unpractical to make any investigation. The matter gave him no concern.

Persons whose sleep is uncertain are apt to have their worst nights when they would like their best. The consciousness of a special need for rest seems to bring enough mental disturbance to forbid it. So on Christmas Eve, in the year 1907, Mr. Batchel, who would have liked to sleep well, in view of the labours of Christmas Day, lay hopelessly wide awake. He exhausted all the known devices for courting sleep, and, at the end, found himself wider awake than ever. A brilliant moon shone into his room, for he hated window-blinds. There was a light wind blowing, and the sounds in the library were more than usually suggestive of a person moving about. He almost determined to have the sashes "seen to," although he could seldom be induced to have anything "seen to." He disliked changes, even for the better, and would submit to great inconvenience rather than have things altered with which he had become familiar.

As he revolved these matters in his mind, he heard the clocks strike the hour of midnight, and having now lost all hope of falling asleep, he rose from his bed, got into a large dressing gown which hung in readiness for such occasions, and passed into the library, with the intention of reading himself sleepy, if he could.

The moon, by this time, had passed out of the south, and the library seemed all the darker by contrast with the moonlit chamber he had left. He could see nothing but two blue-grey rectangles formed by the windows against the sky, the furniture of the room being altogether invisible. Groping along to where the table stood, Mr. Batchel felt over its surface for the matches which usually lay there; he found, however, that the table was cleared of everything. He raised his right hand, therefore, in order to feel his way to a shelf where the matches were sometimes mislaid, and at that moment, whilst his hand was in mid-air, the matchbox was gently put into it!

Such an incident could hardly fail to disturb even a phlegmatic person, and Mr. Batchel cried "Who's this?" somewhat nervously. There was no answer. He struck a match, looked hastily round the room, and found it empty, as usual.

There was everything, that is to say, that he was accustomed to see, but no other person than himself.

It is not quite accurate, however, to say that everything was in its usual state. Upon the tall desk lay a quarto volume that he had certainly not placed there. It was his quite invariable practice to replace his books upon the shelves after using them, and what we may call his library habits were precise and methodical. A book out of place like this, was not only an offence against good order, but a sign that his privacy had been intruded upon. With some surprise, therefore, he lit the candle standing ready in the sconce, and proceeded to examine the book, not sorry, in the disturbed condition in which he was, to have an occupation found for him.

The book proved to be one with which he was unfamiliar, and this made it certain that some other hand than his had removed it from its place. Its title was "The Compleat Gard'ner" of M. de la Quintinye made English by John Evelyn Esquire. It was not a work in which Mr. Batchel felt any great interest. It consisted of divers reflections on various parts of husbandry, doubtless entertaining enough, but too deliberate and discursive for practical purposes. He had certainly never used the book, and growing restless now in mind, said to himself that some boy having the freedom of the house, had taken it down from its place in the hope of finding pictures.

But even whilst he made this explanation he felt its weakness. To begin with, the desk was too high for a boy. The improbability that any boy would place a book there was equalled by the improbability that he would leave it there. To discover its uninviting character would be the work only of a moment, and no boy would have brought it so far from its shelf.

Mr. Batchel had, however, come to read, and habit was too strong with him to be wholly set aside. Leaving "The Compleat Gard'ner" on the desk, he turned round to the shelves to find some more congenial reading.

Hardly had he done this when he was startled by a sharp rap upon the desk behind him, followed by a rustling of paper. He turned quickly about and saw the quarto lying open. In obedience to the instinct of the moment, he at once sought a natural cause for what he saw. Only a wind, and that of the strongest, could have opened the book, and laid back its heavy cover; and though he accepted, for a brief moment, that explanation, he was too candid to retain it longer. The wind out of doors was very light. The window sash was closed and latched, and, to decide the matter finally, the book had its back, and not its edges, turned towards the only quarter from which a wind could strike.

Mr. Batchel approached the desk again and stood over the book. With increasing perturbation of mind (for he still thought of the matchbox) he looked upon the open page. Without much reason beyond that he felt constrained to do something, he read the words of the half completed sentence at the turn of the page—

"at dead of night he left the house and passed into the solitude of the garden."

But he read no more, nor did he give himself the trouble of discovering whose midnight wandering was being described, although the habit was singularly like one of his own. He was in no condition for reading, and turning his back upon the volume he slowly paced the length of the chamber, "wondering at that which had come to pass."

He reached the opposite end of the chamber and was in the act of turning, when again he heard the rustling of paper, and by the time he had faced round, saw the leaves of the book again turning over. In a moment the volume lay at rest, open in another place, and there was no further movement as he approached it. To make sure that he had not been deceived, he read again the words as they entered the page. The author was following a not uncommon practise of the time, and throwing common speech into forms suggested by Holy Writ: "So dig," it said, "that ye may obtain."

This passage, which to Mr. Batchel seemed reprehensible in its levity, excited at once his interest and his disapproval. He was prepared to read more, but this time was not allowed. Before his eye could pass beyond the passage already cited, the leaves of the book slowly turned again, and presented but a termination of five words and a colophon.

The words were, "to the North, an Ilex." These three passages, in which he saw no meaning and no connection, began to entangle themselves together in Mr. Batchel's mind. He found himself repeating them in different orders, now beginning with one, and now with another. Any further attempt at reading he felt to be impossible, and he was in no mind for any more experiences of the unaccountable. Sleep was, of course, further from him than ever, if that were conceivable. What he did, therefore, was to blow out the candle, to return to his moonlit bedroom, and put on more clothing, and then to pass downstairs with the object of going out of doors.

It was not unusual with Mr. Batchel to walk about his garden at night-time. This form of exercise had often, after a wakeful hour, sent him back to his bed refreshed and ready for sleep. The convenient access to the garden at such times lay through his study, whose French windows opened on to a short flight of steps, and upon these he now paused for a moment to admire the snow-like appearance of the lawns, bathed as they were in the moonlight. As he paused, he heard the city clocks strike the half-hour after midnight, and he could not forbear repeating aloud:

"At dead of night he left the house, and passed into the solitude of the garden."

It was solitary enough. At intervals the screech of an owl, and now and then the noise of a train, seemed to emphasise the solitude by drawing attention to it and then leaving it in possession of the night. Mr. Batchel found himself wondering and conjecturing what Vicar Whitehead, who had acquired the close of land to secure quiet and privacy for garden, would have thought of the railways to the west and north. He turned his face northwards, whence a whistle had just sounded, and saw a tree beautifully outlined against the sky. His breath caught at the sight. Not because the tree was unfamiliar. Mr. Batchel knew all his trees. But what he had seen was "to the north, an Ilex."

Mr. Batchel knew not what to make of it all. He had walked into the garden hundreds of times and as often seen the Ilex, but the words out of the "Compleat Gard'ner" seemed to be pursuing him in a way that made him almost afraid. His temperament, however, as has been said already, was phlegmatic. It was commonly said, and Mr. Batchel approved the verdict, whilst he condemned its inexactness, that "his nerves were made of fiddle-string," so he braced himself afresh and set upon his walk round the silent garden, which he was accustomed to begin in a northerly direction, and was now too proud to change. He usually passed the Ilex at the beginning of his perambulation, and so would pass it now.

He did not pass it. A small discovery, as he reached it, annoyed and disturbed him. His gardener, as careful and punctilious as himself, never failed to house all his tools at the end of a day's work. Yet there, under the Ilex, standing upright in moonlight brilliant enough to cast a shadow of it, was a spade.

Mr. Batchel's second thought was one of relief. After his extraordinary experiences in the library (he hardly knew now whether they had been real or not) something quite commonplace would act sedatively, and he determined to carry the spade to the tool-house.

The soil was quite dry, and the surface even a little frozen, so Mr. Batchel left the path, walked up to the spade, and would have drawn it towards him. But it was as if he had made the attempt upon the trunk of the Ilex itself. The spade would not be moved. Then, first with one hand, and then with both, he tried to raise it, and still it stood firm. Mr. Batchel, of course, attributed this to the frost, slight as it was. Wondering at the spade's being there, and annoyed at its being frozen, he was about to leave it and continue his walk, when the remaining words of the "Compleat Gard'ner" seemed rather to utter themselves, than to await his will—

"So dig, that ye may obtain."

Mr. Batchel's power of independent action now deserted him. He took the spade, which no longer resisted, and began to dig. "Five spadefuls and no more," he said aloud. "This is all foolishness."

Four spadefuls of earth he then raised and spread out before him in the moonlight. There was nothing unusual to be seen. Nor did Mr. Batchel decide what he would look for, whether coins, jewels, documents in canisters, or weapons. In point of fact, he dug against what he deemed his better judgment, and expected nothing. He spread before him the fifth and last spadeful of earth, not quite without result, but with no result that was at all sensational. The earth contained a bone. Mr. Batchel's knowledge of anatomy was sufficient to show him that it was a human bone. He identified it, even by moonlight, as the radius, a bone of the forearm, as he removed the earth from it, with his thumb.

Such a discovery might be thought worthy of more than the very ordinary interest Mr. Batchel showed. As a matter of fact, the presence of a human bone was easily to be accounted for. Recent excavations within the church had caused the upturning of numberless bones, which had been collected and reverently buried. But an earth-stained bone is also easily overlooked, and this radius had obviously found its way into the garden with some of the earth brought out of the church.

Mr. Batchel was glad, rather than regretful at this termination to his adventure. He was once more provided with something to do. The re-interment of such bones as this had been his constant care, and he decided at once to restore the bone to consecrated earth. The time seemed opportune. The eyes of the curious were closed in sleep, he himself was still alert and wakeful. The spade remained by his side and the bone in his hand. So he betook himself, there and then, to the churchyard. By the still generous light of the moon, he found a place where the earth yielded to his spade, and within a few minutes the bone was laid decently to earth, some 18 inches deep.

The city clocks struck one as he finished. The whole world seemed asleep, and Mr. Batchel slowly returned to the garden with his spade. As he hung it in its accustomed place he felt stealing over him the welcome desire to sleep. He walked quietly on to the house and ascended to his room. It was now dark: the moon had passed on and left the room in shadow. He lit a candle, and before undressing passed into the library. He had an irresistible curiosity to see the passages in John Evelyn's book which had so strangely adapted themselves to the events of the past hour.

In the library a last surprise awaited him. The desk upon which the book had lain was empty. "The Compleat Gard'ner" stood in its place on the shelf. And then Mr. Batchel knew that he had handled a bone of William Whitehead, and that in response to his own entreaty.

THE RICHPINS

Something of the general character of Stoneground and its people has been indicated by stray allusions in the preceding narratives. We must here add that of its present population only a small part is native, the remainder having been attracted during the recent prosperous days of brickmaking, from the nearer parts of East Anglia and the Midlands. The visitor to Stoneground now finds little more than the signs of an unlovely industry, and of the hasty and inadequate housing of the people it has drawn together. Nothing in the place pleases him more than the excellent train-service which makes it easy to get away. He seldom desires a long acquaintance either with Stoneground or its people.

The impression so made upon the average visitor is, however, unjust, as first impressions often are. The few who have made further acquaintance with Stoneground have soon learned to distinguish between the permanent and the accidental features of the place, and have been astonished by nothing so much as by the unexpected evidence of French influence. Amongst the household treasures of the old inhabitants are invariably found French knick-knacks: there are pieces of French furniture in what is called "the room" of many houses. A certain ten-acre field is called the "Frenchman's meadow." Upon the voters' lists hanging at the church door are to be found French names, often corrupted; and boys who run about the streets can be heard shrieking to each other such names as Bunnum, Dangibow, Planchey, and so on.

Mr. Batchel himself is possessed of many curious little articles of French handiwork—boxes deftly covered with split straws, arranged ingeniously in patterns; models of the guillotine, built of carved meat-bones, and various other pieces of handiwork, amongst them an accurate road-map of the country between Stoneground and Yarmouth, drawn upon a fly-leaf torn from some book, and bearing upon the other side the name of Jules Richepin. The latter had been picked up, according to a pencilled-note written across one corner, by a shepherd, in the year 1811.

The explanation of this French influence is simple enough. Within five miles of Stoneground a large barracks had been erected for the custody of French prisoners during the war with Bonaparte. Many thousands were confined there during the years 1808-14. The prisoners were allowed to sell what articles they could make in the barracks; and many of them, upon their release, settled in the neighbourhood, where their descendants remain. There is little curiosity amongst these descendants about their origin. The events of a century ago seem to them as remote as the Deluge, and as immaterial. To Thomas Richpin, a weakly man who blew the organ in church, Mr. Batchel shewed the map. Richpin, with a broad, black-haired skull and a narrow chin which grew a little pointed beard, had always a foreign look about him: Mr. Batchel thought it more than possible that he might be descended from the owner of the book, and told him as much upon shewing him the fly-leaf. Thomas, however, was content to observe that "his name hadn't got no E," and shewed no further interest in the matter. His interest in it, before we have done with him, will have become very large.

For the growing boys of Stoneground, with whom he was on generally friendly terms, Mr. Batchel formed certain clubs to provide them with occupation on winter evenings; and in these clubs, in the interests of peace and good-order, he spent a great deal of time. Sitting one December evening, in a large circle of boys who preferred the warmth of the fire to the more temperate atmosphere of the tables, he found Thomas Richpin the sole topic of conversation.

"We seen Mr. Richpin in Frenchman's Meadow last night," said one.

"What time?" said Mr. Batchel, whose function it was to act as a sort of fly-wheel, and to carry the conversation over dead points. He had received the information with some little surprise, because Frenchman's Meadow was an unusual place for Richpin to have been in, but his question had no further object than to encourage talk.

"Half-past nine," was the reply.

This made the question much more interesting. Mr. Batchel, on the preceding evening, had taken advantage of a warmed church to practise upon the organ. He had played it from nine o'clock until ten, and Richpin had been all that time at the bellows.

"Are you sure it was half-past nine?" he asked.

"Yes," (we reproduce the answer exactly), "we come out o' night-school at quarter-past, and we was all goin' to the Wash to look if it was friz."

"And you saw Mr. Richpin in Frenchman's Meadow?" said Mr. Batchel.

"Yes. He was looking for something on the ground," added another boy.

"And his trousers was tore," said a third.

The story was clearly destined to stand in no need of corroboration.

"Did Mr. Richpin speak to you?" enquired Mr. Batchel.

"No, we run away afore he come to us," was the answer.

"Why?"

"Because we was frit."

"What frightened you?"

"Jim Lallement hauled a flint at him and hit him in the face, and he didn't take no notice, so we run away."

"Why?" repeated Mr. Batchel.

"Because he never hollered nor looked at us, and it made us feel so funny."

"Did you go straight down to the Wash?"

They had all done so.

"What time was it when you reached home?"

They had all been at home by ten, before Richpin had left the church.

"Why do they call it Frenchman's Meadow?" asked another boy, evidently anxious to change the subject.

Mr. Batchel replied that the meadow had probably belonged to a Frenchman whose name was not easy to say, and the conversation after this was soon in another channel. But, furnished as he was with an unmistakeable alibi, the story about Richpin and the torn trousers, and the flint, greatly puzzled him.

"Go straight home," he said, as the boys at last bade him good-night, "and let us have no more stone-throwing." They were reckless boys, and Richpin, who used little discretion in reporting their misdemeanours about the church, seemed to Mr. Batchel to stand in real danger.

Frenchman's Meadow provided ten acres of excellent pasture, and the owners of two or three hard-worked horses were glad to pay three shillings a week for the privilege of turning them into it. One of these men came to Mr. Batchel on the morning which followed the conversation at the club.

"I'm in a bit of a quandary about Tom Richpin," he began.

This was an opening that did not fail to command Mr. Batchel's attention. "What is it?" he said.

"I had my mare in Frenchman's Meadow," replied the man, "and Sam Bower come and told me last night as he heard her gallopin' about when he was walking this side the hedge."

"But what about Richpin?" said Mr. Batchel.

"Let me come to it," said the other. "My mare hasn't got no wind to gallop, so I up and went to see to her, and there she was sure enough, like a wild thing, and Tom Richpin walking across the meadow."

"Was he chasing her?" asked Mr. Batchel, who felt the absurdity of the question as he put it.

"He was not," said the man, "but what he could have been doin' to put the mare into that state, I can't think."

"What was he doing when you saw him?" asked Mr. Batchel.

"He was walking along looking for something he'd dropped, with his trousers all tore to ribbons, and while I was catchin' the mare, he made off."

"He was easy enough to find, I suppose?" said Mr. Batchel.

"That's the quandary I was put in," said the man. "I took the mare home and gave her to my lad, and straight I went to Richpin's, and found Tom havin' his supper, with his trousers as good as new."

"You'd made a mistake," said Mr. Batchel.

"But how come the mare to make it too?" said the other.

"What did you say to Richpin?" asked Mr. Batchel.

"Tom," I says, "when did you come in? 'Six o'clock,' he says, 'I bin mendin' my boots'; and there, sure enough, was the hobbin' iron by his chair, and him in his stockin'-feet. I don't know what to do."

"Give the mare a rest," said Mr. Batchel, "and say no more about it."

"I don't want to harm a pore creature like Richpin," said the man, "but a mare's a mare, especially where there's a family to bring up." The man consented, however, to abide by Mr. Batchel's advice, and the interview ended. The evenings just then were light, and both the man and his mare had seen something for which Mr. Batchel could not, at present, account. The worst way, however, of arriving at an explanation is to guess it. He was far too wise to let himself wander into the pleasant fields of conjecture, and had determined, even before the story of the mare had finished, upon the more prosaic path of investigation.

Mr. Batchel, either from strength or indolence of mind, as the reader may be pleased to determine, did not allow matters even of this exciting kind, to disturb his daily round of duty. He was beginning to fear, after what he had heard of the Frenchman's Meadow, that he might find it necessary to preach a plain sermon upon the Witch of Endor, for he foresaw that there would soon be some ghostly talk in circulation. In small communities, like that of Stoneground, such talk arises upon very slight provocation, and here was nothing at all to check it. Richpin was a weak and timid man, whom no one would suspect, whilst an alternative remained open, of wandering about in the dark; and Mr. Batchel knew that the alternative of an apparition, if once suggested, would meet with general acceptance, and this he wished, at all costs, to avoid. His own view of the matter he held in reserve, for the reasons already stated, but he could not help suspecting that there might be a better explanation of the name "Frenchman's Meadow" than he had given to the boys at their club.

Afternoons, with Mr. Batchel, were always spent in making pastoral visits, and upon the day our story has reached he determined to include amongst them a call upon Richpin, and to submit him to a cautious cross-examination. It was evident that at least four persons, all perfectly familiar with his appearance, were under the impression that they had seen him in the meadow, and his own statement upon the matter would be at least worth hearing.

Richpin's home, however, was not the first one visited by Mr. Batchel on that afternoon. His friendly relations with the boys has already been mentioned, and it may now be added that this friendship was but part of a generally keen sympathy with young people of all ages, and of both sexes. Parents knew much less than he did of the love affairs of their young people; and if he was not actually guilty of match-making, he was at least a very sympathetic observer of the process. When lovers had their little differences, or even their greater ones, it was Mr. Batchel, in most cases, who adjusted them, and who suffered, if he failed, hardly less than the lovers themselves.

It was a negotiation of this kind which, on this particular day, had given precedence to another visit, and left Richpin until the later part of the afternoon. But the matter of the Frenchman's Meadow had, after all, not to wait for Richpin. Mr. Batchel was calculating how long he should be in reaching it, when he found himself unexpectedly there. Selina Broughton had been a favourite of his from her childhood; she had been sufficiently good to please him, and naughty enough to attract and challenge him; and when at length she began to walk out with Bob Rockfort, who was another favourite, Mr. Batchel rubbed his hands in satisfaction. Their present difference, which now brought him to the Broughtons' cottage, gave him but little anxiety. He had brought Bob half-way towards reconciliation, and had no doubt of his ability to lead Selina to the same place. They would finish the journey, happily enough, together.

But what has this to do with the Frenchman's Meadow? Much every way. The meadow was apt to be the rendezvous of such young people as desired a higher degree of privacy than that afforded by the public paths; and these two had gone there separately the night before, each to nurse a grievance against the other. They had been at opposite ends, as it chanced, of the field; and Bob, who believed himself to be alone there, had been awakened from his reverie by a sudden scream. He had at once run across the field, and found Selina sorely in need of him. Mr. Batchel's work of reconciliation had been there and then anticipated, and Bob had taken the girl home in a condition of great excitement to her mother. All this was explained, in breathless sentences, by Mrs. Broughton, by way of accounting for the fact that Selina was then lying down in "the room."

There was no reason why Mr. Batchel should not see her, of course, and he went in. His original errand had lapsed, but it was now replaced by one of greater interest. Evidently there was Selina's testimony to add to that of the other four; she was not a girl who would scream without good cause, and Mr. Batchel felt that he knew how his question about the cause would be answered, when he came to the point of asking it.

He was not quite prepared for the form of her answer, which she gave without any hesitation. She had seen Mr. Richpin "looking for his eyes." Mr. Batchel saved for another occasion the amusement to be derived from the curiously illogical answer. He saw at once what had suggested it. Richpin had until recently had an atrocious squint, which an operation in London had completely cured. This operation, of which, of course, he knew nothing, he had described, in his own way, to anyone who would listen, and it was commonly believed that his eyes had ceased to be fixtures. It was plain, however, that Selina had seen very much what had been seen by the other four. Her information was precise, and her story perfectly coherent. She preserved a maidenly reticence about his trousers, if she had noticed them; but added a new fact, and a terrible one, in her description of the eyeless sockets. No wonder she had screamed. It will be observed that Mr. Richpin was still searching, if not looking, for something upon the ground.

Mr. Batchel now proceeded to make his remaining visit. Richpin lived in a little cottage by the church, of which cottage the Vicar was the indulgent landlord. Richpin's creditors were obliged to shew some indulgence, because his income was never regular and seldom sufficient. He got on in life by what is called "rubbing along," and appeared to do it with surprisingly little friction. The small duties about the church, assigned to him out of charity, were overpaid. He succeeded in attracting to himself all the available gifts of masculine clothing, of which he probably received enough and to sell, and he had somehow wooed and won a capable, if not very comely, wife, who supplemented his income by her own labour, and managed her house and husband to admiration.

Richpin, however, was not by any means a mere dependent upon charity. He was, in his way, a man of parts. All plants, for instance, were his friends, and he had inherited, or acquired, great skill with fruit-trees, which never failed to reward his treatment with abundant crops. The two or three vines, too, of the neighbourhood, he kept in fine order by methods of his own, whose merit was proved by their success. He had other skill, though of a less remunerative kind, in fashioning toys out of wood, cardboard, or paper; and every correctly-behaving child in the parish had some such product of his handiwork. And besides all this, Richpin had a remarkable aptitude for making music. He could do something upon every musical instrument that came in his way, and, but for his voice, which was like that of the peahen, would have been a singer. It was his voice that had secured him the situation of organ-blower, as one remote from all incitement to join in the singing in church.

Like all men who have not wit enough to defend themselves by argument, Richpin had a plaintive manner. His way of resenting injury was to complain of it to the next person he met, and such complaints as he found no other means of discharging, he carried home to his wife, who treated his conversation just as she treated the singing of the canary, and other domestic sounds, being hardly conscious of it until it ceased.

The entrance of Mr. Batchel, soon after his interview with Selina, found Richpin engaged in a loud and fluent oration. The fluency was achieved mainly by repetition, for the man had but small command of words, but it served none the less to shew the depth of his indignation.

"I aren't bin in Frenchman's Meadow, am I?" he was saying in appeal to his wife—this is the Stoneground way with auxiliary verbs—"What am I got to go there for?" He acknowledged Mr. Batchel's entrance in no other way than by changing to the third person in his discourse, and he continued without pause —"if she'd let me out o' nights, I'm got better places to go to than Frenchman's Meadow. Let policeman stick to where I am bin, or else keep his mouth shut. What call is he got to say I'm bin where I aren't bin?"

From this, and much more to the same effect, it was clear that the matter of the meadow was being noised abroad, and even receiving official attention. Mr. Batchel was well aware that no question he could put to Richpin, in his present state, would change the flow of his eloquence, and that he had already learned as much as he was likely to learn. He was content, therefore, to ascertain from Mrs. Richpin that her husband had indeed spent all his evenings at home, with the single exception of the one hour during which Mr. Batchel had employed him at the organ. Having ascertained this, he retired, and left Richpin to talk himself out.

No further doubt about the story was now possible. It was not twenty-four hours since Mr. Batchel had heard it from the boys at the club, and it had already been confirmed by at least two unimpeachable witnesses. He thought the matter over, as he took his tea, and was chiefly concerned in Richpin's curious connexion with it. On his account, more than on any other, it had become necessary to make whatever investigation might be feasible, and Mr. Batchel determined, of course, to make the next stage of it in the meadow itself.

The situation of "Frenchman's Meadow" made it more conspicuous than any other enclosure in the neighbourhood. It was upon the edge of what is locally known as "high land"; and though its elevation was not great, one could stand in the meadow and look sea-wards over many miles of flat country, once a waste of brackish water, now a great chess-board of fertile fields bounded by straight dykes of glistening water. The point of view derived another interest from looking down upon a long straight bank which disappeared into the horizon many miles away, and might have been taken for a great railway embankment of which no use had been made. It was, in fact, one of the great works of the Dutch Engineers in the time of Charles I., and it separated the river basin from a large drained area called the "Middle Level," some six feet below it. In this embankment, not two hundred yards below "Frenchman's Meadow," was one of the huge water gates which admitted traffic through a sluice, into the lower level, and the picturesque thatched cottage of the sluice-keeper formed a pleasing addition to the landscape. It was a view with which Mr. Batchel was naturally very familiar. Few of his surroundings were pleasant to the eye, and this was about the only place to which he could take a visitor whom he desired to impress favourably. The way to the meadow lay through a short lane, and he could reach it in five minutes: he was frequently there.

It was, of course, his intention to be there again that evening: to spend the night there, if need be, rather than let anything escape him. He only hoped he should not find half the parish there also. His best hope of privacy lay in the inclemency of the weather; the day was growing colder, and there was a north-east wind, of which Frenchman's Meadow would receive the fine edge.

Mr. Batchel spent the next three hours in dealing with some arrears of correspondence, and at nine o'clock put on his thickest coat and boots, and made his way to the meadow. It became evident, as he walked up the lane, that he was to have company. He heard many voices, and soon recognised the loudest amongst them. Jim Lallement was boasting of the accuracy of his aim: the others were not disputing it, but were asserting their own merits in discordant chorus. This was a nuisance, and to make matters worse, Mr. Batchel heard steps behind him.

A voice soon bade him "Good evening." To Mr. Batchel's great relief it proved to be the policeman, who soon overtook him. The conversation began on his side.

"Curious tricks, sir, these of Richpin's."

"What tricks?" asked Mr. Batchel, with an air of innocence.

"Why, he's been walking about Frenchman's Meadow these three nights, frightening folk and what all."

"Richpin has been at home every night, and all night long," said Mr. Batchel.

"I'm talking about where he was, not where he says he was," said the policeman. "You can't go behind the evidence."

"But Richpin has evidence too. I asked his wife."

"You know, sir, and none better, that wives have got to obey. Richpin wants to be took for a ghost, and we know that sort of ghost. Whenever we hear there's a ghost, we always know there's going to be turkeys missing."

"But there are real ghosts sometimes, surely?" said Mr. Batchel.

"No," said the policeman, "me and my wife have both looked, and there's no such thing."

"Looked where?" enquired Mr. Batchel.

"In the 'Police Duty' Catechism. There's lunatics, and deserters, and dead bodies, but no ghosts."

Mr. Batchel accepted this as final. He had devised a way of ridding himself of all his company, and proceeded at once to carry it into effect. The two had by this time reached the group of boys.

"These are all stone-throwers," said he, loudly.

There was a clatter of stones as they dropped from the hands of the boys.

"These boys ought all to be in the club instead of roaming about here damaging property. Will you take them there, and see them safely in? If Richpin comes here, I will bring him to the station."

The policeman seemed well pleased with the suggestion. No doubt he had overstated his confidence in the definition of the "Police Duty." Mr. Batchel, on his part, knew the boys well enough to be assured that they would keep the policeman occupied for the next half-hour, and as the party moved slowly away, felt proud of his diplomacy.

There was no sign of any other person about the field gate, which he climbed readily enough, and he was soon standing in the highest part of the meadow and peering into the darkness on every side.

It was possible to see a distance of about thirty yards; beyond that it was too dark to distinguish anything. Mr. Batchel designed a zig-zag course about the meadow, which would allow of his examining it systematically and as rapidly as possible, and along this course he began to walk briskly, looking straight before him as he went, and pausing to look well about him when he came to a turn.

There were no beasts in the meadow—their owners had taken the precaution of removing them; their absence was, of course, of great advantage to Mr. Batchel.

In about ten minutes he had finished his zig-zag path and arrived at the other corner of the meadow; he had seen nothing resembling a man. He then retraced his steps, and examined the field again, but arrived at his starting point, knowing no more than when he had left it. He began to fear the return of the policeman as he faced the wind and set upon a third journey.

The third journey, however, rewarded him. He had reached the end of his second traverse, and was looking about him at the angle between that and the next, when he distinctly saw what looked like Richpin crossing his circle of vision, and making straight for the sluice. There was no gate on that side of the field; the hedge, which seemed to present no obstacle to the other, delayed Mr. Batchel considerably, and still retains some of his clothing, but he was not long through before he had again marked his man. It had every appearance of being Richpin. It went down the slope, crossed the plank that bridged the lock, and disappeared round the corner of the cottage, where the entrance lay.

Mr. Batchel had had no opportunity of confirming the gruesome observation of Selina Broughton, but had seen enough to prove that the others had not been romancing. He was not a half-minute behind the figure as it crossed the plank over the lock—it was slow going in the darkness—and he followed it immediately round the corner of the house. As he expected, it had then disappeared.

Mr. Batchel knocked at the door, and admitted himself, as his custom was. The sluice-keeper was in his kitchen, charring a gate post. He was surprised to see Mr. Batchel at that hour, and his greeting took the form of a remark to that effect.

"I have been taking an evening walk," said Mr. Batchel. "Have you seen Richpin lately?"

"I see him last Saturday week," replied the sluice-keeper, "not since."

"Do you feel lonely here at night?"

"No," replied the sluice-keeper, "people drop in at times. There was a man in on Monday, and another yesterday."

"Have you had no one to-day?" said Mr. Batchel, coming to the point.

The answer showed that Mr. Batchel had been the first to enter the door that day, and after a little general conversation he brought his visit to an end.

It was now ten o'clock. He looked in at Richpin's cottage, where he saw a light burning, as he passed. Richpin had tired himself early, and had been in bed since half-past eight. His wife was visibly annoyed at the rumours which had upset him, and Mr. Batchel said such soothing words as he could command, before he left for home.

He congratulated himself, prematurely, as he sat before the fire in his study, that the day was at an end. It had been cold out of doors, and it was pleasant to think things over in the warmth of the cheerful fire his housekeeper never failed to leave for him. The reader will have no more difficulty than Mr. Batchel had in accounting for the resemblance between Richpin and the man in the meadow. It was a mere question of family likeness. That the ancestor had been seen in the meadow at some former time might perhaps be inferred from its traditional name. The reason for his return, then and now, was a matter of mere conjecture, and Mr. Batchel let it alone.

The next incident has, to some, appeared incredible, which only means, after all, that it has made demands upon their powers of imagination and found them bankrupt.

Critics of story-telling have used severe language about authors who avail themselves of the short-cut of coincidence. "That must be reserved, I suppose," said Mr. Batchel, when he came to tell of Richpin, "for what really happens; and that fiction is a game which must be played according to the rules."

"I know," he went on to say, "that the chances were some millions to one against what happened that night, but if that makes it incredible, what is there left to believe?"

It was thereupon remarked by someone in the company, that the credible material would not be exhausted.

"I doubt whether anything happens," replied Mr. Batchel in his dogmatic way, "without the chances being a million to one against it. Why did they choose such a word? What does 'happen' mean?"

There was no reply: it was clearly a rhetorical question.

"Is it incredible," he went on, "that I put into the plate last Sunday the very half-crown my uncle tipped me with in 1881, and that I spent next day?"

"Was that the one you put in?" was asked by several.

"How do I know?" replied Mr. Batchel, "but if I knew the history of the half-crown I did put in, I know it would furnish still more remarkable coincidences."

All this talk arose out of the fact that at midnight on the eventful day, whilst Mr. Batchel was still sitting by his study fire, he had news that the cottage at the sluice had been burnt down. The thatch had been dry; there was, as we know, a stiff east-wind, and an hour had sufficed to destroy all that was inflammable. The fire is still spoken of in Stoneground with great regret. There remains only one building in the place of sufficient merit to find its way on to a postcard.

It was just at midnight that the sluice-keeper rung at Mr. Batchel's door. His errand required no apology. The man had found a night-fisherman to help him as soon as the fire began, and with two long sprits from a lighter they had made haste to tear down the thatch, and upon this had brought down, from under the ridge at the South end, the bones and some of the clothing of a man. Would Mr. Batchel come down and see?

Mr. Batchel put on his coat and returned to the place. The people whom the fire had collected had been kept on the further side of the water, and the space about the cottage was vacant. Near to the smouldering heap of ruin were the remains found under the thatch. The fingers of the right hand still firmly clutched a sheep bone which had been gnawed as a dog would gnaw it.

"Starved to death," said the sluice-keeper, "I see a tramp like that ten years ago."

They laid the bones decently in an outhouse, and turned the key, Mr. Batchel carried home in his hand a metal cross, threaded upon a cord. He found an engraved figure of Our Lord on the face of it, and the name of Pierre Richepin upon the back. He went next day to make the matter known to the nearest Priest of the Roman Faith, with whom he left the cross. The remains, after a brief inquest, were interred in the cemetery, with the rites of the Church to which the man had evidently belonged.

Mr. Batchel's deductions from the whole circumstances were curious, and left a great deal to be explained. It seemed as if Pierre Richepin had been disturbed by some premonition of the fire, but had not foreseen that his mortal remains would escape; that he could not return to his own people without the aid of his map, but had no perception of the interval that had elapsed since he had lost it. This map Mr. Batchel put into his pocket-book next day when he went to Thomas Richpin for certain other information about his surviving relatives.

Richpin had a father, it appeared, living a few miles away in Jakesley Fen, and Mr. Batchel concluded that he was worth a visit. He mounted his bicycle, therefore, and made his way to Jakesley that same afternoon.

Mr. Richpin was working not far from home, and was soon brought in. He and his wife shewed great courtesy to their visitor, whom they knew well by repute. They had a well-ordered house, and with a natural and dignified hospitality, asked him to take tea with them. It was evident to Mr. Batchel that there was a great gulf between the elder Richpin and his son; the former was the last of an old race, and the latter the first of a new. In spite of the Board of Education, the latter was vastly the worse.

The cottage contained some French kickshaws which greatly facilitated the enquiries Mr. Batchel had come to make. They proved to be family relics.

"My grandfather," said Mr. Richpin, as they sat at tea, "was a prisoner—he and his brother."

"Your grandfather was Pierre Richepin?" asked Mr. Batchel.

"No! Jules," was the reply. "Pierre got away."

"Shew Mr. Batchel the book," said his wife.

The book was produced. It was a Book of Meditations, with the name of Jules Richepin upon the title-page. The fly-leaf was missing. Mr. Batchel produced the map from his pocket-book. It fitted exactly. The slight indentures along the torn edge fell into their place, and Mr. Batchel left the leaf in the book, to the great delight of the old couple, to whom he told no more of the story than he thought fit.

THE EASTERN WINDOW

It may well be that Vermuyden and the Dutchmen who drained the fens did good, and that it was interred with their bones. It is quite certain that they did evil and that it lives after them. The rivers, which these men robbed of their water, have at length silted up, and the drainage of one tract of country is proving to have been achieved by the undraining of another.

Places like Stoneground, which lie on the banks of these defrauded rivers, are now become helpless victims of Dutch engineering. The water which has lost its natural outlet, invades their lands. The thrifty cottager who once had the river at the bottom of his garden, has his garden more often in these days, at the bottom of the river, and a summer flood not infrequently destroys the whole produce of his ground.

Such a flood, during an early year in the 20th century, had been unusually disastrous to Stoneground, and Mr. Batchel, who, as a gardener, was well able to estimate the losses of his poorer neighbours, was taking some steps towards repairing them.

Money, however, is never at rest in Stoneground, and it turned out upon this occasion that the funds placed at his command were wholly inadequate to the charitable purpose assigned to them. It seemed as if those who had lost a rood of potatoes could be compensated for no more than a yard.

It was at this time, when he was oppressed in mind by the failure of his charitable enterprise, that Mr. Batchel met with the happy adventure in which the Eastern window of the Church played so singular a part.

The narrative should be prefaced by a brief description of the window in question. It is a large painted window, of a somewhat unfortunate period of execution. The drawing and colouring leave everything to be desired. The scheme of the window, however, is based upon a wholesome tradition. The five large lights in the lower part are assigned to five scenes in the life of Our Lord, and the second of these, counting from the North, contains a bold erect figure of St. John Baptist, to whom the Church is dedicated. It is this figure alone, of all those contained in the window, that is concerned in what we have to relate.

It has already been mentioned that Mr. Batchel had some knowledge of music. He took an interest in the choir, from whose practices he was seldom absent; and was quite competent, in the occasional absence of the choirmaster, to act as his deputy. It is customary at Stoneground for the choirmaster, in order to save the sexton a journey, to extinguish the lights after a choir-practice and to lock up the Church. These duties, accordingly, were performed by Mr. Batchel when the need arose.

It will be of use to the reader to have the procedure in detail. The large gas-meter stood in an aisle of the Church, and it was Mr. Batchel's practice to go round and extinguish all the lights save one, before turning off the gas at the meter. The one remaining light, which was reached by standing upon a choir seat, was always that nearest the door of the chancel, and experience proved that there was ample time to walk from the meter to that light before it died out. It was therefore an easy matter to turn off the last light, to find the door without its aid, and thence to pass out, and close the Church for the night.

Upon the evening of which we have to speak, the choir had hurried out as usual, as soon as the word had been given. Mr. Batchel had remained to gather together some of the books they had left in disorder, and then turned out the lights in the manner already described. But as soon as he had extinguished the last light, his eye fell, as he descended carefully from the seat, upon the figure of the Baptist. There was just enough light outside to make the figures visible in the Eastern Window, and Mr. Batchel saw the figure of St. John raise the right arm to its full extent, and point northward, turning its head, at the same time, so as to look him full in the face. These movements were three times repeated, and, after that, the figure came to rest in its normal and familiar position.

The reader will not suppose, any more than Mr. Batchel supposed, that a figure painted upon glass had suddenly been endowed with the power of movement. But that there had been the appearance of movement admitted of no doubt, and Mr. Batchel was not so incurious as to let the matter pass without some attempt at investigation. It must be remembered, too, that an experience in the old library, which has been previously recorded, had pre-disposed him to give attention to signs which another man might have wished to explain away. He was not willing, therefore, to leave this matter where it stood. He was quite prepared to think that his eye had been deceived, but was none the less determined to find out what had deceived it. One thing he had no difficulty in deciding. If the movement had not been actually within the Baptist's figure, it had been immediately behind it. Without delay, therefore, he passed out of the church and locked the door after him, with the intention of examining the other side of the window.

Every inhabitant of Stoneground knows, and laments, the ruin of the old Manor House. Its loss by fire some fifteen years ago was a calamity from which the parish has never recovered. The estate was acquired, soon after the destruction of the house, by speculators who have been unable to turn it to any account, and it has for a decade or longer been "let alone," except by the forces of Nature and the wantonness of trespassers. The charred remains of the house still project above the surrounding heaps of fallen masonry, which have long been overgrown by such vegetation as thrives on neglected ground; and what was once a stately house, with its garden and park in fine order, has given place to a scene of desolation and ruin.

Stoneground Church was built, some 600 years ago, within the enclosure of the Manor House, or, as it was anciently termed, the Burystead, and an excellent stratum of gravel such as no builder would wisely disregard, brought the house and Church unusually near together. In more primitive days, the nearness probably caused no inconvenience; but when change and progress affected the popular idea of respectful distance, the Churchyard came to be separated by a substantial stone wall, of sufficient height to secure the privacy of the house.

The change was made with necessary regard to economy of space. The Eastern wall of the Church already projected far into the garden of the Manor, and lay but fifty yards from the south front of the house. On that side of the Churchyard, therefore, the new wall was set back. Running from the north to the nearest corner of the Church, it was there built up to the Church itself, and then continued from the southern corner, leaving the Eastern wall and window within the garden of the Squire. It was his ivy that clung to the wall of the Church, and his trees that shaded the window from the morning sun.

Whilst we have been recalling these facts, Mr. Batchel has made his way out of the Church and through the Churchyard, and has arrived at a small door in the boundary wall, close to the S.E. corner of the chancel. It was a door which some Squire of the previous century had made, to give convenient access to the Church for himself and his household. It has no present use, and Mr. Batchel had some difficulty in getting it open. It was not long, however, before he stood on the inner side, and was examining the second light of the window. There was a tolerably bright moon, and the dark surface of the glass could be distinctly seen, as well as the wirework placed there for its protection.

A tall birch, one of the trees of the old Churchyard, had thrust its lower boughs across the window, and their silvery bark shone in the moonlight. The boughs were bare of leaves, and only very slightly interrupted Mr. Batchel's view of the Baptist's figure, the leaden outline of which was clearly traceable. There was nothing, however, to account for the movement which Mr. Batchel was curious to investigate.

He was about to turn homewards in some disappointment, when a cloud obscured the moon again, and reduced the light to what it had been before he left the Church. Mr. Batchel watched the darkening of the window and the objects near it, and as the figure of the Baptist disappeared from view there came into sight a creamy vaporous figure of another person lightly poised upon the bough of the tree, and almost coincident in position with the picture of the Saint.

It could hardly be described as the figure of a person. It had more the appearance of half a person, and fancifully suggested to Mr. Batchel, who was fond of whist, one of the diagonally bisected knaves in a pack of cards, as he appears when another card conceals a triangular half of the bust.

There was no question, now, of going home. Mr. Batchel's eyes were riveted upon the apparition. It disappeared again for a moment, when an interval between two clouds restored the light of the moon; but no sooner had the second cloud replaced the first than the figure again became distinct. And upon this, its single arm was raised three times, pointing northwards towards the ruined house, just as the figure of the Baptist had seemed to point when Mr. Batchel had seen it from within the Church.

It was natural that upon receipt of this sign Mr. Batchel should step nearer to the tree, from which he was still at some little distance, and as he moved, the figure floated obliquely downwards and came to rest in a direct line between him and the ruins of the house. It rested, not upon the ground, but in just such a position as it would have occupied if the lower parts had been there, and in this position it seemed to await Mr. Batchel's advance. He made such haste to approach it as was possible upon ground encumbered with ivy and brambles, and the figure responded to every advance of his by moving further in the direction of the ruin.

As the ground improved, the progress became more rapid. Soon they were both upon an open stretch of grass, which in better days had been a lawn, and still the figure retreated towards the building, with Mr. Batchel in respectful pursuit. He saw it, at last, poised upon the summit of a heap of masonry, and it disappeared, at his near approach, into a crevice between two large stones.

The timely re-appearance of the moon just enabled Mr. Batchel to perceive this crevice, and he took advantage of the interval of light to mark the place. Taking up a large twig that lay at his feet, he inserted it between the stones. He made a slit in the free end and drew into it one of some papers that he had carried out of the Church. After such a precaution it could hardly be possible to lose the place—for, of course, Mr. Batchel intended to return in daylight and continue his investigation. For the present, it seemed to be at an end. The light was soon obscured again, but there was no re-appearance of the singular figure he had followed, so after remaining about the spot for a few minutes, Mr. Batchel went home to his customary occupation.

He was not a man to let these occupations be disturbed even by a somewhat exciting adventure, nor was he one of those who regard an unusual experience only as a sign of nervous disorder. Mr. Batchel had far too broad a mind to discredit his sensations because they were not like those of other people. Even had his adventure of the evening been shared by some companion who saw less than he did, Mr. Batchel would only have inferred that his own part in the matter was being regarded as more important.

Next morning, therefore, he lost no time in returning to the scene of his adventure. He found his mark undisturbed, and was able to examine the crevice into which the apparition had seemed to enter. It was a crevice formed by the curved surfaces of two large stones which lay together on the top of a small heap of fallen rubbish, and these two stones Mr. Batchel proceeded to remove. His strength was just sufficient for the purpose. He laid the stones upon the ground on either side of the little mound, and then proceeded to remove, with his hands, the rubbish upon which they had rested, and amongst the rubbish he found, tarnished and blackened, two silver coins.

It was not a discovery which seemed to afford any explanation of what had occurred the night before, but Mr. Batchel could not but suppose that there had been an attempt to direct his attention to the coins, and he carried them away with a view of submitting them to a careful examination. Taking them up to his bedroom he poured a little water into a hand basin, and soon succeeded, with the aid of soap and a nail brush, in making them tolerably clean. Ten minutes later, after adding ammonia to the water, he had made them bright, and after carefully drying them, was able to make his examination. They were two crowns of the time of Queen Anne, minted, as a small letter E indicated, at Edinburgh, and stamped with the roses and plumes which testified to the English and Welsh silver in their composition. The coins bore no date, but Mr. Batchel had no hesitation in assigning them to the year 1708 or thereabouts. They were handsome coins, and in themselves a find of considerable interest, but there was nothing to show why he had been directed to their place of concealment. It was an enigma, and he could not solve it. He had other work to do, so he laid the two crowns upon his dressing table, and proceeded to do it.

Mr. Batchel thought little more of the coins until bedtime, when he took them from the table and bestowed upon them another admiring examination by the light of his candle. But the examination told him nothing new: he laid them down again, and, before very long, had lain his own head upon the pillow.

It was Mr. Batchel's custom to read himself to sleep. At this time he happened to be re-reading the Waverley novels, and "Woodstock" lay upon the reading-stand which was always placed at his bedside. As he read of the cleverly devised apparition at Woodstock, he naturally asked himself whether he might not have been the victim of some similar trickery, but was not long in coming to the conclusion that his experience admitted of no such explanation. He soon dismissed the matter from his mind and went on with his book.

On this occasion, however, he was tired of reading before he was ready for sleep; it was long in coming, and then did not come to stay. His rest, in fact, was greatly disturbed. Again and again, perhaps every hour or so, he was awakened by an uneasy consciousness of some other presence in the room.

Upon one of his later awakenings, he was distinctly sensible of a sound, or what he described to himself as the "ghost" of a sound. He compared it to the whining of a dog that had lost its voice. It was not a very intelligible comparison, but still it seemed to describe his sensation. The sound, if we may so call it caused him first to sit up in bed and look well about him, and then, when nothing had come of that, to light his candle. It was not to be expected that anything should come of that, but it had seemed a comfortable thing to do, and Mr. Batchel left the candle alight and read his book for half an hour or so, before blowing it out.

After this, there was no further interruption, but Mr. Batchel distinctly felt, when it was time to leave his bed, that he had had a bad night. The coins, almost to his surprise, lay undisturbed. He went to ascertain this as soon as he was on his feet. He would almost have welcomed their removal, or at any rate, some change which might have helped him towards a theory of his adventure. There was, however, nothing. If he had, in fact, been visited during the night, the coins would seem to have had nothing to do with the matter.

Mr. Batchel left the two crowns lying on his table on this next day, and went about his ordinary duties. They were such duties as afforded full occupation for his mind, and he gave no more than a passing thought to the coins, until he was again retiring to rest. He had certainly intended to return to the heap of rubbish from which he had taken them, but had not found leisure to do so. He did not handle the coins again. As he undressed, he made some attempt to estimate their value, but without having arrived at any conclusion, went on to think of other things, and in a little while had lain down to rest again, hoping for a better night.

His hopes were disappointed. Within an hour of falling asleep he found himself awakened again by the voiceless whining he so well remembered. This sound, as for convenience we will call it, was now persistent and continuous. Mr. Batchel gave up even trying to sleep, and as he grew more restless and uneasy, decided to get up and dress.

It was the entire cessation of the sound at this juncture which led him to a suspicion. His rising was evidently giving satisfaction. From that it was easy to infer that something had been desired of him, both on the present and the preceding night. Mr. Batchel was not one to hold himself aloof in such a case. If help was wanted, even in such unnatural circumstances, he was ready to offer it. He determined, accordingly, to return to the Manor House, and when he had finished dressing, descended the stairs, put on a warm overcoat and went out, closing his hall door behind him, without having heard any more of the sound, either whilst dressing, or whilst leaving the house.

Once out of doors, the suspicion he had formed was strengthened into a conviction. There was no manner of doubt that he had been fetched from his bed; for about 30 yards in front of him he saw the strange creamy half-figure making straight for the ruins. He followed it as well as he could; as before, he was impeded by the ivy and weeds, and the figure awaited him; as before, it made straight for the heap of masonry and disappeared as soon as Mr. Batchel was at liberty to follow.

There were no dungeons, or subterranean premises beneath the Manor House. It had never been more than a house of residence, and the building had been purely domestic in character. Mr. Batchel was convinced that his adventure would prove unromantic, and felt some impatience at losing again, what he had begun to call his triangular friend. If this friend wanted anything, it was not easy to say why he had so tamely disappeared. There seemed nothing to be done but to wait until he came out again.

Mr. Batchel had a pipe in his pocket, and he seated himself upon the base of a sun-dial within full view of the spot. He filled and smoked his pipe, sitting in momentary expectation of some further sign, but nothing appeared. He heard the hedgehogs moving about him in the undergrowth, and now and then the sound of a restless bird overhead, otherwise all was still. He smoked a second pipe without any further discovery, and that finished, he knocked out the ashes against his boot, walked to the mound, near to which his labelled stick was lying, thrust the stick into the place where the figure had disappeared, and went back to bed, where he was rewarded with five hours of sound sleep.

Mr. Batchel had made up his mind that the next day ought to be a day of disclosure. He was early at the Manor House, this time provided with the gardener's pick, and a spade. He thrust the pick into the place from which he had removed his mark, and loosened the rubbish thoroughly. With his hands, and with his spade, he was not long in reducing the size of the heap by about one-half, and there he found more coins.

There were three more crowns, two half-crowns, and a dozen or so of smaller coins. All these Mr. Batchel wrapped carefully in his handkerchief, and after a few minutes rest went on with his task. As it proved, the task was nearly over. Some strips of oak about nine inches long, were next uncovered, and then, what Mr. Batchel had begun to expect, the lid of a box, with the hinges still attached. It lay, face downwards, upon a flat stone. It proved, when he had taken it up, to be almost unsoiled, and above a long and wide slit in the lid was the gilded legend, "for ye poore" in the graceful lettering and the redundant spelling of two centuries ago.

The meaning of all this Mr. Batchel was not long in interpreting. That the box and its contents had fallen and been broken amongst the masonry, was evident enough. It was as evident that it had been concealed in one of the walls brought down by the fire, and Mr. Batchel had no doubt at all that he had been in the company of a thief, who had once stolen the poor-box from the Church. His task seemed to be at an end, a further rummage revealed nothing new. Mr. Batchel carefully collected the fragments of the box, and left the place.

His next act cannot be defended. He must have been aware that these coins were "treasure trove," and therefore the property of the Crown. In spite of this, he determined to convert them into current coin, as he well knew how, and to apply the proceeds to the Inundation Fund about which he was so anxious. Treating them as his own property, he cleaned them all, as he had cleaned the two crowns, sent them to an antiquarian friend in London to sell for him, and awaited the result. The lid of the poor box he still preserves as a relic of the adventure.

His antiquarian friend did not keep him long waiting. The coins had been eagerly bought, and the price surpassed any expectation that Mr. Batchel had allowed himself to entertain. He had sent the package to London on Saturday morning. Upon the following Tuesday, the last post in the evening brought a cheque for twenty guineas. The brief subscription list of the Inundation Fund lay upon his desk, and he at once entered the amount he had so strangely come by, but could not immediately decide upon its description. Leaving the line blank, therefore, he merely wrote down £21 in the cash column, to be assigned to its source in some suitable form of words when he should have found time to frame them.

In this state he left the subscription list upon his desk, when he retired for the night. It occurred to him as he was undressing, that the twenty guineas might suitably be described as a "restitution," and so he determined to enter it upon the line he had left vacant. As he reconsidered the matter in the morning, he saw no reason to alter his decision, and he went straight from his bedroom to his desk to make the entry and have done with it.

There was an incident in the adventure, however, upon which Mr. Batchel had not reckoned. As he approached the list, he saw, to his amazement, that the line had been filled in. In a crabbed, elongated hand was written, "At last, St. Matt. v. 26."

What may seem more strange is that the handwriting was familiar to Mr. Batchel, he could not at first say why. His memory, however, in such matters, was singularly good, and before breakfast was over he felt sure of having identified the writer.

His confidence was not misplaced. He went to the parish chest, whose contents he had thoroughly examined in past intervals of leisure, and took out the roll of parish constable's accounts. In a few minutes he discovered the handwriting of which he was in search. It was unmistakably that of Salathiel Thrapston, constable from 1705-1710, who met his death in the latter year, whilst in the execution of his duty. The reader will scarcely need to be reminded of the text of the Gospel at the place of reference—

"Thou shalt by no means come out thence till thou hast paid the uttermost farthing."

LUBRIETTA

For the better understanding of this narrative we shall furnish the reader with a few words of introduction. It amounts to no more than a brief statement of facts which Mr. Batchel obtained from the Lady Principal of the European College in Puna, but the facts nevertheless are important. The narrative itself was obtained from Mr. Batchel with difficulty: he was disposed to regard it as unsuitable for publication because of the delicate nature of the situations with which it deals. When, however, it was made clear to him that it would be recorded in such a manner as would interest only a very select body of readers, his scruples were overcome, and he was induced to communicate the experience now to be related. Those who read it will not fail to see that they are in a manner pledged to deal very discreetly with the knowledge they are privileged to share.

Lubrietta Rodria is described by her Lady Principal as an attractive and high-spirited girl of seventeen, belonging to the Purple of Indian commerce. Her nationality was not precisely known; but drawing near, as she did, to a marriageable age, and being courted by more than one eligible suitor, she was naturally an object of great interest to her schoolfellows, with whom her personal beauty and amiable temper had always made her a favourite. She was not, the Lady Principal thought, a girl who would be regarded in Christian countries as of very high principle; but none the less, she was one whom it was impossible not to like.

Her career at the college had ended sensationally. She had been immoderately anxious about her final examination, and its termination had found her in a state of collapse. They had at once removed her to her father's house in the country, where she received such nursing and assiduous attention as her case required. It was apparently of no avail. For three weeks she lay motionless, deprived of speech, and voluntarily, taking no food. Then for a further period of ten days she lay in a plight still more distressing. She lost all consciousness, and, despite the assurance of the doctors, her parents could hardly be persuaded that she lived.

Her fiancé who by this time had been declared, was in despair, not only from natural affection for Lubrietta, but from remorse. It was his intellectual ambition that had incited her to the eagerness in study which was threatening such dire results, and it was well understood that neither of the lovers would survive these anxious days of watching if they were not to be survived by both.

After ten days, however, a change supervened. Lubrietta came back to life amid the frenzied rejoicing of the household and all her circle. She recovered her health and strength with incredible speed, and within three months was married —as the Lady Principal had cause to believe, with the happiest prospects.

* * * *

Mr. Batchel had not, whilst residing at Stoneground, lost touch with the University which had given him his degree, and in which he had formerly held one or two minor offices. He had earned no great distinction as a scholar, but had taken a degree in honours, and was possessed of a useful amount of general knowledge, and in this he found not only constant pleasure, but also occasional profit.

The University had made herself, for better or worse, an examiner of a hundred times as many students as she could teach; her system of examinations had extended to the very limits of the British Empire, and her certificates of proficiency were coveted in every quarter of the globe.

In the examination of these students, Mr. Batchel, who had considerable experience in teaching, was annually employed. Papers from all parts of the world were to be found littered about his study, and the examination of these papers called for some weeks of strenuous labour at every year's end. As the weeks passed, he would anxiously watch the growth of a neat stack of papers in the corner of the room, which indicated the number to which marks had been assigned and reported to Cambridge. The day upon which the last of these was laid in its place was a day of satisfaction, second only to that which later on brought him a substantial cheque to remunerate him for his labours.

During this period of special effort, Mr. Batchel's servants had their share of its discomforts. The chairs and tables they wanted to dust and to arrange, were loaded with papers which they were forbidden to touch; and although they were warned against showing visitors into any room where these papers were lying, Mr. Batchel would inconsiderately lay them in every room he had. The privacy of his study, however, where the work was chiefly done, was strictly guarded, and no one was admitted there unless by Mr. Batchel himself.

Imagine his annoyance, therefore, when he returned from an evening engagement at the beginning of the month of January, and found a stranger seated in the study! Yet the annoyance was not long in subsiding. The visitor was a lady, and as she sat by the lamp, a glance was enough to shew that she was young, and very beautiful. The interest which this young lady excited in Mr. Batchel was altogether unusual, as unusual as was the visit of such a person at such a time. His conjecture was that she had called to give him notice of a marriage, but he was really charmed by her presence, and was quite content to find her in no haste to state her errand. The manner, however, of the lady was singular, for neither by word nor movement did she show that she was conscious of Mr. Batchel's entry into the room.

He began at length with his customary formula "What can I have the pleasure of doing for you?" and when, at the sound of his voice, she turned her fine dark eyes upon him, he saw that they were wet with tears.

Mr. Batchel was now really moved. As a tear fell upon the lady's cheek, she raised her hand as if to conceal it—a brilliant sapphire sparkling in the lamp-light as she did so. And then the lady's distress, and the exquisite grace of her presence, altogether overcame him. There stole upon him a strange feeling of tenderness which he supposed to be paternal, but knew nevertheless to be indiscreet. He was a prudent man, with strict notions of propriety, so that, ostensibly with a view to giving the lady a few minutes in which to recover her composure, he quietly left the study and went into another room, to pull himself together.

Mr. Batchel, like most solitary men, had a habit of talking to himself. "It is of no use, R. B.," he said, "to pretend that you have retired on this damsel's account. If you don't take care, you'll make a fool of yourself." He took up from the table a volume of the encyclopedia in which, the day before, he had been looking up Pestalozzi, and turned over the pages in search of something to restore his equanimity. An article on Perspective proved to be the very thing. Wholly unromantic in character, its copious presentment of hard fact relieved his mind, and he was soon threading his way along paths of knowledge to which he was little accustomed. He applied his remedy with such persistence that when four or five minutes had passed, he felt sufficiently composed to return to the study. He framed, as he went, a suitable form of words with which to open the conversation, and took with him his register of Banns of Marriage, of which he thought he foresaw the need. As he opened the study-door, the book fell from his hands to the ground, so completely was he overcome by surprise, for he found the room empty. The lady had disappeared; her chair stood vacant before him.

Mr. Batchel sat down for a moment, and then rang the bell. It was answered by the boy who always attended upon him.

"When did the lady go?" asked Mr. Batchel.

The boy looked bewildered.

"The lady you showed into the study before I came."

"Please, sir, I never shown anyone into the study; I never do when you're out."

"There was a lady here," said Mr. Batchel, "when I returned."

The boy now looked incredulous.

"Did you not let someone out just now?"

"No, sir," said the boy. "I put the chain on the front door as soon as you came in."

This was conclusive. The chain upon the hall-door was an ancient and cumbrous thing, and could not be manipulated without considerable effort, and a great deal of noise. Mr. Batchel released the boy, and began to think furiously. He was not, as the reader is well aware, without some experience of the supranormal side of nature, and he knew of course that the visit of this enthralling lady had a purpose. He was beginning to know, however, that it had had an effect. He sat before his fire reproducing her image, and soon gave it up in disgust because his imagination refused to do her justice. He could recover the details of her appearance, but could combine them into nothing that would reproduce the impression she had first made upon him.

He was unable now to concentrate his attention upon the examination papers lying on his table. His mind wandered so often to the other topic that he felt himself to be in danger of marking the answers unfairly. He turned away from his work, therefore, and moved to another chair, where he sat down to read. It was the chair in which she herself had sat, and he made no attempt to pretend that he had chosen it on any other account. He had, in fact, made some discoveries about himself during the last half-hour, and he gave himself another surprise when he came to select his book. In the ordinary course of what he had supposed to be his nature, he would certainly have returned to the article on Perspective; it was lying open in the next room, and he had read no more than a tenth part of it. But instead of that, his thoughts went back to a volume he had but once opened, and that for no more than two minutes. He had received the book, by way of birthday

270

present, early in the preceding year, from a relative who had bestowed either no consideration at all, or else a great deal of cunning, upon its selection. It was a collection of 17th century lyrics, which Mr. Batchel's single glance had sufficed to condemn. Regarding the one lyric he had read as a sort of literary freak, he had banished the book to one of the spare bedrooms, and had never seen it since. And now, after this long interval, the absurd lines which his eye had but once lighted upon, were recurring to his mind:

> "Fair, sweet, and young, receive a prize
> Reserved for your victorious eyes";

and so far from thinking them absurd, as he now recalled them, he went upstairs to fetch the book, in which he was soon absorbed. The lyrics no longer seemed unreasonable. He felt conscious, as he read one after another, of a side of nature that he had strangely neglected, and was obliged to admit that the men whose feelings were set forth in the various sonnets and poems had a fine gift of expression.

> "Thus, whilst I look for her in vain,
> Methinks I am a child again,
> And of my shadow am a-chasing.
> For all her graces are to me
> Like apparitions that I see,
> But never can come near th' embracing."

No! these men were not, as he had formerly supposed, writing with air, and he felt ashamed at having used the term "freak" at their expense.

Mr. Batchel read more of the lyrics, some of them twice, and one of them much oftener. That one he began to commit to memory, and since the household had retired to rest, to recite aloud. He had been unaware that literature contained anything so beautiful, and as he looked again at the book to recover an expression his memory had lost, a tear fell upon the page. It was a thing so extraordinary that Mr. Batchel first looked at the ceiling, but when he found that it was indeed a tear from his own eye he was immoderately pleased with himself. Had not she also shed a tear as she sat upon the same chair? The fact seemed to draw them together.

Contemplation of this sort was, however, a luxury to be enjoyed in something like moderation. Mr. Batchel soon laid down his lyric and savagely began to add up columns of marks, by way of discipline; and when he had totalled several pages of these, respect for his normal self had returned with sufficient force to take him off to bed.

The matter of his dreams, or whether he dreamed at all, has not been disclosed. He awoke, at any rate, in a calmer state of mind, and such romantic thoughts as remained were effectually dispelled by the sight of his own countenance when he began to shave. "Fancy you spouting lyrics," he said, as he dabbed the brush upon his mouth, and by the time he was ready for breakfast he pronounced himself cured.

The prosaic labours awaiting him in the study were soon forced upon his notice, and for once he did not regret it. Amongst the letters lying upon the breakfast table was one from the secretary who controlled the system of examination. The form of the envelope was too familiar to leave him in doubt as to what it contained. It was a letter which, to a careful man like Mr. Batchel, seemed to have the nature of a reproof, inasmuch as it probably asked for information which it had already been his duty to furnish. The contents of the envelope, when he had impatiently torn it open, answered to his expectation—he was formally requested to supply the name and the marks of candidate No. 1004, and he wondered, as he ate his breakfast, how he had omitted to return them. He hunted out the paper of No. 1004 as soon as the meal was over. The candidate proved to be one Lubrietta Bodria, of whom, of course, he had never heard, and her answers had all been marked. He could not understand why they should have been made the subject of enquiry.

He took her papers in his hand, and looked at them again as he stood with his back to the fire, having lit the pipe which invariably followed his breakfast, and then he discovered something much harder to understand. The marks were not his own. In place of the usual sketchy numerals, hardly decipherable to any but himself, he saw figures which were carefully formed; and the marks assigned to the first answer, as he saw it on the uppermost sheet, were higher than the maximum number obtainable for that question.

Mr. Batchel laid down his pipe and seated himself at the table. He was greatly puzzled. As he turned over the sheets of No. 1004 he found all the other questions marked in like manner, and making a total of half as much again as the highest possible number. "Who the dickens," he said, using a meaningless, but not uncommon expression, "has been playing with this; and how came I to pass it over?" The need of the moment, however, was to furnish the proper marks to the secretary at Cambridge, and Mr. Batchel proceeded to read No. 1004 right through.

He soon found that he had read it all before, and the matter began to bristle with queries. It proved, in fact, to be a paper over which he had spent some time, and for a singularly interesting reason. He had learned from a friend in the Indian Civil Service that an exaggerated value was often placed by ambitious Indians and Cingalese upon a European education, and that many aspiring young men declined to take a wife who had not passed this very examination. It was to Mr. Batchel a disquieting reflection that his blue pencil was not only marking mistakes, but might at the same time be cancelling matrimonial engagements, and his friend's communication had made him scrupulously careful in examining the work of young ladies in Oriental Schools. The matter had occurred to him at once as he had examined the answers of Lubrietta Rodria. He perfectly remembered the question upon which her success depended. A problem in logic had been answered by a rambling and worthless argument, to which, somehow, the right conclusion was appended: the conclusion might be a happy guess, or it might have been secured by less honest means, but Mr. Batchel, following his usual practice, gave no marks for it. It was not here that he found any cause for hesitation, but when he came to the end of the paper and found that the candidate had only just failed, he had turned back to the critical question, imagined an eligible bachelor awaiting the result of the examination, and then, after a period of vacillation, had hastily put the symbol of failure upon the paper lest he should be tempted to bring his own charity to the rescue of the candidate's logic, and unfairly add the three marks which would suffice to pass her.

As he now read the answer for the second time, the same pitiful thought troubled him, and this time more than before; for over the edge of the paper of No.

1004 there persistently arose the image of the young lady with the sapphire ring. It directed the current of his thoughts. Suppose that Lubrietta Rodria were anything like that! and what if the arguments of No. 1004 were worthless! Young ladies were notoriously weak in argument, and as strong in conclusions! and after all, the conclusion was correct, and ought not a correct conclusion to have its marks? There followed much more to the same purpose, and in the end Mr. Batchel stultified himself by adding the necessary three marks, and passing the candidate.

"This comes precious near to being a job," he remarked, as he entered the marks upon the form and sealed it in the envelope, "but No. 1004 must pass, this time." He enclosed in the envelope a request to know why the marks had been asked for, since they had certainly been returned in their proper place. A brief official reply informed him next day that the marks he had returned exceeded the maximum, and must, therefore, have been wrongly entered.

"This," said Mr. Batchel, "is a curious coincidence."

Curious as it certainly was, it was less curious than what immediately followed. It was Mr. Batchel's practice to avoid any delay in returning these official papers, and he went out, there and then, to post his envelope. The Post Office was no more than a hundred yards from his door, and in three minutes he was in his study again. The first object that met his eye there was a beautiful sapphire ring lying upon the papers of No. 1004, which had remained upon the table.

Mr. Batchel at once recognised the ring. "I knew it was precious near a job," he said, "but I didn't know that it was as near as this."

He took up the ring and examined it. It looked like a ring of great value; the stone was large and brilliant, and the setting was of fine workmanship. "Now what on earth," said Mr. Batchel, "am I to do with this?"

The nearest jeweller to Stoneground was a competent and experienced tradesman of the old school. He was a member of the local Natural History Society, and in that capacity Mr. Batchel had made intimate acquaintance with him. To this jeweller, therefore, he carried the ring, and asked him what he thought of it.

"I'll give you forty pounds for it," said the jeweller.

Mr. Batchel replied that the ring was not his. "What about the make of it?" he asked. "Is it English?"

The jeweller replied that it was unmistakably Indian.

"You are sure?" said Mr. Batchel.

"Certain," said the jeweller. "Major Ackroyd brought home one like it, all but the stone, from Puna; I repaired it for him last year."

The information was enough, if not more than enough, for Mr. Batchel. He begged a suitable case from his friend the jeweller, and within an hour had posted the ring to Miss Lubrietta Rodria at the European College in Puna. At the same time he wrote to the Principal the letter whose answer is embodied in the preface to this narrative.

Having done this, Mr. Batchel felt more at ease. He had given Lubrietta Rodria what he amiably called the benefit of the doubt, but it should never be said that he had been bribed.

The rest of his papers he marked with fierce justice. A great deal of the work, in his zeal, he did twice over, but his conscience amply requited him for the superfluous labour. The last paper was marked within a day of the allotted time,

Mr. Batchel shortly afterwards received his cheque, and was glad to think that the whole matter was at an end.

* * * *

That Lubrietta had been absent from India whilst her relatives and attendants were trying to restore her to consciousness, he had good reason to know. His friends, for the most part, took a very narrow view of human nature and its possibilities, so that he kept his experience, for a long time, to himself; there were personal reasons for not discussing the incident. The reader has been already told upon what understanding it is recorded here.

There remains, however, an episode which Mr. Batchel all but managed to suppress. Upon the one occasion when he allowed himself to speak of this matter, he was being pressed for a description of the sapphire ring, and was not very successful in his attempt to describe it. There was no reason, of course, why this should lay his good faith under suspicion. Few of us could pass an examination upon objects with which we are supposed to be familiar, or say which of our tables have three legs, and which four.

One of Mr. Batchel's auditors, however, took a captious view of the matter, and brusquely remarked, in imitation of a more famous sceptic, "I don't believe there's no sich a thing."

Mr. Batchel, of course, recognised the phrase, and it was his eagerness to establish his credit that committed him at this point to a last disclosure about Lubrietta. He drew a sapphire ring from his pocket, handed it to the incredulous auditor, and addressed him in the manner of Mrs. Gamp.

"What! you bage creetur, have I had this ring three year or more to be told there ain't no sech a thing. Go along with you."

"But I thought the ring was sent back," said more than one.

"How did you come by it?" said all the others.

Mr. Batchel thereupon admitted that he had closed his story prematurely. About six weeks after the return of the ring to Puna he had found it once again upon his table, returned through the post. Enclosed in the package was a note which Mr. Batchel, being now committed to this part of the story, also passed round for inspection. It ran as follows:—

"Accept the ring, dear one, and wear it for my sake. Fail not to think sometimes of her whom you have made happy.—L. R."

"What on earth am I to do with this?" Mr. Batchel had asked himself again. And this time he had answered the question, after the briefest possible delay, by slipping the ring upon his fourth finger.

The book of Lyrics remained downstairs amongst the books in constant use. Mr. Batchel can repeat at least half of the collection from memory.

He knows well enough that such terms as "dear one" are addressed to bald gentlemen only in a Pickwickian sense, but even with that sense the letter gives him pleasure.

He admits that he thinks very often of "her whom he has made happy," but that he cannot exclude from his thoughts at these times an ungenerous regret. It is that he has also made happy a nameless Oriental gentleman whom he presumptuously calls "the other fellow."

THE ROCKERY

The Vicar's garden at Stoneground has certainly been enclosed for more than seven centuries, and during the whole of that time its almost sacred privacy has been regarded as permanent and unchangeable. It has remained for the innovators of later and more audacious days to hint that it might be given into other hands, and still carry with it no curse that should make a new possessor hasten to undo his irreverence. Whether there can be warrant for such confidence, time will show. The experiences already related will show that the privacy of the garden has been counted upon both by good men and worse. And here is a story, in its way, more strange than any.

By way of beginning, it may be well to describe a part of the garden not hitherto brought into notice. That part lies on the western boundary, where the garden slopes down to a sluggish stream, hardly a stream at all, locally known as the Lode. The Lode bounds the garden on the west along its whole length, and there the moor-hen builds her nest, and the kingfisher is sometimes, but in these days too rarely, seen. But the centre of vision, as it were, of this western edge lies in a cluster of tall elms. Towards these all the garden paths converge, and about their base is raised a bank of earth, upon which is heaped a rockery of large stones lately overgrown with ferns.

Mr. Batchel's somewhat prim taste in gardening had long resented this disorderly bank. In more than one place in his garden had wild confusion given place to a park-like trimness, and there were not a few who would say that the change was not for the better. Mr. Batchel, however, went his own way, and in due time determined to remove the rockery. He was puzzled by its presence; he could see no reason why a bank should have been raised about the feet of the elms, and surmounted with stones; not a ray of sunshine ever found its way there, and none but coarse and uninteresting plants had established themselves. Whoever had raised the bank had done it ignorantly, or with some purpose not easy for Mr. Batchel to conjecture.

Upon a certain day, therefore, in the early part of December, when the garden had been made comfortable for its winter rest, he began, with the assistance of his gardener, to remove the stones into another place.

We do but speak according to custom in this matter, and there are few readers who will not suspect the truth, which is that the gardener began to remove the stones, whilst Mr. Batchel stood by and delivered criticisms of very slight value. Such strength, in fact, as Mr. Batchel possessed had concentrated itself upon the mind, and somewhat neglected his body, and what he called help, during his presence in the garden, was called by another name when the gardener and his boy were left to themselves, with full freedom of speech.

There were few of the stones rolled down by the gardener that Mr. Batchel could even have moved, but his astonishment at their size soon gave place to excitement at their appearance. His antiquarian tastes were strong, and were soon busily engaged. For, as the stones rolled down, his eyes were feasted, in a rapid succession, by capitals of columns, fragments of moulded arches and mullions, and other relics of ecclesiastical building.

Repeatedly did he call the gardener down from his work to put these fragments together, and before long there were several complete lengths of arcading laid upon the path. Stones which, perhaps, had been separated for centuries, once more came together, and Mr. Batchel, rubbing his hands in excited satisfaction, declared that he might recover the best parts of a Church by the time the rockery had been demolished.

The interest of the gardener in such matters was of a milder kind. "We must go careful," he merely observed, "when we come to the organ." They went on removing more and more stones, until at length the whole bank was laid bare, and Mr. Batchel's chief purpose achieved. How the stones were carefully arranged, and set up in other parts of the garden, is well known, and need not concern us now.

One detail, however, must not be omitted. A large and stout stake of yew, evidently of considerable age, but nevertheless quite sound, stood exposed after the clearing of the bank. There was no obvious reason for its presence, but it had been well driven in, so well that the strength of the gardener, or, if it made any difference, of the gardener and Mr. Batchel together, failed even to shake it. It was not unsightly, and might have remained where it was, had not the gardener exclaimed, "This is the very thing we want for the pump." It was so obviously "the very thing" that its removal was then and there decided upon.

The pump referred to was a small iron pump used to draw water from the Lode. It had been affixed to many posts in turn, and defied them all to hold it. Not that the pump was at fault. It was a trifling affair enough. But the pumpers were usually garden-boys, whose impatient energy had never failed, before many days, to wriggle the pump away from its supports. When the gardener had, upon one occasion, spent half a day in attaching it firmly to a post, they had at once shaken out the post itself. Since, therefore, the matter was causing daily inconvenience, and the gardener becoming daily more concerned for his reputation as a rough carpenter, it was natural for him to exclaim, "This is the very thing." It was a better stake than he had ever used, and as had just been made evident, a stake that the ground would hold.

"Yes!" said Mr. Batchel, "it is the very thing; but can we get it up?" The gardener always accepted this kind of query as a challenge, and replied only by taking up a pick and setting to work, Mr. Batchel, as usual, looking on, and making, every now and then, a fruitless suggestion. After a few minutes, however, he made somewhat more than a suggestion. He darted forward and laid his hand upon the pick. "Don't you see some copper?" he asked quickly.

Every man who digs knows what a hiding place there is in the earth. The monotony of spade work is always relieved by a hope of turning up something unexpected. Treasure lies dimly behind all these hopes, so that the gardener, having seen Mr. Batchel excited over so much that was precious from his own point of view, was quite ready to look for something of value to an ordinary reasonable man. Copper might lead to silver, and that, in turn, to gold. At Mr. Batchel's eager question, therefore, he peered into the hole he had made, and examined everything there that might suggest the rounded form of a coin.

He soon saw what had arrested Mr. Batchel. There was a lustrous scratch on the side of the stake, evidently made by the pick, and though the metal was copper, plainly enough, the gardener felt that he had been deceived, and would have gone on with his work. Copper of that sort gave him no sort of excitement, and only a feeble interest.

Mr. Batchel, however, was on his hands and knees. There was a small irregular plate of copper nailed to the stake; without any difficulty he tore it away from the nails, and soon scraped it clean with a shaving of wood; then, rising to his feet, he examined his find.

There was an inscription upon it, so legible as to need no deciphering. It had been roughly and effectually made with a hammer and nail, the letters being formed by series of holes punched deeply into the metal, and what he read was: —

MOVE NOT THIS STAKE, NOV. 1, 1702.

But to move the stake was what Mr. Batchel had determined upon, and the metal plate he held in his hand interested him chiefly as showing how long the post had been there. He had happened, as he supposed, upon an ancient landmark. The discovery, recorded elsewhere, of a well, near to the edge of his present lawn, had shown him that his premises had once been differently arranged. One of the minor antiquarian tasks he had set himself was to discover and record the old arrangement, and he felt that the position of this stake would help him. He felt no doubt of its being a point upon the western limit of the garden; not improbably marked in this way to show where the garden began, and where ended the ancient hauling-way, which had been secured to the public for purposes of navigation.

The gardener, meanwhile, was proceeding with his work. With no small difficulty he removed the rubble and clay which accounted for the firmness of the stake. It grew dark as the work went on, and a distant clock struck five before it was completed. Five was the hour at which the gardener usually went home; his day began early. He was not, however, a man to leave a small job unfinished, and he went on loosening the earth with his pick, and trying the effect, at intervals, upon the firmness of the stake. It naturally began to give, and could be moved from side to side through a space of some few inches. He lifted out the loosened stones, and loosened more. His pick struck iron, which, after loosening, proved to be links of a rusted chain. "They've buried a lot of rubbish in this hole," he remarked, as he went on loosening the chain, which, in the growing darkness, could hardly be seen. Mr. Batchel, meanwhile, occupied himself in a simpler task of working the stake to and fro, by way of loosening its hold. Ultimately it began to move with greater freedom. The gardener laid down his tool and grasped the stake, which his master was still holding; their combined efforts succeeded at once; the stake was lifted out.

It turned out to be furnished with an unusually long and sharp point, which explained the firmness of its hold upon the ground. The gardener carried it to the neighbourhood of the pump, in readiness for its next purpose, and made ready to go home. He would drive the stake to-morrow, he said, in the new place, and make the pump so secure that not even the boys could shake it. He also spoke of some designs he had upon the chain, should it prove to be of any considerable length. He was an ingenious man, and his skill in converting discarded articles to new uses was embarrassing to his master. Mr. Batchel, as has been said, was a prim gardener, and he had no liking for makeshift devices. He had that day seen his runner beans trained upon a length of old gas-piping, and had no intention of leaving the gardener in possession of such a treasure as a rusty chain. What he said, however, and said with truth, was that he wanted the chain for himself. He had no practical use for it, and hardly expected it to yield him any interest. But a chain buried in 1702 must be examined—nothing ancient comes amiss to a man of antiquarian tastes.

Mr. Batchel had noticed, whilst the gardener had been carrying away the stake, that the chain lay very loosely in the earth. The pick had worked well round it. He said, therefore, that the chain must be lifted out and brought to him upon the morrow, bade his gardener good night, and went in to his fireside.

This will appear to the reader to be a record of the merest trifles, but all readers will accept the reminder that there is no such thing as a trifle, and that what appears to be trivial has that appearance only so long as it stands alone. Regarded in the light of their consequences, those matters which have seemed to be least in importance, turn out, often enough, to be the greatest. And these trifling occupations, as we may call them for the last time, of Mr. Batchel and the gardener, had consequences which shall now be set down as Mr. Batchel himself narrated them. But we must take events in their order. At present Mr. Batchel is at his fireside, and his gardener at home with his family. The stake is removed, and the hole, in which lies some sort of an iron chain, is exposed.

Upon this particular evening Mr. Batchel was dining out. He was a good natured man, with certain mild powers of entertainment, and his presence as an occasional guest was not unacceptable at some of the more considerable houses of the neighbourhood. And let us hasten to observe that he was not a guest who made any great impression upon the larders or the cellars of his hosts. He liked port, but he liked it only of good quality, and in small quantity. When he returned from a dinner party, therefore, he was never either in a surfeited condition of body, or in any confusion of mind. Not uncommonly after his return upon such occasions did he perform accurate work. Unfinished contributions to sundry local journals were seldom absent from his desk. They were his means of recreation. There they awaited convenient intervals of leisure, and Mr. Batchel was accustomed to say that of these intervals he found none so productive as a late hour, or hour and a half, after a dinner party.

Upon the evening in question he returned, about an hour before midnight, from dining at the house of a retired officer residing in the neighbourhood, and the evening had been somewhat less enjoyable than usual. He had taken in to dinner a young lady who had too persistently assailed him with antiquarian questions. Now Mr. Batchel did not like talking what he regarded as "shop," and was not much at home with young ladies, to whom he knew that, in the nature of things, he could be but imperfectly acceptable. With infinite good will towards them, and a genuine liking for their presence, he felt that he had but little to offer them in exchange. There was so little in common between his life and theirs. He felt distinctly at his worst when he found himself treated as a mere scrap-book of information. It made him seem, as he would express it, de-humanised.

Upon this particular evening the young lady allotted to him, perhaps at her own request, had made a scrap-book of him, and he had returned home somewhat discontented, if also somewhat amused. His discontent arose from having been deprived of the general conversation he so greatly, but so rarely, enjoyed. His amusement was caused by the incongruity between a very light-hearted young lady and the subject upon which she had made him talk, for she had talked of nothing else but modes of burial.

He began to recall the conversation as he lit his pipe and dropped into his armchair. She had either been reflecting deeply upon the matter, or, as seemed to

Mr. Batchel, more probable, had read something and half forgotten it. He recalled her questions, and the answers by which he had vainly tried to lead her to a more attractive topic. For example:

She: Will you tell me why people were buried at cross roads?

He: Well, consecrated ground was so jealously guarded that a criminal would be held to have forfeited the right to be buried amongst Christian folk. His friends would therefore choose cross roads where there was set a wayside cross, and make his grave at the foot of it. In some of my journeys in Scotland I have seen crosses....

But the young lady had refused to be led into Scotland. She had stuck to her subject.

She: Why have coffins come back into use? There is nothing in our Burial Service about a coffin.

He: True, and the use of the coffin is due, in part, to an ignorant notion of confining the corpse, lest, like Hamlet's father, he should walk the earth. You will have noticed that the corpse is always carried out of the house feet foremost, to suggest a final exit, and that the grave is often covered with a heavy slab. Very curious epitaphs are to be found on these slabs....

But she was not to be drawn into the subject of epitaphs. She had made him tell of other devices for confining spirits to their prison, and securing the peace of the living, especially of those adopted in the case of violent and mischievous men. Altogether an unusual sort of young lady.

The conversation, however, had revived his memories of what was, after all, a matter of some interest, and he determined to look through his parish registers for records of exceptional burials. He was surprised at himself for never having done it. He dismissed the matter from his mind for the time being, and as it was a bright moonlight night he thought he would finish his pipe in the garden.

Therefore, although midnight was close at hand, he strolled complacently round his garden, enjoying the light of the moon no less than in the daytime he would have enjoyed the sun; and thus it was that he arrived at the scene of his labours upon the old rockery. There was more light than there had been at the end of the afternoon, and when he had walked up the bank, and stood over the hole we have already described, he could distinctly see the few exposed links of the iron chain. Should he remove it at once to a place of safety, out of the way of the gardener? It was about time for bed. The city clocks were then striking midnight. He would let the chain decide. If it came out easily he would remove it; otherwise, it should remain until morning.

The chain came out more than easily. It seemed to have a force within itself. He gave but a slight tug at the free end with a view of ascertaining what resistance he had to encounter, and immediately found himself lying upon his back with the chain in his hand. His back had fortunately turned towards an elm three feet away which broke his fall, but there had been violence enough to cause him no little surprise.

The effort he had made was so slight that he could not account for having lost his feet; and being a careful man, he was a little anxious about his evening coat, which he was still wearing. The chain, however, was in his hand, and he made haste to coil it into a portable shape, and to return to the house.

Some fifty yards from the spot was the northern boundary of the garden, a long wall with a narrow lane beyond. It was not unusual, even at this hour of the night, to hear footsteps there. The lane was used by railway men, who passed to and from their work at all hours, as also by some who returned late from entertainments in the neighbouring city.

But Mr. Batchel, as he turned back to the house, with his chain over one arm, heard more than footsteps. He heard for a few moments the unmistakable sound of a scuffle, and then a piercing cry, loud and sharp, and a noise of running. It was such a cry as could only have come from one in urgent need of help.

Mr. Batchel dropped his chain. The garden wall was some ten feet high and he had no means of scaling it. But he ran quickly into the house, passed out by the hall door into the street, and so towards the lane without a moment's loss of time.

Before he has gone many yards he sees a man running from the lane with his clothing in great disorder, and this man, at the sight of Mr. Batchel, darts across the road, runs along in the shadow of an opposite wall and attempts to escape.

The man is known well enough to Mr. Batchel. It is one Stephen Medd, a respectable and sensible man, by occupation a shunter, and Mr. Batchel at once calls out to ask what has happened. Stephen, however, makes no reply but continues to run along the shadow of the wall, whereupon Mr. Batchel crosses over and intercepts him, and again asks what is amiss. Stephen answers wildly and breathlessly, "I'm not going to stop here, let me go home."

As Mr. Batchel lays his hand upon the man's arm and draws him into the light of the moon, it is seen that his face is streaming with blood from a wound near the eye.

He is somewhat calmed by the familiar voice of Mr. Batchel, and is about to speak, when another scream is heard from the lane. The voice is that of a boy or woman, and no sooner does Stephen hear it than he frees himself violently from Mr. Batchel and makes away towards his home. With no less speed does Mr. Batchel make for the lane, and finds about half way down a boy lying on the ground wounded and terrified.

At first the boy clings to the ground, but he, too, is soon reassured by Mr. Batchel's voice, and allows himself to be lifted on to his feet. His wound is also in the face, and Mr. Batchel takes the boy into his house, bathes and plasters his wound, and soon restores him to something like calm. He is what is termed a call-boy, employed by the Railway Company to awaken drivers at all hours, and give them their instructions.

Mr. Batchel is naturally impatient for the moment he can question the boy about his assailant, who is presumably also the assailant of Stephen Medd. No one had been visible in the lane, though the moon shone upon it from end to end. At the first available moment, therefore, he asks the boy, "Who did this?"

The answer came, without any hesitation, "Nobody. There was nobody there," he said, "and all of a sudden somebody hit me with an iron thing."

Then Mr. Batchel asked, "Did you see Stephen Medd?" He was becoming greatly puzzled.

The boy replied that he had seen Mr. Medd "a good bit in front," with nobody near him, and that all of a sudden someone knocked him down.

Further questioning seemed useless. Mr. Batchel saw the boy to his home, left him at the door, and returned to bed, but not to sleep. He could not cease from thinking, and he could think of nothing but assaults from invisible hands. Morning seemed long in coming, but came at last.

Mr. Batchel was up betimes and made a very poor breakfast. Dallying with the morning paper, rather than reading it, his eye was arrested by a headline about "Mysterious assaults in Elmham." He felt that he had mysteries of his own to occupy him and was in no mood to be interested in more assaults. But he had some knowledge of Elmham, a small town ten miles distant from Stoneground, and he read the brief paragraph, which contained no more than the substance of a telegram. It said, however, that three persons had been victims of unaccountable assaults. Two of them had escaped with slight injuries, but the third, a young woman, was dangerously wounded, though still alive and conscious. She declared that she was quite alone in her house and had been suddenly struck with great violence by what felt like a piece of iron, and that she must have bled to death but for a neighbour who heard her cries. The neighbour had at once looked out and seen nobody, but had bravely gone to her friend's assistance.

Mr. Batchel laid down his newspaper considerably impressed, as was natural, by the resemblance of these tragedies to what he had witnessed himself. He was in no condition, after his excitement and his sleepless night, to do his usual work. His mind reverted to the conversation at the dinner party and the trifle of antiquarian research it had suggested. Such occupation had often served him when he found himself suffering from a cold, or otherwise indisposed for more serious work. He would get the registers and collect what entries there might be of irregular burial.

He found only one such entry, but that one was enough. There was a note dated All Hallows, 1702, to this effect:

"This day did a vagrant from Elmham beat cruelly to death two poor men who had refused him alms, and upon a hue and cry being raised, took his own life. He was buried in one Parson's Close with a stake through his body and his arms confined in chains, and stoutly covered in."

No further news came from Elmham. Either the effort had been exhausted, or its purpose achieved. But what could have led the young lady, a stranger to Mr. Batchel and to his garden, to hit upon so appropriate a topic? Mr. Batchel could not answer the question as he put it to himself again and again during the day. He only knew that she had given him a warning, by which, to his shame and regret, he had been too obtuse to profit.

THE INDIAN LAMP-SHADE

What has been already said of Mr. Batchel will have sufficed to inform the reader that he is a man of very settled habits. The conveniences of life, which have multiplied so fast of late, have never attracted him, even when he has heard of them. Inconveniences to which he is accustomed have always seemed to him preferable to conveniences with which he is unfamiliar. To this day, therefore, he writes with a quill, winds up his watch with a key, and will drink no soda-water but from a tumbling bottle with the cork wired to its neck.

The reader accordingly will learn without surprise that Mr. Batchel continues to use the reading-lamp he acquired 30 years ago as a Freshman in College. He still carries it from room to room as occasion requires, and ignores all other means of illumination. It is an inexpensive lamp of very poor appearance, and dates from a time when labour-saving was not yet a fine art. It cannot be lighted without the removal of several of its parts, and it is extinguished by the primitive device of blowing down the chimney. What has always shocked the womenfolk of the Batchel family, however, is the lamp's unworthiness of its surroundings. Mr. Batchel's house is furnished in dignified and comfortable style, but the handsome lamp, surmounting a fluted brazen column, which his relatives bestowed upon him at his institution, is still unpacked.

One of his younger and subtler relatives succeeded in damaging the old lamp, as she thought, irretrievably, by a well-planned accident, but found it still in use a year later, most atrociously repaired. The whole family, and some outsiders, had conspired to attack the offending lamp, and it had withstood them all.

The single victory achieved over Mr. Batchel in this matter is quite recent, and was generally unexpected. A cousin who had gone out to India as a bride, and that of Mr. Batchel's making, had sent him an Indian lamp-shade. The association was pleasing. The shade was decorated with Buddhist figures which excited Mr. Batchel's curiosity, and to the surprise of all his friends he set it on the lamp and there allowed it to remain. It was not, however, the figures which had reconciled him to this novel and somewhat incongruous addition to the old lamp. The singular colour of the material had really attracted him. It was a bright orange-red, like no colour he had ever seen, and the remarks of visitors whose experience of such things was greater than his own soon justified him in regarding it as unique. No one had seen the colour elsewhere; and of all the tints which have acquired distinctive names, none of the names could be applied without some further qualification. Mr. Batchel himself did not trouble about a name, but was quite certain that it was a colour that he liked; and more than that, a colour which had about it some indescribable fascination. When the lamp had been brought in, and the curtains drawn, he used to regard with singular pleasure the interiors of rooms with whose appearance he was unaccustomed to concern himself. The books in his study, and the old-fashioned solid furniture of his dining room, as reflected in the new light, seemed to assume a more friendly aspect, as if they had previously been rigidly frozen, and had now thawed into life. The lamp-shade seemed to bestow upon the light some active property, and gave to the rooms, as Mr. Batchel said, the appearance of being wide-awake.

These optical effects, as he called them, were especially noticeable in the dining room, where the convenience of a large table often induced him to spend the evening. Standing in a favourite attitude, with his elbow on the chimney-piece, Mr. Batchel found increasing pleasure in contemplating the interior of the room as he saw it reflected in a large old mirror above the fireplace. The great mahogany sideboard across the room, seemed, as he gazed upon it, to be penetrated by the light, and to acquire a softness of outline, and a sort of vivacity, which operated pleasantly upon its owner's imagination. He found himself playfully regretting, for example, that the mirror had no power of recording and reproducing the scenes enacted before it since the close of the 18th century, when it had become one of the fixtures of the house. The ruddy light of the lamp-shade had always a stimulating effect upon his fancy, and some of the verses which describe his visions before the mirror would delight the reader, but that the author's modesty forbids their reproduction. Had he been less firm in this matter we should have inserted here a poem in which Mr. Batchel audaciously ventured into the domain of Physics. He endowed his mirror with the power of retaining indefinitely the light which fell upon it, and of reflecting it only when excited by the appropriate stimulus. The passage beginning

The mirror, whilst men pass upon their way,
Treasures their image for a later day,

might be derided by students of optics. Mr. Batchel has often read it in after days, with amazement, for, when his idle fancies came to be so gravely substantiated, he found that in writing the verses he had stumbled upon a new fact—a fact based as soundly, as will soon appear, upon experiment, as those which the text-books use in arriving at the better-known properties of reflection.

He was seated in his dining room one frosty evening in January. His chair was drawn up to the fire, and the upper part of the space behind him was visible in the mirror. The brighter and clearer light thrown down by the shade was shining upon his book. It is the fate of most of us to receive visits when we should best like to be alone, and Mr. Batchel allowed an impatient exclamation to escape him, when, at nine o'clock on this evening, he heard the door-bell. A minute later, the boy announced "Mr. Mutcher," and Mr. Batchel, with such affability as he could hastily assume, rose to receive the caller. Mr. Mutcher was the Deputy Provincial Grand Master of the Ancient Order of Gleaners, and the formality of his manner accorded with the gravity of his title. Mr. Batchel soon became aware that the rest of the evening was doomed. The Deputy Provincial Grand Master had come to discuss the probable effect of the Insurance Act upon Friendly Societies, of which Mr. Batchel was an ardent supporter. He attended their meetings, in some cases kept their accounts, and was always apt to be consulted in their affairs. He seated Mr. Mutcher, therefore, in a chair on the opposite side of the fireplace, and gave him his somewhat reluctant attention.

"This," said Mr. Mutcher, as he looked round the room, "is a cosy nook on a cold night. I cordially appreciate your kindness, Reverend Sir, in affording me this interview, and the comfort of your apartment leads me to wish that it might be more protracted."

Mr. Batchel did his best not to dissent, and as he settled himself for a long half-hour, began to watch the rise and fall, between two lines upon the distant wall-paper of the shadow of Mr. Mutcher's side-whisker, as it seemed to beat time to his measured speech.

The D.P.G.M. (for these functionaries are usually designated by initials) was not a man to be hurried into brevity. His style had been studiously acquired at Lodge meetings, and Mr. Batchel knew it well enough to be prepared for a lengthy preamble.

"I have presumed," said Mr. Mutcher, as he looked straight before him into the mirror, "to trespass upon your Reverence's forbearance, because there are one or two points upon this new Insurance Act which seem calculated to damage our long-continued prosperity—I say long-continued prosperity," repeated Mr. Mutcher, as though Mr. Batchel had missed the phrase. "I had the favour of an interview yesterday," he went on, "with the Sub-Superintendent of the Perseverance Accident and General (these were household words in circles which Mr. Batchel frequented, so that he was at no loss to understand them), and he was unanimous with me in agreeing that the matter called for careful consideration. There are one or two of our rules which we know to be essential to the welfare of our Order, and yet which will have to go by the board—I say by the board—as from July next. Now we are not Medes, nor yet Persians"—Mr. Mutcher was about to repeat "Persians" when he was observed to look hastily round the room and then to turn deadly pale. Mr. Batchel rose and hastened to his support; he was obviously unwell. The visitor, however, made a strong effort, rose from his chair at once, saying "Pray allow me to take leave," and hurried to the door even as he said the words. Mr. Batchel, with real concern, followed him with the offer of brandy, or whatever might afford relief. Mr. Mutcher did not so much as pause to reply. Before Mr. Batchel could reach him he had crossed the hall, and the door-knob was in his hand. He thereupon opened the door and passed into the street without another word. More unaccountably still, he went away at a run, such as ill became his somewhat majestic figure, and Mr. Batchel closed the door and returned to the dining-room in a state of bewilderment. He took up his book, and sat down again in his chair. He did not immediately begin to read, but set himself to review Mr. Mutcher's unaccountable behaviour, and as he raised his eyes to the mirror he saw an elderly man standing at the sideboard.

Mr. Batchel quickly turned round, and as he did so, recalled the similar movement of his late visitor. The room was empty. He turned again to the mirror, and the man was still there—evidently a servant—one would say without much hesitation, the butler. The cut-away coat, and white stock, the clean-shaven chin, and close-trimmed side-whiskers, the deftness and decorum of his movements were all characteristic of a respectable family servant, and he stood at the sideboard like a man who was at home there.

Another object, just visible above the frame of the mirror, caused Mr. Batchel to look round again, and again to see nothing unusual. But what he saw in the mirror was a square oaken box some few inches deep, which the butler was proceeding to unlock. And at this point Mr. Batchel had the presence of mind to make an experiment of extraordinary value. He removed, for a moment, the Indian shade from the lamp, and laid it upon the table, and thereupon the mirror showed nothing but empty space and the frigid lines of the furniture. The butler had disappeared, as also had the box, to re-appear the moment the shade was restored to its place.

As soon as the box was opened, the butler produced a bundled handkerchief which his left hand had been concealing under the tails of his coat. With his right hand he removed the contents of the handkerchief, hurriedly placed them in the box, closed the lid, and having done this, left the room at once. His later movements had been those of a man in fear of being disturbed. He did not even wait to lock the box. He seemed to have heard someone coming.

Mr. Batchel's interest in the box will subsequently be explained. As soon as the butler had left, he stood before the mirror and examined it carefully. More than once, as he felt the desire for a closer scrutiny, he turned to the sideboard itself, where of course no box was to be seen, and returned to the mirror unreasonably disappointed. At length, with the image of the box firmly impressed upon his memory, he sat down again in his chair, and reviewed the butler's conduct, or as he doubted he would have to call it, misconduct. Unfortunately for Mr. Batchel, the contents of the handkerchief had been indistinguishable. But for the butler's alarm, which caused him to be moving away from the box even whilst he was placing the thing within it, the mirror could not have shewn as much as it did. All that had been made evident was that the man had something to conceal, and that it was surreptitiously done.

"Is this all?" said Mr. Batchel to himself as he sat looking into the mirror, "or is it only the end of the first Act?" The question was, in a measure, answered by the presence of the box. That, at all events would have to disappear before the room could resume its ordinary aspect; and whether it was to fade out of sight or to be removed by the butler, Mr. Batchel did not intend to be looking another way at the time. He had not seen, although perhaps Mr. Mutcher had, whether the butler had brought it in, but he was determined to see whether he took it out.

He had not gazed into the mirror for many minutes before he learned that there was to be a second Act. Quite suddenly, a woman was at the sideboard. She had darted to it, and the time taken in passing over half the length of the mirror had been altogether too brief to show what she was like. She now stood with her face to the sideboard, entirely concealing the box from view, and all Mr. Batchel could determine was that she was tall of stature, and that her hair was raven-black, and not in very good order. In his anxiety to see her face, he called aloud, "Turn round." Of course, he understood, when he saw that his cry had been absolutely without effect, that it had been a ridiculous thing to do. He turned his head again for a moment to assure himself that the room was empty, and to remind himself that the curtain had fallen, perhaps a century before, upon the drama—he began to think of it as a tragedy—that he was witnessing. The opportunity, however, of seeing the woman's features was not denied him. She turned her face full upon the mirror—this is to speak as if we described the object rather than the image—so that Mr. Batchel saw it plainly before him; it was a handsome, cruel-looking face, of waxen paleness, with fine, distended, lustrous, eyes. The woman looked hurriedly round the room, looked twice towards the door, and then opened the box.

"Our respectable friend was evidently observed," said Mr. Batchel. "If he has annexed anything belonging to this magnificent female, he is in for a bad quarter of an hour." He would have given a great deal, for once, to have had a sideboard backed by a looking glass, and lamented that the taste of the day had been too good to tolerate such a thing. He would have then been able to see what was going on at the oaken box. As it was, the operations were concealed by the figure of the woman. She was evidently busy with her fingers; her elbows, which shewed plainly enough, were vibrating with activity. In a few minutes there was a final movement of the elbows simultaneously away from her sides, and it shewed, as plainly as if the hands had been visible, that something had been plucked asunder. It was just such a movement as accompanies the removal, after a struggle, of the close-fitting lid of a canister.

"What next?" said Mr. Batchel, as he observed the movement, and interpreted it as the end of the operation at the box. "Is this the end of the second Act?"

He was soon to learn that it was not the end, and that the drama of the mirror was indeed assuming the nature of tragedy. The woman closed the box and looked towards the door, as she had done before; then she made as if she would dart out of the room, and found her movement suddenly arrested. She stopped dead, and, in a moment, fell loosely to the ground. Obviously she had swooned away.

Mr. Batchel could then see nothing, except that the box remained in its place on the sideboard, so that he arose and stood close up to the mirror in order to obtain a view of the whole stage, as he called it. It showed him, in the wider view he now obtained, the woman lying in a heap upon the carpet, and a grey-wigged clergyman standing in the doorway of the room.

"The Vicar of Stoneground, without a doubt," said Mr. Batchel. "The household of my reverend predecessor is not doing well by him; to judge from the effect of his appearance upon this female, there's something serious afoot. Poor old man," he added, as the clergyman walked into the room.

This expression of pity was evoked by the Vicar's face. The marks of tears were upon his cheeks, and he looked weary and ill. He stood for a while looking down upon the woman who had swooned away, and then stooped down, and gently opened her hand.

Mr. Batchel would have given a great deal to know what the Vicar found there. He took something from her, stood erect for a moment with an expression of consternation upon his face; then his chin dropped, his eyes showed that he had lost consciousness, and he fell to the ground, very much as the woman had fallen.

The two lay, side by side, just visible in the space between the table and the sideboard. It was a curious and pathetic situation. As the clergyman was about to fall, Mr. Batchel had turned to save him, and felt a real distress of helplessness at being reminded again that it was but an image that he had looked upon. The two persons now lying upon the carpet had been for some hundred years beyond human aid. He could no more help them than he could help the wounded at Waterloo. He was tempted to relieve his distress by removing the shade of the lamp; he had even laid his hand upon it, but the feeling of curiosity was now become too strong, and he knew that he must see the matter to its end.

The woman first began to revive. It was to be expected, as she had been the first to go. Had not Mr. Batchel seen her face in the mirror, her first act of consciousness would have astounded him. Now it only revolted him. Before she had sufficiently recovered to raise herself upon her feet, she forced open the lifeless hands beside her and snatched away the contents of that which was not empty; and as she did this, Mr. Batchel saw the glitter of precious stones. The woman was soon upon her feet and making feebly for the door, at which she paused to leer at the prostrate figure of the clergyman before she disappeared into the hall. She appeared no more, and Mr. Batchel felt glad to be rid of her presence.

The old Vicar was long in coming to his senses; as he began to move, there stood in the doorway the welcome figure of the butler. With infinite gentleness he raised his master to his feet, and with a strong arm supported him out of the room, which at last, stood empty.

"That, at least," said Mr. Batchel, "is the end of the second Act. I doubt whether I could have borne much more. If that awful woman comes back I shall remove the shade and have done with it all. Otherwise, I shall hope to learn what becomes of the box, and whether my respectable friend who has just taken out his master is, or is not, a rascal." He had been genuinely moved by what he had seen, and was conscious of feeling something like exhaustion. He dare not, however, sit down, lest he should lose anything important of what remained. Neither the door nor the lower part of the room was visible from his chair, so that he remained standing at the chimney-piece, and there awaited the disappearance of the oaken box.

So intently were his eyes fixed upon the box, in which he was especially interested, that he all but missed the next incident. A velvet curtain which he could see through the half-closed door had suggested nothing of interest to him. He connected it indefinitely, as it was excusable to do, with the furniture of the house, and only by inadvertence looked at it a second time. When, however, it began to travel slowly along the hall, his curiosity was awakened in a new direction. The butler, helping his master out of the room ten minutes since, had left the door half open, but as the opening was not towards the mirror, only a strip of the hall beyond could be seen. Mr. Batchel went to open the door more widely, only to find, of course, that the vividness of the images had again betrayed him. The door of his dining-room was closed, as he had closed it after Mr. Mutcher, whose perturbation was now so much easier to understand.

The curtain continued to move across the narrow opening, and explained itself in doing so. It was a pall. The remains it so amply covered were being carried out of the house to their resting-place, and were followed by a long procession of mourners in long cloaks. The hats they held in their black-gloved hands were heavily banded with crêpe whose ends descended to the ground, and foremost among them was the old clergyman, refusing the support which two of the chief mourners were in the act of proffering. Mr. Batchel, full of sympathy, watched the whole procession pass the door, and not until it was evident that the funeral had left the house did he turn once more to the box. He felt sure that the closing scene of the tragedy was at hand, and it proved to be very near. It was brief and uneventful. The butler very deliberately entered the room, threw aside the window-curtains and drew up the blinds, and then went away at once, taking the box with him. Mr. Batchel thereupon blew out his lamp and went to bed, with a purpose of his own to be fulfilled upon the next day.

His purpose may be stated at once. He had recognised the oaken box, and knew that it was still in the house. Three large cupboards in the old library of Vicar Whitehead were filled with the papers of a great law-suit about tithe, dating from the close of the 18th century. Amongst these, in the last of the three cupboards, was the box of which so much has been said. It was filled, so far as Mr. Batchel remembered, with the assessments for poor's-rate of a large number of landholders concerned in the suit, and these Mr. Batchel had never thought it worth his while to disturb. He had gone to rest, however, on this night with the full intention of going carefully through the contents of the box. He scarcely hoped, after so long an interval, to discover any clue to the scenes he had witnessed, but he was determined at least to make the attempt. If he found nothing, he intended that the box should enshrine a faithful record of the transactions in the dining-room.

It was inevitable that a man who had so much of the material of a story should spend a wakeful hour in trying to piece it together. Mr. Batchel spent considerably more than an hour in connecting, in this way and that, the butler and his master, the gypsy-looking woman, the funeral, but could arrive at no connexion that satisfied him. Once asleep, he found the problem easier, and dreamed a solution so obvious as to make him wonder that the matter had ever puzzled him. When he awoke in the morning, also, the defects of the solution were so obvious as to make him wonder that he had accepted it; so easily are we satisfied when reason is not there to criticise. But there was still the box, and this Mr. Batchel lifted down from the third cupboard, dusted with his towel, and when he was dressed, carried downstairs with him. His breakfast occupied but a small part of a large table, and upon the vacant area he was soon laying, as he examined them, one by one, the documents which the box contained. His recollection of them proved to be right. They were overseers' lists of parochial assessments, of which he soon had a score or more laid upon the table. They were of no interest in themselves, and did nothing to further the matter in hand. They would appear to have been thrust into the box by someone desiring to find a receptacle for them.

In a little while, however, the character of the papers changed. Mr. Batchel found himself reading something of another kind, written upon paper of another form and colour.

"Irish bacon to be had of Mr. Broadley, hop merchant in Southwark."

"Rasin wine is kept at the Wine and Brandy vaults in Catherine Street."

"The best hones at Mr. Forsters in Little Britain."

There followed a recipe for a "rhumatic mixture," a way of making a polish for mahogany, and other such matters. They were evidently the papers of the butler.

Mr. Batchel removed them one by one, as he had removed the others; household accounts followed, one or two private letters, and the advertisement of a lottery, and then he reached a closed compartment at the bottom of the box, occupying about half its area. The lid of the compartment was provided with a bone stud, and Mr. Batchel lifted it off and laid it upon the table amongst the papers. He saw at once what the butler had taken from his handkerchief. There was an open pocket-knife, with woeful-looking deposits upon its now rusty blade. There was a delicate human finger, now dry and yellow, and on the finger a gold ring.

Mr. Batchel took up this latter pitiful object and removed the ring, even now, not quite easily. He allowed the finger to drop back into the box, which he carried away at once into another room. His appetite for breakfast had left him, and he rang the bell to have the things cleared away, whilst he set himself, with the aid of a lens, to examine the ring.

There had been three large stones, all of which had been violently removed. The claws of their settings were, without exception, either bent outwards, or broken off. Within the ring was engraved, in graceful italic characters, the name Amey Lee, and on the broader part, behind the place of the stones

She doth joy double,
And halveth trouble.

This pathetic little love token Mr. Batchel continued to hold in his hand as he rehearsed the whole story to which it afforded the clue. He knew that the ring had been set with such stones as there was no mistaking: he remembered only too well how their discovery had affected the aged vicar. But never would he deny himself the satisfaction of hoping that the old man had been spared the distress of learning how the ring had been removed.

The name of Amey Lee was as familiar to Mr. Batchel as his own. Twice at least every Sunday during the past seven years had he read it at his feet, as he sat in the chancel, as well as the name of Robert Lee upon an adjacent slab, and he had wondered during the leisurely course of many a meandering hymn whether there was good precedent for the spelling of the name. He made another use now of his knowledge of the pavement. There was a row of tiles along the head of the slabs, and Mr. Batchel hastened to fulfil without delay, what he conceived to be his duty. He replaced the ring upon Amey Lee's finger and carried it into the church, and there, having raised one of the tiles with a chisel, gave it decent burial.

Whether the butler ever learned that he had been robbed in his turn, who shall say? His immediate dismissal, after the funeral, seemed inevitable, and his oaken box was evidently placed by him, or by another, where no man heeded it. It still occupies a place amongst the law papers and may lie undisturbed for another century; and when Mr. Batchel put it there, without the promised record of events, he returned to the dining room, removed the Indian shade from the lamp, and, having put a lighted match to the edge, watched it slowly burn away.

Only one thing remained. Mr. Batchel felt that it would give him some satisfaction to visit Mr. Mutcher. His address, as obtained from the District Miscellany of the Order of Gleaners, was 13, Albert Villas, Williamson Street, not a mile away from Stoneground.

Mr. Mutcher, fortunately, was at home when Mr. Batchel called, and indeed opened the door with a copious apology for being without his coat.

"I hope," said Mr. Batchel, "that you have overcome your indisposition of last Tuesday evening."

"Don't mention it, your Reverence," said Mr. Mutcher, "my wife gave me such a talking to when I came 'ome that I was quite ashamed of myself—I say ashamed of myself."

"She observed that you were unwell," said Mr. Batchel, "I am sure; but she could hardly blame you for that."

By this time the visitor had been shewn into the parlour, and Mrs. Mutcher had appeared to answer for herself.

"I really was ashamed, Sir," she said, "to think of the way Mutcher was talking, and a clergyman's 'ouse too. Mutcher is not a man, Sir, that takes anything, not so much as a drop; but he is wonderful partial to cold pork, which never does agree with him, and never did, at night in partic'lar."

"It was the cold pork, then, that made you unwell?" asked Mr. Batchel.

"It was, your Reverence, and it was not," Mr. Mutcher replied, "for internal discomfort there was none—I say none. But a little light-'eaded it did make me, and I could 'ave swore, your Reverence, saving your presence, that I saw an elderly gentleman carry a box into your room and put it down on the sheffoneer."

"There was no one there, of course," observed Mr. Batchel.

"No!" replied the D.P.G.M., "there was not; and the discrepancy was too much for me. I hope you will pardon the abruptness of my departure."

"Certainly," said Mr. Batchel, "discrepancies are always embarrassing."

"And you will allow me one day to resume our discourse upon the subject of National Insurance," he added, when he shewed his visitor to the door.

"I shall not have much leisure," said Mr. Batchel, audaciously, taking all risks, "until the Greek Kalends."

"Oh, I don't mind waiting till it does end," said Mr. Mutcher, "there is no immediate 'urry."

"It's rather a long time," remarked Mr. Batchel.

"Pray don't mention it," answered the Deputy Provincial Grand Master, in his best manner. "But when the time comes, perhaps you'll drop me a line."

VIII.

THE PLACE OF SAFETY.

"I thank my governors, teachers, spiritual pastors, and masters," said Wardle, as he lit a cigar after breakfast, "that I never acquired a taste for that sort of thing."

Wardle was a pragmatical and candid friend who paid Mr. Batchel occasional visits at Stoneground. He regarded antiquarian tastes as a form of insanity, and it annoyed him to see his host poring over registers, churchwardens' accounts, and documents which he contemptuously alluded to as "dirty papers." "If you would throw those things away, Batchel," he used to say, "and read the *Daily Mail*, you'd be a better man for it."

Mr. Batchel replied only with a tolerant smile, and, as his friend went out of doors with his cigar, continued to read the document before him, although it was one he had read twenty times before. It was an inventory of church goods, dated the 6th year of Edward VI.—to be exact, the 15th May, 1552. By a royal order of that year, all Church goods, saving only what sufficed for the barest necessities of Divine Service, were collected and deposited in safe hands, there to await further instructions. The instructions, which had not been long delayed, had consisted in a curt order for seizure. Everyone who cares for such matters, knows and laments the grievous spoliation of those times.

Mr. Batchel's document, however, proved that the Churchwardens of the day were not incapable of self-defence. They were less dumb than sheep before the shearers. For, on the copy of the inventory of which he had become possessed, was written the Commissioners' Report that "at Stoneground did John Spayn and John Gounthropp, Churchwardens, declare upon their othes that two gilded senseres with candellstickes, old paynted clothes, and other implements, were contayned in a chest which was robbed on St. Peter's Eve before the first inventorye made."

Mr. Batchel had a shrewd suspicion, which the reader will not improbably share, that John Spayne and his colleague knew more about the robbery than they chose to admit. He said to himself again and again, that the contents of the chest had been carefully concealed until times should mend. But from the point of view of the Churchwardens, times had not mended. There was evidence that Stoneground had been in no mood to tolerate censers in the reign of Mary, and it seemed unlikely that any later time could have re-admitted the ancient ritual. On this account, Mr. Batchel had never ceased to believe that the contents of the chest lay somewhere near at hand, nor to hope that it might be his lot to discover it.

Whenever there was any work of the nature of excavation or demolition within a hundred yards of the Church, Mr. Batchel was sure to be there. His presence was very distasteful in most cases, to the workmen engaged, whom it deprived of many intervals of leisure to which they were accustomed when left alone. During a long course of operations connected with the restoration of the Church, Mr. Batchel's vigilance had been of great advantage to the work, both in raising the standard of industry and in securing attention to details which the builders were quite prepared to overlook. It had, however, brought him no nearer to the censers and other contents of the chest, and when the work was completed, his hopes of discovery had become pitifully slender.

Mr. Wardle, notwithstanding his general contempt for antiquarian pursuits, was polite enough to give Mr. Batchel's hobbies an occasional place in their conversation, and in this way was informed of the "stolen" goods. The information, however, gave him no more than a very languid interest.

"Why can't you let the things alone?" he said, "what's the use of them?"

Mr. Batchel felt it all but impossible to answer a man who could say this; yet he made the attempt.

"The historic interest," he said seriously, "of censers that were used down to the days of Edward VI. is in itself sufficient to justify—"

"Etcetera," said his friend, interrupting the sentence which even Mr. Batchel was not sure of finishing to his satisfaction, "but it takes so little to justify you antiquarians, with your axes and hammers. What can you do with it when you get it, if you ever do get it?"

"There are two censers," Mr. Batchel mildly observed in correction, "and other things."

"All right," said Wardle; "tell me about one of them, and leave me to do the multiplication."

With this permission, Mr. Batchel entered upon a general description of such ancient thuribles as he knew of, and Wardle heard him with growing impatience.

"It seems to me," he burst in at length, "that what you are making all this pother about is a sort of silver cruet-stand, which was thin metal to begin with, and cleaned down to the thickness of egg-shell before the Commissioners heard of it. At this moment, if it exists, it is a handful of black scrap. If you found it, I wouldn't give a shilling for it; and if I would, it isn't yours to sell. Why can't you let the things alone?"

"But the interest of it," said Mr. Batchel, "is what attracts me."

"It's a pity you can't take an interest in something less uninteresting," said Wardle, petulantly; "but let me tell you what I think about your censers and all the rest of it. Your Churchwardens lied about them, but that's all right; I'd have done the same myself. If their things couldn't be used, they were not going to have them abused, so they put them safely out of the way, your's and every-body's else."

"I was not proposing to abuse them," interrupted Mr. Batchel.

"Were you proposing to use them?" rejoined Wardle. "It's one thing or the other, to my mind. There are people who dig out Bishops and steal their rings to put in glass cases, but I don't know how they square the police; and it's the same sort of thing you seem to be up to. Let the things alone. You're a Prayer Book man, and just the sort the Churchwardens couldn't stomach. You talk fast enough at the Dissenters because they want to collar your property now. Why can't you do as you would be done by?"

Mr. Batchel thought it useless to say any more to a man in so unsympathetic an attitude, or to enter upon any defence of the antiquarian researches to which his friend had so crudely referred. He did not much like, however, to be antici-pated in a theory of the "robbery" which he felt to be reasonable and probable. He had hoped to propound the same theory himself, and to receive a suitable compliment upon his penetration. He began, therefore, somewhat irritably, to make the most of conjectures which, at various times, had occurred to him. "Men of that sort," he said, "would have disposed of the censers to some one who could go on using them, and in that case they are not here at all."

"Men of that sort," answered Wardle, "are as careful of their skins as men of any other sort, and besides that, your Stoneground men have a very good notion of sticking to what they have got. The things are here, I daresay, if they are any-where; but they are not yours, and you have no business to meddle with them. If you would spend your time in something else than poking about after other peo-ple's things, you'd get better value for it."

This brief conversation, in which Mr. Batchel had scarcely been allowed the part to which he felt entitled, was in one respect satisfactory. It supported his be-lief that the censers lay somewhere within reach. In other respects, however, the attitude of Wardle was intolerable. He was evidently out of all sympathy with the quest upon which Mr. Batchel was set, and, for their different reasons, each was glad to drop the subject.

During the next two or three days, the matter of the censers was not referred to, if only for lack of opportunity. Wardle was a kind of visitor for whom there was always a welcome at Stoneground, and the welcome was in his case no less cordial on account of his brutal frankness of expression, which, on the whole, his host enjoyed. His pungent criticisms of other men were vastly entertaining to Mr. Batchel, who was not so unreasonable as to feel aggrieved at an occasional at-tack upon himself.

A guest of this unceremonious sort makes but small demands upon his host. Mr. Wardle used to occupy himself contentedly and unobtrusively in the house or in the garden whilst his host followed his usual avocations. The two men met at meals, and liked each other none the less because they were apart at most other times. A great part of Mr. Wardle's day was passed in the company of the gar-dener, to whose talk his own master was but an indifferent listener. The visitor and the gardener were both lovers of the soil, and taught each other a great deal as they worked side by side. Mr. Wardle found that sort of exercise wholesome, and, as the gardener expressed it, "was not frit to take his coat off."

The gardening operations at this time of year were such as Mr. Wardle liked. The over-crowded shrubberies were being thinned, and a score or so of young shrubs had to be moved into better quarters. Upon a certain morning, when Mr. Batchel was occupied in his study, some aucubas were being transplanted into a strip of ground in front of the house, and Wardle had undertaken the task of dig-ging holes to receive them. It was this task that he suddenly interrupted in order to burst in upon his host in what seemed to the latter a repulsive state of dirt and perspiration.

"Talk of discoveries," he cried, "come and see what I've found."

"Not the censers, I suppose," said Mr. Batchel.

"Censers be hanged," said Wardle, "come and look."

Mr. Batchel laid down his pen, with a sigh, and followed Wardle to the front of the house. His guest had made three large holes, each about two feet square, and drawing Mr. Batchel to the nearest of them, said "Look there."

Mr. Batchel looked. He saw nothing, and said so.

"Nothing?" exclaimed Wardle with impatience. "You see the bottom of the hole, I suppose?"

This Mr. Batchel admitted.

"Then," said Wardle, "kindly look and see whether you cannot see something else."

"There is apparently a cylindrical object lying across the angle of your exca-vation," said Mr. Batchel.

"That," replied his guest, "is what you are pleased to call nothing. Let me inform you that the cylindrical object is a piece of thick lead pipe, and that the pipe runs along the whole front of your house."

"Gas-pipe, no doubt," said Mr. Batchel.

"Is there any gas within a mile of this place?" asked Wardle.

Mr. Batchel admitted that there was not, and felt that he had made a needlessly foolish suggestion. He felt safer in the amended suggestion that the object was a water-pipe.

An ironical cross-examination by Mr. Wardle disposed of the amended suggestion as completely as he had disposed of the other, and his host began to grow restive. "If this sort of discovery pleases you," he said testily, "I will not grudge you your pleasure, but, to quote your own words, why can't you let it alone?"

"Have you any idea," said Mr. Wardle, "of the value of this length of piping, at the present price of lead?"

Even Mr. Wardle could hardly have suspected his host of knowing anything so preposterous as the price of lead, but he felt himself ill-used when Mr. Batchel disclaimed any interest in the matter, and returned to his study.

Wardle had a commercial mind, which elsewhere was the means of securing him a very satisfactory income, and on this account, his host, as he resumed his work indoors, excused what he regarded as a needless interruption.

He little suspected that his friend's commercial mind was to do him the great service of putting him in possession of the censers, and then to do him a disservice even greater.

Had any such connexion so much as suggested itself, Mr. Batchel would more willingly have answered to the summons which came an hour later, when the gardener appeared at the window of the study, evidently bursting with information. When he had succeeded in attracting his master's attention, and drawn him away from his desk, it was to say that the whole length of pipe had been uncovered, and found to issue from a well on the south side of the house.

The discovery was at least unexpected, and Mr. Batchel went out, even if somewhat grudgingly, to look at the place. He came upon the well, close by the window of his dining-room. It had been covered by a stone slab, now partially removed. The narrow trench which Wardle and the gardener had made in order to expose the pipe, extended eastwards to the corner of the house, and thence along the whole length of the front, probably to serve a pump on the north side, where lay the yard and stables. The pipe itself, Mr. Wardle's prize, had been withdrawn, and there remained only a rusted chain which passed from some anchorage beneath the soil, over the lip of the well. Mr. Batchel inferred that it had carried, and perhaps carried still, the bucket of former times, and stooped down to see whether he could draw it up. He heard, far below, the light splash of the soil disturbed by his hands; but before he could grasp the chain, he felt himself seized by the waist and held back.

The exaggerated attentions of his gardener had often annoyed Mr. Batchel. He was not allowed even to climb a short ladder without having to submit to absurd precautions for his safety, and he would have been much better pleased to have more respect paid to his intelligence, and less to his person. In the present instance, the precaution seemed so unnecessary that he turned about angrily to protest, both against the interference with his movements, and the unseemly force used.

It was at this point that he made a disquieting discovery. He was standing quite alone. The gardener and Mr. Wardle were both on the north side of the house, dealing with the only thing they cared about—the lead pipe. Mr. Batchel made no further attempt to move the chain; he was, in fact, in some bodily fear, and he returned to his study by the way he had come, in a disordered condition of mind.

Half an hour later, when the gong sounded for luncheon, he was slowly making his way into the dining-room, when he encountered his guest running downstairs from his room, in great spirits. "A trifle over two hundredweight!" he exclaimed, as he reached the foot of the staircase, and seemed disappointed that Mr. Batchel did not immediately shake hands with him upon so fine a result of the morning's work. Mr. Batchel, needless to say, was occupied with other recollections.

"I suppose it is unnecessary to ask," said he to his guest as he proceeded to carve a chicken, "whether you believe in ghosts?"

"I do not," said Wardle promptly, "why should I?"

"Why not?" asked Mr. Batchel.

"Because I've had the advantage of a commercial education," was the reply, "instead of learning dead languages and soaking my mind in heathen fables."

Mr. Batchel winced at this disrespectful allusion to the University education of which he was justly proud. He wanted an opinion, however, and the conversation had to go on.

"Your commercial education," he continued, "allows you, I daresay, to know what is meant by a hypothetical case."

"Make it one," said Wardle.

"Assuming a ghost, then, would it be capable of exerting force upon a material body?"

"Whose?" asked Wardle.

"If you insist upon making it a personal matter," replied Mr. Batchel, "let us say mine."

"Let me have the particulars."

In reply to this, Mr. Batchel related his experience at the well.

Mr. Wardle merely said "Pass the salt, I need it."

Undeterred by the scepticism of his friend, Mr. Batchel pressed the point, and upon that, Mr. Wardle closed the conversation by observing that since, by hypothesis, ghosts could clank chains, and ring bells, he was bound to suppose them capable of doing any silly thing they chose. "A month in the City, Batchel," he gravely added, "would do you a world of good."

As soon as the meal was over, Mr. Wardle went back to his gardening, whilst his host betook himself to occupations more suited to his tranquil habits. The two did not meet again until dinner; and during that meal, and after it, the conversation turned wholly upon politics, Mr. Wardle being congenially occupied until bed-time in demonstrating that the politics of his host had been obsolete for three-quarters of a century. His outdoor exercise, followed by an excellent dinner, had disposed him to retire early; he rose from his chair soon after ten. "There is one thing," he pleasantly remarked to his host, "that I am bound to say in favour of a University education; it has given you a fine taste in victuals." With this compliment, he said "good-night," and went up to bed.

Mr. Batchel himself, as the reader knows, kept later hours. There were few nights upon which he omitted to take his walk round the garden when the world had grown quiet, even in unfavourable weather. It was far from favourable upon the present occasion; there was but little moon, and a light rain was falling. He determined, however, to take at least one turn round, and calling his terrier Punch from the kitchen, where he lay in his basket, Mr. Batchel went out, with the dog at his heel. He carried, as his custom was, a little electric lamp, by whose aid he liked to peep into birds' nests, and make raids upon slugs and other pests.

They had hardly set out upon their walk when Punch began to show signs of uneasiness. Instead of running to and fro, with his nose to the ground, as he ordinarily did, the terrier remained whining in the rear. Shortly, they came upon a hedgehog lying coiled up in the path; it was a find which the dog was wont to regard as a rare piece of luck, and to assail with delirious enjoyment. Now, for some reason, Punch refused to notice it, and, when it was illuminated for his especial benefit, turned his back upon it and looked up, in a dejected attitude, at his master. The behaviour of the dog was altogether unnatural, and Mr. Batchel occupied himself, as they passed on, in trying to account for it, with the animal still whining at his heel. They soon reached the head of the little path which descended to the Lode, and there Mr. Batchel found a much harder problem awaiting him, for at the other end of the path he distinctly saw the outline of a boat.

There had been no boat on the Lode for twenty years. Just so long ago the drainage of the district had required that the main sewer should cross the stream at a point some hundred yards below the Vicar's boundary fence. There, ever since, a great pipe three feet in diameter had obstructed the passage. It lay just at the level of the water, and effectually closed it to all traffic. Mr. Batchel knew that no boat could pass the place, and that none survived in the parts above it. Yet here was a boat drawn up at the edge of his garden. He looked at it intently for a minute or so, and had no difficulty in making out the form of such a boat as was in common use all over the Fen country—a wide flat-bottomed boat, lying low in the water. The "sprit" used for punting it along lay projecting over the stern. There was no accounting for such a boat being there: Mr. Batchel did not understand how it possibly could be there, and for a while was disposed to doubt whether it actually was. The great drain-pipe was so perfect a defence against intrusion of the kind that no boat had ever passed it. The Lode, when its water was low enough to let a boat go under the pipe, was not deep enough to float it, or wide enough to contain it. Upon this occasion the water was high, and the pipe half submerged, forming an insuperable obstacle. Yet there lay, unmistakeably, a boat, within ten yards of the place where Mr. Batchel stood trying to account for it.

These ten yards, unfortunately, were impassable. The slope down to the water's edge had to be warily trodden even in dry weather. It was steep and treacherous. After rain it afforded no foothold whatever, and to attempt a descent in the darkness would have been to court disaster. After examining the boat again, therefore, by the light of his little lamp, Mr. Batchel proceeded upon his walk, leaving the matter to be investigated by daylight.

The events of this memorable night, however, were but beginning. As he turned from the boat his eye was caught by a white streak upon the ground before him, which extended itself into the darkness and disappeared. It was Punch, in veritable panic, making for home, across flower-beds and other places he well knew to be out of bounds. The whistle he had been trained to obey had no effect upon his flight; he made a lightning dash for the house. Mr. Batchel could not help regretting that Wardle was not there to see. His friend held the coursing powers of Punch in great contempt, and was wont to criticise the dog in sporting jargon, whose terms lay beyond the limits of Mr. Batchel's vocabulary, but whose general drift was as obvious as it was irritating. The present performance, nevertheless, was so exceptional that it soon began to connect itself in Mr. Batchel's mind with the unnatural conduct to which we have already alluded. It was somehow proving to be an uncomfortable night, and as Mr. Batchel felt the rain increasing to a steady drizzle he decided to abandon his walk and to return to the house by the way he had come.

He had already passed some little distance beyond the little path which descended to the Lode. The main path by which he had come was of course behind him, until he turned about to retrace his steps.

It was at the moment of turning that he had ocular demonstration of the fact that the boat had brought passengers. Not twenty yards in front of him, making their way to the water, were two men carrying some kind of burden. They had reached an open space in the path, and their forms were quite distinct: they were unusually tall men; one of them was gigantic. Mr. Batchel had little doubt of their being garden thieves. Burglars, if there had been anything in the house to attract them, could have found much easier ways of removing it.

No man, even if deficient in physical courage, can see his property carried away before his eyes and make no effort to detain it. Mr. Batchel was annoyed at the desertion of his terrier, who might at least have embarrassed the thieves' retreat; meanwhile he called loudly upon the men to stand, and turned upon them the feeble light of his lamp. In so doing he threw a new light not only upon the trespassers, but upon the whole transaction. No response was made to his challenge, but the men turned away their faces as if to avoid recognition, and Mr. Batchel saw that the nearest of them, a burly, square-headed man in a cassock, was wearing the tonsure. He described it as looking, in the dim, steely light of the lamp, like a crown-piece on a door-mat. Both the men, when they found themselves intercepted, hastened to deposit their burden upon the ground, and made for the boat. The burden fell upon the ground with a thud, but the bearers made no sound. They skimmed down to the Lode without seeming to tread, entered the boat in perfect silence, and shoved it off without sound or splash. It has already been explained that Mr. Batchel was unable to descend to the water's edge. He ran, however, to a point of the garden which the boat must inevitably pass, and reached it just in time. The boat was moving swiftly away, and still in perfect silence. The beams of the pocket-lamp just sufficed to reach it, and afforded a parting glimpse of the tonsured giant as he gave a long shove with the sprit, and carried the boat out of sight. It shot towards the drain-pipe, then not forty yards ahead, but the men were travelling as men who knew their way to be clear.

It was by this time evident, of course, that these were no garden-thieves. The aspect of the men, and the manner of their disappearance, had given a new complexion to the adventure. Mr. Batchel's heart was in his mouth, but his mind was back in the 16th century; and having stood still for some minutes in order to regain his composure, he returned to the path, with a view of finding out what the men had left behind.

The burden lay in the middle of the path, and the lamp was once more brought into requisition. It revealed a wooden box, covered in most parts with moss, and all glistening with moisture. The wood was so far decayed that Mr. Batchel had hopes of forcing open the box with his hands; so wet and slimy was it, however, that he could obtain no hold, and he hastened to the house to procure some kind of tool. Near to the cupboard in which such things were kept was the sleeping-basket of the dog, who was closely curled inside it, and shivering violently. His master made an attempt to take him back into the garden; it would be useful, he thought, to have warning in case the boat should return. The prospect of being surprised by these large, noiseless men was not one to be regarded with comfort. Punch, however, who was usually so eager for an excursion, was now in such distress at being summoned that his master felt it cruel to persist. Having found a chisel, therefore, he returned to the garden alone. The box lay undisturbed where he had left it, and in two minutes was standing open.

The reader will hardly need to be told what it contained. At the bottom lay some heavy articles which Mr. Batchel did not disturb. He saw the bases of two candlesticks. He had tried to lift the box, as it lay, by means of a chain passing through two handles in the sides, but had found it too heavy. It was by this chain that the men had been carrying it. The heavier articles, therefore, he determined to leave where they were until morning. His interest in them was small compared with that which the other contents of the box had excited, for on the top of these articles was folded "a paynted cloth," and upon this lay the two gilded censers.

It was the discovery Mr. Batchel had dreamed of for years. His excitement hardly allowed him to think of the strange manner in which it had been made. He glanced nervously around him to see whether there might be any sign of the occupants of the boat, and, seeing nothing, he placed his broad-brimmed hat upon the ground, carefully laid in it the two censers, closed the box again, and carried his treasure delicately into the house. The occurrences of the last hour have not occupied long in the telling; they occupied much longer in the happening. It was now past midnight, and Mr. Batchel, after making fast the house, went at once upstairs, carrying with him the hat and its precious contents, just as he had brought it from the garden. The censers were not exactly "black-scrap," as Mr. Wardle had anticipated, or pretended to anticipate, but they were much discoloured, and very fragile. He spread a clean handkerchief upon the chest of drawers in his bedroom, and, removing the vessels with the utmost care, laid them upon it. Then after spending some minutes in admiration of their singularly beautiful form and workmanship, he could not deny himself the pleasure of calling Wardle to look.

The guest-room was close at hand. Mr. Wardle, having been already disturbed by Ruhe locking up of the house, was fully awakened by the entrance of his host into the room with a candle in his hand. The look of excitement on Mr. Batchel's face could not escape the observation even of a man still yawning, and Mr. Wardle at once exclaimed "What's up?"

"I have got them," said Mr. Batchel, in a hushed voice.

His guest, who had forgotten all about the censers, began by interpreting "them" to mean a nervous disorder that is plural by nature, and so was full of sympathy and counsel. When, however, his host had made him understand the facts, he became merely impatient.

"Won't you come and look?" said Mr. Batchel.

"Not I," said Wardle, "I shall do where I am."

"They are in excellent preservation," said Mr. Batchel.

"Then they will keep till morning," was the answer.

"But just come and tell me what you think of them," said Mr. Batchel, making a last attempt.

"I could tell you what I think of them," answered Wardle, "without leaving my bed, which I have no intention of leaving; but I have to leave Stoneground to-morrow, and I don't want to hurt your feelings, so 'Good-night.'" Upon this, he turned over in bed and gave a loud snore, which Mr. Batchel accepted as a manifesto. He has never ceased to regret that he did not compel his guest to see the censers, but he did not then foresee the sore need he would have of a witness. He answered his friend's good-night, and returned to his own room. Once more he admired the two censers as their graceful outlines stood out, sharp and clear, against the white handkerchief, and having done this, he was soon in bed and asleep. To the men in the boat he had not given another thought, since he became possessed of the box they had left behind; of the other contents of the box he had thought as little, since he had secured the chief treasures of which he had been so long in search.

Now, Mr. Wardle, when he arose in the morning, felt somewhat ashamed of his surliness of the preceding night. His repudiation of all interest in the censers had not been quite sincere, for beneath his affectation of unconcern there lay a genuine curiosity about his friend's discovery. Before he had finished dressing, therefore, he crossed over into Mr. Batchel's room. The censers, to his surprise, were nowhere to be seen. His host, less to his surprise, was still fast asleep. Mr. Wardle opened the drawers, one by one, in search of the censers, but the drawers proved to be all quite full of clothing. He looked with no more success into every other place where they might have been bestowed. His mind was always ready with a grotesque idea, "Blest if he hasn't taken them to bed with him," he said aloud, and at the sound of his voice Mr. Batchel awoke.

His eyes, as soon as they were open, turned to the chest of drawers; and what he saw there, or rather, what he failed to see, caused him, without more ado, to leap out of bed.

"What have you done with them?" he cried out.

The serious alarm of Mr. Batchel was so evident as to check the facetious reply which Wardle was about to frame. He contented himself with saying that he had not touched or seen the things.

"Where are they?" again cried Mr. Batchel, ignoring the disclaimer. "You ought not to have touched them, they will not bear handling. Where are they?"

Mr. Wardle turned away in disgust. "I expect," he said, "they're where they've been this three hundred and fifty years." Upon that he returned to his room, and went on with his dressing.

Mr. Batchel immediately followed him, and looked eagerly round the room. He proceeded to open drawers, and to search, in a frenzied manner, in every possible, and in many an impossible, place of concealment. His distress was so patent that his friend soon ceased to trifle with it. By a few minutes serious conversation he made it clear that there had been no practical joking, and Mr. Batchel returned to his room in tears. "Look here, Batchel," said Mr. Wardle as he left, "you want a holiday."

Within a few minutes Mr. Batchel returned fully dressed. "You seem to think, Wardle," he said, "that I have been dreaming about these censers. Come out into the garden and let me shew you the box and the other things."

Mr. Wardle was quite willing to assent to anything, if only out of pity, and the two went together into the garden, Mr. Batchel leading the way. Going at a great pace, they soon came to the path upon which the box had lain. The marks it had left upon the soft gravel were plain enough, and Mr. Batchel eagerly appealed to his friend to notice them. Of the box and its contents, however, there was no other trace. The whole adventure was described—the strange behaviour and subsequent flight of the terrier—the men with averted faces—the boat—and the opening of the box. Mr. Batchel tried to shake the obvious incredulity of his guest by pointing to the chisel which still lay beside the path. Mr. Wardle only replied, "You want a holiday, Batchel! Let's go in to breakfast."

Breakfast on that morning was not the cheerful meal it was wont to be. During the few minutes of waiting for it Mr. Batchel stood at the window of his dining-room looking out upon the site of the well which the gardener had now covered in. He rehearsed the whole of the adventure from first to last, wondering whether the new place of safety would ever be discovered. But he said no more to his guest; his heart was too full.

The two breakfasted almost in silence, and the meal was scarcely over when the cab arrived to take Mr. Wardle to his train. Mr. Batchel bade him farewell, and saw him depart with genuine regret; he was returning sadly into the house when he heard his name called. It was Wardle, leaning out of the window of his cab as it drove away, and waving his hand, "Batchel," he cried again, "mind you take a holiday."

THE KIRK SPOOK

Before many years have passed it will be hard to find a person who has ever seen a Parish Clerk. The Parish Clerk is all but extinct. Our grandfathers knew him well—an oldish, clean-shaven man, who looked as if he had never been young, who dressed in rusty black, bestowed upon him, as often as not, by the Rector, and who usually wore a white tie on Sundays, out of respect for the seriousness of his office. He it was who laid out the Rector's robes, and helped him to put them on; who found the places in the large Bible and Prayer Book, and indicated them by means of decorous silken bookmarkers; who lighted and snuffed the candles in the pulpit and desk, and attended to the little stove in the squire's pew; who ran busily about, in short, during the quarter-hour which preceded Divine Service, doing a hundred little things, with all the activity, and much of the appearance, of a beetle.

Just such a one was Caleb Dean, who was Clerk of Stoneground in the days of William IV. Small in stature, he possessed a voice which Nature seemed to have meant for a giant, and in the discharge of his duties he had a dignity of manner disproportionate even to his voice. No one was afraid to sing when he led the Psalm, so certain was it that no other voice could be noticed, and the gracious condescension with which he received his meagre fees would have been ample acknowledgment of double their amount.

Man, however, cannot live by dignity alone, and Caleb was glad enough to be sexton as well as clerk, and to undertake any other duties by which he might add to his modest income. He kept the Churchyard tidy, trimmed the lamps, chimed the bells, taught the choir their simple tunes, turned the barrel of the organ, and managed the stoves.

It was this last duty in particular, which took him into Church "last thing," as he used to call it, on Saturday night. There were people in those days, and may be some in these, whom nothing would induce to enter a Church at midnight; Caleb, however, was so much at home there that all hours were alike to him. He was never an early man on Saturdays. His wife, who insisted upon sitting up for him, would often knit her way into Sunday before he appeared, and even then would find it hard to get him to bed. Caleb, in fact, when off duty, was a genial little fellow; he had many friends, and on Saturday evenings he knew where to find them.

It was not, therefore, until the evening was spent that he went to make up his fires; and his voice, which served for other singing than that of Psalms, could usually be heard, within a little of midnight, beguiling the way to Church with snatches of convivial songs. Many a belated traveller, homeward bound, would envy him his spirits, but no one envied him his duties. Even such as walked with him to the neighbourhood of the Churchyard would bid him "Good night" whilst still a long way from the gate. They would see him disappear into the gloom amongst the graves, and shudder as they turned homewards.

Caleb, meanwhile, was perfectly content. He knew every stone in the path; long practice enabled him, even on the darkest night, to thrust his huge key into the lock at the first attempt, and on the night we are about to describe—it had come to Mr. Batchel from an old man who heard it from Caleb's lips—he did it with a feeling of unusual cheerfulness and contentment.

Caleb always locked himself in. A prank had once been played upon him, which had greatly wounded his dignity; and though it had been no midnight prank, he had taken care, ever since, to have the Church to himself. He locked the door, therefore, as usual, on the night we speak of, and made his way to the stove. He used no candle. He opened the little iron door of the stove, and obtained sufficient light to shew him the fuel he had laid in readiness; then, when he had made up his fire, he closed this door again, and left the Church in darkness. He never could say what induced him upon this occasion to remain there after his task was done. He knew that his wife was sitting up, as usual, and that, as usual, he would have to hear what she had to say. Yet, instead of making his way home, he sat down in the corner of the nearest seat. He supposed that he must have felt tired, but had no distinct recollection of it.

The Church was not absolutely dark. Caleb remembered that he could make out the outlines of the windows, and that through the window nearest to him he saw a few stars. After his eyes had grown accustomed to the gloom he could see the lines of the seats taking shape in the darkness, and he had not long sat there before he could dimly see everything there was. At last he began to distinguish where books lay upon the shelf in front of him. And then he closed his eyes. He does not admit having fallen asleep, even for a moment. But the seat was restful, the neighbouring stove was growing warm, he had been through a long and joyous evening, and it was natural that he should at least close his eyes.

He insisted that it was only for a moment. Something, he could not say what, caused him to open his eyes again immediately. The closing of them seemed to have improved what may be called his dark sight. He saw everything in the Church quite distinctly, in a sort of grey light. The pulpit stood out, large and bulky, in front. Beyond that, he passed his eyes along the four windows on the north side of the Church. He looked again at the stars, still visible through the nearest window on his left hand as he was sitting. From that, his eyes fell to the further end of the seat in front of him, where he could even see a faint gleam of polished wood. He traced this gleam to the middle of the seat, until it disappeared in black shadow, and upon that his eye passed on to the seat he was in, and there he saw a man sitting beside him.

Caleb described the man very clearly. He was, he said, a pale, old-fashioned looking man, with something very churchy about him. Reasoning also with great clearness, he said that the stranger had not come into the Church either with him or after him, and that therefore he must have been there before him. And in that case, seeing that the Church had been locked since two in the afternoon, the stranger must have been there for a considerable time.

Caleb was puzzled; turning therefore, to the stranger, he asked, "How long have you been here?"

The stranger answered at once, "Six hundred years."

"Oh! come!" said Caleb.

"Come where?" said the stranger.

"Well, if you come to that, come out," said Caleb.

"I wish I could," said the stranger, and heaved a great sigh.

"What's to prevent you?" said Caleb. "There's the door, and here's the key."

"That's it," said the other.

"Of course it is," said Caleb. "Come along."

With that he proceeded to take the stranger by the sleeve, and then it was that he says you might have knocked him down with a feather. His hand went right into the place where the sleeve seemed to be, and Caleb distinctly saw two of the stranger's buttons on the top of his own knuckles.

He hastily withdrew his hand, which began to feel icy cold, and sat still, not knowing what to say next. He found that the stranger was gently chuckling with laughter, and this annoyed him.

"What are you laughing at?" he enquired peevishly.

"It's not funny enough for two," answered the other.

"Who are you, anyhow?" said Caleb.

"I am the kirk spook," was the reply.

Now Caleb had not the least notion what a "kirk spook" was. He was not willing to admit his ignorance, but his curiosity was too much for his pride, and he asked for information.

"Every Church has a spook," said the stranger, "and I am the spook of this one."

"Oh," said Caleb, "I've been about this Church a many years, but I've never seen you before."

"That," said the spook, "is because you've always been moving about. I'm very flimsy—very flimsy indeed—and I can only keep myself together when everything is quite still."

"Well," said Caleb, "you've got your chance now. What are you going to do with it?"

"I want to go out," said the spook, "I'm tired of this Church, and I've been alone for six hundred years. It's a long time."

"It does seem rather a long time," said Caleb, "but why don't you go if you want to? There's three doors."

"That's just it," said the spook, "They keep me in."

"What?" said Caleb, "when they're open."

"Open or shut," said the spook, "it's all one."

"Well, then," said Caleb, "what about the windows?"

"Every bit as bad," said the spook, "They're all pointed."

Caleb felt out of his depth. Open doors and windows that kept a person in—if it was a person—seemed to want a little understanding. And the flimsier the person, too, the easier it ought to be for him to go where he wanted. Also, what could it matter whether they were pointed or not?

The latter question was the one which Caleb asked first.

"Six hundred years ago," said the spook, "all arches were made round, and when these pointed things came in I cursed them. I hate new-fangled things."

"That wouldn't hurt them much," said Caleb.

"I said I would never go under one of them," said the spook.

"That would matter more to you than to them," said Caleb.

"It does," said the spook, with another great sigh.

"But you could easily change your mind," said Caleb.

"I was tied to it," said the spook, "I was told that I never more should go under one of them, whether I would or not."

"Some people will tell you anything," answered Caleb.

"It was a Bishop," explained the spook.

"Ah!" said Caleb, "that's different, of course."

The spook told Caleb how often he had tried to go under the pointed arches, sometimes of the doors, sometimes of the windows, and how a stream of wind always struck him from the point of the arch, and drifted him back into the Church. He had long given up trying.

"You should have been outside," said Caleb, "before they built the last door."

"It was my Church," said the spook, "and I was too proud to leave."

Caleb began to sympathise with the spook. He had a pride in the Church himself, and disliked even to hear another person say Amen before him. He also began to be a little jealous of this stranger who had been six hundred years in possession of the Church in which Caleb had believed himself, under the Vicar, to be master. And he began to plot.

"Why do you want to get out?" he asked.

"I'm no use here," was the reply, "I don't get enough to do to keep myself warm. And I know there are scores of Churches now without any kirk-spooks at all. I can hear their cheap little bells dinging every Sunday."

"There's very few bells hereabouts," said Caleb.

"There's no hereabouts for spooks," said the other. "We can hear any distance you like."

"But what good are you at all?" said Caleb.

"Good!" said the spook. "Don't we secure proper respect for Churches, especially after dark? A Church would be like any other place if it wasn't for us. You must know that."

"Well, then," said Caleb, "you're no good here. This Church is all right. What will you give me to let you out?"

"Can you do it?" asked the spook.

"What will you give me?" said Caleb.

"I'll say a good word for you amongst the spooks," said the other.

"What good will that do me?" said Caleb.

"A good word never did anybody any harm yet," answered the spook.

"Very well then, come along," said Caleb.

"Gently then," said the spook; "don't make a draught."

"Not yet," said Caleb, and he drew the spook very carefully (as one takes a vessel quite full of water) from the seat.

"I can't go under pointed arches," cried the spook, as Caleb moved off.

"Nobody wants you to," said Caleb. "Keep close to me."

He led the spook down the aisle to the angle of the wall where a small iron shutter covered an opening into the flue. It was used by the chimney sweep alone, but Caleb had another use for it now. Calling to the spook to keep close, he suddenly removed the shutter.

The fires were by this time burning briskly. There was a strong up-draught as the shutter was removed. Caleb felt something rush across his face, and heard a cheerful laugh away up in the chimney. Then he knew that he was alone. He replaced the shutter, gave another look at his stoves, took the keys, and made his way home.

He found his wife asleep in her chair, sat down and took off his boots, and awakened her by throwing them across the kitchen.

"I've been wondering when you'd wake," he said.

"What?" she said, "Have you been in long?"

"Look at the clock," said Caleb. "Half after twelve."

"My gracious," said his wife. "Let's be off to bed."

"Did you tell her about the spook?" he was naturally asked.

"Not I," said Caleb. "You know what she'd say. Same as she always does of a Saturday night."

* * * *

This fable Mr. Batchel related with reluctance. His attitude towards it was wholly deprecatory. Psychic phenomena, he said, lay outside the province of the mere humourist, and the levity with which they had been treated was largely responsible for the presumptuous materialism of the age.

He said more, as he warmed to the subject, than can here be repeated. The reader of the foregoing tales, however, will be interested to know that Mr. Batchel's own attitude was one of humble curiosity. He refused even to guess why the revenant was sometimes invisible, and at other times partly or wholly visible; sometimes capable of using physical force, and at other times powerless. He knew that they had their periods, and that was all.

There is room, he said, for the romancer in these matters; but for the humourist, none. Romance was the play of intelligence about the confines of truth. The invisible world, like the visible, must have its romancers, its explorers, and its interpreters; but the time of the last was not yet come.

Criticism, he observed in conclusion, was wholesome and necessary. But of the idle and mischievous remarks which were wont to pose as criticism, he held none in so much contempt as the cheap and irrational Pooh-Pooh.

THEY THAT MOURN,
by Juliet Wilbor Tompkins

A woman in black, seeing Eleanor's deep mourning, came and took the chair beside her, as though grief longed to be near grief. The business of the meeting had not yet begun, and after a moment she spoke, impetuously, yet with a tense composure, her eyes straining toward Eleanor's grave, pale face.

"I lost my little girl," she said. "It is just two months today. I had to do something, so I came here. I have two boys, but she was my only little girl."

Eleanor's instinct was to shrink from a grief so nakedly carried; but she made herself bend forward and murmur some word that meant comprehension.

The woman drew out a locket and showed a little face inside.

"She was ill only twelve hours," she went on, with the same strained composure. "Every one loved her, high and low, wherever she went. I don't believe—" The line of her lips broke, drawing down at one side on a sharp intake of breath, but her eyes remained brilliantly dry. The chairman of the meeting mounted the platform and rapped for order.

Eleanor paid little attention to the business that followed. The social demand for reticence seemed, all at once, too trivial to be remembered before this white-hot, world-filling sorrow. The woman had met something too big to be mastered: there was room for nothing else on her horizon. She had no curiosity as to the cause of Eleanor's black garments. After the meeting. Eleanor saw her tell some one else the same simple, breathless tale. A person on whom the actual sky had fallen must have so carried his astounding experience. "That is pure grief—grief without remorse," she decided, as she left the meeting. "She gave everything, she loved wholly; she has no cause for shame." She shivered, and hurried out to her waiting motor. After she had gone, some one told the woman in black that that was Eleanor Searles, whose mother had been lost in the wreck of the *Jessica* last June.

"Ah, I wish I had known," she said, but absently. "My little girl was nine on the 1st of June," she added.

Eleanor's house loomed big and empty that night. The door of the upstairs sitting-room was open, and it seemed as if her approaching step must be met by her mother's welcoming, "Well, Nellie! Got home, dear? Kind o' tired? Want to set a minute?"

She paused in the doorway, looking about the room that was as startling in that harmonious house as her mother's presence had been between her father and herself. Then she went slowly in and threw herself down in the blue brocade armchair that had been her mother's first excited purchase when all the dreams of fairyland had come true and the prince had married her.

The beauty that had driven young Searles to madness and marriage had faded before Eleanor could remember. It had been the temporary bloom of color and curve and joyous country youth; and for any beauty that might have developed later the irritated man had no eyes. But Eleanor, in spite of her slim Searles physique, had not taken her heritage solely from her father. She had gone with him, imitated him in his patient bored courtesy to the woman he had married, learned to scorn what he scorned as soon as the happy nursery warmth had begun to cool. Yet never in all those years had she been perfectly comfortable. And after her father's death, when the charm of his personality was removed and the importance of his approval less compelling, she had reluctantly grown more and more conscious of this cheerful, untutored, busy-handed woman, so appallingly alone in her luxurious house. But she had given no sign, still justified by her father's sanction, and youthfully afraid of committing herself to some bond that should hamper the perfect freedom of her own pursuits and pleasures. When her mother had suddenly decided to go to St. John's and look up a married sister, she had seen her off with a hard, hurried little kiss and a relief that could scarcely await the boat's sailing.

"You wouldn't care to come, too, Nellie, just for the trip?" Mrs. Searles had suggested, but without expressed wistfulness. Eleanor had wished, even before the news came, that she had put her refusal less abruptly. Afterward—

She started up, running from memories. Yet after dinner she came back to the room. She very often sat there now. That young mother whose grief was so pure that it could be spoken of haunted and oppressed her. The wise book she was reading on the economic status of women seemed dusty and remote, and she finally turned to the little, warm-hearted books of her childhood, ranged in a dreadful veneered, glass-doored bookcase, which her mother had bought especially to hold them.

"I kind o' like to see *Dottie Dimple* and *Katy Did* around," she had explained, when she moved them to her sitting-room. Eleanor had missed the under-meaning of that longing. She did not care where the old volumes were kept.

She took down a handful of them, broken-backed and loose-leaved, all with "Nellie from Mamma" written in large, unfluent letters on the fly-leaf. Her mother's voice echoed through the pages that she had read aloud so lovingly and laboriously before her child had learned to wince at her country speech. Only once had this difference between them been put into words. The little Eleanor, studying her mother with puzzled eyes, had suddenly asked:

"Mother, why do you say 'doos' when father says 'does'?" She had been frightened by the tragic change in her mother's face, the force of the hands that closed on her shoulders.

"Dearie, because I ain't had education. It's the only thing in life that matters, except bein' good—and folks'll forgive you for bein' bad before they'll forgive you for not knowin' books. Don't you miss it—don't you let one chanst get by you! It's too late when you're grown up and kind o' brain-stupid and don't know how to learn. You got to get it little. Oh, my baby, don't you miss it! Don't you never shirk your lessons one day! There ain't no happiness on earth without you got education."

She had cried, and they had never spoken of it again; but Eleanor had not forgotten. Her father had been proud of her standing in school and college, of her intelligent reading, quite unaware that the real impetus had not come from his side of the family.

Behind *Dottie Dimple* lay an old copybook. Supposing that it held her own childish work, Eleanor drew it out; then shrank away from its pages in pain and shame. For they were filled with her mother's slow, difficult writing. Spelling lessons, writing exercises, awkward little compositions; stern grammatical warnings, such as, "She and I done it, not Her and me done it," repeated twenty times; and across the end a despairing "It's no use. You can't teach an old dog."

Eleanor thrust back the book, locked the glass doors on it, and tried to get away from it by running to her own quarters. But she might as well have stayed. No chair could hold her still that evening. She longed to go to that woman who had lost her little girl and put fierce, rough questions to her:

"Suppose you had neglected your child, avoided her love, starved her with loneliness—how would you bear that?" But the woman would only have answered that that was an impossible supposition. Other people knew how to love before it was too late.

At last she went to bed; but the dawn found her still wide-eyed and tense. "If I could have her back for just one week!" she said to the creeping light. "I would take anything on earth after that. One week, just to comfort her, to give her something real and warm and rightfully hers! One week—I could make it all up to her." She sat up in bed, stretching out her arms. "Are there no miracles any more? Do we never get a second chance? Just one week?"

* * * *

The woman's name, Mrs. Gannon, was unfamiliar, but hearing that she was dressed in mourning, Eleanor went hurriedly to the drawing-room. Her thoughts had hovered persistently about the mother who had lost her little girl, and could see nothing else in the universe. But it was a person of another class who rose respectfully when Eleanor came in.

"I'm very bold in coming to you, miss," she began, and her pleasant English voice, crisp and honest, was reassuring. Her shabby black had roused fear of some whining tale. "But I'm a good seamstress, and I thought as 'ow, under the circumstances, you might be willing to 'elp me to some work."

"Under the circumstances?" Eleanor repeated. She saw that the woman was not going to cry, and so settled down willingly enough to hear her tale.

"I'm coming to that, miss." Mrs. Gannon returned to her chair and folded her hands self-respectingly at her belt. "You'll forgive me for touching on it, but my 'usband was a sailor, miss, and 'e was lost in the *Jessica* disaster. And so I thought you might be a little interested in 'elping me to get a start. There's three children, and I 'aven't lived 'ere long, so it's not so easy, is it, now?"

Eleanor had started and paled. "In the *Jessica* disaster?"

"Yes, miss." Mrs. Gannon maintained a cheerful, practical impersonality. "'E was a good 'usband, and I 'adn't 'ad to do nothing outside the 'ouse since we was married—"

"Oh, but that is hard," Eleanor broke in.

"Well, yes, miss, it is. With three children. But I'm good with the needle—"

"Tell me, did they—was his body found?" The question forced itself past Eleanor's lips. In the first horror of the news she had been tortured by the thought of helpless voyagers going on and on with the restless tides.

"Oh no, miss. I mean to say, 'e was picked up by a fishing-boat and taken to a village, but 'e died of the hexposure three days later. I 'ave the letter 'ere that told me, so you can know it was all just like I say."

Mrs. Gannon was palpably honest. Eleanor had lifted her hand to motion away the letter, when her eyes fell on its handwriting. She bent nearer to it, clutching the woman's wrist in a grip that hurt. Then, with a cry, she crumpled down on the floor.

Her eyes opened before Mrs. Gannon could run for help. She motioned her back and sat up, dizzily, supported in the other's arm.

"Let me see it again," she whispered, and, with the letter in her hands, began to shake and sob. "It's my mother's writing! Oh, what does it mean? What does it mean?"

"Did she perish from the hexposure, too, miss?"

"But if she could write this letter, why didn't she write to me? Why did I not have one word or sign? Oh, am I mad?" She strained her hands against her throbbing head. "Wait till I get a piece of her writing," she commanded.

She came back with the old copybook, careless now of everything but the truth that layback of that letter; but she scarcely needed the literal confirmation. Though the page was unsigned, through every phrase she heard her mother's voice. Had a letter miscarried? Had she died up there later, in the little fishing-village? Had she died at all?

Faintness came over Eleanor again, but she fought it off. "I will start tomorrow—tonight," she said. "Stay and help me get ready. I must go and see for myself—my mother may be living."

Mrs. Gannon drew off her gloves and folded them with business-like alacrity. "Well, miss, I 'ope you'll find 'er well and 'earty," she said, cheerfully.

The journey was a nightmare of delays and difficulties. The little village on the southern coast of Newfoundland was so obscure that neither maps nor steamships knew of its existence; and when at last, in a red, cold sunset, she stood among the fishing-boats that lined the beach, facing the straggling white hamlet, the hope that had brought her seemed clear madness.

A few battered old seamen, pottering about the boats, looked kindly questions at her, women came to their doors to stare, but she could not ask them anything. Even the hope that her mother might be buried there seemed too fantastic in this chill light of common day. She walked slowly along the beach toward the spire of a church, thinking that she might look among its gravestones and perhaps find shelter in its rectory. She was on British soil, so could count on one spot of order and establishment in the rude little place.

Darkness was closing down with Northern suddenness. Sand grated in her shoes, the bleak wind cut her cheeks, her bag dragged at her arm; but her bodily distress seemed remote and unimportant beside the torment of her exhausted spirit. The end of her endurance had come. She was lost in a bad dream, fumbling through a horror of darkness that had no end. Not till a bar of light struck on her eyes did she know that she had reached the church. The door was open, and she stumbled in.

A hanging lamp had been lit near the chancel, and in its circle of light stood a middle-aged woman busily fitting pew-cushions into new red covers. She moved vigorously, as one who has a great deal to do and is rejoiced to do it. Her worn face had been lined by sadness, but through it a cheerful spirit looked out. Eleanor, still in shadow, crept slowly nearer, pew by pew, till she touched the edge of the lamplight; and still the dream held. She saw her mother. She sank to her knees, hiding her face.

"Who's there?" She heard the old, warm, welcoming voice. "Land sakes, I didn't hear no one come in. You kind o'—" There was a pause, and the scissors fell with a clatter. "Who is it?"

Eleanor could not rise or speak; but she slowly lifted her face. In an instant she felt her mother kneeling beside her, gathering her up as she would have gathered up the little hurt Eleanor of twenty years before. Words came dimly through a thickening mist.

"Why, Nellie—why, my girl, did you come all this—I didn't mean to grieve you, Nellie. I thought you'd be kind o' glad and relieved, dear, truly. I wouldn't have hurt you for fifty million dollars! Why, Nellie, you did care about your old mother! She's worn out, my poor baby! Come and let mother take care of you."

Blinded, speechless, utterly spent, Eleanor let herself be drawn to her feet and half led, half carried to the house next door, where she was put to bed in a clean little whitewashed room, aglow with firelight from an open stove. Neither of them said much; but their hands clung together, and Eleanor's face was often pressed against the helping arms. When she had been made comfortable, she felt her mother standing over her, gently stroking her hair.

"Dearie, I didn't plan to do it," she was saying. "But there was just me and that pore fellow that pulled me up onto his raft — we was picked up together after I dunno how long, and brought here. The mail didn't go out for two weeks, so I had time to think; and, oh, dearie, there was such a lot to do here! They'd had an epidemic, and they was all so sick and weak and helpless. My, but it did seem good to get my hands on a job again! I hadn't had enough to do, dearie, and this was real work. And they was grateful, and loved me. So I kind o' stayed on and on. But I see it wasn't right. I didn't understand, and I ask you to forgive me." She was gone before Eleanor could shape the difficult words in her heart.

There was no need to shape them. Her mother understood. The miracle had happened, and just by being there, helpless and humbled and clinging, she was making up for all those cruel years. Her mind floated dazedly between the present and the past. Several times she started up in distress.

"I have dreamed so often that you came back," she exclaimed. "I wanted it so horribly. And the dreams were just as real as this. How can I know that this is true?" Her mother's hand on hers felt real, but the voice sounded remote and ineffably patient.

"Well, dearie, our hearts have found each other, anyhow. So it's all right."

"Yes, it's all right," Eleanor repeated, and fell asleep.

In the morning she was too ill to get up. Her mother stayed beside her, and would let no one else in, though she herself was called out twenty times. Evidently she was a power in the village, an undisputed authority on things pertaining to ailing babies and grandmothers, young lovers and parish problems. She answered every call with a jump of alacrity, and came back with the shining eyes of happy service. When Eleanor asked her what she had done for money, she laughed.

"My land, dearie, what I had sewed into my petticoat would last an old woman all her life, in this place," she explained.

A fear brought Eleanor up on one elbow. "But you will come back with me!" she exclaimed.

"I'll do whatever is right and best," was the grave answer.

Day and night merged into each other. Eleanor floated between fever and vagueness, and started up at intervals, calling desperately for her mother.

"Am I making it up to you?" she would plead. "Oh, mother, I have suffered so! Is it all right now?"

"It's all right, my baby," the answer would come, strongly, soothing her like a cool hand on her forehead.

One morning she woke up to a world suddenly stilled and exquisitely peaceful. The wind, which had howled for days, was quieted, and sunshine streamed across the bed. A sense of beauty and fulfillment had descended like a blessing. It might have been the earth's seventh day, after the first six days of labor. She and her mother smiled into each other's eyes.

"How long have I been here?" she asked.

"Just a week today, dearie."

"And I have made you happy?"

"So happy!"

"Am I ill?"

"I think you're better. I wish you could get out into this nice sunshine."

"Mother, when can we go hack?"

A shadow fell on the other's face, but she answered cheerfully: "Why, there's a boat coming in this morning with a doctor, but you ain't strong enough to be taken, I'm afraid. We'll see what he says. Now, will you eat some breakfast, like a good girl?"

Eleanor submitted to the spoon at her lips. When her mother, ruddy and smiling in her fishwife's cloak, started for the beach to meet the doctor, she called her back. The fever brightness was coming up in her cheeks.

"I have learned how to love," she said. "All my books and all my teachers never taught me anything so big as what you taught me, mother—just by being you." They clung to each other, smiling through tears. At the door her mother turned back.

"It's all right for ever and ever—remember that," she said, and her voice had a magic beauty.

The sunlight fell on the window like a summons. The churchyard was just beneath, and a confused memory of her need to hunt through its graves goaded Eleanor into dressing. She crept out by a side door, and presently stood in the fresh sunlight among the mounds. She found one with a wooden headboard showing the name "Peter Gannon" and a date. Beside it an oblong had been cut in the sod, and a few spadefuls of earth taken out. Her fevered brain began to conjure up terrors.

"Perhaps that is for me," she thought, and stood as lost and heart-sick as a child that has slipped from a guardian hand in the crowd. The need of her mother's sane, strong presence drove her down the beach road, struggling to run in the unwilling sand. At last, rounding the corner of the school-house, she came in sight of the pier and its moving figures, cut with cameo delicacy on the still brightness of the morning. She saw the sail-boat coming in, and her mother's fluttering cloak, and the excited children scrambling underfoot, all as tiny and brilliant as though she looked through reversed glasses. Her feet had grown very heavy, and she paused, wavering. At that moment a child darted too near the edge, and she saw her mother spring forward.

There was a cry that shattered the scene into a confusion of movement and terror. Eleanor stumbled on until women in the gathering crowd stopped her. By the fright in their eyes she knew.

"My mother is dead!" The words seemed to come from without and to strike her down like a bolt of lightning.

* * * *

When she came out of the darkness and bewilderment, the same words were on her lips.

"My mother is dead," she told the figure beside her. A quieting murmur answered. Looking about, she saw hospital walls. Beyond the windows lay a gleam of roofs and spires, white with snow. She was too tired to wonder. Presently tears began to run down her cheeks. The nurse asked some question, but she could not explain that she was crying for her mother. It was pure grief, grief without shame; she cried longingly, yet with a great sense of peace. She had had no right to cry before. The nurse gave her something to drink, and she fell asleep.

When she woke again it was night, and a different nurse sat by her bed.

"How did I come here?" she asked, and at the quiet, lucid question the nurse started, looking keenly into her face.

"Oh, a doctor brought you, a long way," she said, soothingly. "Don't bother about that now."

"They told you I had lost my mother?" Eleanor went on; and remembered the woman who had lost her child and could speak of nothing else.

The nurse was bent over a chart. "You must try not to think of dreadful things," she said.

"Ah, but this was so wonderful!" Eleanor spoke with sudden strength. "It was like a perfect dream, and yet it was real. Real as my hand here—feel. Sad—oh yes, terribly sad; but she wouldn't call it dreadful. And it makes all the rest of my life possible. But no one will ever understand."

"You are not to talk," the nurse said, gently. "I want you to go to sleep."

Eleanor wound her arms about the pillow and hid her face. "Oh, it is so good to cry for my mother!" she murmured.

GREEN BRANCHES, by Fiona Macleod

In the year that followed the death of Manus MacCodrum, James Achanna saw nothing of his brother Gloom. He might have thought himself alone in the world, of all his people, but for a letter that came to him out of the west. True, he had never accepted the common opinion that his brothers had both been drowned on that night when Anne Gillespie left Eilanmore with Manus.

In the first place he had nothing of that inner conviction concerning the fate of Gloom which he had concerning that of Marcus; in the next, had he not heard the sound of the *feadan*, which no one that he knew played except Gloom; and, for further token, was not the tune that which he hated above all others—the "Dance of the Dead"—for who but Gloom would be playing that, he hating it so, and the hour being late, and no one else on Eilanmore? It was no sure thing that the dead had not come back; but the more he thought of it the more Achanna believed that his sixth brother was still alive. Of this, however, he said nothing to any one.

It was as a man set free that, at last, after long waiting and patient trouble, with the disposal of all that was left of the Achanna heritage, he left the island. It was a grey memory for him. The bleak moorland of it, the blight that had lain so long and so often upon the crops, the rains that had swept the isle for grey days and grey weeks and grey months, the sobbing of the sea by day and its dark moan by night, its dim relinquishing sigh in the calm of dreary ebbs, its hollow, baffling roar when the storm-shadow swept up out of the sea—one and all oppressed him, even in memory. He had never loved the island, even when it lay green and fragrant in the green and white seas under white and blue skies, fresh and sweet as an Eden of the sea.

He had ever been lonely and weary, tired of the mysterious shadow that lay upon his folk, caring little for any of his brothers except the eldest—long since mysteriously gone out of the ken of man—and almost hating Gloom, who had ever borne him a grudge because of his beauty, and because of his likeness to and reverent heed for Alison. Moreover, ever since he had come to love Katreen Macarthur, the daughter of Donald Macarthur who lived in Sleat of Skye, he had been eager to live near her; the more eager as he knew that Gloom loved the girl also, and wished for success not only for his own sake, but so as to put a slight upon his younger brother.

So, when at last he left the island, he sailed southward gladly. He was leaving Eilanmore; he was bound to a new home in Skye, and perhaps he was going to his long-delayed, long dreamed-of happiness. True, Katreen was not pledged to him; he did not even know for sure if she loved him. He thought, hoped, dreamed, almost believed that she did; but then there was her cousin Ian, who had long wooed her, and to whom old Donald Macarthur had given his blessing. Nevertheless, his heart would have been lighter than it had been for long, but for two things. First, there was the letter. Some weeks earlier he had received it, not recognizing the writing, because of the few letters he had ever seen, and, moreover, as it was in a feigned hand. With difficulty he had deciphered the manuscript, plain printed though it was. It ran thus:

"Well, Sheumais, my brother, it is wondering if I am dead, you will be. Maybe ay, and maybe no. But I send you this writing to let you know that I know all you do and think of. So you are going to leave Eilanmore without an Achanna upon it? And you will be going to Sleat in Skye? Well, let me be telling you this thing. *Do not go.* I see blood there. And there is this, too: neither you nor any man shall take Katreen away from me. *You* know that; and Ian Macarthur knows it; and Katreen knows it; and that holds whether I am alive or dead. I say to you: do not go. It will be better for you, and for all. Ian Macarthur is away in the north-sea with the whaler-captain who came to us at Eilanmore, and will not be back for three months yet. It will be better for him not to come back. But if he comes back he will have to reckon with the man who says that Katreen Macarthur is his. I would rather not have two men to speak to, and one my brother. It does not matter to you where I am. I want no money just now. But put aside my portion for me. Have it ready for me against the day I call for it. I will not be patient that day; so have it ready for me. In the place that I am I am content. You will be saying: why is my brother away in a remote place (I will say this to you: that it is not further north than St. Kilda nor further south than the Mull of Cantyre!), and for what reason? That is between me and silence. But perhaps you think of Anne sometimes. Do you know that she lies under the green grass? And of Manus MacCodrum? They say that he swam out into the sea and was drowned; and they whisper of the seal-blood, though the minister is wrath with them for that. He calls it a madness. Well, I was there at that madness, and I played to it on my *feadan.* And now, Sheumais, can you be thinking of what the tune was that I played?
"Your brother, who waits his own day,

"GLOOM."

"Do not be forgetting this thing: I would rather not be playing the 'Damhsa-na-Mairbh.' It was an ill hour for Manus when he heard the 'Dan-nan-Ron'; it was the song of his soul, that; and yours is the 'Davsa-na-Mairv.'"

This letter was ever in his mind; this, and what happened in the gloaming when he sailed away for Skye in the herring-smack of two men who lived at Armandale in Sleat. For, as the boat moved slowly out of the haven, one of the men asked him if he was sure that no one was left upon the island; for he thought he had seen a figure on the rocks, waving a black scarf. Achanna shook his head; but just then his companion cried that at that moment he had seen the same thing. So the smack was put about, and when she was moving slowly through the haven again, Achanna sculled ashore in the little coggly punt. In vain he searched here and there, calling loudly again and again. Both men could hardly have been mistaken, he thought. If there were no human creature on the island, and if their eyes had not played them false, who could it be? The wraith of Marcus, mayhap; or might it be the old man himself (his father), risen to bid farewell to his youngest son, or to warn him?

It was no use to wait longer, so, looking often behind him, he made his way to the boat again, and rowed slowly out toward the smack.

Jerk—jerk—jerk across the water came, low but only too loud for him, the opening motif of the "Damhsa-na-Mairbh." A horror came upon him, and he drove the boat through the water so that the sea splashed over the bows. When he came on deck he cried in a hoarse voice to the man next him to put up the helm, and let the smack swing to the wind.

"There is no one there, Callum Campbell," he whispered.

"And who is it that will be making that strange music?"

"What music?"

"Sure it has stopped now, but I heard it clear, and so did Anndra MacEwan. It was like the sound of a reed pipe, and the tune was an eery one at that."

"It was the Dance of the Dead."

"And who will be playing that?" asked the man, with fear in his eyes.

"No living man."

"No living man?"

"No. I'm thinking it will be one of my brothers who was drowned here, and by the same token that it is Gloom, for he played upon the *feadan*. But if not, then—then—"

The two men waited in breathless silence, each trembling with superstitious fear; but at last the elder made a sign to Achanna to finish.

"Then—it will be the Kelpie."

"Is there—is there one of the—cave-women here?"

"It is said; and you know of old that the Kelpie sings or plays a strange tune to wile seamen to their death."

At that moment the fantastic, jerking music came loud and clear across the bay. There was a horrible suggestion in it, as if dead bodies were moving along the ground with long jerks, and crying and laughing wild. It was enough; the men, Campbell and MacEwan, would not now have waited longer if Achanna had offered them all he had in the world. Nor were they, or he, out of their panic haste till the smack stood well out at sea, and not a sound could be heard from Eilanmore.

They stood watching, silent. Out of the dusky mass that lay in the seaward way to the north came a red gleam. It was like an eye staring after them with blood-red glances.

"What is that, Achanna?"

"It looks as though a fire had been lighted in the house up in the island. The door and the window must be open. The fire must be fed with wood, for no peats would give that flame; and there were none lighted when I left. To my knowing, there was no wood for burning except the wood of the shelves and the bed."

"And who would be doing that?"

"I know of that no more than you do, Callum Campbell."

No more was said, and it was a relief to all when the last glimmer of the light was absorbed in the darkness.

At the end of the voyage Campbell and MacEwan were well pleased to be quit of their companion; not so much because he was moody and distraught as because they feared that a spell was upon him—a fate in the working of which they might become involved. It needed no vow of the one to the other for them to come to the conclusion that they would never land on Eilanmore, or, if need be, only in broad daylight, and never alone.

The days went well for James Achanna, where he made his home at Ranza-beag, on Ranza Water in the Sleat of Skye. The farm was small but good, and he hoped that with help and care he would soon have the place as good a farm as there was in all Skye.

Donald Macarthur did not let him see much of Katreen, but the old man was no longer opposed to him. Sheumais must wait till Ian Macarthur came back again, which might be any day now. For sure, James Achanna of Ranza-beag was a very different person from the youngest of the Achanna-folk, who held by on lonely Eilanmore; moreover, the old man could not but think with pleasure that it would be well to see Katreen able to walk over the whole land of Ranza, from the cairn at the north of his own Ranza-Mòr to the burn at the south of Ranza-beag, and know it for her own.

But Achanna was ready to wait. Even before he had the secret word of Katreen he knew from her beautiful dark eyes that she loved him. As the weeks went by they managed to meet often, and at last Katreen told him that she loved him too, and would have none but him; but that they must wait till Ian came back, because of the pledge given to him by her father. They were days of joy for him. Through many a hot noon-tide hour, through many a gloaming he went as one in a dream. Whenever he saw a birch swaying in the wind, or a wave leaping upon Loch Laith, that was near his home, or passed a bush covered with wild roses, or saw the moonbeams lying white on the boles of the pines, he thought of Katreen—his fawn for grace, and so lithe and tall, with sunbrown face and wavy, dark mass of hair, and shadowy eyes and rowan-red lips. It is said that there is a god clothed in shadow who goes to and fro among the human kind, putting silence between lovers with his waving hands, and breathing a chill out of his cold breath, and leaving a gulf of deep water flowing between them because of the passing of his feet. That shadow never came their way. Their love grew as a flower fed by rains and warmed by sunlight.

When midsummer came, and there was no sign of Ian Macarthur, it was already too late. Katreen had been won.

During the summer months it was the custom for Katreen and two of the farm-girls to go up Maol-Ranza, to reside at the shealing of Cnoc-an-Fhraoch: and this because of the hill-pasture for the sheep. Cnoc-an-Fhraoch is a round, boulder-studded hill covered with heather, which has a precipitous corrie on each side, and in front slopes down to Lochan Fraoch, a lochlet surrounded by dark woods. Behind the hill, or great hillock rather, lay the shealing. At each weekend Katreen went down to Ramza-Mòr, and on every Monday morning at sunrise returned to her heather-girt eerie. It was on one of these visits that she endured a cruel shock. Her father told her that she must marry some one else than Sheumais Achanna. He had heard words about him which made a union impossible, and indeed, he hoped that the man would leave Ranza-beag. In the end he admitted that what he had heard was to the effect that Achanna was under a doom of some kind, that he was involved in a blood-feud; and, moreover, that he was fey. The old man would not be explicit as to the person from whom his information came, but hinted that he was a stranger of rank, probably a laird of the isles. Besides this, there was word of Ian Macarthur. He was at Thurso, in the far north, and would be in Skye before long, and he—her father—had written to him that he might wed Katreen as soon as was practicable.

"Do you see that lintie yonder, father?" was her response to this.

"Ay, lass, and what about the birdeen?"

"Well, when she mates with a hawk, so will I be mating with Ian Macarthur, but not till then."

With that she turned and left the house, and went back to Cnoc-an-Fhraoch. On the way she met Achanna.

It was that night that for the first time he swam across Lochan Fraoch to meet Katreen.

The quickest way to reach the shealing was to row across the lochlet, and then ascend by a sheep-path that wound through the hazel copses at the base of the hill. Fully half an hour was thus saved, because of the steepness of the precipitous corries to right and left. A boat was kept for this purpose, but it was fastened to a shore boulder by a padlocked iron chain, the key of which was kept by Donald Macarthur. Latterly he had refused to let this key out of his possession. For one thing, no doubt, he believed he could thus restrain Achanna from visiting his daughter. The young man could not approach the shealing from either side without being seen.

But that night, soon after the moon was whitening slow in the dark, Katreen stole down to the hazel copse and awaited the coming of her lover. The lochan was visible from almost any point on Cnoc-an-Fhraoch, as well as from the south side. To cross it in a boat unseen, if any watcher were near, would be impossible, nor could even a swimmer hope to escape notice unless in the gloom of night or, mayhap, in the dusk. When, however, she saw, half-way across the water, a spray of green branches slowly moving athwart the surface, she new that Sheumais was keeping his tryst. If, perchance, any one else saw, he or she would never guess that those derelict rowan branches shrouded Sheumais Achanna.

It was not till the estray had drifted close to the hedge, where, hid among the bracken and the hazel undergrowth, she awaited him, that Katreen descried the face of her lover, as with one hand he parted the green sprays, and stared longingly and lovingly at the figure he could just discern in the dim, fragrant obscurity.

And as it was this night so was it many of the nights that followed. Katreen spent the days as in a dream. Not even the news of her cousin Ian's return disturbed her much.

One day the inevitable meeting came. She was at Ranza-Mòr, and when a shadow came into the dairy where she was standing she looked up, and saw Ian before her. She thought he appeared taller and stronger than ever, though still not so tall as Sheumais, who would appear slim beside the Herculean Skyeman. But as she looked at his close curling black hair and thick bull-neck and the sullen eyes in his dark wind-red face, she wondered that she had ever tolerated him at all.

He broke the ice at once.

"Tell me, Katreen, are you glad to see me back again?"

"I am glad that you are home once more safe and sound."

"And will you make it my home for me by coming to live with me, as I've asked you again and again?"

"No: as I've told you again and again."

He gloomed at her angrily for a few moments before he resumed.

"I will be asking you this one thing, Katreen, daughter of my father's brother: do you love that man Achanna who lives at Ranza-beag?"

"You may ask the wind why it is from the east or the west, but it won't tell you. You're not the wind's master."

"If you think I will let this man take you away from me, you are thinking a foolish thing."

"And you saying a foolisher."

"Ay?"

"Ah, sure. What could you do, Ian Mhic Ian? At the worst, you could do no more than kill James Achanna. What then? I too would die. You cannot separate us. I would not marry you, now, though you were the last man in the world and I the last woman."

"You are a fool, Katreen Macarthur. Your father has promised you to me, and I tell you this: if you love Achanna you'll save his life only by letting him go away from here. I promise you he will not be here long."

"Ah, you promise *me*; but you will not say that thing to James Achanna's face. You are a coward."

With a muttered oath the man turned on his heel.

"Let him beware o' me, and you, too, Katreen-mo-nighean-donn. I swear it by my mother's grave and by St. Martin's Cross that you will be mine by hook or by crook."

The girl smiled scornfully. Slowly she lifted a milk-pail.

"It would be a pity to waste the good milk, Ian-gòrach, but if you don't go it is I that will be emptying the pail on you, and then you will be as white without as your heart is within."

"So you call me witless, do you? *Ian-gòrach!* Well, we shall be seeing as to that. And as for the milk, there will be more than milk spilt because of *you*, Katreen-donn."

From that day, though neither Sheumais nor Katreen knew of it, a watch was set upon Achanna.

It could not be long before their secret was discovered, and it was with a savage joy overmastering his sullen rage that Ian Macarthur knew himself the discoverer, and conceived his double vengeance. He dreamed, gloatingly, on both the black thoughts that roamed like ravenous beasts through the solitudes of his heart. But he did not dream that another man was filled with hate because of Katreen's lover, another man who had sworn to make her his own, the man who, disguised, was known in Armandale as Donald McLean, and in the north isles would have been hailed as Gloom Achanna.

There had been steady rain for three days, with a cold, raw wind. On the fourth the sun shone, and set in peace. An evening of quiet beauty followed, warm, fragrant, dusky from the absence of moon or star, though the thin veils of mist promised to disperse as the night grew.

There were two men that eve in the undergrowth on the south side of the lochlet. Sheumais had come earlier than his wont. Impatient for the dusk, he could scarce await the waning of the afterglow; surely, he thought, he might venture. Suddenly his ears caught the sound of cautious footsteps. Could it be old Donald, perhaps with some inkling of the way in which his daughter saw her lover in despite of all; or, mayhap, might it be Ian Macarthur, tracking him as a hunter stalking a stag by the water-pools? He crouched, and waited. In a few minutes he saw Ian carefully picking his way. The man stopped as he descried the green branches; smiled as, with a low rustling, he raised them from the ground.

Meanwhile yet another man watched and waited, though on the farther side of the lochan, where the hazel copses were. Gloom Achanna half hoped, half feared the approach of Katreen. It would be sweet to see her again, sweet to slay her lover before her eyes, brother to him though he was. But, there was chance that she might descry him, and, whether recognizingly or not, warn the swimmer.

So it was that he had come there before sundown, and now lay crouched among the bracken underneath a projecting mossy ledge close upon the water, where it could scarce be that she or any should see him.

As the gloaming deepened a great stillness reigned. There was no breath of wind. A scarce audible sigh prevailed among the spires of the heather. The churring of a night-jar throbbed through the darkness. Somewhere a corncrake called its monotonous *crek-craik*; the dull, harsh sound emphasizing the utter stillness. The pinging of the gnats hovering over and among the sedges made an incessant murmur through the warm, sultry air.

There was a splash once as of a fish. Then, silence. Then a lower but more continuous splash, or rather wash of water. A slow *susurrus* rustled through the dark.

Where he lay among the fern Gloom Achanna slowly raised his head, stared through the shadows and listened intently. If Katreen were waiting there she was not near.

Noiselessly he slid into the water. When he rose it was under a clump of green branches. These he had cut and secured three hours before. With his left hand he swam slowly, or kept his equipoise in the water; with his right he guided the heavy rowan bough. In his mouth were two objects, one long and thin and dark, the other with an occasional glitter as of a dead fish.

His motion was scarcely perceptible. None the less he was near the middle of the loch almost as soon as another clump of green branches. Doubtless the swimmer beneath it was confident that he was now safe from observation.

The two clumps of green branches drew nearer. The smaller seemed a mere estray, a spray blown down by the recent gale. But all at once the larger clump jerked awkwardly and stopped. Simultaneously a strange, low strain of music came from the other.

The strain ceased. The two clumps of green branches remained motionless. Slowly, at last, the larger moved forward. It was too dark for the swimmer to see if any one lay hid behind the smaller. When he reached it he thrust aside the leaves.

It was as though a great salmon leaped. There was a splash, and a narrow, dark body shot through the gloom. At the end of it something gleamed. Then suddenly there was a savage struggle. The inanimate green branches tore this way and that, and surged and swirled. Gasping cries came from the leaves. Again and again the gleaming thing leaped. At the third leap an awful scream shrilled through the silence. The echo of it wailed thrice, with horrible distinctness, in the corrie beyond Cnoc-an-Fhraoch. Then, after a faint splashing, there was silence once more. One clump of green branches drifted slowly up the lochlet. The other moved steadily toward the place whence, a brief while before, it had stirred.

Only one thing lived in the heart of Gloom Achanna—the joy of his exultation. He had killed his brother Sheumais. He had always hated him because of his beauty; of late he had hated him because he had stood between him, Gloom, and Katreen Macarthur—because he had become her lover. They were all dead now except himself, all the Achannas. He was "Achanna." When the day came that he would go back to Galloway, there would be a magpie on the first birk, and a screaming jay on the first rowan, and a croaking raven on the first fir; ay, he would be their suffering, though they knew nothing of him meanwhile! He would be Achanna of Achanna again. Let those who would stand in his way beware. As for Katreen: perhaps he would take her there, perhaps not. He smiled.

These thoughts were the wandering fires in his brain while he slowly swam shoreward under the floating green branches, and as he disengaged himself from them and crawled upward through the bracken. It was at this moment that a third man entered the water from the further shore.

Prepared as he was to come suddenly upon Katreen, Gloom was startled when, in a place of dense shadow, a hand touched his shoulder, and her voice whispered:

"Sheumais, Sheumais!"

The next moment she was in his arms. He could feel her heart beating against his.

"What is it, Sheumais? What was that awful cry?" she whispered.

For answer he put his lips to hers, and kissed her again and again.

The girl drew back. Some vague instinct warned her.

"What is it, Sheumais? Why don't you speak?"

He drew her close again.

"Pulse of my heart, it is I who love you, I who love you best of all; it is I, Gloom Achanna!"

With a cry she struck him full in the face. He staggered and in that moment she freed herself.

"You *coward*!"

"Katreen, I—"

"Come no nearer. If you do, it will be the death of you!"

"The death o' me! Ah, bonnie fool that you are, and is it you that will be the death o' me?"

"Ay, Gloom Achanna, for I have but to scream and Sheumais will be here, an' he would kill you like a dog if he knew you did me harm."

"Ah, but if there were no Sheumais, or any man to come between me an' my will!"

"Then there would be a woman! Ay, if you over-bore me I would strangle you with my hair, or fix my teeth in your false throat!"

"I was not for knowing you were such a wild-cat; but I'll tame you yet, my lass! Aha, wild-cat!" And as he spoke he laughed low.

"It is a true word, Gloom of the black heart. I am a wild-cat, and, like a wild-cat, I am not to be seized by a fox; and that you will be finding to your cost, by the holy St. Bridget! But now, off with you, brother of my man!"

"Your man—ha! ha!"

"Why do you laugh?"

"Sure, I am laughing at a warm, white lass like yourself having a dead man as your lover!"

"A—dead—man?"

No answer came. The girl shook with a new fear. Slowly she drew closer, till her breath fell warm against the face of the other.

He spoke at last:

"Ay, a dead man."

"It is a lie."

"Where would you be that you were not hearing his good-bye? I'm thinking it was loud enough!"

"It is a lie—it is a lie!"

"No, it is no lie. Sheumais is cold enough now. He's low among the weeds by now. Ay, by now: down there in the lochan."

"*What*—you, *you devil*! Is it for killing your own brother you would be?"

"I killed no one. He died his own way. Maybe the cramp took him. Maybe—maybe a Kelpie gripped him. I watched. I saw him beneath the green branches. He was dead before he died. I saw it in the white face o' him. Then he sank. He's dead. Sheumais is dead. Look here, girl, I've always loved you. I swore the oath upon you. You're mine. Sure, you're mine now, Katreen! It is loving you I am! It will be a south wind for you from this day, muirnean mochree! See here, I'll show you how I—"

"Back—back—*murderer*!"

"Be stopping that foolishness now, Katreen Macarthur! By the Book, I am tired of it. I am loving you, and it's having you for mine I am! And if you won't come to me like the dove to its mate, I'll come to you like the hawk to the dove!"

With a spring he was upon her. In vain she strove to beat him back. His arms held her as a stoat grips a rabbit.

He pulled her head back, and kissed her throat till the strangulating breath sobbed against his ear. With a last despairing effort she screamed the name of the dead man: "Sheumais! Sheumais! Sheumais!" The man who struggled with her laughed.

"Ay, call away! The herrin' will be coming through the bracken as soon as Sheumais comes to your call! Ah, it is mine you are now, Katreen! He's dead and cold—an' you'd best have a living man—an'—"

She fell back, her balance lost in the sudden releasing. What did it mean? Gloom still stood there, but as one frozen. Through the darkness she saw, at last, that a hand gripped his shoulder; behind him a black mass vaguely obtruded.

For some moments there was absolute silence. Then a hoarse voice came out of the dark:

"You will be knowing now who it is, Gloom Achanna!"

The voice was that of Sheumais, who lay dead in the lochan. The murderer shook as in a palsy. With a great effort, slowly he turned his head. He saw a white splatch, the face of the corpse; in this white splatch flamed two burning eyes, the eyes of the soul of the brother whom he had slain.

He reeled, staggered as a blind man, and, free now of that awful clasp, swayed to and fro as one drunken.

Slowly Sheumais raised an arm and pointed downward through the wood toward the lochan. Still pointing, he moved swiftly forward.

With a cry like a beast, Gloom Achanna swung to one side, stumbled, rose, and leaped into the darkness.

For some minutes Sheumais and Katreen stood, silent, apart, listening to the crashing sound of his flight—the race of the murderer against the pursuing shadow of the Grave.

THE WERE-WOLF, by H. B. Marryatt

My father was not born, or originally a resident, in the Hartz Mountains; he was the serf of an Hungarian nobleman, of great possessions, in Transylvania; but, although a serf, he was not by any means a poor or illiterate man. In fact, he was rich, and his intelligence and respectability were such, that he had been raised by his lord to the stewardship; but, whoever may happen to be born a serf, a serf must he remain, even though he become a wealthy man; such was the condition of my father. My father had been married for about five years; and, by his marriage, had three children—my eldest brother Cæsar, myself (Hermann), and a sister named Marcella. Latin is still the language spoken in that country; and that will account for our high-sounding names. My mother was a very beautiful woman, unfortunately more beautiful than virtuous: she was seen and admired by the lord of the soil; my father was sent away upon some mission; and, during his absence, my mother, flattered by the attentions, and won by the assiduities, of this nobleman, yielded to his wishes. It so happened that my father returned very unexpectedly, and discovered the intrigue. The evidence of my mother's shame was positive: he surprised her in the company of her seducer! Carried away by the impetuosity of his feelings, he watched the opportunity of a meeting taking place between them, and murdered both his wife and her seducer. Conscious that, as a serf, not even the provocation which he had received would be allowed as a justification of his conduct, he hastily collected together what money he could lay his hands upon, and, as we were then in the depth of winter, he put his horses to the sleigh, and taking his children with him, he set off in the middle of the night, and was far away before the tragic circumstance had transpired. Aware that he would be pursued, and that he had no chance of escape if he remained in any portion of his native country (in which the authorities could lay hold of him), he continued his flight without intermission until he had buried himself in the intricacies and seclusion of the Hartz Mountains. Of course, all that I have now told you I learned afterwards. My oldest recollections are knit to a rude, yet comfortable cottage, in which I lived with my father, brother, and sister. It was on the confines of one of those vast forests which cover the northern part of Germany; around it were a few acres of ground, which, during the summer months, my father cultivated, and which, though they yielded a doubtful harvest, were sufficient for our support. In the winter we remained much in doors, for, as my father followed the chase, we were left alone, and the wolves, during that season, incessantly prowled about. My father had purchased the cottage, and land about it, of one of the rude foresters, who gain their livelihood partly by hunting, and partly by burning charcoal, for the purpose of smelting the ore from the neighbouring mines; it was distant about two miles from any other habitation. I can call to mind the whole landscape now: the tall pines which rose up on the mountain above us, and the wide expanse of forest beneath, on the topmost boughs and heads of whose trees we looked down from our cottage, as the mountain below us rapidly descended into the distant valley. In summer time the prospect was beautiful; but during the severe winter, a more desolate scene could not well be imagined.

I said that, in the winter, my father occupied himself with the chase; every day he left us, and often would he lock the door, that we might not leave the cottage. He had no one to assist him, or to take care of us—indeed, it was not easy to find a female servant who would live in such a solitude; but, could he have found one, my father would not have received her, for he had imbibed a horror of the sex, as a difference of his conduct toward us, his two boys, and my poor little sister, Marcella, evidently proved. You may suppose we were sadly neglected; indeed, we suffered much, for my father, fearful that we might come to some harm, would not allow us fuel, when he left the cottage; and we were obliged, therefore, to creep under the heaps of bears'-skins, and there to keep ourselves as warm as we could until he returned in the evening, when a blazing fire was our delight. That my father chose this restless sort of life may appear strange, but the fact was that he could not remain quiet; whether from remorse for having committed murder, or from the misery consequent on his change of situation, or from both combined, he was never happy unless he was in a state of activity. Children, however, when left much to themselves, acquire a thoughtfulness not common to their age. So it was with us; and during the short cold days of winter we would sit silent, longing for the happy hours when the snow would melt, and the leaves burst out, and the birds begin their songs, and when we should again be set at liberty.

Such was our peculiar and savage sort of life until my brother Cæsar was nine, myself seven, and my sister five, years old, when the circumstances occurred on which is based the extraordinary narrative which I am about to relate.

One evening my father returned home rather later than usual; he had been unsuccessful, and, as the weather was very severe, and many feet of snow were upon the ground, he was not only very cold, but in a very bad humour. He had brought in wood, and we were all three of us gladly assisting each other in blowing on the embers to create the blaze, when he caught poor little Marcella by the arm and threw her aside; the child fell, struck her mouth, and bled very much. My brother ran to raise her up. Accustomed to ill usage, and afraid of my father, she did not dare to cry, but looked up in his face very piteously. My father drew his stool nearer to the hearth, muttered something in abuse of women, and busied himself with the fire, which both my brother and I had deserted when our sister was so unkindly treated. A cheerful blaze was soon the result of his exertions; but we did not, as usual, crowd round it. Marcella, still bleeding, retired to a corner, and my brother and I took our seats beside her, while my father hung over the fire gloomily and alone. Such had been our position for about half-an-hour, when the howl of a wolf, close under the window of the cottage, fell on our ears. My father started up, and seized his gun; the howl was repeated, he examined the priming, and then hastily left the cottage, shutting the door after him. We all waited (anxiously listening), for we thought that if he succeeded in shooting the wolf, he would return in a better humour; and although he was harsh to all of us, and particularly so to our little sister, still we loved our father, and loved to see him cheerful and happy, for what else had we to look up to? And I may here observe, that perhaps there never were three children who were fonder of each other; we did not, like other children, fight and dispute together; and if, by chance, any disagreement did arise between my elder brother and me, little Marcella would run to us, and kissing us both, seal, through her entreaties, the peace between us. Marcella was a lovely, amiable child; I can recall her beautiful features even now—Alas! poor little Marcella.

We waited for some time, but the report of the gun did not reach us, and my elder brother then said, "Our father has followed the wolf, and will not be back for some time. Marcella, let us wash the blood from your mouth, and then we will leave this corner, and go to the fire and warm ourselves."

We did so, and remained there until near midnight, every minute wondering, as it grew later, why our father did not return. We had no idea that he was in any danger, but we thought that he must have chased the wolf for a very long time. "I will look out and see if father is coming," said my brother Cæsar, going to the door. "Take care," said Marcella, "the wolves must be about now, and we cannot kill them, brother." My brother opened the door very cautiously, and but a few inches; he peeped out.—"I see nothing," said he, after a time, and once more he joined us at the fire. "We have had no supper," said I, for my father usually cooked the meat as soon as he came home; and during his absence we had nothing but the fragments of the preceding day.

"And if our father comes home after his hunt, Cæsar," said Marcella, "he will be pleased to have some supper; let us cook it for him and for ourselves." Cæsar climbed upon the stool, and reached down some meat—I forget now whether it was venison or bear's meat; but we cut off the usual quantity, and proceeded to dress it, as we used to do under our father's superintendence. We were all busied putting it into the platters before the fire, to await his coming, when we heard the sound of a horn. We listened—there was a noise outside, and a minute afterwards my father entered, ushering in a young female, and a large dark man in a hunter's dress.

Perhaps I had better now relate, what was only known to me many years afterwards. When my father had left the cottage, he perceived a large white wolf about thirty yards from him; as soon as the animal saw my father, it retreated slowly, growling and snarling. My father followed; the animal did not run, but always kept at some distance; and my father did not like to fire until he was pretty certain that his ball would take effect: thus they went on for some time, the wolf now leaving my father far behind, and then stopping and snarling defiance at him, and then again, on his approach, setting off at speed.

Anxious to shoot the animal (for the white wolf is very rare), my father continued the pursuit for several hours, during which he continually ascended the mountain.

You must know that there are peculiar spots on those mountains which are supposed, and, as my story will prove, truly supposed, to be inhabited by the evil influences; they are well known to the huntsmen, who invariably avoid them. Now, one of these spots, an open space in the pine forests above us, had been pointed out to my father as dangerous on that account. But, whether he disbelieved these wild stories, or whether, in his eager pursuit of the chase, he disregarded them, I know not; certain, however, it is that he was decoyed by the white wolf to this open space, when the animal appeared to slacken her speed. My father approached, came close up to her, raised his gun to his shoulder, and was about to fire, when the wolf suddenly disappeared. He thought that the snow on the ground must have dazzled his sight, and he let down his gun to look for the beast—but she was gone; how she could have escaped over the clearance, without his seeing her, was beyond his comprehension. Mortified at the ill success of his chase, he was about to retrace his steps, when he heard the distant sound of a horn. Astonishment at such a sound—at such an hour—in such a wilderness, made him forget for the moment his disappointment, and he remained riveted to the spot. In a minute the horn was blown a second time, and at no great distance; my father stood still, and listened: a third time it was blown. I forget the term used to express it, but it was the signal which, my father well knew, implied that the party was lost in the woods. In a few minutes more my father beheld a man on horseback, with a female seated on the crupper, enter the cleared space, and ride up to him. At first, my father called to mind the strange stories which he had heard of the supernatural beings who were said to frequent these mountains; but the nearer approach of the parties satisfied him that they were mortals like himself. As soon as they came up to him, the man who guided the horse accosted him. "Friend Hunter, you are out late, the better fortune for us: we have ridden far, and are in fear of our lives, which are eagerly sought after. These mountains have enabled us to elude our pursuers; but if we find not shelter and refreshment, that will avail us little, as we must perish from hunger and the inclemency of the night. My daughter, who rides behind me, is now more dead than alive—say, can you assist us in our difficulty?"

"My cottage is some few miles distant," replied my father, "but I have little to offer you besides a shelter from the weather; to the little I have you are welcome. May I ask whence you come?"

"Yes, friend, it is no secret now; we have escaped from Transylvania, where my daughter's honour and my life were equally in jeopardy!"

This information was quite enough to raise an interest in my father's heart. He remembered his own escape: he remembered the loss of his wife's honour, and the tragedy by which it was wound up. He immediately, and warmly, offered all the assistance which he could afford them.

"There is no time to be lost, then, good sir," observed the horseman; "my daughter is chilled with the frost, and cannot hold out much longer against the severity of the weather."

"Follow me," replied my father, leading the way towards his home.

"I was lured away in pursuit of a large white wolf," observed my father; "it came to the very window of my hut, or I should not have been out at this time of night."

"The creature passed by us just as we came out of the wood," said the female in a silvery tone.

"I was nearly discharging my piece at it," observed the hunter; "but since it did us such good service, I am glad that I allowed it to escape."

In about an hour and a half, during which my father walked at a rapid pace, the party arrived at the cottage, and, as I said before, came in.

"We are in good time, apparently," observed the dark hunter, catching the smell of the roasted meat, as he walked to the fire and surveyed my brother and sister, and myself. "You have young cooks here, Mynheer." "I am glad that we shall not have to wait," replied my father. "Come, mistress, seat yourself by the fire; you require warmth after your cold ride." "And where can I put up my horse, Mynheer?" observed the huntsman. "I will take care of him," replied my father, going out of the cottage door.

The female must, however, be particularly described. She was young, and apparently twenty years of age. She was dressed in a travelling dress, deeply bordered with white fur, and wore a cap of white ermine on her head. Her features were very beautiful, at least I thought so, and so my father has since declared. Her hair was flaxen, glossy and shining, and bright as a mirror; and her mouth, although somewhat large when it was open, showed the most brilliant teeth I have ever beheld. But there was something about her eyes, bright as they were, which made us children afraid; they were so restless, so furtive; I could not at that time tell why, but I felt as if there was cruelty in her eye; and when she beckoned us to come to her, we approached her with fear and trembling. Still she was beautiful, very beautiful. She spoke kindly to my brother and myself, patted our heads, and caressed us; but Marcella would not come near her; on the contrary, she slunk away, and hid herself in the bed, and would not wait for the supper, which half an hour before she had been so anxious for.

My father, having put the horse into a close shed, soon returned, and supper was placed upon the table. When it was over, my father requested that the young lady would take possession of his bed, and he would remain at the fire, and sit up with her father. After some hesitation on her part, this arrangement was agreed to, and I and my brother crept into the other bed with Marcella, for we had as yet always slept together.

But we could not sleep; there was something so unusual, not only in seeing strange people, but in having those people sleep at the cottage, that we were bewildered. As for poor little Marcella, she was quiet, but I perceived that she trembled during the whole night, and sometimes I thought that she was checking a sob. My father had brought out some spirits, which he rarely used, and he and the strange hunter remained drinking and talking before the fire. Our ears were ready to catch the slightest whisper—so much was our curiosity excited.

"You said you came from Transylvania?" observed my father.

"Even so, Mynheer," replied the hunter. "I was a serf to the noble house of—; my master would insist upon my surrendering up my fair girl to his wishes; it ended in my giving him a few inches of my hunting-knife."

"We are countrymen, and brothers in misfortune," replied my father, taking the huntsman's hand, and pressing it warmly.

"Indeed! Are you, then, from that country?"

"Yes; and I too have fled for my life. But mine is a melancholy tale."

"Your name?" inquired the hunter.

"Krantz."

"What! Krantz of—I have heard your tale; you need not renew your grief by repeating it now. Welcome, most welcome, Mynheer, and, I may say, my worthy kinsman. I am your second cousin, Wilfred of Barnsdorf," cried the hunter, rising up and embracing my father.

They filled their horn mugs to the brim, and drank to one another, after the German fashion. The conversation was then carried on in a low tone; all that we could collect from it was, that our new relative and his daughter were to take up their abode in our cottage, at least for the present. In about an hour they both fell back in their chairs, and appeared to sleep.

"Marcella, dear, did you hear?" said my brother in a low tone.

"Yes," replied Marcella, in a whisper; "I heard all. Oh! brother, I cannot bear to look upon that woman—I feel so frightened."

My brother made no reply, and shortly afterwards we were all three fast asleep.

When we awoke the next morning, we found that the hunter's daughter had risen before us. I thought she looked more beautiful than ever. She came up to little Marcella and caressed her; the child burst into tears, and sobbed as if her heart would break.

But, not to detain you with too long a story, the huntsman and his daughter were accommodated in the cottage. My father and he went out hunting daily, leaving Christina with us. She performed all the household duties; was very kind to us children; and, gradually, the dislike even of little Marcella wore away. But a great change took place in my father; he appeared to have conquered his aversion to the sex, and was most attentive to Christina. Often, after her father and we were in bed, would he sit up with her, conversing in a low tone by the fire. I ought to have mentioned, that my father and the huntsman Wilfred, slept in another portion of the cottage, and that the bed which he formerly occupied, and which was in the same room as ours, had been given up to the use of Christina. These visitors had been about three weeks at the cottage, when, one night, after we children had been sent to bed, a consultation was held. My father had asked Christina in marriage, and had obtained both her own consent and that of Wilfred; after this a conversation took place, which was, as nearly as I can recollect, as follows:

"You may take my child, Mynheer Krantz, and my blessing with her, and I shall then leave you and seek some other habitation—it matters little where."

"Why not remain here, Wilfred?"

"No, no, I am called elsewhere; let that suffice, and ask no more questions. You have my child."

"I thank you for her, and will duly value her; but there is one difficulty."

"I know what you would say; there is no priest here in this wild country: true, neither is there any law to bind; still must some ceremony pass between you, to satisfy a father. Will you consent to marry her after my fashion? if so, I will marry you directly."

"I will," replied my father.

"Then take her by the hand. Now, Mynheer, swear."

"I swear," repeated my father.

"By all the spirits of the Hartz Mountains—"

"Nay, why not by Heaven?" interrupted my father.

"Because it is not my humour," rejoined Wilfred; "if I prefer that oath, less binding perhaps, than another, surely you will not thwart me."

"Well, be it so then; have your humour. Will you make me swear by that in which I do not believe?"

"Yet many do so, who in outward appearance are Christians," rejoined Wilfred; "say, will you be married, or shall I take my daughter away with me?"

"Proceed," replied my father, impatiently.

"I swear by all the spirits of the Hartz Mountains, by all their power for good or for evil, that I take Christina for my wedded wife; that I will ever protect her, cherish her, and love her; that my hand shall never be raised against her to harm her."

My father repeated the words after Wilfred.

"And if I fail in this, my vow, may all the vengeance of the spirits fall upon me and upon my children; may they perish by the vulture, by the wolf, or other beasts of the forest; may their flesh be torn from their limbs, and their bones blanch in the wilderness; all this I swear."

My father hesitated, as he repeated the last words; little Marcella could not restrain herself, and as my father repeated the last sentence, she burst into tears. This sudden interruption appeared to discompose the party, particularly my father; he spoke harshly to the child, who controlled her sobs, burying her face under the bed-clothes.

Such was the second marriage of my father. The next morning, the hunter Wilfred mounted his horse and rode away.

My father resumed his bed, which was in the same room as ours; and things went on much as before the marriage, except that our new mother-in-law did not show any kindness towards us; indeed, during my father's absence, she would often beat us, particularly little Marcella, and her eyes would flash fire, as she looked eagerly upon the fair and lovely child.

One night, my sister awoke me and my brother.

"What is the matter?" said Cæsar.

"She has gone out," whispered Marcella.

"Gone out!"

"Yes, gone out at the door, in her night-clothes," replied the child; "I saw her get out of bed, look at my father to see if he slept, and then she went out at the door."

What could induce her to leave her bed, and all undressed to go out, in such bitter wintry weather, with the snow deep on the ground, was to us incomprehensible; we lay awake, and in about an hour we heard the growl of a wolf, close under the window.

"There is a wolf," said Cæsar, "she will be torn to pieces."

"Oh, no!" cried Marcella.

In a few minutes afterwards our mother-in-law appeared; she was in her night-dress, as Marcella had stated. She let down the latch of the door, so as to make no noise, went to a pail of water, and washed her face and hands, and then slipped into the bed where my father lay.

We all three trembled, we hardly knew why, but we resolved to watch the next night: we did so—and not only on the ensuing night, but on many others, and always at about the same hour, would our mother-in-law rise from her bed, and leave the cottage—and after she was gone, we invariably heard the growl of a wolf under our window, and always saw her, on her return, wash herself before she retired to bed. We observed, also, that she seldom sat down to meals, and that when she did, she appeared to eat with dislike; but when the meat was taken down, to be prepared for dinner, she would often furtively put a raw piece into her mouth.

My brother Cæsar was a courageous boy; he did not like to speak to my father until he knew more. He resolved that he would follow her out, and ascertain what she did. Marcella and I endeavoured to dissuade him from this project; but he would not be controlled, and, the very next night he lay down in his clothes, and as soon as our mother-in-law had left the cottage, he jumped up, took down my father's gun, and followed her.

You may imagine in what a state of suspense Marcella and I remained, during his absence. After a few minutes, we heard the report of a gun. It did not awaken my father, and we lay trembling with anxiety. In a minute afterwards we saw our mother-in-law enter the cottage—her dress was bloody. I put my hand to Marcella's mouth to prevent her crying out, although I was myself in great alarm. Our mother-in-law approached my father's bed, looked to see if he was asleep, and then went to the chimney, and blew up the embers into a blaze.

"Who is there?" said my father, waking up.

"Lie still, dearest," replied my mother-in-law, "it is only me; I have lighted the fire to warm some water; I am not quite well."

My father turned round and was soon asleep; but we watched our mother-in-law. She changed her linen, and threw the garments she had worn into the fire; and we then perceived that her right leg was bleeding profusely, as if from a gun-shot wound. She bandaged it up, and then dressing herself, remained before the fire until the break of day.

Poor little Marcella, her heart beat quick as she pressed me to her side—so indeed did mine. Where was our brother, Cæsar? How did my mother-in-law receive the wound unless from his gun? At last my father rose, and then, for the first time I spoke, saying, "Father, where is my brother, Cæsar?"

"Your brother!" exclaimed he, "why, where can he be?"

"Merciful Heaven! I thought as I lay very restless last night," observed our mother-in-law, "that I heard somebody open the latch of the door; and, dear me, husband, what has become of your gun?"

My father cast his eyes up above the chimney, and perceived that his gun was missing. For a moment he looked perplexed, then seizing a broad axe, he went out of the cottage without saying another word.

He did not remain away from us long: in a few minutes he returned, bearing in his arms the mangled body of my poor brother; he laid it down, and covered up his face.

My mother-in-law rose up, and looked at the body, while Marcella and I threw ourselves by its side wailing and sobbing bitterly.

"Go to bed again, children," said she sharply. "Husband," continued she, "your boy must have taken the gun down to shoot a wolf, and the animal has been too powerful for him. Poor boy! He has paid dearly for his rashness."

My father made no reply; I wished to speak—to tell all—but Marcella, who perceived my intention, held me by the arm, and looked at me so imploringly, that I desisted.

My father, therefore, was left in his error; but Marcella and I, although we could not comprehend it, were conscious that our mother-in-law was in some way connected with my brother's death.

That day my father went out and dug a grave, and when he laid the body in the earth, he piled up stones over it, so that the wolves should not be able to dig it up. The shock of this catastrophe was to my poor father very severe; for several days he never went to the chase, although at times he would utter bitter anathemas and vengeance against the wolves.

But during this time of mourning on his part, my mother-in-law's nocturnal wanderings continued with the same regularity as before.

At last, my father took down his gun, to repair to the forest; but he soon returned, and appeared much annoyed.

"Would you believe it, Christina, that the wolves—perdition to the whole race —have actually contrived to dig up the body of my poor boy, and now there is nothing left of him but his bones?"

"Indeed!" replied my mother-in-law. Marcella looked at me, and I saw in her intelligent eye all she would have uttered.

"A wolf growls under our window every night, father," said I.

"Aye, indeed?—why did you not tell me, boy?—wake me the next time you hear it."

I saw my mother-in-law turn away; her eyes flashed fire, and she gnashed her teeth.

My father went out again, and covered up with a larger pile of stones the little remnants of my poor brother which the wolves had spared. Such was the first act of the tragedy.

The spring now came on: the snow disappeared, and we were permitted to leave the cottage; but never would I quit, for one moment, my dear little sister, to whom, since the death of my brother, I was more ardently attached than ever; indeed I was afraid to leave her alone with my mother-in-law, who appeared to have a particular pleasure in ill-treating the child. My father was now employed upon his little farm, and I was able to render him some assistance.

Marcella used to sit by us while we were at work, leaving my mother-in-law alone in the cottage. I ought to observe that, as the spring advanced, so did my mother decrease her nocturnal rambles, and that we never heard the growl of the wolf under the window after I had spoken of it to my father.

One day, when my father and I were in the field, Marcella being with us, my mother-in-law came out, saying that she was going into the forest, to collect some herbs my father wanted, and that Marcella must go to the cottage and watch the dinner. Marcella went, and my mother-in-law soon disappeared in the forest, taking a direction quite contrary to that in which the cottage stood, and leaving my father and I, as it were, between her and Marcella.

About an hour afterwards we were startled by shrieks from the cottage, evidently the shrieks of little Marcella. "Marcella has burnt herself, father," said I, throwing down my spade. My father threw down his, and we both hastened to the cottage. Before we could gain the door, out darted a large white wolf, which fled with the utmost celerity. My father had no weapon; he rushed into the cottage, and there saw poor little Marcella expiring; her body was dreadfully mangled, and the blood pouring from it had formed a large pool on the cottage floor. My father's first intention had been to seize his gun and pursue, but he was checked by this horrid spectacle; he knelt down by his dying child, and burst into tears: Marcella could just look kindly on us for a few seconds, and then her eyes were closed in death.

My father and I were still hanging over my poor sister's body, when my mother-in-law came in. At the dreadful sight she expressed much concern, but she did not appear to recoil from the sight of blood, as most women do.

"Poor child!" said she, "it must have been that great white wolf which passed me just now, and frightened me so—she's quite dead, Krantz."

"I know it—I know it!" cried my father in agony.

I thought my father would never recover from the effects of this second tragedy: he mourned bitterly over the body of his sweet child, and for several days would not consign it to its grave, although frequently requested by my mother-in-law to do so. At last he yielded, and dug a grave for her close by that of my poor brother, and took every precaution that the wolves should not violate her remains.

I was now really miserable, as I lay alone in the bed which I had formerly shared with my brother and sister. I could not help thinking that my mother-in-law was implicated in both their deaths, although I could not account for the manner; but I no longer felt afraid of her: my little heart was full of hatred and revenge.

The night after my sister had been buried, as I lay awake, I perceived my mother-in-law get up and go out of the cottage. I waited for some time, then dressed myself, and looked out through the door, which I half-opened. The moon shone bright, and I could see the spot where my brother and my sister had been buried; and what was my horror, when I perceived my mother-in-law busily removing the stones from Marcella's grave.

She was in her white night-dress, and the moon shone full upon her. She was digging with her hands, and throwing away the stones behind her with all the ferocity of a wild beast. It was some time before I could collect my senses and decide what I should do. At last, I perceived that she had arrived at the body, and raised it up to the side of the grave. I could bear it no longer; I ran to my father and awoke him.

"Father! father!" cried I, "dress yourself, and get your gun."

"What!" cried my father, "the wolves are there, are they?"

He jumped out of bed, threw on his clothes, and in his anxiety did not appear to perceive the absence of his wife. As soon as he was ready, I opened the door, he went out, and I followed him.

Imagine his horror, when (unprepared as he was for such a sight) he beheld, as he advanced towards the grave, not a wolf, but his wife, in her night-dress, on her hands and knees, crouching by the body of my sister, and tearing off large pieces of the flesh, and devouring them with all the avidity of a wolf. She was too busy to be aware of our approach. My father dropped his gun, his hair stood on end; so did mine; he breathed heavily, and then his breath for a time stopped. I picked up the gun and put it into his hand. Suddenly he appeared as if concentrated rage had restored him to double vigour; he levelled his piece, fired, and with a loud shriek, down fell the wretch whom he had fostered in his bosom.

"God of Heaven!" cried my father, sinking down upon the earth in a swoon, as soon as he had discharged his gun.

I remained some time by his side before he recovered. "Where am I?" said he, "what has happened?—Oh!—yes, yes! I recollect now. Heaven forgive me!"

He rose and we walked up to the grave; what again was our astonishment and horror to find that instead of the dead body of my mother-in-law, as we expected, there was lying over the remains of my poor sister, a large, white she wolf.

"The white wolf!" exclaimed my father, "the white wolf which decoyed me into the forest—I see it all now—I have dealt with the spirits of the Hartz Mountains."

For some time my father remained in silence and deep thought. He then carefully lifted up the body of my sister, replaced it in the grave, and covered it over as before, having struck the head of the dead animal with the heel of his boot, and raving like a madman. He walked back to the cottage, shut the door, and threw himself on the bed; I did the same, for I was in a stupor of amazement.

Early in the morning we were both roused by a loud knocking at the door, and in rushed the hunter Wilfred.

"My daughter!—man—my daughter!—where is my daughter!" cried he in a rage.

"Where the wretch, the fiend, should be, I trust," replied my father, starting up and displaying equal choler; "where she should be—in hell!—Leave this cottage or you may fare worse."

"Ha-ha!" replied the hunter, "would you harm a potent spirit of the Hartz Mountains? Poor mortal, who must needs wed a were wolf."

"Out, demon! I defy thee and thy power."

"Yet shall you feel it; remember your oath—your solemn oath—never to raise your hand against her to harm her."

"I made no compact with evil spirits."

"You did; and if you failed in your vow, you were to meet the vengeance of the spirits. Your children were to perish by the vulture, the wolf—"

"Out, out, demon!"

"And their bones blanch in the wilderness. Ha!-ha!"

My father, frantic with rage, seized his axe, and raised it over Wilfred's head to strike.

"All this I swear," continued the huntsman, mockingly.

The axe descended; but it passed through the form of the hunter, and my father lost his balance, and fell heavily on the floor.

"Mortal!" said the hunter, striding over my father's body, "we have power over those only who have committed murder. You have been guilty of a double murder—you shall pay the penalty attached to your marriage vow. Two of your children are gone; the third is yet to follow—and follow them he will, for your oath is registered. Go—it were kindness to kill thee—your punishment is—that you live!"

THE GHOST AT POINT OF ROCKS,
by Frank H. Spearman

As for the country—there is really no end of country around Point of Rocks. When Hughie Morrison asked about the station after he had been assigned to it, he was told that on the north his territory would extend to the pole. He was assured that he would find very little of the country in any direction competitive, and, in matter of fact, he never did find any, though Martin Duffy at one time advised him to circularize the Eskimos with a view of securing any portion of their cold-storage business that might be getting away from Jim Hill.

On the south, while there was no competition in sight, there was even less of business. The southern country for three thousand miles stood on end—at least so Hughie concluded after he had climbed the peak of Point of Rocks to look the field over and make a preliminary traffic survey. After he had climbed down he wrote to his mother that if arrangements could be made to ship all the scenery out of his territory and ship all the unassigned rainbows in, it would make a great farming country. Answering her affectionate inquiries from the East, he wrote that he was making money fast; that he feared, at the moment, to ship it in large sums out of the country, but that she need feel no anxiety; he really had the rocks and would show them to her when she came out.

Point of Rocks has been called everything that is bad because of its reputation for loneliness. The point, a mere speck on a spreading map, set far and singly out on the high seas of the railroad desert, was the dread of all operators on the mountain division, and Hughie Morrison was the first night man sent there after the panic. When there were but two passenger trains a day on the division, and the Government receivers were objecting to these, Hughie, with the rattlesnakes and a worn-out key, was holding down Point of Rocks. Before he and the day man were sent, the Point had long been abandoned. One building, the section house, stood half a mile east of the station, and in this the section men hived. Other than these no human beings lived within miles of Hughie. To the north stretched the forgotten land, on the west rose the point monstrous, and to the south, generally speaking, hell prevailed.

To this spot President Bucks had sent his nephew, Hugh Morrison, to learn the railroad business. Hughie was a Princeton man when he asked his uncle to come through with some sort of job; and his uncle, at that time reorganizing the system, and having troubles of his own, was not disposed to take on any family difficulties. He merely passed the word to Martin Duffy, chief dispatcher at Medicine Bend, to put Hughie through. Accordingly the Princeton man, who had turned twenty, could count to a hundred, and knew that the Rocky Mountains were surrounded by land, was brought to the Mountain Division. Martin soon saw that he could not get rid of Hughie merely by putting him through. Hughie learned the key with facility, ate what was set before him, and looked pleasant when the railroad men set up jobs. Worst of all, Martin Duffy found that he was beginning to like the green one. But orders were orders. Bucks had said Hughie was to be put through, and there was nothing more merciful to Martin's mind for the boy than a quick railroad death. Martin considered that in such a case strong medicine is best, and well knew that to assign a man to a night job at Point of Rocks was equivalent to the knock-out drops.

Hughie never blanched when the orders came. Why should he? He did not know Point of Rocks from Colorado Springs, and made his preparations and departed promptly for the new post. When he asked Duffy where he should board, Martin, a taciturn man, said he might board in Texas if he liked, provided he could make the hours for the job.

Hughie took hold, and the fun began. The trainmen bullied him, called him Hughie and "Nephew," stole his cigars, and made him glad to be left alone with the night, the desert, the coyotes, and the stars. Hughie got used to looking for the constellations of his youth, and to know for a certainty that Orion, calm and immensely dignified, would never fail him and that between freight trains about three o'clock in the morning the red heart of the Scorpion in the south-west could always be counted on, was a mild sort of consolation. Poling at Princeton, they had made, at three in the morning, no impression on him; at Point of Rocks there were absolutely no other associations to suggest God's country.

Besides these there was, in matter of fact, nothing and nobody within measurable distance of the night man. Hughie was a good bit of a philosopher; but even among those of the railroad men who had never been east of the Missouri River a shift from Princeton to Point of Rocks was commonly conceded to be a fright.

When Hugh was told that at one time a colony had existed at Point of Rocks he was unbelieving. Yet an Englishman, fascinated in an earlier day by the mountains, had chosen the wildest spot between Medicine Bend and Bear Dance for a cattle-ranch, and his shipping yards were put in at Point of Rocks. He built for himself in the hills east of the station a great brick house. Deserted and in the slow decay of loneliness, it had stood long after the downfall of his hopes, to serve while a vagrant army of prospectors moved across the country as a quarry for the hammer and chisel of their camp-fires. After they had left it naked in its ruin to the elements it had been struck by lightning and burned. Yet after all of this the house stood. Built in stanch English fashion, its walls remained, and scarred and roofless its height and strength still defied the sun and the sand and the wind.

At one time the Englishman had a hundred men working on his ranches. He founded a colony, planned an abattoir, rode like a fiend, and drank like an engine. The beginning had been ten years before Hughie's day, the end perhaps five. A sheep-herder knew the story. Sitting on the ground one night beside the passing track, a full-moon night with the white streaming through the sightless windows of the ruin on the hill, he had told Hughie about the Swintons—Richard and the bachelor brother John—Hughie, silent, in his belted trousers and bare arms, standing while the wind blew softly, with his back and one foot against the station building, listening.

Once in a month, out of the dreadful south, the sheep-herder, a lost man with sand-burned eyes and sun-split lips, came to hear a human voice. He was the sole caller on the college man at Point of Rocks.

The sheep-herder was pointing in the moonlight to the east. "Dick Swinton built yards from the switch away over to the creek, and from there down to the curve."

"Yards?" echoed Hughie incredulously.

"Cattle yards. He had a barn five hundred feet long the other side of the draw for his Holsteins; another big barn over there to the right for a string of thorough-breds. He run his horses in Denver and Colorado Springs. The whole family used to go down there summers—had a house down at the Springs nigh as big as this one. Mrs. Swinton, she was the thoroughbred, and the governess and the boy and the little girl—she had her own maid—used to go down regular with the China-boy cook and all hands, private car. I seen twenty-two trunks to one time piled up right there where you stand—oh, they were blooded, all right. Champagne right along from New York, twelve cases at a lick, piled up here for the wagons, when their cousins come out from the old country. All gone to hell. Was you ever in England?"

Hughie used to think about the story. He never tired of hearing about the Swintons. They were people, and had done things on a scale, and being the only interest, living or dead, about Point of Rocks, they were naturally matter for re-flection. What if they had sunk their money? They had sunk it royally. The east-bound passenger train was not due to pass Point of Rocks until midnight, and from then until four thirty o'clock in the morning, when the west-bound train was due, the operator had abundance of time to think. Even from sunset until midnight all alone under the lamp in the station, reading, perhaps, or writing, was a good bit of a stretch. But after Hughie got acquainted with the weather-warped sheep-herder he found something to look forward to in the night at Point of Rocks—he was waiting for a storm.

"Wait till you get a good thunder-storm some night," the sheep-herder had muttered. "Then watch them windows over on the hill—you'll see dancing over there yet; I seen it since the house was burned, right along." When he spoke, he was telling of the big dances he remembered in the brick house at times that the New Yorkers and the English cousins came out in the car. The sheep-herder be-lieved that when it stormed in the mountains they still danced through the floor-less halls. Hughie wanted to ask a lot more questions when he heard of this: it was a story different from the others. But the passenger train in the west was whistling, and when it had come and gone the sheep-herder had disappeared. He blew in from the south like the wind, and died as silently away.

Night after night Hughie waited for him to come back; night after night, at sunset, he scanned the vanishing point of the track, looking in vain for the stunted figure and the sidewise, twisted shamble. The silence of the place with the long hours of twilight and dark outside his window began to grow on Hughie, and one evening he walked across the creek for a change and up the hill to the ruin.

He had not realized before how large the house had been. Standing under the brick entrance arch where double doors had enclosed a deep vestibule, he saw how heavily every part of the house was built. The timbers that had crashed through the floors when the roof fell were like bridge stringers. The floors them-selves had been framed like decks, and their charred debris lay in a forbidding tangle just as the storm drowning the conflagration had left it. The blackened walls gaped; the parting light streamed through vacant casements, and above the arches of the tower—which had suffered least from the fire—stars twinkled. The desolation was complete.

He climbed into the tower. A stairway still remained, and, climbing higher, he found intact a half-story, once a child's playroom. Prints pasted on the walls hung in tatters. A little scrap-heap of rusty tin cars lay under the window opening. The sheep-herder had said the little girl was wild about engines and often used to ride with the enginemen on the passenger trains when the family were travelling. In a corner Hughie saw a Japanese doll, weather-beaten, but still lying where it had been left to its last sleep, with a battered locomotive for pillow. The frock was faded, and the pink cheeks and almond brows of the doll were blanched. He stooped to lift it from its long nap and something fell from its bosom. Hughie picked the something up. It was a broken ivory miniature, but the colors cunningly laid in still preserved the features of a little girl. Nearly half of the oval had been broken away, but the child's face remained. Under his lamp that night, Hughie examined it. Brown hair fell over the temples and the high cheeks were touched with pink. The eyes deep-set and the nose straight and determined, looked boyish, but below it the face narrowed to a mere dimple of a girl's mouth; the chin was gone.

That night the east-bound train was an hour late. The operator, idle in his solitude, studied the miniature. He wanted to know more about the children that had played in the tower and ridden the desert on their ponies—he had heard something about it—and wished continually for the sheep-herder to come back. The old fellow had been gone this time for weeks. While Hughie was reflecting, the train whistled, and he was still in a study when the engineman, Oliver Sollers, walked into the office for orders.

"I struck a man tonight, Hughie," said Oliver, sitting down as he drew off his heavy gloves.

"Where?"

"Somewhere the other side of Castle Creek. He's back in the baggage-car. I didn't see him. It's bad luck, too, to strike a man that you don't see; leastwise, it never happened to me before. He must have been walking ahead of us, I guess, and the pilot picked him up. When we stopped at Castle Creek for water I got down to oil around and found him on the front end. He was an old man, too," added the engineman moodily. "We will have to leave him here with you, Hughie, for Number One to take back to Sleepy Cat. Well, it can't be helped. Got any orders, boy?"

The trainmen brought in the body. They laid it on the waiting-room floor and Hughie, busy with his orders, did not look at the man. After the train pulled out and the dull red of the tail-lights had disappeared in the east he sat down under his lamp at the window table, the telegraph key in front of him clicking vagrant messages, to wait a few minutes before stepping out of the office to close the waiting-room door. The door was left open at night, but tonight it must not be, because the coyotes had long noses for blood. When Hughie went at length to bolt the outside door he took the lamp in his hand and, coming back, stooped to lift the newspaper from the dead man's face. It was the sheep-herder.

The operator let the newspaper drop. He went slowly back into the office. He remembered now that he had never asked the man his name. If he knew it he could perhaps notify relatives somewhere—at the very least supply a name to go on the coffin.

Dismiss the shock as he would, he realized that he was unnerved. He sat down with his head in his hands, thinking over it, when he heard thunder in the mountains; the sky had been overcast when the train pulled in. Soon rain began to fall in great drops on the roof above his head, and within a few moments in the land of no rain it was raining a flood. For a long time the storm hung above the peaks in the Mission range. Presently the wind shifted and shook the little station building with a yelp. Then, with the shock of an earthquake, the lightning claps of a cloudburst, and the pent-up fury of a long, dry summer, down came the storm from the high mountains.

The wind whipped the water in sheets against the window-panes, and little gusts, exploding in the downpour, rattled the sash viciously. If the wind abated the rain plunged on the roof, and when it blew, water poured in at every joint and crevice of the dried-out building. Hughie turned down the lamp, cut in the light-ning arrester, and sat down with his hands in his pockets.

He knew now what the sheep-herder had meant when he talked of a storm. The lightning ceased to crash very soon and the thunder that shook the earth for a few moments abated, but great electric waves played almost silently and in a terrifying way through the deluge of falling rain. The desert rippled and swam in the dance of waters, the far mountains were strangely lighted, and above them distant thunder moaned unceasingly.

Hughie unaffectedly wished himself away from Point of Rocks. He swore mentally but savagely at everything about the place except his dead companion, and when he could sit still no longer he began to walk around with his hands in his pockets. As he passed the waiting-room door he saw that the rain was driving in at the open window above the head of the sheep-herder. He resisted an inclina-tion to turn away, for the window ought to be closed. Above the roar of the rain he heard now through the open sash the roar of the water foaming down Dry Bit-ter Creek. Hughie walked out into the dark waiting-room to close the window. As he stepped toward it he saw the play of the storm in the ruin on the hill.

From the heavens to the horizon the naked basin of the desert trembled in the shock of the storm. Through the deluge great curtains of light, shot from horizon to horizon, threw the landscape up in fanciful, quivering pictures. Water leaped on arid slopes, hills floated in falling rivers, rain fell in never-ending sheets, and above all played the incessant blaze of the maddened sky and the long roll of the far and sullen thunder.

He looked at the old house. Like a lamp set within a skull, lightning burned and played about it. Through the casements he saw the staring walls lighted again. The words of the dead sheep-herder came back and he waited for graceful figures to weave past the burning windows to the trembling rhythm of the storm. He stood only for a moment. Then he lowered the sash, stepped away from the dead man and going back into the office, sat down at his table with his head be-tween his hands.

Chapter II

The chief dispatcher, Martin Duffy—this is the same man who is digging the Panama Canal—called Hughie up on the wire and began talking with him as soon as he received his letter of resignation. "You don't know your own mind," declared Martin Duffy, sending his annoyance fast, because the furtive liking he had for the boy made him the more solicitous. "Take off your head and pound it, Hughie. Your uncle won't like this. You are in line for a better thing. Just as soon as we can get a man to take Point of Rocks you are to come in and take an East-end trick under me. I've been keeping it as a surprise. Just hold your horses thirty days, and see what will happen."

"It may well be," returned Hughie over the wire in dry reply, "but that is just the point: I don't want anything to happen—leastwise, not anything at Point of Rocks."

"Hold your horses thirty days, will you?" retorted Martin Duffy, who when incensed always said "horses" with a hiss.

"I can hold my horses for thirty days," returned Hughie, always impudent and already clever at a key, "but who will hold them for thirty nights? Forty-second Street and slavery for life for mine, Mr. Duffy, if I can't get away from this job."

However, Hughie held on as he had been told to and nothing whatever happened either at Point of Rocks or elsewhere. But he realized uncomfortably that Point of Rocks was getting on his nerves, and when the desert really does get on a man's nerves, it is time to get out. He was already conscious that he was overstaying his leave, and but for Duffy he never could have been persuaded to hang on. The nights grew lonelier and lonelier. But just as they had become unbearable he got the long-awaited reprieve—orders to report at Medicine Bend on the 1st of September for the dispatcher's trick. It was then the 30th of August.

Since the storm the desert nights had seemed never so peaceful. Hughie felt ashamed of himself almost as soon as he knew he was going to leave. For nearly a month there had not been a cloud in the evening sky—just the clear lilies or roses of the sunset streaming into a high salmon field; then, purple; gray patches of dusk, and over all a lighting of stars.

At dawn it was the very same: one morning prettier than the other. Hughie began to realize he should lose something in leaving the desert. That night, the last but one, he was sneakingly sorry to go. The whole evening went to getting up his reports, and when he looked at the clock the east-bound passenger was due. Hughie had no orders for it, but the engineman stopped that night to tighten a nut, and the conductor came in to congratulate the boy on his promotion; also to give him a cigar instead of stealing one, and to beg Hughie to remember him when he came into the seats of the mighty—not to leave him lying out long hours at Point of Rocks on cold nights waiting for orders. Hughie had already promised everybody the best of every thing, and after the conductor signaled and the long string of Pullmans drew past the station into the eastern night, he watched the lights vanish upon the distant tangent feeling content with himself and the world.

Chapter III

The lamp had burned bad all evening. After the train was gone Hughie stopped poking at the wick. His reports were up and signed, and he had finished a long letter home when he remembered that in his report to the express company he had forgotten, under the head of "Unusual Incidents," to note the death of the sheep-herder and the fact of the body's being brought in to the station and left all night in the waiting-room. By keeping a record of such events the company sometimes developed clues to thefts, robberies, and other unpleasant happenings. While Hughie felt certain that there could be no after-clap to this affair, since the dead man had been taken away and duly buried, it was a part of the routine work to make up the record, and he began a brief account of the matter.

As he wrote, the night of the death came back. The storm presented itself, and so vividly that he hesitated at times for words. His thoughts crowded fast one on another. It was what there was in his recollections to leave out that bothered him; things indefinable but things creepy to think about. He stopped his writing for a moment and took the chimney from the lamp to poke the ill wick with his pen. Through the open doors the south wind, fanning the uncertain flame, caused it to flare suddenly, and as he put back the chimney he heard the office door behind him close. The wind often closed or opened the door and the south wind was a kindly companion, blowing for hours together with the same gentle swiftness over the desert wastes. Hughie wrote the last words of his report. Just as he pressed the blotter down upon the signature he became aware of an odd sensation; an impression that he was no longer alone in the room.

He passed his fingers mechanically across the blotter-pad waiting for the impression to pass. Instead, an almost imperceptible shiver ran up his back. He rubbed the blotter more firmly, almost officiously, but with the growing conviction that someone else was in the room, and soon the difficulty was to stop the rubbing. When he did lay the pad aside a faint moisture suffused his forehead. He wanted then to open the door that he had heard close, but to do it he should be compelled to turn around. This required an effort, and he tried to summon the resolve. He looked at the lamp—it burned brightly. The moisture cooled on his forehead; the signature he had just blotted lay under his eyes. He recognized it perfectly and felt sure he was awake. He was even conscious that his hands were growing cold, and he put them up to his head; what it cost mentally to do even this surprised him. He could not look around. He attempted to whistle softly and had almost shamed himself out of a fear he felt to be ridiculous when he was stunned by a voice at his very side: "Should you like to have your grave dug out here under the stars?"

The words were distinct. Hughie froze to his chair. If the tones were soft they were perfectly clear, and the words were already stamped on his consciousness. What did it mean? Could it be the voice of a living creature? Of a woman? No woman lived within twenty miles of Point of Rocks—no living creature with a voice such as that within a hundred miles. He heard it again:

"Your grave will be under the stars." Hughie's fingers moved, but beyond that he sat paralyzed, and his tongue clove dry to the roof of his mouth. He knew now that an unreal presence had come upon him. He knew, too, that in the mountains men went mad of mere loneliness, and faint with horror, he clutched his temples, waiting every instant for reason to leave.

"The stars are singing for us tonight." With these words, spoken softly and almost in his ear, something touched his shoulder. The touch went through him like needles, and he sprang like a madman from his chair.

He whirled and cried out in a cracked voice. A figure shrank quickly away—a woman's figure, seemingly, with a shadowy face and loosened hair. When he could realize that he really saw something the head was averted and he could remember only a glimpse of startled eyes. The apparition, with hands outstretched, was moving toward the door. He heard a suppressed utterance, "I cannot find my grave."

The voice was too human. "Who are you?" cried the operator in desperation. "Why are you here?"

"I cannot find my grave."

"I—I haven't got it," stammered Hughie, with hair on end.

The figure shrank farther away. In the dim light he could see outlines of loosened draperies and falling hair. It already seemed as if the ghost were more frightened, if possible, than he, and his scattered faculties began to act. The figure moved toward the door and laid a white hand on the knob, but could not turn it. Hughie saw that the spring lock would hold the door and the helplessness of his unreal visitor inspired courage. If it was a woman she was trying painfully to open the door. Hughie took a cautious step. There was no longer any thought of a vision in his mind; the clock was ticking loudly, the sounder clicked at intervals on the table and his heart beat fast and heavily. He was awake, and whether living or dead, a woman was standing before him. If she had not dropped from the stars, how could she have come? There had not been the slightest warning of an approach save the closing of the door—no wagon rattle from some far-off ranch, no sound of horses' hoofs, and as for walking, there was no place to walk from. Even believing her to be a living creature, there was something unnatural in her manner. She inspired fear. When she put her hands to her face a shiver passed over him. When she moved, her feet gave forth no sound. Hesitating between the fear of what the wildest surmise could not explain and the conviction that this must be a reality, Hughie heard a sob and pity moved him.

"I will let you out," he exclaimed unsteadily. Watching his visitor narrowly as he stepped forward, he released the spring-bolt. In doing so he saw her face. A shock checked him and a new fear overcame him. What mystery could this be? It was the face of the broken miniature. The head, as he now saw it, was bent and the eyes were drooping, but the high cheeks, the lines of the hair falling over the temples, the straight nose, and the curving side mouth. With the certainty of an acute memory the operator knew it all. He collected himself and spoke again. "Shall I let you out?"

Failing to see that he held the knob in his hand, she put forward her own to reach it. Her fingers touched his, and he knew that he faced a creature of flesh and blood. He released the lock. "Shall I let you out?" She looked helplessly before her and her voice trembled. "It is cold."

He closed the door. "It is cold," he echoed. "How did you come here?"

She drew timidly back. "What is your name?" he persisted.

"It is so cold."

To none of his questions could she give an answer. She spoke like one in a trance; at times trying pathetically to put back her loosened hair, pleading at times to be let go and shrinking in fear from her companion, who found himself now the protector of his unaccountable apparition. He continued to speak and with growing excitement, to all of which the strange visitor appeared insensible. He saw very soon that he was unnecessarily frightening his ghost, and he presently stood silent with his hands on the back of a surprised chair, waiting for his visitor to make the next move herself.

She had, so far as he could ever remember afterward, but two coherent movements; either her eyes sought in hope the light of his lamp or turned from it in despair. This much, at least, was intelligible, even if incomprehensible. Not until he saw her falter, put her hands blindly out and sink to the floor did he realize that she was ill and in distress. Too excited to breathe as he took her in his arms, he lifted her up and placed her inert upon a chair. She opened her eyes in a moment. A chill passed over her. Hughie threw open the drafts of the stove and chafed her hands. Something of gratitude seemed to move her, for as she shrank into the chair she looked at him with less of fear. He sat down then himself, and facing her, tried with his hands on his knees to inspire confidence. She would not talk. Instead, as the fire in the stove blazed up and the heat diffused itself she showed unmistakable drowsiness and added the last straw to Hughie's embarrassment by asking him why he did not go to bed. He tried to explain that he went to bed in the daytime. His apparition was too far overcome by the warmth to comprehend, but an inspiration seized him. He asked if she would rest for a while on the long table at the back of the room. She opposed nothing that he suggested, and he took the cushion of his chair for a pillow and helped her as well as he could to lie down on the table. When he had done this he went back to his end of the room and watched the dim corner beyond the stove. His charge, for he now made her such, lay perfectly quiet, and when she breathed regularly he took his overcoat from the nail behind the door, tiptoed over to the corner, and laid it across her shoulders. It had been a swagger coat at school, but was short for a coverlet. Still, it served, and as he walked back better satisfied to his chair he heard a rapid clicking from the sounder. The train dispatcher at Medicine Bend was sending the 19—the imperative call from headquarters to clear the line for the dispatched office—and every night operator on the division was getting out of his way. As soon as the wire was free a station call came, and to Hughie's surprise it was for Point of Rocks. He answered instantly, and the message came so fast he could hardly write it.

"Passenger missing from Chicago sleeper on Train Number Two—a young Englishwoman. Is believed to be somewhere between Castle Creek and Point of Rocks. Get your section men out quick with lights and hand-cars and with orders to stay out till they find her. Name, Grace Swinton. Answer quick."

The chief dispatched initials were appended. Hughie Morrison sent his answer straightway.

"Unnecessary to call out the men. I have the missing passenger. She is asleep here in the office. Instruct."

"Good boy, Hughie," returned the pleased dispatcher. "Hold her for special car and engine from here running as second Number One. Make her as comfortable in every way as possible. Get whole story. If injured in any way notify office of Whispering Smith."

Hughie Morrison, turning from the key, drew a breath. It was his last night at Point of Rocks. He looked with curious feelings into the dim corner where the missing passenger lay. He turned in his chair again and again, but she did not move. He adjusted and readjusted the drafts of the stove, noisily and at times officiously, but her soft, regular breathing never varied and day broke on a face upon the table as delicate as ivory and the operator in despair for a sign of awakening.

First Number Two, the regular train, came and went, with every man of the train and engine crews peering furtively into the shaded corner at Hughie Morrison's ghost, but Hughie waved them away and knew that the Special to bear her away would follow all too soon. When it drew in, bringing the superintendent's car, he was ready to rebel against his orders and disposed to hold the ghost against all comers. But with careful tread they brought in heavy blankets, and as Grace Swinton lay wrapped her in them and carried her, sleeping heavily, to the car, regardless of Hughie's protests that they ought at least to wait till he had got her story from her own lips. They asked for orders, got them almost at once, and puffed noisily away for Medicine Bend. When they were gone Hughie folded his papers; he was all ready to say good-by to Point of Rocks.

Chapter IV

The promotion had come. After all, it was not exciting. Indeed, nothing excited Hughie any more. Martin Duffy was the most crestfallen man, save one, on the division over having picked Hughie for a dispatcher, that one being the new dispatcher himself. The change that had come over the president's nephew was the common talk of the trainmen. His alertness, the light play of his humor, the grasp that met the little desert emergencies at Point of Rocks with the ease of a veteran—where were they? As to the night with the ghost, nobody gave that any consideration, because where things happen all the time, and where everything that happens is unusual, an incident holds the stage only for its fleeting instant. Hughie himself felt the situation keenly. He even asked to be relieved, but Martin Duffy was above all things not a quitter. "Don't commit suicide," he growled. "You're in a funk, that is all. I pulled a woman once from in front of a locomotive. What do you think she did? Sent me a cross-stitched waistcoat and a copy of 'The Simple Life.' Wouldn't that kill you? And I've wanted a meerschaum pipe for twenty years."

The advice was good, and Hughie swallowed it, as a fool should, with disgust and humility. But Martin Duffy usually caused things to happen, and this time proved no exception. When the new dispatcher walked into the office just before twelve o'clock that night for his trick, the mail from Number One was being distributed and a letter, small but plump-looking, bearing a foreign postmark and addressed in a clear, firm hand to Hughie Morrison, was laid before him. He cut open the envelope with feverish haste and began to read. Line after line and page after page slipped past the lightning of his eyes, and one would have said that the play of his mental fire had quite come back. This was the letter that it should be. This was the story, her own story with its frank account of the long illness that had first shown itself during an overland railroad journey in America; here were the prettily chosen expressions of gratitude—all that the greediest Princeton man could ask for, and Hughie was greedy—thanking him for the delicate kindnesses she said he had shown to her during her night of trance and terror on the desert. Hughie, unable to read and breathe at the same time, sat down. The desert came back; the stillness of the wind and the glory of the stars, the stealing fear, the shock, and now the grip of the eagerly waited letter.

"I had come from the coast," she wrote, "and was bringing home from California my invalid brother. He was then, and is still very ill. The worry of providing for his journey and the fear that I might not be able to bring him home alive had worn upon me until I was in but little better condition, I fear, than he.

"How I ever came to leave my berth in my sleep and to walk asleep straight out of our sleeping-car when the train stopped that night at Point of Rocks I cannot, of course, explain. But the doctor has since told me that in crossing the Rocky Mountains the altitude is often accountable for strange things that people do. When I reached home after the ocean voyage I was already ill of brain fever —less, I suppose, could hardly have been looked for—and my recovery has been very slow. But for your delicate consideration in that night of delirium I should probably never have recovered at all. Wandering as I did over the open country around the station in the cold of those dreadful hours of unconsciousness, I seem faintly to remember seeing the light in your window—the only light, I was afterward told, within many, many miles. And I want now to apologize with all humility for breaking in upon your solitude at so unearthly an hour and in so forlorn a condition. If at any time hereafter, you should ever be in England, I hope you will surely come to Ormonde Road, Richmond. You will find us at The Knolls, and it will give me a chance to tell you in person how grateful I am for all you did for me. It will surprise you very much, I know, to learn that I myself once really lived at Point of Rocks, but it was years ago, during my childhood. An uncle of mine had cattle ranches in that country, and built a large house near the Point, which afterward burned. As a little girl I lived with my aunt, and I often played with my dolls among the very rocks near the railroad station.

The letter bore the signature of Grace Swinton. Hughie Morrison brought his hand down on the table and a new light shone in his face. His resolve was taken. Saint George and Merry England was the watchword, whether it forever blasted hopes of promotion or not. He began his eight-hour trick on the instant that night and did the best work with the trains he had done since his promotion. Moreover, he found time to write a letter and start it at six o'clock that morning on Grace Swinton's own train, as he called Number Two, to The Knolls, in Ormonde Road, Richmond, explaining how he had happened to be sent to Point of Rocks —with incidental mention that he had long known of her having lived there. And mention, too, of a broken miniature and of one surviving doll that she might, he hoped, still be interested in.

Inquiries mutually began could not, of course, be satisfied at so long distance with a single exchange of letters. When Bucks heard the story he seemed more pleased than he ever had been with a relative in his life, and to Hughie's surprise, gave the six months' leave asked for the trip to England and The Knolls without a word of reproach. But an account of that trip with its surprises, with the international complications that followed, with Hughie's questions as to whether the stars really had sung on the desert that night and Grace Swinton's denials as to ever having said anything about their singing; the journey made by President Bucks to inspect the English railways and to be present at The Knolls at his nephew, Hughie Morrison's, wedding—all this would make a chapter told too often in the traditions of the Mountain Division. What is of importance is that Hughie, being now general manager of the coast lines, is stationed where his English bride—having lived in the Rocky Mountains as a little girl—professes to feel entirely at home.

ABOUT THE AUTHORS

JOHN YONGE AKERMAN (1806–1873) was an English antiquarian specializing mainly in numismatics. He also wrote fiction under the pseudonym Paul Pindar.

JACK BRANT was a pulp writer who appeared in such magazines as *All-Story*. Little is known about his life.

ARTHUR WILLIS COLTON (1868-1943) obtained his Ph.D. in literature from Yale and was a popular magazine writer, known for his romanticism, humor, and sarcasm. His notable works include "Tioba" (1903), "The Belted Seas" (1906), and "The Cruise of the Violetta" (1906).

BITHIA MARY CROKER (née Sheppard, 1849–1920) was a prolific Anglo-Indian novelist. Very little is known about her life. She was the only daughter of Rev. William Sheppard, Rector of Kilgefin Church in County Roscommon, Ireland. She married Lieutenant Colonel John Stokes Croker (1844-1911 CE), an officer in the Royal Munster Fusiliers in 1871. Soon after their marriage she followed her husband to Madras where he worked, then went to Bengal. She lived in India for fourteen years, and spent some time in a hill station in Wellington. There she wrote many of her works. After her husband's retirement in 1892, the couple went to live in County Wicklow, and finally settled in Folkstone. She had one daughter who was educated at Rockferry, Cheshire. She was immensely interested in reading, travelling, and theatre.

Her literary career spans 37 years, from 1882 when she was 33 years old, until 1919. She wrote nearly 46 works of which some are short story collections dealing with variety of themes. In the stories and also in the novels she occasionally employs a Gothic element for which she seems to have had a special infatuation. Most of her works were set in India and other parts of the Empire, including Africa and Egypt. They usually deal with Indian military life. Most of her novels reveal the troubles and tribulations of unswerving and dedicated lovers who are destined to unite after a considerable delay. Her works have been compared to those of her Victorian contemporaries like Thomas Hardy.

CHARLES DICKENS (1812–1870) was an English writer and social critic. He created some of the world's most well-known fictional characters and is generally regarded as the greatest novelist of the Victorian period. During his life, his works enjoyed unprecedented popularity, and by the twentieth century he was widely seen as a literary genius by critics and scholars. His novels and short stories continue to be widely popular.

SIR ARTHUR CONAN DOYLE (1859–1930) was a British writer and physician, most noted for his fictional stories about the detective Sherlock Holmes, which are generally considered milestones in the field of crime fiction. He is also known for writing the fictional adventures of a second character he invented, Professor Challenger, and for popularizing the mystery of the *Mary Celeste*. He was a prolific writer whose other works include fantasy and science fiction stories, plays, romances, poetry, non-fiction and historical novels.

OLIVIA HOWARD DUNBAR (1873-1953) was an American author most remembered for her body of supernatural fiction. Her work also appears in *The Second Ghost Story Megapack*.

AMELIA B. EDWARDS (1831–1892) was an English novelist, journalist, traveller and Egyptologist. Born in London to an Irish mother and a father who had been a British Army officer before becoming a banker, Edwards was educated at home by her mother, showing considerable promise as a writer at a young age. She published her first poem at the age of 7, her first story at age 12. Edwards thereafter proceeded to publish a variety of poetry, stories and articles in a large number of magazines including *Chamber's Journal*, *Household Words* and *All the Year Round*. She also wrote for the *Saturday Review* and the *Morning Post*.

ELLEN GLASGOW (1873–1945) was an American novelist who portrayed the changing world of the contemporary south.

LILLIAN B. HUNT published a small number of supernatural stories in the early part of the 20th century. Little is known about her.

JEROME K. JEROME (1859–1927) was an English writer and humourist, best known for the comic travelogue *Three Men in a Boat* (1889). Other works include the essay collections *Idle Thoughts of an Idle Fellow* (1886) and *Second Thoughts of an Idle Fellow*; *Three Men on the Bummel*, a sequel to *Three Men in a Boat*; and several other novels. His supernatural work tends to be humorous in nature.

SARAH ORNE JEWETT (1849–1909) was an American novelist, short story writer and poet, best known for her local color works set along or near the southern seacoast of Maine. Jewett is recognized as an important practitioner of American literary regionalism.

RUDYARD KIPLING (1865-1936) was a British writer born in India, and heavily influenced by his experiences there. He's best-known today for such soldiers' stories as "The Man Who Would Be King" (1888), and for his children's tales, especially *The Jungle Book* (1894), *Just So Stories* (1902), and *Kim* (1901). He was the first English-language author to win the Nobel Prize for Literature (1907).

WALTER E MARCONETTE is primarily remembered these days for his fanzine editing. As editor of *Scienti-Snaps* in the 1930s and 1940s, he published a mix of fiction, columns, and articles by fans and professionals.

H. B. MARRYATT is better known as Frederick Marryatt, famous for his novel *The Phantom Ship*.

BRANDER MATTHEWS (1852–1929) was an American writer and educator. He was the first full-time professor of dramatic literature at an American university and played a significant role in establishing theater as a subject worthy of formal study in the academic world. His interests ranged from Shakespeare,

Molière, and Ibsen to French boulevard comedies, folk theater, and the new realism of his own day.

FIONA MACLEOD was the pseudonym of **WILLIAM SHARP** (1855–1905), a Scottish writer, of poetry and literary biography. In 1893 he began also publishing as Macleod, a pseudonym kept almost secret during his lifetime.

MARY NOAILLES MURFREE (1850–1922) was an American fiction writer of novels and short stories who wrote under the pen name Charles Egbert Craddock. She is considered by many to be Appalachia's first significant female writer and her work a necessity for the study of Appalachian literature, although a number of characters in her work reinforce negative stereotypes about the region. She has been favorably compared to Bret Harte and Sarah Orne Jewett, creating post-Civil War American local-color literature.

FRANK H. SPEARMAN (1859–1937) was an American author best known for his books in the Western fiction genre and especially for his fiction and non-fiction works on the topic of railroads.

EDMUND GILL SWAIN (1861–1938) was an English cleric and author. As a chaplain of King's College, Cambridge, he was a colleague and contemporary of the scholar and author M. R. James, and a regular member of the select group to whom James delivered his famous annual Christmas Eve reading of a ghost story composed specially for the occasion. Swain collaborated with James on topical skits for amateur performance in Cambridge, but he is best known for the collection of ghost stories he published in 1912, entitled *The Stoneground Ghost Tales*.

JULIET WILBOR TOMPKINS was a popular author at the turn of the 20th Century, known for romances such as *A Girl Named Mary* and *Pleasures and Palaces*.

HENRY VAN DYKE (1852–1933) was an American author, educator, and clergyman. Among his popular writings are the two Christmas stories, *The Other Wise Man* (1896) and *The First Christmas Tree* (1897). Various religious themes of his work are also expressed in his poetry, hymns and the essays collected in *Little Rivers* (1895) and *Fisherman's Luck* (1899). He wrote the lyrics to the popular hymn, "Joyful, Joyful We Adore Thee" (1907), sung to the tune of Beethoven's "Ode to Joy."